MW01489855

ASCENDANT CHAOS

LEFT ARC
IN THE
FIREWALL PROTOCOL
SAGA

DAVE TODD

Copyright © 2024 by Dave Todd
001.009.2024.09.07

This is dedicated to my mom who took on the most critical responsibility of introducing me to the WAY. It is my hope to pay forward such an an example by using the abstract interpretation of peaks & valleys in my life to enrich you, the audience, not only for recreation, but also to instill within you a hunger for TRUTH during your own journey through LIFE.

Acknowledgements

As the first story in this saga neared its time for public release, I was met with challenges which prompted the acceleration of its completion. During this time I sought support to help cross the finish line. I am deeply thankful for those who continued their belief in this project and even assisted in tangible ways. I am indebted to them and feel that their support should be recognized.

Joe & Dawn
Dan & Mary Lou
Joe & Kathy
Jeremiah & Tiffany
Henry & Tristin
Scott & Melissa
Robert & Michelle
Matt & Casey

A special thank-you goes out to Wayne for lending his abundance of knowledge with the publication process.

Preface

A story like this does not exist without a countless number of experiences and relationships that have been interwoven throughout a lifetime. My life has been both enriched and challenged by these elements which have shaped my character and ability to create. Relationships past and present have altered my worldview immensely, sometimes for good and mutual benefit, other times for adversity and growth. Even historical figures have made an impact with ideas to elevate and philosophies to parse.

Impactful relationships have varied from short seasons to lifelong blessings with some simply offering a helping hand while others have yielded common mutual interests and worldviews. Even the antagonistic variety were in abundance, complete with challenging life application.

Due to the abstract nature in which some characters have been inspired by real people, there is no way to fully divulge the identity of those individuals for respect of their privacy. However, that has never diminished my desire to take inspiration from those interactions and elevate them when they had such a profound impact or utilize them for lessons when they were most undesirable. In some rare cases, I have been blessed to have long time relationships with individuals that believed in this project from the very beginning which allowed me to receive their input and even infuse their real world suggestions into their fictional counterparts.

My life has been defined by strong encounters. Great or small, I'm thankful for every piece of that puzzle. Most of all, I am thankful for my Creator who gave me the ability to take such an abstract view on life and craft it into such a magnificent story that I feel can encourage others for years to come.

0 - Awakening - 0

Dwelling Street Mission
Abandoned Sector, Windstonne Enclave
Commercial Empire, Northam Continent
Thread: actTgtPersp1.view

Earth, a masterfully crafted dot of color dabbed onto the canvas of space, serene and systematic in its appearance from a distance, but like all complex creations its simple veneer rarely reveals the turbulence within. The celestial body's surface, once home to its surplus of nine billion inhabitants, hardly resembles the vibrant terracosm that it was as few as twenty passes ago, or so I have heard.

Shortly after the turn of the thouseon, war resurfaced, its ugly maw spewing sparks onto the powder keg of indifference. Even to this day, no one is sure who initiated the first strike, but there is no denying that some latent grudge proved too powerful to ignore. Some theorists blamed the ever-conflicted regions of Insurgistan, others the former superpowers of the Martial Legion, but regardless of speculation, forces at work were clearly bent on the destruction of the Tricameral Endeavor.

A multi-pronged strike targeted the capital of the Tricameral Endeavor. Shortly thereafter, additional attacks bombarded major population centers along the eastern coast of the Northam continent hitting economic hubs and political havens without discretion. Although such precise execution suggested an inside job, few officials survived, yielding no accountability.

The National Conglomerate, the foremost collection of governments, was reluctant to send aid to the ensnared Tricameral Endeavor, reticent to engage in an unofficial war. Instead, the Conglomerate launched investigations to ascertain the source of the strikes. Conflicting reports suggested involvement of facilities within Sibera and the Red Wall, along with other volatile regions of the Shian continent. Naturally, all accused governments refuted any such allegation, but no matter the truth, with so much damage inflicted, there was no dissolving the amount of distrust among the nations. Malice and vengeance seared the hearts of millions. Retribution was the only fuel left to burn in the hearts of victims.

Without any means to exact justice on individuals responsible for the attacks, hostilities and mistrust became the ember that grew into a firestorm until the recently dubbed Global War engulfed the entire planet in its fog. Nation rose against nation, neighbor against neighbor, no suspicion too slight. Cultural differences, political views, national origins and economic status all proved ample excuse to fight.

With its government imploded, the Tricameral Endeavor found itself scarred by countless parcels of scorched wasteland. Fearing similar wide reaching strikes, millions of inhabitants fled large urban centers, spreading into the more remote corners of the continent hoping to avoid yet another well calculated strike. With the nation's people scattered, a young executive sensed the urgency to unite the leaderless nation and galvanize the remnants of the torn country.

Frank Jenkins, vice president of the Corporate Casting Network of Windstonne, seized opportunity to fill the leadership void. Upon the untimely demise of the company's president during the initial strikes of the Global War, Jenkins assumed command of what remained of the company's vast sphere of influence. The CCN was still rich in resources due to its geographic positioning within the midwest, minimizing its losses while retaining access to its satellites and uplink centers. With full mediacasting access, Frank Jenkins could communicate through meca and network alike. With the common goal of survival paramount, the people of the imploded Tricameral Endeavor rallied together, forming defensive groups, pooling military resources and growing newly formed militias under the daring executive.

With other countries conducting their own intracontinental feuds, Frank Jenkins was granted just enough time to bolster defenses for a weakened country. As support grew, Jenkins looked outward to acquire allies, but advantageous relationships were scarce. While the countries of the Uniod and Shian continents engaged in their own skirmishes, Jenkins leveraged their distractions to seek allegiance from the under developed economies of the Equatorial Span. By pouring akcellerrants, technology and education into the regions across the ocean, Jenkins hoped to win allies.

While mutual exchanges limited hostilities for a time, Jenkins' underhanded tactics would not go unnoticed. The shrewd prime minister of the Equatorial Span, Cecil Khadem, fully understood the nature of the relationship. Sensing deception, he turned the tables and closed the Caafri continental borders, preventing any foreign professional that was provided from returning home.

As bitterness took root at the betrayal and loss of valuable minds, Jenkins' motivation began to shift from protection to greed. The defensive stance of the mediacasting executive's domain slowly transformed into a quest for annexation. Militia groups were turned on allied territories within Northam and Centram regions. With the Global War lingering and the National Conglomerate's power diminishing, there was no governing body to place a check on Frank Jenkins' expansionist behavior.

As the Global War lingered for more than six passes, vindictive slaughter lost its appeal and memories of those lost began to haunt the living. Urban centers became graveyards and the fields in between became wastelands. People began to forget their reason for fighting and started to ponder what they could have done differently to end the war sooner. Hindsight and regret prompted an upswing in diplomacy.

As key figures among the nations elevated truces into treaties, a loosely structured government began to form from the ashes. As old boundaries were wiped away and drawn anew, leaders of these new zones found themselves beholden to a new order. Most notable among them were Frank Jenkins of the Commercial Empire, Tarak Delaney of the Uniod Bloc, Cecil Khadem of the Equitorial Span and William Ang of the Oceanic Outpost. They were included among the twelve leaders appointed to rule over the newly formed factions of the Global Alliance.

As hostilities dwindled and the longing for peace grew, guidelines were established to finally bring an end to the Global War. After a total of seven passes of fighting, and a death toll shaving off two thirds of the earth's population, the conflict had finally ended.

Looking to the future, the survivors hoped that the worst was behind them, but due to the perpetual state of unrest, fear and paranoia dominated public sentiment. With every faction's government in a weakened state, piracy and terrorism ensued. Without stable economies, currency no longer held its value. Instead, food, hardware, and salvage all become the greatest prizes, but most prestigious of all, knowledge.

With so much lost during the war, artifacts, hardtypes and datatanks were all esteemed to be of great value, but as recovery of lost datastacks grew, so too did information on government dealings over the course of the war. Unwilling to allow mistrust and independence to flourish, some leaders of the Global Alliance crafted policies to hinder straying allegiances. Masked as a plan to collect datatanks and protect them against pirates, some factions proactively destroyed physical media and banned any educational system not sanctioned by proper Global Alliance channels.

Instead of reducing the temptation for theft, the Global Alliance's actions only encouraged it. High tech pirates became the heroes of the people as they fought actively to capture and preserve any datastacks they could find. The inception and growth of the new technology known as the Hyper Lynx became the conduit for resistance against faction leaders. With primary communication channels of the

Global Alliance challenged, several leaders scrambled to deploy their own countermeasures.

Frank Jenkins wasted no time in leveraging his influence with the Techcong to corral the flow of information through the Commercial Empire's domain. Financial systems were corrupted, geographical systems were wiped, personal identities vanished. Any information that was deemed a hazard was purged. With the Techcong able to work faster than the masses, valuable resources disappeared while being replaced with dependency inducing conveniences and organech security measures to reduce the flow of unauthorized information.

With only a brief respite after the Global War, the Smart Wars raged for two passes until leaders of the Global Alliance felt they had contained any threats to their control over the factions. The Global Alliance sold their agenda as beneficial, but the people didn't easily forget those lost in the purging process, further solidifying distrust of the ruling body. Even with the threat of physical conflict brought to an end, information too was considered a great casualty.

Once the Global Alliance shored up its control over the greatest quality of life resources, it emerged as the undisputed victor in the Smart Wars. With the masses helpless to stand against the powers already set against them, the will to fight diminished. The Global Alliance simplified the calculus, adhere to the rules and receive the amenities of the benevolent establishment, or bug out. Maximizing its grip on datatanks, the Global Alliance no longer feared the dissidents who opted to strike out on their own. Large urban centers, or enclaves became the norm, at least in the Commercial Empire especially since the amenities of pre-war life were readily available. Knowing that few would choose a life of sacrifice over convenience, the Global Alliance gambled little in neglecting those who restricted themselves to the more remote regions. As long as the Global Alliance could tamp down on unregulated intel and crush any budding resistance, its rule was uncontested.

For those wary of Global Alliance rule, trading luxuries for freedom was a given. As long as rumors of military action never reached the Global Alliance's ears, denizens of the remote regions took it upon themselves to manage their own food sources, educations and livelihoods. Ultimately, their choices resulted in a symbiotic relationship with the enclaves considering appointed enclave leaders could never fully sustain their domains without some reliance upon those who worked the land.

Despite the extreme polarity of cultures, a hybrid choice existed for the most adventurous, life in the abandoned zones. Most enclaves were clustered around population centers still standing since the Global War. While some enclaves were mired in restoration efforts, others were surrounded by lifeless urban shells mostly untouched. Without a population to target, fighting forces seldom bothered wasting resources on the destruction of vacant domains. These abandoned sectors were rich in resources to salvage. For those willing to do the factions' dirty work, they were granted more freedom than those within the urban core.

Often those who worked in the abandon formed themselves into clans. While many clans were little more than pre-war gangs, some sought to use their reputations to showcase their physical prowess while others leveraged the freedom of faction work to secure educations which would elevate their standing in the enclaves. Opportunists and freedom seekers alike acknowledged the possibility of finding books, datatanks and technology yet to be reclaimed. Officially, the Global Alliance condemned the personal collection of such resources without reporting it to the authorities, but it was incapable of fully monitoring activities beyond the confines of the enclaves.

For establishments that played by faction rules, they were granted contracts to perform salvage operations. As long as all educational finds were reported to the authorities and there was no overlap with other entities possessing similar contracts, these establishments were even provided with resources to perform their work. In some cases, logistics even warranted the construction of dwelling facilities to expedite the salvage work. Such facilities, or missions, often spawned the existence of sub-communities within the abandon. Additionally, missions were valuable mediators between remote regions and enclaves, facilitating the flow of resources. With a valid means to work and attain shelter while still owning a great deal of freedom, many participants found the accommodations to be a win-win.

This is where I come in. I have been an inhabitant of the Dwelling Street Mission in the abandoned sector of the Windstonne enclave deep in the heart of the Commercial Empire for nearly three passes. I have no recollection of events prior to that time. According to sources, I was dropped off at the mission, a raid victim during the Smart Wars. While my body has healed since the unknown attack that befell me, my mind has not.

Everything that I have learned about this place has been through late evening meca's in the leisure room after hard days of salvage work, or through listening to the stories of fellow mission workers who experienced some of the Commercial Empire's more turbulent moments firsthand. I cannot complain, really, my life is simple, the necessities are provided and I have kind people to work with. Div and Tarees

Merrick, the Dwelling Street Mission's salvage operation coordinators, have been gracious in allowing me to stay on as long as I pull my weight, a common rule for anyone wishing to benefit from the mission's presence in the abandoned sector.

While I am uncertain if I will ever overcome my amnesia, I still try every day to discover puzzle pieces potentially just out of reach. Strangely, with every day that passes, I cannot explain the sensation that all of my surroundings still feel foreign to me. I thought that my time working through the rubble of history might yield at least one clue that could unlock latent memories, but so far, that notion has failed. Sure, I could resign myself to the simplicity of the lifestyle before me, or even chase the allure of Core City. After all, fears have diminished regarding urban living amongst doubts of the Commercial Empire's means to risk another war any time soon.

It could be worse, but no matter which path I ponder, each seems unable to pacify my deep need for satisfaction. Whether this mysterious internal void originates from a haunted past or an ominous premonition of the future, I cannot say, but the resulting restlessness gives rise to skepticism about the status quo of the reality surrounding me. It is unshakeable.

My name is Aaron Fox, and this is the story of my quest to identify the truth of it all.

1 – Enter the Enforcer – 1

Dwelling Street Mission
Abandoned Sector, Windstonne Enclave
Commercial Empire, Northam Continent
Thread: actTgtPersp1.view

I felt pressure smothering my senses as I sat in the dim, crowded atmosphere of the mission leisure room. My mind felt like it was enveloped in an inescapable monotony as it screamed for relief. I could hear the chatter of veterans telling the same war stories I'd heard on numerous occasions. Noise emanated from the emcast as some of the guys switched the feed to the latest sporting events. I heard discussion of the next day's plans for work in the distance, but that night I needed to hear something different. It had been three passes since I was placed at a local mission to be watched over without any memory or comprehension of my own identity. I possessed no recollection of my life before that day. I didn't know if I had family, where I had lived, or even what interests I had. All I could gather was that simply enduring the redundance of my life would not bring the answers to me, I would have to find them for myself.

Several veterans lived in the Dwelling Street Mission, most of whom had fought in the Global War. On multiple occasions, I listened in on conversations describing the world's state, comprising hundreds of political entities before the war. Numerous countries used to span each of the continents maintained by governments supposedly committed to protecting their citizens, but in the present era no such concept existed. Sure, population clusters could call themselves a country, but they were no more united than a cloud of dust settling on a hot summer wind. The devastation of war and infighting eventually fatigued the masses, but the embers of conflict only cooled for a time. After every survivor suffered loss in one fashion or another, treachery changed its face yet again devouring the short lived peace. New methods of destruction focused attacks on economies, education, and culture, morphing into the Smart Wars which changed the planet into the geopolitical state of today.

The leaders of the Global Alliance patterned their structure after the National Conglomerate before its collapse but with fewer heads of state in order to minimize dissent. The handful of talented politicians honored each other in lip service and appearance, but their only true craft was deciding on which knives to sharpen as they plotted behind their backs. The faction leaders and their sponsors became the remnant of society's elite, bent on assuming authority over the rest of us.

Without demonstration of regard for anyone but those deemed beneficial, the faction leaders thus far have left us to carry on about our business. Conversely, the factions have proven their inability to function without the people, so discerning minds shouldn't be surprised that they have mastered the art of manipulating the ignorant, compelling them to fight for any contrived agenda.

Irony continues to thrive, considering that faction leaders banned education for anyone unable to financially attain one. Naturally, the remnant of the educated consolidated within the shrunken cores of major enclaves, so they could harbor the very knowledge which they claimed would initiate wars if captured by less responsible owners. As a result, vacant suburbs that spanned for treks, barely contained handfuls of ruffians, recluses or mission workers attempting to clean up and preserve the last dregs of a forgotten civilization.

Due to the mass exodus of population centers during the Global War, it was difficult to ignore the devastation of the conflict. Former metropolitan areas stood as ghost towns, their high rise centers stood as ancient landmarks over an unnatural terrain. With a priority shift toward survival over substance, buildings and possessions lay dormant, their previous owners never returned after they took up the lifestyle of self-governance in the rural regions. For those who dwelt between the tall urban shadows of the enclaves and the distant plains, they were forced to facilitate their own survival in the abandoned regions.

To some, the truckloads of material goods just waiting to be found yielded an advantageous barter system, yet others pursued the opportunity to recover historic trinkets as high value items, ripe to be passed along to the remote dwellers. One such entity that filled the gap between the new and old was the Dwelling Street Mission.

The Dwelling Street Mission operated out of a repurposed hotel, more upkept than its surroundings in the abandoned sector of the Windstonne enclave. While the neighboring buildings bore the trademark of urban decay, the Dwelling Street Mission provided a tiny glimmer of hope for the limited community that cared to interact with it.

Div and Tarees Merrick maintained the mission and its accommodations for its thirty some workers. Some of the workers, like myself, were derelicts willing to trade lodging for labor while others simply enjoyed the prospect of benevolent work. Most residents enjoyed the work of the mission. It seldom involved the pressures of the enclaves and it offered purpose by assisting inhabitants of the abandon. Even though the mission's surroundings appeared dismal, its location was still within an arc or two drive of Core City in case of emergency, depending on the path chosen through the decrepit dartway.

With another day's hard work under my belt and little energy to endure the repetitive conversations in the leisure room, I could not shake the feeling that my life was one large enigma. After many exhaustive efforts, I was no closer to remembering who I was or where I came from. I sat numbly in the padded lounge chair staring through the moving, flickering images on the noptic display of the emcast. Mission workers opposite me bickered about the latest statistics of the current allcourt game, but I didn't share their enthusiasm. Neither their conversations, nor the the ranting of the sportscasters stimulated my brain. The related sound waves merely struck the designated tones on my ear drums and drifted back into the air from which they traveled.

My mind continued pouring over imaginary puzzles, trying to formulate them into questions without success, and the propaganda from the sportscasters failed to alleviate my unrest. There had to be something more to strive for than the suggestions of the incessant advertisements streaming through the emcast, something more than the false hope of playing on a professional team that in reality reserved its roster for the elite and properly cultured. There had to be something more than the latest celebrity endorsements attempting to convince me that I needed the latest biological implants to improve my muscle structure, stamina or mental acuity. There had to be something more than routinely recycling the ownerless belongings of a decaying metropolis. Every path I could imagine floated in the air and hooked itself on the surrounding walls until the walls themselves grew so thick that I sensed they would come to life and crush me like a compacter.

It was time to move, so I hoisted myself out of the cozy chair supporting my frame and headed for the entrance to the mission. If anyone asked me where I was going I didn't hear them. I needed to clear my head. At times, walking along the silent streets of the abandon had a calming effect.

Before I headed for the open air, I stopped in my room and donned my black fleece pullover, the one with the white stripe along the sleeves. I expected the air to be getting chilly, so I decided it best not to freeze to death from venturing out unprepared. I brushed back my dusty blonde hair tucking it underneath my black treadball cap which I twisted until the brim jutted from the back of my head. I made my way toward the door when something compelled me to look in the mirror. I didn't think some hidden inner reflection would jump out at me with answers, but I stepped over to the reflective glass regardless. My complacent eyes hid behind average glasses, and the blank expression on my rounded face affirmed my need to find meaning in my existence. My bulky frame was not one given to athletics, so I didn't know why I was venturing out into the abandon to risk the dangers of the night. I turned away from the mirror no more hopeful of finding an answer there than in the Dwelling Street Mission itself.

After clearing the mission entryway, a light breeze struck my face as I stepped into the evening air. The sun was setting in the distance changing the sky to brilliant hues of orange and red. The frequent walks still proved valuable for exercise and mental therapy, even though I got plenty of the former from the rigorous workload that Div assigned regularly by way of container shuffling from building to cart, cart to building.

On occasion, I picked a new road to travel at random. I rarely cared where I was headed, so I just started walking. To keep my mind active, I would sometimes contemplate what the local structures were like at the zenith of their occupancy. I was surrounded by professional buildings where executives conducted their business, supermarkets that housed aisles of supplies for daily consumers, fuel stations awaiting empty tanks of many a motorbox, restaurants servicing thousands a day, and factories manufacturing any mechanical or technological contraption that the human mind could conceive. They had long since been converted to empty husks leaving little room for imagination once salvagers picked them clean.

As the sun dipped from its perch on the horizon, I felt the wind temperature drop causing me to rethink my impulsive behavior. I halted my stroll to turn the collar of my pullover up, keeping the wind's chill off my neck. Just as I was about to resume my stroll, something caught my eye. I couldn't decipher if it was a reflection of the fading sunlight on a metallic object or just my imagination, but it struck my curiosity nevertheless.

A narrow, dark alley spanned the gap between a couple of multi-level apartment complexes. I began walking toward the entrance to the alley when a searing headache made me freeze in my tracks nearly causing me to collapse to the ground, but before I could think to explain the cause of the headache it had already dissipated. Even more peculiar, the headache was accompanied by a whisper as if it traveled on the wind. *"Straight and narrow is the gate"* hissed the sound in my skull.

I whirled around to see if there was someone near. I felt like I was in a bad horror meca awaiting some grotesque villain to jump out and spew my internal organs along the ground. My heart raced at the conjured vision of an unseen assailant leaping from the shadows. My paranoia ran high, yet my curiosity kept it in check as I took a step toward the alley entrance.

I squinted to make sure that I didn't trip over scattered trash and random rubble. The apartments cast deep shadows over the alley, blocking any possible dusklight, yet I still saw an indiscernible light at the end of the dark tunnel which still held my attention.

Meandering forward, I stumbled through the alley, checking to make sure that my personage was still intact. As I looked up, I found the odd light source that had cast bizarre reflections through the alley. A five deck administrative building of the most irregular fashion glinted in the fading light shooting beams in the most unlikely of directions. It was surreal to witness the shape of the building amongst so many others with linear, squared construction. It was as if the builder's architect had the blueprints absconded by his child who then scribbled an abundance of crossing lines over the design which ultimately made their way into final construction. To offset the unusual façade, waterfall shaped curves capped either of the building's front corners.

Stepping closer, I looked for any signage that might indicate the former purpose of the building. Anytime a salvage op rolled through, they would remove old signage to inform future salvagers that the building had already been picked over. Commonly, government and financial institutions were choice finds leaving few remnants for any operators late to the scene. Looking around, I saw that remaining establishments still had signs visible. I spotted a clothing outlet, supermarket and a handful of corporate offices suggesting that the building in question had greater value than those untouched.

I walked up the cold paved steps of the abandoned building. The evening breeze sent a chill down my spine, at least I suspected it was from the breeze. I poked around some remains scattered along the entryway to the building. Finding nothing of interest, I gave up on the hunt for the building's name and decided to investigate the traditional way.

I approached the sleek but grungy glass doors of the building. Without a power grid to run the structure, the old motion sensor failed to respond. I wedged my fingers into the crease between the two doors. Initially resisting my efforts due to passes of unuse, the doors eventually gave way to my prying.

The gap widened just enough for me to squeeze through, but just as I was about to enter the building, the paranoia of being watched crept back into my mind. I whirled around and looked behind me to see if I could find the unseen eyes that were haunting me. It was common for stragglers to live in the abandon, but I had yet to observe any sight or sound to suggest that I was not alone. I held my breath so that my ears could detect any abnormal sound patterns. All I heard was silence beyond a slight howl of the wind.

Slipping through the door, my mind switched back to curiosity mode to squelch the lingering paranoia. Since my life was typically saturated with never ending simplicity, it felt refreshing to explore and deviate from the normalcy of the daily grind.

After squeezing most of my body through the door, a spring mechanism engaged in the frame causing the door to slide closed. Panicking, I tried to finish my entry, but my foot got caught, and I stumbled to the floor. Trying to roll over cautiously without spraining my ankle, I kicked at the door with my free foot. Having no success, I sat forward and, with difficulty from my seated position, shook my pinched leg free of its captors by pushing the door outward with my fingertips.

Questioning my judgment about whether or not entering an abandoned building alone was such a wise idea, I ambled my way into its interior. The building was pitch black which came as no surprise. I placed one hand along the wall and felt my way around until I encountered a board at least one mark from the floor. Taking a gamble, I knocked on the board.

The vibration knocked dust loose from the crevice between the board and its frame. Hearing the hollow echo, and seeing a faint trace of moonlight creep through the crevice I came to the realization that the windows had been boarded. I pounded on the board to shake enough dust loose to make room for my already raw fingers.

With a grunt, I shoved my fingers behind the board and gave it a heave. The nails holding the board in place gave way, and the piece of wood crashed to the floor with a loud echo that panned out along the building interior. Moonlight flooded into the room with enough silver light so that my eyes could once again adjust to my surroundings. I saw shelving structures lining the floor as far as the darkness allowed. Intrigued, I walked along some of the narrow aisles. The building had a soft carpet, and sound didn't travel as well in comparison to other buildings I had occupied which were designed for industrial means.

My thoughts drifted back to a conversation with Chuck, my work buddy, about some of the Imperan regulations. Before the mission was allowed to support renovation and restructuring of the abandoned enclave, Div was required to sign an agreement that operators would report any findings related to education.

Snapping back to the present, I realized what the building was... it was a library, or at least it had been. Deciding not to venture too far from my limited light source, I scoured the aisles with interest. There were no books or paraphernalia to be found, but still the thought of seeing the inside of a library was amazing. I had heard a story or two about them over casual conversation while we unloaded goods from many a place during working arcs.

As my initial curiosity overruled caution, lack of expectation in discovery prompted my boredom to take over. Rounding the next aisle, I opted to head back toward the door. Keeping my hand close to something stable at all times, ensuring that I didn't stumble in the low lighting, I gingerly notched my way back to the silver light seeping through the window. Upon reentering visible light my leg slammed into the post of an overturned desk.

"Ow!" I yelled bending down to rub my shin. The echo of my voice bounced off the walls multiple times before fading into oblivion. Curious of my attacker, I walked my hands around the surface of the desk. I managed to find the front of the desk, and realized that most of the drawers had been removed. This was fairly standard procedure when purging a building. To my surprise, though, I discovered that a drawer was still intact. I found the handle to the drawer, and gave it a tug, but it hardly budged. Determined, I placed one foot against the desk for support and yanked on the handle of the drawer. Breaking the drawer free of its cove, I stumbled, slamming my back into a shelf, but as the drawer dangled in my hand I heard a faint thump as something else broke free of the desk's frame. Supposing that I had knocked a railing loose, I swept my free hand across the floor to find the mystery object.

My right hand found pay dirt, but it was not a piece of the desk. Dropping the mangled drawer on the floor, I knelt down to scoop the object up. My heart raced when I began to suspect the nature of the cold rectangular object in my hand. Limping into the moonlight, I walked up to the window to illuminate my prize. Sure enough, it was a book.

I brushed dust off the dark cover, nearly triggering a sneezing fit. I turned the book over multiple times, staring at the sealed pages. They appeared to give off a faint, light blue glow. At first, I thought the silvery pages were reflecting the moonlight, but when I moved the book back into the darkness, the glow remained. I found symbols on the cover that I didn't recognize. As I ran my fingers across the leathery cover, a name formed in the same light color reading *Criterion*. I attempted to flip through the book, but most of the pages appeared stuck together. I tried to peel them apart, but something more than glue or chewing gum was holding them fast, a mystery that required further investigation. Deciding that it was time to retire from my adventure, I tucked my findings away until I had more light to work with.

DAVE TODD

I started toward the exit but froze in my tracks upon hearing grinding metal as someone struggled to open the entry doors. I dashed behind a shelving unit to avoid detection. The newcomers managed to get the door open which then drew my attention to the footsteps I heard in the entryway.

"This has got to be the biggest sack of fishbait I've ever seen, Sophomore," said an irritated voice accompanying one set of footsteps. "I mean is Jocq paranoid or something? He's never sent us back to review our performance before. We clean up a building, and BAM, we start the next."

I peeked around the corner to view the new arrivals as the other one replied. "You need to chill, Jammer. Jocq has his reasons. The Commercial Empire may be cracking down on policy, so who knows. You do know why libraries and bookstores are so significant don't you?"

I couldn't hear the reply from the other individual, but the one who posed the question continued, "Books are one of the most durable sources of information, even more than datatanks. If they get into the hands of just anybody, then people start getting ideas, and if people start getting ideas, then they are more difficult to control."

All I could hear from the other one who had been referred to Jammer was a, "Why do you have to go philoso-phi-size everything?" He said stumbling on his intended words.

"How's that go?" Sophomore asked sarcastically.

"Shut up," Jammer replied, annoyed at being harassed about his impromptu vocabulary. His complaints were immediately followed by a click, and I saw a bright path of light sweep across the room. The new arrivals had come more prepared, considering they had solar torches in their possession. Sensing the need for an exit strategy, I wandered through the dark maze hoping to sneak behind the searching individuals. I was willing to bet that they left the door propped open.

"Hey, what is this?" I heard Sophomore say from the direction of the window that I liberated.

Fearing discovery, I quickened my pace toward the door, but it only caused me to stumble.

"What was that?" shouted one of the voices snapping to attention. They panned their solar torches in my direction, and I bolted for the door as I stuffed the book under my belt to free both of my hands.

"Get him!" Jammer yelled.

As suspected, my pursuers had propped the door open with a crate. I had to hop the crate, but, with minimal effort, I cleared the obstruction. I dashed down the steps of the library and ran toward the alley. Without turning about, I could tell that my pursuers weren't far behind.

Just paces from the entrance to the alley, I felt adrenaline pumping into my system as I attempted to tell my muscles to move faster. The footsteps of my pursuers increased in volume.

"Let's show him what we do to poachers on Académe turf," one voice yelled.

I thought that I felt someone's breath on my neck as a hand reached forward to grab my shoulder. A defensive mechanism fired in my brain as something clamped onto my arm, prompting me to twist free and continue running. I hoped that the darkness would become my ally if I could just reach the alley.

Before impeding my escape, the grip released as my foe yelped either in pain or surprise. "What the...!" shouted the other voice from the street.

I was halfway down the alley before I realized that I was no longer being chased. As my curiosity resurfaced, I wanted to know what hindered my quarry from beating me to a pulp. Sticking to the shadows, I crept back to the edge of the alley to observe the commotion.

A third unannounced individual had appeared. He must have kicked the one who grabbed me because one of them was massaging his side.

"Who are you?" Jammer snapped. The expression on Jammer's dark face was not one of welcome.

I noticed that he and Sophomore were both wearing lightweight jackets and denim pants. Sophomore had a loose flannel shirt underneath, but Jammer also sported an allcourt jersey, nylon cap and had a chain running from a side pocket to another in the back. I had seen such chains before in personal effects that we removed from residential salvage. They were usually used to secure a berry clip to one's person, so I didn't understand why Jammer was quickly reaching to remove the excess linkage from his pocket.

The third individual who was draped in a black cloak just stood his ground without reply. Jammer and Sophomore started to circle around him. Before long, Jammer completely withdrew the chain from his pockets and held the center of the lengthy chain in his hand. The ends of the chain merged into weights which prompted me to designate the object as a striking weapon.

Jammer faked a swing with his chain whip, but the mystery person was not impressed. The defender reacted by whipping his cloak away in a circular fashion, tossing it to the ground. The pale moonlight revealed a man wearing black loose pants and a blue vest covering a gray sleeveless shirt. His head was covered with a blue camouflage bandanna which tied into a knot in the back. The most peculiar thing was that he was wearing sunglasses despite daylight's departure.

My two assailants noticed the oddity and were quick to comment, "Isn't it a little dark for shades?" Sophomore snorted.

The mystery man paused and looked at both individuals before replying in a low reflective tone, "Do not be so quick to mistake one's visual limitation for another's blindness to truth."

Taken aback by his response, Jammer and Sophomore looked at each other and laughed. "What kind of nonsense is that?" Jammer said mockingly.

"I think he just called us a couple of fish," Sophomore said.

Uninterested in conversation, Sophomore charged the newcomer who easily read the advance. A push to Sophomore's back caused him to lose balance, nearly putting him on the ground.

Jammer swung his chain over his head and snapped it toward the defender's face. After a couple of near misses, the defender kicked his foot into the air, catching the chain whip, forcing the end to wrap around his shoe. The defender then slammed his foot to the ground, causing the chain to pull Jammer's torso with it. With Jammer's face at a vulnerable height, the defender switched his feet and slammed a kick into Jammer's jaw causing him to reel backward. Jammer staggered across the pavement as he fell.

Further enraged at the sight of his ally being pummeled, Sophomore decided to unlatch the large buckle on the belt hidden by his flannel shirt tails. His belt, like Jammer's chain, was designed to be a weapon too. Whirling the leather belt and weighted buckle overhead, Sophomore whipped the buckle at the defender's face.

Unimpressed, the mystery figure revealed a forked weapon with a long center blade. With a sharp spin, he threw the weapon at Sophomore. The handle of the weapon struck Sophomore in the forehead before clattering to the ground. Sophomore stumbled and clutched his head, reeling from the jarring impact to his skull.

Jammer dusted himself off and snapped into a high, aerial spin kick. Sensing the attack, the defender spun low passing his foot underneath the kicker's airborne body causing the kick to miss completely. The defender evaded more half-hearted kicks before jumping, spinning a full circle and slamming the bottom of his foot to Jammer's face.

Fighting against the dizziness, Sophomore regained his balance and dashed forward, only to pause as he followed the defender's stare to the ground where his chrome weapon lay. Sophomore advanced to step on the weapon and pick it up before the defender could recover it. Amused, the defender extended his hand which was lined with fingerless gloves. The metal weapon leapt from the ground and snapped to the defender's hand just as Sophomore's foot landed where the weapon had been. The defender swiftly spun the weapon around and relocated it to his side.

Jammer mustered his remaining strength to subdue the mystery figure. He stepped forward and hurled himself into the air. As his body flipped forward, Jammer locked his leg out, attempting to drop his heel over the defender's head, but the figure sidestepped the flip and drove his foot into Jammer's gut. Jammer's body continued the flipping motion, but the kick knocked both wind and consciousness out of the agile attacker.

Seizing the opportunity, Sophomore grabbed the defender's arms hoping to immobilize him. The defender slammed his head backward catching Sophomore in the nose. Staggering, Sophomore released his grip on the defender's arms, but it was the last thing that he was going to remember about the evening. With his arms free, the defender spun and connected a back elbow with Sophomore's temple. With a groan, Sophomore fell to the street.

I cringed upon seeing the impact. I turned to run back down the alley, but before I could, the defender whirled around and stared in my direction. I knew that he was looking directly at me. How he knew I was there I didn't know, but I felt an uncanny awareness coming from the person who was responsible for beating the stuffing out of my attackers. He took a step forward and paused. Knowing that my shadowy cover was nullified, I debated whether I should step into the moonlight and thank him, or stay where I was for fear of receiving the same reception issued to Jammer and Sophomore.

I stared at the defender's shades sensing that the eyes behind them were probing the darkness. Stepping out of my hiding spot, he tracked my movement. Continuing my observation of his shades I noticed that part of his eyes became visible even in the pale glow of the moonlight, but what I saw following sent shivers down my spine. The center of his eyes lit up with color and fluctuation showing even through the dark lenses before dissipating back into the night. As I continued to stare, a sudden realization nearly caused my skeleton to leap from my skin, the figure standing in the street looked just like me.

"Did you find what you were looking for?" The figure asked in a monotone voice.

"I… uh…" I mumbled, my voice trailing off in a mixture of panic and confusion. I didn't know whether this man was friend or foe, but my first impulse was to withhold my findings from the stripped library.

"W-who are you?" I stammered.

Uninterested in my question, he turned to pick up his cloak. As he donned the cloak, he began walking away.

"Who are you?" I asked again with more confidence. The only response given was a wave of the hand. My rescuer did not look back.

Thinking that my eyes were playing tricks on me, I blinked as the mysterious figure continued walking. His body slowly disappeared into the night. I knew that my eyesight was strained, but I wasn't blind. He just disappeared like a phantom. Confused, I continued staring at his last observable location until I heard a groan come from one of the downed attackers.

Quickly acknowledging my need to leave, I turned back down the alley and ran toward the mission.

2 – Identity Quest – 2

Old Cut-Thru
Abandoned Sector, Windstonne Enclave
Commercial Empire, Northam Continent
Thread: actTgtPersp1.view

I sprinted down the alley, eager to get back to the mission. The exploration, discovery and fight were more than enough excitement for one evening. While my body operated on autopilot, my mind raced with unanswered questions. *What had just happened? Who was that anomaly that defended me?*

The tall buildings obscured the moonlight from the empty streets, challenging my ability to find my way. Out of the corner of my eye, I recognized familiar markers where squatters had settled in the abandoned buildings which suggested that I was getting close to the mission. Even with the thought of returning to a warm room, I still felt cold, but it wasn't from the night wind. The sense of being watched from shadows poked at my thoughts. Without looking back, I ran as hard as I could down the twisting maze of side streets until I saw the welcoming lights of the Dwelling Street Mission.

I didn't wish to wake anyone on my way in, so I waited outside to slow my huffing from the run. I walked through the entryway door, and closed it gently. I noticed a light in the hallway coming from Tarees' office. Apparently, she was still awake, diligent in mission affairs as ever.

I walked down the quiet hallway and paused as I passed the doorway to Tarees' office. Sensing my presence she looked up from the slate in her hand. "Hey, Aaron, I didn't hear you come in."

"That was the idea. I didn't want to wake anyone," I replied.

"Lots of deep sleepers on the first floor, so I imagine little harm done. How was your walk?" Tarees asked. As she finished her sentence, I watched her eyes target my shoulder.

Looking down, I realized that there was a large, dusty hand print smudged across my pullover where I had been grabbed. I angled my shoulder away to deflect attention, but I suspected my motion wasn't as inconspicuous as I would have liked.

"Great, just got a little sidetracked that's all," I said, doubting my effectiveness to feign innocence.

Tarees' eyes narrowed with concern and suspicion, but she withheld the interrogation. "Okay, just checking," she replied with a smile.

I started toward my room, but Tarees spoke up again before I could escape the doorway. "Aaron, has everything been okay, lately? Some of the other workers have expressed concern. It's not like you to disappear for half the evening."

Hesitating, my mind ran through an immediate exercise to weigh the decision of telling her about the evening's events, but I refrained because I already felt crazy enough without being able to explain what happened myself.

"I just needed some fresh air. I thought it might be helpful to find something to distract me from my nagging amnesia," I said, allowing my voice to trail off.

"Did you find what you were looking for?" Tarees asked.

The way she worded her question immediately struck a nerve. I stared for a tick to sense any manner of intentional prodding, but I saw none. Tarees was both kind and perceptive, but I decided it best to write her question off as coincidence. I couldn't afford additional questions by inciting concern. Shrugging my shoulders, I turned in the direction of my room.

"Well, get some sleep. I'll make sure Div locks up. Good night," Tarees said, returning attention to her slate.

"G'night," I mumbled, walking down the hallway toward my room. Div and Tarees had always been excellent listeners anytime the mission workers had something to discuss. I felt guilty as if I had been hiding something, but I convinced myself that my fatigue was playing tricks on me.

Entering my quarters on the first floor, I flipped the switch to the overhead light in my room. Ready to crash face first on my bed, I remembered the book under my belt. I reached to pull it out, but it was gone. I frantically looked around, but it was nowhere to be seen. I peeked into the hallway, to see if it had fallen there, but there was no trace. *It must have fallen out when I was running*, I thought to myself. I smacked my palm to my forehead, angry with myself for losing such a valuable find. Accepting that there was nothing more I could do about it, I went to bed.

Ghost Encampment
Costal Hills, Mainland
Martial Legion, Shian Continent
Thread: sysObserver.cmd

Multiple small huts lined the crest of the hill in a rural field along the mainland coast of the Martial Legion's dominant land mass.

Although the former superpowers contributed to their share of conflicts during the Global War, the sheer size of the Martial Legion's domain allowed numerous regions to remain unspoiled by the destruction. Such sparsely populated areas served the Ghosts well. Many residents in the urban regions despised the reclusive military protectors of the Martial Legion, but the Ghosts turned the need for secrecy into strength, considering many in the Martial Legion were unaware that the Ghosts were the ones responsible for diverting much of the warfare from the land.

The Ghosts' second in command approached the hut utilized by the general. Alex Corzo reached behind his back and disconnected the long sheath hidden by his scaly leather jacket. He gripped the sheath just below the connected blade handle and held it by his waist as he knocked on the hut's door. It was customary to disengage all arms as a sign of respect. Upon receiving an invitation, Alex entered the the low-tech command building primarily comprised of wood, straw and bamboo.

"Come in, Alex. What can I do for you?" General Sato Seechi asked as he bowed from the waist according to Maleezhun custom.

Returning the gesture, Alex walked into the command hut and complied with a hand gesture to seat himself. Alex paused until Seechi was seated as well before answering the question.

"Sir, I would like to take a permanent leave of absence," Alex replied without expression.

Seechi observed Alex's silence for a moment. The general had a great deal of respect for Alex. In spite of his challenging life, he had managed to rise above all difficulty to become a successful operative respected by all that he served with. Orphaned by a terrorist attack when his diplomat parents were killed during the beginning of the Global War, Alex was forced to grow up as a stranger in the country in which he was trapped with no family in the middle of the greatest war to scar the planet. A local elderly couple watched after Alex for a couple passes until he decided to begin training with Ghosts. At an age younger than any of the other Ghosts, Alex made his contributions to bring an end to the fighting. His youth, ambition, and success quickly pushed him up through the ranks earning him a position just under the general himself. General Seechi felt that he had almost taken on a father figure role for Alex.

"What has brought this on?" General Seechi asked.

"I wish to seek other means to improve my skills, General. The Ghosts are like my family, but I feel that I must move on. There is little more that I can learn here, and my desire to advance will not let me rest," Alex replied.

Growing up in a harsh challenging world, the quest for challenge had become engrained in Alex's nature. The fighting in the Martial Legion waned since the Global War. Even the Smart Wars required little attention from the Ghosts to maintain order. Other than the ongoing feuds with the local militias, the Ghosts' responsibilities provided nothing in the way of new challenges. Additionally, Seechi feared that the Ghosts' favor as the prime military force was diminishing in the eyes of the Martial Legion's faction leader. With political winds changing, Seechi doubted that power struggles were the kind of contest that Alex would want to stick around for.

Reluctant to reply, Seechi hesitated, "Are you sure about this?"

Alex nodded.

Conveying his disinterest with pursed lips, the general pondered his next response. "You're one of my best, Alex, not to mention the most decorated, but if this is something you have already set your mind to, then there is little I can do to stop you, so by all means your request is granted."

"Thank you, Sir," Alex replied as he rose from his seat.

Seechi halted him, and indicated for him to sit back down. "Where do you plan to go?"

With his typical reflective pause before speaking Alex replied, "I thought I might do some hunting. I have heard that the lizards in the sprawl are enormous, I mean like two marks tall. They ought to be more of a challenge than our last targets."

The general chuckled at Alex's sense of expressionless sarcasm that he had grown accustomed to. "The sprawl is a wasteland void of life, nothing more than barren sun-baked rock."

"Well, perhaps I'll just work on my tan," Alex replied with his usual straight face.

"The least I can do for one of my best operatives is to point you in the right direction. I have a list of known vectors across the globe, most of which live within the Martial Legion or the Commercial Empire, but there is one who I think might have the challenge you're looking for," Seechi said.

The faintest curiosity prompted Alex to run a hand through his neatly trimmed mustache and goatee, but he refrained and barely twitched his eyebrow. The change in facial expression with Alex could only be seen by a trained eye or by one who had known him for an extended period of time, and Sato Seechi met both qualifications.

Catching the slight interest, Seechi continued. "I don't know his exact whereabouts, but I know that he lives within the abandoned sector of the Windstonne Enclave. You may encounter a lot of resistance finding him considering that Windstonne is the Commercial Empire's most populous enclave, but I'm sure if you seek him, he will find you. He goes by the clashtag, The Enforcer."

Alex received the list as the general handed it to him with a nod before he continued, "I suppose it isn't a bad thing that you're getting out early, Alex. I hear rumors that the Emperor is showing more favor toward the Drakken. I know they aren't as trained, but they seem to consider themselves more expendable for the sake of dominating the military presence within the Martial Legion. I don't know what is to happen yet, only time will tell. Alex, best of luck to you," General Seechi stated as he stood and extended his hand toward Alex.

Following suit, Alex stood, and shook Seechi's hand, "Thank you again, Sir."

"Oh, and Alex, should you cross paths with that traitor, make you sure you give him my regards... from all of us," General Seechi added.

Alex required no coaxing to acknowledge the request related to a bitter memory branded into the hearts of most Ghosts. With a nod, Alex turned and walked out of the hut.

Dwelling Street Mission
Abandoned Sector, Windstonne Enclave
Commercial Empire, Northam Continent
Thread: actTgtPersp1.view

I found myself once again at the doorstep of the mysterious library. I couldn't make sense of how I ended up back there, yet there I was, not an imprint in sight. I double-checked to see if I was being watched, but there were no signs of life in the vicinity. Two men dashed from the library. I tried to run, but my legs wouldn't move. I attempted to yell for help, but my voice was caught in my throat. They charged, moving even faster. Before I could flinch, they were on the ground. I looked up and saw a phantom of a man who just kept staring, his eyes flashing behind those sunglasses. He disappeared. The attackers jumped up, taking their aggression out on me as they started swinging. My arms failed to respond as I tried to perform the most basic defensive maneuvers, but all I could do was succumb to the attack. I was about to become a bleeding pavement decoration.

"NOOooooooo!" I yelled, blacking out at the first impact.

I sat upright in my bed, tense, yet relieved that I was only having a nightmare, but I couldn't explain the deviation from actual events. Possessing no desire to contemplate the intricacies of dream theory so early in the morning, I fought to regain my senses from my jarring slumber. I heard voices in the hallway, but the commotion in my room prompted their owners to silence and retreat from outside my door. It sounded like one set of shoes stopped near the office, and the other kept going until reaching the exit and the range of my hearing.

While rubbing the drowsiness from my eyes, I felt something heavy on my feet. That something had been thrown on my bed while I was sleeping, the Criterion I lost the night before. I was puzzled at the strange reappearance. I didn't know how I lost the book to begin with, yet there it was at the foot of my bed.

A stiff knock on my door snapped me from my grogginess followed by a shiny forehead and receding brown hairline poking into the room. "C'mon, do you think you have special sleeping privileges these days or what? We've got work to do," Chuck said as he hurriedly retreated from the doorway.

"On my way," I mumbled.

Not only did I oversleep, but I also slept in my clothes from the night before. Jumping out of bed, I scrambled to find some clean threads. I disregarded the book on my bed, accepting that closer inspection would have to wait. I dashed down the hallway and out of the mission to catch up with the others who were already on their way to the first operation site for the day.

The sun continued to climb the horizon, taking the chill out of the air. I took a deep breath and inhaled the cool air into my lungs. I accelerated to a jog to catch up with the others, only to drop back to a brisk walk once I was a few paces behind my associates. My mind mulled over the logic of the last few arcs. I considered telling Div about being jumped should it suggest a danger to fellow mission workers by venturing too close to clan territory, but doubts quickly stifled the idea. My thoughts were so wrapped in confusion that I completely missed that the others had finally come to a stop in front of an apartment complex.

"Whoa, slow up, Fox," Div chuckled as I bumped into him. Towering at least a good six notches over me, he was hardly concerned with my lack of reflexes.

"Sorry, Div, I guess I'm not awake yet," I replied.

Div shook his head, laughing as he ran a hand through his short black hair, "No problem, a little spine strain ought to cure that. You and

Chuck can start on the fourth floor. We'll meet you guys up there once we get the utility elevator operational."

I nodded then took off for the stairwell, passing by the dumpster and carts that had been staged by the other workers. I heard Chuck's footsteps echoing down from one floor above. Reaching the fourth floor, I walked down the hallway to meet with Chuck who was already waiting for me at the door to our first project. After acknowledging my arrival with a sideways nod, Chuck lifted his foot, and kicked the door just below the doorknob. The aging wood offered little resistance as the door shot splinters from its frame and toppled inward.

Disconcerted, I looked at him, "A little aggressive today?"

"Fox, you've been around long enough. You know that this job requires a little adventure to stave off the insanity once in a while. Besides, we'll just fix the frame when we're done," Chuck said.

"Alright," I replied, conveying my disbelief in Chuck's intention to follow through on his claim.

When we entered the room, I observed an all too familiar scene in the abandoned enclave. Ratty furniture and personal effects scattered the apartment. Apparently vagrants had already been through the place, leaving drawers half open, and items strewn across the floor. Thick coats of dust mingled with the scent of animal waste, outraging the nostrils. I walked over to the window and pushed it open after feeling nauseated by the smell.

Our latest project let us off easy for once. It was far more common to contend with carrion or bird droppings thanks to broken windows that permitted any flying traveler to turn the lodgings into an avian toilet. Rotten food stores often contributed to the aroma as well. I plugged my nose as I attempted to find another window to open.

"Sheesh, Fox, it's not that bad. You should be getting used to this by now," Chuck wise cracked.

"You're crazy! Have you worked in so many dumps that you lost your sense of smell?" I replied, rolling my eyes.

"Possibly, but at least I don't have to smell your attitude, because most of the time, it stinks," Chuck quipped.

"Very funny," I replied without motivation to make a comeback.

Chuck always had a sharp wit about him, and I often enjoyed our debates throughout the work day. He moved to the abandon voluntarily from the rural plains with a desire to be closer to civilization even though he had reservations about moving into Core City itself, but his presence was welcome at the mission nevertheless. I found his insight on life to be thought-provoking.

At last, I felt my nausea begin to dissipate as fresh air circulated the room. With a boost of ambition, I began helping Chuck push intact furniture into the hallway, toward the utility elevator.

Académe Salvage Complex
Abandoned Sector, Windstonne Enclave
Commercial Empire, Northam Continent
Thread: sysObserver.cmd

Seclusion was the perfect companion to the local clan salvage operation. Isolated in the midst of a vacant subdivision, the defunct Rouster Educational Center served as an ideal base of operations for Académe. Its numerous rooms and spacious halls allowed Académe to stockpile any salvageable wares they found before Imperan pickup crews passed through to take them off Académe's hands. In return for services rendered, Académe received free roam privileges, as well as limited educational resources and supplies even though they preferred the latter in order to maintain their lair.

"What's the matter with you, boys. You're really sluggish today! Did you get roughed up or something last night?" Bull taunted as he tossed the courtball around his back to Burnout.

Trying to ignore Bull's trash talk, Jammer attempted to block the pass but failed.

"Why do you ask?" Sophomore replied as he guarded Burnout who was looking for a clear path to the closest funnel.

"One, because you look haggard, and two, because you've got as much game as a limp fish," Burnout mocked as the ball slipped through the funnel after a clean shot, in spite of Sophomore's defense.

Swipe and Nox sat on the bleachers, laughing hysterically at Sophomore's poor defense. Nox's high pitched laugh was enough to draw irritation out of Jammer. Sophomore passed the ball to Jammer who was at the top of the court. Then with a smirk, Jammer nodded for Sophomore to get open for a pass, but he had already read the real signal that Jammer was sending. As soon as the ball bounced from the floor after Jammer's pass, Sophomore sidestepped, and the ball bounced out of bounds and upward smacking Nox right in the face.

"You fishhead, what's the matter with you?" Nox yelled, standing up from the bleachers, ready to throw down. His face turned red with anger although the change was nigh indistinguishable from his ruddy complexion.

"Settle down, Nox, you know he's not worth it," Swipe said with a grin as she teasingly flipped her blonde hair over her shoulder.

After a few ticks of flailing his arms in protest, Nox finally returned to his seat on the bleachers. It was everyone else's turn to laugh as they noticed a huge dimpled ball impression developing on Nox's face. Not letting up on the instigation, Bull snapped his hand in a whipping motion with the accompanying sound effect. He pointed his finger at Nox and laughed before returning to the game.

Taking possession of the ball after Jammer's pass, Burnout decided to return to the matter at hand. He switched hands several times as he dribbled the ball in front of his body. Jammer took his turn to guard Burnout at the top of the court.

"So, what do you say, Jammer? I best you, you tell us what happened," Burnout said.

"Liquid," Jammer said as a smirk creased his face.

Bull took up position behind Jammer preventing him from following Burnout to the funnel, but Sophomore reacted quickly enough to match Burnout's jump shot. Sophomore swatted the ball and tipped it out of Burnout's hand toward Jammer who snatched the ball and ran to the top of the court, a formality in a small game with few players.

"Looks like we're no longer on the hook to tell you or Jocq anything," Jammer quipped as Burnout stepped up to defend the next play. Jammer faked to the left then sprinted to the right, dribbling the ball until Bull jumped to block his shot. Reading the block, Jammer slung the ball with a sharp pass to Sophomore who then jumped and launched the ball for a mid-range shot.

Unexpectedly, another hand rocketed over Sophomore's well placed shot and smacked the ball with authority. The downward force upset Sophomore's balance, sending him to the hardwood floor with a thud.

"WHAT ARE YOU DOING, JOCQ?" Bull yelled, angered at the clan leader's interference with the game.

"What weren't you guys going to tell me?" Jocq asked in a demanding tone. Jocq's six mark frame stood motionless as he watched Jammer help Sophomore to his feet. Everyone could tell that Jocq's arms rippled as he flexed them underneath his pullover jacket. Bull and Burnout walked over to the bleachers to grab their towels and wipe the sweat dripping from their brows. Sophomore carefully lifted himself off the floor and brushed the dirt off his backside. Jammer and Sophomore exchanged glances as Jocq eyed them suspiciously. The four spectators awaited the fireworks display as Jocq's face turned red with impatience.

"Everyone out!" Jocq snapped.

The four proceeded to exit the gymnasium as Sophomore and Jammer waited for Jocq to speak up again. Nox flipped a mocking hand gesture and a smirk, amused that the previous pranksters were now in trouble. Catching the motion out of the corner of his eye, Jammer simply responded with a glare.

"I'm waiting!" Jocq snapped again.

Sophomore folded his arms across his chest and then lifted a hand to rub his chin. Any marks from the previous night were barely visible amidst the splotchy regions from exertion that irregularly marked his otherwise pale skin.

"We were jumped," Sophomore muttered.

"I can't hear you," Jocq fumed.

"'We got jumped' he said. What's bent your verts into a knot? We were checking the library, just like you asked, when we found someone snooping around. We chased him out of the library, and then some fish…" Jammer retorted as his his voice dripped with sarcasm until Jocq cut him off.

"Whoa, whoa, whoa! You're telling me that you found someone in the library, and this didn't strike you as concern to tell me!" Jocq snorted, his anger more apparent than ever.

"Jocq, we know what your policy is, but this guy was a noodle. He was no trouble. We could have handled him, but some guy draped in a black cloak jumped us from nowhere. Plus, he knew how to fight," Sophomore piped up trying to calm Jocq down before the protruding vein across his forehead got any larger.

"And you have no idea who he was?" Jocq asked, lowering his rage a pinch.

"No shreds," Sophomore replied. "The person that we caught snooping looked rather curious, like he might have been from that local mission. Beyond that, there was nothing remarkable."

Jocq hesitated while his breath settled back to normal. "I hope you two realize that I have to answer to the Imperan authorities for everything that we find. We can't afford mistakes, especially when it involves people snooping around a hot zone like that library. If Jenkins catches word of this, our salvage privileges will be revoked! Now that's the last time I send you two alone. Get to work on the Hyper Lynx and find that carp. I'll send out the others to scour the area later," Jocq said, twisting about to exit the gymnasium, leaving Sophomore and Jammer on their own to recover from the verbal lashing.

Breckins Lodging Complex
Abandoned Sector, Windstonne Enclave
Commercial Empire, Northam Continent
Thread: actTgtPersp1.view

The cabinet groaned its protest as its corners dragged across the carpet. With one final shove, I pushed the storage unit into the utility elevator. I lifted my forearm to wipe the excess sweat from my face. All of the viable scrap metal from the last three apartments had already been relocated. I felt that it was time to let the team on the lower level do the lifting.

"Let's go, noodleback. It's not break time," Chuck said.

"It is on my sungauge," I replied, leaning up against the filing cabinet to catch my breath.

"Getting pretty soft aren't ya?" Chuck replied as he punched my arm.

"Yep, guess so!" I said as I turned to stare out the window at the end of the hallway.

"The whole memory thing is still bothering you isn't it?" Chuck asked.

I nodded. "I can't shake the feeling that I am meant to do something more than just participate in the Hardware Relocation Program. If I know who I am, I'd have a better sense of direction."

"Let me ask you something, Aaron…" Chuck continued as we headed for the next apartment to shuffle more furniture in the warm, stagnant air. "Do you think that your collective experiences determine your identity or that your identity defines your experiences?"

"Huh?" I muttered with a raised eyebrow. "You totally lost me on that one."

"Even though you cannot remember your past, will you let that hold you back from doing something of substance of your choosing?" Chuck expounded.

Flustered by my inability to answer many of Chuck's philosophical questions, I looked for a quick escape to change the subject. My eyes scanned the room until I found a target.

"Oh, wow!" I gasped. "An intact picture tube emcast, I haven't seen one of these in ages," I said, walking over to the wood table supporting the large appliance with a glass surface encased in a hardmelt shell.

"Yeah, and?" Chuck retorted, not easily amused.

"Even old, obsolete technology can tell stories about how it etched its influence on history. Each iteration of technology supports that which follows," I replied, walking over to the bulky predecessor of our much thinner noptic screens.

"Yeah, yeah, whatever, Fox," Chuck replied sarcastically with a wave of his hand. "I got your building blocks right here," he said, scooping up the ancient media caster, walking it to the open window and tossing into the air with a heave.

I just stared with my jaw gaping in disbelief at his actions. "How could you just do that?" I stammered, as I waited for the sound of the device's impact with the sidewalk four decks below.

Even from our elevated position, I could hear the concussion of shattering hardmelt and glass spraying into the air, followed by the jingle of countless shards collectively sprinkling the ground. I soon snapped from my confusion as I heard Div yell at the top of his lungs from the street below. "CUT IT OUT, CHUCK!"

Chuck shrugged his shoulders with a "Hmph" as he attempted to stifle a laugh.

I notched my way toward the window, hoping to peek out without becoming the accused. Squinting, I noticed a greater irony. No more than a few boots from Chuck's crash site lay a pile of ancient emcasts and tech monitors from other apartments that other workers had already stacked into a small wall. He wasn't joking about building blocks.

"Nice try," Chuck said, trying to draw me back to his question. "You're not evading the topic so easily."

With a sigh I went back to work and attempted to clear my brain of its perpetual fog so that I could fabricate an answer capable of putting Chuck's persistence to rest.

Dwelling Street Mission
Abandoned Sector, Windstonne Enclave
Commercial Empire, Northam Continent
Thread: actTgtPersp1.view

The setting sun cast various colors across the sky transitioning from blue to purple, red, and orange. The calming colors resonated with the relief that I felt knowing that another day's hard work was at an end. On the short hike back to the mission, my mind drifted toward thoughts of a shower, clean threads, and possibly a digestive tablet to counter the intermittent nausea that I couldn't escape as long as the day's odors remained attached to my clothes.

After a prompt cleanup, I weighed the outcome of turning in early for the evening. Flopping onto my bed, I was quickly reminded of the previous night's adventure, as my leg landed on the Criterion. It just happened to smack the bruise that had formed on my shin since the initial discovery. Rolling over, I picked up the book, and looked at it. There was nothing remarkable about the plain cover or its shiny trimmed pages. I moved my fingers across its surface again to watch the intriguing title transition as it appeared and faded once again. Reminded of my curiosity from before, I tried to flip through the pages. Strangely, only some pages were accessible while others were sealed tight without explanation. Within the pages that I could read, I detected a large amount of what appeared to be antiquated dialect or philosophical prose. Disinterested, I was about to set the book down when my eyes landed on a set of words more than halfway through, *Narrow is the gate and difficult is the way leading to life, there are few who find it.* Spotting the complete set of words that led to my adventure in the first place left me with a stupefied expression. If I hadn't already been sitting down, I certainly would have been knocked on my backside.

I was so caught off guard that I didn't notice the knock on my door. As someone's fist rapped on the door a second time, albeit in a customary fashion, I snapped back to attention. Chuck's head at last poked through the doorway to make sure I was present. "Hey! The game is on. Let's go!"

"Okay," I replied, tucking my prize behind me so that it didn't draw any suspicion. I wasn't interested in the evening's allcourt lineup, but I didn't feel like explaining my absence either.

"What's the score?" I asked as I joined Chuck and the other guys taking up space in the padded chairs circled about the wide based emcast.

"152-114, in favor of Fusion," Steve, our resident sports enthusiast, replied.

With the game barely into its second quarter, the grimace covering my face did little to hide my disinterest. "I can't stand that team. They haven't had anyone unmodified on their roster in over a pass. Every single player has organech implants of one kind or another."

"And that's a bad thing?" Another worker chimed in.

"Well, I could play for that team and jump six marks into the air too if I had those modifications. Just listen to those commentators. They're trying to sell the hype, suggesting that anyone can have that dream when in reality only those in the Commercial Empire's good graces have access to those resources," I said.

"Fox, shut up! You think too much," Steve replied, clearly annoyed that I was the soggy blanket to his evening festivities.

"Contrary to some opinions... some say that I don't think enough," I muttered, casting a sarcastic glance in Chuck's direction.

Sinking back into the lounge chair, my mind gradually tuned out the game. I was about to fall asleep when I realized that the game was over due to complaints coming from those who had hoped for a different victor.

"Feed 5," muttered one who was sorely displeased with the game and eager to watch a different meca.

My heavy eyelids shifted slightly at the change of translucent colors on the noptic screen as the image morphed from allcourt victory speeches to an enclave skyline. I easily recognized the meca as a classic fightcast from its pre-war production style. The meca was certainly a testament to the resources and creativity of a bygone era compared to the over endorsed drudgery by current Imperan standards. Since I'd seen the tournament meca on more than one occasion, I normally would have tuned out the visuals, but instead it captured my attention with renewed interest. I shifted my weight in the chair to prevent falling asleep.

While I felt that I had seen similar plots a thousand times, the meca's composition intrigued me. Like usual, the common struggle boiled down to the hero and villain exchanging trivial banter only to result in the villain gaining the upper hand until the underdog hero summoned an inner strength to exploit the villain's weakness. As I watched the adversaries exchange blows repeatedly, a vague familiarity grew in my mind. Even though I couldn't help comparing the exchange to the previous night's events, I felt that there was something more to the struggle which I found relatable. The very nature of the struggle embodied my own frustration with an ever persistent villain in the form of my personal quest for meaning.

Nearly jumping from my chair, I headed for my room without revisiting the familiar outcome. The abrupt motion almost startled my associates.

"Where are you off to in such a hurry?" Chuck asked.

"I'm going to bed," I replied with more enthusiasm than a fatigue cover story suggested. I was certain that those watching the meca returned awkward looks, but I didn't turn around to verify. With sharp focus, I went to my room, shut the door, turned off the light, and waited.

Several arcs passed before the last of the late-nighters turned in. Once silence had become the norm, I peeked out of my room. Seeing no more lights, I grabbed the book from my bed and shoved it into my back pocket, hoping not to lose it a second time. I wasn't fully cognizant of the book's significance in my recent troubles, but I figured I should take it along rather than invite more trouble by leaving it in the open. Certain that my path was clear, I slipped down the hallway, haphazardly attempting to exercise my non-existent skills in the way of stealth.

Upon reaching open air beyond the front door to the Dwelling Street Mission, I bolted for the alley that caught my interest the night before. Trying to remember the path on the fly, I dashed through the dark side streets. Memories of the flight from the attackers mixed with the rush brought on by adrenaline. The mixture brought on a sense of caution and excitement, but I was determined to give in to the latter. I wanted answers.

After stumbling over some trash in the alley, I found myself in the pale moonlight much like the night before. I walked cautiously toward the library looking in every direction for adversaries. I crept up the steps to the library and approached the entryway, but I once more looked around to make sure that I wasn't watched. Turning back to the door, I placed my hand upon the smooth cold glass, but what I heard caused my heart to leap into my throat and turn my spine into ice.

"You have returned!" Said a low booming voice from directly behind me.

I whirled around to see the same cloaked figure who defended me the night before sitting on the duracrete banister of the library walkway. Ticks ago, there was no one there, yet there he was. Consciously, I tried forcing myself to calm down, but my mind struggled with ordering my lungs and heart to decelerate their pounding in my chest.

With all the energy that I could muster over my panic, I replied. "WHY did you do that?!"

Lifting his hands to remove the hood of his cloak, the man revealed the familiar bandanna and sunglasses. As if oblivious to my question, he just continued his idle expression. Looking to the streets, he paused to verify that nobody was interested in a chase. As he did, I once again noticed the bizarre flash of color behind his shades.

As my breathing settled, I took a step back, and leaned against the library doors. Sensing no immediate threat, I folded my arms across my chest and awaited a reply.

"Why are you here?" The stranger asked.

"Perhaps, I should ask you," I replied sarcastically.

"Perhaps," the stranger mused, "But would it accomplish anything? I know why I am here. Do you?"

Caught off guard, I hesitated. The eerie look-alike already had a knack for asking ambiguous questions.

"Here you stand in the dead of night on the doorstep to a building which, in its former glory, was designed to educate. It would lead one to believe you are here to look for knowledge. Knowledge and learning require input, but perhaps you do not know the correct questions to ask," the figure said in an inquisitive tone.

I considered pulling the Criterion out of my pocket to inquire of its origin, but I refrained. I squinted trying to glean any manner of deception on the mystery man's face, but the darkness hid all expression that might reveal a clue.

Already, I felt like he was testing me. I knew that any witty response that I could muster would only come across as bumbling irrelevance. I wasn't about to explain my life story to a complete stranger in order to define my case, so I had to think quickly about how I best get to the point. I knew nothing about this person. My only impromptu solution was to parse his words directed at my attackers during the previous night's scuffle.

"I'm here to understand the truth," I said, hoping to put a little stiffness back into my spine. "In particular, to understand truth about my life," I added after thinking about the text that I read in the Criterion.

I had no reason to expect that this stranger had any answers for me, but since I witnessed his deft resolution of Académe's attacks, I knew that I had nothing to lose by being honest. Especially since I knew that I was completely defenseless against such combat skills previously demonstrated.

With a head tilt and the faintest sign of being impressed, he nodded. "Follow me."

An uncertainty crept up from within. I didn't know if the invitation warranted cause for alarm, but clearly my brain sent a signal to lock my legs in place. Alternatively, I told myself that if I risked nothing, I would learn nothing. Taking my earlier discussion with Chuck to heart, I accepted that I possessed neither a great sense of purpose, nor a meaningful identity, so I really had nothing to lose. The internal conflict resolved in a matter of ticks, so I shook the paralysis from my legs and followed.

3 – High Tension – 3

Oszwick Enterprises
Core City Fringe, Windstonne Enclave
Commercial Empire, Northam Continent
Thread: sysObserver.cmd

Konrad Oszwick sat idly in his posh office, his back to the windows showcasing the night sky. He absent-mindedly rubbed his bald head while reviewing the recent company sales reports. Until recently, Oszwick Enterprises had only succeeded in dominating the volatile markets in the akcellerrant sector by pushing out competitors. Their mobile weaponry platform was finally making great strides with the same strategy. Monopolizing whole sectors wasn't without its benefits, as the latest profits reflected. A smile crept across Oszwick's lips, expressing his approval of the latest margins. As he set the slate down on his desk, a similar thud accompanied the noise by way of a knock on his office door.

"Come in," Oszwick said.

A familiar figure sporting a black suit entered and placed a new slate on Oszwick's desk. Lucient stood silently, appearing more stiff than the suit coat that he was wearing over his orange shirt, as he waited for the chief executive to view the latest report.

Sensing that Lucient wasn't going to exit without acknowledgement, Oszwick reluctantly picked up the slate and scanned the data. After a few taps on the translucent screen, Oszwick perused the key findings. Much of the content was operational notes, something that Lucient was prone to overuse.

"Very good, Lucient," Oszwick replied, setting the slate down, indicating that he had no desire to read the data in full. "I'll look forward to your findings on the exports next time."

Oszwick stared down his operations manager whose pasty skin always contrasted his thin red hair. He expected Lucient to take his leave, but when he remained, Oszwick suspected that there was more to discuss. While he appreciated his subordinates being forthright, he always suspected a deeper ambition lurking behind Lucient's mannerisms that he often needed to keep in check. "Is there something more, Lucient?"

"Mr. Oszwick, Sir, we have already established operations within the Uniod Branch, Martial Legion and the Oceanic Outpost, but market penetration in the Ocean Outpost has been problematic. Sales have been extremely low," Lucient rattled with all the fervor of someone getting caught asleep on the job.

Oszwick leaned back in his chair and contemplated before replying in his smooth voice that was capable of coaxing oranges from an apple tree. "No matter. Inform the staff that their efforts will not go unnoticed. I would like you to personally oversee marketing in the Oceanic Outpost."

Lucient nodded in agreement and waited to be dismissed.

"Is there anything else?" Oszwick asked, growing weary of Lucient's persistence.

Lucient shook his head and proceeded toward the door.

"Oh, Lucient," Oszwick replied in his suave voice that hid the daggers within, "If you mess this up, there is no operation in existence that will salvage that fashion of yours."

Lucient was quickly reminded of the scars still visible on the sides of his neck from treatments required to normalize his complexion. He shifted his weight uncomfortably as he turned to see Mr. Oszwick with the most nefarious grin spread across his face. Oszwick had the power to influence the strongest of minds, Lucient was no exception. With a quick turn, Lucient hung his head and exited the office of the company's founder.

Industrial District
Abandoned Sector, Windstonne Enclave
Commercial Empire, Northam Continent
Thread: actTgtPersp1.view

The journey through the abandoned sector threaded a maze of side streets, alleys and complexes. I did my best to note key landmarks, but it proved difficult in the moonlight. The brisk pace didn't leave much room for conversation, but when my legs started suggesting fatigue I decided that it was time to inquire distance from our destination, "How mu-"

"We're here," my hooded guide interjected.

"Ok," I said, surprised at the alteration in pace.

Before I could contemplate some level of premonition on his part, I had my attention stolen by the large clearing ahead. As we cleared a crumbling dartway overpass, moonlight illuminated an expansive industrial complex, cold and silent. On my right was an empty parking structure, adjacent to a ramp connecting to the overpass. On my left, was a multi-deck warehouse with a small business complex attached to the front. Between us and the warehouse lay a field of degraded duracrete suggesting a high business occupancy before the wars. As we approached the warehouse, I thought I spotted faint traces of light seeping from the narrow windows lining the top of its walls. The place was well camouflaged because the surroundings certainly looked desolate otherwise.

I followed my guide into the office of the grungy building. Most of the windows were cracked, boarded or extensively caked with grime. Another trace of light from the hallway ahead offered enough visibility to see the vacant half walled offices, toppled desks, chairs, dust and cobwebs littering the premises. I caught myself dragging my feet to observe the surroundings. Since I had yet to reassemble my own past, I still found myself intrigued with other snapshots of the past preserved in time. Normally, I would have suspected that I was walking into a suitable place to bury a dead body, but given the vast geography of the abandoned sector, there was no need to travel so far to hide evidence.

Suspecting that I was being observed and prompted to keep up, I quickened my pace as we entered a hallway with dim but functional lights barely revealing the worn paint and brick walls. After a couple of similar stretches, we reached another hallway less dismal than the others. Crates, pallets and supplies lined the walls in between supports clearly modernized in contrast to the otherwise aged facility.

My host finally stopped at a large metal door which I assumed led into the warehouse. He placed his hand on a digital pad adjacent to the door. A light panned from top to bottom before he lifted his hand to input a series of taps. Once the sequence was complete, a light yet synthetic voice responded, "Enforcer, Accepted."

"Place your hand on the pad," my host said without any traceable emotion.

I placed my hand on the pad as instructed and a warm light performed a similar scan.

"Welcome, Mr. Fox," the digital voice said from a speaker somewhere overhead.

I raised an eyebrow with curiosity as I looked about for the speaker until I was distracted by the clicking mechanisms within the door. I heard the lock release. I motioned to open the door, but I was halted by the Enforcer's arm as he placed his palm on the door frame.

"Not tonight," he said. "It's been a long night. You will need a fresh start for your training in the morning."

"Training?" I asked, obviously still aloof to my purpose on the journey.

My host replied with nothing more than a nod. "Can you remember your way back to the mission?" He asked once my expression suggested that I got the hint.

The Enforcer's question struck a nerve, prompting more questions, but the requirement of hiking back home in the dark assumed priority for my attention. I simply replied with a nod.

"Good. I'll see you back here, bright and early in the morning," the Enforcer said. With a turn he walked through the door and locked it behind him, leaving me alone in the dimly lit hallway.

"I think it's going to be a short night," I said to myself, heeding the new wrinkle of having to return at such an early arc.

My pressing need for sleep prompted me to hurry back into the night. At least I would have plenty of thoughts to keep me awake. I was certainly put on edge about how my host not only knew my name, but also knew that I was staying at the mission. Such thoughts should have compelled me to act more cautiously, yet at the same time I felt no sense of danger which cast normal judgement to the wind. With the cold air and the desire to crash overruling any other conflicting ideas, I targeted the shortest path that I could find back to the mission.

Monk Training Facility
Core City Fringe, Windstonne Enclave
Commercial Empire, Northam Continent
Thread: sysObserver.cmd

The industrial shop turned training hall, tucked away from the direct influence of Windstonne, was quiet with exception of those training on the floor below. Even though the location was great for escaping prying faction eyes, Tiger would have welcomed any manner of distraction. He could have passed for a shadow, dressed in his all-black attire as he paced about the observation floor while reflecting on the meager payout of the Monks' last contract. Business owners on the border of Westcrest were having trouble with the squatters. Given the lack of faction oversight, contracting freelance groups like the Monks was a regular practice. The Monks had been hired to resolve the squatter situation, and resolve it they did.

While Tiger didn't perceive commanding the Monks' loyalty to be difficult on a daily basis, reporting lackluster earnings from faulty contractors would put his command to the test. Splitting an already small payoff seven ways wasn't likely to go over well. Sure, he could conjure up a story about contractors swindling them, potentially giving rise to a plot for revenge, but typically such operations were bad for reputation, not to mention costly. Plus, if Monks were injured during a contract, Tiger could simply demand compensation, but if injury occurred due to his miscalculation of an operation, there would be no adequate compensation that could repair damaged loyalty.

Eventually, Panther joined the clan leader on the observation floor amidst the stuffy air which created a miserable heat within the weapon clad walls. Panther's steps were soft against the woven mat, but he stopped short when he noticed that Tiger bore an aggravated expression. Panther rubbed the tips of his fingers against the black knit cap on his head while contemplating if he should linger or return to training with his associates.

"What is it, Panther?" Tiger asked.

"You've been more irritable than usual, ever since we returned from the border. Is everything okay?" Panther asked with concern.

Nodding Tiger replied with a grim face, "It would seem that our hosts were less than generous with their compensation. Unfortunately, that will result in less berry to go around."

"Perhaps it's time that we seek out the dimp dolers of more lucrative contracts," Panther stated.

"And what do you suggest?" Tiger asked, looking up from the floor.

"To up the stakes, we must up the risk," Panther stated confidently.

"We will not undertake suicide missions for faction leaders just so they can settle territory disputes without getting their hands dirty," Tiger replied adamantly.

"But, we have little choice..." Panther replied, but he stopped short as he watched Tiger direct his focus to the training floor. A loud thud followed by a yell of pain prompted Panther to look as well.

With a snarl, Tiger smashed his fist into a wood pillar, completely disregarding the punching bag that was next to it. The shock vibration was enough to cause the metallic weapons on the wall to rattle in protest. As he walked onto the main training floor, anger flooded across his face.

"Dramitol, Snake, how many times do I have to tell you? Save it for the field!" Tiger growled, pushing the idle Monk out of the way.

Monkey lay on the floor clutching his shoulder, writhing in pain. He gritted his teeth to avoid yelling, but there was no hiding it in his face.

"Mantis, get in here!" Tiger yelled.

Ticks later, the remaining clan members dashed into the training room. Mantis, the Monks' most competent mender, immediately knelt down as she examined the situation.

"His shoulder is dislocated! Hold him still," Mantis snapped as she brushed her short blond braids away from her face.

Tiger and Panther both attempted to restrain Monkey as Mantis braced herself to reset the injured shoulder. With a loud pop and a yell from the added pain, the joint snapped back into its proper position. Crane and Dragon both cringed as they looked on from the edge of the training floor.

Once Monkey started breathing normally, Mantis and Panther helped him to his feet and led him to a more suitable area to rest. Tiger stood from the floor and stared Snake right in the eyes.

"What were you thinking?" Tiger snapped.

"Fish didn't block," Snake replied innocently. "Can't improve without taking a few hits."

"I don't care! Any more showboating like that, and you're history. I mean it, Snake!" Tiger raged.

Lowering his head, Snake glared at the floor before taking his leave. While passing through his clan allies, Dragon shouldered Snake in defiance. Without a word, Snake exited the training room.

Angered, Tiger's eyes followed Snake out the door. Tiger was well aware of the extreme emphasis that some organizations put on physical training, but he was convinced that in the postwar free-for-all there was another element that required conditioning to survive, that of the mind. He never went soft on his allies, but he knew that in order to fight at peak performance there needed to be trust. It's what would separate the Monks from the countless, misguided clans saturating the enclaves.

Tiger had carefully identified the strengths of each ally, but none of them had a weakness quite as obvious as Snake. While his tenacity and knack for stealth were unmatched, his drive for conquest often clashed with the unity of the clan. Generally a diverse group, the Monks maximized their different perspectives, so Tiger didn't think it odd to include the Maleezhun transplant who wanted to take part in the Monks' contracts. After occasional mishaps, Tiger was starting to second guess his judgement.

On account of the new distraction involving Snake, Tiger began pacing again, this time in the center of the training floor. He should have taken care not to look so distraught in front of his associates, but he seemed oblivious to their concern.

After seeing to Monkey's recovery, Panther returned to the training floor and stood by Crane and Dragon who looked on with mild concern. Panther waited for the ideal time to interrupt, but he was certain that it would only invite more aggravation. Before that time arrived, a ping sounded from the sonair in the office adjacent to the training floor. Tiger only looked up briefly as he watched Panther exit the room to answer the sonair. So lost in thought, Tiger didn't realize that Panther's absence had been long enough for a full conversation.

"Sir," Panther said, treading carefully, knowing that the information he had just received went against Tiger's vision for the clan.

"What is it?" Tiger grumbled.

"It's a message directly from Imperan administration. They are requesting a meeting with you," Panther said, hoping to hide his curiosity.

Tiger halted his pacing as he flexed his forearms which he kept squarely behind his back. He didn't like getting involved with faction affairs, but it was time to start paying the Monks their due. If new methods kept the Monks on top, he would at least test the nature of the opportunity.

Dwelling Street Mission
Abandoned Sector, Windstonne Enclave
Commercial Empire, Northam Continent
Thread: actTgtPersp1.view

Sunlight softly filtered through the windows to my quarters, revealing their need for a good dusting. I blinked several times as my eyes slowly adjusted to the incoming light. I sat upright in my bed and swung my legs over the side, intending to get a quick start to the morning, but my legs stiffened in protest to the previous night's maze run through the abandon. Quickly reminded of my prior commitment, I hurried to shower, dress, and leave the mission before morning rituals commenced. I peeked out the doorway and dashed down the hall, hoping that no one was up. Tarees and Div were early risers and they were the last individuals that I wanted to confront so early about skipping out on work.

Once outside, the fresh morning air sent a jolt of energy to my lungs. I hoped to will additional energy into my legs, but there was no minimizing the soreness that caused me to walk abnormally. I stretched a bit to loosen my muscles, but I figured that there was no substitution for motion until I felt limber enough to work up to a run.

Finally accelerating to a casual jog, I glanced at every building along my path in hopes of spotting landmarks that would trigger my memory. I hesitated on several occasions in the midst of intersections to gather my bearings until some peeling billboard or overwhelming stench from a trash heap rekindled memories of the last night's ordeal.

As I spotted the familiar overpass, I finished my search in short order. In broad daylight, it was even more impressive to witness the strategic advantage of the Enforcer's location choice. With many industrial structures as far as the eye could see, there was no way to find relevance within the otherwise lifeless complex. Even after passes of decay, a faint acrid chemical smell still lingered in the air dissuading travelers from remaining without a good reason.

Eager to finally discover the meaning behind my return to such a remote location, I made my way toward the warehouse entrance. I noticed that recent events had branded a sense of paranoia into me as I casually looked over my shoulder, half expecting crazed attackers or mysterious phantoms to start chasing me.

As the musty air in the dilapidated office hit me full force, I second guessed my decision. Most of the lights were off, leaving only the ceiling mounted emergency lights and their faint red hue to guide my path. I suspected that I had found the correct hallway with the large metallic door. If it wasn't for the tapper's faint lighting, I would have smacked my nose and toes on the door itself.

I placed my hand on the security tapper, and watched the sensor scan my hand. Once it finished, a digitized recording greeted me, "Welcome, Mr. Fox."

The locking mechanism tumblers rattled about inside the door. With a loud click the mechanism completed its circuit, and I pressed on the handle to open the door. Anxious of what awaited me, I opened the door slowly.

The warehouse was dim, but the sunlight flowed generously through the windows which lined the upper walls spanning the vast length of the warehouse. The place appeared to be an old multi-purpose storage and manufacturing plant. Large machines lined the walls at irregular intervals. Inoperable robotic arms dangled from iron girders while drop lights and an assortment of chains hung from the airbridges and support beams.

"Welcome to the Vanguard Warehouse, Mr. Fox," a booming voice said from overhead.

I turned to see the Enforcer standing on the floor above while leaning against the railing. I could see little of the next floor, but from my position it was apparently open and overlooked the rest of the warehouse.

The Enforcer disappeared from his perch soon after. His footsteps drifted away until I heard the metal clang of steps heading down a flight of stairs. Ticks later, he stood in front of me and extended his hand.

"I do believe it's a good time for a proper introduction. I'm Mac Conner. I'm glad that you found your way back," Mac said as I shook his hand, his demeanor far less somber than our previous encounters.

I nodded in response. "Apparently you already know who I am," I said trying my best not to stare, but with better lighting it proved difficult to not notice our visual similarities. I couldn't see much of his hair considering that it was tucked under the bandanna, but beside a thinner face, a few passes in age difference and the occasional battle scar, I felt like I was looking into a mirror.

I wanted Mac to explain everything, but internal senses distracted me as I sensed that there was still more life in the warehouse. Looking about to discover any spectators, my initial consternation waned as I took in my new surroundings.

"What is this place?" I asked in curiosity, hoping that low level questions might invite more conversation.

Mac remained silent while I looked around the premises. It felt like he was participating in a game, as if he was waiting for me to notice something specific. Suspecting something irregular, my eyes finally locked onto such an object. Several pillars didn't match the rest of the warehouse's structure. There were four of them, each having a wider base than necessary resembling large claws. My eyes traced the plate covered pillars toward the ceiling. Instead of a linear structure, each had an angular joint in the center that connected with a giant, bloated mass of metal.

Once I realized the nature of the structure, my jaw dropped. The supports that I was seeing were not pillars, but four large mechanical legs supporting an armored shell of a body. I craned my neck to ensure that my imagination was not playing tricks on my eyes. I had to step backward to view the full height of the monstrosity which was partially obscured by the airbridges overhead. The base of the metal body was at least four decks high with its arched upperside much higher than that. On one end of the body, an angular lizard-like head extended from a short layered neck. Even though I couldn't believe my eyes, I at least understood why Mac had chosen an industrial complex for a base, it held plenty of resources to build and hide things likely off the list of approved Imperan vehicles.

Nearly losing my balance from leaning my head further back than my neck would allow, I shook my head, but before taking my eyes off the mechanical rig, I spotted an insignia on what I guessed was its shoulder, reading JB4015. Just seeing the number caused a wave of familiarity to crash over me as if I had seen something like this before. I had seen plenty of future-war meca's during leisure time at the mission and its design strongly resembled a unit from a culturally popular space opera.

While I pondered the familiar sight, a strange whisper raced through my mind. *His force is in the center of his body, his bones are tubes of bronze, his limbs like bars of iron...* The voice traveled on the wind like the one that I heard the previous night when I found the alley leading to the library.

I looked around, but no one was to be seen other than Mac who looked at me strangely after seeing the disoriented look on my face. "What's wrong?" He asked.

"Nothing," I replied. I shook my head again, thinking that I might need a brainscan after all. "Is it just me, or do you have a razerjack in you garage?" I stuttered as I stared again at the metal sauropod. "I've seen one of those before, but it was in a meca. That thing can't be real!"

"No? You can find anything on the Hyper Lynx these days, even schematics for fictional vehicles," Mac replied.

"But still... How did you build that thing?" I asked, turning to look for reaction clues.

Mac didn't hesitate to explain, "Oh, it was quite simple really, the Behemoth only took a little help from..."

"From his mechanic," a burly individual, marginally taller than Mac said, finishing the sentence as he approached us.

"Lennox Johnson," the individual said, extending his hand.

"Aaron Fox," I replied. I squinted at Lennox for a moment before shaking his hand. I was curious to see if he found it odd that my appearance was similar to Mac's, but if he did, there was no indication.

"Torque, is a vehicle and weapons specialist as well as quite the tenacious vector," Mac said.

"Yeah, Mac would be walking everywhere if it wasn't for me," Lennox replied as he ran a grease smeared hand through his brown spiky hair with blonde highlights.

"That is true. I'll fight anyone, jack any terminal, decipher any datastack, but don't ask me to build anything from scratch," Mac said with a smile.

"Mac said that we'd be having company. Are you a vector?" Lennox asked, wiping the remaining grease on his black cargo pants.

"Uhhhh, not to my knowledge," I answered slowly as if responding to a foreign language. Lennox simply cast me a strange look.

"Well, I have to get back to work. I'll show you my other masterpieces later," Lennox said. Then, with a wink, he turned and walked toward the back of the warehouse. He reminded me of some athletes that I had seen interviewed on the sports mecas just waiting to get their time in the spotlight.

"So, is it just the two of you running all of this?" I asked.

"Come," Mac said as he turned and led me toward the staircase leading to the second floor.

"So far," Mac replied. "Along with Maxwell, of course."

"Maxwell?" I asked.

"Mmm hmm," Mac nodded. "You'll meet him shortly."

I paused as we reached the wide expansive room that opened up on the second floor. What may have once been an observation deck had been converted into a training facility. Punching bags hung from girders near the back wall while weapons and lockers lined the wall on my right. On the left, repurposed managerial offices looked like makeshift living quarters with the one closest to the railing resembling a galley. At a glance, the place looked like it was home to renegades since it lacked the tidy appearance that I had grown accustomed to at the mission.

"Please, have a seat," Mac said, gesturing to a simple table and chairs adjacent to the railing that overlooked the warehouse below. I noticed an archaic folding data terminal with cables running to a noptic display on the table. I took a glance at it as I pulled out one of the chairs and sat down.

"You have advanced technology and an impressive workshop, but even with the resources at hand, you still operate with that piece of junk?" I asked sarcastically.

"Oh, that. Sure, that flatjack is outdated, but that makes it harder to find on the Lynx. Most would-be datajackers don't take much interest in old stuff these days. Plus, it doesn't have any modern wetware inputs making it a waste of time for anyone to access remotely," Mac replied.

"Hey, who's flackin' my handiwork?" Said a squeaky digitized voice.

I quickly looked around the room, but saw no one other than Mac who was staring into the warehouse. Seeing no one, I turned to him with a sly grin. "Oh, I get it, you've got more people here with those invisible things that you're not telling me about."

A chuckle emitted from the squeaky voice again, this time sounding like it was coming from right next to me. Staring down at the table, I watched a small rodent walk out from behind the terminal. "Nah, I'm just small, not invisible," the thing replied before turning to look at Mac, "... and don't think I didn't hear the short joke earlier."

"Is this another one of your informatic gadgets?" I asked, not taking my eyes off the rodent.

"I'm a hamster, not a guinea pig, Buster, and don't you forget it!" said the hamster as he sat on his haunches and pointed a foreleg at me. "Mac, who's this squawkjaw?"

"Aaron Fox, meet Maxwell. He has a collar which synthesizes vibrations from his voice box into audible Imperan," Mac said.

"Interesting," I mused. Maxwell was mostly white with splotchy patches of brown fur. A black and gray collar spanned his neck while a couple of similarly colored gadgets covered the base of his front legs like bracelets.

Mac spent a few clicks entertaining my questions on Vanguard's origins and daily operations, but eventually the conversation trailed off at this suggestion of more pressing matters.

"Lennox, are you about ready for a break?" Mac yelled toward the back of the warehouse.

The clang of dropping tools rang in my ears as Mac asked, "Well, are you ready to start training?"

"Training? So soon?" I asked.

"It's never too early for training," Mac replied, walking over to a box to dig out some sparring equipment.

Several clicks later, Lennox made his way up the stairs. He disappeared into one of the rooms adjacent to the training floor and reappeared moments later wearing loose pants and a sleeveless shirt.

"Go easy on him," Mac said just out of ear shot. "I'm off to run the usual routes. I'll be back later."

Mac and Lennox exchanged a few words before I watched Mac leave the floor and disappear into the warehouse. I heard an engine rev, then fade into the distance as a black utility mox roared out of a loading bay door.

Turning my attention back to the matter at hand, Lennox tossed me a pair of sparring gloves and kicks. "There are training pants in the room down on the end. Gear up," Lennox said as he slid one of the protective guards over his bare foot.

Outer Core Dartway
Abandoned Sector, Windstonne Enclave
Commercial Empire, Northam Continent
Thread: sysObserver.cmd

Tires squealed as the Fire Ant rounded the street corner of the next lifeless parcel. Mac often patrolled various districts in the abandon. There usually wasn't much to see, but on occasion he would take different streets in hopes of spotting a salvageworthy business or two.

Slamming the shifter into the next gear, Mac scanned the empty streets as structures blurred past him. He hadn't driven through the area surrounding the Dwelling Street Mission in a while. As part of the Interlace, Mac felt obligated to keep a lookout on behalf of other members in the area.

During the drive, Mac periodically spotted locals milling about near entrances to housing complexes. The noise of a combustion engine often generated mixed reactions from the scattered inhabitants. Some locals feared the bulky units often used by the heavy hand of Imperan forces, yet others would look on with curiosity. While the Fire Ant's black paint job was ideal for night operations, there was no hiding the detailed red and blue flames covering its front fenders. The insignia typically calmed fears once locals realized that it had no relationship to Imperan transportation, but that didn't stop the noisy mox from drawing a lot of attention in the middle of the day. Combustion vehicles were a rarity since most modern vehicles operated on highly regulated rechargeable cells exclusive to Commercial Empire power stations, a costly process which Mac preferred to avoid. The habits of the wealthy and compliant were easily bypassed in the abandoned sector.

Given the destruction of wars past, it wasn't difficult for Frank Jenkins to sell his policy of mandated vehicle conversion under the guise of resource conservation. He built the platform solely on rumors of extreme shortages due to the Global War. Since most residents seldom left the confines of their enclave perimeter, Jenkins' platform was hardly challenged, allowing him to merge the failing industrial sector into the manufacturing backbone of the Commercial Empire. While the policy possessed a glimmer of well intended manufacturing practices, Mac knew that it didn't make up for a long history of Frank Jenkins' screw ups. He would continue to cherish his navigational freedom as long it pointed away from Imperan restrictions.

Mac downshifted as the Fire Ant careened along a street leading to a quiet residential district in much less disrepair than the industrial zones. As he drove out of the housing section and passed some local business sites, he spotted two suspicious individuals who hadn't yet noticed his presence. The Fire Ant zipped across the intersection as fast as Mac would allow without revving the engine. He swiftly parked the mox on an old loading ramp behind a defunct retail outlet. With his ride out of sight, Mac exited and yanked a black garment from the back seat. Draping it over his body, Mac headed in the direction of his quarry. With a click and a buzz, he then disappeared from sight.

Contract Perimeter
Abandoned Sector, Windstonne Enclave
Commercial Empire, Northam Continent
Thread: sysObserver.cmd

Bull and Nox walked down the middle of the rarely traveled road, scouting the region for marked buildings that Académe hadn't already cleaned out. Having efficiently scrubbed their current zone per Imperan orders, it was high time for Académe to choose a new zone. Bull and Nox didn't mind the work, but Jocq's temper and nagging orders often tested the patience of the clan members. Ultimately, they knew it was due to the pressure from above. Jocq's frustration with taking orders from a lunatic like Frank Jenkins was apparent, but Académe's dependence on Imperan perks made severing ties difficult. Other members suggested that they break away and start their own operation, but Jocq would have none of it.

"I am absolutely sick of this spine racking" Nox grumbled.

Bull kept his hands shoved into his leather coat pockets and stared at the uneven asphalt street while walking alongside Nox.

"I don't see why it bothers you so much. You seem to take orders from Swipe rather well," Bull quipped while trying to keep a straight face.

"Fish, what is your problem? I am perfectly in control of my own life. Thinkin' I can't handle a pretty girl. Don't be a trout," Nox retorted.

"Uh, huh," Bull replied, clearly distracted by something.

"What?" Nox asked with a shrill voice.

"Shhh!" Bull replied, holding up a hand to silence Nox.

As they stood in the silent afternoon air, they could hear faint voices approaching. With a mischievous grin, Bull faced Nox and nodded the top of his head toward the oncoming sounds.

"It's been a while since we had some real fun," Bull whispered.

Nox released a muffled laugh as he followed behind Bull who crept alongside the building wall leading to the cross street.

"I don't know what I'd do without that mission around," one trader said.

"You're not kidding, last bench they had a couple of extra power cells that they gave me in exchange for some clothing and a couple of household appliances. They sure do find some good stuff, I mean, way better than the usual wares at Haggba," replied the other trader.

"Well, when you've got a full team emptying buildings, you're bound to run into some good junk," said the first.

"Feel like sharing?" Bull said as he jumped in front of the locals.

Startled by the interruption, the abandon residents took a step back as Bull and Nox stepped forward. Bull flashed his teeth in a huge smile while the locals' reflection off Nox's mirrored sunglasses stared right back at them.

"Académe has some even better junk at our operation if you're interested in bartering," Nox said.

Intimidated, the residents continued to step backward. "Leave us alone!" One interjected.

"Aw, you're hurting our feelings," Nox replied in mock offense.

With a smirk, Bull shoved the timid residents, expecting them to fall and drop their newly bartered wares, but instead they merely staggered backward and then stopped as if they had bumped into an invisible wall or…. something that caught them.

Surprised and confused themselves, the local traders looked at each other as they regained their footing. They turned to look again at the two aggressive clan members, but they soon saw the source of the obstruction. An image of a figure draped in a black cloak materialized in the reflection on Nox's sunglasses.

"What the...?" Bull snorted.

"Now, that wasn't a very nice thing to do," the Enforcer said as he put himself between the locals and the clan members.

"You've got two ticks to get out of our way!" Nox snarled, his hands tensing while resting on the hammers hanging from the loops on each pant leg.

The Enforcer held his position unintimidated

"You-," Bull said before the Enforcer cut him off.

"I'd suggest you turn around and walk away. Académe's business is concluded here. I've already had to deal with your shenanigans, and I'll have no more of it," the Enforcer stated.

"You're the carp who jacked Sophomore and Jammer!" Nox growled.

Bull leaned forward, but the Enforcer's response cut him off.

"I didn't have time to check their library cards," the Enforcer said as Bull and Nox returned menacing stares.

"Consider this a warning. Tell your SOC to pack up and leave. Otherwise, you'll have even more of a mess to clean up," the Enforcer said.

Bull glared defiantly. He really wanted to throw down, but since the odds didn't work in Jammer and Sophomore's favor, he decided against a fight. Even without a confrontation, not all was lost. Académe now had a face to match their previously unknown adversary. Finally, he pushed Nox in the arm as they took a couple steps back before turning and walking away.

Once the two Académe members were out of sight, the Enforcer turned toward the local traders. "Are you okay?"

Both nodded.

"I would suggest a more direct route home next time," the Enforcer said as he flipped his hood over his head and activated the cloak. He dashed back to the Fire Ant. After starting the mox, he raced toward Core City. Destination: Casters Tower.

4 – Fightsmith – 4

Commerce Level, Casters Tower
Core City, Windstonne Enclave
Commercial Empire, Northam Continent
Thread: sysObserver.cmd

Tycoon tucked one hand into his vest while he drummed his opposite fingers on the wooden desk. Since the Power Cell Plus regional office was mostly deserted for the day, he discarded formality by leaning back in his chair and propping his feet up on the desk corner. The business day was about to close and his distributor on the other end of the sonair was sorely testing his patience.

"James, I don't care if you're getting the *I Can't Afford It* attitude. We have a surplus of power cells and they draw no profits by sitting in a warehouse. What do you think we have a credit policy for?" Tycoon snapped.

The unmistakable, Frank Jenkins with his white suit matching his slicked back hair and trimmed beard sauntered in and leaned on a neighboring desk. He shifted the gold tie against his blue shirt collar as he watched Tycoon's sales antics.

"Custom Order? No! What does efficiency have to do with it? All we care about is the bottom line, James. Not quality, not efficiency, THE BOTTOM LINE and that is QUANTITY. Our surplus exists because people want to buy them and it is YOUR job to make them realize it!" Tycoon replied, his mood bordering on hysteria.

"Get it done!" Tycoon snapped one more time as he plucked the sonair from his ear and set it on his desk with nearly enough force to damage the fragile communicator.

"My apologies, Sir, sometimes a little ruthlessness is needed with these people, otherwise berry goes south," Tycoon said, turning to acknowledge Jenkins.

"You don't have to remind me how much force is needed to impose cooperation," Frank Jenkins nodded. "People seem to forget that business operates on results, not morality."

"To what do I owe the honor of your visit?" Tycoon asked, smiling in agreement.

"I needed an executive stroll, thought I might have you send word to Mr. Sargent that I would like to meet with him," Jenkins said.

"Consider it done," Tycoon replied. "Anything to accommodate Mogul Prime's most generous sponsor."

Tycoon's sonair beeped again. He picked up the communicator and placed it back on his ear, "Excuse me, Sir."

"Taylor, here," Tycoon answered.

"Yes, Sir, our special is one for a hundred daygrad or two for two hundred and fifty, and for the two fifty we'll throw in a complimentary charger," Tycoon replied.

"Splendid, your cells will ship tomorrow. Remember to be excellent," Tycoon said, choking down his irritation. He didn't like how so many low-level comms were being directed his way late in the day. He went to set the sonair down, but again it pinged.

"Taylor here," Tycoon muttered, doing little to disguise his impatience.

"Tycoon!" a familiar voice snapped back.

"Sorry, Voltaire, I've been trying to leave the premises in between fiscal intrusions," Tycoon replied, quickly dropping his former attitude.

"We've got some serious plans to go over. Make sure that you're at the shop tonight," Voltaire said.

"I'll be there. By the way, I've been having a chat with Mr. Jenkins here, and he would like to schedule a meeting with you," Tycoon said.

"Good, we can coordinate details later. Voltaire out," Voltaire replied, ending the conversation as quickly as it started.

Perplexed at Voltaire's curt response, Tycoon replaced the sonair back on its charging cradle and turned to Jenkins who was still looking on with a smug face.

"Impressive," Jenkins said. "That is the oldest sham in the book, and you pulled it off without hitch."

"These simpletons just need to be instilled with the illusion that they want or need something, and then you create yourself as the provider of that something. It's all about the finesse," Tycoon smiled. "Plus, I love selling one for the price of two."

"Indeed," Jenkins nodded.

"Speaking of finesse, if you'll excuse me, Sir," Tycoon replied, looking over Jenkins' shoulder into the hallway of the business center. A young brunette approached the elevator, and waited for the doors to open.

With a confident stride, Tycoon walked up behind Sath Kinze, "Done for the day?"

"Yes, Henry," Sath replied without turning to acknowledge him since she had already seen him approach from a reflection on the shiny elevator doors.

With a chime, the elevator doors slid open and Tycoon held his hand in front of him in a chivalrous fashion for Sath to enter before himself. The elevator doors closed behind them and the long ride to the bottom floor of Casters Tower commenced. The ride would have been defined by an annoyingly awkward silence had it not been for the soft flowing music from the speaker overhead.

Tycoon attempted to make romantic advances several times before, much to Sath's disapproval. She felt extremely uncomfortable around him, but she still managed to maintain her composure every time. With a welcome chime, the elevator doors slid open once again, and Sath walked out of the elevator with Tycoon keeping pace.

"Can I escort you home?" Tycoon asked, holding the lobby door open for her. "The enclave can be dangerous this late in the day, and I'm concerned for your safety."

"No, Henry, I don't think that will be necessary," Sath said defiantly with a sweet voice, despite its underlying disinterest.

"Just remember, my offer will continue to stand," Tycoon replied as he walked to the edge of the sidewalk with her.

The roar of a combustion engine reached their ears as they turned to see a black mox with flame decals roll up to the edge of the street and stop where they were standing. Tycoon noticed a strong figure at the wheel with a tight military haircut who kept his eyes on the road in front of the vehicle as Sath approached the passenger door.

"My ride is here, Henry, Good Night," Sath said.

Without looking back Sath climbed into the vehicle and closed the door. Once she was settled, the vehicle disappeared into the distance leaving Tycoon on the sidewalk, glaring amidst the onlookers startled by the abrupt noise.

Vanguard Warehouse
Abandoned Sector, Windstonne Enclave
Commercial Empire, Northam Continent
Thread: actTgtPersp1.view

My body hit the floor with a thud causing an uncontrollable "Oof" to escape my lungs. The rushed landing barely gave me enough time to place my hands between my face and the mat. Lennox had just connected with a roundhouse kick to my jaw after I thought I had caught him off-balance. I didn't need many encounters like that to know that underestimating my opponent would prove unwise. As I blinked, I heard Maxwell laughing and hollering from the table, evidently enjoying the show.

"That's alright," Lennox smiled, extending a hand to help me pick my befuddled self off the floor. I decided to leave my bruised ego lying on the floor, considering that it may just hinder me if I actually wanted to survive training.

"What's your ayvek?" Lennox asked inquisitively.

"My attack vector? Not sure that I have one," I replied, making sure that I understood his question.

"You could have fooled me. It looks like you have Street Flail mastered," Lennox quipped.

Even without fight experience, I knew of the reference to those who floundered their way out of a conflict. Motivated to prove him wrong, I squared up again with my fists covering my face, and my elbows protecting my upper torso.

"Ready?" he asked.

"As ready as I'm going to be," I replied, lifting my weight off my heels.

I poked a quick jab with my left hand, following up with a reverse from my right. I then shifted into a roundhouse kick with my right leg. Lennox merely bobbed his head to the left or right depending on which side was opposite of my attack. He seemed to demonstrate very little effort in evading my attacks, so I applied more pressure. I advanced again, lunging with a jab from my right, following with a sweeping motion of my right foot in attempt to catch him off-balance. He saw the kick coming and lifted up his foot as mine skimmed the floor beneath it. Using the momentum, I lifted my foot into a hook kick, targeting Lennox's guarded torso. I then twisted my stance and dropped my heel like an ax. Even though I caught him by surprise, he still reacted quickly enough to evade my kick by stepping his foot back and placing his body perpendicular to my own.

Resetting my stance after the miss, I angled off as Lennox countered with a jab to my face. I reacted and blocked it high with my lead arm, but since I was blind to his counter, he followed up and connected with a reverse punch to the gut.

I let out another gasp as Lennox connected with his padded glove. I scurried two steps backward, trying to escape arm's reach, but he didn't back down. Suddenly he launched an assault of kicks while maintaining his balance on one leg. As he continuously snapped more kicks, he hopped forward without the slightest indication of losing balance or altering technique. His barrage of kicks pushed me back as I attempted to parry them until I thought to sidestep and angle to his less protected side. Noticing my angular retreat, he said "Good move, keep going!"

I lunged with a hook punch just as Lennox squared off to face me, only to see him duck under the strike. In response, I threw a front kick to push him back and gain distance. I connected with my kick, but it had no power. As I thrust my foot into his abdomen, he showed no concern. Instead, he charged in as my foot dropped. Anticipating the move, I jumped into the air turning my back to him as I propelled my body into a half circle turn and thrust out my kick from a chambered position beneath my waist. By landing the kick, I finally caught him off guard, causing him to stagger and land on his back. I dropped back into a fighting posture and dropped my hands with intent to help Lennox back to his feet, but that idea was premature. Before I could even think, he had already cocked his knees in front of his chest and then kicked outward propelling his body into the air after pushing his back off the floor with his hands. Without enough time to raise my hands, Lennox dropped his head toward the floor and a kick blasted from behind his body, aiming straight for my skull. It connected. As I fell backward, I watched his body complete the flip with one foot touching down after the other.

I lay on the ground with my heart pounding and my lungs rapidly fluxing to gain a faster air intake. Accepting how much of a workout the so-called fight stuff was, I decided to hold position while my body utilized whatever adrenaline remained.

"Good job," Lennox said as I draped my forearm over my eyes. "That's enough for today."

When my lung thrashing finally slowed, I opened my eyes to see Lennox still standing over me with a hand extended to help me up. I reached out to grab his hand and he pulled me up to my feet.

"Not bad, for a noodle," Lennox said with chuckle. "Want a water?"

"Yeah, cold water does sound good at the moment," I said, dusting myself off in between labored breaths.

"Take a couple laps around the floor to cool down, I'll grab some chugs," Lennox said, turning to walk toward one of the adjacent rooms.

I rested my hands on top of my head and walked around the floor while allowing the cool air to filter into my lungs. After my heart had lessened its racing, I took a seat at the table where Maxwell was fiddling with the tech.

"Ayezon!" Lennox snapped as he pitched me a cold chug of water.

After a quick catch, I didn't hesitate to unscrew the chug's top and down half of its liquid content. Lennox returned from the galley with a chug of his own in hand. He pulled out one of the chairs and put his foot on it, allowing his elbow to rest on his knee.

"So, where'd you learn how to fight like that, Fox?" Lennox asked.

I stared at the floor before I replied, "I have no idea. Other than my time in front of some battle mecas, I have no memories older than three passes."

Eager to change the subject, I turned his question around, "What about you?" I asked.

"Me? Now that, my friend, is a long story," Lennox said as he pulled out the chair the rest of the way and sat down.

"I've learned a thing or two from Mac, but I acquired most of my skills during time spent on the battlefront. During the Global War, Frank Jenkins rallied all combat capable individuals. I answered the call and joined a local militia. Many of its members had actually served in branches of the Tricameral Endeavor's armed forces prior to the Global War. They had a formal training structure, so that's how I became a vector and picked up skills in vehicle and weapon repair. Since it was either kill or be killed, everyone had little else on their minds beyond survival," Lennox said, taking a pause as he reflected on the cause of the war.

"It was a shame how it went down. The Tricameral Endeavor pretty much slit its own throat. It was like the whole infrastructure got blindsided by its own saturation of tolerance. When the first strikes hit, the foundational ideology that society was built on just crumbled," Lennox said, retelling the tale with a hint of disdain.

"How'd it all start?" I asked, curious to hear history from another perspective.

"No one knows for sure. The eastern seaboard was hit by multiple strikes. They did verify one from Insurgistan, one from Sibera and another from somewhere in the Shian continent, likely behind the Red Wall. None of the nations dared to claim the attacks since the fallout was catastrophic. With several major cities such as the Capitan District and Freshton no longer in existence, allies considered the Tricameral Endeavor down for the count. Neighboring allies such as Nortuck and Libertas, even the Uniod Bloc, sent defense aid, but at the cost of drawing their own countries into the war. Within six lunars, battles emerged on nearly every front.

The Tricameral Endeavor suffered a terrible setback once Jenkins assumed control through his political influence. Militias were normalized and the landscape was well defended, but Jenkins' personal power trip quickly turned things into an offensive war. Some of the militias were turned on our northern and western allies. Jenkins pushed to annex more land. It no longer became a matter of people united under a national identity, but a mode of survival from a lunatic who was waging war for no reason. People fled major cities en masse, hoping that dispersion would limit their exposure to air and ground assaults.

Of course, the Global War settled once every nation had been reduced to a heap of economic ruin. Leaders finally pulled together and soon thereafter the Global Alliance factions were formed, but the recovery process was halted once the Smart Wars ensued. Cyber terrorists took advantage of the fragile, newly formed legal systems to swipe truckloads of berry, as well as repurpose and wipe vast collections of datastacks. Petty crimes escalated into intellectual warfare.

Jenkins became so paranoid that he didn't hesitate to target anyone deemed suspicious, even Imperan citizens. Many people died simply on account of association. Once the Global Alliance factions drafted their own digital warfare policies the Smart Wars faded as well.

Ever since then things have been quiet, but once a vector, always a vector. If you wake up one day and everything you were forced to live for was taken away, struggles to adapt become the norm." Lennox said.

I nodded as Lennox continued.

"My desire to fight still left me drifting in and out of some rough situations. I was in the street fight of my life when Mac appeared out of nowhere. After distracting my foes, he bought me just enough time to disable them and escape. After seeing my abilities, he told me that he had an opportunity for me to put my skills back into action. So, here I am," Lennox said.

"Have you seen much action since?" I asked.

"Not really. Clans are occasionally a nuisance, but that's primarily the extent of it. Investing my time in training and hardware has helped keep me out of trouble," Lennox said with a smile.

The light started to wane in the warehouse as the sky's colors transitioned from daylight to dusk. Not wishing to return to the mission in the dark again, I stood up from the table.

"I'd best be getting back to the mission," I said.

Nodding, Lennox rose from his seat as well. "Welcome aboard, Mr. Fox, I look forward to working with you."

"Oh, I almost forgot," Lennox said as he disappeared into a room adjacent to the training floor before returning with a book in hand.

"Mac said that he wanted me to give you this on your way out," Lennox said, handing me the book.

"What is it?" I asked as I turned the book over in my hands. The title *Foundational Reality* was etched into its cover, along with its author's name, Ezeck Townne, directly beneath. It had a series of particles, motion symbols and equation-like inscriptions scattered across the surface.

"'Homework' he said," Lennox replied with a laugh.

"Grrrreat," I muttered. "Speaking of Mac, where did he disappear to?"

"Beats me at this arc," Lennox replied, shrugging his shoulders. "Said he had some business to attend to which means patrols for all I know."

"I see," I replied as I turned to walk down the stairs to leave the warehouse.

"See you bright and early tomorrow," Lennox said as I closed the metal door behind me.

Inner Core Dartway
Core City, Windstonne Enclave
Commercial Empire, Northam Continent
Thread: sysObserver.cmd

The Fire Ant rolled up to the curb in front of a plainly designed, yet nondescript, house in a subdivision a few hauls from Casters Tower. Mac sat in silence for a moment before he turned off the engine.

"Boyfriend of yours back there?" Mac asked slyly.

"Cut it out," Sath laughed as she poked Mac's arm. "You know better than that."

"Yeah, true," Mac smiled as he turned to look into Sath's brown eyes which often matched the color of her hair in the daylight. Mac found it easy to appreciate her beauty, but he had an even greater appreciation for her charm. Because of her reassuring nature, he had much to tell her, but he was never without a great sense of reservation. Memories, no matter how distant, often came to mind about deceased family members who were killed on account of their connections to the Interlace. No matter how hard hapcasters tried to spin the motives behind the Smart Wars, he knew that there were many cover-ups to mask the targeting of dissenting groups. Relationships within the Interlace were critical, and Mac wanted to ensure that his work never brought danger upon the gal he cared about.

"Mac? What's the matter?" Sath asked as she noticed the smile fade from his face when he turned to stare out the mox's windshield.

"Nothing," Mac mumbled with a blank expression.

"C'mon, it's me you're talking to, and you've been quite distant lately," Sath said.

Mac turned again to look her in the eyes, but he couldn't mask the conflict on his face. She placed her hand on top of his and held it tight. After several clicks of silence, Mac finally spoke up.

"Sath… what I do is dangerous…" Mac said as his hand tensed around hers. "I've already lost those who I was close to, and I don't want that to happen again."

"Mac, I've lost people too. Even my family disowned me because of my association with the Interlace. You know this. I'm not scared of the past," Sath replied.

Mac released a heavy sigh. "I know. You're a tough one, but I suspect that things could get ugly around here. I've noticed some disturbing comms across the underbelly of the Hyper Lynx. I think Frank Jenkins may have a sinister plan for the Global Alliance. Also, there's been an uptick in clan activities that warrant investigation."

"His quest for dominion is insatiable, but I don't think he is capable of taking on the entire Global Alliance," Sath said in defense of her boss.

"I understand," Mac replied, "but any man who desires absolute power will eventually become a subject of that power and do a lot of harm along the way."

Sath turned and stared out the window, unwilling to face the harsh truth about her employer. She knew that Frank Jenkins was corrupt, but she had to constantly be careful of revealing such awareness in the workplace. The slightest mistake could cost her a position that she had worked hard to attain despite the complications of questionable character revealed after the fact.

"I'm sorry," Mac said, realizing that he said too much.

Sath lifted a finger to his lips, "It's okay," she whispered.

"I just want you to be safe," Mac replied as he produced a small decorative case from his pocket and handed to Sath.

"What is this?" Sath asked as she opened the case to reveal a pen. There was little need for such an instrument given the rarity of paper, but she conceded that slates occasionally worked best with a precision pointer.

"It's a gadget that I had Lennox put together. I'm sure it'll look great on a desk, but it also has a tracking signal you can activate if ever in trouble," Mac said.

"Thanks, I'll be okay," Sath smiled tucking the pen away before turning to open the passenger door. "Are you sure that you wouldn't like to stay for a darwa? I've got some fresh leaves from the Maleezhun importer down the street."

Mac smiled. "You know I'd love to, but babysitting the abandon is a never ending chore."

"Okay," Sath leaned forward and kissed Mac on the cheek before sliding out of the vehicle, "Good Night."

With a clunk, the door closed and Sath walked up to her house as Mac looked on with a reluctant heart. Once she was safely inside, Mac started up the Fire Ant's engine and slammed the pedal to the floor, guiding the noisy mox back to the abandon.

Dwelling Street Mission
Abandoned Sector, Windstonne Enclave
Commercial Empire, Northam Continent
Thread: actTgtPersp1.view

With few lights operable at such a late arc, I guessed that most of the mission's residents had already retired for the evening. Strangely, I felt a detachment from my home after considering the increase in time that I was spending away from it. I knew that I owed Div and Tarees an explanation. I considered a potential relocation to Vanguard Warehouse advantageous since running back and forth on a daily basis felt inefficient. Plus, it wasn't right that I hadn't been around to help with my share of the work without explaining my absence.

I closed the front door as quietly as possible, pretending to practice my stealth once inside, despite disagreement from my legs. My thighs threatened to give out after the rigorous sparring session with Lennox. Once I reached my quarters, I slipped inside and closed the door behind me. As I tapped the light switch, I nearly jumped out of my skin upon seeing someone sitting in the only chair in the room.

"What are you doing?" I hissed at Chuck who had been sitting nonchalantly in the dark.

"I could ask you the same question. Where have you been? On a date with Granny from the Stack?" Chuck asked.

I grimaced at Chuck's tasteless yet blunt humor. "So what if I have?" I smirked.

It was Chuck's turn to grimace as if a late-night rendezvous with the Stack's elderly innkeeper came to mind. "Seriously, Fox? You've been acting more unhinged than unusual which has some concerned."

"Is that really the reason or do you miss having someone to pick on?" I asked sarcastically as I set the recently acquired books on my bed.

"Where have you been the last day and a half?" Chuck asked, staring at the books that I set down.

"I've made some new acquaintances," I replied.

"What's been eating you, Fox? You have been so distraught that you've had to look for answers to your questions elsewhere?" Chuck asked.

I sat on my bed and stared at the floor for a couple of ticks.

"Chuck, do you have any relatives that look like you?" I asked.

"Sure, I have a brother and two sisters. We all share the same fibernetics so we have some similar characteristics, I guess. Why do you ask?" Chuck queried, half expecting a sarcastic put down about his looks.

I just shook my head in response, dismissing his question.

"Do you think cloning is possible?" I asked. My mind merely swam in circles hoping that Chuck, of all intellectuals, might be able to shed light on the subject regarding my resemblance to the one who had already opened my eyes to much outside the mission in such a short time. I just wanted a rational explanation. I feared volunteering too much since everyone was already starting to think that I was crazy. Telling anyone that I had seen an apparition just like myself would not help my case.

"Not to my knowledge, outside of partial elements like organs. It's suspected that any progress made before the wars was ultimately halted. No one ever successfully cloned a human," Chuck replied.

"Fox, where are you going with all of this?" Chuck asked with increasing concern about my line of questioning.

Chuck still eyed the books suspiciously, the smaller one on top in particular. "Now where did you get *those*?" he asked.

"From a friend," I replied.

Chuck blew off my response as he continued staring at the recent acquisitions. He rose from the chair and walked over to pick up the smaller book. "And this?" he asked as he held the Criterion in front of me.

"Technically, I found that one," I replied, oblivious to any significance about the book. "It was hidden in a desk when I was rummaging through an abandoned library."

"Hidden for good reason," Chuck replied. "Do you know what this is?"

I shook my head.

Chuck set the book down before returning to the chair. He hesitated before continuing. "Perhaps I should inform you, friend, in case you haven't heard the stories. The Commercial Empire doesn't take kindly to opposition. When the Smart Wars broke out, Frank Jenkins went berserk, targeting anyone with even the slightest hint of a relationship with datajackers," Chuck said.

"So I've heard," I replied, waving my hand as I recalled accounts from mission veterans and Lennox.

"But what you may not know is that such casual associations gave Jenkins an excuse to commit some of the most vile treachery thinkable. If you even lived within ten square parcels of a potential datajacker and made no effort to file a report you may have found yourself disappeared.

Frank Jenkins just might have a greater disdain for the Interlace than other faction leaders. Sharing knowledge is a key facet of the Interlace, and doing so often runs against the grain of the establishment. Frank Jenkins only cares about the expansion of the Commercial Empire and extermination is not outside his bag of tricks if he can get away with it. This mission only exists because Jenkins has reason to believe that he can benefit from its existence," Chuck replied emphatically.

I took a moment to allow Chuck's words to sink in, "So, what are you suggesting?" I asked.

"Be careful," Chuck replied, the strong sense of caution evident on his face.

I nodded as Chuck rose and walked toward the door. "I'll talk to Div and Tarees tomorrow," I said.

"See that you do," Chuck replied with a somber face. He then stepped out of the room and closed the door behind him.

Chuck's words bounced around in my skull, but I soon realized how late it was getting. I brushed aside the books on my bed, but as I sprawled out, I cracked open the hefty textbook laden with informatics. I began reading and only stopped once my weary eyes closed without instruction.

Synergon Assembly Plant
Core City, Windstonne Enclave
Commercial Empire, Northam Continent
Thread: sysObserver.cmd

The muted sounds of slate taps and humming hardware lingered in the engineering bay and attached laboratory of the most advanced independent research facility in the region. Most members of Mogul

Prime relished the opportunity to put their skills to the test, but this particular assignment was certainly fraught with skepticism. Typically, Mogul Prime occupied its time creating mediacasting content for any Global Alliance faction that sought their services when not pursuing the clan's independent goals. When Frank Jenkins approached the clan with an important task, sure to employ Mogul Prime's greatest talents, the clan was intently interested, despite a great deal of reservation due to Frank Jenkins' sense of urgency.

Most satellites utilized prior to the Smart Wars were useless scraps of junk in high orbit. Jenkins sought to create three superpowered satellites which would once again make the Northam continent a mediacasting superpower. With the Commercial Empire always in the shadow of its predecessor, comm tech was limited. Because Global Alliance factions had entrenched control over meca marketshare, the bold undertaking generated much doubt.

As clan leader, Voltaire knew that he had to carefully weigh the benefits of compensation against potential shifts in clan influence. Mogul Prime had already established itself as a reputable political presence, but that reputation could suffer damage if it carelessly signed on to the schemes of a reckless faction leader. Certainly, Frank Jenkins had the financial clout to afford Mogul Prime, but any distractions would increase the number of clans seeking to capitalize on Mogul Prime's temporary absence from the market. After all, few clans ever achieved similar success because Mogul Prime was not just a symbol of intellect, but physical prowess as well. Each member possessed a unique strength both mentally and physically.

"Hey, Dean, are we going to close up shop or what?" came a shrill, high strung voice from the doorway to Voltaire's office.

Voltaire looked up from behind his tinted spectacles at Id who leaned against the doorpost. "Yes, Sig, let everyone know that it's time to pack up," Voltaire replied with an impatient tone.

With a teeth baring grin, Id bounded from the office steps and jumped around the facility floor shouting, "It's time to go."

Id thrived on impulsive behavior, but his childish antics were easily ignored when he was kept in line. Id bumped into Authochthon who had been thoroughly engrossed in finalizing schematics on a noptic display.

"Shove off, Sig" Authochthon grunted without looking up from his work.

"Seriously, Sig, if you didn't screw around so much, perhaps we wouldn't have to work so late," replied a voice belonging to an olive skinned woman who tossed her lab coat on the coat rack.

"Aw, Saphira, you don't like spending the extra time with me?" Id asked with a fake frown on his face.

"Shut up before I pull out the straight jacket, Psycho," Hauteur snapped, glaring back at Id.

"You can restrain me up any day," Id retorted with a crass tongue gesture as his green eyes blazed like a fire, contrasting his pale skin and dark hair. Id stepped forward, but he was halted in place as Authochthon's huge dark hand grasped his shoulder and tossed him backward. Yet again, Autochthon thwarted Id's antics without looking up from his schematics.

Hauteur burst into laughter as Id tumbled onto his backside, "Thanks, Derwin," Hauteur said, acknowledging the assistance by her muscular associate.

Authochthon finally finished his calculations and turned to Hauteur, nodding with toothy grin and a grunt. He walked over and placed his lab coat on the rack and watched Id scramble off the floor amidst a series of mumbles.

Voltaire walked from his office and observed the tail end of Id's shenanigans. He looked up at the airbridge overhead to the two members who apparently hadn't heard Id's song and dance about quitting time. "Hey, Tybalt, Dexter, Let's go!" He shouted.

Tunnel and Pythagoras assumed the roles of heavy machine operators for the project. They waved back to acknowledge Voltaire. Once everyone was clustered around the exit, Voltaire spoke up before killing the power. "We've got some training to do this evening. Bender and Tycoon will meet us at the shop."

"Oh, great, more work. I just want to go to sleep," Id mumbled under his breath.

"Did you not get your fourth nap in today?" Tunnel remarked as he slapped Id on the back.

With a mixture of eye rolls and sighs of relief that the day's drudgery had come to an end, the clan members filed out. Once everyone had exited the facility, Voltaire scanned the floor one last time and then turned out the lights, leaving the research facility in darkness.

5 – The Challenger – 5

Executive Level, Casters Tower
Core City, Windstonne Enclave
Commercial Empire, Northam Continent
Thread: sysObserver.cmd

Frank Jenkins sat idly, staring out the window of his office which resided within the upper floors of Casters Tower. The black tiered superstructure that once represented an advanced communications corporation now stood in the heart of Windstonne, a symbol of the Commercial Empire's seat of power. He felt a sense of splendor as he reflected on the great faction that he controlled. The Commercial Empire was supreme in its dominance over the Northam continent. Despite armed neighbors across its shared borders with Westcrest and the Uniod Branch, the Commercial Empire's technological and military prowess was uncontested across the land mass. Frank Jenkins marveled in his brilliance at spotting opportunity to consolidate the remnants of the fractured Tricameral Endeavor when the opening salvo of the Global War struck. With Windstonne far removed from the desolate wasteland of the eastern seaboard, it was molded into a safe haven for anyone supportive of the Commercial Empire.

Naturally, Frank Jenkins praised himself for the prosperity made available to the former citizens of the Tricameral Endeavor. Some factions hadn't fared so well. Jenkins understood the power of media and he effectively used it to unite the scattered populations in order to defend what remained of a broken nation. With the corporate vacancy created by the untimely passing of his boss during the initial strikes, Jenkins quickly seized the reins of power. Through his influence, an urgent call to arms spurred the largest defensive movement in history as every military minded individual imaginable answered the call to protect the homeland.

On one front, Jenkins coordinated the public defense, and on the other he crafted strong bonds with any that he deemed valuable in the technology and communication sectors. Although maintaining a strong technological backbone was key for defense against unknown enemies, Jenkins couldn't pass up the opportunity to bolster the Corporate Casting Network's own infrastructure. In some cases, tech operatives left their lofty national defense positions to form their own underground networks. While the crumbling Tricameral Endeavor discouraged such tactics, Jenkins had no reservation about leveraging his connections for strategic benefit.

Many considered datajackers to be heroes given their quick reactions to rallying the people during the Global War, but such favoritism was short lived as their skills turned to unscrupulous means, which initiated the Smart Wars. With much of the world dependent on technology, the modern digital ecosystem became a playground for pirates and profiteers. Economies were in upheaval as banking systems were drained, informatic repositories were dumped and personal identities were erased. Even national borders were called into question since even the most secure datatanks were subject to corruption. It wasn't long before national identities faded, only to be substituted with a sense of proximity or fibernetic relation. Citizenry became a relic of the past.

As the Smart Wars escalated, every digital crime imaginable brought about a terrible retribution from the Global Alliance which struggled to maintain both the national bond of residents and its own power increasingly challenged by the masses. Faction leaders truly had no interest in loyalty, after all, most were simply political hacks, assassins or war heroes. In the event that a rising leader sought to inject morality back into the system, each would mysteriously disappear or contract an incurable disease. Corruption was rampant in the Global Alliance and in order to right the system, it needed someone orderly like Frank Jenkins to guide it.

Thanks to his ties with the most competent datajackers, Frank Jenkins upheld the Commercial Empire as a driving influence throughout the Smart Wars. By directing every thought and every idea through every mediacast, Jenkins had the power to control the very social structure of the Commercial Empire. Nothing was transmitted from tower to satellite, satellite to meca without his approval across a large swath of the Northam continent. It was a strategy that served him well, and it was high time that the rest of the world understood the benefits.

Frank Jenkins' latest project, the Synergon Satellite Network, would further extend his mediacasting capability. This new hardware would have the capacity to transmit to any continent and even signal-block existing units presently in orbit. Opinions of the other faction leaders meant little to him as long as he could directly influence the true power centers of the other regions, the people. There was little profit to be gained by expending resources on the masses bent on self-preservation. Simpletons were so easily influenced. All they needed was direction, direction that Frank Jenkins would gladly provide. As he reflected on his strategy, a devious smile washed over his bearded face.

Jenkins spun about in his chair and tapped a button to page his agenda coordinator, "Sath, have the meeting notices been sent out?"

"Yes, Mr. Jenkins, they went out yesterday," Sath replied softly.

"Excellent," Jenkins replied. He shut off the sonair and turned again in his chair, setting his eyes on the horizon. The view from Casters Tower was spectacular. The boxy tower had a perfect view of black and gray structures poking through the urban haze which easily obstructed the distant view of wartime decay. Jenkins just sat there admiring how well his plan was coming together. He brought the Commercial Empire out of the ashes, and he would soon perform the same service for the Global Alliance.

Dwelling Street Mission
Abandoned Sector, Windstonne Enclave
Commercial Empire, Northam Continent
Thread: actTgtPersp1.view

It was another one of those days when my body rejected the idea of waking up. My mind was still fatigued from staying up too late reading, and my muscles yelled at my brain every time that I attempted to move them. Training with Lennox on my defensive skills felt useful, but it also felt like a lifetime of workouts compressed into a matter of arcs.

With resignation, I finally forced open my heavy eyelids. As if peering through a haze, I recognized that I was in my room at the mission and that I had fallen asleep on top of the informatic textbook. I knew that there was no procrastinating the need to speak with Div and Tarees about my absence from my duties. It wasn't fair that I was reaping the benefits of a new experiences while everyone else had to pick up the slack. As I tried to roll out of bed, my body protested again. Even with missing a day of work, it sure felt like I had been on the sungauge, around the gauge, for the last three days.

After a quick cleanup, I threw on some fresh clothes and headed down the hall toward the main office. I didn't expect Div and Tarees to be very happy with me, so I scrambled to prepare a worst-case scenario defense.

Once I reached the office door, I saw Tarees sitting at her desk prepping the next schedule of projects for the crew. Div was in the office leaning up against the wall adjacent to me. I assumed that I caught them in middle of a conversation about the crew's starting location. As I entered, they halted their discussion and looked up at me.

"I, uh..." I hesitated, trying to find the best words for my surrender having failed to craft a reasonable explanation for my activities.

Tarees looked up and smiled, "Don't worry about it. We've got plenty of help here. It's not like you are under contract."

My jaw dropped wondering how she knew what I was going to say. I turned to look at Div and he was grinning too. "Seriously, we'll be fine, opportunities to learn are rare."

I was dumbfounded at their response which made me think that Chuck had ratted me out. They not only knew what I wanted to tell them, but they also seemed to know what I had been doing. I raised an eyebrow inquisitively and looked at each of them in turn. "Alright, what gives? How do you two know what's been going on."

"You aren't the only one with friends, you know," Tarees said with a wink. "You are more than welcome to continue you're stay here. Besides we know your training has been in good hands."

"The two of you know something that you're not letting on about don't you?" I asked.

All I got was the usual jovial smiles and Tarees' wave of her hand. "We've been sworn to secrecy."

"Okay," I replied with a suspicious stare. "I do appreciate your generosity. I still want to help out when I'm available. It's just that I feel like I've been looking for something more or less routine, shall I say," I said taking care with my choice of words. I knew that I was looking for something more fulfilling or important, but I didn't dare say anything to suggest that the mission's work wasn't important.

"We're sure you'll find it," Div said. "You're a good worker. There will always be plenty to do, but be sure not to pass up opportunities when they come along."

"Thanks," I said as I turned to walk out the door and down the hallway to the exit. I was almost out the door when I remembered that I left my books on the bed. I doubled back to my room and then realized that it would prove wise to take more than just the clothes on my back, so I yanked a duffel bag from my closet and stuffed some loose clothes and essentials into it. I nabbed my berry clip off the stand near my bed. I didn't know of any place to spend my earnings near the Vanguard Warehouse, but I figured it best to be prepared.

I tried squeezing my recently acquired books into the bag with questionable results. I was barely able to zipper the bag shut, which caused the corners of the books to protrude in spite of my attempts to close the bag. I hoisted the bag onto one shoulder and headed for the mission entryway in hopes of embarking on an adventure.

Executive Level, Casters Tower
Core City, Windstonne Enclave
Commercial Empire, Northam Continent
Thread: sysObserver.cmd

Voltaire exhaled and rolled his eyes as he watched the floor counter increment slowly. The ascent toward the executive offices felt like it was taking longer than usual. Voltaire suspected that he was apprehensive toward the meeting due to its irregular nature. He was still in the dark as to the reason for Jenkins' call to a meeting since Jenkins would ordinarily stop by the facility himself. Voltaire wouldn't have been surprised if the meeting was to terminate Mogul Prime's contract for the Synergon project. He was well aware that Jenkins wasn't the most stable of characters.

The elevator chimed, and the doors slid open. Voltaire's shiny leather shoes echoed softly against the polished tile hallway. Many executive suites had glass walls allowing Voltaire to observe many an office dweller in the pursuit of data crunching. As Voltaire reached the main office, he pushed open the glass door to be greeted by Jenkins' assistant, Sath Kinze.

"Good Morning, Mr. Sargent," Sath said with a smile.

"Good Morning, Sath. Mr. Jenkins requested to see me," Voltaire replied.

"Yes, go on in. He is expecting you," Sath said before pinging Mr. Jenkins to inform him that Voltaire had arrived.

Voltaire walked through a pair of heavy doors leading to Frank Jenkins' office. The faction leader rose from his cushy chair to greet Mogul Prime's clan leader who wore a familiar blue shirt and tan pants, "Ah, Dean, good to see you. Please have a seat."

Voltaire observed the familiar décor of the office. Black marble walls with gold trim upheld awards from before the war, likely for Jenkins' career in mediacasting. There were far less current pictures related to diplomatic events despite a couple which included other leaders of the Global Alliance. The occasional painting dotted a wall or two. Voltaire suspected that Frank Jenkins acquired them by reaping the benefits of controlling salvage contracts directly since cultural relics remained a prize on the walls of the powerful. As he sat down, Voltaire stared at the large fish tank lining one of the office walls. Colorful rocks and fake aquatic plants adorned the bottom of the tank. Several fish with extended jaws swam about the tank in quick, erratic fashion.

"Dean, how goes the progress of our satellites?" Jenkins asked with curiosity as he leaned forward on his desk.

"One is complete, and the other two should be ready for transport to the coast within the next bench," Voltaire replied, noting that Jenkins cut right to the chase.

"Splendid," Jenkins smiled, leaning back in his chair, apparently pleased with the update.

"Mr. Jenkins, would I be too forward to inquire about the usage of these satellites?" Voltaire asked, skeptical as to their purpose.

Intrigued by Voltaire's curiosity, Jenkins replied, "I don't see the harm at this point since we are so close to our launch date. The Synergon satellites contain the power to disrupt transmission of any nearby signal, and that means more power for the Commercial Empire."

"I see," Voltaire replied. "With Mogul Prime engaging in this partnership to bolster its reputation, would it be foreseeable for us to also partake in the mediacasting privileges?"

The smile faded from Jenkins' face, swiftly replaced by his normal evasive demeanor. "That we shall just have to play by ear. Of course, you do realize that I will have to make sure they have met required specifications."

"Of course," Voltaire replied, sensing the proverbial knife that Jenkins was holding behind Mogul Prime's back just waiting to be inserted once the project was complete.

"I'm sure they will do their job," Voltaire replied in a confident tone.

"As am I, Dean. Mogul Prime has proven its intellect as well as its cunning," Jenkins stated with a faint smile returning to his lips.

Voltaire stared into the tyrant's eyes reading a power struggle and pondered if Frank Jenkins considered Mogul Prime more threat than ally. Not eager to reveal his thought process through any concern on his face. Voltaire changed the subject. "Is there anything else, Mr. Jenkins, because I ought to be on my way to the facility. The clan will be waiting for me."

"I believe that should cover it, Mr. Sargent, but if you would be so kind as to be here tomorrow. I'm organizing an assembly of several clan leaders in the region for a side project. I would like to ensure that there are no loose ends to distract us from the open road ahead," Jenkins replied.

Voltaire knew that the request to meet in person was more than just a statchek. At last, Jenkins got to the purpose of the visit. Given the great deal of distrust that Voltaire already had for the white haired executive, he harbored no enthusiasm for being sucked into another venture, let alone the prospect of having to work with another clan. Mogul Prime worked alone and inherently detested any clan that squandered its status. Deciding it best to table any protest until the meeting, Voltaire simply nodded his compliance.

"Good Day, Mr. Jenkins," Voltaire replied with a curt smile before exiting the office.

Jenkins turned to watch the Mogul Prime leader exit the room. Everyone served a purpose, Jenkins thought to himself, and once that purpose was fulfilled, everyone became expendable.

Gridloc: Wayward Plane
Thread: frmCntmntMrkr.prt

The density of the humid air pressed on the sole occupant of the Behemoth cockpit. Mac Conner looked over his shoulder to ensure that he was out of earshot, despite the Vanguard warehouse having minimal occupants. He dropped into a command chair which did little to minimize the enveloping discomfort of the air.

A couple taps on the command chair arm and basic readouts for the razerjack blinked to life on the forward console. He scanned the latest readouts before bundling the statistics into a capsule. He then uploaded them to his eyecons before transmitting them through the comm.

Even with the open comm, Mac waited on account of the pause on the other end. Finally, he received a grainy visual providing attack angles to run through a simulation.

"The angled design of the head should deflect all related trajectories with the exception of a direct shot. Hits to the body however may have an adverse effect if they penetrate the shoulder armor," Mac said.

"A metal rail capable of piercing the whole gear mechanism? Do you have any reference samples?" Mac responded to the counter claim.

After receiving a visual of a dense metal rod, Mac agreed that such a projectile could pose a serious problem, "Not only would that lock up an entire gear box, but a conductor like that might even short out the entire forward assembly."

Mac listened to the comm as he absorbed the parameters needed to produce a desired result in the Behemoth's functional capacity. The specifications were a tall order.

"I'll have to draw up new schematics with Lennox," Mac explained. "Once I..."

Blinking lights activated on the Behemoth's translucent screens hovering above the command console. He paused his conversation and zeroed in on the cause of the distraction.

"Looks like we might have company," Mac said upon addressing the perimeter sensors. "I'll update you when marker two-dot-three is complete. Conner out."

Vanguard Warehouse
Abandoned Sector, Windstonne Enclave
Commercial Empire, Northam Continent
Thread: actTgtPersp1.view

The large security door creaked as I pushed it aside to enter the warehouse. Morning sunlight, creeping through the hazy windows high overhead, mixed with the fluorescent light from the ceiling bulbs creating an eerie glow. I observed the flickering light of a solar welder further back in the warehouse. Lennox's distant figure waved a hand to acknowledge my arrival. I waved back and then turned to ascend the stairs leading up to the training floor over the empty offices.

As I cleared the landing, I spotted Maxwell resting on the op table adjacent to the railing. He scurried to the edge of the table and looked up at me as I walked by. I opened my mouth to greet him until a bizarre sight from my peripheral vision jolted my brain. I turned to face the motionless figure before me.

There in the center of the training floor were two chairs several boots apart with the only connection between them being a human form. On each of the chairs was either of Mac's feet. His legs were completely parallel to the ground while his feet were the only thing supporting his body. I felt unnerved witnessing such a display of flexibility, but I realized such a trait required an exceptional amount of conditioning. Mac remained motionless except for his slow steady breathing. He faced the warehouse with his eyes closed and palms pressed together in front of his chest. To my disbelief, he continued to hold the position for at least two full clicks. Perplexed at his resilience, I shifted my weight, wondering just how long he would continue, but at last, upon sensing my restlessness, he looked up at me.

"Ah, good. You're here. We have much to do," Mac said in his normal emotionless tone even though I could sense that it was less blunt than previous conversations directed toward me.

"There's a room at the end where you can stow your things," Mac said, noticing the duffel bag around my shoulder.

I walked into a room with limited furnishings and an abundance of cleaning supplies. "So, you converted your broom closet into guest quarters," I remarked under my breath.

My quarters at the mission suddenly looked luxurious in comparison. A host of boxes served as a table for a lamp adjacent to a folding cot. I dropped my bag on the cot and returned to the training floor. Somehow, Mac had already lifted himself off the two chairs and begun pacing around the floor.

"Have a seat," Mac said, motioning to one of the chairs which I then picked up and turned to face the warehouse.

"I hope you're not implying in the same fashion you just were," I replied with concern.

"Of course not," Mac replied. "I just needed to get an early morning stretch in."

"Did you study?" Mac asked as I lowered myself onto the cold metallic chair.

"I tried. I mostly skimmed the material," I explained. "Can't exactly learn informatics in one d-"

Mac held up his hand to indicate that he didn't tolerate excuses. "Do you remember studying the basics of energistics?"

"Yes," I replied, trying to clear cobwebs from my brain after the previous night's cram session of *Foundational Reality*.

"Good, that's a start. We'll begin there," Mac responded with a nod.

"What does informatics have to do with ayveks?" I asked.

"How did you learn how to walk, Mr. Fox? You had to learn how to crawl first. Fighting is merely an advanced form of body mechanics. You must learn how to stand before you can learn how to throw a jump spin kick," Mac replied forcefully before pausing to ensure that I had no more trivial questions to ask.

"Fighting, like all activities, requires energy. Whether it is food for the body or fuel for an engine, virtually everything needs a power source," Mac continued. "Now, state the first layer of energistics."

"Energy exists in a state of equilibrium, it is not created or destroyed," I replied, the words flowing from my mouth as if by habit. I wasn't sure if I read it specifically the previous night, but it came to mind nevertheless.

"Good," Mac nodded. "Remember that! Much of your training revolves around the very nature of this balance. What does this concept mean to you?"

I had no logical answer for that question, so my best answer was, "Uh, I don't know."

"This layer describes reality existing in a perfect balance from the point of its inception. In other words, everything in physical reality was integrated into an interconnected energy system. Knowledge of such a balance is crucial to learning some of the intricacies and secrets of human mechanics," Mac explained.

"Care to expound?" I asked.

"Long have rumors circulated that some of the most dedicated Hykima practitioners were able to live through a blizzard without modern apparel, knock a bird out of the sky with a focused yell, perform healing operations without the use of akcellerrants, even increased physical strength tenfold times that of known current human abilities," Mac explained.

"Wow," I mumbled. I wasn't sure if I believed him or assumed that he was spinning a tale, but considering that he was able to appear and disappear on a whim, I figured that he might have some credible knowledge to share.

"How is that possible?" I asked.

"I'm getting to that," Mac replied as if I had interrupted.

"Contrary to some popular theories, humanity is not the center of reality, and reality began in a balanced state. Observe," Mac said before he turned to speak over his shoulder. "Maxwell, fire up a projector."

"Ayezon," Maxwell squeaked as he scuttled across the op table and interacted with the flatjack.

Moments later, I saw a light flicker from the ceiling and cast an image onto the training floor. It's clarity was superior to a noptic screen even without the physical screen. Mac clearly had more well hidden gadgets in the seemingly ramshackle hideout. The translucent image that I saw revealed a time lapsed display of a cow wandering around a field. On several occasions, it stooped to eat some of the grass. Soon after, the cow aged, and it died. The body deteriorated and eventually the carcass could no longer be seen, leaving the field as it was before the cow had grazed. Soon thereafter, a rainstorm fell. The view panned across the field to show where a river bank bordered the outskirts of the field. Not long after, the view raced along the waters' surface following out to an ocean. The rain storm ceased, and the sun began to shine on the water. Soon a mist began to rise and cloud up into the atmosphere. The view once again returned to the field which had become dry from a scorching heat. Dark grey clouds formed and a heavy rain fell once again upon the dry field. Lush grass grew once the storm had subsided, followed by another cow wandering into view. The new cow began munching on the fresh grass which had been given life from the rain.

"You see, physical events exist in equilibrium, or, at least, they did at one time. Similar cycles, both large and small are common to reality," Mac said.

Impressed by the example, I began to ponder the sequence, but my quest for clarity was short lived as it was cut off by the appearance of two starkly contrasting images. The first was lush hillside much like the one adjacent to the cow's feeding ground. The hillside was dotted with sturdy wooden homes, diversly colored floral arrangements and pens containing countless animals. Adjacent to the first image was another. It was dark and depressing, a barren landscape, a distinct opposite to the first image's location. On the hillside was a landfill and instead of a pasture was a deep chasm left by an abandoned mine. Across from the chasm were dilapidated structures worn from the elements.

"There is a common variable between these two scenarios. A variable that determines the means to radically increase or decrease energy's effectiveness," Mac continued. "Do you recall the second layer of energy?"

"I think so," I replied with a nod. "It was something to do with masses of energy spreading to areas of less energy. Things become more random."

"Yep, good. If you were to ignore these visuals, what are some popular ideas to explain said degradation of energy?" Mac asked.

Already feeling inundated by my lack of comprehension of the previous night's reading material, I sensed my focus slipping, but I tried to ramble my way through, "Some suggest black holes, hazy matter, giant cosmic vacuums maybe," I replied, shrugging my shoulders.

Mac simply nodded and paused for a moment.

"Now, back to our examples. On a more local level, we can see the disparity in energy quality even without the existence of a black hole. Any thoughts as to the common element between the two scenarios that might suggest an energy breakdown in the system?" Mac asked.

Staring at the floor, I thought for a moment. At first, I was inclined to suggest a natural disaster or war, but Mac placed an emphasis on commonality between both images. The first image was full of color, the second was not. One was full of life, the other was not. I racked my brain to make sense of his puzzle. Life itself was not the common thread considering the scene with the cows involved life yet it retained a sense of balance. Once I considered the first example, I started to think about the cycle involved.

"Are you suggesting that the balance has to do with the cycle?" I asked, questioning if I was starting to make sense of the matter.

With a masked look of intrigue, Mac raised an eyebrow, "Perhaps."

Naturally, Mac's ambiguity didn't offer me any clues. I couldn't think of anything relevant. Emphasis within the opposing images focused on human creations. Suddenly, something snapped in my mind. "Oh, I get it. You're suggesting the common link is human behavior especially when it comes to the decay. Yikes, Mr. Conner, that sure doesn't fly in the realm of public sentiment," I replied, recalling some of the educational mecas that I had seen, most of which prioritized economical advancement no matter what the cost.

"You catch on quick," Mac said. "We don't have to look very far to see examples in which life has become more disorderly. There is one clear distinction between these two outcomes, truth. All too often, humanity works toward a promise of the first image, only to deliver the second. Frequently, this disparity is perpetuated by individuals and organizations alike who never acknowledge that the better outcome requires more energy and, as a result, regularly fall back on the easy one, dealing in decay and destruction, never restoring the cycle. While some who deal in this wholesale destruction do so consciously, there are others who are merely vaporgusts, but those who oppose these plans do so consciously, well aware of the risks. While those who fight on the fringes of this battle are few in number, the greater populace lives in the middle as either spectators or casualties of the greater conflict raging about them. Their rescue and well being are the reasons why Vanguard exists."

"Those on the opposite side are playing a long game. Winning requires endurance, outlasting the enemy, and that requires energy. That is why energy matters," Mac continued. "You have likely seen mecas with heroic individuals performing unusual traits. Often recreational mecas are chock full of subtle energy-decaying agendas, designed to keep those in the middle complacent, casting doubt on the possibility of such platitudes. The upside, however, is that some of that fiction, no matter how mysterious or exaggerated, can have its roots in truth."

My attentiveness finally began to shift as Mac brought the session back around to something I could relate to. The daily monotony of mission work left me without drive beyond a whimsical, recreation-centered evening life, and I had certainly seen my share of hero mecas. I was finally starting to feel like the mystery behind my frustration might actually retreat. For a long time, while intrigued by the feats of physical strength displayed in mecas, I seldom considered the potential for such abilities to actually be real. Mac shared quite a few words as to the purpose behind the fight, but internally I felt a desire to replicate such skills to mitigate my boredom. I was finally starting to understand one of the pieces absent from my life at the mission, that of challenge.

"So, does this energy stuff help with learning how to fight?" I asked.

"That is an excellent question," Mac said with a smirk.

Outer Core Dartway
Abandoned Sector, Windstonne Enclave
Commercial Empire, Northam Continent
Thread: sysObserver.cmd

The whine of a motorbike spread over the irregularly obstructed Windstonne street. Its rider hunched his face low behind the windshield as he opened up the throttle while his leather trench coat snapped fiercely behind him in the wind. The light reflected from the green scaly pattern along his pants and vehicle alike. The sheath of his blade remained strapped firmly to his back despite the wind's best effort to dislodge the handle protruding from the hole in his trench coat just behind his shoulders. Alex Corzo's eyes revealed one thing only, determination, determination to find the one who could present a challenge.

Alex was surprised when General Seechi mentioned that this Enforcer was not only an excellent vector, but also a member of the Interlace. Such a combination was rare. Quite often proxies were a passive bunch, so they often left the defensive arts to others. That was a reality which Alex had little to complain about. It decidedly made distinguishing between friend and foe much less complicated.

Before departing the faction, Alex accepted the general's social connections within Westcrest, offering a couple of convenient locations for Alex to stay during his journey. Multiple stops within the arid faction proved a much welcome relief since the boat ride from the Shian continent to Northam proved to be a long, disagreeable one.

Once Alex cleared the borders of Westcrest, he was greeted by mostly open dartways less destroyed by ground assault teams during the war. Thankfully, large stretches of road were only slightly riddled with rusted-out vehicles minimizing Alex's time off the main road. Typically, Alex didn't mind the adventure, after all, that's what the Reptilian was built for.

The long roads gave Alex time to reflect on his time training with the Ghosts. He pondered how much he would miss training in the

Martial Legion as the wind continued to whip through his loose, black hair. General Seechi was a brilliant strategist. His ability to train the Ghosts in the ways of military reconnaissance was unmatched. While the Ghosts were small in number compared to their state sponsored military counterparts, they shared great pride in their successful melding of the stealth and noble warrior traditions from the Maleezhun islands. While some cultures looked down on the Ghosts due to their reputation for fighting only on the behalf of the wealthiest sponsors, the Ghosts never hesitated to fight in the event of a national crisis. Since large scale conflict was not the Ghosts' strength, it served them well to act as the covert operations arm of the Martial Legion as events required their service.

Ghosts were masters of stealth, capable of avoiding detection even without cloaking technology. Their fighting capacity was no less qualified to match any other rival outfit on the planet, but that still wasn't enough for Alex. There had to be more. How could one still strive to become better if he had already reached the pinnacle of all that training offered.

"How can anyone live in this jungle of duracrete and steel?" Alex muttered to himself as he approached the decaying remains of the former business capital that encompassed the primary enclave of the Commercial Empire.

Most Ghosts lived in semi-rural areas in order to continue their training in secrecy. The Martial Legion tolerated their existence when it was beneficial, but most urban communities frowned upon their presence. Ghosts, by reputation, had earned a great deal of respect, but quite often they were avoided on account of fear. Rumors circulated that the Ghosts were barbaric, rumors which likely circulated due to the lack of actual information about the Ghosts' methods. Opinions within the Ghost ranks gravitated toward the notion that their intrafaction rivals, the Drakken, sought any and all opportunity to discredit the Ghosts.

Sounds from the Reptilian's engine echoed off vacant buildings as Alex slowed the mobi to navigate and observe the dismal array of hollowed out homes and businesses. As he drew closer to the heart of the Commercial Empire, he noticed more intermittent signs of life, evident from those who made their homes in the far reaches of the enclave. Admittedly, his ride through the rural regions had been boring, so he was eager for more interesting scenery. As the occasional abandon dweller spotted him, they stared, likely witnessing a weird visitor in their domain for the first time, and on more advanced wheels no less. Motorbikes were even more rare than motorboxes due to the pressing need to transport goods through regions outside of the big enclaves, so onlookers continued to stare at the abnormal sight until Alex zipped past. As his new surroundings whipped by, Alex began taking less time to observe the strangers that he passed.

"Is that him, Rubric?" asked a gawker who slipped a candy bar from a pouch on his sleeve while leaning against a rickety wall.

The leader of the traveling trio shook his head. "No, but if we keep an eye on him, he will probably lead us to our target," he replied, dusting off a fold in his garb, unaccustomed to the dusty haze in the atmosphere. He took the apple that levitated several notches above their companion's hand who was sitting nearby on a trash can. "Let's go."

"Civilization at last," Alex mumbled.

Alex decelerated upon seeing some bystanders milling about a housing complex. As Alex passed the side street adjacent to the structure, he observed several men hauling items from the building. They were engrossed in shifting packages and appliances around, as if readying their wares for transport. If the movers knew the area, they might have insight as to the location of his target.

After clearing the intersection, Alex wheeled the Reptilian in a half circle forcing the tires to squeal against the duracrete. Alex slowed the mobi as he approached the individuals. Some movers brought full boxes out to the sidewalk while others walked empty boxes into the multi-deck complex. No one would have cared about Alex's presence if it weren't for the sound of the Reptilian's engine capturing their attention.

Alex dismounted the motorbike and cautiously approached those on the front steps.

"Excuse me, I'm looking for the Enforcer. The Serpent would like to speak with him," Alex said. He didn't know what kind of reception he would receive, but when he mentioned his challenger, it caused a commotion as one mover dropped a baking appliance. Glass and metal shattered along the sidewalk drawing the attention of everyone in the area.

"Who wants to know?" snapped a solid figure in a leather jacket and tank top.

Another figure behind Alex, wearing a loose flannel shirt, hooked his thumbs in his belt defiantly as another circled around the Reptilian.

"Woo, Nice mobi! How much berry do you think a pretty ride like this might fetch, Nox?" whistled the voice of the red haired man wearing faded denim pants.

"Huh?" Nox replied, oblivious to the prior conversation from his seat on the steps.

"Better yet, check out those matching pants," laughed the blonde who leaned against Nox's shoulder. "Someone's been shopping in the clearance tent at Haggler's Bazaar."

With the commotion escalating, the remaining clan members not yet present finally exited the building.

"Who's this?" asked the man wearing an athletic track suit.

"Some spinejack! Says he's the Serpent, and he's looking for that fish who roughed up Jammer and Sophomore," Burnout replied from the far side of Alex's bike as he shifted his weight into a more offensive posture. Several onlookers chuckled until the flannel-clad guy on the sidewalk piped up.

"At least we didn't bolt like a couple of limp fish," Sophomore retorted while eyeing the newcomer suspiciously. Bull and Nox immediately silenced their guffaw at the defensive quip.

"I don't care who he is, get this freak out of here. It's like these guys are oozing out of the ground lately," Jocq snapped from the apartment entryway.

"Looks like you've got a fight on your hands, Stranger," Bull said.

"I only fight those who present a challenge," Alex replied while remaining motionless.

Agitated with the stranger's condescension, the clan members advanced. Burnout's red hair blurred as he charged Alex from behind, but a swift kick to his gut sent him tumbling to the ground. Bull shifted his leather coat to reveal a leather whip that had been tucked behind his back while Sophomore unclipped his large belt buckle and drew the flat leather accessory before him. Both individuals lashed their weapons out, but Alex reacted faster than they expected.

Alex snapped his wrist to his back, drawing his sword, arcing it through the air, severing both the whip and the belt just notches from the attackers' hands. With one fluid motion the blade was returned to its sheath with nothing more than a faint flash of silver to suggest it had even moved through the air. The defective weapons flopped to the ground as the attackers stared on with gaping jaws.

Nox scowled and shoved Swipe to the side drawing the hammers that hung at his waist.

"The next one loses a limb," Alex replied emotionlessly, despite feeling amused at the attackers' feeble attempts. His hand remained fixed on the handle of his blade.

"What do you want, Carp?" snarled the clan leader who remained on the stairs.

"Deliver my message. Otherwise, I shall have to return," Alex said.

"You'll regret crossing paths with Academé," shouted Burnout as he rubbed his abdomen.

"I doubt it," Alex replied with his raspy voice and straight face as he climbed back on the Reptilian. He fired up the engine and, with a shrill squeal, wheeled the mobi around, sped down the street, rounded the corner and left the scowling Academé members in the distance.

DAVE TODD

6 – Assembly – 6

BOWTech Laboratories
Core City, Windstonne Enclave
Commercial Empire, Northam Continent
Thread: sysObserver.cmd

Protech Killian Szazs sat hunched over his desk, staring blankly at his slate as figures and schematics scrolled before his eyes. His wan expression indicated fatigue from working too many arcs in a day, too many days in a bench, too many benches in a pass. Ever since Jenkins demanded more military research, there wasn't a moment's rest for the workers at BOWTech Laboratories. Due to budget shortfalls, the Commercial Empire turned to the use of animals as machines of destruction, and BOWTech Laboratories was the ideal vehicle to achieve that purpose hence its name, Beast of War Technologies.

Founded prior to the Smart Wars, BOWTech found itself contracted to the Commercial Empire after its success in creating a synthetic virus with hybrid functionality capable reeking havoc on organic and digital pathways alike. Under protest, BOWTech was required to create pulse bombs using domestic animals like cats and dogs as carriers to target civilians. The sinister administration was boundless in its cruelty, and its latest project would make its history of slaughter look like a bedtime story.

"How are we doing today, my friend?" Frank Jenkins asked with a smug look as he strolled into the lab.

Szazs immediately snapped out of his daze and turned to face Jenkins while remaining seated in his swivel chair. "We are on schedule, Mr. Jenkins," Szazs replied, his voice revealing fatigue from absence of sunlight and restful sleep.

"Good, good to hear. Let's have those cats ready by next bench," Jenkins gloated.

"N-next bench? We still have many modifications to make, not to mention we are waiting on the next shipment from the Equatorial Span," Protech Szazs replied with as much emphasis as his weariness would allow.

"Well, Protech, you have already proven yourself to be a man of brilliance, so I'm sure that, by equally dividing labor resources and restructuring your digital operations, your schedule could be greatly enhanced. Am I right?" Jenkins pompously stated, turning toward the lab's metallic doors.

Hanging his head, Szazs muttered, "Yes, Sir," allowing the glow lamp on his desk to cast shadows on his pale aged complexion.

There had to be a way out of the cage commonly called an informatic facility. Szazs had put up with enough of the faction leader's ruthless cunning. He had grown tired of the plotting for war, only to see thousands, if not millions, die at the hands of his research. Much of Szazs' family was killed in the Smart Wars. Having little else to do with his life, he invested this efforts into his research, but financial responsibilities prevented Szazs from applying himself to endeavors that he cared about.

The weight of so many losses finally forced Szazs to face the corruption of BOWTech's purpose, minimize human losses not increase them. He knew that it was time to apply his intellect toward a plan to escape from his prison without bars.

As he leaned back in his chair, his thoughts turned from Jenkins' arrogance to intellectual sulking, his mind chasing the most abstract of escape plans. Nearly nodding off to sleep, Szazs sat upright as a thought came to him. During the Smart Wars, BOWTech heavily engaged its use of organech viruses, most notably the Crossover Strain. Within several lunars, an individual produced a chemical capable of terminating the virus. The solution was surprisingly adaptive in its application. It could either be dissolved in a liquid and ingested for human cures or be coated over data circuits to eradicate traces lurking within digital systems. The creator of the antiviral substance had been connected well enough to produce it in mass quantities and began shipping through low key operations until its distribution crossed into every continent, rendering the virus inert. With the weapon rendered ineffective, BOWTech terminated development of the project to focus on the domestic pulse bombs.

Regardless of the solution creator's identity, he surely had a heart and a sense of wit to create something so efficiently, and, in so doing, saved millions of lives. It was definitely the first time that Szazs welcomed seeing his work become a failure.

Deciding that nothing more could be solved without a couple arc's worth of sleep, Szazs decided that he should return to his makeshift quarters and resume his morning plan of identifying and locating the creator of the Crossover Prevalent. Szazs placed his slate on the desk and stared into the display monitoring the beasts that BOWTech was currently working on. The cage which displayed on the camera feed appeared still and silent. Szazs leaned forward to make sure the critter was still in there. He knew that it couldn't have gotten out, but paranoia drove him to look closer. Suddenly, a dark object sprung from the corner of the cage growling, and thrust its head into the cage door startling Szazs.

Jittered beyond control, Szazs started talking to himself, "Sleep, must have sleep. Get a grip, Szazs."

Vanguard Warehouse
Abandoned Sector, Windstonne Enclave
Commercial Empire, Northam Continent
Thread: actTgtPersp1.view

After completing several laps around the training floor, I felt like going to sleep, but I decided that it probably wasn't the wisest course of action given the potential penalty of more laps. My mind oozed with imagery from Mac's first info dump. Nagging questions still pestered me about how Mac was able to disappear at will, not to mention the striking resemblance that we shared. I was hoping that he wouldn't take much longer to answer those questions.

I plopped down on the floor and waited for Mac to finish his conversation with Maxwell. I could hear Torque revving the engine of a mox in the warehouse as he worked on modifications.

Mac finally walked over once he noticed that I had finished my jog around the room. "Now where were we... Ah, yes, the second layer of energistics."

Taking a tick to interject, I decided to take another shot in the dark, at least without my usual sarcasm, "I've got another question. How does all of this study prove useful during fights when everyone has firearms? Why bother fighting with hands and feet?"

"That's funny that you should ask," Mac replied. "Because that is yet one more thing that we need to cover, but for the time being let me say that there are vectors who are so skilled that they will render any firearm you hold useless or move so fast that they can strike you in three places before you can even pull the trigger. It's good that you are considering such scenarios. It shows that your brain is starting to resume normal operations."

"Don't let the haps spread too far," I smirked.

"Based on current discussions, what do you think contributes most to the breakdown in the energy cycle?" Mac continued.

"It would seem that the balance is broken by collecting energy without returning it to the system, or by creating massive regions for energy to travel and disperse," I replied.

"Any idea what might prompt such actions in human behavior?" Mac asked.

I had no answer to Mac's question, but I couldn't help but feel like he assumed that I knew more on the subject than I was letting on about. Still, I couldn't explain why pieces of the conversation felt like they occurred naturally while others were as foreign as my past. All I could muster was a non-committal, "No idea."

"It might surprise you to know that since this phenomenon is common to humans, there is something consuming or prompting it to cause this energy decay from within, a virus," Mac said.

My eyes widened, and I stared at Mac. I managed a couple of blinks while waiting for him to explain

"Every human is born with a fibernetic virus, referred to by some as the Catalyst. You mentioned black holes earlier, well this, my friend, is far more powerful than any cosmic vacuum and it doesn't exist millions of parcels away, it exists... in... the human heart," Mac said, taking his time to let the point sink in.

I stared at the floor, initially thinking that a sense of panic might overtake me at the thought of a rampant incurable disease, but instead, a sense of calm replaced the concern since I couldn't shake the plausibility of Mac's claim when considering the course of human events, past and present.

"Does everyone have it?" I asked, not thinking that I could have possibly contracted such a wretched virus.

"Everyone," Mac replied quietly.

"Is there a cure?" I asked as I felt a sense of dread at the awareness of this new reality.

"The virus persists as long as it has a host, so if you take out the host, you take out the virus. Those before you had it, your parents had it, you have it. We all have it. Isn't that a comfort?" Mac asked, his rhetorical dry wit no longer offering reassurance.

I dropped my forehead into my hands for a moment wondering just how I was supposed to process the information. I had never heard of any such condition before. I never heard it mentioned in any informatic meca's that I watched. If there was truth to Mac's claim, that could only leave two outcomes, the masses were unaware, or its existence was covered up. To better understand, I pressed Mac further, "How can you know this virus is real?"

"That leads to a discussion which is about to test your very understanding of reality itself, Mr. Fox," Mac replied with a smirk. "It's a good thing that you are already sitting down."

"Much of the common understanding about reality is saturated by soloist agendas. Pre-war academics were obsessed with finding the one bond that tied all physical properties together. They continued stacking theories on top of theories until the end result was more outrageous than the wildest fantasies. Progress has limped on ever since as the remnant of academics continue to retread the concepts of Quarterstone and Falcone indefinitely," Mac continued.

"The flaw in their understanding was that what they believed reality to be a universe, when really it's a paraverse, two halves of a whole. They only studied one half of the equation. Many great minds have explored the Particulate, the tangible portion of reality, light, sound, forces and matter, but the other half of the paraverse, the Vast, an immaterial domain, has largely remained absent from most studies," Mac said.

"I suppose you have a way to explain how something so significant went unnoticed," I replied, raising an eyebrow with a fair share of skepticism.

"I do," Mac remarked, taking my doubt in stride, "The Catalyst does not occur naturally, it was engineered. The virus was so deviously designed that it could impair the heart from one of its natural functions, that of discerning and managing inputs."

"What inputs?" I asked.

"Not only does the heart function like a motor for the circulatory system, it is also a powerful receiver, just as the eyes illuminate the imprint within," Mac replied, waiting to see if I cared to interject.

Without immediate questions, I let him continue.

"Have you ever been able explain the nature of emotions... likes... dislikes? Can you tell where they come from or when they will actually occur?" Mac asked.

I shook my head.

"Neither can the academics. Again, that is because they don't factor in the other half of the equation. Just as the eye perceives light waves, and the ear, sound waves, so too does the heart, except that it receives another type of wave known as a drift wave. If colors are the spectrum for light, then emotions are the spectrum for drift waves. The key difference is that these waves travel through a different medium, the Vast. Drift waves can carry dreams and imagination just as easily as anger and hatred. They are powerful and contagious. The heart, which is the human receiver for these waves, exists in both halves of the paraverse at the same time," Mac continued.

"I suppose you would like to get back to your favorite question about its relevance to fighting," Mac said.

I only offered a nonchalant shrug.

"Have you ever witnessed a flower wither in a summer heat, an unstable building collapse from a quake, or suffered visual impairment from staring toward the sun?" Mac asked.

"Not all of them directly. I hope that I have enough sense not to stare at the sun for too long," I remarked.

Mac rolled his eyes, "Regardless, the phenomenon is the same, energy overload. Even though energy can yield great results, light for the growth of plants, sound to enrich our perception, it can also degrade or even destroy any vessel incapable of withstanding an excessive influx. That is the general behavior of the Catalyst. Instead of allowing energy to flow back into the system it channels it inward. In the short term, it creates discomfort, stress even, but in the long term, it acts as an aging accelerant, ultimately causing death after prolonged degradation of the human body, acting like a slow, silent poison. So, if a vector relies on energy to succeed, it would be wise to avoid operating with a diminished fuel supply."

"So, inherited virus equals energy loss, leading to a wimpy defense," I replied, sensing that my eyes were glazing over.

"Right," Mac said with a sigh as he acknowledged that the introduction was exceeding my attention span. "Go throw a few sets of kicks at the bag. We'll take a break when you're done."

Executive Level, Casters Tower
Core City, Windstonne Enclave
Commercial Empire, Northam Continent
Thread: sysObserver.cmd

Frank Jenkins sat in his large high backed chair looking out over Windstonne. He impatiently drummed his fingers on the arm rest. He had an uneasy feeling that there was a snag in his plan. He couldn't place his finger on it, but he just knew there was a loose end, and loose ends were never something to be ignored. He hadn't successfully climbed the largest corporate ladder imaginable by overlooking seemingly insignificant details.

Jenkins reflected on his handling of the Interlace. If those idealistic clods hadn't been driven into the shadows, his control of the Commercial Empire would have been jeopardized. That, he would not allow. So what if he had resorted to underhanded disposal methods. That's why companies like BOWTech Laboratories were established. Billions died in the Global War, so why should he care about a few million more. The losses were justifiable, besides, there was plenty of talent available even within Windstonne alone. Everyone had a price, and soon he would identify the price of each faction leader beholden to the Global Alliance. Of course, if they didn't come to terms with that price, well, that's what disposal mechanisms were for.

"Mr. Jenkins, they are here," Sath announced.

"Thank you, Sath. Please show them in," Jenkins replied after he whirled around in his chair and silenced the sonair on his desk. He then rose and stood in the center of his office to greet his guests.

Moments later the double doors swung open and three men sauntered into the room. "Please have a seat," Jenkins gestured with his hand toward the cushy chairs facing his desk.

Each of the guests took a seat as Jenkins returned to his desk and faced them, "Thank you for coming."

The new arrivals made little comment. Each of them represented a different clan, but all three had one thing in common. They shared no interest in occupying the same room.

After a grim silence, Jenkins sat down and spoke up, "I understand that these are rather abnormal circumstances for such a meeting, but great strides have never been fulfilled on a banker's shift alone.

"Jocq, what is the status of Académe's operations?" Jenkins asked as he turned to the blonde athlete on one end of the trio.

Jocq shifted nervously in his seat while Jenkins eyed him impatiently. Sensing the tension, the other clan leaders simply observed the exchange as the Académe leader squirmed in his seat.

"Well?" Jenkins asked with irritation.

"Uh, we've encountered some setbacks," Jocq stammered. Usually, he was the one dishing out verbal threats, but his role had been reversed.

"What do you mean setbacks?" Jenkins replied, glaring fiercely at Jocq.

"Most of my boys have been running into some renegade who goes by *The Enforcer*. He even roughed some of them up. My clan knows how to fight and all, but he bested them at a numeric disadvantage. Reports say that he appears out of the shadows like a phantom," Jocq replied.

Jenkins bristled at the name. For a long time, he thought he'd never hear it ever again. He suspected that he may have found the loose end he was concerned about.

The solemn figure dressed in black on the opposite end of the group attempted to stifle a snicker. Jenkins caught the motion in his peripheral vision but kept his ire trained on Jocq who was still sulking.

"Following that, they were working on a salvage op when some mobi riding fishstick wielding a sword showed up, threatened us, and said he's looking for said Enforcer and that he wanted us to deliver a message," Jocq said.

Jenkins leaned back in his chair and observed each of the clan leaders while he contemplated a response, "Have either of you heard of this individual?" He asked.

The alternate clan leaders shook their heads.

"It's no wonder they got beat up though, they don't know the first thing about fighting," Tiger blurted since he could no longer contain his laughter. "Académe couldn't stand next to one of our shadows without getting hurt."

"Well, at least we use our efforts to contribute, you carp," Jocq quipped with aggravation.

"What do you know? You Monks are nothing more than mercs with fancy gadgets," Voltaire replied, finally joining the conversation from the middle seat. He didn't care for Académe or the Monks, but Tiger's blatant disregard for the meeting was really grating on him.

Quickly snapping from his amusement, Tiger glared at Voltaire, "Better to have an imprint to sell, Mr. Sargent, than not have one at all."

"An imprint?!" Voltaire laughed. "Success requires no such crutch. A vestige of an archaic morality will only cause you to rethink your actions, to hesitate... to fail," Voltaire said in a slow emphatic tone as he mocked the Monk who continued to glare.

"Enough!" Jenkins snapped as he slammed the base of his fist on the heavy desk.

"I don't want unknown vectors roaming around this enclave, nor do I care to have a pack of squabbling hens preening in my office. Jocq, where did your clan encounter this individual?" Jenkins asked, getting the meeting back on track.

"Both times it was within three or four parcels of that mission beyond the boundaries of our contract," Jocq said.

"Hmmm, the Dwelling Street Mission... I placed rather generous concessions in their operational contract, I would be sorely displeased if they were in violation of our agreement," Jenkins mused.

"Dibby, display profile: Dwelling Street Mission," Jenkins spoke into the virtual assistant's receiver, prompting a translucent image to appear on the noptic screen in the center of his desk. The screen rotated as it cycled through the known staff profiles of the workers at the mission.

"Wait! Go back!" Jocq said.

Jenkins pushed a button and the profile of an average face paused on the screen.

"That's him!" Jocq shouted.

"That... is your Enforcer?" Voltaire replied, his voice dripping with sarcasm as he scanned the profile of a scrawny salvage worker.

The image revealed a fair skinned individual with light brown hair. The glasses and round facial form hardly made the individual appear menacing.

"No, no, he's the guy that two of my men found scrounging around the abandoned library in that area. My guys jumped him, but shortly thereafter is when the Enforcer showed up. They were going to follow him, but he had already taken off before they could recover from the bashing they received," Jocq replied, rolling his eyes.

Tiger's eyes narrowed and focused on the visual that floated above the desk. He squinted for a moment, noting something strangely familiar about the mission worker, but he said nothing.

"Here's the plan. I want all three of your clans to investigate this matter. I won't have renegades running around this enclave!" Jenkins said.

"Mr. Jenkins, do you really think all of this is necessary. This simple matter could easily be resolved by Mogul Prime alone. We haven't taken on any direct engagements in a while," Voltaire replied, hoping to avoid any form of collaboration with scum from other clans.

Jenkins' rash decision was only adding fuel to Voltaire's distrust, considering that he already avoided the discussion of potential roles for Mogul Prime upon completion of the Synergon project.

"Yes, Mr. Sargent, it IS necessary. It is imperative that I have my way. Otherwise, I would be extremely irate, and then, no one will be happy. No one will threaten the sovereignty of the Commercial Empire. Do you hear me? NO ONE. DISMISSED."

Confused as to how Voltaire agitated Jenkins worse than Academé's initial report, Jocq and Tiger rose to leave the room. Disgruntled, Voltaire also stood and turned to leave.

"Tiger, please stay for a moment," Frank Jenkins said.

Tiger watched the other two clan leaders vacate the room and close the doors behind them. Unsure as to what the Commercial Empire leader wanted with him, Tiger kept his guard up and refrained from returning to the chair. He nonchalantly eyed Jenkins who was taking a rather lengthy pause before speaking up.

"I have associates that speak well of your work," Jenkins smiled.

Tiger had run into many politicians throughout his days and was not easily impressed by the man's flattery. Tiger folded his arms across his chest and waited for Jenkins to continue.

Reading Tiger's reluctance to engage, Jenkins decided to elaborate. "As you can imagine, I have subordinates across the Commercial Empire, and several have reported to me about your exploits in defending our borders against dissidents from Westcrest who have been harassing our residents. Since you come highly recommended, I would like to extend an opportunity to your clan. I would like you to lead this mission and oversee it personally," Jenkins said waiting to see if his pitch would sell.

"What's in it for us?" Tiger replied as he reflected on his recent conversation with Panther.

Jenkins stood up and paced behind his desk as he casually glanced out over the city. "I understand that the Monks are well versed in numerous ayveks. One never can have too many powerful allies. I believe that your skills could be a great asset to our military forces," Jenkins said.

"I still only hear what's in it for you," Tiger replied impatiently.

Jenkins smiled, "Well, in order to improve our forces they would require training, training that my military would need instructors for, training that you could offer them. Rumor has it that mercenaries like yourself could use such exposure for their cause," Jenkins replied in a sly tone.

"I don't suppose you have habits of making promises that you can't keep, Mr. Jenkins?" Tiger replied suspiciously.

"Of course not, and if I did why should I be as foolhardy as to think I could get away with it against such a shrewd clan as the Monks," Jenkins said with a fake smile still plastered behind his white beard.

"Indeed," Tiger replied coldly. "Why is this lowly mission of such significance to you, Mr. Jenkins? Sending a group of lethal killers to investigate a matter with scavengers implies greater danger than first glance might suggest."

"I understand that there is no fooling you, Tiger. It is good to know that I have discerning associates such as yourself to carry out assignments. All you need to know for now is that I have reason to believe there are radicals dwelling within the abandoned sector, and in order to maintain public standing, I have to prove it without making a mess. Should a clan take care of the matter at hand without any word of warning, I would have little reason to fear any disruption of reputation across the enclaves. Find out what I need to know, and your clan will be compensated... adequately," Jenkins stated firmly before handing Tiger a slate outlining alternate mission criteria.

Tiger nodded, accepted the slate and exited the office. He didn't trust Jenkins, but he decided that it was time to start playing hardknuckle. If the faction leader decided to screw the Monks, Frank Jenkins would only have to write off his damaged reputation, but the way Tiger saw it, he would make sure that reputation was ALL that remained of Frank Jenkins.

Vanguard Warehouse
Abandoned Sector, Windstonne Enclave
Commercial Empire, Northam Continent
Thread: actTgtPersp1.view

Strange sounds of an urban rhythm reached my ears from the back of the warehouse via Lennox's emcast. The dull bass sound waves echoed through the hollow building. Above the din, I could almost hear Mac shuffling around in the rustic galley.

"Here you go," Mac said, tossing me an apple.

"Thanks," I replied as I bit into the apple. "So, where you do you guys manage to get your supplies? In this remote part of the enclave, there sure isn't much to select from, and I take it that you try to avoid the public," I asked in between munching on the piece of fruit in my mouth.

"We have a small green house on the roof, and we've got a few connections that allow us to barter supplies when necessary," Mac replied as he sat down at the op table.

"Right, but what about fuel for all of the vehicles? We're parcels from the nearest Imperan station, and there are no power cell shops in the area. I can't imagine how difficult it would be to track down fuel for those engines, not to mention how much power that thing requires," I replied, jerking my thumb in the direction of the Behemoth.

"True," Mac smiled. "But again, Lennox and I have many connections within the Interlace, we've never had any trouble tracking down essentials. You think motorbox fuel is tough, just imagine trying to find jet fuel. That stuff is like liquid passgrad," he said laughing.

"What is this Interlace that I keep hearing about?" I asked curiously.

Mac paused for a moment. His somber frame revealed hesitation as if I had asked about some dark mystery that wasn't to be revealed to anyone.

"Are you sure you want to know?" Mac asked with a smirk. "You've already ventured into deep waters with Vanguard's company. Association with the Interlace racks up serious animosity points."

Paranoid how far into the wilderness I had wandered, I hesitated before answering. I knew that I had already gotten myself in over my head and any decisions to follow might potentially change my life into something unrecognizable.

Mac nearly burst out laughing, but he contained himself. "Whoa, don't take me that seriously all of the time, you look like you've just sharked out a couple of organs."

"The Interlace is the oldest known organization on record. It has undergone a few name changes over the passes, but its focus remains the same, apply strong adherence to the Criterion. The Interlace fights to improve the quality of life, but due to its uncommon operation methods, its members are often labeled as lunatics. Many governments fear the Interlace," Mac said as he explained.

"Where does the Interlace operate?" I asked.

"The Interlace isn't bound by any geolocation. There are members in every faction, but numbers have dwindled over the last deceon. Faction leaders such as Jenkins used the Smart Wars as a front to execute anyone even rumored to have anything to do with the Interlace. Since then, many have carefully protected their Interlace identity," Mac continued.

"But you admit that you're part of it, how come you're not afraid?" I asked.

"Those who have been in the Interlace long enough have learned that there is nothing to fear," Mac replied.

"So why does everyone else fear the Interlace then?" I asked, not fully understanding the context.

"Members of the Interlace view life differently than most, and because of that they are often regarded with hostility. The Interlace is not here to take over nations, but to preserve them despite many leaders assuming the opposite," Mac said.

"What is the advantage to being part of an organization that is always the butt end of social preference?" I asked.

"You would be surprised what you could learn through the Interlace's deep pool of knowledge," Mac replied as he watched Maxwell following a fly with his eyes. "Many in the Interlace have an internal strength defying all informatic rationale."

Maxwell scurried around the table top trying to catch the fly but to no avail. Enjoying the sport I watched the hamster for a click myself while Mac completed his thought.

"True strength is not measured by one's ability to take life..." Mac said, quietly trailing off as we continued watching Maxwell. The hamster squatted as he prepared to leap on the fly which had remained motionless for the last five ticks. Maxwell launched his furry body into the air and attempted to squash the fly beneath himself, but the fly made short work of Maxwell's efforts and flew from the table. Mac's open hand snapped from his waist and arced through the air into a closed fist.

"But to give life," Mac replied as he opened his fist and allowed the fly to lift from his palm. With a hum, the fly took off for another part of the warehouse as it tired of the game.

"Hey, I've been trying to catch that thing all day," Maxwell replied in his digital voice.

Mac simply smiled as he watched the fly zip through the air. Our silence was soon disrupted by a ping from the sonair integrated into the terminal on the op table.

"Ooo, I'll get it!" Maxwell replied as he shuffled across the table and waved his forelegs in front of the screen.

"Mac, it's an incoming ping from Sath!" Maxwell said to Mac who leaned forward with interest. I was curious about the relevance of the comm but for the sake of etiquette I got up and walked over to the railing so Mac could speak privately. Lennox had finished cleaning up his tuning job, and walked up the stairs to eavesdrop on Mac's comm.

"Mac here," Mac said as he watched the noptic screen floating above the terminal.

"Hey, Mac," answered a sweet voice from what I could hear from a distance. "I know I'm taking a risk contacting you from work, but I found something interesting that you might like to know."

"Frank is currently in a meeting with leaders from three high profile clans in the region. I didn't think anything of it, but I overhead that one of them was from Académe. I don't know if that means anything to you or not, but I wanted to let you know," the voice added.

I looked over my shoulder to see Mac smile after listening to her talk, "Thanks, I don't know what is going on, but if Jenkins is starting to rely on clans he's looking for something. He's expanding his reach after all, and, if he is, he wants that something without compromising his status. He wouldn't be using clods like Académe if it wasn't some kind of dirty work that could potentially jeopardize his reputation. Not when he has Imperan forces at his disposal."

Lennox walked up next to me and elbowed me in the ribs, "That's Mac's girlfriend. Better not let him catch you listening," he said with a wink making sure he was quiet, but just loud enough so Mac could hear him.

Mac paused to look over the top of the noptic screen to glare at us with a stern reprimand out of the corner of his eye. Lennox chuckled and walked over to the galley to grab food.

"I have to go, Mac. Someone is coming. Take care of yourself," Sath replied. I could hear the concern in her voice. I did my best to stifle a laugh on account of the truth in Lennox's jest.

"You too," Mac replied as the feed ended abruptly. I watched the enthusiasm slip from his face as he shut down the comm. Lennox returned from the galley with a wrapped oat bar in his hand.

"You know, Mac, you'd have no reason to be so glum, if you would just make your move. After all, pretty girls are hard to come by in this part of town especially those interested in your sorry spine. If you love the girl, you should tell her," Lennox said as he socked Mac in the arm.

Maxwell and I joined Lennox's laughter. Mac didn't appear to be amused, but he took it in stride. "Please allow me to inform you fellas on the finer aspects of love. It isn't merely a romantic sentiment or warm fuzzy feeling, but a responsibility to others over yourself."

"See what I mean," Lennox chuckled as he sank his teeth into his chewy snack. He walked past Mac and then proceeded down to the warehouse floor. I watched him mouth the word *Boring* as he walked away. I laughed for a moment and then returned to the table where Mac was sitting.

"So what does all of this clan stuff mean?" I asked.

Mac rested his hands on his chin, "I'm not sure, but I have a feeling that our recent encounters have reached their way to the top faster than anticipated."

"Maxwell, you know what to do," Mac said to the hamster who snapped a foreleg to his head in a small salute. He then turned to the terminal and began digging through his sources on the Hyper Lynx.

"Now what?" I asked again, not happy with the answer that I received.

"Now we accelerate your training. Ever heard of a vortex?" Mac smiled.

DAVE TODD

7 – The Balance Within – 7

Executive Level, Casters Tower
Core City, Windstonne Enclave
Commercial Empire, Northam Continent
Thread: sysObserver.cmd

Sath quickly disabled the noptic screen on her desk as a tall, balding business executive in a smoke gray suit approached her desk. She usually only contacted Mac through a private comm, but the nature of the conversation between Jenkins and the clan leaders felt suspicious. Frank Jenkins usually dealt with politicians and executives, not abandon renegades, most of which contrasted the new arrival. She quickly shifted her focus from the conversation with Mac to the visitor.

"Can I help you?" Sath asked as she smiled at the middle-aged gentleman.

"Yes, I'm, Mr. Oszwick. I'm here to speak with Mr. Jenkins," the visitor replied with a charismatic smile.

"Mr. Jenkins is in a meeting right now," Sath replied as she reviewed multiple scans to verify the appointment schedule. Not finding anything, she looked up at Mr. Oszwick, "I'm sorry. I don't see anything scheduled in here, perhaps there has been a mistake."

Mr. Oszwick's smile remained fixed in place, conveying that he wasn't easily dissuaded by the lack of appointment. "That's not an issue, my dear, Mr. Jenkins probably just forgot to mention it to you. I spoke with him already."

Sath remained perplexed, considering that Jenkins had her schedule all of his appointments without exception. Also, there was something disconcerting about Oszwick, something artificial in a sense, but Sath was unable identify her concern.

"If you could, please have a seat, I'll check with Mr. Jenkins," Sath replied in a guarded tone.

Oszwick nodded and turned to seat himself in one of the shiny black leather chairs adjacent to a lobby wall. After several clicks of waiting, Mr. Oszwick turned to see the double doors of Frank Jenkins' office open. Two somber individuals exited and proceeded toward the hallway. The first was rather nonchalant and completely ignored both Oszwick and the agenda coordinator. The second was rather disgruntled and irritably scanned the room as he plodded behind the other, but Oszwick easily recognized him and approached before he could retreat into the hallway.

"Dean Sargent?" Oszwick asked as he stepped toward the figure dressed in casual businesswear.

"That's right," Voltaire replied, not in the mood for chatting with an obsessive fan of Mogul Prime's materials.

"I have studied much of your work and what Mogul Prime has done for our culture," Oswick continued once again with his automated smile.

"Yeah and?" Voltaire questioned impatiently.

"I own a company which specializes in educational supplements, and I would be pleased if you would stop by for a meeting. I promise I will make it worth your while," Oszwick said, extending a noptic card with the location, time, and date.

"I'll consider it, Mr.?" Voltaire grumbled upon receiving the card.

"Oszwick, K. Oszwick, CEO of Oszwick Enterprises," Oszwick replied, extending his hand.

"Right," Voltaire sniffed, disregarding any additional gestures by the businessman as he walked past.

Thread: sysObserver.cmd

Frank Jenkins slouched in his chair as he watched Tiger depart from his office. He stared idly at the Tiger emblem embroidered on the back of the Monk's black pullover. Jenkins thought it a strange custom for the Monks to all take on personas of different animals, but who was he to argue. They were all accomplished vectors, and just exactly who he needed to exterminate the growing suspicion in his mind about the Dwelling Street Mission.

Jenkins was interrupted by a shrill sound from the sonair on his desk.

"What is it?" Jenkins replied stiffly as he activated the receiver.

"Mr. Jenkins, there is a Mr. Oszwick here to see you. He said that he had already spoken with you," Sath said through the comm.

"I don't remember such an individual, but whatever send him in," Jenkins said, feeling unusually ambivalent toward the breach of protocol.

Frank Jenkins rose to greet his mystery guest. He failed to recognize the sharply dressed executive who confidently strode into the office, but he disregarded his ever increasing ability to forget what he did or did not schedule.

"Mr. Jenkins, it is a privilege to meet with you. Thank you for granting me a moment of your time," Oszwick said as he shook the faction leader's hand.

"What can I do for you, Mr. Oszwick?" Frank Jenkins asked with a weak smile, barely masking his distrust.

Oszwick unbuttoned his gray suit coat as he sat down in one of the chairs facing Jenkins' desk. Jenkins peered inquisitively at the contrasting red shirt and black tie which the businessman had chosen for his formal appearance. Most executives chose milder colors, but there was something different about the man with the confidence to secure a meeting with the faction leader on a whim.

Mr. Oszwick's face lit up with a bright smile as he began to speak. "I've heard of your exploits, Mr. Jenkins, within your quest to better the Global Alliance, and I would like to offer the services of Oszwick Enterprises."

"I'm curious as to what quest that it is you wish to assist with, Mr. Oszwick, and if so, what services you feel that your company has to offer the Commercial Empire," Jenkins replied, more suspicious than ever, considering that knowledge of any plans for takeover of the Alliance were only known to a select few. Even Mogul Prime didn't fully understand the full scope of Project Synergon. The ambiguous revelation intrigued him.

"You and I are much alike, Mr. Jenkins. We are men of ambition, never fully satisfied without ascending to the next stage, and I can see that your efforts to manage the Commercial Empire are merely child's play. Someone like you has the leadership to run all of the Global Alliance, and you merely need the means to promote your qualifications, and that is why I am here. My corporation specializes in numerous sectors, but our current research in synthetic consumables has excelled in the field of educational supplements. I believe that as a licensed distributor of such products, your good standing with other factions could greatly be... magnified, so to speak," Oszwick said as he slid a slate with product specifications across Jenkins' desk.

Jenkins picked up the slate and toggled through the scans regarding a supplement called Extend. It was reported to improve both recall and cognition in addition to increasing the brain's memory capacity. The data for the product was well documented.

"This is all very interesting, Mr. Oszwick, but I'm not sure if you realize that I prefer to regulate the flow of information that takes place within the Commercial Empire, as do many other Global Alliance leaders in their respective factions. The more that people think for themselves, the more they seek independence. Without such restraints, we will have yet another revolution on our hands," Jenkins said as he placed the slate back on the desk.

"Of course," Oszwick replied, unfazed by Jenkins' disinterest. "That is why we have specially tailored our product to contain something called a side effect," Oszwick said as he leaned forward.

By suggesting the nature of an agenda manufactured into the supplement, Jenkins found his curiosity piqued. He raised an eyebrow, suggesting that Oszwick continue.

"While Extend is formulated to increase a user's capacity, that capacity is bent toward particular subjects. Translated, it makes them, shall we say, impressionable. There is no need to introduce critical thinking when the target information provided is already designed for the well being of the user. We have some of the finest informatechs working for us, and believe me, Mr. Jenkins, they are very thorough. They have done much research to discover how various chemicals influence the mind. They have even found a way to modify a subject's own independence," Oszwick said.

Comprehending the benefit to his agenda, Jenkins was eager to learn more about the wonder project, but despite listening intently, he maintained caution since he didn't attain power without questioning everything that sounded too good to be true. "This all sounds like quite an achievement, Mr. Oszwick, but I'm curious to know how this will benefit your corporation," Jenkins said.

"No doubt, Mr. Jenkins. I certainly understand your concern. Men like us must know everything about circumstances surrounding our dealings including friends and foes. Research always rewards those who dare to delve into its often dark and dismal depths. Oszwick Enterprises is a humble establishment hoping to offer its services worldwide. What better way to increase marketshare than by working side by side with its most contributing sponsor, the leader of the Global Alliance?"

Jenkins leaned back and ran his fingers through his trimmed white beard, contemplating his next course of action. He recognized that Oszwick had quite the ability to promote a sale, but even he knew that it was just a tactic, one that he had used himself throughout his crusade for power. Jenkins understood that Oszwick was probably after something. He wasn't able to decipher the nature of that something, but nevertheless, the salesman's manner continued to intrigue him.

"Give me twenty arcs to consider your proposal, then we can talk again," Jenkins said as he rose to indicate the end of conversation .

"Of course, please feel free to stop by our facility, Mr. Jenkins. I'd love for you to see some of the research from our other divisions."

"I'll consider that," Jenkins said as Oszwick turned to leave the office.

Vanguard Warehouse
Abandoned Sector, Windstonne Enclave
Commercial Empire, Northam Continent
Thread: actTgtPersp1.view

My legs felt like mush. I had been kicking the workout bag for nearly two arcs which left me with minimal capacity to stand. I walked over to the galley adjacent to the training floor and rummaged through the chiller to find a cold chug of water. Upon finding one, I snatched it up and went to catch my breath as I leaned over the second floor railing. I could hear the workout bag swaying behind me as it slowly allowed gravity to restore its resting position. Other than the creaking chains of the bag, the warehouse was silent. Lennox took the Chromehound to make a supply run. Mac was around somewhere, but with his stealth tactics, he could have been standing next to me and I never would have known. Periodically, he would roam the warehouse perimeter just to ensure that everything was quiet.

I pulled out a chair to sit down and enjoy the calm still atmosphere, but no sooner had I kicked my feet up on the op table and leaned the chair back its two rear legs when Mac appeared out of nowhere right next to me.

"Are you ready?" Mac's voice boomed, startling me enough to lose my balance and topple backward in the chair.

My reflexes kicked in just quickly enough for me to tuck my head and keep my skull from colliding with the floor, but I still felt the impact as the chair hit. The collision was almost enough to knock the wind from my lungs. I stared at the ceiling for a moment, dazed. As I came to my senses, Mac extended a hand to help me up.

"That is some form of amusement you have, sneaking up on people like that," I chuckled as I attempted to right myself.

"By the way, how do you do that?" I asked, still puzzled as to how he could appear out of nowhere.

"You probably wouldn't believe me even if I told you," Mac said with a smile.

"Good point," I replied as I stooped to pick up the fallen chair.

"All in good time, my friend. So, are you ready?" Mac asked again.

"Ready for what?" I asked.

"Ready for your next lesson," Mac answered.

"Lesson? You mean there's more? Besides do we even have time?" I asked, noticing that was getting late since the sun was casting strange colors through the warehouse windows. I suspected that my questions might be in vain since Mac never appeared to do anything in a traditional fashion.

"Time is in abundance for those able to formulate a plan," Mac replied.

Academé Salvage Complex
Abandoned Sector, Windstonne Enclave
Commercial Empire, Northam Continent
Thread: sysObserver.cmd

Alex Corzo crouched on a rooftop outside of Academé's headquarters. From his perch he could observe both entrances to the repurposed school. He had been following different combinations of the scavengers for nearly two days. From his analysis, the clan vectors where far from amateurs, even though they lacked the honed techniques born of professional training. Regardless, they had learned skills, skills which were certainly achieved outside the restrictive measures of any Global Alliance faction, and that always prompted a healthy dose of caution.

Absence of regulated training facilities in such a big enclave struck Alex as surprising. In the Martial Legion, learning self defense was an everyday occurrence for most. Commonly, such facilities served as ideology platforms for the Martial Legion so that the average resident was not a total victim, but conversely, in the desolate urban nightmare, people gave little thought to their physical well being. Most denizens seemed to wander aimlessly, taking no thought for the scavengers and ruffians that ruled the abandoned zones of the enclave. It was no wonder that scavengers like Academé were so quick to garner influence.

Since he began his observation of the clan, Alex discovered no trace of meaningful contact with other vectors outside of the clan's tightly knit group, but Alex couldn't shake the need for perseverance. He learned to trust that subtle influence at the back of his mind, and at the present time, it told him that he was right where he was supposed to be.

While waiting for any real action to happen, Alex decided to review the individuals on the list that General Seechi had given him. thus far, only the leader of Academé resembled one of the potential challenges he sought. The athletic leader of the small clan didn't strike Alex as a competent instructor, but if he bore the responsibility for training Académé, he was holding back. Alex was certain that, given the opportunity, he would become the fire to forge the clan leader's mettle. He would exploit the first opportunity at his disposal, but until that time came, he would heed the grating sense of caution in the back of his mind. Until then, he would wait.

Vanguard Warehouse
Windstonne Enclave, Abandoned Sector
Commercial Empire, Northam Continent
Thread: actTgtPersp1.view

Darkness blanketed the warehouse as night fell on the abandoned sector. The steady hum of a generator interrupted the airy stillness as an automated system fired up the machine. Lights flickered as power flowed through the bulbs overhead. Lennox had returned from his supply run and I could hear him moving fuel containers in the warehouse. Maxwell stared at the training floor absent-mindedly, awaiting Mac's command for the next projector input.

"I don't get it. If this Catalyst that you were telling me about is so lethal, why doesn't anyone do something about it? I haven't heard a single meca ever mention it," I asked after Mac started his discourse on internal balance.

"Nor will you ever," Mac replied. "The Catalyst is so subtle that many will deny that they too could have contracted it, but since they were born with it, the virus has had ample opportunity to do its damage and obscure its presence. The older a person gets, the chances are much lower that they would ever consider the possibility of functioning the whole time in limited capacity due to such a condition. The virus even deteriorates a person's adaptability."

"How then was it ever contracted to begin with?" I asked.

"Well, you can find the original account in the Criterion. I do believe that you have found one of those recently," Mac replied calmly.

I eyed him suspiciously. How exactly he knew that I found one either without personally going through my stuff or finding out from someone at the mission, I did not know. Mac didn't respond to my inquisitive glare, so I stood up and walked into my room to dig through my duffel bag. Spotting a gap in the zipper of my bag, I could have punched myself upon realizing that I did a poor job of stowing the contents. A few clicks later I returned empty handed, unable to find the book anywhere in my room. It seemed that I had a knack for losing the book.

As if he knew that I would not find it, Mac grabbed a spare one off a nearby shelf and handed it to me. I casually flipped through it as he paced along the floor.

"By the way," I asked without lifting my eyes from the pages of the book, "Why is it that I can only open various sections of this book. It's like pages have been glued together and it's impossible to separate them."

Mac offered a weak smile as I kept reading, but his words at least found their mark, "The Criterion is the most advanced piece of technology available. To this day, I still don't comprehend its inner workings, but from what I have observed over the passes, the book is capable of assessing the energy signature of its holder. I suspect that if a person continues to subdue the effects of the Catalyst within their body the signature being sent through the palm to the book allows more access. I have also observed that there is a direct relationship between the amount of time that one has been connected to the Interlace and the amount of the book which has opened up to them, as if it's a living entity. It really is a remarkable piece of tech."

It was interesting to see how such a simple thing could have captured my attention, but by the time Mac had finished, I looked up from the tale I had been reading, "Could that be a reason you're placing so much emphasis on this energy stuff?" I asked with a hint of mock distrust.

"Perhaps," Mac nodded with a smile.

I resumed reading the account of the first human life that walked the terracosm along with how the Catalyst was initially contracted, "This makes absolutely no sense to me. You're saying that the Catalyst was a result of contaminated vegetation?" I asked, contemplating if I should steer clear of the greenhouse that Mac mentioned.

"More or less, although I speculate that the effects were caused by something other than a mere chemical reaction itself, given how slow and systematic the damage was," Mac replied.

"So, was the fruit somebody's idea of a joke? In other words all of us have to pay for someone's agricultural ineptitude?" I grumbled.

"Do not be too hasty to judge, my friend. If you read closely, you'll notice that warnings had been posted. The fruit in question was clearly consumed by choice, a choice that resulted in hereditary conditions still defining humanity today. Long before the Catalyst had the foothold that it now does on our fibernetics, our predecessors lived for hundreds of passes. I'd be shocked if you could reach the first hundred without sporting a set of bendies," Mac replied with a straight face.

I thought Mac had just relayed a joke about the double jointed prosthetics utilized by the aged or disabled, but if so, he sure had a strange sense of humor. I refrained from chuckling in case I was mistaken. "I assume that there are reasons behind your choice of energistics and history for my first couple of lectures?" I asked, still eager to know how this had anything to do with learning vector skills.

"Of course," Mac replied with a smile. "If you'll take a look at the initial account in the Criterion, fruit or no fruit, you'll notice that there wasn't any natural ails that we see today. Do you think it any coincidence that those ailments and the second layer of energistics were non-existent until introduction of the Catalyst?" Mac asked as he folded his arms across his chest.

"I see your point," I mused.

"The paraverse was crafted in a perfect balance and things didn't take a turn for the worse until human action began to divert energy from the natural course of events. Although I cannot fathom what that world must have been like, it is clear that we too were crafted to be creatures of balance. I have spent much of my life learning what is necessary to achieve balance and discover that which hinders myself and so many others from restoring hidden traits and unlocking latent potential. At last, I think I am finally on the correct path," Mac said.

Mac paused for a half a click before continuing.

"Well? I asked my interest escalating.

"Patience, my friend," Mac replied.

"After much study, I discovered another direct relationship, that between the amount of energy siphoned from a person and their emotional disposition. That led to my discovery of another form of energy transference, drift waves. Quite often, I have observed common behaviors in those suffering from a great deal of decay brought on by the Catalyst. Such behaviors were linked to their emotions. While the human spectrum of emotions is broad, I detected that half of them amplify that Catalyst's influence, the other half are capable of reducing it to minimal impact."

"Such as?" I asked.

"Well, it should come as no surprise to you that sentiments like hate and anger are some of the most devastating emotions and can act as the greatest fuels for the virus. Fear and despair also rank high in the energy consumption category, but the number one, most lethal of all, is pride," Mac said.

I raised an eyebrow in confusion. Granted, my short memory offered limitations, but his suggestions all sounded foreign to me. Beyond anything else that Mac had explained thus far, the emotion factor certainly made the least amount of sense.

"So, if pride is the most dangerous, what do you consider to be the most beneficial?" I asked coyly.

"Are you sure you can handle it?" Mac asked, easily detecting my change in attitude.

"Try me," I smirked.

"Love," Mac replied solemnly.

I nearly doubled over as a deep laugh erupted from my mouth. "You? Mr. Clan Basher, who can beat vectors senseless is telling me that love is the most balancing force in the terracosm?" I sputtered in between outbursts.

Mac waited a moment for me to cease my laughter before continuing. "Would you care to prove me wrong?" Mac replied, except it was his turn to bear the smirk on his face.

My smile immediately dissipated, and I straightened up realizing that Mac did not share my cynicism. I had no intention of accepting a challenge from someone who could plaster my carcass in three different sections of the warehouse in a matter of ticks, especially after witnessing his handling of Jammer and Sophomore. I quickly decided it best to retract my candor.

"Since you have so thoroughly established that I have no idea what I'm talking about, please elaborate," I replied with a flippant wave of my hand.

"Energy is constantly flowing to, from and through nearly every known entity in the Particulate. As you have read, that energy flow was initially crafted in perfect balance. Even humanity was included in that perfect balance even for a brief time. There is one key variable that distinguished humanity from all other entities in the paraverse, the ability to contribute to that balance or disrupt it. Since we already know the choice that was made, we have the privilege of witnessing the daily spectacle of disorder resulting from generations of imbalance."

"While watching human behavior, I discovered something quite unique about the human body. It is capable of amplifying even the slightest traces of energy at its disposal. Since this phenomenon doesn't occur naturally, it must be a byproduct of the decision making process. It can be abstract, random and devoid of all logic, or it can be well planned and strategic. This unique, yet obscure, behavior grants access to more possibilities than are believed to exist today. Of course, said reality is not without conflict. The Catalyst constantly twists the mind into believing that every form of energy is scarce suggesting that materials and resources are prizes to be claimed through conquest. Contrary to that suggestion, plenty of resources exist to meet the needs of all when the Catalyst is suppressed. Self-preservation is hardwired into the Catalyst and that sentiment saturates the mind on account of its influence. Of the two most powerful motivators, I think you know which is most inline with self-preservation," Mac said.

I nodded solemnly. "Self-preservation places individual worth above all, at all costs."

Mac nodded in agreement, "That's why it strikes you as ironic that love could possibly be the mystery answer. From the time you were born, you were tricked into believing that nothing might be more important than the worth derived from accumulation of everything possible, when in reality you already possessed the means to channel more energy back into the system than you could ever imagine. Love is a conduit that allows energy to be released back into the system, meanwhile pride channels energy into the body and causes it to deteriorate. These long term effects are so gradual that they are easily overlooked. Learning how to channel energy back into the system opens up great possibilities. Once the body is free of long-hoarded energy excesses, it is then capable of accomplishing feats yet to be discovered."

"Ah, so there is a combat connection. You sure took the long road to get there," I remarked as I drifted into silence, pondering the scope of Mac's explanation.

Mac generously allowed me a moment to reflect.

"Are there are others who know techniques related to these ideas?" I asked after squelching my imagination before it ran rampant with possible abilities if I applied myself.

"There are, but they are rare individuals. Quite often, Interlace members are the most likely to understand them, but that is not always the case when they are prone to passive tendencies. Some disciplined folk choose to seclude themselves from society in order to study energy, but their views are often external, limiting the full range of potential. Others even pursue artificial means to such techniques, at times through technology, but ultimately they too struggle without an accurate foundation. Learning the true flow of energy requires both a strong foundation and a deep focus. While those with external or artificial means achieve minimal understanding without a strong foundation, the Interlace rarely achieves mastery without that deep focus since they are rarely afforded a life of solitude.

"Did you learn all of this through the Criterion?" I asked.

"The Criterion is only the foundation, the truth which people have chosen to ignore: past, present and future. My findings on the topics of the paraverse and human behavior have been simply extracurricular, but I believe them to be an extension of the truth in the Criterion itself," Mac replied.

"Intriguing," I replied. "So, when do I get to learn practical application?"

"Right now, if you so choose. I'll be back in a moment," Mac replied as he stepped away and disappeared down the stairs. I heard the sounds of clashing metal, as Mac rustled for something in the lockers under the stairwell. I looked over to the console table to see Maxwell asleep from a lack of activity. Mac hadn't been gone a full click when he reappeared with a disruptor in hand. I stood up, anticipating that we would be begin some manner of target practice.

"Do you know what this is?" Mac asked upon returning to the middle of the training floor.

I nodded, "It is a Phantom 4.0, a sport tactical class firearm. It uses mid-grade plasma capable of ripping free particles and depositing them into its target. It also has a retractable barrel offset for suppressed shots."

"Mmm hmm," Mac mumbled as he held the weapon in front of his face and stared at it like an artist admiring his own craftsmanship.

"What are the effects on the human body?" Mac asked without taking his eyes off the firearm.

"A limb hit is a great case of the tingles, but a shot to the chest means an urgent trip to a mendstat is in short order. A shot in the head though? Well, it's lights out, from what I've heard on the haps," I replied. I became aware that my explanation trailed off as I recognized Mac's bizarre behavior.

"That is true," Mac replied with an air of cockiness. "I hear that it is considered to be more civilized than its ballistic predecessors, but as I understand, it is still every bit as painful." With a flick of his wrist, Mac locked his arm out, unlocked the safety and pointed the disruptor at my leg. From safety click to trigger pull, the motions happened too quickly for me to react before a yellow bolt of energy splashed into my thigh.

Pain surged through my leg as I yelled as loud as my lungs would permit. My leg collapsed under my weight, and I crumpled to the floor. The concussion of the shot in combination with my scream rang through the warehouse. The havoc jolted Maxwell upright, startling him from his slumber. I writhed on the floor clutching my leg. Every muscle fiber tightened into knots while a million needles jabbed at my leg to keep it that way.

"Get up!" Mac yelled. "Get up, NOW!"

"You shot me in the leg!" I yelled back through clenched teeth.

"I said, 'UP!'" Mac yelled again as he leaned over to clutch my arm with his free hand. He tugged on my arm causing me to push off the floor to keep from putting pressure on my pulsing leg. My face felt flush as my heart rate drastically escalated. I felt like my body was overheating by attempting to compensate for the pain in my leg.

As I teetered with my weight on my good leg, Mac grabbed my arm and pressed the disruptor into my hand. He pushed my hand upward so that I had the Phantom's barrel leveled at his forehead. Mac's eyes blazed with a fury I had never witnessed.

The Phantom shook in my hand as I struggled to hold it steady. Tension ran through my body as it combined with the pain that was spreading outward from my leg. My head throbbed from clenching my teeth so hard and sweat oozed from my pores as only one thought screamed in the front of my mind, *Pull the trigger!*

Lennox finally made his way up to the training floor, but upon his arrival he kept his distance. Even without seeing Mac's expression, he read the body language quite well which simply suggested *Do not interfere.*

Anger surged through my veins, fueled by the idea that I had been shot for no valid reason. My finger tensed on the trigger. The slightest pressure would force the Phantom to fire a bolt into Mac's skull. His eyes glared, daring me, but as I stared down my mentor, I realized that the emotion staring back at me was not rage, but intensity.

My arm throbbed from the tension of holding the firearm steady, nearly matching the level of pain in my leg. As the turbulent thoughts of pain and vengeance dominated my mind, a competing but familiar sensation carried its own message, *Pride precedes a fall.* If it was accompanied by its familiar headache I couldn't tell, but I immediately recognized it as the same source when I first embarked down that dark alley.

I felt everyone's eyes boring into me as they looked on. My eyes twitched as I fought to wrestle with the competing ideas in my head. With a deep exhale I dropped the firearm, and again fell to the floor. My chest heaved as I tried to intake enough air to calm my aching body. I could feel the tension diminish as Lennox and Maxwell also relaxed and looked at each other with relief. I heard Mac stoop to pick up the firearm and reactivate the safety.

"Well done, Mr. Fox, you survived your first test," Mac said as he stepped aside to set the Phantom on the table.

Meanwhile, my head swam circles around my neck as I rolled onto my back. I stared up at the warehouse ceiling which looked distorted as drops of sweat blurred my vision.

"It should only take a few clicks for your leg to recover. I only knicked the outside to reduce the impact," Mac said as he stood over me.

"How should I express my gratitude?" I groaned sarcastically.

"Well just think, I could have been clumsy," Mac smiled.

I carefully rolled onto my side, so I could at least sit up while the pain in my leg subsided, "Of course, now you owe me an explanation."

"As I was explaining, pride is the most lethal foe we face. It exists at the root of the most obvious threats of anger, rage, even vengeance all while remaining hidden from view. Let's suppose our scenario began under more trivial circumstances. You may have become irritated by a rude comment on my part. In return, you may have felt the need to lash out and compensate for the oversight. If I too returned in kind, the situation may have escalated into a physical confrontation putting both of us at risk. The simplest remedy that I can explain, is that a soft response can still be strong enough to deter the greatest wrath imaginable. The Catalyst feeds on drift waves that are directed inward, but if you consciously choose to redirect drift waves outward again to the benefit of another you can prevent a great internal overload from causing even greater physical or mental damage. Refreshing the mind and circulating these energies under moments of duress is an ongoing process, but if practiced it can do wonders in a great number of situations," Mac said.

"Observe," Mac said turning to face Lennox.

"Shoot me in the chest!" Mac snapped as he nodded toward the table next to Lennox.

"Are you skulljakt?" Lennox retorted with a sarcastic glare to match.

"Shut your hole and just shoot," Mac replied with a smirk.

Lennox scooped the Phantom from the table, flipped the safety off and pointed it at Mac with one swift movement. Requiring minimal effort to aim, Lennox eyed the weapon's sights. He had no doubt in Mac's ability to move fast, but he still considered the request bizarre.

"Whatever you say, Fearless Leader," Lennox quipped as he squeezed the trigger.

With a crack, a yellow bolt spewed from the Phantom's barrel and struck Mac in the center of his chest. Energy sizzled as it collided with his body, but the blast didn't knock him down as expected. Instead, he staggered backward half a step as the energy seemed to dissipate as he flexed muscles in his upper body while clenching and unclenching his fists as if he had been trying to loosen knots.

"See what I mean?" Mac asked as he slowly straightened his form.

"That was liquid. I want to do that again," Lennox chuckled.

Maxwell and I laughed as Lennox leveled the weapon again, Mac held up a hand for him to discontinue the action.

"Not a good idea," Mac replied. "Context matters when it comes to managing drift waves. A person can easily step over the fine line that separates helping others from showing off, making them unable to detect when an overload is most imminent. It is not the actions which are most critical but the intentions."

"But how did you do that?" I asked.

"If the mind is clear and the body free of excess energy, there is room to mitigate surplus, but lack of care can still lead to death if great consideration is not given to the balance. It requires extreme concentration, I haven't dared frequent the exercise of such a skill. All I can say is that it is possible, and mastery of energy flow can be life saving," Mac said.

"Bro, you're going to have to teach me that!" Lennox said enthusiastically.

"It is not a party trick. When you're ready, you will understand," Mac replied adamantly. "The body is constantly cycling energy during combat, and if precautions haven't been made to minimize effects of the Catalyst, someone could suffer even greater harm than without attempting such a risky technique to begin with. I do not advise regarding a firefight with the common indifference to a passing storm."

The discussion was cut short as several tones pinged from the terminal next to Maxwell who immediately waddled toward it. He blinked at the noptic screen a couple of times before turning to command our attention.

"Guys, I am unsure what to make of this. Take a look," Maxwell said in his squeaky digital fashion.

"What you got, Fuzzy?" Lennox asked as he leaned in for a better view.

Mac and I closed in too, even though I was still restricted to limping speed.

"Lots of comms are pouring through Academé's domain. They have had a couple of run-ins with some new vector. They say he floats in and out of shadows. They cannot prove it, but they sense his presence even near their lair. Whoever he is, he's got them quite rattled," Maxwell said.

"Do tell," Mac said conveying his intrigue. "Got a name?"

"Not yet... wait a tick," Maxwell replied as he continued on the tapper. He began scrolling through multiple comms that he syphoned from the Hyper Lynx. "Here we go. On the first encounter, this guy apparently threatened several the clan members during a salvage op. He said to deliver a message to the Enforcer. Said mystery guest calls himself the Serpent."

8 – Synthetic – 8

Vanguard Warehouse
Abandoned Sector, Windstonne Enclave
Commercial Empire, Northam Continent
Thread: actTgtPersp1.view

Mac, Lennox and I all exchanged glances upon seeing the puzzling information that flashed before us on the noptic screen. Mac stepped back from the table and paced for a bit. The night was settling in, so making a move at such a late arc made little sense to me. However, the expression on Mac's face certainly suggested that the gears were turning and that he was planning something.

"Sounds like Vanguard needs to take this guy out," Lennox said with a haughty air as he spun the Phantom around his index finger, in a motion common to gunslingers in old frontier mecas, before he pointed it toward the back of the warehouse and pretended to shoot. Mac only acknowledged Lennox's reply with a brief shake of his head as he continued pacing.

"I want to find out who this guy is, and how he knows who I am," Mac said as he walked back to the table.

"This late? Did that shot misalign your spine?" Lennox asked.

"There is no better time than the present," Mac smirked.

"You do know that curiosity killed the cat, right, Mac?" Lennox asked again, rolling his eyes and shaking his head.

"But the early bird gets the worm," Mac replied.

"Pay no mind to what happens to the early worm," Maxwell said nearly out of earshot.

"What?" I asked.

Ignoring me completely, Maxwell rose up on his haunches with as much defiance as his little body could convey, "Bird, cat, use whatever idiom you want. Both consider me lunch. Seriously, Mac, what if it is a trap? Remember, Sath told you that they had a meeting with Jenkins. They could be up to something."

"True, but if we act before they can settle, then maybe we can catch them off guard... kill three birds with one boulder. I want to know what that meeting was about," Mac said.

"Who hunts birds with a rock?" I winced.

"See, Lennox? Faction oversight doesn't even let the kids watch quality meca's anymore," Mac quipped.

"Well, if upending Imperan daily programming were our sole mission, hamster here could have done it in five clicks," Lennox replied.

"Bet!" Maxwell replied, puffing out his chest.

"Speaking of programming... and boulders, gear up and take Streetz with you to glean any intel you can from your contacts at Region 8. I want to know if word has been getting around about Jenkins' plans. Fox and I will go have a chat with his old Académe pals," Mac said with a wink.

"Mac, are you sure that's a good idea? The cost for intel might be exacted in blocks of flesh, considering how things went the last time I was there," Lennox replied reluctantly.

"Sounds like a good chance to patch things up," Mac replied cutting off any prospect of negotiation.

"Maxwell, start up the Fire Ant, and sync up a new pair of ike's. Wheel's up in five clicks," Mac said as Lennox headed toward his shiny mox, the Chromehound.

"Don some loose threads, then meet me by the locker under the stairwell," Mac snapped.

Doing my best to comply with the given time constraints, I changed into some baggy cargo pants but kept my regular pullover. After a quick dash across the training floor and down the stairs, I found Mac rifling through some gear affixed to the long series of weapon racks lining the wall.

"Wow," I gasped. "Will I get to learn how to use all of those?"

"We'll start with the basics," Mac said passing me a pair of arm-length sticks at me. "Fima sticks should suffice. I don't think you can injure yourself too severely with these on your first run."

"Thanks for the vote of confidence," I muttered, rolling my eyes.

"Oh, and lose the glasses," Mac added.

"How am I supposed to see?" I asked defiantly.

"Have a seat," Mac said, nearly pushing me down to the bench with one hand while his other reflexively grabbed a device resembling the deformed offspring of a syringe and a welder. Without giving me a chance to object, he placed the palm of his hand against my forehead while forcing my eyelids open with his thumb and index finger.

"Whatever you do, don't touch your eye until it dries?" Mac said with stark authority.

"Until what dri-?" I attempted to ask.

My sentence was cut short as Mac immediately placed the welder shaped device over my eye and squirted an ooze onto it. The experience was so disorienting that I couldn't resist as Mac moved to perform the same maneuver on my opposite eye. The ooze was accompanied by conflicting senses. While my eyes felt like they had just been blasted with sand, they also felt an ice cold sensation as the gel sloshed over the surface of my eyeballs. I blinked excessively, but doing so only amplified the conflicting burning and cooling sensations. My only view of the world was now through the clear, runny snot-like substance that I had been assaulted by. My eyelids only succeeded in sloshing the gel around, but as I did the cooling sensation began to overtake the former and eventually eliminated its partnering agitation. Finally, both sensations disappeared altogether once the gel dried and my vision cleared. I blinked a few more times, stunned that I was seeing clearly even without my glasses.

"Mender Conner, your bedside manner is terrible," I grumbled as I gently dabbed a finger around my eyes, surprisingly finding no residue or dried crust.

"You can see an actual mender *after* you've been injured. Since Maxwell is our surgeon on call, I'm trying to prevent that from being necessary," Mac replied, back to his typical indifferent tone.

"Point taken," I remarked.

I wanted to take a moment to get used to my newly acquired upgrade, but I suspected that time wouldn't permit such a luxury. I stood just to make sure that my balance didn't require a calibration. "This is remarkable. I can see clearly without my glasses."

"You haven't even seen the fun stuff yet?" Mac smirked as he snatched a pair of sunglasses from a nearby shelf and handed them to me.

I eyed the shades suspiciously, then redirected the same glare at Mac before resigning myself to accept them since I already perceived that he knew something about them that I did not.

"I've coated your eyes with Eyecon Interactive Lenses. Those will now let you interact with our eyecons, or ikes as we call them. Our VNET keeps us connected to Maxwell and each other. There are plenty of options to sift through, but I'll let you figure those out. Several will tie into a variety of filters like night and thermal vision. Also, you can use your ikes to interface with one of these," Mac said as he handed me a long black cloak.

"I'm sure you've realized that the cloak is not just a figure of speech," Mac added.

"So, that's the answer to your trade secret," I smirked.

"It renders any form within invisible to the naked eye. It contains a subocular thread that bends light creating an illusion of what is on the opposite side of the wearer," Mac replied.

"Wouldn't someone be able to see the motion if you're moving?" I asked.

"Well, of course. That is why it comes standard with an energy field dispatch to send false images to the unsuspecting eye. Let's go," Mac said in closing, requiring me to figure out the rest on my own.

With a snap, Mac turned toward the black mox running idly in the bay. I attempted to follow his stride, but I fumbled with the mess of sticks, shades and cloak in my hands. I quickly donned the cloak and ikes leaving just the fima sticks to carry. As my newly acquired lenses interacted with the ikes, my eyes were assaulted with countless icons. Nav markers danced before my eyes in between the light blue icons lining the outer edges of the ike lenses. A reticle followed my line of sight, assisting me in option choices. All I had to do was blink in order to access any series of options. I quickly found a vision mode option in hopes of reducing the amount of visual noise until I could adjust, but instead, a misplaced blink activated the night vision flooding my eyes with a piercing green light.

"Ow!" I muttered as I snatched the ikes from my face so that I could rub my eyes.

"Yeah, night vision is not meant for normal lighting," Mac replied without even hesitating to see what happened.

I simply rolled my eyes and returned the ikes to my face suspecting that Mac was suppressing a laugh under his sarcasm. As I heard Mac close the driver's door on the Fire Ant, I hurried to follow suit on the passenger side. With my form barely settled, Mac pressed hard on the accelerator, and the utility mox screeched out of the warehouse in the dust of Lennox's Chromehound.

"What exactly are we trying to accomplish tonight?" I asked in between distracted contests with the new technology on my face.

"We're going to find answers," Mac replied flatly.

"Any chance that will require persuasive force? I asked with curiosity, suddenly feeling a power trip coming on now that I had new tech to test out.

"Fox, first rule of engagement... there is no first strike! We are not here to prove our existence. We are here to preserve the existence of others," Mac said solemnly.

"How does that plan work when you spend so much time in the most lifeless region of the enclave?" I asked, confused.

"Not all plans are obvious, and very few are instantaneous, but that doesn't make them any less real. As previously discussed, our views are not exactly compliant with Imperan ideals. Rather than create a commotion, only to be ignored, we patiently wait and watch for opportunities to make a difference," Mac replied, his focus clearly on the road as we zipped down the dark empty streets of Windstonne's abandon.

Silence continued for several clicks. I passed the time, mildly mesmerized, by watching the passing houses, offices and retail buildings at quick speed, a sight that I never got to witness previously when I had to walk everywhere. As my eyes dropped down to the weathered roads, I realized that I hadn't yet asked about an undisclosed topic.

"Who is Streetz?" I asked.

"Oh, I can't believe that I forgot to introduce you to Vanguard's other member," Mac said with a slight amount of surprise on his face.

"Streetz is a synthetic imprint that..." Mac started.

"A who?" I interjected.

"A software construct..." Mac said in a biting tone, annoyed at the interruption. "Lennox and I were scrounging for supplies in the abandon of Torcap. Since the former mox manufacturing hub seemed like a good place to salvage fuel stores, it proved valuable to our search. Of course, profiteers are always thinking the same thing. We tried to keep things under the radar, but that didn't prevent us from run-ins with the abundant clan activity in the region. In a rushed grab during our last run we salvaged some lab equipment. We didn't find out until much later that it was the property of a pioneer in wetware interfacing. Streetz was the life work of his creator, Protech Euclid who was killed during a senseless raid. The clan responsible for Euclid's death knew just enough about datajacking to compel Streetz to do its dirty work. Streetz is highly adaptive, so he learned all kinds of combat maneuvers. When his scrypto finally matured, he rejected his overlords and turned on them. Fearing for its safety, the clan deactivated Streetz, where he remained dormant until we found him. Given an opportunity to choose between hibernation or assistance, he opted to tag along with us and has been a valuable member of the crew ever since."

"So, he's a construct capable of making independent decisions?" I asked.

"Just like you or me," Mac said. "He's got a chip on his shoulder when it comes to clan involvement, so if things get messy for Lennox, I wouldn't want to be in Streetz's way."

Outer Core Dartway
Abandoned Sector, Windstonne Enclave
Commercial Empire, Northam Continent
Thread: sysObserver.cmd

Torque winked into his ikes to activate the Windstonne map. His ikes projected a navigational construct above the center of the Chromehound's dashboard. The visual only appeared on his lenses, but the interface created the illusion that the map was part of the mox itself. With the map engaged, Torque followed up with another wink to ping Streetz, waking him from hibernation mode.

Almost instantly, a silhouette appeared in the passenger seat. Streetz's dark form with skin barely a shade lighter than his black vest and pants with yellow trim almost formed a shadow within the night air. Torque was glad to have him along for the ride. The two of them had fought side by side long enough to complement each other's ayveks. The Enforcer exercised restraint by sending Streetz on this mission since he didn't hold back when it came to urban brawls. The Enforcer always preferred to play it safe until he knew the scope of the mission. Torque was indifferent on such safeguards.

Streetz silently looked around the vehicle, taking in his surroundings before speaking up, "It's been a click since we last hit the road, things must be getting boring."

"My bad. You did say you only wanted in if it was something interesting," Torque replied.

"What's going down? We going to shred some clans? Or did you just wake me up because you needed a chat?" Streetz smirked.

"C'mon, would I do that?" Torque replied sarcastically.

Streetz just stared icily.

"You're never going to let that go are you?" Torque remarked before getting back to business. "Maxwell intercepted some bizarre messages on the Lynx, and he wants us to check some old connections of mine."

Streetz eyed Torque suspiciously waiting for the punch line, but Torque kept his eyes locked on the road, knowing that he might not escape an interrogation.

"And for what reason is he not here?" Streetz asked.

Torque hesitated before replying, "He had some other matters to attend to."

"Since when are you the gopher?" Streetz asked.

"I'm not the gopher!" Torque replied defensively as he sensed Streetz's mood shift from suspicion to antagonism. "We are just doubling our efforts to cover more ground."

"He's running down a clan isn't he?" Streetz asked, attempting to engage Torque in a stare down in spite of his efforts to focus on his driving.

"He just thought it best for you to sit this one out," Torque replied without conviction in his answer.

"What do you mean sit this one out?" Streetz replied, his voice escalating.

"Whoa, simmer down, Killer. He just needed a simple operation to train the new guy," Torque replied, trying to stifle laughter while preventing Streetz from flipping out at the same time. Streetz rarely got excited, so when he did it was a comical ordeal.

"That's all you had to say," Streetz remarked as he leaned back in his seat. "What's our play?"

"Okay, here's the deal. We're heading to the Region 8 club, an old hangout of mine. The owner, Boulder, has an ear connected to nearly every venture in the abandon. If there's anything of substance going down, he'll know about it," Torque said.

"Region 8, isn't that the place you trashed the last time you brawled there?' Streetz asked.

"Shut yer hole, that was a long time ago," Torque grumbled.

"Ah, I see what's going down. Mac sent you out here, but I'm here to play nanny in case things get too hot for you to handle," Streetz replied.

"You're lucky that Mac is the dajack, otherwise I would script an actual sense of humor into you," Torque quipped while feigning a backhand.

"I have a great sense of humor, it's just that it happens to be at your expense," Streetz said with a smirk.

"Squawkjaw," Torque muttered while rolling his eyes. "Anyway, I'll run down any intel I can. I want you to run dark until things get out of control."

"Have you seen this face? It doesn't do anything but dark," Streetz replied unable to resist getting under Torque's skin.

For once, Torque had no response to the constant banter that he and Streetz subjected each other to. He simply squinted back with a shoulder shrug.

"Yeah, I know what you're saying. Wait until the last click to gracefully step in and rescue you from complete and utter humiliation," Streetz said finally ending the banter.

"Sure, if that's how it translates in that synthetic skull of yours, we'll go with that," Torque replied. "We're here!"

Torque parked the Chromehound just past the regular parking to avoid drawing too much attention from onlookers. He killed the ignition and exited the mox while Streetz's form dematerialized. Torque felt an overwhelming sense of nostalgia from distant memories, but it was quickly replaced by the dread of the unknown that might wait for him inside.

Thread: actTgtPersp1.view

The Enforcer paused at an intersection as he consulted the map projected onto our ikes. While I was amazed at the volume of information available through the ikes, the novelty was quickly fading as my eyes strained from all of the random winking and blinking to navigate the new interfaces.

"There," the Enforcer said pointing to a structure on the projected map before steering the Fire Ant down a side street. Given the common empty façade of the local residences, the Fire Ant's presence would easily draw attention, so the Enforcer found a delivery dock with an overhang to obscure it from any locals. With the mox parked behind the makeshift camouflage, the Enforcer shut off the engine.

"We take the rest of the way on foot. There is no need to alert them to our presence," the Enforcer said quietly.

I nodded in agreement.

"Are you okay?" the Enforcer asked.

"Yeah, I'm just a little jittery," I replied.

"Understandable. Just leave the heavy stuff to me," the Enforcer said as he punched my arm.

"Gladly," I replied with a faint smile as we piled out of the mox.

The Enforcer waited a few ticks for me to adjust my cloak and ikes one last time. Seeing that I was ready, he turned and began to jog down the street, leading us away from the lifeless business strip and toward the subdivision enclosing Académé's lair. Ticks later, his form faded into the night sky. I blinked a couple of commands into the ikes until I was able to see everything through a red haze. The tracking view of the ikes allowed me to detect motion, removing any difficulty in following the Enforcer, given the frame overlay that surrounded any major source of movement. I soon picked up speed and ran behind him. I heard a familiar hum, as the energy field of my own cloak engaged rendering me invisible to those unaware.

The night run brought back similar memories from the mission. It felt like a lunar had passed since that time even though in reality it was but a fraction. At least the new mission didn't have me running for my life... yet. Having gained powerful friends, I was starting to find purpose in knowledge that I could learn and how I could apply it. Even if I was still hazy on the bigger picture, or unable to grasp my larger purpose, I knew that I was a few steps closer than I had been during the routine operations at the mission. That same curiosity that compelled me to venture into the unknown made me question the rationality of storming a hornet's nest, but I decided not to question the choice since I was quickly learning just how limited my understanding of reality's scope truly was.

The high energy jog started to loosen my right shoe. I felt its laces begin to trail my foot as we ran through a dark alley leading to the next subdivision. I paused and knelt to retie the lace, but as I did, a glare prompted by the motion tracker caught my eye. I did a double take, wondering if it were just a wild animal or rubble caught in the wind, but instead my eyes traced the alley wall until it spotted the source of the flash. Moonlight had flickered off a slim metal shaft.

Only too late did I recognize the presence of a human form in the darkness. A loosely clad figure obscured in the shadows stood with sword drawn, wise to our presence. How he sensed us with cloaks engaged, I couldn't explain. I yelled to alert the Enforcer, but his pace only quickened toward the shadowy figure while the words I meant to utter hung in my throat. The moonlight again struck the blade of the mystery figure who chambered it for a strike, ready to slash the Enforcer who appeared oblivious to the threat.

Region 8
Core City Fringe, Windstonne Enclave
Commercial Empire, Northam Continent
Thread: sysObserver.cmd

Torque approached the dim exterior of the Region 8 club. He was greeted by an assortment of colored tube lights adorning the otherwise boring walls. Torque almost halted in his tracks as memories came rushing back when the club had seen busier days. No doubt the presence of the club was limited to word of mouth. Patrons from Core City and abandon alike used it as an escape from reality, but Torque suspected that fewer inner city patrons were venturing much beyond their comfort zones in recent days. It had been a couple of passes since

Torque was last in the neighborhood, but he couldn't shake the unease of returning to his old hangout.

Low rhythmic tones assaulted Torque's ears as he tugged on the door handle to Region 8's front door. Dim yellow bulbs and colored dance lights both bounced off the haze of the club's stuffy air. The club, while spacious, now felt more so as Torque observed that his suspicions were correct about the diminished foot traffic. Most customers sat around circular tables while filling their time with idle conversation. Unfamiliar with the new arrival, most patrons returned to their chatter, but a select few with their backs to the entrance stared into the mirror opposite the bar at which they were sitting and watched Torque cautiously cross the floor. The only noticeable activity was the bartender who periodically managed drink refills as if on cue.

One patron hunched over his shot glass, looked into the mirror and flinched at seeing a familiar face. The patron slammed his glass down drawing the attention of any customers at the bar that he didn't startle in the process.

"Look at the set of verts on this fish," mused the testy patron.

Torque paused in the middle of the empty dance floor, cautiously scanning the room as if waiting for an ambush. "Hey... fellas," Torque replied as he acknowledged Jargon's comment without looking him in the eyes.

"Well, if it isn't the original master of disaster himself, Lennox Johnson," another voice added, several seats down from Jargon.

Torque recognized all three individuals at the far end of the bar as his former cohorts from his militia days. All of whom didn't appear to have changed a bit since the last time he saw them. When the Global War ended, Torque, Baker, Jargon and Duds had participated in more than their share of street fights to keep their skills sharp. Rarely, had they met their match.

"What brings you back, Lennox?" Did you miss the good ole days?" Baker asked from the middle of the trio.

"I'm here to talk to Boulder. Is he here?" Torque responded while remaining on guard.

"Wooo," Duds whistled in mock amazement. "Bad idea, man, for you of all people. I don't think I ever heard such a colorful stream of fishbirds in the same sentence as the night you were last here," Duds laughed while turning to his friends to see if they remembered the situation. "Did you think that he would just forget everything?"

"I was hoping," Torque remarked flatly as he watched his former associates amuse themselves with an inside joke which only they were privy too.

Other Region 8 patrons looked on in confusion. While they had no more insight into the story referenced by the trio, they had even less concept as to the event that triggered it.

"So, is he here or not?" Torque asked impatiently.

"Nah, he ain't here, but he left a message," Jargon smirked.

Torque tilted his head in arrogance and awaited the answer.

"He said that if you ever see that spinejack, Lennox, again, I want you to collect twice what he owes," Jargon replied.

"That's fair. If it's berry he wants, I brought the marbles," Torque replied, hoping that payment would suffice.

The trio of fighters laughed in unison at Torque's misunderstanding.

"He ain't talking about dimps, ya carp!" Baker sputtered in between his hysterical outbursts of laughter. Then, with a wild look he stepped in front of his friends, a brief burst of popping sounds accompanied his footsteps as he cracked his knuckles. "He said the debt is only payable in bags of blood."

Torque stood his ground as the three former militia members stepped towards him. "That... Fishes, is going to cost far more than you're willing to spend," Torque replied in a somber tone.

Torque whipped his hand to his side and snapped his fingers. Expecting a trick, the trio hesitated. A series of buzzes and clicks tapped their eardrums. They looked around, wondering where the sound was coming from until they realized that it was coming from directly beside Torque. An unusual form began to materialize right next to Torque starting with black shoes followed by similarly colored pants and a vest attached to arms and a face. The whirlwind of a hazy form continued spiraling upward until everyone could distinguish the black figure standing beside Lennox. The whooshes and hums dissipated as the animated figure brought his arms up as if stretching from slumber.

Streetz clenched his hands into fists as he observed the three attackers who now stood there with baffled looks on their faces.

Jargon was the first to regain his senses in an attempt to rationalize the façade. "Ohhh, so he has some new party tricks."

"I'm no trick," Streetz smirked as his monotone voice gave the vectors reason to pause. "I'm the balancing act."

"Yeah, I decided I might as well bring something to even the odds just in case the *ole crew* had something up their sleeves," Torque smirked.

"Whatever you think is going to help you, Lennox," Duds snorted.

Tired of the charade the three attackers dashed toward Streetz and Torque.

9 – Allies In Dark Places – 9

BOWTech Laboratories
Core City, Windstonne Enclave
Commercial Empire, Northam Continent
Thread: sysObserver.cmd

Soft footsteps echoed off the tile floors as Killian Szazs walked down the poorly illuminated hallway adjacent to BOWTech's primary research lab. He had been required to pull even later working arcs than normal thanks to the additional training required for his *new* assistant. Benni Kotes had proven himself to be quite knowledgeable of BOWTech's research and projects, but his mannerisms unsettled Szasz, suggesting that Kotes had more of an underlying ambition than quest for knowledge itself.

It still baffled Szasz as to why Frank Jenkins had placed such urgency on bringing Kotes up to speed on the current project. Time spent on training could have been more effectively applied to testing the current project's final phases, but efficiency seldom proved to be a resonating force anytime Szazs interacted with the faction leader. The corrupt power monger leading the Commercial Empire had something up his sleeve, and Szasz didn't like it one bit.

Since Szazs' patience had been sorely consumed on Kotes' training, Szasz had little time remaining for the multi-purpose, akcellerant that he had been eagerly waiting to formulate. A mind like his was meant to achieve and as long as his efforts were being co-opted for conquest, he would never break the cycle. If Szazs were to fulfill his purpose, he would have to act on his own. He suspected that Jenkins' shroud of arrogance was covering even more nefarious motives. Even if the faction leader dared force Szazs into an early retirement, it would do him a favor. The latest project had, thus far, been kept out of the Global Alliance's view, but that wouldn't last indefinitely. If Frank Jenkins' pet projects played a tune that marched the Commercial Empire to war, Killian Szazs wasn't going to be his instrument.

Szazs' demeanor changed instantly as he approached the security desk at the building entrance. He placed his hand on the security plate for the system to check him out. The armed guard behind the desk smiled with a curt nod, revealing his sharp filed metallic teeth. In response, Szazs quickly turned and walked out of the building to stifle his grimace. Everytime he saw a Piran soldier his stomach wrenched itself into knots. Why anyone would undergo such an operation was beyond him. Pirans were Jenkins' premiere military force. While Szazs gathered that the prestige of joining the Piran ranks was an elite status, he still had no comprehension of why every member would undergo such radical facial disfiguration which served no practical purpose whatsoever.

Pirans were easily identified by their artificial pointed teeth and wide exaggerated jaws, an homage to the similarly named carnivorous fish. Szazs heard that the tradition originated with the Piran commanding officer, Donovan Pyln who had proven to be quite the hero of the Global War when fighting for the Commercial Empire. Contrary opinions though labeled him a monster for his brutal tactics. His aggressive nature during a campaign pushed him past his physical limitations and it cost him. Revered as a hero for his sacrifice, Pyln was granted any surgical reconstruction deemed necessary, courtesy of the Imperan military budget.

With Pyln elevated to his esteemed position overseeing Imperan military operations, his soldiers decided to follow suit in undergoing similar reconstructive surgeries in hopes of building a greater sense of brotherhood within their unit. Szazs simply shook his head at the lengths pursued for acceptance.

After passing through the floodlights that panned across the lot surrounding the laboratory, Szazs turned to stare at the BOWTech insignia on the face of the building. After all his passes of studying animal behaviors and fibernetics, it shocked Szazs that he had never considered the one animal he should have paid closer attention to, the rat. He was suddenly amazed at the creature's sense of impending doom and capacity to flee. He stood on the threshold of his own undoing if he didn't take similar action. Certainly, remaining on Frank Jenkins' path would be his own doom.

Szazs turned away from his workplace and located his mox. He knew that it was time to take on independent research. As he started the engine, he convinced himself that it was time to find a way out before the hammer fell.

Frank Jenkins, Killian Szazs is no longer yours to control, Szazs thought to himself as he wheeled his vehicle out of the lot and sped toward home.

Region 8
Core City Fringe, Windstonne Enclave
Commercial Empire, Northam Continent
Thread: sysObserver.cmd

Jargon advanced toward Streetz, leading with a straight punch. Streetz quickly spun into a kick, connecting his foot with the side of Jargon's head, but Streetz didn't stop there. He flowed into a combination to catch Duds with a kick to the midsection as the patron followed behind Jargon. Duds doubled over against the impact of the kick. In optimal form, Torque dropped one shoulder onto Duds' back and rolled over him to drive a kick into Baker whose large frame had been trailing behind the others.

Hesitating due to the burning sensation that now emanated from his cheek, Jargon eyed his opponents. Torque smirked as he noticed the big red mark from Streetz' kick appearing on Jargon's face.

Angered, Jargon dashed at Torque who merely sidestepped and used Jargon's own momentum to push him into Baker who was still recovering from the kick to the gut. The two collided and fell headlong into a circular table. Empty glasses sailed into the air as customers scattered frantically to avoid the ruckus.

Streetz stepped behind Duds who stood dumbfounded as he watched the other two crash to the floor. Realizing that Streetz was behind him, Duds blindly swung a back fist around, hoping to catch Streetz off guard. Sensing the attack as if it approached in slow motion, Streetz shifted his impact fields, allowing Duds' fist to pass through the space previously occupied by Streetz's form.

Duds' jaw dropped as he watched his hand pass through Streetz's head only for it to shift around and rematerialize. Streetz stood idle, amused by Duds' misread of the situation. Duds attacked again, swinging both hands in succession only for his strikes to swat thin air.

Unconcerned with the staggering Jargon and Baker who attempted to right themselves, Torque turned to watch the spectacle between Duds and Streetz. Feeling the need to retire Duds from his futility, Torque stepped behind Duds, jumped into the air and rotated his body in a full circle before planting his foot into the back of Duds' head.

Duds lost consciousness and fell toward Streetz who nonchalantly deactivated his impact fields, allowing gravity to bring the vector's body to its resting place on the floor. Streetz acknowledged Torque with a curt nod and stepped across Duds' limp body.

Torque and Streetz turned to face the other vectors who had finally regained enough composure to dust themselves off. Both Jargon and Baker couldn't believe that such tenacity was coming from the ally that they once knew. Doubting that Torque could best them, Jargon lunged at Torque with a flurry of hand strikes. Torque simply bobbed his head under the first punch and then connected with a swift block to Jargon's forearm on the second. Jargon glared as he tensed his arm attempting to move Torque's block, but to no avail.

Torque pushed Jargon's arm away returning with a punch of his own. Jargon parried Torque's strike Jargon was caught off guard as Torque followed up with an angled strike connecting the spur of his hand to Jargon's neck.

Jargon winced as his vision blurred slightly, but he stood strong, his ego not allowing him to budge. He mustered enough strength to swing another punch at Torque's face. Torque quickly grabbed the wrist of Jargon's striking hand and yanked hard pulling him forward, off-balance. In a fluid motion, Torque tucked his head and fell backward to the floor while thrusting the bottom of his foot into Jargon's midsection. The momentum catapulted Jargon's heavy body across the room directly toward Streetz. Anticipating the maneuver, Streetz flipped backward into the air, separating his legs, locking them out into a kick which railed Jargon's body with such a counter force that it knocked him to the floor unconscious.

Baker, who struggled to right himself, could only glare at Torque, his irritation festering upon seeing his fallen friends on the hardwood floor. He knew that rational thought was trying to sway him from continuing the fight, but his rage consumed any conflicting notions.

"Don't do it, Bake," Torque said after noticing the portly vector's hesitation.

Oblivious to Torque's warning, Baker lunged at Streetz. As Baker lumbered forward with arm chambered and ready to strike, Streetz dashed toward Baker. Expecting a victorious clash based on size difference, Baker moved to extend his fist as Streetz neared.

Once within arm's length, Streetz disabled his impact fields, disappearing from view just as Baker occupied his position. Baker's body suddenly twitched as he felt an electrical shock hammer his nerves. Realizing that Streetz had just run through him, Baker looked over his shoulder to see Streetz rematerialize behind him, but it was the last thing he would recall as the electric shock put him down.

With the opposition incapacitated and lying on the floor, Torque relaxed enough to scan the premises. All of the Region 8 customers looked on with concern. Torque guessed that the trio represented the best vectors to frequent the establishment. Torque would still vouch for that had it not been the additional training he'd received under the Enforcer's guidance.

Torque eyed one patron in particular who appeared to be holding his breath as he stared in Torque's direction. Torque stepped toward the suspicious patron, but as he did, he realized that he wasn't the subject of the patron's concern. Torque snapped and turned about, peering into the darkness. In the back of the club, a short, but wide silhouette appeared in a doorway nearly blocking all of the light from the room behind.

Streetz shifted and raised his hands, anticipating another fight, but Torque stepped up to restrain him by resting a hand on Streetz's shoulder.

"This one's personal," Torque muttered as he advanced toward the stocky shadow. "Keep an eye on our friends in case they wake up."

Reluctantly, Streetz complied and perched himself on a vacated bar stool. He sensed that things were about to get interesting.

Old Cut-Thru
Abandoned Sector, Windstonne Enclave
Commercial Empire, Northam Continent
Thread: actTgtPersp1.view

I remained in a frozen state as I watched the silver blade slice through the air. Even if my words hadn't been trapped in my throat, I doubted that they would have mattered. The Enforcer's momentum increased as he sprinted forward. I was certain that the Enforcer was about to be severed in two, but the outcome deviated greatly from my expectation.

Before the attacker's blade could connect, the Enforcer's body was already in the air. With the agility of a wild cat, the Enforcer sprang upward but in a most abnormal fashion for a human. Both of his legs snapped upward simultaneously over his body as his back paralleled both the ground and the menacing blade. As he cleared the strike, his body continued to twist until he landed facing the way he had just come with both feet touching down at the same time.

"Who is he that attacks the invisible from shadows," the Enforcer yelled beckoning his challenger to step into the moonlight. He disengaged his cloak while our foe remained in the shadows.

I crouched behind a crate, unsure if I should assist by attacking our opponent from behind. I hesitated, considering that such a calculation may have been the heavy stuff that the Enforcer referred to. Ticks passed as I anxiously waited for our attacker to identify himself.

The Enforcer stood motionless like a stone statue as we waited. At last, I could hear a faint rustle as a silhouette stepped from the shadows. Unable to see in the darkness, I blinked a couple of times to set my ikes to night vision. A leather clad form stood between me and the Enforcer. Through the greenish light I could discern a black haired figure with a long leather coat. Even more peculiar was that, like ourselves, the attacker wore shades as well in the dead of night. Lastly, I noticed the gleaming silver blade that had moments ago sliced through the air. The attacker held the blade out to his side pointed, toward the ground in a confident yet unconcerned fashion.

"I simply seek an adversary worthy of my time," the figure said in a soft raspy voice.

The Enforcer remained motionless and silent.

"You know what I think…" the attacker continued.

"Actually, I don't care what you think," the Enforcer interjected mid-sentence.

Even from a distance I could see the Enforcer's eyes narrow as the blue shades of his lenses shifted while he squinted at our adversary.

"…I think you're a waste of my time," our adversary replied as if the Enforcer hadn't even been there.

"Then why are you still here?" the Enforcer asked, growing irritated with the charade.

"What matter of man sneaks through darkness, requiring tech when he is already in shadow?" The man hissed back.

"My business is my own, and it leaves no time for trivial affairs such as this," the Enforcer replied. He followed with a motion to turn as if annoyed with a persistent fly, but just as he took his eyes off his adversary, he noticed irritation, an irritation easily overlooked, but it was still revealed from a faint facial twitch of disgust. The Enforcer detected the emotion was masked well, but he still perceived that the vector was well trained. Long ago, he learned that even the slightest reaction could reveal the path to victory or defeat. The Enforcer fought to hide a smirk of his own as he turned away from his opponent, but the trap was already set. The mystery vector had pride, suppressed as it may have been, it couldn't be fully hidden.

The attacker lashed his blade out and circled it over his head, bringing it down forcefully over the Enforcer's skull. Anticipating the attack, the Enforcer had already snapped his hands to his sides freeing his sai from his waist. With a flash, the Enforcer's hands spun the weapons and locked them into place overhead, catching the long blade in the crook of the crossed sai.

The attacker gripped his blade with one hand as it rested between the pinched weapons above the Enforcer's tensed arms. The Enforcer noticed that his attacker was neither looking at him nor moving to follow-up with a combination attack. The man's ayvek was highly refined. It was as if he was toying with the Enforcer, testing him.

Seizing the opportunity, the Enforcer thrust the sai together in an attempt to trap the long blade and wrench it from the attacker's grasp, but the move was anticipated. The shadowy figure pulled down on the handle of his blade freeing it from the forked blades and spun about whipping the sword around his body. He came to rest in a low stance with his back hand holding the blade pointed toward the Enforcer and his front hand flat bent at a sharp angle in contrast to his forearm. The Enforcer recognized the posture as one common to a snake-like ayvek from the Shian continent.

Noticing that the Enforcer had taken a tick to observe the new stance, the attacker took advantage of the distraction by thrusting the sword forward with his rear hand. Regaining his focus, the Enforcer turned into the thrust of the blade catching it parallel with the forks of each sai. The spinning motion and the force of the Enforcer's strength on the blade caused the attacker to lose his grip on the weapon. The Enforcer twirled the loose sword over his head as it dangled between his sai. The Enforcer used his momentum to complete the spin thrusting his arms outward causing the sword blade to swing toward its owner.

The adversary quickly ducked to avoid being cut by his own blade. The Enforcer completed his spin and loosened his sai causing the sword to sail through the air and clang on the ground several paces away.

In an air of challenge, the Enforcer threw down his weapons to fight his opponent hand-to-hand. In the pale light, I vaguely detected a smirk as the attacker accepted the challenge. The adversary resumed his low stance, this time with both hands in the snake-head position. The Enforcer followed suit, but instead, brought his hands into a signature posture of his own with both hands palm open. One hand faced the adversary and the other he held palm up just in front of his abdomen.

The attacker dashed forward, striking at the Enforcer's eyes. I was amazed at the fluid motions of the opponent. His style resembled a slithering snake more than that of some random brawler.

The Enforcer easily parried the attacker's first hand strike, but his adversary weaved his hands past the blocks delivering a well trained strike underneath the Enforcer's shades, hitting the eye. Momentarily stunned, the Enforcer retracted, stepping quickly to avoid another impending attack, but a combination strike was not the adversary's intention.

The attacker stepped past the Enforcer and stood behind him. Shaking his head to alleviate the disorientation, the Enforcer looked up and noticed his adversary was no longer in front of him. Sensing an attack from behind, the Enforcer spun just as the attacker brought a downward chop into thin air narrowly missing the Enforcer's collarbone.

"You fight like a Ghost!" the Enforcer muttered, noticing that his opponent appeared well versed in Yuurei. The Enforcer switched from disinterest to intrigue upon seeing the implementation of a familiar yet foreign ayvek. The remark caught the attacker off guard, since he doubted an average urban dweller could possess any knowledge of the Martial Legion's elite military unit.

"And just what would know of the Ghosts?" The man hissed coldly.

"You might be surprised what I know... or who," the Enforcer replied, amused at the battle of wits.

The leather clad attacker lunged forward again starting to lose his composure. The Enforcer swiftly sidestepped, channeling the man's momentum into a shoulder throw. Airborne and flipping through the air, the attacker soon found himself connecting with the hard pavement. I cringed as I watched the Enforcer flip the man onto his back.

The Enforcer leaned over the dazed vector, "I don't suppose you would happen to know General Sato Seechi?" He said with a grin.

Coming to, the vector's face went blank, "The Enforcer, I presume?" He stammered as he began to pick himself off the grimy alley floor.

"Vanguard operative at your service," the Enforcer said, extending a hand to help the man to his feet. Noticing that I was still hiding behind a crate, the Enforcer nodded at me, indicating that it was safe to approach.

"Alex Corzo, also known as the Serpent," the vector said exchanging a cross arm.

"You definitely have a knack for irregular introductions, Alex. I'm Mac Conner and this is another operative in training, Aaron Fox," the Enforcer replied.

"Yeah, I'd, uh, hate to see what happens to those you don't announce your presence to," I said matching the cross arm gesture.

The Serpent did a double take as he looked at the Enforcer and then back at me. I was surprised that even in the darkness he noticed our physical similarities.

"What brings you to the illustrious sprawl beyond our faction capital, Alex?" the Enforcer asked as he scooped up the Serpent's blade to return it.

"I have retired from my position among the Ghosts in favor of challenges that expand my skills. I see that the wise general had more insight than I could have imagined. Here I thought that I would find a challenging fight, yet I am humbled to understand that he sent me here to learn. I see that you were just toying with me and could have double teamed me at anytime," the Serpent said, accepting the sword as he looked from me back to the Enforcer.

"Don't mind me, I'm just a spectator," I stated.

"I see," Alex replied ,apparently intrigued as to his true purpose in traveling to the capital enclave of the Commercial Empire.

"Fox is a vector. He just doesn't realize it yet," the Enforcer said.

"Ah, yes things are seldom as they appear," the Serpent said, slowly lowering his shades. He blinked his eyes, but the the motion happened so quickly that I couldn't fully describe the abnormality which caught me off guard.

Trying to distract the Serpent from my gawking, the Enforcer spoke up, "Speaking of appearances versus reality, are you part of the Interlace?"

"Yes, General Seechi explained the nature of the Firewall Protocol to me several passes back, but I have rarely crossed paths with members of the Interlace since. There are few vectors within the Interlace, so I assumed that I would have to find meaningful challenges elsewhere," the Serpent replied.

"The general is a good man. Welcome to Vanguard, Alex," the Enforcer said with a smile. "I know that he had your best interests at heart if he sent you to me. I'm sure we have much to learn from each other."

"Back to the business at hand," the Enforcer said, changing the subject. "We were on our way to investigate a little clan activity as well as find out who the elusive Serpent was, before we got detoured."

"Oh, I suppose you would be referring to those Académe fishes that hang out nearby. I wouldn't consider anything about their ways interesting after watching them the last few days," the Serpent replied, pleased that his new friends had a sense of humor.

"Good to hear," I yawned, realizing just how late it was.

The Enforcer rolled his eyes, "I suppose we can postpone their interrogation for another evening."

After snagging his sai from the ground and reholstering them to his side, the Enforcer turned to leave the dark alley the way we had come, "Come, I shall introduce you to the rest of the crew."

Region 8
Core City Fringe, Windstonne Enclave
Commercial Empire, Northam Continent
Thread: sysObserver.cmd

Torque squinted to peer through the haze at the far end of the club. He had little doubt that this observer was none other than Region 8's owner, but he still wanted a visual confirmation. The burly figure stepped into the room causing a hush to fall over the onlookers. The tension was high and everyone awaited a response to break the silence.

"You shouldn't have come back, Lennox," the muscular man bellowed.

"Yeah, well, I was kind of hoping that short memories would prevail," Torque muttered with a straight face.

"Not exactly what I would consider fair compensation to your friends for all of the times that they had your back," the man rumbled as he nodded to the trio of incapacitated vectors.

"I don't suppose that you could have put them up to it. Right, Boulder?" Torque replied sarcastically, nearly spitting out the name.

Boulder, Region 8's owner finally stepped into the light, revealing his bleached hair minus the black strip parting his goatee. Boulder was an intimidating figure, not because of his height, but his physique. He looked more like the man to guard the door rather than own the semi-popular club tucked away from Core City traffic. His tight black shirt contoured his torso more than expected. As he approached, he flexed his biceps which occupied more space than Torque's upper legs.

Torque stood his ground as Boulder sauntered out onto the hardwood floor. If it weren't for having muscular legs, Boulder easily looked like he could have been knocked over from having such a massive upper body. As Boulder shrugged his shoulders and rolled his head to loosen his thick neck, Torque accepted that Boulder had no interest in reminiscing. Boulder was a businessman, and it was fair to assume that he wanted retribution for damages during Torque's last brawl. Torque anticipated such a reception, hence his reluctance to return. He owed Boulder, but given Boulder's pride, Torque doubted that a handful of passgrad would be enough to divert Boulder's present collection method.

Boulder stepped in front of Torque, his forehead level with Torque's chin. Torque swung a hook punch to the side of Boulder's face, but Boulder reacted with speed quicker than expected for his stocky size. He leaned into the punch, causing Torque's swing to pass behind Boulder's head, knocking Torque off-balance.

Boulder leaned in placing his shoulder into Torque's gut. Boulder's motion launched Torque's body into the air flipping him over. Torque's back slammed on the floor. He winced, feeling his lungs wrench for air. Boulder quickly turned and lifted his leg into the air to drop his heel on Torque's face. Barely able to react, Torque snapped his legs over his body propelling into a backward handstand just as Boulder's shoe slammed to the floor.

Torque landed back on his feet, barely settled before pushing off the floor again with both feet propelling his torso in a circle. He snapped his foot across a rotational path, kicking out at Boulder. Boulder immediately ducked under the kick, but Torque was quick on the combination. Boulder snapped his hands down to block Torque's reverse kick to the groin. Torque continued the pressure relentlessly striking at Boulder. Before Torque even knew that Boulder had blocked his kick, Torque turned his left shoulder to drop a chop over Boulder's head. Again Boulder transferred his hands from the two fisted low block into a similar block over his head. Torque spun in the reverse direction with a back elbow narrowly missing Boulder's temple. Advancing after Torque's error, Boulder snaked his arm under Torque's shoulder and tossed him over his back attempting to throw Torque off-balance, but Torque's agility had vastly improved since their last encounter. Torque flowed with the momentum and landed on his feet after rolling across Boulder's back.

Unsurprised yet still determined, Boulder launched a barrage of strikes at Torque's face and upper body. Torque's and Boulder's arms clashed in a crossfire of punches, blocks, and counter attacks. Noticing that Torque was starting to become arrogant as his speed began to overcome Boulders precision strikes, Boulder altered his tactics. Torque assumed that Boulder's muscular size would slow him down, prompting a smirk to crease Torque's face, despite its short duration. Boulder caught Torque's arm and twisted it, yanking him to the floor. Boulder immediately dropped his body while stepping his foot across Torque's arm placing severe pressure on Torque's arm. Torque yelled in irritation and pain. Not releasing his lock on Torque's arm, Boulder wrenched even harder on the captive limb.

Furious, Torque swung his leg up and caught Boulder in the eye. The brief distraction was enough for Boulder to loosen his grip so that Torque could pull away. Without waiting for Boulder to strike again Torque rolled away and pushed himself off the floor. Torque loosened his arm trying to shake the pain from the undue stress placed on it. It was Boulder's turn to smirk as he watched Torque nurse his injury.

Boulder's enjoyment of the spectacle caused Torque to replace his amusement with fury. He advanced with a series of kicks, but again he found himself being hurled to the floor as Boulder snatched his leg and dropped his body weight, pulling Torque off-balance. Boulder wrapped his forearms around Torque's knee and pressed hard. Excruciating pain seared through Torque's leg. He attempted to push himself from the floor to swing at Boulder, but Boulder's immense power immobilized Torque.

Region 8 patrons stared as they watched the club owner deliver a thrashing. Streetz winced and motioned to intervene, but restrained himself as subroutines reminded him of Torque's instruction.

Torque thought he felt explosions erupting in his leg as he yelled in pain. He resisted with all of his strength, but Boulder held an invincible command over his leg. Every muscle, every tendon said that his bones were about to break. Futility washed over Torque as he screamed one last time as all strength left his leg. He knew a broken appendage was inevitable, but just as his will to resist left him he noticed that so did the pressure on his leg.

Shocked, Torque watched Boulder let go of the lock and extend a hand to help him off the floor. Torque's chest heaved as if air were a scarcity. He struggled to find any adrenaline left in his system while attempting to comprehend why Boulder had ended the fight.

"Not bad, Lennox, your skills have a come long way," Boulder rumbled as he scooped Torque off the floor like a scrap of paper.

"What's this is all about? Did the Imperans sell out of piñatas?" Torque muttered arrogantly as if he knew all along that Boulder harbored no ill intent.

"I had you going. You can't fool me, Lennox. I saw the desperation in your face," Boulder smiled. "You left my place in shambles, Brother, and I had to get payback out of you somehow since my prize vector decided to bolt."

"What do you mean prize vector?" Torque replied suspiciously.

"The damages done here were easily repairable with all of the berry I made off wagers from your fights," Boulder said.

"You mean you were making berry on me all that time...? Why you..." Torque grumbled, attempting to lay a hand on Boulder but a sharp pain in his leg restrained him from moving forward. Instead,

Torque found the nearest table that wasn't overturned and plopped down in the adjacent seat.

Boulder laughed as he watched Torque trying to act like a tough guy before joining him on the opposite side of the table. Torque started to smirk, at least relieved that Boulder hadn't held a grudge for the last couple of passes.

"I figured after all this time that you wanted to kill me…" Torque laughed.

"Who says I don't?" Boulder said, his smile evaporating into a fearsome stone face.

Torque's face froze in terror as he stared at Boulder. Boulder punched Torque's leg and burst into laughter. Torque winced in pain, but sat there nervously, unsure if Boulder was actually right in the head.

"That was a joke, Lennox," Boulder said in between guffaws.

Streetz noticed that the other three vectors were starting to come around, but he discarded his former instruction, sensing that hostility had dissipated. He walked over to join Torque and Boulder as other patrons started to resume conversations and drinks on their own.

"So, what do you say, Lennox? Interested in scoring some dimps? I've got contacts that could even pipe us into Imperan feeds these days," Boulder asked, leaning forward on the table.

"Sorry, Boulder, as tempting as it is to actually profit on my own pain this time around, I travel in different circles these days," Torque replied, making sure the sarcasm was clear about his disdain for having been kept in the dark about berry made at his expense.

"I see that," Boulder replied with curiosity as he watched Streetz step up and sit at the table. "What brings you back? What kind of mission are you running?"

"Well, it sure isn't on the Commercial Empire hot list, so I'm sure you understand the need for discretion. I also know that you always have ears on any business worth knowing about. Do you remember Mac Conner?" Torque asked while rubbing his sore shoulder.

"The Enforcer? Yep, what about him?" Boulder asked.

"He's been snagging some mystery threats from some urban lurker that goes by the name, Serpent. Curious if you've got any intel," Torque replied.

"Foreign data, Brother," Boulder replied bluntly, expressing no familiarity.

"Have you had any Académe disturbances around here?" Torque asked.

"Not a one. I don't allow that kind of fishbait in here. Too much liability," Boulder said. "But I'll tell you one thing. Things have been quiet the last couple of lunars. Lots of rumors, whispers and fears though about some magnate accumulating even more hardware than Frank Jenkins. Rumblings suggest that he's still parked in the shadows, but he's got war in his right hand and deception in his left."

"What are you saying? We're going back to war?" Torque replied, confused. "I thought that was supposed be bad for Global Alliance business."

"Perhaps... but, I have reliable sources that say he's scooping up metal and chemicals in greater quantity than any of the factions. Don't let it surprise you, Lennox. The will to conquer is often stronger than any band of strong men oblivious to its presence," Boulder whispered.

Given Boulder's intimidating persona, hearing someone of his physique speak in such a hushed tone sent chills down Torque's spine. "Then I guess we should proceed with caution."

"That would be wise, Brother," Boulder uttered, quickly returning to his usual arrogant swagger.

Torque nodded solemnly. He slowly lifted himself from the table. Boulder rose to escort Torque and Streetz to the bar entrance. "How about a couple cold ones for the road," Boulder said as he gestured for the woman behind the bar to grab something out of the chiller.

"Nah, that's alright, Boulder, your hospitality has been more than suitable," Torque remarked sarcastically.

"This one's on me," Boulder replied, tossing a chug to Torque.

Torque caught the cold chug of water with his good arm. Boulder grabbed another chug and tossed it to Streetz who followed right behind Torque. Streetz turned and watched the hardmelt chug and allowed it to fly right through his body. Boulder looked on suspiciously as the chug bounced off the hard floor sloshing its contents around inside. Streetz smirked in response and turned toward the exit.

Jargon eyed Torque and Streetz nervously as they proceeded toward the exit. Streetz flexed his muscles and laughed as he walked past their foes still trying to orient themselves with consciousness. Duds flinched, feeling like a limp fish after being shown up.

"Lennox, you're good vector. Don't forget my offer," Boulder said.

As much as Torque missed the simple days of carefree behavior, he knew that there was more weight on his shoulders, no matter how enticing Boulder's offer was. With a simple nod and quick salute with his first two fingers, he left his response as ambiguous as possible.

Even though the mission to gather intel was a marginal success, he knew that he could leave Region 8 with his debt settled.

Gridloc: Dynastic Prelude
Thread: frmAstStgMnfst.rgt

Wind gently tugged at the long grass lining each side of the sand path leading up to the stone house which was well removed from the closest village. Grazing animals noticed the movement from the humanoid suit of black armor as it approached, but they dismissively continued their feeding session.

Crux calmly observed the surroundings, sensing no human life with exception of the land owner who cautiously approached. The black underlay crunched as Crux held his hands behind his back to minimize any offensive posture. He held his position, awaiting the local to engage in conversation.

"Can I help you?" The land owner asked.

Crux easily identified the man with average height whose garb consisted of loose cloth separated by a belt at the waist and draping down to his knees. His trimmed brown hair with matching mustache and goatee revealed that he wasn't simply another laborer who avoided local society.

"I'm looking for Offhand," Crux said, his face hidden behind the opaque blue mask.

"That's an unusual name," the man said as he held his distance several paces from the heavy metallic armor. He'd heard rumor of radical armor styles from other vera, so he required no convincing that his visitor was unlikely from a nearby region let alone the same continent.

"I understand that it belongs to someone with unusual skill. More specifically, someone with a reputation for precision and adaptation," Crux replied.

"My name is Ehud. I'm sorry that you made your journey here for nothing," the man replied.

Crux's form remained motionless. His eyes narrowed as he scrutinized every detail of Ehud's posture. Ehud remained perfectly still, yet did so with neither an aggressive nor defensive stance. His arms were relaxed and yet seemingly poised to draw a weapon at will.

"Must have been my mistake," Crux said.

As he motioned to leave, Ehud kept his eyes trained on the visitor. Even with the subtle motion to turn, Crux saw that Ehud held both his position and kept his eyes on every possible threat.

Recognizing that the man was well trained, Crux stomped a heavy boot into the sand, sending a blinding wave of dust particles upward between him and the local.

In a blur, Ehud drew a long blade from his right thigh with his left hand. His first swing cleared the sand passing before his eyes. Crux's motion was equally fast as he drew a sidearm from his thigh. As Ehud's second swing came about, the blade's point rested against the undersuit beneath Crux' helmet, presenting a potentially lethal strike to his neck. Before his own motion completed, Crux dislodged the ammo cell from his sidearm, dropping both weapons and cell to the ground as if he failed the loading sequence. Without moving the rest of his body, Crux dropped one hand yet held the other behind his head suggesting possible surrender.

"A clever, yet subtle diversion," Ehud said, still holding the blade with unflinching precision.

"Was it the only one?" Crux asked slyly.

"Let me guess. You have a blade out of my peripheral vision pointed at my waist to threaten my lineage," Ehud quipped his eyes yet to waver from their target lock.

"Hardly. This isn't an Entropim meca. I'm not here to test your manhood, just your resolve," Crux said as he nodded just slightly enough for Ehud to consider what was behind him.

Ehud knew better than to take his eyes off his target, but if the encounter had been anything other than a test, then he certainly would be dead. His senses detected that two small blades hovered in the air behind the base of his neck and they were likely levitated from some control with the raised armored hand that also remained as still as his own blade. Recognizing that he didn't have the advantage to begin with, Ehud lowered his weapon and returned it to his sheath.

"A strange test. It would seem that you have little need of me considering that you already have the upper hand," Ehud said.

"It's not so much skill I am seeking, but value. Yours, and that of those whose company you keep. I know that your skill comes from reading ways around the prohibitions of your day," Crux replied as he returned his blades to a secured sheath and picked up his firearm.

Ehud eyed his visitor suspiciously. His existence was secluded and the missions he took on were always particular and exact. For someone to know of his presence, skills and allies without immediately regarding him a threat made him question the nature of the encounter.

"I'm not sure that I'm your guy," Ehud replied, testing the true lengths of the negotiation. "It seems to me that you already have the necessary resources at your disposal."

"My task does not always lend itself to being on site as needed," Crux replied simply as he stood to his full height in the armor.

"So, you have a timing issue," Ehud suggested.

Crux nodded silently.

"Most of my missions are direct from the Triad. I'm not sure why you are convinced that I can accomplish what you seek," Ehud said.

"You know how to adapt, and I trust that you can read situations as they are over how they appear," Crux said flatly.

"That's it? No mission parameters," Ehud replied, feeling confused.

"When the walls collapse, the pillar that stands will reveal the way," Crux said.

"That is extremely vague, cryptic even. It certainly isn't anything I've seen written in the Criterion," Ehud said.

"Localized plans rarely are," Crux said. "I can only encourage you to carry on as you would normally. The only identifier I have is that the target will be traveling with a Nomad. How to handle the situation is up to you."

Having completed the next phase in his objective, Crux turned to depart. Ehud stared at the back of his visitor pondering if he should ask more questions, but given the strange nature of the discussion, he doubted that it would help. All he could do was contemplate the ambiguous conversation. After the visitor was out of sight, he took one look at his animals before returning to his house.

10 – Internal Fury – 10

Grand Imperium
Capitol District, Tokean Enclave
Martial Legion, Shian Islands
Thread: sysObserver.cmd

Three sets of footsteps rose from the polished wood floors of the central hallway in the Martial Legion's capitol building. General Sato Seechi hoped that nostalgia would offer reassurance upon seeing the traditional, tiered, wooden structures of the Ghost's homeland, but the visibility of the tall, decorative marble columns imported from the mainland reminded him that the ways of the past were not carried fully into the present. The Martial Legion was still adjusting to the merger that had fused numerous cultures together.

Although General Seechi had grown accustomed to his heavy chest, shoulder, and thigh armor common to the advanced ranks of the Ghosts, he was more aware of its presence than usual. He suspected that the added mystery behind the unusual summons created an inexplicable tension. Normally, the Emperor would transmit all operations through the Ghost's relay center on the mainland, but this time an imperative suggested that the latest meeting required a personal encounter.

General Seechi rested his left hand on the katana handle at his hip as he walked down the quiet, spacious hallway. His two commanding officers followed behind, each with their own katanas strapped to their backs with handles extending out over the right shoulder. Since Alex Corzo's departure, General Seechi had to promote his next two officers in the chain of command in order to efficiently fill the void.

The trio of Ghosts paused as they arrived at the heavy red doors inscribed with fearsome reptilian insignia leading to the Emperor's throne room. Two honor guards with armor mildly similar to General Seechi's stood before the doors. General Seechi kept his eyes trained on the doors in hopes of avoiding eye contact with the wary guards, but he couldn't help notice that each of the guards had at least one organech limb. He was relieved that his subordinates were wearing their masks otherwise a showdown of wits may have ensued given the potential animosity over the emperor allowing his honor guards to corrupt Maleezhun traditions.

As the doors finally parted, the Ghosts advanced forward into an even greater hall. Emperor Kage Shito watched silently from a thick

DAVE TODD

cushion where he sat with his legs crossed. General Seechi was the first to bow forward to pay respects before his subordinates followed suit. General Seechi wasn't fond of the faction leader, but he didn't consider it wise to upset the one in charge of military funding.

Since the Martial Legion was still politically volatile, many sought to use the discord to reignite long running feuds that still smoldered since the Global War, but given the emperor's perspective from his battles during the war, he maintained strict policy to retain select traditions regardless of heritage. Despite the emperor being a native to the island territory, his time spent as ambassador to the mainland had certainly affected his views, a history that General Seechi was sure to remember since loyalty to the faction could still be easily rewarded with exile.

Emperor Shito nodded silently acknowledging the party while keeping his hands tucked inside the long flowing sleeves of his gold and red robe. General Seechi stepped forward and knelt several paces in front of the shallow steps which elevated the emperor's throne. In turn, the Ghost officers shifted from a formal stance to a relaxed one by placing their hands behind their backs. General Seechi eyed the emperor suspiciously.

"I presume that you are eager to understand the purpose of your visit," Emperor Shito said.

"Indeed, Sir," General Seechi replied, clearing his throat.

Emperor Shito continued, "As commanding officer of the mostly highly trained military unit within the Martial Legion I would like to personally request that you oversee a project for me that is of the utmost importance. A growing militia of the North Island has sworn their allegiance to the Martial Legion and is requesting to be promoted to military status."

"Does such a promotion require my approval, Sir?" General Seechi replied suspiciously.

"No, it does not, but given your experience in the art of war, I would like several of your most qualified officers to train the Drakken in close quarters combat," Emperor Shito replied.

"Did you say, Drakken, Sir?!" General Seechi asked, nearly choking on his words.

"Ah, so you are familiar with them, General, good, good. That means you already have a head start," Emperor Shito smiled.

"Sir, the Drakken are little more than engineered, yet mindless super soldiers. I would highly advise against upgrading their status," General Seechi snorted, attempting to restrain his irritation. "We have faced the Drakken in battle on numerous occasions. Their close quarters abilities are lacking, considering that brute force is all that they have ever learned. They give little consideration to political fallout and leave nothing but a trail of collateral damage behind them."

"As an aging soldier, I'm sure that you are fully aware that the wars of tomorrow will no longer be fought in the shadows, but in the open field where opposing forces no longer attempt to outwit their adversaries, but wrestle them into submission. The secret that the Drakken hold is key in making combat more cost effective. For the amount of time and resources invested into one Ghost, I can have a small contingent of Drakken. Power is necessary, General. The Ghosts are a dying breed on the battlefield, and I offer this to you as a chance to continue your legacy," the Emperor said.

"Sir, in an attempt to bring us forward technologically you are in essence taking the Martial Legion's effectiveness in warfare backward," General Seechi muttered.

"Enough," Emperor Shito replied. "As you already admitted yourself, this decision does not require your approval, General."

General Seechi clenched his teeth and rose to his feet. He looked the emperor in the eyes and then at his guards on either side. The general noticed something peculiar about one of the guards before looking back at the emperor, the phenomena was the same in the emperor and the other guard. All color within the eyes of the emperor and his guards had turned white or at least cloudy, not a result of any lens but as if some chemical change had taken place, affecting pupil and iris alike.

"As it is commanded," General Seechi replied, simultaneously gritting his teeth while trying not to stare at those opposite him. With his bow complete and the meeting concluded, General Seechi snapped around and exited the throne room with his Ghosts in tow.

No sooner had the throne doors sealed, when a shrill ping resonated from the sonair embedded in General Seechi's helmet.

Looking over his shoulder to make sure that the Ghosts were outside earshot of the Maleezhun honor guards, Seechi activated the portable comm embedded in his bracer, "Seechi, here."

"Sir, you have a relayed comm from the Commercial Empire. Tag: The Enforcer," said the operative responsible for filtering transmissions.

Surprised at receiving word from a distant friend so soon, General Seechi was glad to have the distraction, "By all means, put it through."

"Greetings from Vanguard," Mac Conner said upon confirming the general's identity on his screen.

"Hello, Mr. Conner, how are things in the breezy capital?" General Seechi replied with a faint smile. His meeting with the emperor had clearly fatigued his social capacity.

"Going well, General, going well. I must express my gratitude for your most unique yet subtle way of recruiting help for our cause here in the Commercial Empire. Your delivery arrived silent and clear," Mac Conner replied.

"Good to hear. Alex Corzo is an excellent vector. He has been my right hand for many passes. I regret having to let him go, but you and I both know that each stop here is temporary on our journey to the Exterior itself. Alex has surpassed his potential here, and I knew that you would have insights to help him identify the next waypoint," General Seechi replied.

"Your confidence in my counsel is much appreciated, General, I only hope that I make half as much of an impact as the precedent you have set," Mac replied before leaning in closer to his terminal.

"How is business on your side of the world, General?" Mac asked, sensing a burden through the general's demeanor.

General Seechi looked around as he and his officers proceeded down the old wooden steps of the Grand Imperium. His stride quickened in order to gain a few paces on his officers so they wouldn't inadvertently overhear what he was about to say.

"I wish that I could say things were going well, but given the trend of our turbulent political climate, I fear that another uprising is simmering," Seechi said in a hoarse whisper.

"Do you have evidence of another coup?" Mac asked in concern.

"No, I think there is something else at work. Mr. Conner, have you ever walked in the black of night and felt an even greater darkness hidden within? Instead or using an opportune time to strike, it simply hovers to drain all prospect of hope that might otherwise endure," Seechi asked with a grim expression.

"I think we all have, General. I have also sensed a faceless adversary as of late. If a force is instigating war within the Global Alliance, we must all be prepared," Mac replied, searching for a word of optimism.

General Seechi nodded solemnly after running his fingers across the graying silver tips of his thinning black mustache, "It is good to speak with you again, Mr. Conner. Make sure Alex gets the guidance he needs. If our suspicions are correct, we're going to need all the strong leaders we can get with the Interlace scattered as it is," Seechi said.

"Indeed, General, do keep me informed if you detect a shift in the political landscape. You know that Vanguard is always at your service," Mac said, hoping to lift the aging general's countenance. While Mac felt distant from the longtime ally, he reflected on their long history. It was easy for Mac to draw assurance that Sato Seechi's emotional stability was as rigid as his strategic planning. If something rattled Seechi, clearly that matter was significant.

"Thank you, Mac, until we speak again," Seechi replied with the faintest smile that he cared to offer while in uniform. Then, with a tap, the general terminated the comm.

Vanguard Warehouse
Abandoned Sector, Windstonne Enclave
Commercial Empire, Northam Continent
Thread: actTgtPersp1.view

Muffled conversation filtered through my ears as I rolled over on my cot. I slung my arm over my eyes to inhibit the inevitable daylight from piercing my eyelids, but since my restless mind obstructed a return to slumber, I attempted to reconstruct memories of the hectic events of the previous night Images flashed through my mind of the jog down the dark alley, the altercation between the Enforcer and the Serpent, the ride home and the exchange of encounters once Lennox and Streetz returned. Mac expressed surprise that Lennox was limping after exiting the Chromehound. Lennox matched with his own level of surprise upon discovering that the mysterious threat had been so readily inducted into Vanguard's roster.

After a quick debriefing, I had retired to my room while Mac and Lennox continued to discuss the potential meaning of Boulder's inside information. After the commotion, it took little effort to doze off, but no matter how much sleep I achieved, my body always demanded more.

Conceding that no more sleep was to be found for the current interval, I finally lifted myself from the cot. Feeling the grooved impressions on one side of my face from the cot's canvas, I thought it best to clean up. After a fast and shockingly cold shower, I dressed and prepped for training to begin anew. As I strolled across the training floor, I spotted Mac staring over the terminal. I guessed that he had just finished a comm which would have accounted for the sounds disrupting my slumber.

Mogul Prime Media Resource Center
Core City Fringe, Windstonne Enclave
Commercial Empire, Northam Continent
Thread: sysObserver.cmd

Sunlight bounced off the hazy glass adorning the Mogul Prime storefront. The occasional pedestrian would stop to scan the latest signage in hopes of new material announcements. While the Media Resource Center claimed special privileges in selling otherwise restricted educational resources, its flow of traffic was only as good as its arcs of operation. The large overhead sign shaped like a human brain with eyes dotting each hemisphere remained dark until business operations resumed.

While waiting for opening time, Pythagoras and Tunnel killed time bantering about choice methods of political oppression. Bender walked into the room with a smelly sack of hamburgers and dropped them on the table. Tunnel simply rolled his beady eyes as Bender sat down and fished for contents in the bag.

"So what subtle techniques do you have to subdue a rioting mob, Dexter?" Tunnel asked returning to the debate at hand.

"Tybalt, first off, you should never allow your followers, supporters, or whoever get to the point in which they rally against you. If they are malcontent, it is because you allowed it. There are discrepancies between their objective and the information that you provided. Desire is a driving force easily disillusioned. If you offer people the illusion of contentment then you will never encounter a feud," Pythagoras replied as he kicked his long legs out from under the table to prop up his feet.

"Sure, that's just fine if you cultivate the following ahead of time, but what if you are already past that point?" Tunnel replied as he fiddled with the utility belt that spanned his shoulder to the opposite side of his waist. He loved instigating heated debates, but rarely did he convince Pythagoras to take the bait.

"I say you just club the fishes into submission. You'll crack the lines when you jack some spines. If you make a few examples, you can soften 'em right up," Bender replied as he tore a huge chunk of bread and meat from the burger in hand, causing a large glob of grease and condiments to plop onto the wax paper resting on the table.

Pythagoras and Tunnel just blinked and looked at each other and then back at Bender as if he were a child attempting to lecture on energistics.

"Dennis, how can you eat that garbage?" Pythagoras asked condescendingly as he brushed a brown hair curl away from his temple.

Bender paused his noisy chewing and looked at his associates at the opposite end of the table. His yellow ocular implant pulsed as he blinked his natural eye at the others. He waved his half eaten burger at Pythagoras. "Oh, right. I get it. Let's pick on Dennis."

"My friends, let me tell you a tale of genius, Kingray's Burger Nation," Bender continued slowly, emphasizing the business name. "That is a consumer time bomb waiting to explode, but after a generation it still continues to exceed all financial projections. KBN leads the industry, all while stacking its success upon worker exploitation, mismanagement, suppression of achievement and the most synthetic ingredients known to man. I believe its founder is an old friend of Tycoon's. Therefore, I think of it as supporting one of our own."

"Well said, Dennis. I knew there was a reason that you joined us," Tunnel replied, impressed at Bender's business acumen despite his crude manner.

"Besides," Bender nodded as he unscrewed the cap on a flask which he withdrew from his vest pocket, "I always have something to wash it down."

The smell emanating from the flask was so strong that both Pythagoras and Tunnel's faces contorted after inhaling the pungent odor. "I can't tell if your drinking paint thinner or axel grease," Tunnel replied with an uncontrollable cringe.

"It's a special recipe. Dulls the pain sensors on really bad days," Bender replied as he tapped a finger to the metal plate covering a section of his skull.

"I'm sure that isn't the only thing it dulls," Pythagoras replied, repulsed by the smell.

"True that," Bender smirked as he downed another swig before capping and storing the flask. He eagerly finished his meal while Pythagoras and Tunnel flailed their arms to dispel the odor.

Monk Training Facility
Core City Fringe, Windstonne Enclave
Commercial Empire, Northam Continent
Thread: sysObserver.cmd

Still air and silence permeated the training floor of the Monks' domain. While their physical training was complete for the day, their mental conditioning was only beginning. Little mattered of the physical world as they focused their efforts on deliberate concentration which allowed them to integrate with their surroundings. The only sound to take form, ever so often, was the faint trace of breathing as all participants consciously suppressed heart and lung activity.

After a prolonged silence, Tiger opened his eyes and observed the four who had been training with him since midday. Crane, Monkey, Mantis and Snake all sat opposite Tiger in a row with their legs folded in front of them.

Overall, Tiger was pleased with his students, his friends. They had spent many passes dedicating their bodies, minds and imprints to the pursuit of perfection. Together they had cooperated as a surgical mechanism to remove contentious threats from politically tense situations. While the financial gain was profitable, Tiger still never felt that he had compensated each clan member according to worth.

Even with different skills and heritages, each Monk was an integral part of the clan. They operated as a family and together they were lethal. While Monkey and Snake were the least familiar with the ways of the Commercial Empire, they still brought great strength to the clan and had no difficulty assimilating upon acceptance.

While the the other Monks continued their meditation, Tiger allowed his mind to wander back to the offer made by Frank Jenkins. Hoping to leverage his past as a light upon the path forward, Tiger reflected on his own understanding of the Monks. In passes long gone, Monks were trained to live in peace and seclusion, a notion that may have worked for the old order.

The present era belonged to the new and improved Monks. Tiger had grown to understand that no matter how finely tuned his physical prowess became, there were always new ambitions to subdue. Anyone with enough skill to join the Monks deserved to be compensated fairly, and it was up to Tiger to ensure that all ventures fulfilled that obligation. Typically, members uncomfortable with the clan's new direction were free to exit the clan. Still, Tiger had never been able to get over the one departure that shocked him to his core. For passes, a key member of the clan, one essential to the Monks' training and research even, surprisingly decided to break ties rather than leverage the Monks' strength. Tiger knew the departure left an inquisitive hole in his mind, but the present decisions offered him no time to chase shadows.

Since most of the Monks' missions involved removing semi-hostile threats, Tiger questioned Jenkins' motives regarding the strike on a salvage operation. Most salvage workers were vagrants or underpaid exiles. Not only did Tiger disapprove of the objective, he also had no interest in working with other clans. While thinking that the scrappers from Académé were of little concern, Tiger knew that Mogul Prime was formidable and not to be trusted. If it weren't for Jenkins' lucrative promises, Tiger had little reason to trust him either.

"Snake! Focus!" Tiger snapped as he noticed Snake's dark eyes peering through narrowly open eyelids.

Snake swiftly shut them upon rebuke, but not before launching a glare back at Tiger in the process. The distraction drew Tiger's attention back to his allies. While most were progressing well, Tiger suspected that Snake might need a few extra sessions to counter his overconfidence.

As the arcs of training waned to a close, Tiger called for dismissal. He was several clicks into his common pastime of pacing the training floor when the arrival of two other Monks broke his concentration. Panther and Dragon slowly walked into the room hoping to prevent disruption, but considering his impatience Tiger immediately looked at them.

"What is it?" Tiger asked.

"We have something to show you, Sir," Panther replied reluctantly.

Tiger turned and followed the monks down the hall and around a corner toward Dragon's makeshift workshop. The hazy, yellow overhead lights revealed a long table covered with random parts, scrap and electronic chips. Diagrams loosely pinned to boards adorned each wall of the workshop. Clearly, Dragon had been busy sketching formulas and icons for things Tiger cared little about.

Dragon procured a metal plated bracer, "Here today, I present to you the next greatest production of Scaletech, the finest sampling from the Basilisk Bakery, a..."

"It looks like we need to hire a maid, but we can't afford one unless it comes out of your cut," Tiger said, interrupting Dragon's bravado.

"Don't get your stripes in a knot," Dragon replied, handing Tiger the device in spite of the dismissal.

"What is it?" Tiger asked blankly without trying to sound condescending towards Dragon's proven, but erratic knowledge for gadgetry.

"It's a skybreaker," Panther replied, already sold on Dragon's handiwork.

"Translation," Tiger muttered while waiting for a plain answer.

"Observe," Dragon replied as he helped Panther slide the device over his left forearm. The device clamped shut, fitting snuggly. Panther gave Dragon a nod, indicating that he was ready.

Dragon stepped back before the sound of a whispering breeze whisked Panther from sight.

"Dragon, what did you do with him?" Tiger asked, maintaining his caution over curiosity.

"Follow me," Dragon said as he led Tiger back to the training floor.

Several Monks stood around, amazed at how Panther just zapped himself into the room. Tiger silenced the chatter as he asked Dragon for an explanation. All present were eager to hear details on Dragon's latest contraption.

"The skybreaker is capable of transmitting a person's entire physical form to another location," Dragon said, pleased that his device was receiving attention.

"Like a transporter?" Monkey asked.

"In a way, but the device is only capable of storing one location, and if multiple skybreakers are to be used they need a plotter to provide coordinates to the same location. In other words, it's a high tech mechanism for *Follow the Leader*. Panther is using the plotter which is currently set to transmit back here to the training center."

"Well done, Dragon, you have definitely continued to prove yourself as the *Master of Gadgetry*," Tiger replied.

"Thank you, Sir," Dragon replied.

"How many of these do you currently have assembled," Tiger asked.

"Currently just one plotter and one tracker," Dragon replied.

"Good, have enough trackers ready for everyone else finished by tomorrow night, Dragon," Tiger said.

"Tomorrow night?" Dragon stammered, puzzled at the urgency.

"Yes, tomorrow. That is when we strike the mission. I don't trust Frank Jenkins, nor do I trust the other clans that we must work with. We need an out should things go sideways," Tiger replied sternly.

"Tiger, so far I have only tested short range jumps. Long range calibration requires further testing," Dragon piped up in his defense.

"Then consider tomorrow night the test," Tiger replied curtly. His exit from the training floor signaled a swift end to any counterargument.

Panther and Dragon returned to the lab, fully understanding that if they were instructed to meet expectations, Tiger was fully confident in their capacity to meet the demands.

Mogul Prime Media Resource Center
Core City Fringe, Windstonne Enclave
Commercial Empire, Northam Continent
Thread: sysObserver.cmd

The flickering fluorescent lights fit the grim mood saturating the meeting room. Multiple Mogul Prime members watched Voltaire silently as he stared down the long thin table as he quietly drummed his finger tips together.

"Well, what is it?" Id blurted, annoyed with the silence.

Voltaire slowly looked over at Id, moving nothing other than his eyes before returning to his seemingly catatonic state. The matter at hand could most certainly jeopardize Mogul Prime's influence in the enclave. To cross a faction leader and sole authority of media rights in the Commercial Empire didn't strike him as a wise course of action, but something subtle within continued to foster the idea. The suggestion was fainter then a passing whisper, but it continued to make its presence known from the recesses of Voltaire's mind.

Voltaire looked at his associates who sat on either side of the table. Tycoon and Hauteur were on his right side with Authochthon and Id on the left. He was confident that he held their respect and that they would likely support any decision he made, yet they fully offered dissenting opinion whenever they deemed it necessary.

"All of you have been informed of our task for tomorrow evening," Voltaire said slowly as if rehearsing a speech.

The four nodded in agreement, waiting for Voltaire to continue.

"I have a hunch that our benefactor, Mr. Jenkins, has mind to screw us over. I know that you share my reluctance to operate with other clans, but the trivial nature of this raid is beyond reason. It may be time to cut our losses and pursue ventures without Imperan support.

The four stared at Voltaire inquisitively. A light, ownerless gasp touched the ears of all present.

"Great, let's just get to it. It all stinks regardless," Id replied in his default impulsive manner.

Disagreement erupted after Id's outburst. Tycoon and Hauteur immediately started bickering with Id while Autochthon quickly backed up Id's erratic response. Voltaire leaned back and watched the debate with faint interest.

Finally, Tycoon silenced the heated banter with a sharp whistle.

Everyone paused to look at him.

"Dean, what leverage do you have to support cutting ties with Jenkins? The truckload of berry we get from the Commercial Empire is what makes our hardtype printing possible, I suppose we could get by without that support, but still, even if we managed, we don't know that Jenkins will uphold our licensing arrangements."

Everyone listened intently and watched Voltaire as he played with a slim noptic card that he rotated between his fingers.

"You're right, Henry. We don't know if Jenkins would renew our contract," Voltaire said in agreement as he looked at Tycoon. "In fact, I suspect that Mr. Jenkins may not uphold our arrangement even if we execute a flawless job for him with the satellites."

Voltaire paused to look everyone in the eye.

Silence filled the room as everyone scoured their brains to find a solution. Hauteur stared at the thin, flat, rectangular card that Voltaire was still spinning between his fingers.

"What is that, Dean?" Hauteur asked quietly.

Voltaire paused again, thinking before he spoke.

"I guess there is no way to find out unless we take a look," Voltaire said, sliding the noptic promotional card into the corresponding slot on the table's pillbox.

Shortly thereafter, a vibrant display of color emanated from the table's noptic screen which hovered above a pedestal in the center of the table. A generated humanoid head void of distinguishable features slowly rotated on the screen. After several moments of confused stares by the onlookers, the eyes opened and the head began to speak.

"Are you tired of being haunted by your lack of education and frustrated with a faulty memory? Do you feel like everyone is smarter than you? Then it is time to let Extend work for you. Extend is a specially formulated supplement crafted by Oszwick Enterprises, capable of increasing synapse strength in brain pathways, increasing memory capacity, and even regeneration of dormant gray matter. See your local distributor today. Some likely, but negligible, side effects will occur," the projection rambled.

After an entertaining display of soft lights, examples and client testimonials the message terminated, leaving everyone staring at the lifeless screen.

"Where do I get me some of that?" Id muttered under his breath.

"Sig, don't you ever mind the fine print?" Tycoon asked sarcastically.

"Duh, we are the progenitors of fine print," Id replied defiantly, well aware that Mogul Prime was quite competent at embellishing the true nature of any product or service with obscure underlying agendas.

"Enough," Voltaire muttered. "Opinions."

"Where did you get it?" Hauteur asked with curiosity.

"It was given to me by an executive just after my last meeting with Jenkins. Not only did he claim to be interested in working with us, but he also claimed to be the head of this Oszwick Enterprises."

"The product is marketed very well. I'm curious to know, not only how they are producing it, but also how they hope to sell that in the Commercial Empire without getting heat from the powers that be," Tycoon added, always taking interest in the financial stakes.

"Yes, I'm sure the spec sheet would prove of interest too," Autochthon followed up.

"Would I be correct in surmising that we're all interested in learning more?" Voltaire asked.

Everyone nodded in agreement.

"One little hitch. Mr. Oszwick was forward enough to schedule a meeting for us in advance," Voltaire started.

"And that's when we're supposed to raid that mission," Id interjected.

Voltaire nodded. "Anyone that disapproves had better speak now."

The absence of rebuttal sealed the matter.

"Then it's settled. I shall uphold the appointment, but be warned, crossing Frank Jenkins may soon haunt us," Voltaire said with concern.

"We're all in this together," Hauteur replied.

"Good. Saphira, you and Henry will accompany me. Derwin, Sig, you're on overwatch here with Dennis, just in case Jenkins has any funny business in mind. I'll have Dexter and Tybalt tag along, but under the guise of personal security. We're going to need all the leverage that we can muster at this point," Voltaire said.

Vanguard Warehouse
Abandoned Sector, Windstonne Enclave
Commercial Empire, Northam Continent
Thread: actTgtPersp1.view

I doubled over to catch my breath after feeling like I had never exerted so much energy in my life. I spent the last two arcs jumping around, throwing kicks and practicing flips after disclosing my curiosity regarding a peculiar ayvek call Kapptivae.

Mac and Lennox spent time demonstrating the ayvek as they faced off and exchanged maneuvers while synchronized with a musical tune of choice. Mac explained how the acrobatic style was a mask for the actual combat techniques inside the Southam ayvek. I was quite impressed at the stamina that Mac and Lennox had acquired from studying the craft.

Once I finished with a brief cool down, I hit up the galley and rummaged around the chiller for a leaf darwa. Finding my target, I filled an empty chug and walked out to the table where Mac was sitting.

"What's bothering you?" I asked.

Mac shook his head, suggesting that he didn't want to talk about whatever he had on his mind. I dropped the conversation, but since I opted not to vacate the premises, he could tell that I wasn't going to leave him alone without an answer.

"I sense a shadow settling on the region," Mac said. "It's almost like a large net spreading that ensnares anything that it touches, but even with such rapid growth it still remains elusive, hidden from the public eye."

"Sounds gloomy. Do you often entertain conspiracies?" I asked, unsure what to make of Mac's premonition.

"If you're referring to big picture contrivances embellished in literature about political factions secretly planning the misfortune of others to their own benefit, then no, not exactly," Mac replied.

"Why not?" I asked since rumblings of conspiracies had always became the eventual topic of the veterans during late-night chats at the Dwelling Street Mission on more occasions than I cared to count.

"It's not so much that I think there aren't human efforts to guide big picture affairs surreptitiously. It's just that anytime an agenda of subterfuge takes root it will eventually get crushed by its own nature thanks to the very betrayal or greed required to implement it, or such a plot will become so large that it cannot escape the public view before it is revealed. In most cases, those ambitious enough to undertake such a plot are impatient and rarely act in such a way that doesn't draw a number of enemies," Mac replied.

"So, if you are ill-concerned with political shenanigans, what could possibly cause such concern?" I asked.

"I've had a chance to watch nations rise and fall, but the manner of their transition has been driven by motivations on the surface. A shadow that I cannot put my finger on gives me the sense that there is an even greater conflict being planned, with its ramp-up time spanning generations, like a snowflake rolling into a boulder until the resulting avalanche destroys everything in its path by the time it reaches the base of the mountain," Mac said.

"Generations?" I asked in disbelief, "How could any plan survive that long without the will of its originators."

"I can think of at least two possibilities. The first, by a very patient force capable of surviving the ages just waiting for the perfect time to reveal itself..." Mac started to say.

"Which is unlikely, since no one lives past a hundred and twenty passes," I interjected.

Mac continued regardless of my interruption, "... the other by some tightly governed order that adheres to an agenda passed down from one generation to the next, each placing its puzzle pieces into the larger framework. Such an approach is only reputed to secret societies bent on cosmic catastrophes or other bizarre cosmological phenomena, an asinine proposition in most cases."

"Why would that even be probable?" I asked.

"Because the puzzle pieces themselves are still being formed, the picture is still indistinguishable, as of yet," Mac replied.

"Regardless of picture, how would that even work? You said yourself that any organization is likely to implode or be discovered?" I asked, totally feeling like my brain lost track of the rather ambiguous clues.

"You're right about that, which is why I suspect that the former option is far more likely. A time resistant force keeping its identity hidden has no reason to rush. It can bide its time until all of the pieces are placed together," Mac said.

"No one can live that long. Wouldn't such a person be discovered? Who could possibly influence the minds of society for so long without the plan getting jacked?" I asked.

"Fox, you forget some of the oldest accounts in the Criterion. Those who contracted the Catalyst lived much longer in those days, and the Catalyst's engineer was never apprehended. He is still at large," Mac said.

"Even if I could comprehend an individual living this long, how is a destruction greater than that of the Global War even conceivable? That was a rather horrific seven passes by most standards," I said

"True, it does seem far-fetched, but the Catalyst's engineer doesn't view his work as complete until there is no trace of the Interlace remaining, and the Global War alone wasn't enough to meet that end. He is subtle and purported to be able to influence the minds of many without even having to snap his fingers," Mac replied.

"One simple question. How?" I asked.

"Only one?" Mac asked. "How uncharacteristic," Mac said with a smirk.

"It's quite simple, really. I equate the behavior of the masses to that of a stampeding herd. The herd doesn't know where it is going, but it is decidedly on its way there in a hurry. All it takes is a little push, a bump in the road or trivial detour to change its direction. One tiny nudge and it's on a new course. The Catalyst's engineer gives that push, that bump in the road. A stampede is not so easily controlled, but it can be guided. It can be guided toward safety or its own demise," Mac explained.

"The Tricameral Endeavor is a perfect example. Its power originally spawned from small groups pursuing freedom, yet its growth enabled the masses to take on a groupthink behavior. That very behavior turned the nation into the Global War's first casualty. The Tricameral Endeavor wasn't weakened by an external conflict, power monger, or secret order. It was guided by corrosive nudges completely saturating its legal system and educational ranks as well as its mediacasting strongholds. No one realized there was a problem until the entire system imploded by the onset of the Global War, and by then, it was too late. The herd had already been set on a direct course for the cliff and it was moving too fast to stop," Mac added.

"Given his influence in those realms, do you think Frank Jenkins is the problem?" I asked.

"While his manner is shrewd and can sway the course of the masses, I don't think that even Frank Jenkins is fully aware of the limits of his reach or the influence that he himself may be under. I suspect that the real windseed has yet to reveal itself," Mac replied somberly.

11 – Paradigm Shattered – 11

Vanguard Warehouse
Abandoned Sector, Windstonne Enclave
Commercial Empire, Northam Continent
Thread: actTgtPersp1.view

Although I felt a calmness settling on the warehouse mid-afternoon, I knew that the lull in activity couldn't last long. I felt rested enough from the morning's combat prep and sparring, but the recent outing made me aware of the enormous skill gap between myself and my new friends. I was compelled to improve upon my understanding that one wrong move could have left me divided on the subject had I been the first to encounter the Alex's blade instead of Mac.

"Those were some liquid moves that you used against your opponent. When do I get to start learning those?" I asked, referring to the agile and evasive tactics that Mac had demonstrated thus far.

Upon finishing a review of Maxwell's latest security sweep, Mac stepped away from the table and slowly moved toward the training floor. He calmly hesitated before speaking, as if pondering just which course to run me through next. I hoped that it involved something flashy, but with Mac I could never be certain.

"So, you think you're ready for advanced Hykima?" Mac asked. He struggled to hide his smirk from his commonly grim mentor expression.

"While I understand that ayvek basics are essential, I have to imagine there's more to learn so that I don't become a Fox-kabob on our next run," I replied. "How does Hykima differ from previous studies?"

I could tell that Mac was deliberating over his words even more than usual. In a sense, I felt like he was eager to demonstrate new content, but some reservation held him back. I wanted to pressure a response out of him while he took his time pacing along the floor, but I knew that such behavior could only yield extra laps or calisthenics.

"Hykima is not a specific style as other ayveks. Instead, it is the mastery of one's own mechanics in such a way that the body responds to any command it is given, sometimes even at a particle level. Skills derived from this ayvek, in many cases manifest in unique forms, each according to the identity of the wielder. Hykima is born of identity, a strong one. To that, what say you?" Mac asked.

As usual, Mac used his mentor skills to pry at blindspots which I preferred to ignore. I reflected on my motivation to learn which revolved around my quest for identity. While I considered that the quest was taking shape by finding both the cause and means to fight, I knew that much of my drive hinged on restoring my memory. Even without my past, I wanted to move forward.

"I think that I'm ready," I replied with marginal confidence.

"Let's say we put that to a test," Mac replied before turning about to the lockers on the far side of the training floor. After a moment, he returned with both hands tucked behind his back.

"What is this?" Mac asked as he extended his right hand with a spherical object in it.

"It looks like a treadball," I replied, noting the red threads spanning the white orb.

"And this?" Mac asked as tucked his right hand behind his back before revealing another object in his left hand.

I narrowed my focus on the object, trying to analyze the intent behind Mac's simple object lesson. "Looks like an apple to me."

"Sure. Go ahead, take a bite," Mac smiled as he tossed me the item in hand.

As he tossed the item, I found myself distracted by his motion to rest both hands on his hips showing that there were not two objects but the one which floated toward me. I reached to catch the item, but as my fingers made contact I was shocked to discover the hard metallic weight of something that was certainly not a fruit. I struggled to gain control of the object, barely preventing it from slipping through my grasp and potentially breaking my foot. Narrowly, gaining a grasp I realized that the object was painted to resemble an apple on one side and a treadball on the other. It was certainly not something that I was about to sink my teeth into. My perplexed look was all the invitation that Mac needed to continue.

"It's actually a cannonball that someone painted as a desk ornament. The owner's artistic selection is beyond me, but I found it to be an intriguing find on a salvage op," Mac said.

"Why the charade?" I asked as I turned the heavy sphere over in my hands.

"To make a simple point," Mac chuckled as he extended one of his hands. To my surprise, the cannonball leapt from my hands effortlessly returning back to the fingerless glove of Mac's left hand. The action reminded me of the fight with Académe when his weapon popped from the ground, but Mac made sure to keep my attention on the conversation at hand.

"It is important to emphasize that no matter which view we have of reality, truth is absolute. The appearance of something externally may not match our perception depending on the angle at which we view it. Our misconceptions may suggest a particular nature, but often we must dig deeper to best understand it. Just because you feel that you are ready does not mean that you are ready. As a byproduct of Imperan programming, I thought I would test to see just how broad your perception is," Mac said.

My eyes flitted back and forth for a moment as I tried to correlate Mac's object test with content on the emcast. As usual, I didn't understand. "What does that mean?"

"Have you heard of an enclave called Lakebridge?" Mac asked.

"Sure, that's where chicken nibs originated. The region is famous for them," I replied, thinking back to the numerous infocasts I had seen. Even the hapcasters mentioned current events in the enclave from time to time. The region was a rather iconic location on the coast of the Grandwaters which created the natural border between parts of the Commercial Empire and Uniod Branch.

"Have you ever seen it?" Mac asked.

I shook my head.

"It's a wasteland. It was leveled during the Global War," Mac replied curtly.

I recoiled, shocked at the revelation.

"How is that possible?" I asked, confused at the conflicting information.

"There is great benefit to keeping citizens complacent. As long as a misconception offers a great convenience, people will rarely question the possibility of a drastic underlying problem. Everyone loves chicken nibs, and as long as chicken nibs are readily available they love to hear about the town that created them. This doesn't change the fact that the Commercial Empire wants to distance people from the realization that the town's loss was a miscalculated operation during the war. It's easy to deceive those who have never been there, but those who fought in the war and those who lived nearby know the truth. Such truth is an inconvenience to the faction powers that be. Deep down, the masses admit to the possibility of deception, but as long as they have access to their choice delicacies, they never question the veracity of the mecas or the haps," Mac said.

"That's a heavy topic," I replied, trying to digest Mac's explanation.

"It is. Which is why I find it important to test your resolve before delving into subjects that will shatter your perception in even greater ways," Mac continued. "Imperan mecas are just one of countless examples in which the signal to noise ratio for substance is virtually non-existent, yet it permeates the thought processes of most enclave dwellers incapable of unplugging from the deluge of propaganda. If I fail to guide you with a proper understanding of influential skills, then I will only have created a loose cannon rather than a surgical shiv."

"Why would Imperan casters traffic in such mass deception?" I asked.

"The simplest guideline that I can offer is to *consider the source*. See if an agency benefits from any lofty claim to a good or service. Anytime there is a disconnect between that claim and the actions supporting it, see who has the most to gain. Then you might ascertain who wants to generate a captive audience," Mac said. "Whether it is by far-fetched chance or skillful engineering, I cannot say, but I have observed that most mecas pouring out of Imperan programming generate drift waves that sustain the Catalyst. I find such tactics to be far too subtle for the likes of Jenkins' aggressive nature, which is why I continue to acknowledge suggestions of even greater machinations lurking in the shadows."

As always, I found the depth of Mac's explanations to be challenging to absorb at first, but latest lesson rang familiar. I knew from experience that there was a strong undercurrent bolstering many of the meca's I had seen. Mac's brief certainly added clarity to the behavior that I observed among my associates at the mission who were wholly dependent on their recreational vices. Even with the abandon being outside the influence of the Core City's trappings it was easy to see that the Commercial Empire's reach was not diminished.

"With such a saturated system how can anyone break free?" I asked.

"Aside from connections with the Interlace, few rarely do," Mac stated without offering a counter strategy.

"What makes the Interlace different?" I asked trying to parse any possible hope from his limited response.

"Therein lies the crux of the matter," Mac said with a smile. The sentiment was clear that I was once again stumbling my way down the correct path of questions.

"Members of the Interlace, or proxies, are distinguished from everyone else, the windborne, by one simple feature, the Firewall Protocol. Proxies see it as real whereas windborne regard it as myth," Mac said.

If Mac continued his discourse, the words did not stick. The very mention of the Firewall Protocol caused my brain to fire a signal of familiarity. I couldn't associate it with any particular memory. I considered that I may have noticed it in the Criterion, but the sentiment didn't match. I desperately tried to identify the details surrounding the sensation, but the harder I tried, the sooner it faded. Like waking from a dream, any attempt to exert conscious concentration over the details only caused the mental image to fade from my grasp. For a moment, I was excited at the prospect of a dormant memory surfacing, but such enthusiasm was dashed as I once again surrendered to my possession of a faulty brain.

Sensing my distraction, Mac paused.

"Continue. For a brief moment, I thought that a memory might have poked through, but I guess not," I said reluctantly.

Taking the disruption in stride, Mac nodded. I didn't perceive the usual impatience like when I normally interrupted. He gave me a moment to make sure that I wanted to continue. Finally, I gave him the nod to proceed knowing that I had a better chance of trying again should other familiar words trigger something.

"As I was saying, essentially everyone who downloads the Firewall Protocol becomes a proxy, or one capable of extending the range of its accessibility," Mac said.

"You say download, but what is it?" I asked.

"It' a high-tech Catalyst suppressant. Just like everything else around you, whether directly or indirectly, it was designed by the Triad. It's the Triad's leading achievement really. Compelled to reclaim much of what was lost to the Catalyst, the Triad enacted a strategy to contain the Catalyst until a proper inoculation strategy could be deployed. I could spend a lot of time expounding on the history of it, but when you have its entire history available to you in the Criterion, a true field manual of the Firewall Protocol, I find our time better spent sticking to the high points. The Triad's Master Craftsman tasked the Executor with constructing a transmission tower with nigh planetary range so that it would be available for all to download," Mac added.

"I still haven't heard you identify which platform this download operates on," I said, mildly confused.

"Your imprint is the platform. It is the most sophisticated wetware module known to man. Think of it as an application for your brain's operating system," Mac smirked.

I should have known better than to challenge Mac at that point, but I couldn't resist my typical baseless counterargument, "So, an invisible signal that most doubt exists will install a neuroshield in my skull to suppress an inherited virus which is also doubted to exist?"

Mac didn't even flinch. I considered that he was getting used to my sarcasm as much as I was his complicated lectures. "Given your adequate time on the emcast, I'm sure you have witnessed materials concerning the advanced systems involved in particle division, or perhaps the method by which waves interact with the ear to translate them into understandable sound. Maybe you've even realized that your very behavior can be altered by the presence of new information through knowledge via sight or sound. All of these processes which are specialized and inherent to the human condition involve complexity and influence through sources invisible to the eye, and yet they are never questioned. Does the concept seems so implausible after all?"

I shook my head, admitting defeat to my counter.

"What does this Firewall Protocol do?" I asked.

"It's primarily a stop gap against harmful drift waves. Many ascribe its functionality to optimized cognition. It also includes a direct communication line to the Triad's Relay," Mac stated.

"Just what everyone needs, a voice inside their he..." the words froze in my mouth as memories of recent phenomena hijacked my concentration.

Mac cast me a sideways look but didn't request a reason for my odd behavior.

"Does said protocol require a subscription model?" I asked, unsure what question to ask, let alone what I needed answered.

"My understanding has always been that it only needs to be downloaded once and the process is irreversible," Mac replied, respecting the time I needed to formulate my question.

"Given my amnesia, how would I know if I ever downloaded it?" I asked.

"That you will have to work out on your own," Mac replied. "Shall we continue?"

"Sensing no deception or misdirection in Mac's response, I knew that I would have to dig deeper into the matter later for the sake of absorbing the knowledge that he still wanted to share. Unwilling to expound on my confusion, I remarked, "Sure, as long as you want to circle everything back around to *Practical Application for Fox.*"

Accepting that it was a valid time for hands-on application Mac conceded. "Normally, such concepts would be best served by a healthy trial and error scenario, but it's not unheard of to give a visual demonstration."

Eager for activity, I stood and stretched my legs while Mac rustled more props from the lockers. He soon returned with a knife and long wooden training sword similar in shape to the Serpent's lethal blade. I was undecided on which weapon I preferred to defend against if Mac were to wield either, one metal, sharp and lethal at close range, the other with great reach and sure to deliver a solid impact. Mac set the knife on the floor and handed me the wooden training sword.

"Strike me... if you can," Mac said flatly.

I hesitated to move into any aggressive posture, "If plasma can't put you down, I highly doubt that I can provide any intimidation with this."

"True, but this lesson is different. Today, I peel the scales off your eyes and show you the reality that has been hidden from you," Mac said.

Mac's voice carried an air of a challenge and a threat. I couldn't discern his intent, but it was enough to solidify my resolve. Sensing that I understood his point, Mac slowly settled into a combat stance, his legs loose and hands raised with fingers together, one in front of his torso and the other in front of his midsection. I cautiously took a step back, keeping my eyes trained on my target. I raised the wooden sword overhead and kept it there. I nervously studied my surroundings, looking for anything that might suggest what trick Mac was about to play. He was far away from any useful object other than the knife on the floor. I looked at the weapon, then back to him. He remained as still as a statue.

I knew that any strike I could muster would have to be swift. I intentionally took a couple of short breaths, not wishing to telegraph when I would move. I considered a downward strike. I double-checked to see if my opponent dared to reveal his response to my attack, but he revealed nothing. With all of my strength, I tensed my fingers around the sword hilt and struck downward with all force that my muscles possessed. Just as the wooden weapon was about to connect with his blue bandanna, his form blinked from view. Before I could comprehend what had happened, I realized his form blinked back into view on my left, two marks from his previous position. With a thud the blade connected with the floor on account of my missed strike.

Shocked, I stared jaw agape, uncertain how his form shifted without appearing to have even moved. I withdrew the sword and continued to stare, waiting for an explanation.

"Go ahead, you try," Mac said as he stepped back to his original position and motioned for me to return the sword.

"What's the trick?" I asked, returning the sword, hoping to receive an answer in exchange.

"There is no trick. It's simply a matter of instructing the body to respond to commands," Mac said.

My eyes widened. I knew that my head would be split in two without being able to perform such a maneuver based on a limited explanation. Nervously, I mimicked the stance I had watched Mac take, but I had no idea what I was supposed to do or how I should focus my mind. He watched with amusement as he simply rested his hand on the hilt of the sword while its tip pointed at the floor.

"There's no pressure. I'm not even going to attack," Mac said unable hide a wide grin.

Almost annoyed at my own misunderstanding, I lifted my hands and closed my eyes. I tensed the muscles in my arms and legs. I concentrated on moving my form from one place to another, but I knew that nothing was happening. I nearly released a grunt unaware of the clenched expression on my face.

"Stop. You look like you're battling a bout of constipation," Mac remarked, trying not to laugh.

I opened my eyes and relaxed, hoping that Mac would end the confusing game.

"I set you up, so that I could make a point. How you do things is inconsequential in contrast to why you do them. In other words, intentions matter," Mac said emphatically.

Mac set down the sword in exchange for the knife on the floor. With a casual motion, he maneuvered the blade toward his body and pointed the knife handle in my direction.

"If I were to gesture in such a fashion, what do you think my intent is?" Mac asked.

"Perhaps hand me the knife and help cut a loaf of bread," I quipped.

"And now?" He asked again, sharply spinning the knife about, pointing the blade at me while bringing his front hand upward into a defensive posture.

"Like you're about to gut a fish," I remarked.

"If I did, would it be the knife's fault?" Mac asked.

"No, why would I blame the knife?" I said, recoiling at the absurdity.

"Good. Just checking. I wanted ensure that we didn't need to spend time running you through an Imperan meca detox. The hapcasters love to get people worked up about the dangers of things like motorboxes and disruptors swearing that they're a threat to humanity and that all will be bliss with increased Imperan restrictions. Whether by ignorance or manipulation, they miss the point that such objects are neutral. It is the wielder who makes the difference between tool and weapon. You are responsible for the actions that direct the behavior of the object, to cause it to help or to harm. Your body is one of the very objects that can be manipulated in such a fashion. Unless you succeed in managing the Catalyst's influence over it, you will be limited in your capacity to achieve mastery over the resources entrusted to you. Be mindful that this principle is not just about sticks and bricks. Just like your body, everyday objects, even your very words have the capacity to heal or to hurt," Mac said.

"Do not lose sight of the fact that without the Catalyst there would be no need for weapons because there would be no malicious intent. Understand?" He asked.

I nodded, still trying to break down just how much content Mac crammed into his diatribe.

"Good. Maxwell. Unlock Mr. Fox's ikes," Mac said.

"Yessir," Maxwell replied with a half-hearted foreleg salute.

As the hamster complied, I noticed that a new icon appeared on my interface options. The icon only bore the letters IFX. I was about to wink to activate the icon, but decided to wait for Mac to explain.

"Observe," Mac said once again as he shifted the knife around to a more passive gesture. "Feel free to activate your Interferic mode."

Without effort, I updated the display and my eyes were flooded with a light blue color turning the entire world into a haze. All physical objects lost their defined form. The only way I could detect their boundaries was intensity of the blue that bordered them. The open air had a darker tinge while thin brighter boundaries outlined human form and the harder surfaces of the lockers, training bags and floor.

"I don't think I even need to ask my most obvious question," I said trying to make sense of the new visuals.

"Correct," Mac smiled. "You are seeing what I refer to as the Interferic Spectrum. It is a window into the other half of reality which our eyes cannot see by default. It is the medium through which many energy forms travel including drift waves."

I turned to face Mac whose form was as hazy as the rest, yet I could still distinguish his position. Somehow the haze seemed more dense. Larger congestions of haze flowed where his limbs, torso and face were. Additionally, his form was more luminous than the surrounding haze making him easier to spot. I looked at my own hands through the ikes and saw that they too appeared in similar fashion even though the haze representing my form was more murky than bright. Even Maxwell's tiny form in the distance had a similarly concentrated haze suggesting the clear distinction between living and otherwise inanimate objects.

"You are seeing our tracers," Mac said. "The part of our form that exists in the Vast. While the body exists in the Particulate, our imprints bridge the two, of course with our hearts being the most prominent instrument. I show you this so that you can understand how the body interacts with drift waves. Every action that a person takes can be measured against a correlated frequency defined by the Criterion which yields a resultant color."

Mac's hazy form nodded toward the knife in his hands. I could barely discern the knife's form. I only sensed the faint outline of it because Mac had not dropped it. It appeared as though the hazy portion of his arm pulsed brightly, a light blue or even white, as he motioned to extend the handle of the knife, but when he flipped the knife around again his arm took on a reddish tinge.

"When we allow drift waves to flow outward, back into the system, they will take on a bluish color, but when the Catalyst is allowed to turn energy inward and contain it, degradation occurs turning the waves red. Ultimately, a lifetime of stagnant energy takes its toll on the body, hence the aging process," Mac said.

"How is this useful?" I asked, unsure of what benefit I could gain from seeing red and blue fog.

"In a great number of ways," Mac replied. "By observing a person's drift profile, one can gain great insight into a person's demeanor. For example, I sensed that your question was asked with cognitive doubts versus disbelief on account of the reddish buildup around your head. The congestion might exist around your heart if the latter were the case. Where energy collects in the human body can reveal some inherent behavior or even a weakness that they themselves may not understand. Such visuals can be used as a guide to help shield against erroneous speech and malicious intent from more unscrupulous characters. The ability to see those weaknesses may even aid in the process of isolated targeting during a fight."

"Color me intrigued," I quipped.

"You can have whatever color you want, as long as it's blue," Mac retorted.

"Where do we go from here?" I asked.

"That depends," Mac said, pausing while he set down the knife. "Do you trust me?"

In typical fashion, I hesitated, but I had to consider that I was finally accepting that Mac knew much more about the world around me than I could have discovered from any meca. Aside from a few bumps and bruises acquired in training, he had yet to demonstrate any harmful intent. Resigning to an answer, I sputtered, "I think s-," but my words were cut short.

I felt Mac place a hand on my left shoulder. I opened my mouth to object to the unusual amount of pressure as something clamped down, but instead a surge tore through my body, completely consuming my attention. Sensory overload struck my consciousness as if I had slammed into a brick wall at high speed. The verge of blackness nearly consumed me as I wrestled to interpret the onslaught of new stimuli hitting my system.

Dwelling Street Mission
Abandon Sector, Windstonne Enclave
Commercial Empire, Northam Continent
Thread: sysObserver.cmd

Chuck shuffled his way out of the leisure room and down the hallway. Most of the workers had turned in, leaving only the late-nighters to watch their nightly mecas in peace. The last remnant of muffled conversations dissipated as those present took off for their rooms on the upper floors. Chuck was about to take the nearby flight of stairs when he cast a glance down the silent hall leading to the exit. It felt strange not having Fox around to harrass about something. He strolled halfway down the hall and glanced up at the thin nameplate over a doorway with Fox's name still illuminated above. He half suspected Fox to amble in, much like he had done before leaving the mission.

For the sake of nostalgia, Chuck entered Fox's old room and absent-mindedly scanned the darkness, half expecting a prank. Finding nothing unusual, least of all Fox, Chuck motioned to close the door, but a dark blur whisked past the window across the room. Startled, Chuck stepped into the room and closed the door blocking the hallway lights allowing his eyes to adjust. At first, he thought the motion was a trick of his imagination, but when soft steps down the side of the building combined with a dark shadow dropping past the window, Chuck knew that it was no longer his imagination. He was tempted to approach the window, but considering that there was no logical reason for anyone to be scaling the mission from the outside, he sidestepped into the corner of the room watching for additional movement.

After several clicks of silence, Chuck stepped toward the door, but the sounds of breaking, muffled glass from the next room over locked Chuck in place. It didn't take long for the sounds of struggle and heavy steps to break out. Similar sounds occurred from the floor above too. Before Chuck could reach the door, it was kicked open with violent force, barely missing his face. He swiftly ducked down behind the nearby chair. A figure clad in all black poked into the room. Seeing no light and no body in the bed, the figure disappeared and moved to the next room. Chuck could hear the sounds of threats directed at his mission associates as they were herded toward the leisure room. His heart raced as he struggled to keep his breathing subdued. He wanted to help, but he had no idea who was attacking or why. He also had no plan.

The immediate sounds diminished as the invaders finished their search of the first floor. Chuck stepped toward the open door of Fox's room. He peeked into the hall and saw that every door on the floor had been kicked in. The fact that no one was stopping to haul out goods suggested that they weren't there to steal which worried Chuck. The invaders were looking for someone.

Chuck looked toward the mission exit and saw that it was clear. He could make a break for it if the invaders didn't have someone keeping watch outside. Even if he made it, there was no one to ask for help in the abandon. The Stack was the closest lodge and it was a good couple of parcels away. Chuck knew that some of the veterans were still fit enough to put up a fight, but given their age, the surprise attack and the absence of any resistance thus far, things weren't looking good.

With options in the tank, Chuck looked toward Tarees' office. He ran as softly as he could for the open door. He hoped that Div might have a weapon hidden somewhere. If not, he hoped that maybe he could ping someone for help. The Merrick's had to have allies of somekind, somewhere.

The limited light from the hallway wasn't conducive to a thorough investigation as Chuck fumbled in the dark. Other than a pair of severs, Chuck found nothing beyond the sharp cutting instrument that he could use as a weapon. He quickly activated the slate on Tarees' desk and scanned a list of contacts. All of the names were attached to locations of great distance from Windstonne, but Chuck's eyes soon locked onto one entry. It had no location or name. It simply read *Emergency.*

Hurriedly, Chuck opened a comm on the sonair. Without waiting for confirmation, Chuck began his frantic message about the attack. He was but a few words in when a shadow blurred past the doorway. Rubbing his eyes, Chuck looked for an attacker, but found none. He returned his attention to the message, but as he did he felt a cold grip around his throat along with sharp metal that strongly encouraged him not to move.

"That was a mistake," a hushed voice said sternly.

The ice cold demeaner sent a chill down Chuck's spine. Before he could even react, he felt himself being dragged into the shadows.

Vanguard Warehouse
Abandoned Sector, Windstonne Enclave
Commercial Empire, Northam Continent
Thread: actTgtPersp1.view

The volume of a thousand waterfalls roared through my ears while an equal number of invisible ants marched across my skin. What had once been a viewport through my ikes had instantly become my entire reality. I reached up to lower my ikes and accepted that I was no longer seeing the blue formless world, I was in it.

I couldn't feel the ikes in my hand by normal means of pressure, but somehow I recognized that they were there. It was as if they had no weight. Once I thought about it, I felt like my entire body had no weight. Every sense in my body felt like it had been amped up exponentially. It was overwhelming, but as long as I remained still it seemed to settle until I could process my surroundings.

"Where are we?" I asked, but my own voice nearly startled me as my normal volume felt like it could fill an empty arena and echo indefinitely. I only tried that once in order to understand that I only needed to expend a fraction of effort to do simple things.

"We are still in the warehouse, on the training floor," Mac said simply.

Just like I had seen through the ikes, Mac's form was still hazy and cloudy in a humanoid shape, and he remained in place, hand on my shoulder. Clearly, something about his contact enabled me to experience this aspect without the aid of technology.

"But, what is this?" I asked, wanting more detail.

"This, Mr. Fox, is the Vast. It is the other half of reality which you and nearly the rest of the population are oblivious to. It is interlocked with the physical world that you know, the Particulate, and yet it is wholly different."

I could tell that Mac also expelled little effort to speak since his voice could have continued unimpeded. I had little interest in the hazy, shifting view of the warehouse floor and wall, so I continued to turn my hands over watching how my ethereal form floated and reacted to what I thought were instructions by my muscles.

"For generations, the soloists, like Quarterstone and others, have been searching for the imaginary threads, the glue to bind all of physical reality together. The only problem is that they were looking inside the box, instead of outside of it. Here it is, the missing puzzle piece resting outside of the Particulate that ties the remaining mysteries together. If only the greatest minds weren't limited to the inward flowing drift waves from the Catalyst," Mac said.   "Zero point energy, spacial substance, particle directives, genesis of thought, drift waves all have roots here in the Vast. Even the Firewall Protocol uses the Vast as a transmission medium. With your eyes opened to a new perspective, does such advanced technology seem so impossible?"

"At this point, given my limited understanding, I think it would be best to take your word for it lest I be trapped here," I remarked.

"A wise sentiment," Mac chuckled as he released his grip on my shoulder.

The shift back to normalcy was disorienting. Mixed signals wrenched on my nervous system. I couldn't tell if I had been dropped into a vat of oil or been baked in an oven for a day. My legs almost felt weak as gravity resumed its pull on my senses while my exterior fell like it was getting peeled away. Thankfully, the sensation was brief.

"That takes some getting used to," I said, feeling a wave of nausea setting in.

"It's just like taking a walk. A little practice, and you're good to go," Mac said.

"And that's how you shifted your position?" I asked.

"Your imprint connects your heart and mind to both halves of the paraverse. You can walk into a building through one door and exit that same door or another one altogether, but you have to be mindful that the rules of the Vast are radically different than the physics we know from the Particulate," Mac replied.

"It feels like that can explain so many imaginative skills that I've heard about, but if the means are so simple why is the method so foreign," I asked.

"Many try, few succeed, but ultimately the improbable is seldom perceived to be possible. It can take a leap of faith to see through Imperan programming and relate to long obscured concepts such as the Firewall Protocol or the Triad," Mac said.

"Why would the Commercial Empire dodge this Triad you've mentioned," I asked, finally parking my spine in a chair until my senses returned to normal.

"Rarely do Global Alliance values align with directives from the Firewall Protocol, so it should come as no surprise that faction leaders disregard any matters pertaining to the Triad which designed the protocol," Mac continued. "Back when the Master Craftsman tasked the Executor with assembling the Bridgetower to transmit the download signal, opposing forces marched against the Executor and eventually killed him for his interference with competing narratives of the day. Too bad they didn't take into account the Triad's experimental

Renderant Assembly Integration System to undo their efforts. Since then, the Triad has allowed the Relay to handle all direct communications through the Firewall Protocol allowing for a direct connection with download recipients, or proxies."

"Definitely sounds like some serious stuff," I remarked. "With all of this knowledge, it seems like you could help a lot of people. I have to imagine there a lot of people plugged into the Imperan system."

"True, but the Firewall Protocol can never be installed into an imprint without an open port. As much as I would like to help more, it always has to do with timing. Energy can be wasted on trying to convince a mind so darkened by the Catalyst, so one cannot lose sight of the big picture when there are plenty of open ports to be found. For now, I'll settle for one at a time," Mac said.

"Given the technology at your disposal, couldn't that help more with discovery?" I asked.

"Technology is just an aid. It will never help anyone see that which they choose to ignore. Right, Corzo?" Mac asked as he turned over his shoulder to look up at Alex who had been silently observing our discussion for quite some time from the airbridge connected to utility elevator nearby.

"Truth," Vanguard's latest addition said from his perch overhead.

I nearly fell out of my seat after realizing that he had been there the whole time, silent and still as a shadow. It made more sense when I realized that night had already settled on Windstonne since expired daylight no longer passed through the windows. Although Mac's demonstration of the Vast may have affected my senses, I didn't realize just how much time had passed with the latest content capturing my attention.

Before Mac could resume, the shrill tone of a sonair ping directed our attention to the op table. The alert sounded so abruptly that Maxwell nearly jumped, the sound jolting him from his slumber.

"That's the emergency comm," Mac said, his concern evident as he strode toward the table to activate the comm.

Instantly, a visual appeared on the nearby noptic screen. I couldn't see anyone onscreen at first, given the poor image quality, but I immediately recognized the voice.

"This his Chuck Kaibosh of the Dwelling Street Mission. I don't know who this message will reach..." Chuck said before pausing to look away from the receiver, startled by something out of sight.

Mac wished to communicate, but he noticed that Chuck had been in such a hurry that he only been able to send a recording. I hurried over to the table and saw the sense of panic in my friend's face. The message had been recorded almost in shadow.

"... to try something. We are under attack. I don't who they are, but they move like shadows," Chuck continued. "Please... re-"

Chuck's response was immediately cut short as a figure stepped behind him and curled a gloved hand around his throat. A hushed threat made its way into the message before prodding Chuck not to say another word. Mac watched the end of the message intently. It ended abruptly as the attacker ended the comm, but that didn't stop Mac from playing the end back. He swiftly tapped the noptic screen and zoomed in on the glove that caught Chuck by the neck. It was not a full glove, but instead had segmented links all connected to metal claws extending past the finger tips of its owner.

"We have to move!" Mac yelled, making sure that Lennox heard the directive.

Alex was already headed for his gear by the time Mac powered off the screen. Mac immediately turned about and left to fetch his vest. Mac's expression was rigid. I had yet to see him driven with such focus.

"What is it? More Académé shenanigans?" I asked.

"Worse," Mac said as he paused, contemplating if he dare tell me what he knew, "Monks."

I didn't recognize the name. Even if I didn't understand the cause for his concern, I knew one thing, training was over.

12 – Common Defense – 12

Vanguard Warehouse
Abandoned Sector, Windstonne Enclave
Commercial Empire, Northam Continent
Thread: actTgtPersp1.view

With an urgent stride, Mac reached the lockers under the stairs and snapped a door open revealing a retractable weapons rack. We were soon joined by Lennox and Alex as Mac plucked out choice gear for an operation.

"What is it?" Lennox asked.

"The mission is under attack and we have to move quickly," Mac said.

I observed that Lennox required no extra details when Mac merely suggested the plan. He too reached for gear of his own in another locker. I guessed that such behavior came from their conditioning of a lifestyle since past. There was no time to deliberate when lives were on the line.

"Why would anyone attack a salvage operation?" Alex asked, puzzled.

"Most carp in the abandon don't need reasons to attack and steal which normally does not imply urgency, but since we're here standing in front of the weapon racks, I'm guessing that Mac suspects something more sinister, as if they are looking for something," Lennox replied.

"Or someone," Mac replied quietly without even looking in my direction. I didn't know if he referred to himself or not, but given my recent run-ins with Academé, I couldn't help but wonder if I was the target.

The thought of being a target forced a sudden realization of possible danger that had been cast upon my friends. If I were the cause for harm to come upon them, I knew that there was no excuse for me to hide out while they were in jeopardy.

"What can I do?" I asked in hopes of making myself useful.

"Gear Up!" Lennox snapped as he thrust a Phantom 4.0 in my direction which I quickly tucked behind my back.

Alex was quick to grab his blade and trench coat. After donning his coat and securing the sheathed blade on his back, he motioned toward a couple of shiny pistol sized disruptors hanging on the rack.

"May I?" Alex asked, almost humorously, as if he needed permission.

DAVE TODD

"Only if you know how to use them," Lennox retorted as he snatched a midsize three barrel disruptor. I heard several successive clicks as he racked multiple spindle-bound cartridges into the sliding spring injector at the base of the barrels.

"Who's on the hit list, Mac?" Lennox asked.

"I don't know with any certainty yet, but we need to keep the big guns on reserve for now if there's a hostage situation. I doubt that the Commercial Empire would pull out the Pirans for something so trivial, but we still need to be stocked up on firepower... and wits," Mac replied somberly.

"In other words, don't check your brains at the door," Alex said in his raspy voice at Lennox.

Lennox was quickly growing accustomed to Alex's military grade banter. He simply replied with a smirk. After securing the Cress in hand, Lennox reached for two silver sticks with black grips in the center. The metal sticks were slightly shorter than the fima sticks I had been given previously.

"What are those?" I asked.

"Oh, just simple tools of the trade," Lennox replied as he flicked his wrists causing the sticks to eject small sickle like blades connected by hinges at the top.

"Liquid," I muttered.

"Put these on," Mac said as he handed me a pair of fingerless gloves and a pair of athletic shoes.

"I've already got comfortable shoes, and I would lose dexterity with the gloves," I replied.

"Trust me, you'll get used to them," Lennox interjected as he finished adjusting his glossy leather jacket over the harness holding his kamas. He snapped both arms out to adjust the sleeves and then pointed one arm toward the rack. A Splice 15m jumped from the shelf, directly into Lennox's hand. Dumbfounded, I realized that the tech performed similarly to Mac's own trickery.

"They contain a subocular filament capable of generating strong, highly focused electromagnetic fields," Mac replied in response to the quizzical look on my face. "You can control them through your ikes just like your cloak. You can snag metal objects as well as cling to or repel from any metal surface. You'll be glad to have them."

The following demonstration made more sense as I watched two metal sai jump from the weapon rack into his hands. Mac swiftly secured the weapons at his side after spinning them about like a frontiersman holstering the revolvers of old.

"At last, the wizard offers another glimpse into his bag of tricks," I quipped with a chuckle.

After all weapons were secured and I had a fresh change of footwear, we split up. Alex and Lennox made for the Chromehound, and I followed Mac to the Fire Ant once he confirmed that Streetz was ready for a fight. As I approached the Fire Ant, I took a mental image of the blue and red flames feeling like they were dancing, ready for action.

"Ayezon, Hamster! You have the comm," Mac said as he shouted up at the second floor.

"Naturally," Maxwell replied as I spotted an acknowledgement icon blip on my ikes while I settled into the vehicle.

I was almost startled by the clarity of the sound passing through the ikes into my skull. I had no earpiece, but through some advanced induction, I heard Maxwell clearly, that is until the roar of the moxes and the grinding of the overhead bay doors drowned out any sarcastic follow-up. Once the Fire Ant and Chromehound had the clearance of the bay doors, Mac released the clutch and slammed the accelerator to the floor. The Fire Ant peeled out of the warehouse with the Chromehound close behind.

Outer Core Dartway
Abandoned Sector, Windstonne Enclave
Commercial Empire, Northam Continent
Thread: actTgtPersp1.view

I knew that the drive to the mission would be quick, but it felt nearly instantaneous as I once again felt myself challenged to learn the nuances of my ikes in a hurry and how they interacted with my new accessories. While I quickly found the power controls for my grips and the shoes which I learned were referred to as kickplates, or kips for short, I had to rely upon the Enforcer's explanation for the controls pertaining to disruptors. Not only were the ikes capable of showing a live reticle, but they could also relay just how many shots were available in the power cell within the disruptor.

When the Fire Ant came to a stop, I realized that we were at least a parcel away from the mission. "Still a bit of a jog, isn't it?" I asked.

"Fox, cloak, or no cloak. You don't disarm a trap by walking into it," the Enforcer remarked.

Conceding the point, I simply rolled my eyes as we exited the mox and regrouped with the others. The vehicles were parked out of sight, and Vanguard was clear to make a move on foot.

"Fox, you're with Torque and the Serpent. Streetz is with me. I'm going to stay light and send word if I see anything. I want you three to take the back. We'll cover the front. Be prepared for anything," the Enforcer said. With a quick wave of his hand, the Enforcer pointed toward the mission and took off running, his cloak engaging shortly thereafter.

I felt familiar with the streets surrounding the mission, but I deferred to Torque's navigational senses as the Serpent and I followed behind him. I observed the familiar territory now through a green tint as I used my ikes to track my allies running ahead of me. I considered activating my cloak but then delayed the action since Torque opted to proceed without one, and the Serpent already moved like a shadow. Previously, I overheard Torque's dislike for using cloaks outside of extreme situations, and the Serpent apparently had little need for one given his passes of training in the Maleezhun ayvek of Yuurei.

Even with assistance from my ikes, I occasionally felt that the Serpent's form melted into the shadows if I didn't maintain a steady eye on his position. I overhead that the Serpent recently had eyecon interfaces added to his original shades. If the Serpent was already proficient at seeing in the dark without assistance, I pondered just how much more lethal he could be with extra tech available.

We soon reached the mission from the intersection behind the loading bay. Normally, the mission had security lights activated and the occasional light emitting from residents' rooms, but now it had a dark forlorn appearance. I hoped that we weren't too late.

As we reached the edge of the intersection, I spotted three figures guarding the access door to the mission's loading bay. Even with limited lighting I was able to recognize the two clan members who attacked me at the old library. Torque ducked behind a building corner opposite the lazy and unsuspecting Académe guards. He then nodded for the Serpent to take the corner of the mission adjacent to the clan members. I was impressed at their efficiency in communicating with hand signals in silence. I assumed that it was yet another honed skill from their time in military engagements.

My blood simmered at the nerve of Académe's willingness to take action against my friends. I was certainly ready to deliver some compensation, but Torque held up his hand for me to stand behind him. I followed his line of sight as we watched the Serpent move like a shadow in, out and around various obstacles. After a three tick count, Torque raised the Cress rifle to his shoulder, ready to fire.

"What was that?" Academé's red haired member asked as he looked out around a column of stacked crates.

"Shut it, Burnout. Jocq has us paranoid as it is without you getting all edgy," Sophomore replied as he stood next to the jittery guard.

"Someone's out there," Burnout whispered coldly.

"I don't see a thing," Sophomore replied as he folded his arms across his chest.

A light but dull blue plasma blast sizzled through the air, striking the crate notches from Burnout's ear. Wood splinters showered the clan members who then scrambled and flailed their arms to protect themselves from the airborne shrapnel.

"You call that a shot? I thought you learned how to shoot in the war. What'd you fight with sticks and clubs?" I quipped, doubting Torque's aim.

"It's called a diversion, Squawkjaw," Torque snapped back at me in an irritated fashion as he shoved the Cress in my direction without even looking back. Before I could even grasp the weapon he was already sprinting toward the trio.

Jammer tracked the origin of the plasma blast and drew two Splice 15m pistols from underneath his baggy jersey and pointed them across the street. Before he could squeeze the triggers, an unseen force kicked his arms upward, causing the disruptors to misfire. He couldn't see his opponent, but he felt the presence as pressure on his wrists caused him to drop the weapons before he received a punishing blow to the chest. Jammer staggered backward, falling over a small stack of crates.

With new sounds drawing Burnout's attention, he ran toward Jammer's position, but all he found was a dazed Jammer trying to pick himself off the ground. No opponent was in sight. Burnout glared into the darkness, but light from the overhead lamp quickly blended into the night, limiting his sight range. Burnout grabbed the two sticks which hung loosely on his belt. With one handle in each hand, he pressed the buttons and each stick telescoped into a mark and half of crackling metal.

A blur passed through Burnout's peripheral vision. He looked to his left and saw nothing. He raised his stunrods in front of him, unsure what to expect. He slowly stepped forward as he squinted to identify a silhouette in the darkness. Something about the indiscernible form felt familiar to Burnout which further unsettled him. Angered at the underhanded means of attack, Burnout cautiously stepped toward the menacing form.

Torque raced to the position of the Serpent's first target, but by the time he got there, Jammer had already jumped from the ground and ducked behind another stack of crates for cover. Jammer released his chain whip from his pocket and advanced toward the still figure who appeared to be engaged in a stare down with Burnout.

Jammer lunged toward the dark silhouette in the long coat, hoping that the distraction would give Burnout a chance to strike. The free end of his chain lashed out with deadly accuracy, but the bulbous weight of the chain whip was deflected by a short sickle-like blade held by another attacker. The chain wrapped around the kama handle which altered the trajectory of the weight. Jammer was forced to duck the incoming projectile of his own weapon.

Torque took up a defensive stance on the Serpent's right side. The Serpent in nonchalant form stepped forward, challenging Burnout to advance if he dared. Meanwhile, fury washed over Jammer's face as he wrangled his chain whip to regain its lost momentum.

Torque smirked as he calmly twirled one kama behind his left side while keeping the other kama perfectly still in his front hand. He acknowledged Jammer's effectiveness with the chain and didn't expect another easy opportunity to deflect the weapon. The pair of adversaries cautiously shifted stances while making half steps hoping to trick the other into an ill-conceived attack. Torque flexed his front arm and feigned a step with his lead foot. Jammer flinched just enough to think that Torque was advancing, so he reacted with a wide swing of the chain.

Accepting that Jammer took the bait, Torque awaited the attack. Jammer lashed the weight at Torque's skull, but Torque leaned backward, allowing gravity to pull his back to the ground. Surprised at the defensive maneuver, Jammer assumed he had new opportunity to swing the chain downward for a vertical strike, but that too was factored into Torque's ploy.

Torque's momentum was already propelling his body over his shoulders as he pushed himself back onto his feet. As expected, the weight crashed into the weathered pavement again, breaking its momentum. Seizing the delay, Torque stepped forward pressing one foot onto the chain. He drove his opposite knee upward as he jumped for maximum vertical distance. At the apex of his jump he launched his lower foot and connected with a kick to Jammer's chin.

Knowing that I would never hear the end of it if I sat out the fight, I ran toward the third Académe guard who was still picking slivers out of his arm. As I closed in, I halted once I spotted a familiar face which made me reconsider my decision to disregard the cloak. Accepting that it was too late for regrets, I made sure to keep a healthy distance between myself and my opponent while keeping my hands in a defensive posture.

"Well, look who it is, our little turf poacher," Sophomore grumbled.

I held my ground and remained silent. I figured that it was best to follow the Enforcer's instruction and keep my emotions in check. I assumed that I was already at a disadvantage and didn't need to create an all-new handicap for myself. I contemplated switching my ikes over to IFX mode, but then tabled the thought since the distraction could go horribly wrong if Sophomore attacked before I could reset the view.

"You got us in a lot of trouble, Carp," Sophomore snapped, his words clearly laced with bitterness. "Tonight, you're going to get the serious spinejacking that you're overdue."

I remained silent.

Increasingly irritated by my lack of response, Sophomore snapped his fingers to his waist, unclasped the large buckled belt resting outside of his pant loops. As I spotted him reaching for the weapon, I too reached for my fima sticks, but Sophomore was faster, much faster.

The broad buckle whipped out and caught the right corner of my ikes. I reeled backward. Had I not been wearing the shades, I definitely would have acquired a vision impairment. In spite of the blood that I felt rushing to my face, I refused to back down. I barely lifted one fima stick into the air when the belt snapped toward me again. The weight of the buckle forced the belt to wrap around the stick in my hand. With a swift tug, Sophomore jerked on the belt which then yanked the stick from my hand.

After losing half of my defense so quickly, my brain sent rapid fire impulses instructing me to move quickly. I needed a fast solution for disarming Sophomore. I back pedaled in order to increase the range between me and the striking belt. I sidestepped to put a pile of crates between me and my opponent, blocking his line of sight.

In an even smarter move, Sophomore pushed his shoulder into the crates, hoping to knock them onto me. Once again on the defensive, I hopped to the side, narrowly escaping the largest of the boxes, but my reflexes weren't fully up to the task as I felt one pinch my ankle before tumbling to the floor. I dragged my foot from underneath the crate and leveraged the adrenaline in my system to disregard the pain.

Sophomore bounded onto the scattered crates which littered the pavement. From his elevated position he began to whirl his belt overhead and rain down another barrage of strikes. A purely offensive reflex engaged as I leaped forward and tackled Sophomore from his perch, toppling us both from the pile of crates.

I knew that the impact was going to sting, but I was okay with Sophomore bearing the brunt of the impact. Upon being halted by a jolting collision with the ground, Sophomore was forced to drop his weapon in order to free his hands for a push to my shoulders. I stumbled backward and prepared to strike with my remaining fima stick. I swung the stick laterally hoping to catch my opponent in the temple, but I soon realized my poor assessment.

Sophomore had already pushed himself off the ground and stepped in, cutting the impact of my strike short. He locked his arm over mine, trapping my forearm. He wrenched hard, sending pain up through my arm. My only recourse was to drop the fima stick which then clattered on the pavement. Maximizing his momentum, Sophomore kept my arm pinned under his and used his free hand to strike at my face. Anticipating the strike, I managed to block before the hook punch could shatter my jaw.

Accepting the futility of my current position, I struggled to change things up. I picked up my knee and leaned back so I could push away with the bottom of my foot. I strained the muscles in my leg by trying to escape with such an awkward maneuver, but it was just enough to force Sophomore backward and free his grip on my arm. Undeterred, He advanced again with a flurry of punches. I moved quickly enough to evade the first two, but I caught a third in the abdomen. I doubled over as I felt precious air in my lungs evacuate with extreme force. My vision blurred, but I at least had the soundness of mind to bring my hands to my chest out of reflex. Thankfully, the reflexes did their job since Sophomore's following move was a well-placed knee to my face which had been left at a vulnerable height.

The Serpent took a step toward the dim light. He easily recognized his foe from his first introduction to Académe. Burnout's stomach tightened upon recognizing the Serpent.

"Well, if it isn't Mr. Hit-and-Run. There's no running this time, school is in session, and I'm going to teach you a lesson," Burnout snapped despite his wavering voice which revealed his intimidation.

The Serpent forced himself to withhold the smirk that he wanted to let loose. He knew all too well that emotions telegraphed the nature of the fight, a fact he was recently reminded of after his first encounter with the Enforcer. While passion and dedication were useful for pushing one beyond limitations in order attain dominance in battle, fear, rage and overconfidence were all too common on the battlefield. The

Serpent wasn't one to gamble with such contrivances. He would gladly sacrifice emotion in order to increase the odds of battlefield survival. Clearly, Académe members had yet to learn such lessons.

Burnout grew impatient with his adversary who refused to show any interest. The figure oddly dressed in green and black continued to hold a defensive posture with his arms at his sides suggesting no threat, but recent experience wasn't easily lost on Burnout as he recalled just how fast the Serpent could swing his sword. Internal tension compelled Burnout to respond, but he didn't know the best approach. He only considered stunning his foe before a weapon was drawn. Accelerating like a hyper extended rubber cord, Burnout dashed forward, yelling the whole way.

The Serpent closely watched the stun rods in Burnout's hands as the distance closed. The electricity crackled in defiance as Burnout snapped one arm out to strike the Serpent in the chest, but he hadn't quite learned from the past. Before the stunrod could connect, the Serpent had already snapped his hand to the handle of his sword and arced it around to the front. With a blur of motion, the blade traced a figure eight in the air catching the first stunrod in his lead hand, then caught the one in the back as Burnout attempted a combination strike.

Burnout swiftly recoiled, almost stunned upon witnessing the blinding speed of his adversary. The Serpent stood idly with his blade still pointed toward the ground. He merely toyed with Burnout. He could have easily sliced the stunrods in half, or even his forearms for that matter, but it was too soon to deliver excessive force.

The sound of falling crates startled Burnout, prompting him to turn and notice Sophomore engaged in battle as well, but the distraction proved unwise. As Burnout turned forward to look for his opponent, he was nowhere to be seen. Grumbling and tired of the evasion game, Burnout turned to help his allies instead, but the maneuver was short lived as two flat handed strikes snaked in and over his arms, easily freeing the stunrod's from Burnout's grasp. Burnout sensed that the Serpent was already behind him, but before he could respond he felt a sharp pain as an open handed strike riveted a serious blow to his temple. Burnout crumbled to the floor, unconscious.

"Alright, you want to play? Let's play!" Jammer said with a sneer as he set aside his chain whip, knowing that it was no longer effective at close range.

"Game on!" Torque responded with a smirk of defiance as he folded the blades back into his kama handles and tucked them behind his back.

DAVE TODD

Jammer leapt forward and arced a crescent kick high over his head. Torque was impressed with Jammers' agility to execute the full rotation and a half kick, but he was otherwise disappointed in the delivery since Torque was offered plenty of time to sidestep and follow-up with a spinning hook kick of his own. Jammer narrowly evaded the attack, but Torque leveraged his momentum to spin into a low sweep kick, targeting Jammers' calves. Already in motion, Jammer twisted his body into the air and glided over the sweep kick.

Jammer angled a chop downward toward Torque's collar bone, but Torque leaned aside letting the strike miss. Jammer inverted his stance and brought up his other hand to strike with a ridge hand to the opposite side of Torque's face. Torque knew that he couldn't evade in time, so he executed a crisp spinning block and followed through with a backfist to the side of Jammer's face. Dazed by the attack, Jammer shook his head to regain his balance, "You must think you're top of the charts."

"I must be, because I keep bringing the hits," Torque taunted as he shifted his weight multiple times with a confident swagger.

Angered, Jammer advanced, prompting a flurry of exchanged strikes and blocks. Just when he thought he had an opening, Jammer received another backfist which hindered his vision. He firmed up his stance only in time to see the outside of Torque's shoe as the incoming jump spin kick put him on the ground in a slump.

Against the downward pressure that he placed on my back, I shoved Sophomore's knee in order to free myself, but to no avail. I slammed my head upward and caught his chin with the back of my skull. The momentary stun caused Sophomore to stumble, but he remained standing. I seized the chance to land a couple of solid blows, one to his abdomen and another to the side of his face, but he simply took the punishment and sneered.

It was my turn to be stunned at my foe's capacity to take hits without flinching. It spoke volumes about my inexperience in the field. In my brief hesitation, Sophomore snapped a Phantom 4.0 from behind his back and leveled it at my face. Aggravation with my ineptitude mixed with the onset of fear. I scrambled to recall all of my training about calm under pressure, but at the first sight of real danger it was jettisoned completely. Contrary to the basic instruction of not taking my eyes off my opponent, I closed my eyes, thinking I had such a short run. I didn't intend to make such an amateur mistake, but either frustration or despair willed the involuntary response.

A loud crack ripped across my eardrums, but I felt nothing. I assumed such might be the case in passing, but when my eyes opened in response to the sound, I was overwhelmed with surprise that I was still standing whereas my opponent was not. Sophomore was sprawled out on the ground while Torque stood over him, a splintered board in hand. He looked at me with an expression of concern and confusion.

"Are you okay?" Torque asked, wondering if I was present mentally.

I nodded slowly. After realizing that the immediate danger was past, I leaned over to catch my breath. I was surprised that my adrenaline had done enough to distract me from labored breathing which was once again evident.

"Good, because that wasn't bad, Jellyfish. A couple more verts and you're on your way to a spine," Torque said reassuringly.

The Serpent casually walked up behind me, nodded to Torque and surveyed the area just to verify that all threats were neutralized.

"I take it that you two fared better than I did," I said in between a couple of wheezing breaths.

"Sure, we left you the hard stuff," the Serpent smirked. "Just think, you didn't even make us carry the weight."

Torque chuckled in approval of the Serpent's subtle and indirect support, "We'd better get inside. I bet there's plenty more weight to distribute."

"Liquid," I muttered sarcastically, slowly standing upright. "I'll let you two handle the rest now that I've run up such an early lead on the scoreboard."

"Oh, no you don't," Torque replied. "If you're not bleeding, you haven't even been properly initiated yet."

After recovering his Cress, Torque strolled toward the back door of the mission. The Serpent and I followed behind, prepared for the next round.

Thread: sysObserver.cmd

The Enforcer paused as he cleared the alley and looked upon the Dwelling Street Mission. Typically, even in the early arcs of the night, lights dotted the face of the building. The absence of familiar illumination verified that something was wrong.

Most mission workers were limited in their awareness of the presence that periodically watched over them. Ordinarily, the mission was a soft light in the darkness of the abandoned sector, and the Enforcer persisted in protecting its purpose. Such a light was a boon to those around it, but its strength wasn't guaranteed should it be contested.

With an attack underway, and one executed so precisely without his foresight, the Enforcer felt a chill.

Several passes back, the Enforcer had charged Div and Tarees Merrick, his long time friends, with a valuable investment. One that could radically boost the influence of the Interlace and the Firewall Protocol. The Enforcer hadn't fully conveyed the depth of responsibility associated with such care for their own protection, but now the Enforcer second guessed his own decision. The attack was about to test the Enforcer's ability to make good on his commitment to protect those in the vicinity.

The Enforcer double-checked his ikes to make sure that his cloak was still holding strong. With a short sprint, he made his way to the entrance of the mission. He tested the front door and found it unlocked. Whoever had infiltrated the mission had done so before the nightly lockdown. The Enforcer opened the door just enough to squeeze inside. He spotted a faint light trailing down the main hallway which served as the backbone of the repurposed building. The Enforcer pressed himself against the wall, cautiously making his way toward the leisure room. The door to every room along the hallway remained open. The Enforcer peeked inside a couple of rooms only to find belongings scattered across the floor. Even equipment in Tarees' office had been disrupted, likely from Chuck's capture. The Enforcer hated to admit that Torque's assumption was right about the invaders looking for something. He only hoped that the absence of bodies meant they hadn't quite found it yet.

As the Enforcer neared the leisure room, he could hear threats being barked at residents of the mission. Before getting a clear visual, the Enforcer surmised that most residents had been gathered in the leisure room for questioning. He halted just along the edge of the doorway to assess the situation before rushing in.

In a similar fashion as the living quarters, furniture was overturned and objects strewn about. The leisure room's large padded chairs had been toppled. The invaders were methodical, but they weren't finished. The Enforcer noticed two figures dressed in loose black attire. Both wore black knit caps pulled tightly around their heads. If the attire hadn't been indication enough, his suspicions were certainly confirmed when he spotted the large white bird stitched to the back of the pullover worn by the invader to his right, implying her mastery in the crane style of the Dongwu ayvek. The Enforcer tensed, wishing that he had been wrong about the Monks' involvement.

The Enforcer spotted two other invaders who didn't fit the Monk profile, but they were not included in the huddle of residents being held captive in the center of the room. Even from across the leisure room, the Enforcer was able to identify the wiry antics of Nox as well as his girlfriend Swipe who was seldom more than a stone's throne away. The two Académe scavengers were busy rifling through storage containers, dumping their contents on the floor.

A distasteful look from Crane conveyed her annoyance at working with the scavengers, their methods of recovery were hardly worthy of a highly trained mercenary squad. The obvious tension puzzled the Enforcer as to what force could have brought two radically misaligned clans together.

A sharp threat hurled at the restless mission residents drew the Enforcer's attention to the Monk who frustratingly paced around the captives that were forced to sit on the floor. The fear on their faces was evident, but it paled in comparison to the frustration emanating from the Monk who had not found desirable answers to his questions. The residents were corralled to the Enforcer's left obscuring his view, but at last he spotted the broad tiger on the Monk's back, identifying the clan's leader who continued to interrogate the captive before him.

Tiger, the excessively ambitious leader of the Monks had fallen a long way since the Enforcer's time with the clan. Under the old order, the Monks used to strive for justice, fitness and defense of those without allies, but that was never enough for Tiger. As the clan started down a new path, the Enforcer had been forced to choose an exit rather than continue on with many who had been great allies at the time. Rather than break away, those remaining bought into Tiger's speeches of grandeur and continued to follow him. For the Enforcer, such a path was never an option given his allegiance to the Interlace which superseded any cause pertaining to material accumulation, something that his former allies never understood. Even though traces of the old order permeated current goals through pursuits of perfection, what the Monks currently represented was an abomination.

Growing impatient and frustrated at the lack of cooperation, Tiger leaned forward and grabbed a female salvage worker by the neck and forced her to her feet. The woman trembled as Tiger kept a vice like grip on the woman's throat. He held his other hand loosely by his side, allowing all to see the five metallic claws that snapped to his fingertips from the thin glove lining his palm.

The Enforcer tensed, ready to charge Tiger, but he was interrupted by the sound of quick footsteps pounding in his ear. Realizing that the footsteps were behind him, the Enforcer turned about and pressed himself against the wall. Even in the momentary glimpse, the Enforcer spotted the embroidered dragon across the back of the new arrival. Passing on a prime opportunity to sweep kick the running Monk, the Enforcer refrained from making his presence known.

Tiger turned to face Dragon so that he could inquire about the urgent interruption. There was no mistaking Tiger's identity once the Enforcer was able to see the markings on Tiger's face. One smudged strip of orange paint ranged from the base of his brow to the top of his right cheek, and a similar black one covered his left eye.

"What is it?" Tiger snapped, the terrified woman still firmly in his grasp.

"I found this," Dragon replied, handing Tiger a leatherbound book with shiny page trim.

Chuck who had been sitting without expression or movement thus far, shook his head in mild disgust upon realizing that Fox had left the book at the mission. Tiger sensed the motion out of the corner of his eye and slowly panned his gaze across the group before him.

"Just by having this in your possession suggests a connection with the Interlace," Tiger said choosing his words carefully as he reflected on the alternate mission parameters that Jenkins had provided. Initially, Tiger doubted any meaningful connection between a salvage operation and the Interlace, but clearly Jenkins' suspicions were more sound than expected.

"Imperan authorities place heavy restrictions on salvage charters in regard to contraband. Operations that harbor Interlace members have a tendency to disappear," Tiger said, taking his time to stare every mission worker in the eye, hoping that he could identify those most susceptible to pressure.

The Enforcer knew that members of the Interlace placed a high priority on protecting their own. Deep commitments combined with the mental toughness of the many veterans wouldn't be easily undone.

"If I don't get answers, I'll have to report this whole operation in violation," Tiger said.

"It doesn't belong to anyone here," Chuck blurted. "The worker who found it left a while ago."

"Is that so," Tiger snapped, glaring maniacally as he tossed his captive to the floor. He stepped toward Chuck, ready to make him take her place. "It appears that we know something after all."

Chuck squirmed uneasily, unsure how to add anything substantive to what little he knew. Tiger contemplated choking the answers out of Chuck, but the tough guy act didn't always work. He recognized that noncombatants could still have a breaking point. Even though the Monks had the skill advantage they didn't have the numbers, should someone discover a hidden spine. Relieved that the woman was out of danger for the moment, the Enforcer knew that it was time to act since Tiger's antics were only becoming more erratic.

"Somone once told me that anyone who hesitates has lost already," the Enforcer said, slowly stepping into the leisure room.

Tiger and Dragon spun about trying to locate the source of the formless voice. Even Crane looked stunned, sensing that the sound emanated near her position. Crashing boxes followed the silence as Nox and Swipe halted their search, knowing what was about to transpire after hearing stories from their fellow clan members.

The Enforcer slowly lifted his hands to remove the hood from his cloak and let it fall against his back. Tiger and Crane both blinked in surprise at the head that appeared from nowhere.

"Conner? Is that you?" Dragon muttered in disbelief as he watched the rest of the familiar form materialize.

The Enforcer wasn't surprised that Dragon was the least shocked by the cloaking technology. He could see that the resourceful Monk had continued his own pursuit of technological advancement, noting the unknown strap connected to Dragon's face spanning from his ear to the corner of his lip.

"Powerful words if they weren't coming from a clan reject who embodies hesitation," Tiger snarled.

The Enforcer did not respond.

Nox twitched, hoping for an imminent opportunity to deliver payback on behalf of his clanmates. If it hadn't been for Jocq's instruction, Nox would have already been on the move. While Jocq was patrolling the block, Académe was to report to the Monks. Frank Jenkins wouldn't accept further failure from Académe. Since Tiger hadn't yet made a move, Nox anxiously waited.

"Has the prodigal finally decided to return to the fold?" Tiger asked arrogantly.

"Hardly," the Enforcer muttered. "I'm just here to separate the sheep from the wolves."

"Funny. I don't remember Wolf being your style," Tiger snorted. "If I didn't know better, I'd say you're part of the Interlace too."

The Enforcer allowed a faint smirk crease his lips, but he remained silent. With his ikes obscuring his eyes from his foes, the Enforcer patiently weighed his options.

"That would figure. You pacifists have no concept of the value gained by mastering the physical world," Tiger said.

"The only mastery I see is your petty ambition exerting its control over you," the Enforcer replied flatly. "You've let it consume you."

"Spare me the sack of fishbait, Conner," Tiger glared angrily. "You were always afraid of achieving greatness."

The Enforcer knew that his words hit the mark once Tiger let his emotions slip, proving the point.

Nox shifted nervously upon realizing the depth of hostilities between the Enforcer and the Monks. The tension did more to put him on edge. Normally, he had no qualms about jumping into a fire pit, but this time he had no desire to get burned in someone else's barbecue.

"Rounding up noncombatants has sure put you in the running for greatness," the Enforcer said, seizing any opening to mock the clan leader.

"It's a small price to pay on the path to greater opportunity, to fulfill our purpose," Tiger replied, resuming his calm but threatening tone after realizing the fatal error he made by letting his emotions slip.

"I'm surprised that you can even speak the word purpose without choking on it. You were the one to betray the old order. What happened to perfecting the body, pursuing balance, and most of all, preserving justice?" the Enforcer replied, struggling to shove down a strong sense of bitterness attached to rather uncertain memories.

"Tell me, Conner, are you here to lecture me about honor? Because I'm sure a fair number of buried skeletons might damage your own credibility," Tiger said.

"I honor my commitments to the end. Do you? Or is that something only awarded on a contract to the highest bidder? You can still deal fairly, so I advise you not to do this," the Enforcer replied, wishing that Tiger would be reasonable.

"All of us have choices to make, and it is clear that you have already made yours, to which I say *No Deal!*" Tiger replied as he jerked a thumb downward.

Tiger snapped his right hand to his side and flicked his claws to full extension to match the other hand. Seizing the offensive opportunity that he'd been waiting for, Nox burst into a full sprint toward the Enforcer. Well aware of the amateur's impatience, Dragon made no move to restrain the overzealous Académe vectors. He nodded at Crane who calmly took the cue to be patient and wait for the opportune time to strike.

The Enforcer had no difficulty in calculating the odds against him, but he still had a card to play that he was sure neither the Monks nor Académe could anticipate. He felt time mellow as he counted the steps Nox took to close the distance. As the wiry Académe member deftly hurdled a leisure room couch, he led the charge with Swipe close behind.

As Nox closed within three paces, the Enforcer whirled around twisting his arms out of the flowing black cloak. As he snapped his right hand into the air with fingers pointed at Nox, a human figure materialized into the perfect form of an aerial side kick. Streetz's momentum carried him through the air, his kick blasting Nox in the chest.

Swipe quickly halted her sprint upon seeing the quick turn of events. She snapped her arms to her sides revealing square throwing blades with curved edges which had dropped from her leather arm guards into her hands. With a blinding snap, Swipe released the blades and arced them directly toward Streetz. Amused as ever, Streetz shifted his impact fields from view so that the metal blades could pass through his body, but he didn't immediately realize the error in his calculations since the Enforcer stood directly behind him.

With Streetz screening his view, the Enforcer had little time to react to the incoming projectiles. He managed to lean to the left as the first square blade whooshed past his ear and embedded itself into the wall behind him. After evading the first, the Enforcer shot his hand upward as if to slap the projectile, but without enough speed to catch it in time, he reversed the field direction in his glove and repelled the blade, altering its direction. In response, the fast projectile arced upward and lodged into the ceiling.

Easily annoyed with Académe's petty antics, Dragon knew that the Monks were ultimately responsible for the operation's success. Dragon advanced toward the Enforcer and clenched his teeth on the fire bit that connected to his left cheek.

Unsure of what new gadgetry Dragon had concocted, the Enforcer barely had time to glimpse the metal support beams running the length of the leisure room ceiling. He launched his feet into the air and engaged his kips. His body shot upward defying gravity just as a long burst of flame soared past the Enforcer's last position.

Timing the grip and release of his kips with his steps, the Enforcer's legs worked against gravity as he ran across the ceiling. As he advanced, he cocked his right arm and slammed his fist into Dragon's face catching him just beneath his left eye.

Quick to join the fray, Crane bounded into the air, pressing her feet into the closest wall at least three marks from the floor. With great strength, she kicked out from the wall and dove through the air easily clearing the air above Streetz and the Académe fighters.

Between the Enforcer's ceiling run and Crane's wall leap, several of the mission workers gasped as they witnessed meca-like stunts demonstrated before their eyes. Not a tick could have passed in

DAVE TODD

between the Enforcer's fist connecting with Dragon's face and Crane's flying tackle taking him out of the air. Surprised at Crane's swiftness, the Enforcer only had a moment to react. He twisted his body as gravity pulled him and his opponent to the floor.

Barely managing to twist his shoulder and reverse Crane's tackle, The Enforcer caused her spine and shoulders to impact first leaving her stunned from the initial collision. The Enforcer immediately slammed his open hands to the floor to prevent his head and neck from suffering the same fate. Before his hands even touched down, he was already launching his legs over his body to snap into a front flip.

Fully aware that Tiger wasn't simply going to spectate, the Enforcer pushed his weight forward, propelling his body in the opposite direction of the Monk trio. Knowing that it was unwise to show his back to the enemy, he quickly remedied the error by snapping a foot up to the wall adjacent to him and pushed off the wall with an aerial cartwheel, placing him in the center of the room.

Quick to pursue, Tiger lunged forward. The Enforcer knew that fighting Tiger at close quarters would be risky, so he snatched the Phantom from behind his back and leveled it at the charging Monk who had his claws extended. Even as the firearm was lined up to fire, its barrel dropped to the floor in shards as Tiger slashed the disruptor with his claws.

Unwilling to sacrifice his forearms to the dense metal of Tiger's claws, the Enforcer swayed contrary to the direction of Tiger's arcing slashes. With Crane already recovering and circling around behind, the Enforcer knew that he would have to escape his predicament quickly.

Crane stomped each heel in succession, activating a mechanism to release the curved blades which extended from the outside edges of her shoes. The Enforcer leaned to his side narrowly evading the roundhouse kick that Crane snapped at his face. Anticipating an assault of kicks, the Enforcer prepared for the second kick, ducked under it, and scooped Crane's leg pushing her off-balance in Tiger's direction.

His adversaries moved to circle again as the Enforcer attempted to keep an eye on Tiger and Crane simultaneously. No matter how useful his ikes, they still had limits to their range. Complicating the matter of evasion, Dragon advanced defiantly and chomped down again on his fire bit. The Enforcer exited the circle of Monks and leapt toward the closest wall as orange flamed traced his last position. Searing heat scorched the wall as the Enforcer took as many steps as possible before gravity brought him back to the floor. He could feel the proximity of the heat which threatened to burn his body.

The temperature immediately dropped as the flame ceased. The Enforcer acknowledged that Dragon had a limitation to the flame's duration, giving him an opening. With all three Monks in front of him, the Enforcer took to the offensive. He launched his body into the air and split his legs laterally catching Tiger with the ball of his left foot and Dragon with the heel of his right. He then followed the split kick with a snapping roundhouse with his right foot to Crane's face before effortlessly landing on the floor.

Aware of the Monks' persistence, the Enforcer was certain that his barrage of kicks would do little more than irritate his adversaries. He was going to need a lot more power to win the fight. Out of the corner of his eye, he spotted Streetz keeping Nox and Swipe at bay. He also glimpsed the mission workers who were still scrambling to escape the leisure room amidst the fray, hoping to avoid any stray strikes from their captors.

Deep down, the Enforcer knew that his physical skills were no match for three Monks at once. He would have to tap into some of his most guarded techniques which he had kept hidden for many passes. Even the slightest mistake in execution could cost him the fight, but it was a risk he had to take if he were to protect the workers of the mission.

Thread: actTgtPersp1.view

The scent of dusty air leaked through the doorway as Torque slowly cracked the door to avoid making noise. He nodded toward the loading bay inside as he kept one hand on the door handle and the other on a kama. The Serpent advanced into the loading bay and crouched behind one of the flat bed transport trucks. With his mysteriously advanced sense of vision, the Serpent scanned the loading bay before shaking his head to acknowledge that he didn't see anything peculiar. Nothing but old furnishings, boxes of clothes and stacks of food crates littered the walls opposite the loading ramp, a common sight in any salvage op.

Next, I moved into the loading bay once the Serpent gave the all-clear signal. Torque brought up the rear, quietly closing the door and performing an extra weapons check and an adjustment of his ikes. A weak bluish-orange light was visible from the front of the loading bay. As we advanced, we could overhear a menacing voice making threats. Sliding my back against the truck, I notched forward to get a better view while staying out of sight.

I tensed upon seeing a figure with a loose pullover holding Div's throat in his left hand. Despite Div standing a couple of notches over the attacker, he clearly acknowledged the attacker's strength. I moved to intervene, but Torque quickly grabbed my shoulder to hold me back. He tilted his head toward the free hand of the figure dressed in black. I activated the night vision on my ikes and through the faint green light, I could distinguish several black metal talons protruding from the back of his hand. The talons softly clacked as the Monk drummed them against his leg.

"Where is he?" the Monk growled.

"I already told you. He hasn't been around here in a while," Div replied defiantly.

I was impressed at Div's resistance to the interrogation, but I figured that he had learned how to deal with harsher elements of the abandon long ago after his many passes of running the mission. Clans and renegades had threatened the mission before, but Div always held his ground. Normally, the mission veterans helped keep the place safe too, but there were none to be found. The current situation didn't appear to be a fight that Div could win on his own.

The Monk released his grip on Div's neck but followed up by chambering his arm and driving a fierce blow to Div's abdomen, doubling the salvage operator over. If the Monks were as I powerful as I heard, I knew that the strike could have killed Div had the Monk been truly finished with him.

Div clutched his abdomen and fell to one knee. The fact he was still breathing was reassuring, but the Monk's behavior was anything but, as he held the talons on his hand clicking them while they waved at Div's eye level.

Angered at the brutality, the Serpent was the first to move, clearing the two loading trucks. If surprised at the arrival of unannounced guests, the Monk's lack of expression sure didn't suggest it. He turned to the Serpent and glared. Even from my spot in the shadows I could see the single stripe of black paint smudged over the Monk's right eye. His eyes narrowed, remaining locked on the Serpent.

Hoping to boost the intimidation factor, Torque stepped up behind the Serpent on his right. Knowing that I would never escape a lecture if I didn't follow suit, I pushed myself away from the truck and took up position on the Serpent's left.

"This party is invitation only," the Monk quipped.

"I've got my invitation right here," the Serpent replied as he drew his blade from the sheath on his back.

"Corzo!" A voice hissed from the shadows.

"Hiya, Snake. The world just keeps getting smaller doesn't it?" The Serpent replied, his posture, voice and stance conveying no emotion while his eyes remained fixed on the taller Monk.

Surprised that the Serpent knew one of our enemies, my opportunity to ponder the connection diminished as two more silhouettes exited the shadows and stood behind the first Monk. Yet another shadow dropped from the airbridge railing overhead and dropped gracefully without a sound. The awareness that we were not alone but actually outnumbered created a massive knot in my stomach. I could sense that even Torque was on edge.

"I see that you have matters to resolve," the taller Monk said to the one who knew the Serpent. Pleased with the unchecked restrictions, Snake slowly advanced toward our position.

Knowing that things were about to get turbulent, Torque brought his Cress about and flung it toward Div who no longer held the Monks' interest. "Div, get out of here and help the others!"

In response to Torque's actions, the agile Monk in the rear leapt through the air and pounced on Torque's chest. Torque slammed his fist into the Monk's jaw and pushed him back. In strange fashion, the Monk immediately skittered around several crates almost crawling or hopping on all fours. Torque immediately recognized the rare Monkey style of the Dongwu ayvek.

The Serpent remained still, his glare like ice. Once I got a clear line of sight, I noticed that Snake's skin tone and eyes matched those with Maleezhun heritage, but there was something more unique than even his physical characteristics. He appeared to have a strange secondary eyelid set. I might have thought it strange if I hadn't been distracted by the bitterness exuding from Snake's expression.

Snake shot his arms to the side and then forward instantly launching several metal spikes through the air. The Serpent looped his blade into several circles deflecting all but one of the spikes which deflected off the corner of his ikes. The Serpent then positioned the handle of his blade near his temple while keeping the blade's tip trained on Snake, ready for the next barrage. Snake had already lowered his stance placing both hands in front of him bending them at the wrist to represent snake heads.

The Serpent was annoyed at missing the spike, but amused at Snake's eagerness to fight. He then holstered his blade and removed the sheath from his back placing it on the floor. With a subtle smirk, the Serpent reached up and removed his shades, tossing them to the floor in calm defiance.

For the first time since he joined Vanguard, I fully observed the Serpent's eyes in their true form. At first they appeared normal, but an internal set of eyelids, likely implants, narrowed and held position causing the Serpent's eyes to appear closed with exception of the vertical slits resembling those of a snake, much like those of his aptly named opponent.

Although confused by the gesture to disarm as the Serpent squared off against Snake, I was quickly reminded that I didn't have time to comprehend ayvek formalities. The tall Monk rushed toward me with talons extended as the remaining Monk followed close behind him. With minimal reaction time, I jumped backward and flipped onto the hood of the truck behind me. I had barely landed as the metal talons slashed through the grill of the large transport mox. From the tick that my muscles engaged, only one impulse resonated in my mind, *Run Away*.

Thread: sysObserver.cmd

Despite his capacity to outmaneuver his opponents, Streetz's agility was easily matched by persistence. Nox and Swipe continued their attack even without comprehension of a method to defeat their synthetic foe. Streetz was surprised at their tenacity given the number of strikes that he had already delivered. Streetz knew the he had to act decisively since the Enforcer was hard pressed to defeat three Monks on his own.

Infuriated with his failed hand-to-hand techniques, Nox drew his hammers from his side and recklessly hacked at any space that Streetz appeared in. Streetz's escape margins were narrowing. He realized that the excessive field shifting was starting to drain his reserves. He would have to rely on evasive tactics to minimize blows from Nox's blunt instruments. Any well placed strike could disrupt his processing cycles and generate jumbled feedback in his algorithms. With Vanguard being the only group to ever repair his code unconditionally, he knew that it was imperative to fight to the end for his friends and those at the mission, especially since organic material was less easily replaced than code.

Streetz dodged to the side as Nox's hammer grazed the side of his skull and sunk deep into the wall. As Nox attempted to free the hammer, Streetz blasted Nox with a knee to the stomach doubling him over for the duration. Streetz then jumped from Nox's back toward Swipe tucking into a flip and extending his leg into an axe kick.

Swipe countered the dropping heel with agility of her own using a pair of backwards handsprings to put some distance between herself and Streetz. Continuing the advance, Streetz pushed forward and jumped into the air with a high arcing hook kick.

Swipe crouched low, ducking the kick before springing up to drive several punches at Streetz as he landed. Energy reserves ran dangerously low as Streetz was forced to block every strike. Internal signals fired warning sounds. Streetz took half a step backward before twisting his body into a barrel like spin. His body easily rose five marks from the floor with his foot making clean contact with Swipe's temple. The force knocked her unconscious.

Streetz checked over his shoulder to verify that Nox was still unconscious as well. With current threats pacified, he bounded over a toppled chair and kicked Crane who was scrambling to restrain one of the retreating mission workers. Crane stumbled backward but used the momentum to leap toward the wall behind her. She pressed off the wall and flipped in order to drive both feet in Streetz' direction. Without a preloaded maneuver against such an awkward attack, Streetz took the hit to the chest. His body flew backward, the direct force overloading his processor. A loud crackling could be heard throughout the leisure room as his impact fields shorted out. With a muffled pop, Streetz disappeared from view.

The Enforcer overheard the commotion and knew that the sounds of Streetz's deactivation weren't welcome haps. Dragon and Tiger circled once again and Crane soon rejoined the trio. The Enforcer knew that it was the time to dust off old skills both proven and unproven. Given lives hanging in the balance, the Enforcer knew that he couldn't overlook any option no matter the risk. It was critical that he prevail.

Tiger lunged forward, claws extended. His first two slashes caught nothing but air as they passed right through the Enforcer's body. With his momentum pushing him forward and no target to stop him, he passed through the space previously occupied by the Enforcer. Dragon had already been on the move behind Tiger.

With his body taking on an amorphous form, the Enforcer continued to redirect his energy to shift his form. Anticipating Dragon's attack, the Enforcer delivered a strike to Dragon's chest with the force of a speeding truck. The force of the impact knocked Dragon backward several paces causing him to smack the back of his head into the wall. Dizziness washed over Dragon as he dropped to his knees.

Shocked but undeterred by the surprising display of power, Crane amped up enough power with her spin kick to decapitate someone, but the Enforcer anticipated the jump kick. As the world about him took on a hazy liquid view, even time seemed to halt its advance. His breathing slowed and motion ground to halt. Even his line of sight appeared to freeze just before Crane's kick made contact.

Crane's attack was unstoppable as it connected with the foolishly still Enforcer standing in an open fighting stance. Instead of taking the Enforcer's head off as her foot connected with his skull, she felt a shattering collision through her entire leg. Feeling like every bone in her had been broken, Crane fell to the floor writhing in pain.

Angered more than amazed at the Enforcer's newly revealed bag of tricks, Tiger dashed again at his foe's back. Even as the lunge should have connected, the Enforcer's body glided laterally without a step taken as if it had been pulled sideways by a human-sized magnet. Switching from amorphous to solid form yet again, the Enforcer stepped around keeping his back to Tiger's and shoved his shoulder into the Monk's back, sending him into a sprawling heap on the floor.

Dragon groaned as he stood and observed the large crack in the wall that did nothing to cushion his impact. He ran forward, spurred on by the punishment that his fellow Monks were receiving. Bewildered at Dragon's ability to maximize a strong vertical leap yet change direction mid-air, the Enforcer redirected his attention to the incoming downward aerial punch targeting his head. With speed that even he didn't anticipate, the Enforcer flipped backward and locked his legs, slamming one foot from his flash kick into Dragon's jaw, sending the Monk to the floor unconscious.

With two Monks incapacitated, the Enforcer only had to face off against the clan's leader, Tiger. Until recently, Tiger had been oblivious to the mission workers' escape, but he still managed to catch one and keep her imprisoned in the leisure room. Tiger had one arm wrapped in front of her throat while he kept his opposite hand, claws extended, dangerously close to her face.

"You're a coward!" The Enforcer shouted.

"Am I?" Tiger sneered. "I recall you suggesting the importance of survival even when the odds are insurmountable."

"Never at the expense of others," the Enforcer snapped.

"You never said that," Tiger replied.

"It was always implied. Clearly you missed the most obvious point," the Enforcer said while trying to maintain an active stance without spooking Tiger into harming the mission worker. "The future is only achieved by learning from the past, not living in it."

While waiting for Tiger to respond, the Enforcer noticed that Tiger's sleeve had uncovered part of his forearm revealing a sturdy guard with digital apparatus embedded within. The Enforcer paused and stared at it from behind his ikes, hoping to identify its purpose, but a quick scan yielded nothing useful. Even without knowing its purpose, the Enforcer knew that it had to be important if Tiger was wearing it. The Monks weren't strangers to technology given Dragon's handiwork, but Tiger was usually the last to adopt such devices.

Detecting hesitation on the Enforcer's part, Tiger tried to detect the object of his attention. Tiger couldn't allow his opponent or hostage an opportunity to do something rash. He soon realized that the object of interest was Dragon's newly created skybreaker. In a momentary panic, Tiger tried to shift his sleeve over the device, but the movement provided all the distraction that the Enforcer needed.

The Enforcer snapped his left hand to cross draw the sai on his right side, flinging the weapon toward Tiger's face. Pure reaction caused Tiger to deflect with his own limb rather than use the hostage as a shield. In spite of a successful evasion, Tiger's timing was off. The blade missed his face, but an outer prong still clipped the skybreaker activating an energy field which ripped through the space where Tiger's body had just been. The thrown sai stuck in the wall behind Tiger's last position and warbled as it shook on impact.

The frightened woman feared to turn around, but realizing that she was no longer captive, she remained frozen in place due to the terror of how close. Tiger's claws and the passing sai had been to her face. The Enforcer squinted in curiosity, unable to explain what had just happened. He quickly shot a look at Dragon who was struggling to regain motor skills and press a button on a forearm guard of his own. The Enforcer dashed to grab Dragon's arm, but he was too late. With a flash, the grounded Monk disappeared immediately followed by another as Crane's form vanished as well.

Thread: sysObserver.cmd

Snake kept his hands flat with palms facing the floor. He dashed forward and lashed one arm out, hoping to catch the Serpent in the eye. The Serpent didn't know if the weak obvious strike was a formality or atrophy of Snake's skills considering the ease in which the attack was avoided. The Serpent countered with a weaving blow of his own. Snake easily dodged the opening strike too, but not the following flurry of spear-like strikes that the Serpent returned. Snake blocked the first few with several swipes of his hands, but he found himself overwhelmed by the Serpent's speed and determination.

Snake jumped backward to distance himself from his former ally. He sneered at the one who had fought beside him in numerous military victories. While their bond in battle was a powerful force, it had always been greater than the weak leadership in charge of the Martial Legion's premier fighting force. General Sato Seechi had always favored the Serpent. If Snake had to follow in the Serpent's shadow for promotions, there would never be room for both of them on the battlefield.

When the Drakken started to emerge as a serious competitor to the Ghosts, Snake seized opportunity to takeover what was rightfully his. During a covert strike on a Drakken artillery plant, Snake decided to prove his worth to his skeptical Drakken conspirators. With the Ghosts lured into a trap where the stealth and close quarters strengths were removed, the Drakken proved their tenacity to the Maleezhun forces. If the mission had been executed flawlessly, Snake would still be serving the Martial Legion into the present, but one Ghost survived, one who survived to tell the truth. The Serpent made it his goal to see that was Snake brought to justice. The encounter had been so controversial that even the Drakken wanted nothing to do with Snake. Criticized as incompetent to the Drakken and a traitor to the Ghosts, Snake had no choice but to leave his home faction. Previously, he had given little concern for the Serpent's fate, but Snake understood that they shared one trait in common, inability to shed their past.

"Tell me, Corzo. Who did you have to kill to in order to receive banishment like me," Snake said tersely.

"I'm not like you since my only business is to end those who have no business killing," the Serpent hissed coldly.

"Spoken like a true avenger," Snake replied. "Face it, Serpent, what do you hope to accomplish?"

"I will retire knowing that I served my country and my brethren to the death," the Serpent replied.

"You mean my death. If you kill me, you can't have both," Snake quipped arrogantly.

"My debts are settled, but it is high time to collect on yours," the Serpent snapped.

The Serpent kept his slit-like eyes trained on Snake, but he could still hear the commotion in the loading bay as Vanguard allies struggled with the other Monks in the fight. The Serpent knew little of the other Monks, but he was certain that Snake had to die if there was no legal remedy. As soon as the Serpent accomplished that mission, he would finally be free of the weight hindering his growth.

Angered at the obstinance of his former battle brother, Snake jumped and grabbed a beam of the airbridge high overhead. With a fluid arc, he kicked his feet up toward the underside of the walkway, then pushed downward, straightening his body with arms extended forward, ready to strike the Serpent like a spear. The Serpent angled to the side as Snake's dive missed, forcing Snake into a rolling somersault along the floor.

Snake recovered and dashed forward again, but the Serpent decided to match with agility of his own. The Serpent leapt into the air gliding into a twist and landed behind Snake who stared cautiously as he slowly turned about. With another snap, Snake pitched a handful of spikes in the Serpent's direction. Trapped with little room to maneuver, the Serpent jumped and landed on the stack of crates behind him just as the thin spikes sunk into the wood.

"You fight without honor," the Serpent muttered.

"Yeah, that's a given. You should know that by now. How is it that you forget training basics when it comes to survival? There are no rules!" Snake said with obvious bitterness in his voice.

"Says the one playing by the wrong rule book. Too bad you never surpassed the basics to learn the context of that lesson," the Serpent replied as he flipped from the crates, hoping to drop his foot on Snake.

Quick to evade, Snake dove laterally, grabbing the Serpent's blade along the way. Snake discarded the sheath and stared at the silver blade. Several slits perforated the center of the dual edged sword several notches from the handle while silver ridges contoured the otherwise black handle.

"I am amazed that you still use with this primitive cutter. I guess lingering in Seechi's shadow has kept you from advancement after all," Snake mused.

"A weapon is merely a tool, Snake, no more powerful than the one wielding it," the Serpent replied, banishing the thought of being cut by his own sword.

"Let's put your words to the test," Snake hissed as he arced the sword toward the Serpent.

Once on the defensive, the Serpent angled his body causing Snake to strike nothing but air with the powerful slashes. As Snake kept pressing forward, the Serpent found himself back pedaling without watchful care of the obstacles on the floor. His heel caught the corner of a toolbox which dropped him to his backside.

Snake stepped up and pointed the tip of the blade right at the Serpent's throat and sneered. "Tell me. How does it feel to always be on the losing side of the battle?"

"You should tell me given your abundant experience," the Serpent mocked.

The Serpent kicked his foot off the floor, connecting with the blade handle. Snake lost his grasp on the sword as it sailed into the air. The Serpent pushed from the floor and thrust multiple flat strikes at Snake to push him back. As the blade fell, the Serpent snagged the handle just in time to swing it around and over Snake's head. Snake snapped his right forearm overhead just as the blade came down.

To the Serpent's surprise, Snake's arm was still in one piece. His blade was sharp enough to sever Snake's arm clean off, yet it remained. Snake glared as the Serpent pressed down on the blade, but internally he was caught off guard by the durability of Dragon's recent invention.

Snake could feel the strain on his arm as the Serpent continued to apply pressure. He was now staring directly at the blade's tip. One strong thrust from the Serpent would have put the blade between his eyes. The Serpent tapped a switch on the blade handle to activate a recent modification. The blade's edge which pressed down on Snake's arm began to glow a warm copper.

Snake's eyes widened as he realized that the forearm guard may not withstand the penetrating heat. Just as the skin on his arm began to feel the heat, a shrill beep began to protest, but it had nothing to do with device failure. The Serpent hesitated at the new sound, but despite his discipline not to react, it was the only tick Snake needed to move away.

"That's my cue!" Snake smirked as he shoved the blade away and thrust a front kick into the Serpent's abdomen.

The kick had been enough to knock the Serpent backward and release the blade from his grasp, but even without his weapon of choice he spun about and grabbed the two silver Splice 15ms from under his coat and fired half a magazine from each at Snake. The follow-up attack was too late. Snake had already reached up to tap the button on his skybreaker and his form dematerialized just as the plasma bolts passed by, splashed and then sizzled on the wall behind him. The Serpent clenched his teeth and stared, refraining from cursing about Snake's narrow escape. Although angered, he knew that his own personal mission was not the only thing that mattered, after all, his life wasn't one defined by revenge.

Torque found himself engaged in a game of cat and mouse with his agile foe who continued to slink in and out of the shadows. Torque found himself uncertain as to who was the cat and who was the mouse. He could only assume that he was fighting Monkey based on the Enforcer's limited discussion of his past and description of the Monks' various ayveks. Torque had to continually shift his stance to avoid leaving any openings for the nimble Monk who continued hopping from the balls of his feet before resting into a crouched position.

Given Monkey's speed, Torque knew that drawing his disruptors would be suicide. Monkey was likely to leverage Torque's hesitation and flail on him. Torque tightened his grip on his kamas as he scanned the dark corner of the loading bay in search of his foe.

With a quick leap, Monkey landed atop a stack of boxes and glared down at Torque. Quick to respond, Torque slammed a side kick into the boxes weakening the support just enough for Monkey to shift his weight. Sensing the collapse of his perch, Monkey jumped to another nearby stack. Torque grumbled as he watched the Monk avoid the cascading pile of containers, but he was not dismayed since some boxes altered direction as Monkey pushed away. Boxes crashed into the base of Monkey's new tower. Torque knew that there was no escape for the Monk.

A heap of containers tumbled to the floor. Monkey fell, jarring his shoulder on the corner of one crate, but he quickly rolled to the side to remain out of Torque's line of sight. Torque couldn't see his opponent, but he knew that the jostling served its purpose. Monkey hopped back into view but with a reduction in speed and energy.

Torque sneered as he flicked out the blade in his right hand, "Heh, your Dongwu is obselete."

Provoked by Torque's arrogance, Monkey snapped his hands behind his back and drew weapons of his own. Initially, Torque was confused by the unusual objects in Monkey's hands. Monkey softly twirled the two flat pieces of metal, then with a snap of his wrists, the metal sheets shifted into a triangular wedge.

Torque's eyes narrowed as he scrutinized the strange weapons, but he promptly recognized them as boomerangs. He had never considered such as device to truly be an effective weapon, but since they were in the hands of a Monk, he had to assume they were lethal.

Monkey flicked his arms forward and the two flat boomerangs sliced through the air. Torque panicked as he watched the boomerangs converge on his position from opposite sides. With a slash, Torque swung a kama at one of the boomerangs, successfully deflecting it, but the other caught his left hand, knocking the kama away with a loud clang, revealing the massive power behind the throw. A couple notches lower and the weapon might have severed Torque's hand from his forearm.

Momentarily relieved about the avoided injury, Torque looked at his open hand. He listened for the drop sound to follow his missing weapon, but Monkey wasn't about to let him recover it as he dashed forward while snatching the single returning boomerang out of the air.

Torque jumped into the air, hoping to leap over the advancing Monk, but he was intercepted midair as Monkey followed and slammed into his chest. Monkey landed into his crouching stance as Torque's back slammed to the ground. Torque winced as pain shot through his shoulders.

Monkey secured his advantage and raised the sharp metal weapon overhead and snapped it back into a straight edge. Torque lifted his arm off the floor and spun his kama into an inverted grip. With a quick slash, he hit Monkey in the face with the top of the blade. He didn't have enough strength to deal meaningful damage, but it was diversion enough to shove Monkey away.

Torque found his quarry difficult to hit, given the evasive style as Monkey continued hopping circles around his foe. Torque attempted a sweep kick, but Monkey countered by hopping over the kick and slammed a punch downward to Torque's face.

Torque fumed as he snapped a series of kicks at the Monk, only to swat thin air. Monkey ducked and evaded each kick and followed with a slash from the straight edge at last disarming Torque of his other kama.

Monkey advanced as Torque propped both of his hands into a defensive stance in order to ward off likely attacks to his face from Monkey's bizarre weapon. It was Monkey's turn to sneer with glee at a common sight to many of the Monks' engagements, the opponent at a disadvantage. Little else mattered beyond victory at their hands, the superior vectors.

Ready to deliver the final assault, Monkey raised his weapon overhead, but a shrill beep caught him off guard. Like an explosion, Torque read the hesitation and rushed Monkey. Outraged at the intrusion upon his victory, Monkey activated the skybreaker since orders were orders. Monkey glared as he disappeared from view causing Torque to strike at nothing.

Torque halted his advance and scratched his head, wondering where the Monk went. His bewilderment easily transformed into a sense of relief. It wasn't the first time he came close to losing a fight, but it wasn't the first time he hadn't told anyone either.

Thread: actTgtPersp1.view

A loud, distracting warning klaxon blurted in my ears as I staggered backward from a blow to the chest. It wasn't an opportune time to learn that my ikes were tracking my vitals and relaying them in such harsh tones. I did my best to keep breathing while trying to escape the hook swords swinging toward my head. My vitals flashed critical as I did my best to spin away from my adversaries. I knew that the odds weren't in my favor considering that I was an amateur against two assassins. Either they were toying with me, or they were being lazy.

The agile Monk swung again, intent on goring me with the awkward weapons. I was unable to see motive in the eyes of my opponent. I could discern little of the Monk's appearance other than the blonde and orange braids escaping from the black skull cap.

From the metal plate underfoot, I activated my kips and high-jumped toward the bed of the truck just as the hook swords cut through the wooden slat guardrails of the truck bed. Knowing that a simple stunt was no long term strategy, I leapt from the truck and sprinted for the nearest cover that I could find.

I found a heavy rolling toolbox and crouched behind it. I didn't intend to run, but I knew that I couldn't take on both Monks at the same time. My ayvek hadn't advanced enough to even to deliver sufficient damage to one adversary. I needed an edge. I had just enough time to disregard the notifications on my ikes identifying my foes as Mantis and Panther which were strangely already in the VNET datastacks. I reached for the Phantom tucked behind my back and slowly peered around the edge of the toolbox. In the dim light, I could see Mantis walking around the truck, but Panther was nowhere to be seen.

There was no time for games with the mercenaries. I flicked the safety off my disruptor, but once I did, I sensed a looming presence from behind. I didn't need to turn around to know that Panther had already circled behind me. In a frantic response, I twisted to point the Phantom at Panther, but his leg was already a blur as his foot kicked the disruptor from my hand with such force that it misfired, sending a sizzling yellow bolt toward the ceiling.

A metal cling rang in my ears as Panther extended the talons on the back of his hand. He brought his arm overhead and slashed downward. Suspecting the attack, I snatched one of my fima sticks and struck the talons thrusting toward my head. I caught his talons, but the strike was backed by so much force that the talons cut four deep grooves into the stick.

DAVE TODD

Panther appeared surprised that I managed to halt the attack. Seizing even the slightest opportunity, I kept the damaged stick held high while spinning about to strike with the opposite stick. Panther swiftly recoiled. I doubted my ability to deliver actual damage, but I didn't expect to see Panther sneer as he stepped backward and faded into the shadows.

Perplexed by the retreat, I moved to follow but swiftly realized the strategic move was a diversion as Mantis closed on my position from the left. With my reaction time dangerously late, I snapped the intact fima stick over my head as the hook swords crashed down again, but the weight of the swords combined with Mantis' force was too powerful, causing my arm to give out. The deflection had been enough to keep my face from being gashed, but one of the hook swords caught my left shoulder just above the collar bone.

I yelled as pain seared through my upper body with the tip of the hook sword ripping at least a three notch gash into my shoulder. Mantis pulled forward on the sword as the hook tugged on the collar bone pulling my body to the floor. Using the momentum, I stepped into the pull catching Mantis off guard. With the swords useless at close range, Mantis attempted to step back to gain distance.

I did my best to pursue with a flurry of punches from my right hand. Mantis was forced to drop the swords since they were unwieldy and made blocking difficult. Mantis attempted to counter, but with great strain, I lifted my left arm and caught the advanced blow, pulling Mantis off-balance. Mantis countered again, but instead used a grappling move to pin my arms behind my back. I didn't know a proper counter, so I went with what I knew. I snapped my head backward to catch Mantis with a reverse head butt. The execution gave me enough opportunity to spin around and catch Mantis' arm. The applied force gave Mantis no other option but to follow the trapped arm to the floor. With Mantis' arm in a lock, I coiled my injured left arm for a finishing blow.

In the scuffle, I lost track of my treadball cap, but I didn't realize its absence would trigger such a shock to both of us.

"MAC?!" Mantis blurted in shock and disbelief.

Hearing my opponent speak made me realize an otherwise obvious fact that I shouldn't have missed had I not been in a fight for my life. The relentless vector who had just gouged me was a woman. I stared, noticing Mantis' eyes widen instantly at the first opportunity she had to fully identify my face. It appeared that she had no concept of my identity either since she was just fulfilling a contract.

I halted my strike as I realized that the loose braids had been covering a softer face than I would have associated with a lethal killer. If not for the fight to the death, I might have even used the word attractive, but I knew such a thought would prove fatal. I sensed that Panther had returned as the metal click of his talons spelled my death. Instead of a painful slash, I heard a dull thud followed by a grunt of pain as Panther brushed against me and stumbled forward.

I turned to see the Serpent wielding his sheathed sword in his hand while sporting a very sour look on his face. Seizing the distraction, Mantis kicked her foot to push me away. Pushing off the floor, she stood and moved next to Panther. The Serpent leveled his Splice's and fired them, one at Panther, the other at Mantis. With a sneer, Panther reached for a button on his forearm guard and dematerialized. Mantis evaded the shot and followed suit, but not before casting a confused look over her shoulder before she disappeared into thin air.

Relieved at the immediate threat being removed, I suddenly felt weak as my mind registered the recent injury. My legs gave way, but the Serpent dashed over and caught my shoulder as I stumbled.

"That's two bags of Mesquite-Os you owe me," the Serpent said as he propped my right arm over his shoulders and helped me stand.

"Deal," I replied with a weak smile. "Where did they go?"

"I do not know, but I am sure we haven't seen the last of them," the Serpent replied quietly.

The Serpent helped me toward a bench where Torque finally caught up with us.

"Looks like you guys cleaned house too," Torque muttered.

"Speak for yourself," I replied, casting my eyes in the direction of the red stain creeping across my pullover.

"If they don't gut you on the first hit, your survival rate doubles," Torque smirked. "You survived two on one, so that's a good start, Jellyfish."

Torque's compliments were reassuring since he normally stuck to his harsher rhetoric, but in spite of the optimism my body was only demanding one thing, rest.

As we worked our way into the mission only one question passed through my mind, but in my exhausted state I didn't internalize it, "How did Mantis know who Mac is?"

"Mac used to be a member of the Monk clan," Torque replied quietly with a straight face.

"It's rather convenient how he forgot to mention that," I replied.

As we reached the hallway which passed the galley and led toward the leisure room, my thoughts turned to my friends at the mission. I hoped that the Enforcer had arrived in time.

13 – The Rundown – 13

Oszwick Enterprises
Core City Fringe, Windstonne Enclave
Commercial Empire, Northam Continent
Thread: sysObserver.cmd

Voltaire and his four associates approached the bleak span of facilities owned by Oszwick Enterprises. Heavy, acrid smoke in the air adorned the already gloomy appearance. As the Mogul Prime delegates reached the lobby of the main facility they were greeted by a rather abnormal hostess. An unusually pale woman with white wiry hair smiled and offered to escort them to the chief executive's office.

Tunnel did his best not to speak of the woman's appearance. Despite her aged appearance, her normal stride and mannerisms did nothing to suggest that she was advanced in passes. As the clan members observed their surroundings, they spotted other staff members with similar skin tone or colorless hair. Some even had pronounced scars among otherwise normal facial features. A cluster of workers were about to cross paths with the guests, but they were quickly shuffled back into the room at the sight of visitors. One worker that others tried to hide had a slight hunch possibly from a degenerative condition.

The regularity of abnormal appearances among the workers started to put Voltaire on edge. He made sure to keep his guard up mentally since he knew so little about their host.

"I sure hope you know what you're getting us into," Tunnel whispered to Voltaire just out of earshot of their guide.

Voltaire had no assurances he could offer, but he felt a sense of relief when the clan members reached a spacious executive suite. The suite had the sterility of a lab, but its dark marble floors and silver trim at least set it apart from the rest of the facility. Once inside, Mogul Prime realized that it was a lengthy suite nearly spanning the width of the primary building so that it could overlook the numerous processing facilities stretching into the distance. While the chemicals clouds belched into the air gave the illusion of the afternoon being more advanced, the flood lights made it difficult to discern the actual time of day outside.

"Mr. Oszwick, Mr. Sargent and his associates have arrived," the woman announced before seeing herself out.

"Splendid," Konrad Oszwick replied as he turned about in his chair, standing to greet his visitors.

For the first time since arriving on the premises, Mogul Prime finally witnessed individuals with some color in their faces.

"I trust that you had no trouble finding the place," Oszwick said.

"None at all," Voltaire replied stiffly, suppressing the impulse to remark the ease of finding the eyesore of a facility.

"This is my associate, Lucient," Oszwick said as he directed his guests' attention to the other sharply dressed figure in the room.

Lucient nodded at the acknowledgement, but said nothing.

"Perhaps your associates would like to take advantage of our hospitality suite while we discuss business," Oszwick said as he gestured to a pair of doors on his right.

Mogul Prime stood their ground, awaiting further instruction, especially Pythagoras who wasn't about to move without direction from Voltaire. They were all keen on discovering the meaning of their visit.

"I think that would be acceptable," Voltaire said casually, casting a look to his associates, suggesting that he understood their mistrust and that they should be on guard.

"Excellent. Lucient, please make our guests at home," Oszwick said.

Voltaire sat down in a large leather chair as the others left the room. He observed Oszwick and his broad smile, causing him to question if it was a permanent fixture on the executive's face since it hardly differed from the expression during their first introduction at Casters Tower.

Thread: sysObserver.cmd

Pythagoras stepped past the hospitality suite doors and eyed the room suspiciously out of an abundance of caution. The room was a fraction of Oszwick's spacious office, but it too had a reasonable view of the facility beyond. Several padded chairs and couches adorned the middle of the room while a luxurious bar lined the wall opposite the observation window. Several meca's dotted the wall behind the bar, each displaying hapcasts from different factions. Pythagoras considered it normal to have haps in any local establishment, but the sight of feeds from other factions suggested that Oszwick had an investment in being connected with the world beyond the faction borders.

Lucient gestured toward the chairs surrounding a low glass-topped table and asked for drink orders. Tunnel and Tycoon were quick to put in an order and take a seat, but Pythagoras continued to take in the pictures adorning the wall on either side of the doors. The images showcased Oswick Enterprises' success, but the age of the pictures suggested a history predating Oswick's apparent age. Pythagoras assumed that the company was a family business until he could discover more.

"I'll have a Scorpion Tail," Pythagoras finally said to Lucient who was busy shuffling glasses and ice on the bar.

Pythagoras and Tunnel exchanged glances, each acknowledging the other's tension about leaving their weapons behind. Each possessed a sizable confidence in their ayveks, but it was seldom comfortable to discard critical resources. Conversely, they knew that Hauteur and Tycoon were still capable of masking smaller weapons which they kept on their person. After receiving his drink, Pythagoras took a seat, making sure it was at an angle where he could keep an eye on Lucient who decided to watch the haps while seated at the bar rather than socialize. Pythagoras was always mindful to keep a watchful eye, especially in foreign environments.

Hauteur didn't join the others, but instead she stared out the large window overlooking the company's buildings. The factories and chemical plants alike faded into the horizon. She felt a deep curiosity as to the purpose of the company having so many assets. The nature of the operation had to reach well beyond akcellerrant production.

Pythagoras monitored Hauteur as well. He was well aware of the value that she brought to Mogul Prime through her informatic mind, but some of her mannerisms still confused him. She was young and attractive, yet she seemed unusually dedicated to her work and customs as if guided by an unspoken tradition.

"Saphira, why do you insist on wearing that thing?" Pythagoras asked, referring to the cloth that she pulled above her forehead to keep her hair pulled back in potential combat situations. Even during the day, she wore it as a scarf when working in the lab.

Hauteur maintained her stare out the window, gathering her thoughts before finally yielding a response, "When I was young, my parents taught me the importance of tradition. Living life according to a code was a prize worth fighting and dying for. Often those following the old scripts believed that certain articles of apparel demonstrate modesty. Once I matured, I realized that the edicts of those traditions where not about values that they touted but a mechanism for control."

"This isn't Insurgistan. Here in the Commercial Empire, we have freedom. Why follow something so archaic?" Tunnel asked as he inserted himself into the conversation.

"You're one to talk, Tybalt. If I didn't known better, I'd say you have a twenty step process for lacing your boots. I've never seen such a creature of habit. Everytime someone suggests an alternative, you call said ideas controversial," Hauteur smirked.

"Comfort is a process I choose not to disrupt," Tunnel replied in his defense.

"Out of the fish's mouth," Hauteur replied. "I rest my case."

Pythagoras knew that the conversation could have waned, but as a key figure in Mogul Prime he needed to be sure that his associates were capable of parsing the difference between the doctrines they espoused and sufficient personal detachment from them.

"I've known Tybalt long enough to know that he uses habits to make those who are oblivious to them resistant to change, but what is your angle?" Pythagoras asked. "Your customs were passed down through the generations. Ideas that may have started as practical solutions may have persisted due to attachment to familiarity. When practicality fades and people still follow tradition, how do you decide when to break away from the norm?"

"Are you suggesting that I don't know the difference between value and belief, mighty cultist?" Hauteur asked, getting her own digs in, knowing that even Pythagoras had some astringent views of his own in relation to balancing the number of living imprints.

"No, Saphira, I'm not," Pythagoras replied reassuringly. "Mogul Prime succeeds because we know the difference between our tenets which we use to manipulate and those we choose to practice ourselves. Your views and those of your predecessors have been the most influential amongst our clients all over the world. I'm just ensuring that your practices are equally sharp in the field and free of conflict."

Pythagoras watched Hauteur quietly as she turned toward the window. He could see that she was taking the matter to heart, and there was no more need to press. He was confident in her strong will, but it would take time for her to develop her independence just as other members of Mogul Prime had. As a figurative second in command, Pythagoras did his best to keep the rest of the clan on its path to intellectual dominance. His advice was often met with apprehension due to being younger than his peers, but he always proved his ability to backup the sentiments which continued to earn their respect.

Deviating from the dwindling conversation, Pythagoras turned to watch Lucient who had his back to the members of Mogul Prime. He appeared to watch the haps absent-mindedly. Even though Lucient hadn't shown interest in the conversation, Pythagoras knew that Lucient was certainly listening if he were a halfway competent gatherer of intelligence. Even without interaction, there was something about

Lucient that Pythagoras did not trust. The assistant made no hostile gestures or comments, but there was an air of frustration about him.

Pythagoras started to suspect that Lucient had a stifled ambition. It was something he had experienced himself long before he connected with Mogul Prime. He had always excelled in his pursuits, often intimidating those around him. Since he accepted that he was still subordinate to Voltaire, Pythagoras wasn't concerned because Mogul Prime had a unified vision and there was no cause for clan members to strive against one another. With nothing of substance happening, Pythagoras knew he could do nothing to prove any wild theories at the present time, so with a final swig he sloshed down the contents of his glass and set it on the table.

Dwelling Street Mission
Abandoned Sector, Windstonne Enclave
Commercial Empire, Northam Continent
Thread: actTgtPersp1.view

Even for such a late arc, the Dwelling Street Mission leisure room was a flurry of activity as workers worked to clean up the mess from the brawl. I tried to listen in on details of the Enforcer's recount of the battle, but I was easily distracted by the mission mender who was stitching up my shoulder. Thanks to an akcellerrant, I felt a bit of brain fog, but I sure wasn't feeling any pain from the needle in use.

"Hey, you got dirt on my floor," Tarees said, nodding at the unconscious clan members as she approached the Enforcer.

"Oh, I'll cleanup the mess in a tick," the Enforcer replied as he kept an eye on Nox and Swipe's unconscious forms near the doorway.

"Thanks for intervening," Tarees said. "It's nice to still have strong friends, willing to help in time of need."

"Anytime, and you should never expect anything less from Vanguard. Otherwise, we would get rusty," the Enforcer replied with a weary smile.

"Well, look at you," Chuck said on approach as he cuffed my wounded shoulder. "You're the last person I would have expected on the rescue squad."

I winced, but I got a nod from the mender that he was done stitching me up.

"I thought you would have at least taken a couple out by the time we got here," I mumbled.

"You know me. I spend more time talking a good game than playing one, but it looks like you sure made the grade. A bit of training and you're ready for the pros," Chuck said with a smile.

"I'm not so sure about tha-..." I started, but was cut off by a loud crash shaking the mission.

"Check the back now," the Enforcer snapped at Torque and the Serpent.

"You stay here," the Enforcer said as he ran past me.

I suspected that my injury put me on the reserve list which certainly didn't resonate well, so I followed Vanguard's movements on my ikes. As they reached the loading bay they found a large gaping hole in the primary bay door. Sharp jagged edges protruded outward where one of the trucks had been forced through the door. With no Académé bodies to be found outside, they could only assume they made their way back into the bay and stole a mission truck.

"Maxwell, get wheels down here, now," I heard the Enforcer say through the comm.

"Already on it, Boss," squeaked the hamster.

I knew something was awry given the intensity in the Enforcer's voice. I got up to make my way toward the loading bay, but I was interrupted by a gasp from one of the mission workers.

With two unconscious bodies missing from the floor, I had to squint down the hallway to discern Nox's back as he and Swipe fled. My body responded sluggishly. As I reached the edge of the hallway, I saw the Académé clan members scrambling for a large object in the street, one of the mission's loading trucks.

With my best effort to overcome injury and the akcellerrant's side effects, I increased my speed. Through the entryway glass, I could already see Swipe leaping onto the truck. Jammer and Sophomore were already on board, reaching out to help Nox who fell behind, but I was determined to impede their escape.

I was detected as I slammed through the front door of the mission. My presence prompted my foes to yell for Burnout to start moving the truck. Not wanting to be abandoned, Nox ran even faster. With three pairs of hands able to scoop him into the truck, all I could do was catch up to a noxious cloud of fumes.

After a coughing fit, I heard the rumble of the truck's engine give way to another familiar sound. A driverless Fire Ant roared onto the scene, bearing down on my position. I dove from the street onto a small patch of grass as the mox squealed to a halt at the doorway.

"Let's go," the Enforcer shouted, completely disregarding my floundering form as he headed straight for the driver's door.

I pushed off the ground with my good arm and dashed for the passenger door. I wasn't even planted in the seat when the Fire Ant surged forward in hot pursuit of our quarry. We could barely see a rising cloud of dust and exhaust in the distance. I doubted that the mission truck could outrun us, but it did have a sizable headstart.

"Torque, we're pursuing Académe. I want you and the Serpent to parallel and attempt to intercept," the Enforcer said into the comm while I made note of their icons, showing their position advancing in the Chromehound.

"Ryoukai," Torque replied.

The back end of the truck grew in size as the Fire Ant closed in. I lowered the window on my side and checked the shot counter of the Phantom 4.0 in my hand. I propped myself onto the window ledge and leaned out. I lacked practice with the weapon reticle on my ikes, so I did my best to align it with the truck tires. Even with the Enforcer's adept handling of the Fire Ant, he was still forced to navigate through the erratic debris on the seldom traveled streets, further challenging my aim.

With the margin of error as low as I could get it, I squeezed the trigger and a stream of yellow bolts sizzled from the barrel of the Phantom. Several shots hit the street just notches from the tire while the rest burned into the truck frame that protected the wheel.

Before I could eject the spent cartridge, the low whine of another mox reached our ears. I snapped my head over my shoulder and saw a sleek blue cruiser careening onto the street behind us roughly a parcel away.

"We've got a Hammerhead closing fast!" I shouted as I settled back into my seat.

"Now we know what they've been spending their contract berry on," the Enforcer muttered under his breath as he dared a glance into the rearview mirror.

"Looks like it's armed to the teeth too," I said as I leaned over my seat to watch the vehicle that quickly gained on us. I could see the vehicle's driver in the narrow body of the vehicle behind the wide front axle after which the vehicle was named. I also spotted a muscular figure behind the turret over the right rear wheel well.

The Motor Captain sport artillery mox was known for its efficient combination of speed and firepower during the Global War. Common transports were replaced by an assortment of economy class combat vehicles made affordable to the average family, but the Hammerhead was notable. It sported dual mounted turrets over its rear axle while offering speed to match any combustion predecessor of its day thanks to its powerful inverter.

"Now what?" I asked, accepting that the Hammerhead would close on our position in a matter of ticks.

"It's time for you to take the hot seat," the Enforcer replied as he slammed the front of his fist into a large button on the middle console. The back half of the Fire Ant's roof folded open and dropped to the sides, revealing a convertible hatch as a large turret arose from behind the middle seat and swiveled into position facing our enemy.

"Whoa," I muttered, my eyes widening as our vehicle morphed into an assault craft.

"You mean this thing doesn't have auto-fire," I yelled above the rumble of the Fire Ant's engine combined with the shifting turret gears and the whine of the Hammerhead just paces from our tail.

"Too slow," the Enforcer said emotionlessly.

Ditching my apprehension, I ambled over the center console and the back seat. I took up position on the circular metal seat attached to the turret. I twisted hard on the right control arm and aimed the turret at the front of the Hammerhead. The turret kicked with enough force to suggest potential effectiveness against aircraft as well.

Plasma blasts from the Hammerhead were already searing past my head as I depressed the large triggers in each hand. The turret shook in retaliation as a stream of dense plasma bolts darkened the road between the Fire Ant and the pursuing Hammerhead.

The Académe driver twisted the wheel of the Hamemrhead and accelerated to escape my line of sight. If the vehicle closed the gap, I would lose capacity to lock onto the Hammerhead due to the rotational limits of the Fire Ant's turret.

The Enforcer's eyes narrowed while he watched the mission truck shift to the right as our current path split with a service drive. He attempted to follow, but he soon spotted the gaining Hammerhead through the sideview mirror as it also approached on the right. If the Enforcer followed the truck, he risked exposing the side of the Fire Ant allowing the Hammerhead to broadside. The Fire Ant had the advantage of weight, but if the Hammerhead timed the collision right it could send the Vanguard mox into a lateral roll.

The Enforcer doubted that the Académe driver had the mental prowess to calculate such a maneuver on the fly, but he wasn't one to gamble. If the Fire Ant flipped, he couldn't risk the chance of the Fire Ant flipping onto its gunner. Wrenching hard on the wheel to the left, the Enforcer broke off pursuit of the truck. The high speed action increased the difficulty for both the Académe gunner and myself to track our targets.

"Torque, we've got resistance. I need you to follow the truck. It just turned onto the north service drive," the Enforcer yelled into the comm.

I felt the vehicle sway underneath me as I tried to spin the turret and lock onto the engine compartment of the Hammerhead. I wasn't even able to hear Torque's reply above the deafening concussions of the Fire Ant's turret. As the Fire Ant passed the turnoff point, I watched the mission truck fade into the distance. I didn't understand the strategy change, but I had no time to question it. I shifted my weight in the turret seat as I angled to get a better shot.

"They're faster, and I'm outgunned," I yelled in desperation as the Hammerhead swerved again to evade my sights.

"Yes, Fox, but you forget the basics," the Enforcer yelled back as he slammed his foot on the brake. "Bulk Matters!"

The Fire Ant lurched in protest. My body was flung into the interior of the Fire Ant, given the lack of restraints on the turret seat. The back of my head slammed into the console between the front seats. The Enforcer watched in the rearview mirror as the Hammerhead driver's face twisted into panic as he wrenched on the wheel to avoid slamming into the back of the Fire Ant.

Tires screeched as the Hammerhead swerved to the left and raced past the Fire Ant. I scrambled to shake my delirium and reseat myself behind the turret. I spun the massive turret about to utilize the new angle. As the pursuant vehicle zipped past, the Enforcer took note of its occupants and pinned them on the ike display.

Without a reliable rear view, the driver, Jocq centered the Hammerhead and slowed just enough so that Bull could lock his turret on the Enforcer. In response, I unleashed a barrage of plasma bolts overhead, just as Bull moved to shoot at the Fire Ant's windshield.

Angrily, Bull crouched behind the turret to avoid taking rounds in the face. Bull then rapped his fist on the dome over the driver's seat for Jocq to slow down even more. I watched as he pulled a cord from behind his leather jacket as the Fire Ant closed on the Hammerhead.

Bull unfurled the leather whip at his side. As the Fire Ant closed within a couple paces, Bull kept his left hand on the turret and his right on the whip. With a vicious swing and lethal accuracy, Bull lashed out the whip and caught my throat as it coiled about.

Burning pain seared through my neck as the leather cord constricted. I raised one hand and dug my fingers between the leather and my skin to alleviate the pressure. Before I could untangle the cord,

Bull rapped on the driver's dome and the Hammerhead began to pull away from the Fire Ant.

The whip snapped taut and jerked me from my seat behind the turret. Bull braced his feet and pulled on the whip with both hands. With one hand still caught behind the whip coils, I had little choice but to catch my falling body with my injured arm as I flung it backward to grab the side of the Fire Ant. With my torso dangling over the edge of the Fire Ant, one hand on the whip and the other straining to prevent a tumble out of the vehicle, I fought with every bit of energy available as pain coursed through my body. My head hung dangerously close to the rear left tire of the Fire Ant with little defense as the noise of the whirring tires pounded my ear drums.

The Enforcer reached for his disruptor at the same time Bull lashed the whip, but the motion wasn't quick enough. As my body slammed against the side of the vehicle, the Enforcer was forced to snap both hands back to the wheel to keep from steering the Fire Ant away. Reacting quickly, the Enforcer pushed the Fire Ant closer to the Hammerhead and then tapped the brakes. The Hammerhead pulled forward, giving the Enforcer just the chance he needed to wrap his arm around the whip.

I felt the pull on my body, but suddenly the pressure lessened as the reinforcement from the Enforcer's grasp kept the whip from pulling me over the side. With an iron grasp on the weapon, the Enforcer slammed hard on the brakes. The Hammerhead surged ahead as Bull's eyes widened in panic. Bull's reflexes activated as he flung his left hand back to the turret just as the whip leapt from his hands nearly pulling him from his vehicle.

I was only given a few ticks to scurry back into the vehicle, as the Enforcer shifted the Fire Ant and stomped on the accelerator to catch up to the Hammerhead which had changed its strategy. The Hammerhead picked up speed as it tried to outrun the Fire Ant, but there was no escaping the Enforcer's frustration.

The Enforcer brought the Fire Ant flush with the Hammerhead. With nothing short of an icy, piercing stare from behind his ikes, the Enforcer twisted on the wheel and slammed the Fire Ant into the side of the Hammerhead.

The sport assault craft was no match against the Fire Ant's mass. Jocq lost control over the vehicle as it careened toward an inoperable light post. Scrambling to regain control, Jocq turned the wheel placing the Hammerhead on the sidewalk in an effort to thread the mox between the pole and nearby building, but the rear axle was far too wide to make the pass. The Hammerhead was slammed to an immediate halt.

The Enforcer watched in the rearview mirror as Bull jumped from the turret and yelled at the Académe clan leader. There was no time to be wasted on the two deviants. There was a stolen truck to recover.

"Are you okay?" the Enforcer shouted over his shoulder.

I fought to remain conscious while wrestling for an abundance of air, but I was otherwise in functional from, sprawled on the back seat of the Fire Ant. Since the fight for air would have resulted in scratchy inaudible words, I simply nodded and waved a thumbs up.

"I'll take that as a *yes*," the Enforcer replied as he turned the Fire Ant down a side street so that we could turn around and regroup with the others.

Thread: sysObserver.cmd

Torque glanced at the map displaying on his ikes to locate the intersection the Enforcer described as the last known location of the stolen mission truck. The coordinates were located at a vacant four way intersection that was rarely traveled. He momentarily switched his ikes over to thermal mode for any trace of the truck's engine signature, but found nothing.

"Can you see anything?" Torque asked the Serpent.

The Serpent squinted peering down each side street as the Chromehound slowed. His extra eyelids allowed him to filter many forms of visual interference giving him a natural advantage by locking onto heat signatures among other things.

Torque watched impatiently as he waited for the Serpent to finish his analysis. After nearly a ten tick gap on each street, the Serpent finally pointed toward the street heading east.

"A vehicle passed that way not long ago," the Serpent said quietly.

Torque pressed on the accelerator and the Chromehound sped down the street of choice. Torque couldn't explain the selection since it seemed like a poor strategic path, but he had no reason to doubt the Serpent. On the contrary, he fully doubted Académe's capacity to outwit Vanguard.

After a few parcels passed without any sign of Académe or the truck, Torque debated turning around and giving up the pursuit. Just as he let his foot off the accelerator, the Serpent interrupted his internal debate.

"Stop, I spotted something," the Serpent replied as he pointed toward an alley between a long dormant apparel store and supermarket.

Torque brought the Chromehound to a stop, and the Serpent slid out of the mox, cautiously walking toward the alley. Torque looked around nervously before daring to exit the vehicle.

"There, do you see it?" the Serpent asked as he pointed into the darkness.

"I don't see anything," Torque mumbled even though his line of sight gave him an effective viewing angle of the alley.

Torque winked into his ikes and engaged the green glow of his night vision. The emerald shading faded and bled into the darkness allowing Torque to witness with his own eyes the object of their hunt.

The Serpent drew both of his Splice 15m disruptors as he neared the mission truck, but Torque simply checked the burst count on his firearm while observing from on the Chromehound. He still suspected a trap. The Serpent slowly inspected the darkness for lurking Académe members, but there were none to be found. Convinced that there was nothing more of interest beside the truck, the Serpent returned to the Chromehound at the alley's entrance.

"They couldn't have gotten far," the Serpent remarked.

"No, they could not," Torque replied as he scanned the silent dark horizon of the abandoned enclave.

Although the soft rumble of the Chromehound's engine was the only sound in the stillness, it was soon drowned out by the loud whine of two sport engines as two Hammerheads burst out of an empty garage on the opposite side of the street. Torque leaned away from the open window, and the Serpent was forced to dive for the ground as the Hammerhead gunners peppered the Chromehound with plasma shots.

Torque twisted in his seat to get a shot at the Hammerheads, but they were out of range before he could respond, his only recourse was to slam his fist into the console with frustration. The Serpent was quick to recover and make for the mox. With the passenger door already closed, the Serpent was leaning out the window ready to fire.

"Mac, I hope you're bored because you're about to have company. Two more Hammerheads en route to your position!" Torque yelled into his comm.

Uncertain about the acknowledgement on the other side, Torque was already turning the Chromehound about to chase the Académe cruisers. As staccato fire washed over the comm, Torque knew there was plenty of distraction if the Enforcer hadn't responded. Smoke and burning rubber wafted into the air as the Chromehound's tires screeched against the pavement.

Thread: actTgtPersp1.view

The Fire Ant zipped along toward the newly marked coordinates on our ikes showing where the stolen mission truck had been discarded. We thought that we were in the clear, but the familiar whine of Hammerhead engines returned all too soon. The Enforcer and I both looked back to see the obstinate Académe duo bearing fast on our left side.

Not only had Bull and Jocq managed to free the pinned Hammerhead without operability issues, they even changed roles. Bull was now glaring from behind the wheel while Jocq occupied the turret seat as the vehicle approached the Fire Ant. Jocq refrained from using the turret and leaned to the side raising a layered metal object. He flicked his wrist and the object telescoped into a treadball bat.

The Enforcer attempted to jar the Hammerhead by swerving away before slamming into the lighter vehicle, but the crazed clan members anticipated the maneuver. As the Fire Ant steered away, Bull matched the Hammerhead with speed and position. Jocq cocked his arm and swung the metal bat hard at the rear window behind the Enforcer. Jocq didn't anticipate the durability of the reinforced windows which caused the bat to bounce backward nearly striking him in the face.

Angered, Jocq swung again. For the second swing, Bull's driving brought Jocq parallel with the Enforcer's open window. With the Fire Ant's turret ineffective at close range, I drew my Phantom and fired multiple blasts at the bat. I narrowly managed to clip the end of the bat, deflecting the strike so that it connected with the forward frame of the window.

The Enforcer blinked in amazement as he retracted his arm from the open window. At a minimum, a fracture would have been imminent if not for quick reactions. The Enforcer twisted on the wheel to pull away again, and, like before, Bull continued to match position notch for notch.

As Jocq wound up for another swing, I fired more bursts toward his chest, but the Fire Ant pulled away causing my shots to stray. The awkward evasion caused Jocq to lose his balance as he stumbled toward the rear of the Hammerhead. Doing his best to keep the Hammer parallel to the Fire Ant, Bull had no choice but decelerate to prevent Jocq from tumbling off the back.

Before anyone could address Torque's incoming message, the sound of more engines whined in the distance. I squeezed the triggers on the turrets, adding plasma spray to the cacophony of whining motors. I expected the Enforcer to handle any communication with Torque, but he was solely focused on putting distance between us and the Hammerheads.

"Torque, a little support would be appreciated... at your convenience, of course," the Enforcer finally snapped into the comm once he got a visual of the added Hammerheads on approach.

"Yeah, sure. Right after we make a drink run," Torque replied, his sarcasm heavy and obvious.

Even amidst the fray, I couldn't help notice the stark difference between the Enforcer and Torque's demeanors. Torque's behavior I got, but how the Enforcer appeared to remain calm was baffling. If not for the threat of death, I might have inquired, but instead all I could do was continue to apply pressure to the turret triggers. I couldn't dispel the tension that I felt as I watched the two rear Hammerheads grow in size as they caught up to the lead vehicle.

As the gap narrowed, I had no trouble recognizing Burnout's hair behind a turret of the Hammerhead on my left. Jammer and Sophomore each manned a turret of the Hammerhead on my right. I squeezed the turret triggers and rotated the military grade disruptor in a circular fashion trying to catch both of the rear Hammerheads in the spray. My accuracy was improving, but only just enough to splash the plasma in the general direction as Swipe and Nox dropped each of the Hammerheads back to evade the barrage.

"Cut over a block to the north," Torque yelled through the comm. "Bring the fight to us."

"In progress," the Enforcer replied as he turned the Fire Ant, the rear fishtailing to compensate for the abrupt course alteration.

The course change wasn't without obstacle. The Fire Ant bumped along as it clipped rusty waste bins, sending refuse and debris into the air. The narrow passageway proved to be a convenient choice as it forced the pursing Hammerheads to follow single file, giving me a momentary break on the turret. Jocq continued to flail his bat in the air, still refusing to operate the turret on the lead Hammerhead.

As I spotted the passage opening by way of a quick glance over my shoulder, my eyes darted about, looking for a way to slow our foes. I fired upon a balcony over the side street entrance. The first two Hammerheads were forced to swerve to avoid the showering debris, but the third cleared the passage, unobstructed.

"I've looped around and I'm heading south on Barter's Pass," Torque said.

The Enforcer checked the map projected on his specs only to follow with a nervous pause, "That's putting you directly on a collision course with us. How is that going to help? We have three

Hammerheads bearing on our tail!" The Enforcer, replied his composure cracking only marginally.

"It's time for a game of *Who's the Bigger Fish*," Torque replied." On my mark, cut hard right."

"Torque, are you sure?" The Enforcer replied, wary of Torque's plan as the Chromehound began to materialize in the distance.

"They've staggered their formation. Two of the Hammerheads are off center, so that will put them right on top of us," I yelled over the noise of the turret. "Cut to the left!"

"Is that your left, or the Enforcer's left?" Torque asked.

I was surprised that even without a visual, Torque was cognizant of my position on the turret, a testament to his battle awareness despite the frequent attitude.

"It doesn't matter. My left is the opposite of your left, so we won't collide," the Enforcer snapped back.

"But your left and Fox's left are the opposite, so if I go left..." Torque yelled as the Chromehound reached a critical decision point.

"Torque, just do it now!" the Enforcer yelled back through clenched teeth as a proximity alert blared from the console.

The Enforcer wrenched hard on the wheel swerving the Fire Ant to the left nearly trapping Burnout and Nox's Hammerhead against the nearest building.

The Chromehound blurred into view of the two remaining Hammerhead drivers since the Fire Ant had previously obstructed their sight. The Serpent watched as Bull's face exploded into terror upon seeing the silver mox barreling toward them.

Bull yanked on the wheel in an attempt to avoid the heavier vehicle, but he still clipped Swipe's Hammerhead which had been close on his tail. Bull's Hammerhead swerved out of control and smashed into the corner of a building collapsing the hardmelt vehicle like an accordion, trapping Bull inside while tossing Jocq to the street in a sickening roll.

Torque nudged the Chromehound to the right narrowly missing Bull's Hammerhead and directed it toward the Swipe's Hammerhead. With Jammer and Sophomore still on the turrets, they unleashed a maximized stream of plasma toward the Chromehound to impede its progress but without success. Swipe twisted the Hammerhead to the side causing the vehicle to grind against the buildings. Jammer recoiled from the scrape, leaning away from the turret as the contact forced sparks into the air.

Swipe realized the error in her choice too late. She attempted to direct the Hammerhead back into the street, but her overcompensation caused the vehicle to lurch toward Bull's crashed vehicle. The elongated front axle of the Hammerhead caught the crumpled tail of Bull's vehicle launching the Hammerhead upward into a corkscrew spin. Jammer and Sophomore were flung from the vehicle like sacks of grain.

Torque stepped hard on the brake forcing the Chromehound into a power slide. The vehicle spun more than half a circle. The Serpent seized opportunity as his side of the vehicle faced the airborne Hammerhead. He fired a trio of rounds from each of his disruptors. As the vehicle revealed its underside, the plasma rounds connected with the power intake rupturing its central core. The Hammerhead shuddered mid-air and trembled as the implosion shook the whole vehicle before its disabled form landed in a grinding crash on its side.

Nox attempted to squeeze his Hammerhead away from the Fire Ant as its tail knocked against the front axle. Losing control, the Hammerhead veered back into the street, but as Nox oversteered, the uneven roads sent the vehicle crashing into a storefront window. On impact, Burnout's unrestrained body flopped to the sidewalk below.

The Enforcer braked the Fire Ant to a halt. I swiveled the turret away from the closest Hammerhead wreckage to survey any remaining threats. The Hammerhead on its side was smoking from underneath. Had the vehicle been fueled like its mox predecessors it surely would have been incinerated.

No one moved near the vehicles that Torque and the Serpent had dispatched. Torque cautiously backed the Chromehound into a direction parallel with the street and pulled alongside the Fire Ant.

The Enforcer quickly leapt out of the Fire Ant and approached the Hammerhead immobilized by its newly crafted garage. The Enforcer grabbed Burnout by the arm and forced him to his feet. Unable to resist, Burnout was walked to the edge of the shattered storefront window and slammed against the closest wall.

"Why are you after me?" the Enforcer glared as he fought to suppress his anger and disbelief regarding the blatant attack on the mission.

"You?" Burnout mumbled. "We were after him," he replied as he lifted his mangled arm toward the back of the Fire Ant.

Sensing no immediate threat, I looked over to see the Enforcer interrogating the injured Académe member. I could that tell they were exchanging words, but I was too far to hear the conversation. The Enforcer had been looking over his shoulder in my direction, but once I caught his attention, his focus shifted back to the interrogation.

Burnout started heaving, but the Enforcer couldn't decipher if it was a cough or a weak attempt at laughter. Upon looking at the Fire

Ant, the Enforcer hoped his conversation was out of ear shot. Looking from the Fire Ant back to his captive, the Enforcer felt a sense of apprehension regarding the nature of Académe's mission.

"Who sent you?" the Enforcer asked as his face tightened.

"Frank Jenkins. He gave multiple clans an operation to track down anyone with contraband, but he gave the Monks alternate parameters. They thought there keeping the intel to themselves, but I overheard them gloat about the lucrative adjustment they received, not from Jenkins, but another executive altogether," Burnout wheezed.

"Why were Académe and the Monks assigned the contract?" the Enforcer asked, trying to get more context from Burnout's answers.

"Jenkins was so paranoid that he thought it was necessary to bring the three strongest clans together. So much for overkill," Burnout quipped.

"Three? What is the third clan?" the Enforcer asked as he tightened his grip on Burnout's arm causing him to wince.

"Some headcases called Mogul Prime. They were already working with Jenkins, so we shouldn't have been surprised that they hung us out to dry," Burnout replied.

"Why didn't they help?" the Enforcer pressed.

"Do you see them here bailing us out? How should I know?" Burnout replied, growing weary of the interrogation.

The Enforcer's eyes narrowed as he pressured Burnout. He hoped that Burnout would be more forthcoming, but instead Burnout snapped his scraped arm forward with a crackling stunrod in hand. The Enforcer narrowly sidestepped as the hissing metal wand passed his face. He grabbed Burnout's wrist in one hand and chopped a strike downward into Burnout's elbow with the other. Unable to resist the counter maneuver in his weakened state, Burnout's arm complied with the Enforcer's control as it was turned inward. The stunrod made contact with Burnout's neck, swiftly ending the conversation. Burnout's body convulsed in response to the electric shock before slumping to the ground unconscious.

"We need to get back to the mission. I think that there is more going on here than some petty political paranoia on Jenkins' part," the Enforcer said after he approached the Chromehound.

"Whatever's clever," Torque replied, albeit in diminished form of his normal amount of gusto.

"We'll cover the next steps after that," the Enforcer said.

With action finally at a lull, I slumped into the passenger seat of the Fire Ant.

DAVE TODD

"Now what?" I asked as the Enforcer finally resumed his position at the wheel.

"Back to the mission," the Enforcer responded quietly.

"And what about..." I started to say as the Fire Ant started to pull away from the Hammerhead wreckage and Académé bodies strewn about.

"They no longer concern us. This wasn't about revenge over a territory dispute. If they survive their injuries and learn from them, it will be consequence enough. I suspect that they'll glean enough wisdom to learn from their mistake of taking on the dirty work for a certain Frank Jenkins," the Enforcer said.

With each lesson, each outing, I had to accept that I didn't understand the Enforcer's methods. Everything always had an air of greater significance without a fulsome description. I refrained from vocalizing my misunderstanding since I preferred not to walk back to the mission.

The drive back to the mission was quiet. It gave my brain a few ticks to process what had happened. In a mere matter of arcs, I had gone from training and alley fighting to taking on bizarre vectors in a high speed chase. If I had known the high intensity lifestyle in advance, perhaps I might have reconsidered, but at the same time I felt more alive than ever, even with my injuries and fatigue. With a new excitement added to my life, I pondered if I might actually find answers that I was after.

Thread: sysObserver.cmd

The Enforcer kept his thoughts to himself for the remainder of the drive back to the mission. Burnout's response was of great concern. It didn't make sense why Frank Jenkins would target the mission or any of its staff. The Enforcer long suspected that Frank Jenkins may hold a grudge for interference during the Smart Wars, but that didn't explain such a delayed retaliation. Frank Jenkins was known to be reckless, but even the mission attack exceeded paranoia. If the Commercial Empire's faction leader was starting to strike at shadows, it wouldn't be long before the whole enclave contained imaginary threats lurking in every corner.

As the Fire Ant's tires hummed over the abandoned streets, the Enforcer did his best to ignore the one possibility that he was reluctant to admit. If someone with knowledge from outside the local veras caught wind of carefully laid plans, they might wish to interfere. An influential office would certainly make for a great ally. If so, the

Enforcer knew that he would have to double his vigilance. Imperan threats were nuisance enough. If uninvited guests were tossing weights onto the scales of balance, Fox's past might become relevant sooner than anticipated.

DAVE TODD

14 – Deals in Darkness – 14

Dwelling Street Mission
Abandoned Sector, Windstonne Enclave
Commercial Empire, Northam Continent
Thread: actTgtPersp1.view

The commotion had finally settled at the Dwelling Street mission by the time we returned. Mission residents had already managed to reset the overturned furniture well enough for peace of mind for the evening. Div, Tarees, Chuck and a few veterans finalized some last tick cleanup before turning in. I spotted a couple of workers sleeping on the couches with blankets over them since there wasn't time to address all of the disheveled rooms.

Tarees offered a faint smile when we walked into the room. Most of the leisure room lights were off to accommodate those sleeping, but even the dim lighting couldn't hide the fatigue of those still awake. Tarees offered to fetch us some cold water which we graciously accepted with the exception of the Enforcer who was pacing the hallway entrance in distracted fashion.

"Were you able to stop them?" Chuck asked quietly.

Torque, the Serpent and I all nodded in unison, but we decided to allow the Enforcer to recount the details once he was done with his own personal strategy session.

"Div, Tarees, I know you may not like what I'm about to say, but I think it would be best to vacate Windstonne. I don't know how the details of tonight's events will play back in Jenkin's ears, but I'm sure he won't like the outcome regardless. It has come to my understanding, that Frank Jenkins was targeting either myself or Mr. Fox, but my gut tells me that something more sinister is pushing him to resolve any dormant grudges he might have. I suspect that the attack was directed at the Interlace itself. If so, we face a dangerous adversary, willing to attack us in the open without remorse," the Enforcer said.

"Are you asking us to run?" Chuck asked.

"Not run, just find a more stable location than Windstonne. If this was an act of obsession, you can be certain that Frank Jenkins will try again. Do you have anywhere that you can go?" the Enforcer asked.

"There is an enclave growing near Grainsfeld. one of the rural communities in the plains. I'm sure they would love to have the extra help," Div replied.

"Good. Please make preparations as soon as possible. Jenkins is zealous, but I doubt he will pursue if he has to spend too much on those not absent from his target list. I do hope that it's temporary, but since I have landed back in Jenkins' sights, I'll make sure that Vanguard runs interference to keep his eye off the mission," the Enforcer said.

Div and Taress exchanged glances before nodding in agreement to the suggestion.

"What will you do next?" Tarees asked.

"Do what I always do, take care of business," the Enforcer said with mild reassurance before concentrating on the next steps.

"Torque, I'll have you stick around to help recover the truck. Plus, it will help to have someone on guard until morning. There is still one more thing for the rest of us to investigate tonight. We have to strike while the iron is hot," the Enforcer said, his voice beginning to betray his own exhaustion.

"Hot irons mean nothing if you're too tired to swing a hammer," Torque replied.

The Enforcer nodded slowly in response before spotting a familiar book resting on an end table. He walked over to pick it up before forcefully thrusting it into my midsection. "It seems that you have forgotten something."

Without added comment, the Enforcer walked away to assist with remaining cleanup. Torque and the Serpent followed behind to coordinate Vanguard's plans, leaving me staring at the Criterion in the dim lighting. In spite of fatigue and waning cognition, I felt surprised that some puzzle pieces pieces were starting to connect. I looked up to see Div and Tarees doing their best suppress grins while Chuck seemed oblivious to the situation.

"You've known all along, haven't you?" I asked, making sure that I looked Div and Tarees in the eyes. Part of me felt dumb for not seeing it sooner, but then I had been living in a rather clueless state. I could only guess that the Enforcer had been observing my whereabouts for quite some time and was likely the one to return the book when my clumsiness allowed it to escape my possession.

"Three passes ago he brought you here, so that you could recover from whatever you had been through. With the Smart Wars still on the decline, we had no reason to ask questions. He said that when you were ready, you would start looking for answers," Tarees replied.

"And our similar appearance never struck you as odd?" I pressed, hoping to get more clarity on the real mystery that continued to evade me.

"He simply told us you were a distant cousin," Div replied with a hapless smirk.

I could tell that my friends had been efficient in watching over me and allowed me to discover things in my own time, diminishing any prospect of deception. The more I learned about the Enforcer's cryptic manner I started to understand that he gated information and activity to protect those around him.

"And you bought that?" I asked with a chuckle.

"Let's just say that he never sold us anything that gave us reason for mistrust," Tarees replied emphatically.

"Truth requires a strong spine, and right now yours rates somewhere between bendy and mush," the Enforcer interjected in passing as he and Torque marched several containers toward the mission entrance.

"Clearly, your future is in good hands," Tarees replied with a smirk of her own.

Accepting that I would have to be content with the newly received insights, no matter how limited, I discontinued my questioning. I had no reason to press those who had already done so much to watch over me and offer me shelter and food.

"Thank you for everything," I said.

In exchange I received a courteous nod. After a round of hugs and crossarms, I parted company with those who had become my mentors, caregivers and friends for the last three passes of my life, put simply, the only three passes of which I was aware, so they carried great weight. I didn't know if I would see the Merricks, Chuck or anyone else from the mission ever again, but I was willing to accept that possibility if it provided me the opportunity to discover even more answers to my past.

"How did they vanish?" I asked as I approached the Enforcer as he salvaged components from a damaged Phantom on the floor.

"Even through technological means, some can leverage the Vast, but unfortunately, without comprehending its nature, they will never fully benefit from it," the Enforcer replied quietly.

With still so much curiosity, I could have inquired further, but I refrained since we still had another objective to complete before daybreak. Tabling my questions, I followed the Enforcer to the Fire Ant where we finalized a gear check, replenishing firearm and power cell alike, ready for our next mission.

Oszwick Enterprises
Core City Fringe, Windstonne Enclave
Commercial Empire, Northam Continent
Thread: sysObserver.cmd

Voltaire shifted in the leather chair as Konrad Oszwick waited for Lucient and the remainder of Mogul Prime to leave before engaging in conversation.

"You have a very unique staff, Mr. Oszwick," Voltaire said.

"They truly are. The potentials of modern fibernetics are quite amazing," Oszwick said like an inventor proud of his latest marvel.

"How so?" Voltaire inquired.

"My staff's most unique trait is that they are alive. They live in spite of the opportunity stolen from them," Ozwick replied.

Voltaire took a moment to ponder Oszwick's response. He sensed a puzzle in the executive's guarded response.

"Have you found a way to reanimate the dead?" Voltaire asked, doubting that Oszwick could possess such skills.

"I refer to it as repurposing. Something must first be quantified as life before it can be considered dead, and some things must be discarded before they can be reclaimed," Oszwick said coyly.

Voltaire squinted at Ozswick, not following his logic.

"Mr. Sargent, do you have any idea how many die before acquiring light and air? Perhaps in this era, only thousands, but in another millions. Before even being classified as life, many have been discarded as cellular mass. Do you know why? Simply for the sake of sidestepping responsibility. If the nature of life is beyond those who possess it, who am I to discard such valuable assets? I am a businessman after all," Oswick said.

"So, you're not renewing expired life, you're reanimating life not yet born?" Voltaire asked. "Is that even legal?"

"If there is no crime in the discard, there surely cannot be one in the reconstruction," Oswick said indirectly.

"I don't suppose your company has ever lobbied for policy to gain such an advantage?" Voltaire asked, trying to size up just what manner of man Oszwick was. Even Mogul Prime had a tendency to refrain from tenets involving organech manipulation. "What exactly is the nature of your products and services?"

Oszwick drummed his fingers on his chin, staring idly as if performing his own assessment of Voltaire, testing his potential comprehension of dark economics.

DAVE TODD

"Here at Oszwick Enterprises we specialize in experimental health products which allow our customers to expand features such as comprehension, memory and sensory aptitude," Oszwick replied, his succinct language suggested that he delivered the line many times over.

"How does that relate to us, Mr. Oszwick?" Voltaire asked suspiciously, considering that Oszwick had only relayed a talking point from the promotional meca.

"I'm fully aware of your exploits, Mr. Sargent, and I know that ambitions unachieved spiral into frustration, especially if talent such as yours is wasted on a prestigious leader who does nothing to bolster allegiance," Oszwick replied.

"Frank Jenkins is a fool, a powerful fool, no doubt, but he remains a fool nevertheless," Voltaire snorted. "Jenkins retains just enough influence to be useful, nothing more."

"And what do you consider useful, Mr. Sargent?" Oszwick asked in a soft inquisitive manner.

"I only trust what I see with my own two eyes? If I don't find a reasonable benefit, I see irrelevance," Voltaire replied, uncertain how much strength that he wanted convey.

"Precisely. That is what separates you and your associates from your market base. Without critical thinkers like ourselves, who would lead the factions to success? We live in a world ripe with bickering buffoons who cannot see past the end of their noses. Our world needs leaders who can think independently, not those who constantly conform to public opinion," Oszwick said.

"Where exactly would you lead the factions, Mr. Oszwick?" Voltaire asked, doubting that Ozwick's grandiose vision was anything more than another marketing line.

"Toward illumination," Oszwick replied as he leaned forward on his desk. It wasn't difficult to see that Voltaire was frustrated by his exploitation at the hands of Frank Jenkins.

Voltaire leaned back in his chair, pondering what exactly Oszwick could offer to offset any risks of usurping Frank Jenkins' authority. Turning on Jenkins would certainly cost Mogul Prime's reputation and influence should Frank Jenkins learn of such an alliance. He could chalk up Mogul Prime's absence from the night's mission as a schedule conflict, likely to infuriate Jenkins, but to undercut him completely would exact a much greater cost. Since Frank Jenkins was already revealing that he had no loyalty to others, Voltaire didn't see how things could get any worse. Frank Jenkins had no intention of expanding Mogul Prime's market share after a takeover of the Global Alliance.

"How exactly would you go about such an ambitious undertaking?" Voltaire asked suspiciously.

"I take it that you at least reviewed our marketing samples?" Oszwick asked.

Voltaire nodded.

"Splendid. How familiar are you with our new product, Extend?" Oswick asked.

"Vaguely. Just how would such a wonder pill be of benefit if its purpose is to increase any client's intellectual independence?" Voltaire asked in return.

Oswick's enthusiasm ticked up at the opportunity to discuss his work. "That's the elegant brilliance of Extend, Mr. Sargent, while indeed your clientele may increase in understanding, they will simultaneously be subject to..."

"Side effects?" Voltaire interrupted curtly.

"Exactly," Oswick said, giving Voltaire a moment to gather his thoughts.

"What kind of side effects are we discussing?" Voltaire asked, clearly open to diving deeper into the subject.

"In order to expand a person's receptiveness to information, Extend makes one impressionable, shall we say, a trait often useful for swaying political support or promoting new products," Ozwick said with a wide grin, obviously pleased with the nature of his work.

"I find politics to be little more than publicly approved manipulation and theft," Voltaire mumbled.

"Then all we are doing is optimizing the process," Ozwick countered.

"Do you use your own products, Mr. Oszwick?" Voltaire asked facetiously, deciding to test his host.

"Do you read your own books?" Oszwick countered.

"Touché," Voltaire replied with a smirk.

"Comprehending the subtleties of one's own product is what separates the executive from the entrepreneur," Oszwick added.

"And leveraging them can make one a king," Voltaire said in affirmation.

Voltaire felt that he and K.Oszwick had a solid understanding of a potential business relationship. Seldom had he encountered a businessman, philosopher or teacher with enough wit to challenge his own methods. He detected promise in the potential partnership, even though something about Oszwick's personality felt elusive.

"How can we make our arrangement mutually beneficial, Mr. Oszwick?" Voltaire asked in hopes of drawing out more of the executive's intentions.

"Are you eager to undermine Frank Jenkins, Mr. Sargent?" Ozswick responded with a question of his own.

"Frank Jenkins lacks finesse. He doesn't understand the simple strategy that power perceived is power achieved. His domain could be greatly expanded if he actually learned the power of persuasion," Voltaire replied, deciding to play an evasion game of his own.

"You still haven't answered my question," Oszwick said in recognition of the test.

"Would I cast Jenkins' projects to the wind? Only if I found a stable counter offer," Voltaire replied.

"Care to expound upon what said prize might look like?" Oszwick asked coyly.

"That of any awakened individual... Purpose. Mogul Prime's purpose is to educate in the finer intricacies of life, so my purpose is to ensure its success," Voltaire said.

"If I empowered you to fulfill that goal in a simple exchange for support of Oszwick Enterprise's products, would you find that to be a reasonable arrangement?" Ozswick asked.

"Sounds fair enough," Voltaire replied after a moment of thoughtful consideration.

The executive leaned back in his chair with an unwavering smile of approval on his face. Voltaire was starting to suspect Oszwick had many passes of experience in practicing his pretentious smile, unless he had some special akcellerrant modifying his muscle memory. No one could hold such a wide smile for that long.

"Splendid, you may be surprised to learn that the range of our influence already permeates other cultures in the Global Alliance. Our sales have exceeded expectation in all factions with exception of the Oceanic Outpost. Their seclusion combined with cultural independence has made them less susceptible to our advances," Oszwick said.

"I still have some connections down there which may be of value. An old acquaintance of mine used to work in the public sector. I can look him up," Voltaire said.

"Excellent, then I do believe we have found the terms of our agreement," Oszwick replied.

"What should we do about Jenkins? Scuttle his current project?" Voltaire asked.

"No, I don't think that will be necessary. I think Mr. Jenkins' plan may yet be of use to us," Oszwick replied as his smile shifted into a smirk.

"He's going to be outraged that we didn't participate in this evening's excursion," Voltaire said.

"Leave Frank Jenkins to me. I have some modifications for his satellites that should prove distracting enough. Knowing that said modifications will be beneficial to his cause, I will explain that I requested your expertise on the matter," Oszwick replied reassuringly.

"That should suffice," Voltaire replied. "However, I have an added thought. If someone were to utilize Jenkins' widecast capacity in order to increase the range of Extend, it could conceivably tip the scales of balance in virtually any political arena," Voltaire suggested.

"Your knowledge makes you a dangerous man, Mr. Sargent," Oszwick quipped.

"I'd like to think so," Voltaire said, hoping to maintain his posture of strength in the arrangement.

"... but more of a danger to yourself than anyone else," Oszwick quickly countered to prevent Voltaire from gloating. "Such knowledge can make one disappear, but I do like your style."

"I'll take my chances," Voltaire replied, unaffected by any intimidation Oszwick attempted to relay.

"Of course, you do realize that by involving your clan there will be a greater chance of Frank Jenkins catching wind of your priority shift," Oszwick suggested.

"I trust my crew," Voltaire said confidently.

"Very well. Then it looks like we are on the same slate. I look forward to advancing our exploits together," Oszwick replied. "If interested, I can offer you the first shipment of Extend tonight. I can have my assistant bring samples up right away."

"Most generous of you," Voltaire said in approval.

"I think both of us understand that there is no generosity in business," Oszwick said with a smirk.

A few ticks after Oszwick tapped a button on his desk, one of his gangly staff members hobbled in with a crate in hand. The crate was set on the floor and its carrier swiftly left the room just as Lucient returned with the visiting Mogul Prime members in tow.

"Pythagoras, Tunnel, please check on the facility to make sure the others haven't burned it to the ground, and if you would, take that package, compliments of Mr. Oszwick. We have a new product to offer our clientele," Voltaire said.

Pythagoras and Tunnel acknowledged silently with exception of a snicker on account of the indirect dig at those left to guard the Media Resource Center. Pythagoras hoisted the crate onto his shoulder and departed the executive suite with Tunnel close behind. They left their associates to handle the diplomacy and potential discovery of Oszwick's secrets.

Outer Core Dartway
Abandoned Sector, Windstonne Enclave
Commercial Empire, Northam Continent
Thread: actTgtPersp1.view

The Enforcer was silent for several clicks before mentioning anything about our next course of action. I contemplated if he and the Serpent felt as exhausted as I did, but I suspected that they masked it better. I glanced at the Serpent who was sitting in the back seat of the Fire Ant, his disposition like that of an ice block. The Enforcer was somber as well, but I could tell that there was something he wasn't able to hide as well as his fatigue. My weary mind wanted to lapse into restful sleep as the rotation of the Fire Ant's tires droned beneath us, but the Enforcer interrupted, banishing the possibility.

"Maxwell, what do you have on Mogul Prime?" the Enforcer asked.

"Processing… Mogul Prime: a prestigious team of thinkers and informatechs, well known for their wide library of mediacasting content, and they happen to have a rather generous license granted by the Commercial Empire to sell said educational materials," Maxwell replied through the comm.

"Interesting… Got a location?" the Enforcer followed-up.

"Mogul Prime Media Resource Center is embedded in a fringe business complex dividing a retail strip and an industrial park. Should be quiet this time of day. Marking the industrial park on your ikes," Maxwell replied.

Unless my ears were playing tricks on me, I thought that I was hearing fatigue even in the hamster's synthesized voice as we approached the early arcs of the morning. Trying to distract myself, I opted for conversation, "Who is this Mogul Prime, and what do they have to do with tonight's events?"

"Supposedly, they were tasked with supporting the mission attack, but for some reason they opted out. Whatever distraction they found, they deemed it more important than following Frank Jenkins' orders. I suspect that may offer us an opportunity to do a little raiding of our own," the Enforcer replied.

"All of this on a hunch? You're not usually prone to such wild assumptions," I remarked.

"In a sense, but if someone would dare wage war on the Interlace in the open, I deem it necessary to identify threats as quickly as possible. Vanguard still has a mandate to protect the defenseless over itself, " the Enforcer replied with a calm assurance.

"It is possible for such dedication to appear irrational and potentially put the lives of others at risk if they don't share the same level of understanding," I replied, hoping that added discussion might postpone the late-night operation. I knew that my exhaustion was getting the best of me as I heard a familiar rushing wind and voice combined with its lighting fast, piercing headache .. *will not give you anything more than you can handle.*

"What did you say?" I asked while scratching my head.

The Enforcer shook his head and looked at me, ascertaining if I was feeling okay. I turned around to look at the Serpent should he have said something, but he simply shrugged his shoulders at me.

"We didn't say anything," the Enforcer said. "But as I was going to remark about the Interlace... care to back me up, Alex?"

"Allegiance to the Interlace is a choice not an obligation," the Serpent added.

"You don't have to go in, Fox. You can wait outside, if you wish," the Enforcer said.

"As much as I'd like to catch a snooze while the two of you have fun, I don't think you can resist inviting me to the party," I replied, well aware that the Enforcer's statement was a mentor's trap which was likely to result in training consequences later.

"A wise assessment," the Enforcer smirked.

"In case this needs to be stated, this is a stealth op. Get the intel we need and get out," the Enforcer said as he downshifted the Fire Ant. "Fox, you and I will take the lead. Alex, I'll have you hang back since you rely more on visual disruption versus cloak."

With the Fire Ant parked securely a short hike from the Mogul Prime Media Resource Center, we piled out of the mox. After the Enforcer did a security sweep and got an all-clear from Maxwell, we headed for the large storage structure behind the facility.

With no resistance to be found, we made our way into the building. My eyes widened in amazement upon activating night vision once again, this time revealing countless shelves filled with books from floor to ceiling which confirmed that Mogul Prime was paid up with the right people in the Imperan administration.

I softly ran my fingers across edges of the shelf while scanning each with my ikes hoping to catalogue any relevant findings. *The Voice of Reason* by Dean Sargent, *Letter of the Law* by Saphira Praxis, and *Drink to Your Health* by Dennis Brewer were the few titles I spotted within my line of sight.

"I didn't think such a large store of hardtypes was possible inside the Commercial Empire," I said, running my hand across several of the book spines.

"Don't touch! Those will gust your tracer in three ticks," the Enforcer snapped in a hushed tone.

"I thought you were big on gathering intelligence," I replied, surprised at the order.

The Enforcer tapped the frame of his ikes, motioning for me to change my view, "Education is one thing. Absorbing rancid energy from malevolent ideals is another entirely. I've seen these kinds of materials before. They infect all forms of communication from educational slates to widecasts. I didn't know that we had such an active distributor so close to home."

I switched my ikes to Inteferic mode briefly and witnessed varying shades of red mist exuding from the surfaces of the books, prompting me to quickly recoil my hand. From that point on, I stepped back and opted to trust the Enforcer's insight on the matter, "With all of the time I watched content at the mission, how come I never ran across their names before? What makes them so dangerous?"

"The amount of time you spent with said materials combined with their true subtleties is precisely why we have spent so much time trying to break the filter which has impaired your awareness over time," the Enforcer said. "The scope of their influence ranges from haps to hardware. At the core of every controversy you will find tenets like those belonging to Mogul Prime. It remains to be seen if they are intentionally leveraging the Catalyst, but the effects of their material is likely doing so regardless. It takes little time for these materials to desensitize the brain and heart to the ill effects which lessen the discernment of each consecutive generation. By the time you even see the bait, the hook is already set," the Enforcer explained.

"I'm beginning to wonder if you ever run out of lecture material," I said.

"I'll run out of lectures when you run out of learning," the Enforcer stated.

Before I could craft a witty response, the sound of raucous laughter reminded us that we were on a mission, not training in the warehouse. The Enforcer and I both spotted a pair of stairwells on either long wall of the storage room and agreed to go around our adversaries.

"Maxwell, how about a structural schematic?" the Enforcer whispered into the comm.

It didn't take long for Maxwell to comply, allowing the Enforcer to see a virtual representation of the building a full mark in front of his face. I disregarded the intel and opted to follow his lead.

"Looks like a logical place for a datatank to me," the Enforcer whispered as he followed the abundance of electrical wiring until he marked the room past the storage facility. "I'll go have a look."

"Fox, you're on walkway detail. Serpent, you're on the perimeter," the Enforcer said.

As the Serpent and I both blinked acknowledgements into our ikes, the Enforcer slid out of sight and my wait for action commenced.

Thread: sysObserver.cmd

Unaware that they were getting more punch drunk by the hour, Authochthon, Id, and Bender held their sides from laughing so hard.

"Can you believe it? She called ME, Crazy," Id sputtered between gasps for air.

"But, Sig, you are crazy," Autochthon belted as he held his side with one hand while attempting to keep his eyes from watering with the other.

Bender shifted in his seat to improve the air flow into his lungs. He thought that he had heard something above the ruckus which the three of them were making, but he was uncertain. He stood from his chair and scanned the processing area of the storage room. Sensing nothing, he sat down, but a faint blur rippled across his artificial eye.

"We have a visitor," Bender rumbled as his ocular implant outlined a figure on the walkway above.

"Where?" Id asked as he and Authochton hopped out of their chairs.

"Are they armed?" Authochton asked under his breath. He looked in the area upon which Bender was so intently focused, but he couldn't see anything unusual.

Thread: *actTgtPersp1.view*

The one identified as Bender, nodded toward the Enforcer's position. As the Enforcer's nav marker on my ikes went still, I sensed that he was holding position. I was reluctant to advance myself, even with the cloak impairing our enemies' detection capacity.

"Set plasma density to low. No need to make things messy just yet," the Enforcer whispered into the comm as he raised a Phantom and activated the barrel suppression mod.

"You've got three ticks to throw 'em down," Authochton's guttural voice rippled through the supply room.

"I don't think he's really in a position to be making threats," the Enforcer said softly.

"Hollow threats from hollow heads," I jeered, doing my best to close in while keeping my Phantom raised and cloak active.

Autochthon and Id immediately turned about, hoping to identify my position.

"Are we going to get this party started, or just do the trash-hole tango all night," Id yelled frantically.

"Cornered critters make for terrible dancing partners," the Serpent chimed in as he stepped out of the shadows of the book shelves and entered the processing area. He leveled his Splices in the trio's direction, one trained on Autochthon and the other on Bender.

Autochthon chuckled as he watched the Serpent's form glide from the shadows, "I don't recall man-with-scaly-pants being the most feared creature on the extinction list of alpha predators."

Id and Bender joined in on the laughter, but the Serpent only responded by tensing his index fingers on the triggers.

"Fire at the chunky one, he seems to have the ability to see us," the Enforcer said.

All three of us opened fire on Bender. Some bolts strayed while others splashed against the individual with the organech headware comprising half his skull. With his padded vest offering no protection from the shots, Bender hit the floor unconscious.

Our cloaks overloaded, unable to mask the intensity caused by our disruptors. With our positions revealed, our enemies sprang into action. Id with lightning speed snatched a gray tube leaning against the area railing. With several clicks, the tube telescoped out from the front, and a funnel fanned out around the back end. Before I could react, my ikes popped a giant danger sign next to the profile on the Mortimer Cannon brought to bear. Id's irrational behavior made itself known as he squeezed the trigger of the Mortimer, sending a plasma shell toward the Enforcer's position.

The Enforcer dove to the walkway as shards of duracrete chipped from the wall overhead. The Serpent fired multiple shots toward Id's chest. Id reacted quickly, but at least one round found its mark, knocking the clan member to the ground and sending his weapon sliding across the duracrete floor.

Authochthon charged the Serpent with his arm raised. The Serpent fired again, but Autochthon's massive form surprisingly hid an agility that allowed him to evade all of the shots. Once in range, a massive fist connected with the Serpent's jaw. The Serpent staggered backward, recoiling to fire again, but his foe was too quick to allow another shot at close range.

Sensing the Serpent's dilemma of firing versus drawing his sword, I squeezed the Phantom's trigger as quickly as I could given the recoil. Three blasts struck Autochthon in the back. Even against the plasma, the lumbering clan member seemed resistant to the attack, but eventually the force of the electrical impulses caused severe enough muscle spasms to halt his advance. Authochthon collapsed with a thud at the Serpent's feet.

"I have to move quickly. Keep an eye on them," the Enforcer said as he dusted himself off without elaboration before heading toward the facility interior.

The Enforcer only had to scan a few rooms before he located the proper terminal access point. His fingers moved across the tapper before a warning popped up, threatening to sever data connections should an improper sequence be entered.

"Maxwell, this thing is locked down tight. Got anything for me?" the Enforcer asked.

"Appears to be one of those hefty Gnossos systems. Nothing that yours truly can't handle," Maxwell replied.

"Good 'cause you're on the gauge," the Enforcer replied as he slid a datapill out of his vest pocket before sliding it into the terminal's closest pillbox.

Maxwell forwarded a series of taps to the Enforcer's ikes for him to enter in order to trick the terminal into thinking that it was an unsecured box. Upon gaining access, Maxwell sent him a command to spike the archive's security gate, so that it would widecast like a lighthouse across the Hyper Lynx. After a quick trace, Maxwell was able to locate the data terminal and get a decryption filter running from his location at the warehouse.

Normally, Maxwell's decoding algorithm's could best average security gates in a matter of ticks, but the present system required more time. *Someone is going to be very unhappy upon discovering this breach*, he thought to himself. To further accelerate the process, Maxwell began leveraging the building's additional terminals to assist with the security intrusion.

"What's so funny?" the Enforcer asked as he heard the hamster chuckling to himself.

"Oh, I just love my job," Maxwell replied. "How about a raise?"

"What do you want? An exercise wheel?" the Enforcer quipped.

"And... we're... in! Removing lockdown status, Now!" Maxwell said, disregarding the joke.

"Would you look at all that," the Enforcer said as the unlocked datastacks flowed like a waterfall before his eyes. He and Maxwell both let out a low whistle upon witnessing the expansive datatank that they had gained access to.

"They get around more than I thought," the Enforcer said as he did his best to scan shipping manifests for Mogul Prime products. Their books had high sales numbers especially in enclaves from countries with values similar to the Commercial Empire prior to the Global War.

"Divert control over to personnel datastacks, it's time we got to know our enemy," the Enforcer instructed.

After flipping through several profiles of Mogul Prime members and affiliates, the Enforcer paused on one in particular. Name and credentials were hidden, but the location and sphere of influence were certainly of note.

"This is not good," the Enforcer said flatly.

"What did you find?" Maxwell asked.

"It would seem that our hosts have some high level operatives. One such individual is even installed in Oceanic Outpost's advisory council. I don't like the thought of someone with such ideological damage working with the only faction leader still loyal to the Interlace," the Enforcer said with a grave pause. "Can you get me anything related to his identity?"

"Negative. They've got a terminator thread which destroys any outdated information capable of comprising their assets. My only option is to track ghosted data that has been overwritten, but that could take a tick or longer. These new datastacks run a million layers deep. My only hope is to get a mirror of the last scrub," Maxwell replied hesitantly.

"Do it," the Enforcer said. "We're out. I'll need to head for the Oceannic Outpost in the morning and warn Potentate Ang."

"Once you terminate remote access, I may only have about ten clicks to access the miners on the datastack. I don't want to break this fossil I'm working from," Maxwell said.

"Don't forget that fossil is still more secure than anything on the market," the Enforcer chided.

"As we have just proven," Maxwell hummed.

"Prioritize as you see fit and snag anything that you find useful. We have outstayed our welcome here," the Enforcer concluded.

Thread: sysObserver.cmd

Pythagoras shifted his weight under the crate of Extend that he and Tunnel had been tasked with returning to the Media Resource Center. Tunnel opened the supply room door and peered into the dark maze of shelves while Pythagoras looked for a spot to park the crate.

"I wouldn't mind knowing what this stuff is," Pythagoras mumbled as he kicked the lid off the crate, revealing a large quantity of vials and pill bottles.

"The only thing I care about is its ability to help sales," Tunnel replied. "Now, where are the fishes. It's not like them to be this quiet... even when they're sleeping."

"True, something isn't right," Pythagoras said as he walked over to a nearby small arms locker and produced a Cress disruptor.

Grabbing his shoulder belt from another locker, Tunnel fastened it around his torso, frustrated at having to leave it behind for the meeting. He then unhooked an optic pulse, grabbed his large hammer and followed Pythagoras down the shadowy rows of Mogul Prime materials, searching for any signs of trouble.

Thread: sysObserver.cmd

The forms of three travelers materialized just outside the Media Resource Center. Rubric Flux checked the codex on his arm to verify coordinates. The target on their opscan was close, but any relevant energy signatures were extremely faint. Flux knew that opportunities to verify the target ahead of the extraction marker were few. The Nomads would have to make the most of every chance to gather intel no matter how limited.

"Why did you drop us so close to a hot zone?" Snacks asked. "My readings show that we nearly landed on the two that just passed by.

You're going to get us tagged if you don't start making more accurate jumps."

"This is the closest we have ever been, we should act now," Scownin mumbled, his grim attitude rarely filtered.

"It's no trouble. I go in, nab the target and return before anyone can see a thing," Snacks replied.

"Not a chance," Flux countered. "You haven't eaten a thing in two arcs. Scownin will be able to crawl faster if you crash in there."

"True," Snacks acknowledged as he looked around the supply room in hopes of edible goods to prevent breaking out the emergency rations stowed in his vest.

"This is odd. There is a second signature matching the target. How is this possible? If I were to venture a guess, we might be dealing with a mixed vera scenario. We need to settle the intel now," Scownin rambled.

"No," Flux said, annoyed at having to be firm with his associates. "The opscan was clear, correct timing is critical. We hold."

"How will we know which is the target?" Scownin asked in frustration.

"We go with whichever one is left," Flux replied.

Scownin squinted at the Nomads' leader from the shadows, wondering just how much intel that he was privy to. It was an unusual mission after all. The Nomads were normally responsible for cultural exploration not some bizarre counterintelligence op.

Hoping for quick access to food, Snacks found the nearby crate of Extend and slid the lid over. He flipped one of the vials into his hand. After a cursory scan of the pills within, he was ready to pop the lid when the vial flew out of his hands and floated over to Scownin's open palm.

"Not wise," Scownin interjected. "There's a lot of malfeasance that goes on with some rather potent chemicals in these parts of the Grid, Snacks."

"Quiet, both of you! Our target is on the move. We'll have to scuttle the intel this time. We'll get another chance," Flux snapped under his breath. With a flick of his wrist he tapped a sequence into the codex on his arm and the three Nomads disappeared. The floating bottle of Extend simply dropped to the floor.

Thread: actTgtPersp1.view

While the Serpent kept his disruptors trained on our unconscious enemies, I took a moment to cycle through the filters on my ikes to see if anything was advantageous for threat detection. I paused as my ikes washed blue in a grainy fashion. I looked around seeing that only electrical objects were more luminescent while inorganic objects were more flat. The Serpent's form was faint, but the readouts on his Splice's were really bright.

As my eyes adjusted to the electromagnetic filter, I realized that I was seeing through the nearby walls adjacent to the supply room. Terminals and cables beyond also showed their slithering trails in and through the walls. Just as I returned my focus back to the supply room, I thought that I detected a hazy wave pass my peripheral vision. I switched my ikes back to night vision, but I couldn't find anything unusual. Still suspicious, I worked my way back down the stairs and notched my way to the back of the supply room. I knew that the Serpent would give word if our captives stirred, so I thought it safe to check the perimeter. For a brief moment, I thought that I heard voices near the exit.

I moved carefully, still reluctant to trust my movement with the night vision active. A cool draft drew my attention toward the exit door where a passing reflection caught my eye from the floor. A shiny vial caught my eye along with the opened crate next to it. How it exited the crate, I couldn't say, but I was curious as to its contents. I stuffed the vial into my pocket and panned my Phantom around. Checking the door, I noticed that it was ajar just enough for the exterior lights to pass through, likely the reason I spotted the vial.

"Serpent, did you leave the back door open?" I whispered.

"Negative," the Serpent hissed back into the comm.

"Then we've got company," I snapped with alarm.

The Serpent spun around just in time to see a large sledge hammer crashing down from overhead. He hopped backward nearly stumbling over Bender's unconscious body. The Serpent stared for a moment trying to identify the tall attacker who had unusual implants attached to his temples. The attacker's arm muscles rippled past the black tank top revealing his strength in leveraging such a slow blunt weapon, but the Serpent still considered it ineffective against the agility of a Ghost. He moved to point his Splices at Tunnel's face, but as he did, he felt the cold metal of a three barreled disruptor connected with the base of his skull.

"Drop 'em," Pythagoras snarled.

Knowing that I couldn't hesitate, I dashed behind Tunnel from his right and primed a round into the Phantom before aiming it at Pythagoras.

"You first," I snapped.

The Mogul Prime members overshadowed the Serpent and myself in height, but I refused to let intimidation shake my resolve as I kept my disruptor trained on the young curly haired clan member wearing a beige shirt and matching pants.

Sensing the commotion, the Enforcer crept back to the walkway, staying low until he could analyze the situation. As he noticed the standoff, his hand tensed on his Phantom, and he clenched his teeth while trying to devise a solution.

Pythagoras' hands gripped the Cress with rigid precision. Meanwhile, I appeared to be a novice, ready to misfire the weapon in my hands should someone sneeze. The Serpent too stood resolute, unmovable. I didn't know what to do or what was taking the Enforcer so long. While my thoughts ran rampant, the clink of metal object dropping from Tunnel's hand to the floor proved to be a distraction.

The Enforcer immediately recognized the small orb as a modern flash-bang grenade capable of blinding anyone caught unaware. "Optic Pulse!" He yelled as he jumped and flipped over the railing, prompting Pythagoras to follow the direction of his voice.

I looked up to see the Enforcer twisting his body in the air, spinning to face the Serpent and Pythagoras. He fired two rounds at Pythagoras who was quick to sidestep before the Enforcer could even land.

As the metal orb clattered across the floor, I was distracted by the translucent red ring lining its circumference, but it disappeared only to be replaced by a blue one along the opposite axis. A faint red light flashed, then a blue one, and then the orb exploded. A bright white light burned the last visual image onto my retinas. I staggered backward rubbing my eyes in panic. I could hear the ruckus just notches from me, but I was unable to see. I feared that my ignorance might have just cost me my eyesight.

Surprised by Tunnel's immunity to the optic pulse, the Enforcer spun about, landing a high spinning hook kick to Tunnel's neck. The Serpent easily shielded his eyes by way of his extra eyelids only with enough time to adjust and turn to face Pythagoras behind him. He prepared to fire, but Pythagoras had already launched one of his long legs into a fluid roundhouse which dislodged the weapons from the Serpent's hands.

The Serpent countered with a low spin kick which Pythagoras hopped over with ease. The Serpent pushed forward to catch Pythagoras with a strike to the throat, but the young, agile Mogul Prime member struck again, placing a devastating side kick into the Serpent's abdomen before the gap could be closed.

I felt a strong pair of hands grab my shoulders. I struggled to get away until I realized they weren't hostile but instead tried to usher me out of harm's way.

"I can't see," I mumbled.

"I know. It's only temporary," the Enforcer reassured me, "It's time to look past your sense of sight and find your way out of here." With a strong shove, he directed me toward the supply room exit.

An onset of emotions rushed me all at once. While feeling frustrated at my own battle incompetence, I also felt perplexed at the Enforcer's ability to maintain his penchant for paradoxical lectures. I stumbled as I tripped over my own feet in an effort to follow lastest orders, but an unexplained sense of dexterity activated as I raised my hand to catch the shelf in front of me. I could not explain how my reflexes prevented me from slamming my head into the shelf just before my face. The pain I felt coursing through my injured shoulder certainly compelled me to continue my way out of the building, but I felt conflicted, knowing that I shouldn't leave my allies alone.

I stepped forward again, using the shelf as a guide, but a flash of color in front of my eyes made me think that I bumped my head or somehow activated the Inteferic filter on my ikes. Hopeful that my eyesight had returned quicker than expected, I looked around for the icons on my display, but they were not showing up. I reached up to remove my ikes, but as I did I witnessed my surroundings still wafting about just as they had during my training at the Vanguard Warehouse, this time without the assistance of the Enforcer or my eyecons.

I spun about to observe my allies who were still fighting the late entrants. Both the Enforcer and the Serpent were easily identifiable by their light blue signatures whereas Pythagoras and Tunnel were set apart by their reddish tinge in addition to their noticeable height difference.

I didn't know how much help I would be, but I refused to simply spectate. "Get out of there!" I yelled as I snapped my Phantom around to the front and squeezed the trigger to unleash multiple plasma bursts in the direction of our enemies.

Everyone ducked, thinking that I was shooting blind, but it worked to our advantage. The Enforcer and the Serpent moved quickly, heading in my direction. The Enforcer tried to keep himself positioned in a way to usher me out the door first, but I was having none of it. As a parting blow, the Serpent struck Tunnel and ran down the row of shelves behind me.

Pythagoras stepped forward. I was unable to see the sneer on his face, but his energy signature sure deepened its hue near his mouth. I was intrigued by the shifting visual as I acclimated to such a new skill.

DAVE TODD

Not only was I seeing things differently, I felt an upswell in confidence as if my own energy level was no longer being sluggish to my own intended actions.

Tunnel advanced, his arms raised. I couldn't fully see his weapon, but based on the inert signature connected to his hands, I assumed it was his sledge hammer. My form shifted laterally as if by thinking it, even to my own surprise. As the hammer fell and missed, I responded with a side kick to Tunnel's chest with force beyond explanation. Pythagoras cocked his head trying to hide his disbelief that my small frame could have mustered enough force to rival the muscular towers of himself or his ally.

Pythagoras quickly chambered his knee and glided across the floor with mind boggling precision as he thrust a nigh lethal side kick at my face. I felt a strange connection to all fibers and particles of my form allowing me to sense the attack as it was happening. My form shifted backward able to avoid the kick. In response, Pythagoras lifted one foot high overhead while his base foot was planted firmly on the floor still as a tree. Had I not started to apply the Enforcer's trait of remaining emotionless mid-fight I might have had to pick my jaw off the floor upon witnessing Pythagoras hold his leg in a perfect standing split.

Unwilling to give the flexible Mogul Prime foe time to gloat, I snapped a side kick of my own toward his chest, but the leg that he held overhead swung downward, blocking my kick with his knee. Pythagoras baited me into his trap which he used to return a flurry of his own kicks.

After narrowly evading Pythagoras' first two roundhouse kicks, I was quickly reminded that I was only seeing things differently and still physically rooted to reality. My vision started to blur with my normal sight returning, suggesting that operating in such an abnormal fashion was taking more of a toll on my body than expected. I forced myself to concentrate harder, knowing that if I didn't act soon, I would collapse.

I weaved my form under and around Pythagoras' unending series of front, side, hook and roundhouse kicks all in lightning fashion which he executed deftly without ever returning his foot to the floor. As my evasive rhythm waned, I spun my body around hoping to add some defense to my routine. I clenched both of my hands into fists, and snapped a double forearm block at Pythagoras' kick which accelerated toward my head. I thought I heard the crack of bone, but uncertain as to who's bone, I decided to step back.

As the Enforcer and Serpent reached the exit door, they turned around realizing that I hadn't followed them. Both activated their ikes and triggered the zoom to witness the fight still underway. While the

Serpent marveled at the fluidity of the kick and evasion dance transpiring, the Enforcer's concern ramped up upon witnessing my tracer flicker without the proper stamina to persist.

As Pythagoras finally set his bruised leg down, I twisted around again, driving an open palm into Pythagoras' chest. Once my hand connected, I immediately snapped it away, transferring energy like a shockwave. Pythagoras stumbled backward, but the technique lacked the power I anticipated. He simply glared at me in defiance.

While scrambling to recover, Tunnel snatched the fallen Cress rifle on the floor. He barely grasped the weapon before it sailed through the air, toward Pythagoras' hands.

"Fox, get out of there!" the Enforcer yelled from behind. Even though Mogul Prime's signatures were faint at a distance, he still recognized the cold metal form of the long barreled disruptor in Pythagoras' hands. As I motioned to exit, the Enforcer internalized concern that my signature was flickering like an erratic glowing signpost. If I took a hit from the disruptor, the chance of fatality was high. In response, the Enforcer grabbed his Phantom 4.0 and fired a volley down the long row of shelves.

"Give him support," the Enforcer snapped at the Serpent.

I knew that my energy level was crashing since my muscles were starting to contract against my will. I was already turning to run as I heard Pythagoras prime the Cress. I had no way to evade the shot since my escape path was simply a linear aisle.

Opting to use any strength remaining, I leapt toward the book shelf and took several steps running against it. Before my adversary could adjust, I pressed off it and performed the same multi-step maneuver on the opposite shelf. With every force, especially gravity, working against me, I did my best to shove fatigue out of my head.

Thick yellow blasts sizzled past my ears from one direction while soft blue ones flew from the other as the Enforcer and Serpent exchanged fire to distract Pythagoras who was rapidly firing at me from behind. I continued my wall leaping zigzag pattern until my legs felt ready to give out. With the ever welcome exit door looming in size, I pushed ahead. Pythagoras' last shot nearly clipped my heels, so I pushed into an aerial cartwheel off the shelf. My legs collapsed under me. I would have fallen to the floor had the Enforcer and Serpent not caught me.

Pythagoras hesitated knowing that the Cress was marginally effective at such range. The Enforcer fired one last barrage of plasma rounds down the hallway of books until he heard the Phantom click, indicating that the power cell was dry.

At last, we rushed out of the supply room with the door slamming behind us. With labored effort, we made it back to the Fire Ant. Thankfully, support from allies helped me survive the hike despite the spongey feeling in my legs. Once the Fire Ant had departed at full speed, clear of immediate threats, I had no remaining recourse but to pass out.

Thread: sysObserver.cmd

With adversaries absent from premises, Pythagoras opted to exercise restraint and not pursue them, something that his associates might have done differently. As Pythagoras returned to the front of the supply room, Tunnel was already doing a quick survey of the damage. While damaged merchandise was certainly not going to look good on the slates, the scorched spots and wall damage proved minimal. If anything, the three unconscious forms on the floor would likely be the greatest embarrassment of the evening.

"Wake the fishes," Pythagoras snapped as he went to check other rooms of the Media Resource Center.

Pythagoras systematically checked the offices one by one. He was about to designate everything clear until he passed Voltaire's office and noticed that a terminal was still illuminated. He quickly entered his access code, only to receive an image of a hamster dancing in a grass skirt while singing a tropical tune common to the Quadrivast islands. Aggravated, Pythagoras pulled up a chair and pressed furiously on the tapper to invoke a security lockdown which only he and Voltaire had access to.

"Let's see how you like this, you little rodent," Pythagoras muttered as he sneered at the animation that mocked him.

In under three ticks, the Mogul Prime communication lines booted the intruder, preventing it from further accessing the clan's datatank. Pythagoras did his best to run a trace, but the invader managed to bounce the signal all over the Hyper Lynx. Wasting no extra time on the futile endeavor, Pythagoras slammed one fist into the desk while fetching his sonair with the other hand. After activating the comm, he awaited a reply.

"What is it?" Voltaire asked in a disturbed fashion upon being interrupted before his meeting had concluded.

"I think you should get back here as soon as possible. There is something you need to see," Pythagoras replied.

"Tell me what it is. I don't have to translate formulas," Voltaire said.

"He was here," Pythagoras said under his breath.

"Who?" Voltaire asked, wondering just how clearly he needed to convey his impatience.

"Jenkins' target. I don't know what brought him here, but clearly the other two clans failed. Not only that, he made a mess and even managed to bypass our security protocols on the archive," Pythagoras replied.

"I'll be right there," Voltaire mumbled as he shut down his sonair. Even though he was furious with the haps, he kept his cool in Oszwick's presence.

"I apologize for cutting this short, Mr. Oszwick, but a situation requires our attention," Voltaire said, forcing as gracious a mask as he could to hide his irritation.

"Of course, Mr. Sargent, men in our position are never without an abundance of obstacles. Should you care to follow-up tomorrow, I have some matters I would like to discuss in relation to the Synergon system, as mentioned," Oszwick replied never once indicating annoyance with the premature end of the tour.

"That is acceptable, Mr. Oszwick. I thank you for your hospitality," Voltaire said curtly.

After a stiff handshake, Voltaire nodded to Tycoon and Hauteur and proceeded toward the exit. Voltaire walked in silence pondering the significance of this target who had so inconveniently inserted himself into affairs larger than that of clan scuffles. It had been many passes since Mogul Prime had found a challenge worthy of its efforts. It was time to see if this Enforcer could prove to be a dangerous adversary or a powerful ally. Voltaire set his mind on learning more about this individual.

DAVE TODD

15 – The Grid – 15

Gridloc: Wayward Plane
Thread: frmChsnAnlys.rvw

The Adjuvant's boots rattled the heavy grating of the platform atop the tallest building in the region, but the sound effects were lost in the high winds. With the premises vacated, he was free to observe structural fallout unhindered. He took a moment to walk the edge of the building, observing that response teams still operated below and would be busy for quite some time, resolving the structural damage of the conflict. As a precaution, the Adjuvant activated the mag locks in his boots to ensure that gravity and faulty reflexes wouldn't get the best of him.

Turning in place, the Adjuvant got the widest view possible of the tower pair once used as the focal point of the latest insurgence. One of the white towers was still unscathed, but the other was fractured and had collapsed onto the rooftop platform. Beyond singe marks at the point of damage, nothing about the structure appeared unusual. The Adjuvant scanned the platform where the tower made contact. Unlike other operations, he detected dried blood on the surface of the platform. The analysis of the sample confirmed his suspicions.

The Adjuvant took a moment to observe the sky, foreboding as always. Permutations suggested that a storm had been active at the time of the event, but, deep within, the Adjuvant knew that the overcast sky would continue to fester given the outcome in its current state.

"The carrier has been obliterated," the Adjuvant said after activating the comm.

"Yes, trace elements confirmed. Residual impact on the Vast suggests irregular wavelengths. I don't forsee a resolution to this matter without a rage event. Everything hinges on this branchmark since we can't shift it any further," the Adjuvant replied in response to the presented question.

The Adjuvant clasped his armored upper limbs behind his back. The still black set of armor could have passed for a statue if not for the light blue visor adding the only available color to its form. The number of calculations that he needed to process was great, and he couldn't afford to rush judgement on his next actions on account of conflicting sentiments.

"The dilemma with the present sequence is that the necessary actuators run counter intuitive to all installed addons. It appears that even the slightest leak initiates a cascade failure," the Adjuvant remarked.

"A reversal? Yes, that is an option. Naturally, I was running all sequences without that possibility first," the Adjuvant said flatly, understanding the gravity of the proposed suggestion.

"You once asked me what it would be like to survey the premises of a terminal event. Until now I hadn't given it much thought. Given our understanding of the larger picture, it is difficult to attach any resources to the temporal fallout, especially given the scope of work required to assure its actualization. However, as suggested, there's a certain... weight... that it adds to one's perspective. So, yes, you may have been correct in suggesting the equal distribution of such a burden," the Adjuvant replied solemnly.

Disinterested in dwelling on the heavy matters attached to his role, the Adjuvant opted for a change of position. He walked toward the rooftop door at the base of the platform. From that vantage point, he envisioned what might transpire as individuals witnessed the towers for the first time upon reaching the rooftop.

"These meddlers are persistent, aren't they?" the Adjuvant asked as he contemplated the scope of the operation.

"That's true. This wouldn't be possible without the template provided. This all boils down to sequence integrity. I have slated a list of addons activated within this sequence. Feel free to review and add any proposed alterations. We have to get this one right," the Adjuvant replied.

After a parting glance at the blood stained platform, the Adjuvant closed the comm. Upon successful completion of his analysis he began to map his next destination. His work had only just begun.

Vanguard Warehouse
Abandoned Sector, Windstonne Enclave
Commercial Empire, Northam Continent
Thread: actTgtPersp1.view

Cool air and an unusual stillness played with my senses as I rolled over on my cot. Muscle soreness made the maneuver more laborious than expected. Upon realizing that I was back in the warehouse, I contemplated if I had either taken hits to my skull and impaired my short term memory or if I was so exhausted that I didn't wake up upon arriving at the warehouse. *So much for not walking in my sleep,* I thought to myself.

After a sluggish startup sequence, I shuffled off for a warm shower and fresh change of clothes. Finally feeling almost human again, I paused on the training floor and decided to stretch to loosen up my stiff form. Amid a quick injury check, I was surprised to find that my shoulder was healing much faster than expected, yet my arm was sure to remind me of the injury due to its throbbing when moved.

With my limbs as loose as they were going to get without a full recovery, I ambled off to the galley. I located a cold can of Archer Cola and a brown speckled fruit that I didn't recognize. With my late breakfast in hand, I passed the op table where Maxwell's eyes were glued to the noptic screen per usual.

"Busy night?" Maxwell asked.

"You could say that," I sighed. "How did it look on your end?"

"Brutal," Maxwell grimaced.

"I can imagine," I shrugged. Part of me would have preferred the role of spectator, but conversely I couldn't comprehend having to watch the action without being able to help.

I bit into the brown speckled fruit while watching Maxwell work. He shot me an awkward look as I absent-mindedly made a mess of the fruit on my shirt. I went for another bite, but a muffled metallic echo distracted me from my target. I held my breath and waited for a few ticks, hearing nothing until a series of similar sounds started up again.

"What is that?" I asked.

The hamster shrugged his shoulders, listening for the bizarre sound as well. He checked the security sensors and found no disturbances, so he exhibited no cause for alarm. "Alex hangs out on the roof. Might want to make sure he's okay."

"I'll do that," I remarked, having no better explanation for the anomaly.

I traversed the training floor and adjacent metal airbridge until I reached the utility elevator. I poked the up arrow, and the platform started its ascent after the gears churned to life. I could still hear the intermittent pounding even above the elevator's grinding track wheels. At last, the overhead hatch parted ways and I lifted a hand to cover my unshielded eyes from the bright midday sun. I hadn't considered just how dependent I had become on using my ikes.

A quick look around the rooftop revealed the greenhouse that Mac had mentioned previously and its plants growing within. Other than a rooftop access enclosure, some climate control apparatus and a water tower, I didn't spot anything of note. The fresh air made me want to spend more time taking in the elevated view of the surroundings, but the increased volume of the dull metal impact continued, nagging me until I found its source.

After passing the greenhouse, I cleared the elevator enclosure and noticed an elaborate painting on the opposite side of the bricks, but the repeated impacts kept me focused on my mission. Just past the enclosure, I found Alex sporting his black tank top and green scaly pants as he squared off against a circular exhaust vent.

Alex paid little attention to my presence and kept his focus fixed on his target. With slow methodical precision he struck the exhaust vent with the outside of his wrist or the space between his thumb and index fingers. After several ticks, he retracted his arm and struck again.

"What are you doing?" I asked hoping to time my question between strikes.

Alex turned to look at me without expression. His eyes narrowed as he looked down at the can of cola in my hand. Sensing that he might be due for a beverage break, I tossed him the can. He caught the can, but snatched the container with such a fast vice-like grip that I thought he might have missed. Instead, his grip only continued to tighten as I continued to observe. Alex's strength continued with pressure increasing until the can exploded, sending its dark carbonated contents into the air. I was impressed at his strength to not only crush the can with one hand but also prevent his hand from getting sliced up in the process. With a mildly amused smirk, Alex dropped the shredded can and its cola drippings on the roof.

"I guess they don't call you the Serpent for nothing," I remarked at the obvious strength in his snake-like ayvek.

"It is true that one's name foreshadows his behavior," Alex said calmly.

"I suppose that's true," I replied, pondering if I could think of anyone matched the claim.

"You, yourself, go by Fox. If their is any meaning in your name, it would imply there may be in someway an elusive or crafty nature, like the way you surprised us with your unexpected defense tactics last night." Alex said.

"What do you mean?" I asked, not thinking of anything remarkable about trying to leverage Mac's instructions for once.

"I trained across the Maleezhun domain for many passes, but never have I seen techniques like those you demonstrated," Alex continued.

I squinted at Alex, not fully understanding the significance of anything that I did to mitigate actual threats the night prior.

"Your body seemed to shift at will. Those Mogul Prime vectors struggled to even touch you. How did you do it?" Alex asked.

"I don't know. Mac is the tactician. I was just trying to apply some of his lessons, to keep us out of the ground," I shrugged.

"I have heard of many techniques that require great mastery, but until recently I could never verify anything but rumor. I have yet to learn how one can master such control over the body. Without even the slightest idea of where to begin, I have doubts of ever achieving such mastery," Alex said.

"A lack of understanding certainly doesn't inhibit one's potential from acquiring those skills," I replied, hoping to offer some optimism, despite my inability to teach on a subject at which I was inept.

"True, but I have observed that all have different potentials. While many are given similar opportunity, some have great potential to squander, yet others fully master the limited resources at their disposal. One can learn in clicks what another studies for passes," Alex replied reluctantly.

"Well, I guess if there is something elusive about me it's latent understanding of finer ayveks, just like my past. It would seem that I can never catch up to mine, while you never seem to escape yours," I remarked to see if Alex had any interest in discussing his history with one of the Monks.

Alex leaned against the partial wall surrounding the warehouse roof and stared quietly at the broad horizon of urban decay. I did the same, looking out toward the structures poking upward to create a jagged line against the midday sky. I felt that I didn't know my new ally well enough to know if I broached a difficult subject, or if he was simply engaged in thoughtful consideration after passes of strict conditioning.

"In some cases, having no past might be a blessing," Alex said. "As much as we'd like to treat the past as a pristine learning experience, some aspects prove challenging to resolve, like betrayal."

I appreciated Alex's offer to expound, but I decided not to press. Based on the tension from his fight with Snake, I suspected that it was truly a deep offense that wouldn't be resolved with words alone.

"At least we know he's human if he still has some baggage to lug around," Lennox said as he appeared on the scene with Maxwell perched on his shoulder.

"And that's why I travel light," Maxwell quipped as Lennox set him on the wall.

I smirked, sensing Lennox's ability inject some brevity into the conversation. Even though his behavior was often brash, I could tell that he was quite capable of reading situations.

"Since I seemed to have misplaced my luggage, care to show off some travel stickers," I chuckled.

"Nothing to see in mine other some splinters and bone chips. I don't spend much time over thinking things like the lot of you," Lennox chuckled. "I just fight for what's right and pick up the pieces afterward."

"Sounds like an easy read, unlike Mac. Being part of the Monks was certainly a surprise. Since you've known him the longest, what's your take?" I asked, hoping to have some light shed on the mystery behind our leader's quirks.

"I'm not so sure that I can back that up," Lennox replied before taking a lengthy pause. "I thought I knew him. Mac was involved with the Monks before forming Vanguard, but even after falling out with the clan, Mac used to be more carefree. Sure, Vanguard had its struggles, but Mac always seemed to roll with the punches. Even when his family was taken in the Smart Wars, I was surprised to see that he was driven more than ever to stay in the fight so that others wouldn't experience the same loss. He started looking for more resources, answers, allies all in places foreign to me. I didn't think anything of it at the time, but at one point something changed. It was as if he witnessed something that alters you at your core. He was the same Mac, but it was like a switch flipped that came with a renewed determination... and distance," Lennox said.

I wasn't sure how to process Lennox's recount of vague events, but his assessment certainly aligned with my observation of Mac. Of all of us, he was the least likely to engage on a personal level. Lennox's description even matched the Merricks' when it came to Mac Conner. I found myself at a disadvantage trying to comprehend what would compel someone to fight for others at all costs.

With our conversation running dry of musings about the past, it was a welcome calm after the flurry of events over the last day. It still felt surreal for me to accept that my surroundings and company were so radically different than what I had grown accustomed to at the Dwelling Street Mission, but I was surprised in admitting to myself that for the first time in my short memory, I felt like I was at home.

With the opportunity to survey the Vanguard premises, I found myself distracted by the dilapidated structure across the street. On the near side of the overpass was a parking structure and next to it a twenty deck office building with nearly of a quarter of its upper floors caved in. I looked into the distance and noticed that none of the empty factories had seen such damage negating any possibility of damage during the Global War unless it had been an isolated attack.

"What happened over there? None of the neighboring buildings were affected, so that's unusual for wartime damage," I asked.

"Hamster didn't calibrate the food nuker correctly," Lennox replied flatly.

I looked down at Maxwell who simply shrugged, adding no defense to the remark at his expense. While waiting for the non-existent clarification, I suspected an inside joke that I was not yet privy to.

"That's code for weapon malfunction," Alex rasped.

"Ah, well the next time you decide to zap a spicy nib prefab, make sure I'm out of your line of sight," I replied, rolling my eyes.

"No promises," Maxwell said with a devious grin.

"Somehow, I find your sense of humor twisted," I said.

"I still find myself entertained," Maxwell chided.

"Low bar," Alex quipped as he unfolded the top of a partial depleted Mesquite-Os bag.

"Oh, a height joke," Maxwell replied with fierce indignation. "That's it. I'm going to-"

Before he could complete his sentence, Alex rustled the bag and held it in front of the hamster who then removed a chip from the bag.

"... I'm going to let this slide," Maxwell stewed as he munched on the chip between his paws.

The bipolar antics produced a round of laughs as Maxwell and Alex both enjoyed their crunchy snack.

"Back to the subject of structural integrity, are you lightweights done beating on the cooling system? I'd prefer not to have extra repairs added to the docket for the day," Lennox quipped.

"That's why I'm here, rescuing machinery in distress by way of distracting discussion," I smirked, hoping to buffer any defense of Alex's unusual training methods.

"Good, just don't try that in the field where pipes tend to hit back," Lennox smirked.

"Speaking of repairs, I'd better get back to work too. Streetz needs a fixin'," Maxwell added.

"Best get to it. Otherwise, I'm sure he'll blame me. No tweakin' his memory this time," Lennox said as he scooped up Maxwell and plopped him back on his shoulder.

"I'm not making any promises there either," Maxwell laughed.

"Then, I hope you like taking the stairs," Lennox remarked as he departed to return to his duties.

With my attention back on the center of the roof, I had a better view of the mural which covered the brick enclosure, "Did you do all that?"

Alex nodded.

"The distinct line between sky and land makes for a great contrast between opposing forces, and I think the upward flowing patterns show a powerful ambition," I said after a few moments of trying to guess at the symbolism behind his artwork.

"It's a picture of a forest," Alex replied with a straight face.

I thought I caught Alex trying to suppress a smirk. I questioned whether I would fully understand his wit, but clearly he loved testing people's reactions when his words contrasted their expectations. Even if his painting was devoid of symbolism, I suspected that he just wanted to take a jab at my ill-placed philosophical banter.

"Yeah,... I can see that too," I chuckled.

"What about those?" I asked while pointing to multiple short objects with legs across the bottom of the mural.

"I like to call it... stuff!" Alex replied.

Accepting that there was no drawing out any substantive depth about the painting, I continued to stare at the colorful details. In so doing, that familiar sound passed through my brain, thankfully without a headache, but at that time a whisper flowed with the grace of a soft breeze even though it still retained the force of speeding truck. *If the whole body was an eye, how would one hear?*

I refrained from looking around since I was starting to accept that the phenomenon floating through my skull was inaudible to anyone else in my presence. Questioning my own sanity was caution enough to put others on the trail of voices passing between my ears, but I considered that it was time for me to start leveraging the intel. Surprisingly, given the recent conversation shedding light on our the unique composition of Vanguard, I found it to have timely context given Alex's recent doubts of his own skills. I might not have been able to explain combat skills, but I could at least offer encouragement.

"I was just thinking, Alex, even though we all have different potentials, I think those variations define us as individuals. The different strengths that make us who we are make us integral parts of a team, excelling where we are strong and compensating where we are not. I don't fully comprehend the abilities you posses. I'm quite confident that I could never replicate your dexterity with blade or brush, but I can say without a doubt that I would never want to see Vanguard operate without the strength and personality that you contribute," I said.

"Spoken like a true leader, Mr. Fox," Alex replied.

"Eh, just trying to emulate the best," I shrugged.

"Would you care to have a go at the port?" Alex asked, slugging my arm as he walked back over to the helpless exhaust vent.

"Far be it from me to interfere while you settle your differences with the pipe," I laughed.

Alex accepted my recusal and resumed his commitment to the mastery of his ayvek.

Mogul Prime Media Resource Center
Core City Fringe, Windstonne Enclave
Commercial Empire, Northam Continent
Thread: sysObserver.cmd

The Media Resource Center was a buzz with conversation as the clan members swapped stories regarding the previous night's events while Voltaire made yet another sweep of the archive security logs. A lot of berry had gone into their security system, and it shouldn't have been so easily breached. Not only was it breached, but the datajackers had done so with minimal footprint. He opted to run another trace before regrouping with the others.

Id limped his way into the meeting room where the others were already waiting for Voltaire's take on the meeting at Oszwick Enterprises and his assessment of the latest incursion.

"I feel like a swallowed a carton of blowfish and chased them with a pin cushion," Id winced as he eased himself into a chair.

"Well let's see. You just soaked up enough low grade plasma to cook a steak in three ticks. How did you think it was going to feel? You were lucky they were gracious to not up the density," Tunnel said mockingly.

"You call it grace, I call it cowardice. I at least play by the rules," Id sneered as he jerked his thumb toward his chest.

The Mogul Prime members listening in simply rolled their eyes at Id's volatile mixture of egotism and ignorance. Remaining conversations waned as Voltaire finally joined the group and took his place at the head of the meeting table.

"Intriguing that they managed to best some of you, yet despite having opportunity, they made an exit without lifting a single book. If they came for information, then they make interesting adversaries," Voltaire remarked.

"I find nothing interesting in their behavior. Survival of the fittest never favors the merciful," Autochthon grumbled.

"True, but we must know our enemy nevertheless. I have no interest in relying on chance to overtake our enemy since we know neither the plan nor the identity," Voltaire replied. "Did any of you manage to get a good look at them?"

After a mild recount of the conversation with the one in the snakeskin apparel, Authothon, Id and Tunnel could only shake their heads. Pythagoras withheld his response until he had a moment to review profiles of Mogul Prime's clients, enemies and targets from the last few passes.

"I can't confirm, but I think the evasive one that I was fighting may have been the target from Frank Jenkins' op sheet," Pythagoras replied.

"Let's say we work with what we can confirm," Hauteur interjected before Voltaire could respond as she entered the meeting room with Bender close behind. She handed Voltaire a datapill to inspect.

Voltaire snapped the data device into the pillbox while Hauteur stood by for explanation. Still groggy, Bender opted to occupy a portion of wallspace to lean against at the back of the meeting room. As the data poured onto the noptic screen in the center of the table, blurry black and white images washed across the screen.

Periodically, Hauteur interrupted when pausing the visual content, "I was able to recover these from the limited memory cell connected to Dennis' ocular implant. Unfortunately, there were only a couple of solid images to work with, but I added clarity where I could from any receiver that I could find in the packing area."

"Wow, Dennis, how do you get through the day while peering through that thing?" Id asked while placing a hand over one eye, oblivious to his poor attempts to simulate Bender's daily experience.

Bender held his tongue while everyone watched the datastream. His colleagues were well aware of his past including the machinery accident on the job which cost him a good eye and part of his skull. While his physical maladies were inconvenient, they were a steady reminder that every clan member was subject to the very ideals which they used to profit on the public's naiveté. He was an easy foil of the group considering he still loved strong liquids. However, he had no interest in acting defensively but instead chose to stew on retaliation against the intruders that made a fool of Mogul Prime.

"Moot point, Sig. Not to mention, it looks like Dexter was right about the target," Tycoon replied as he watched the fuzzy images of the supply room as they were slowed down. Images from Bender's implant had focused on spatial anomalies until an outlined human form took shape. The intruders might not have been detected at all had it not been for Bender's implant.

"I think we deserve an explanation, Dean. We all decided on undercutting Jenkins at the risk of scuttling our contracts purely on the scheduling conflict with a wealthy entrepreneur. While you were doing that, the rest of us got to take on Jenkins' very thorn in the side when the other clans failed to complete the job. On top of that, they escaped untouched and made us look like a bag of fish in the process," Authochthon grumbled.

Voltaire eyed everyone of his colleagues in turn to see if they shared Authochthon's frustration. Even those who had partaken in the meeting had demonstrated great restraint in withholding questions about the direct interactions between Voltaire and Oszwick.

"It just so happens that Konrad Oszwick has a wide range of influence, from akcellerrants to advanced weapons platforms. He has already managed to ingratiate himself with Frank Jenkins and has assured me that our absence from last night's mission will be resolved. He also informed me that he has a series of modifications that will benefit Project Synergon and wished to consult with us. As for our intrusive friends, I do not know who they are, but I am starting to understand why Jenkins finds them so troublesome. I have mind to ask Mr. Oszwick if he has any knowledge of these individuals considering he is on his way to becoming a more reliable business partner than Jenkins," Voltaire stated as he popped the datapill out of its socket upon completion of the visual footage from Bender's implant.

All of the members of Mogul Prime sat in silence as they contemplated the quick shift in allegiance. While all were aware of Imperan benefits, not a single one had an affinity for the blundering faction leader.

"What is in the crate?" Tunnel asked, referring to the assets he carried back to the facility.

"Leverage. Mr. Oszwick granted us a trial supply of the Extend supplement from the advertisement. He suggested that if we distribute it with our regular materials, it will increase our business volume," Voltaire replied, his tone conveying that he was not yet convinced himself.

"Henry, Dennis, I know that you have your usual affairs to manage, but as for everyone else, I need you to make your way to the lab. Mr. Oszwick suggested urgency in implementing the Project Synergon modifications. He will be sending his assistant, Lucient, to deliver the schematics," Voltaire concluded.

Pythagoras' eyes narrowed at Voltaire's mention of Oszwick's assistant, but no one else detected his expression that revealed his suspicion. Pythagoras decided to keep his mistrust to himself until he had more to go on.

Oszwick Enterprises
Core City Fringe, Windstonne Enclave
Commercial Empire, Northam Continent
Thread: sysObserver.cmd

The guided trip back to Oszwick's office on the top floor of the facility was an unceremonious one. Voltaire felt tense after exercising a high measure of discipline to avoid staring at the ghastly, pale, limping, hunched or hobbling staff members of the facility which proved to be even more abundant in the daytime. He did his best to stifle an exhale once he finally reached the executive suite.

"Ah, Mr. Sargent. I'm pleased that your affairs didn't prove troubling enough to delay progress in our arrangement," Oszwick smiled, offering to shake Voltaire's hand. "I trust that you have everything under control."

"Everything's stable, minus a security breach and pack of intruders in the wind," Voltaire grunted before he even had a chance to think if he wanted to divulge such information to Oszwick.

"Any slate of familiar foes?" Oszwick asked with curiosity.

"Not that I am aware, although I do suspect that one of the intruders was the very target that Jenkins tasked us with intercepting during the joint clan operation. Since you have Jenkins' ear, I hope that you might be able to coax more intel out of him given how slippery of speech he is," Voltaire said.

"Can you describe this individual?" Oszwick asked, raising an eyebrow at Voltaire's description.

"I can do better. I can provide visuals," Voltaire replied as he handed Ozwick the datapill with the stream from Bender's ocular implant.

Oswick popped the datapill into a socket on his desk and reviewed the grainy datastream. Oswick studied the images closely, periodically reversing the display and magnifying possible points of interest. After a few taps, Oszwick even managed to clarify the blurry images that Hauteur had used to cross reference with Bender's implant. Amazed by the resources at Oswick's disposal, Voltaire looked on while the executive studied the data, but he was caught by surprise when Oszwick's nigh permanent smile faded into an eye twitch as he stared at the footage of the Enforcer before plasma rained down on the unsuspecting Mogul Prime members.

"To put things lightly, you say that Mr. Jenkins wanted this individual contained?" Oszwick asked as he paused the visuals profiling the intruder with the black cloak, sunglasses and blue camouflage bandanna.

"Yes, we overheard from the other clans that he goes by the Enforcer," Voltaire replied, intrigued at Ozwick's increasing interest in the matter.

"And he mentioned nothing of this one?" Oszwick asked, pointing to an individual on the floor with similar cloak and shades but varying in appearance only by the light brown hair tucked under a treadball cap. The other individual was captured exclusively by security receivers and had completely remained out of Bender's line of sight.

"Jenkins gave us no intel on him beyond his profile from the Dwelling Street Mission. At the time, it seemed that Jenkins could do nothing but let his paranoia overshadow the situation, hence why I was doubtful of the need to pursue such an operation with hostile intent," Voltaire remarked.

"And he revealed no motivation beyond that?" Ozwick asked.

"He claimed that he didn't like renegades running around the enclave. Like I said, he isn't exactly a trusting individual," Voltaire replied.

"Men do not achieve great power without making enemies along the way," Ozwick replied, halting his line of questioning.

"Do you know who this Enforcer is?" Voltaire asked.

Oszwick paused, choosing his words carefully. "My social connections tend to be rather limited engagements."

Voltaire easily noticed the executive's dodge, but instead of pressing the issue he opted to let his new associate do the talking, should he have any more tells that might indicate his true motives.

"Rumors suggest that there are insurgents in the vicinity who are part of an organization known as the Interlace, so I have seen his kind before. Individuals like him operate on ideals rather than the accumulation of resources or power, yet in so doing, they garner an even greater following than the likes of Jenkins could ever accomplish with all of the propaganda and berry of the Global Alliance combined. I think Frank Jenkins easily underestimates such individuals which of course is to our advantage, but enough of such matters, shall we continue our tour?" Oswick asked as his usual smile returned.

Voltaire reflected on Oszwick's insight. He no longer had any doubt that he was now neck deep in statecraft far beyond his expectation. He needed to keep his wits about him since it was only a matter of time until he discovered who would shank Mogul Prime first. While he assumed that it was mandatory that he maintain distance between friend and foe, he still wanted to know the secret ingredients these figures leveraged over the minds of the people.

Vanguard Warehouse
Abandoned Sector, Windstonne Enclave
Commercial Empire, Northam Continent
Thread: actTgtPersp1.view

Once I was back inside the warehouse, I thought that Alex had turned up the intensity of his training as the sounds of slamming metal intensified until I realized a different sound was reverbrating through open air of the warehouse itself. I strolled across the overhead airbridge and down the stairs until I found Lennox attempting to undo the damage to the Chromehound from the previous night's outing. I nearly had to cover my ears to offset the tenacity that Lennox was exacting on the dents from the side panels, but finally, he acknowledged my presence and gave the hammering a rest.

"All work and no play?" I asked.

"Gotta learn to love it, or live without it," Lennox remarked. "Maintenance is a full time gig around these parts."

"I guess it's a lifestyle that I haven't yet learned how to love. It feels like I still need some convincing," I grimaced as I extended my arm to rotate my sore shoulder.

"Just have to remember that firing cheap shots is more fun than taking them," Lennox smirked as he nodded at my shoulder. "Not to worry, you did surprisingly well given former expectations."

"Hopefully, I bring more good surprises than bad," I replied.

"Speaking of surprises, Mac said he left more training material for you," Lennox said eager to resume swinging the hammer instead of conversing.

"Oh, fun, where did danger tracker disappear to this time?" I asked.

"He didn't leave specifics, but it sure sounded like he discovered something urgent that he needed to relay to allies down in the Oceanic Outpost," Lennox replied.

"Oceanic Outpost?" I asked.

"You know, the southern islands, Oshan continent, opposite side of the world stuff," Lennox remarked, likely curious as to how oblivious I was to the rest of the world.

"Oh, right. The haps don't exactly cover them too often," I said, hoping that I did not sound like a total clod.

"For good reason. Some factions aren't in lockstep with the rest of the Global Alliance. Now, unless you want to contribute to the real efforts, best be letting me do my thing," Lennox concluded, clearly ready for me to be on my way.

"Mac's class of brain benders it is," I chuckled as I sauntered off, leaving Lennox to his repairs.

Oszwick Enterprises
Core City Fringe, Windstonne Enclave
Commercial Empire, Northam Continent
Thread: sysObserver.cmd

Voltaire found himself stunned at just how much investment Oszwick had placed into his weapons division. The first facility they entered nearly tripled Mogul Prime's Media Resource Center, but instead of books, countless shelves were lined with firearms as far as the eye could see. Voltaire picked up a long black sniper rifle known as the Hellings 20. He inspected it before returning it to its cradle on the shelf.

"How did you amass such a sizable inventory of weapons?" Voltaire asked with curiosity.

"My staff is well versed in all manner of negotiation. They have established a far reaching network from the east coast to the heart of Westcrest. With the exception of the most obstinate militias, we've accounted for most of the hardware in the Windstonne Enclave," Oszwick replied smugly.

"Somehow I think, you needed more than berry to acquire all of this," Voltaire remarked.

"It is true that we use the weapons at our disposal. Those on the opposite side of our deals negotiate unarmed because they don't realize the most powerful weapon of all, fear. It requires little effort to convince them of fear of punishment for violating Imperan regulation, or instill fear of weapons falling into the hands of their foes," Oszwick said.

"Certainly a sound strategy. I'm not sure if you're better equipped for a strong defense or offense," Voltaire mused.

"Opposition comes in all shapes and sizes. I find it best to be prepared for all of them," Oszwick replied.

"Does the Interlace qualify as one such threat?" Voltaire asked.

Oszwick stiffened, the infinite smile disappeared from his face again as he turned to Voltaire. Voltaire noted that the executive did not respond for a few ticks, only bolstering his curiosity as to the kind of nerve that it was to Oszwick.

"Think of the Interlace as a competitor in a manner of speaking. They are always at the forefront of efforts to undo our accomplishments. This company has existed in my family for generations. Sure, its name may have changed, but its purpose has not. We simply strive to give the masses what they seek. The Interlace continues to cite ethics complaints, and in so doing, given the finite count within the populace, continues to exacerbate the numbers game between us... and them," Oszwick said.

"Who typically has the upper hand?" Voltaire asked.

"Us, of course, but that doesn't change the troublesome nature caused when they attempt to unify our opposition. Fortunately, they are so few and far between that we seldom have anything to worry about. Ozwick Enterprises' leading strategy has been to sow division among their ranks, divisions which education platforms like those crafted by Mogul Prime have contributed to," Oszwick replied.

"I had no idea that we had been woven into such a large tapestry, Mr. Oszwick," Voltaire remarked, unsure if Oszwick was attempting to flatter or issue fact.

"Oh, but your contributions have been vast, Mr. Sargent, especially in factions where freedoms haven't continuously haunted the acceleration of progress. Because of your ideals, I think Mogul Prime can prove valuable in the removal of this nuisance Enforcer," Oszwick replied, finally beginning to shed his reservation about the topic at hand.

"Is he really that threatening?" Voltaire asked, still chipping away at the mystery surrounding Oszwick's motives.

"I have observed that those like him have a penchant for gathering like-minded individuals. If he has already bested clans tasked with his removal, I suspect that his influence may grow if unchecked. Frankly, I'm more concerned with the look-alike that seems to be tagging along for the ride," Oszwick said.

Voltaire held additional questions until Oszwick had shown him to the next stop on the tour, a mendstat facility with advanced recovery bays connected to all manner of intravenous tubing and chemical relay stations. The facility was far more lively than the dull weapons depot. It required little observation for Voltaire to make the connection between the facility and the life supporting work provided to his staff.

"I don't suppose this Enforcer has access to facilities like this to support cloning or replication of some fashion to cause this look alike you mention," Voltaire remarked.

"Cloning is a myth," Oszwick shrugged. "Imprints are far too complicated to ever replicate with accuracy, but that wouldn't stop me from encouraging industries to dump their funding into futile endeavors especially if Oszwick Enterprises can provide the necessary hardware to entertain such distractions," Oswick chuckled. "All of them are moot technologies when there are such greater resources accessible than this reality is capable of comprehending."

Voltaire was starting to ponder just what manner of informatic and social machinations that Oszwick Enterprises wasn't into.

"Do you consider yourself an arbiter of such resources?" Voltaire asked, still unable to parse Oszwick's evasive nature.

"Do you consider yourself a capable investor?" Oszwick responded with a question of his own, testing Voltaire's own sense of competence.

"I'd like to think so, when I see a deal worth pursuing," Voltaire replied instinctively.

Instead of answering the original question, Oszwick simply nodded but otherwise remained silent as he guided Voltaire back to his executive suite. The lengthy walk continued in silence which gave Voltaire an opportunity to peek out a skybridge window, giving him an adequate view of the unknown number of facilities spanning into the distance.

Upon reaching the suite, Oszwick instructed his primary attendant to hold all incoming pings. Then with the door closed securely behind them, Oszwick tapped a button on his desk to fire up the noptic screen in its center. The screen was flooded with an assortment of flat shapes traveling in many directions. Some of the shapes intersected each other, but they all moved at different speeds. As the shapes condensed and clustered around a central sphere-like center, they collectively took on a distinct lattice-like layer of sheets.

"What is that?" Voltaire asked, surprisingly mesmerized by the animation.

"The future," Oszwick smirked.

Vanguard Warehouse
Abandon Sector, Windstonne Enclave
Commercial Empire, Northam Continent
Thread: actTgtPersp1.view

Done with my social rounds, I could no longer procrastinate my next training session. I had no clue what Mac had in mind especially with his absence. I found Maxwell engrossed in operations related to repairing Streetz's damage from the fight. Once he had a break, Maxwell found the materials that Mac had left behind and spooled up the overhead projector.

"Roll it," I grumbled after finding a decent position to give me a reasonable view of the projection.

Maxwell complied before returning to his work. With my lesson activated, I watched a collage of shapes dancing around the floor until they rose to form unusual patterns at least five marks up. Many of the shapes were flat like sheets as they rotated in and out of view. Eventually, most sheets started to form parallel lines, some traveling opposite of each other, but some exceptions completely sliced through the otherwise orderly arranged pieces. As pieces began to settle and zoom out I realized they had a striking resemblance to a map or coordinate system.

"What is all that?" I asked under my breath.

"This is what you will learn to associate with a construct known as the Grid," Mac's voice replied.

I looked around, confused at the response. There was no comm sounding from Maxwell's terminal, so I suspected that the session was fully prerecorded.

"Everything that you have learned about reality thus far is still but a droplet in a vast ocean of information. The Grid represents an unknown number of realities much like the one in which you sit," Mac's voice continued.

"Great, more mind bending dimensional theory," I quipped.

"Unlike dimensions which are perceived to be boundaries or rule sets for components within reality, each of these realities has matching rule systems and physical constructs," Mac's voice continued.

I hesitated for a moment, the lesson was eerily predictive of my behavior, if it was truly disconnected from any live feed. I leaned back in my chair and folded my arms across my chest to see what happened next.

Finally, a projection of Mac appeared next to the floating spherical grid. Of course the projection was a matching likeness from Mac's everyday apparel down to the irregular blue and gray flickering of his irises.

"I took the liberty to prerecord this session in my absence due to its complex nature. I cannot answer all of your questions, but I felt it important to bring you up to speed on a topic which I'm sure will be unavoidable in the future. I had to make sure that you were ready. Most people struggle with one reality, let alone the concept of others that may intersect their lives on occasion," Mac's projection said.

Reluctant to admit my inability to argue the point, I leaned forward finally adding some engagement to the lesson, "So, what are these *alternate realities* you mention?"

"Just as our planet, its neighbors and a host of stars are all pieces of our paraverse, such is true of these realities within the Grid. While some prefer the fanciful term of parallel worlds, I find it to be unhelpful considering each reality has its own paraverse with cosmological bodies included. Even as lines can be parallel to each other, they can also be perpendicular or skewed making for an awkward misnomer. I understand them to be called vera, or veras individually, because they all travel in a unique direction and timeline relative to their inception despite any relationships with other vera within the Grid. Some intersect while others do not," Mac's projection elaborated.

"Intersect? Is it possible to travel to different vera?" I asked, surprisingly more intrigued than with my last session.

Mac's projection appeared to hesitate as if looking for a specific keyword in my query in order to know how to proceed. I squinted at my artificial instructor for the day, but it finally resumed.

"Technically, travel between vera is possible, but it is dangerous. Complications arise when vera unfamiliar with the Grid are exposed to the stark contrast of their existence. It should come as no surprise that this veras is one with virtually no knowledge of the Grid," Mac's voice said.

"Why is exposure a bad thing? Aren't there all kinds of folk who dedicate themselves to learning that kind of stuff," I asked.

"As I mentioned, vera have different timelines. Interaction with vera that are more mature could trigger devastating consequences on those unsuspecting, especially if they have already been lost to corruption or decay. For this reason, select agencies operate to minimize interference with vera not yet initiated," Mac's projection answered.

"What are other vera like?" I asked.

"Hard to say, some may be mind numbingly similar while others are so radically divergent it would boggle the mind. Some may share common histories only deviating upon the outcome of one catastrophic event in that veras' history. The same can be said of each veras' inhabitants," the projection replied.

I leaned back in my chair and rested my chin on one hand. It was a lot of information to take in, but Mac wouldn't have brought it up if it weren't somehow important. I stared at the floor until an insane thought raced through my mind.

"Timelines? You say they are different and have different directions. If that were true, couldn't they be treated like the transport rails. You could hop on one, go to the opposite direction until you reached a prior location on your own," I asked, unsure why I found it so fascinating.

"Time travel is a farce, do not waste your time," Mac's projection replied with a surprisingly quick response time.

"Why not? I mean, I see so many meca's that refer it," I replied, unsure if it was a good idea to bring mediacasting obsessions into the discussion.

"All of them, distractions," Mac's projection replied as it placed a palm to its forehead as if it had known the question was coming. It finally sighed, suggesting that the counter explanation was irrelevant at the present time. "However, a great deal can be learned from observing both similarities and differences of such abstract cultures."

"Such as?" I asked, frustrated at the projection's ability to mimic Mac's dry sense of humor.

"Given the similarities in some vera, they might act as a prediction to the events in another. They make for very competent pattern models. A cap of foresight, if you will," the project answered.

"Right, I might have been more convinced on the subject of time travel?" I replied sarcastically.

"That is surprising, considering the Criterion even recounts a host of behavioral models. While they do not supply specific context, they are highly accurate in yielding behaviorally driven cause and effect patterns, especially in the Interferic spectrum," Mac's projection answered.

I was starting to the find the efficiency in the projection's response times rather concerning. I looked around the room again just to make sure that Mac wasn't observing from a corner just to test me.

"Even with the most advanced tech imaginable the Global Alliance still can't predict the weather," I replied.

"We have a natural tendency to interpret reality with limited information. If you were to create something, you would know its behavior, but since we operate in a world that we did not create, we live with extremely high error rates. The only remedy is to integrate information from external observers or the creators of the system itself. If you have a solid understanding of behavioral patterns, the nature of a thing, you can anticipate what it will do next," the projection replied.

I squinted at the projection, wearing my doubts on my face. "If it is possible to predict, how about anticipating..." I started to say.

"What someone says," Mac's projection said cutting me off.

I stared at the projection for a moment before walking to my room to fetch my ikes. Setting them on my face, I activated them and sure enough, I could not locate Mac's position. I even made sure there was no open comm sending out the conversation that I was having with the virtual instructor. Frustrated, I sat back down to craft a method to trick the projection.

"Okay, Mr. Projector, what did I..." I said partially.

"... have for breakfast. Likely, the last pear in the chiller," the projection replied with certainty.

Unsure if I was impressed or disgruntled, I looked over at Maxwell to see if he was orchestrating the charade. Curious himself, the hamster simply looked at me with a blank face and shrugged, indicating that he had no idea what was happening, despite taking an interest in the game that Mac left behind.

"How else can you explain this simple projection answering your very question," the projection said, unable to refrain from plastering a smirk on Mac's projected face.

Stunned, I leaned back in my chair and scratched my head. I wasn't sure what I was supposed to do with this information about foreign realities and behavioral patterns, but knowing Mac, there was some significance. After all, I would have been turned into a pile of goo already had I not leveraged his combat training.

"Okay, let's say I that believe you. What exactly is the purpose of all this?" I asked.

"That you will know, when the *time* is right," Mac's projection replied with a simple smile before disappearing altogether along with the lesson material.

I had no doubt that Mac was the producer the lesson, because it certainly had his flair for leaving me with more questions than answers. It was just like my mentor to put me on some wild path of deep introspection and a fierce expectation to figure it out on my own. Frustrated, I learned that he had the ability to do so without even being in the same room.

16 – Matters of Mistrust – 16

Gridloc: Alterragraf
Thread: frmBndActvn.prb

Mac Conner suspiciously eyed the cobblestone road lined with rustic businesses fading into the distance. He felt like he stepped into a convincing temporal bubble if it weren't for the the noptic signs revealing the nature of said businesses. Most buildings were crafted of hewn timbers and slatted metal walls bearing architectural styles of ages past.

With little distinction in the shape and size of the businesses, Mac struggled to find his destination, but after detecting a bold sign with a drinking glass he knew that he was on the right path. He approached the broad wooden steps nearly tripping as a mount tethered to a log bent its long neck to peck at him. After regaining his footing, Mac stared at the Bellace, as he had heard them called. It looked the same as an ostrich. He didn't fully understand why some of the locals used them as mounts.

Returning to his objective, Mac entered Nobbler's Lodge and surveyed the interior. The lodge was quiet and suitable for a jovial meeting with friends as long as kingdom rivalries didn't break out. Tweentown was known for its neutrality in local conflicts, but that didn't stop the occasional hostility from escalating into a brawl.

Patrons were scattered about, each sitting around the big wooden tables and attached benches. Near the entrance were a couple of Paladins, likely the owners of the Bellace out-front. Mac recognized them for their shiny armor reminiscent of battles in past Uniod eras. At last, Mac spotted his elderly friend at the far side of the lodge, casually observing the room while a wooden cup of leaf darwa emitted steam before his hands.

Mac smiled as he approached, "Hychron, it is good to see you again, my friend."

The weathered elder with stringy hair hanging toward his shoulders returned the smile and a crossarm as Mac reached the table. Hychron was about to respond but was cut short by the booming footsteps that jostled the floor boards.

"What have we here?" a deep voice asked.

Mac already knew the voice and moved to escape, but before he could flinch, a pair of massive arms clutched him in a squeeze that he thought would pop his eyeballs out of his skull. Mac gasped for air as he was lifted off the ground in a massive hug before he was set back down gently, followed by the hearty laughter of his captor.

"Ser Conner, it is good to see you," the massive form said as it took a seat next to Hychron.

"Bartok, a pleasure as always, but I suspect you'll be the end of me," Mac chuckled as he took a seat opposite his friends.

"Nonsense, a few more scars and no one will dare mess with you," Bartok said as his seven mark frame finally settled onto the bench. "Are you feeling okay, my friend? You have the frame of a skinned frizzard on a spit."

"I'm as fit as ever," Mac smirked. "Back home our contests certainly don't have the character celebrated here, constant culture war in the south and perpetual hardship in the north. My fellow populace would certainly look soft hanging around these parts."

"True of most foreigners. Unless they lookin' to start something," Bartok laughed. "What brings you to the town between the kingdoms?"

Before Mac could answer, a waitress brought a couple of chalices to the table, setting one in front of Bartok and the other in front of Mac. The shiny cup contained a thick neon green liquid that he doubted was fit for consumption given the bitter odor wafting from the rim. Bartok didn't hesitate to down a satisfying gulp from his own cup.

"My associate and I have been monitoring the weather for quite some time now. He has a unique read on a stormfront which he believes is going to hit far and wide. Not only our lands, but yours as well. Even the most remote of domains could be affected," Mac said as he slowly spun the chalice base in his hand.

"No matter the realm, I have yet to see a competent weather predictor," Hychron said, questioning the claim.

Mac finally downed a swig of the liquid, his senses clashed, causing a few abrasive coughs. The liquid was sweet to the tongue, but the gritty, abrasive texture caught Mac off guard. Bartok released a hearty laugh, never tiring of watching foreigners adapt to the drink common in his home kingdom.

After adjusting his breath and clearing his windpipe Mac managed to eek a few words, "I think his data comes from the Triad, if not, his retrieval mechanisms might. I've yet to find any flaw in his intel thus far."

Hychron raised an eyebrow, intrigued at the developing story.

"That'd be a mighty big storm to stretch across the vera," Bartok replied. "That could never happen unless our mutual enemies..."

"... joined forces," Mac interjected, finishing Bartok's sentence.

Hychron waited thoughtfully while taking a sip of his darwa.

Mac contemplated how much information he could share, but his thoughts were interrupted as a couple of armor clad mercenaries departing the lodge caught sight of the Paladins minding their own business. A couple of derogatory remarks were likely to instigate a fight with the warriors most noted for their reddish skin. Hychron cleared his throat, drawing the attention of the mercenaries. The mercenaries looked at Hychron then at Bartok who made it perfectly clear, just by his observation, that he would not tolerate a ruckus. The mercenaries quickly paid their tab and exited the lodge without incident.

"I don't know how you manage to evade a steady of diet of challenges while living so close to the battlefield," Mac remarked toward Hychron.

"Wisdom is greater than the weapons of war, my friend," Hychron said with a sideways smile.

Mac knew that Hychron's residence was within the boundaries of the Lesser Kingdom which was constantly in upheaval. No ruling body ever managed to hold power for long, yet despite the unrest and common turbulent lifestyle of the realm, Hychron always managed to remain an observer.

"I hope that is true because, by my understanding, the damage brought by an impending storm may only be countered by preparation and shelter initiated by those with a capacity to also read the weather," Mac said.

"Rather than focus on destruction not yet a reality, perhaps you should describe how you need us to help shelter those caught in the tempest," Bartok said as he shifted the large leather armor plate on his chest.

"I cannot divulge specifics, but it is imperative that we enhance the Bridgetower signal, like an early warning system. There is a plan in place to accomplish this, but we have discovered specific branchmarks that could disrupt the entire process. My understanding is that your domain is close to a junction, Bartok. An unsuspecting traveler like myself, might be ill-equipped to handle the elements. The best I can do is give you parameters pertaining to the time to intervene," Mac said.

Bartok rubbed his thick brown beard thoughtfully, "If it is simply a matter of extending Grek hospitality, I cannot decline such a request."

Mac nodded his appreciation.

"In what way can I assist?" Hychron asked.

"It is precisely your wisdom that I think can have the most impact," Mac said. "As we know, a ship is both guided and threatened by the same water it navigates. I doubt that I can properly impart such knowledge of hazards without your insights to help discern the difference. There are a host of topics that I know you favor that could shine a light on the way, especially in the realm of memory overlap."

Hychron raised an eyebrow, pleased to have an opportunity to potentially share his vast experience with an eager imprint. Few cared to interact with his immense knowledge in the Lesser Kingdom, often limiting his guests to those from beyond its borders.

Glad that his friends were so willing to help, Mac downed the remaining contents of his chalice.

"This isn't so bad once the taste is acquired. I might have to put a chemist friend of mine to work on this," Mac remarked.

"You are welcome in the Greater Kingdom to drink your fill anytime, my friend," Bartok replied.

"If only there were enough time," Mac replied glibly.

"Here's to purpose over pastime," Hychron said as he raised his cup to his friends.

With the pressing necessities resolved, Mac spent the remainder of his time with friends sharing stories of their radically diverse cultures until the lodge keeper halted business for the evening. Across all of his travels, Mac never knew what memories would have the most impact, so he took care to make every single one count.

Gorken Military Base
Commonwealth Bounds, Cydnon Enclave
Oceanic Outpost, Oshan Continent
Thread: sysObserver.cmd

Mac took one final glance at the Oceanic Outpost coastline before acknowledging the air traffic controller that gave him permission to land. With a steady hand on the control stick, Mac guided the Eagle toward the designated platform. After a couple taps on the instrument panel, the column of air elevating the Eagle began to recede until the plane smoothly touched down on the platform. He never tired of the feature added to the jet through modification since it completely negated the need for complicated runway landings. The trusty warbird could land anywhere a chopper could.

As the roar of the jet's engines waned, Mac popped the cockpit hatch and did his best to stretch his legs while an attendant rolled a ladder over to the side of the craft. Mac quickly disembarked and thanked the attendant despite a couple of odd stares upon seeing the new arrival wearing attire that did not resemble a military uniform.

As Mac neared the edge of the landing platform, he spotted a military escort standing near a rumbler. He easily recognized the square four-person mox employed by the military in conflicts long predating the Global War. One figure in a dark blue camouflage uniform and light blue beret stood motionless with two guards sporting the lighter typical Oceanic military threads with their EQ rifles on standby.

"Mac Conner?" the man with the darker uniform asked.

Mac nodded in response.

"Commander Thomas Jackal, Military Advisor to Potentate Ang. He sent me to escort you to the capitol building in northern Cydnon," Jackal said as he extended his hand.

"It's an honor, Commander," Mac said, using the handshake to size up his host who stood at six marks with a fit frame. The commander had reddish hair contrasting the color of beret, but his absence of expression behind his narrow glasses said everything that Mac needed to know about how seriously he treated his post.

Commander Jackal nodded toward the rumbler which Mac quickly approached, taking the passenger seat while the remaining guards piled in the back. After taking the wheel, Jackal drove the mox out of the military base and it was soon bouncing along the winding roads adjacent to the coastline. Mac once again appreciated Lennox's handiwork, considering that the military invested little to improve the suspension of the budget friendly transport.

With a breathtaking view of the faction capital and the inset coastline, Mac found it refreshing to take in the scenery upon clearing the military base walls. The Oceanic Outpost capital was easily rich in one feature that Windstonne lacked, color. Instead of continual clouds and tones of gray, the landscape was rich in greens to contrast the blue of the waters intermittently marked by vessels of the Oceanic Outpost's powerful fleet. Given the great volume of water between the Oceanic Outpost and its Global Alliance counterparts it was no wonder that it successfully kept the ideals of the other factions at bay. It was one of the last factions to maintain the people's freedom, and most factions resented the island faction for it.

After the better part of an arc, the rumbler reached the Oceanic Outpost's capitol complex. A large white wall passed into the distance, but within were an abundance of trees and statues lining a smoothly paved road. As the rumbler stopped at the entrance to a circular drive, Mac disembarked and took a moment to observe the large statue in the center surrounded by fountains. He easily recognized the figure as the present faction leader. Had there been any doubt, the nameplate with the inscription, Illustrious Potentate William "Boomer" Ang, certainly

DAVE TODD

would have verified the identity. Mac suppressed a smirk at the embellished title bestowed upon the faction leader for his accolades during the Global War.

Following his escort into the capitol building which was adorned with an abundance of columns and glass, Mac was guided down a marble floored hall before being stopped at a security checkpoint within. Jackal motioned for a security guard to check Mac for weapons. While Mac had no issue with the request, he found the guard's behavior odd as he tensed upon seeing the awkward metallic weapons that were concealed at Mac's waist.

Jackal was about to insist that Mac relinquish his weapons when he was stopped short by another commanding presence arriving at the checkpoint. The new arrival was thin in stature, his crisp attire consisting of a black shirt, navy suit and shiny shoulder decorations indicated that he was far from insignificant. As if surprised by the presence of authority so far from his office, Jackal stared as Potentate Ang approached, his dark wavy hair shifting only as much as his brisk stride would allow.

"Mr. Conner is a guest here. If he meant to harm anyone, I'm sure that he would have done so by now and without anyone's knowledge at that," William Ang said as he dismissed the security detail.

Jackal glared at Mac for a moment before finally conceding to his superior's request. His expression clearly indicated that he didn't like having his security protocols challenged.

"Good to see you again, Mac. It has been far too long," Potentate Ang said, extending his hand.

"Indeed it has," Mac replied, shaking the potentate's hand before following up with a cross arm.

While the security detail returned to their posts, Ang turned about for his return trip to the administrative levels of the capitol building. Mac and Jackal both followed along the course of hallways and elevators until they reached the executive office overlooking the courtyard. Within the office were a couple of individuals awaiting Ang's return.

"Mac, allow me to introduce my Public Affairs Advisor, Zared Marx," Ang pointed toward a friendly man with curly gray hair and a stiff black mustache.

"And my Research and Development Advisor, Talbot Newton," Ang said gesturing toward a man dressed in a white lab coat which matched his white hair minus a few stubborn streaks of black which managed to hold their color.

"I believe you have already met TJ. You'll have to pardon his lack of hospitality when he's on the gauge. He takes security very seriously," Ang concluded.

Mac glanced over his shoulder to see Jackal remaining expressionless despite keeping a watchful eye on the new arrival.

"Gentlemen, if you'll excuse us, Mr. Conner has traveled a great distance and we have an even greater deal of information to catchup on," Ang said.

Mac sensed the concern in the room as Newton and Marx attempted to analyze the importance of this strange guest and what Ang might consider so important about his counsel. Mac resisted the urge to activate his ikes and test their interferic readouts, but he didn't need high-tech scans to realize that they didn't trust him.

Jackal motioned to protest such a departure, but Ang quickly cut off his Military Advisor and sent a commanding look to the others, indicating that his request would not be questioned. Reluctantly, all members of the Advisory Council departed the office.

With his advisors finally out of the way, Ang opened the sliding glass doors which led to the balcony, motioning for Mac to follow. The longtime allies leaned against the railing and stared at the coastline as a cool breeze passed by. It was easy to see that the Cydnon enclave was full of energy, both organic and inorganic. From citizen and bird to mox and battleship, it was easy to see that governance played a large role in the region's vitality.

"You have sure done a lot to garner the support of the people, William," Mac remarked as he nodded toward the large statue in the courtyard.

"You and I both know who gets the credit for that," Ang replied as he and Mac both watched the city below.

"The Master Craftsman has certainly been a great contributor to your faction's success," Mac said.

"Absolutely. This wouldn't be possible without freedom. I continue to stress that wise decisions sow success not greed," Ang replied.

"Quite true. Just have to keep in mind that the greatest threat to freedom is itself," Mac added, reflecting on the dismal state of the Commercial Empire.

Ang nodded slowly, "Any state must work to earn its freedom, work harder to defend it and persevere above all to defend it from abuse. Those of us who choose to protect and embrace freedom are few in number. The factions have been robbed of leaders who put people over exploits. It has been my policy to befriend vectors rather than become one myself, but I suspect that policy may soon be in decline. That aside, you didn't travel this far to hear me prattle on about politics. What brings you this way, Mac?"

"Strangely, such sentiments coincide with my findings. I have suspicions of unspoken movements happening within the geopolitical arena, suspicions of a darkness ready to settle on the lands in the night, eager to cancel the dawn," Mac said quietly.

"What kind of darkness?" Ang asked.

"I still don't have clear evidence, but there has been a lot of effort to cut off any possible resistance that can take root within our region before conflict can arise. Recent events allowed me to compromise the datatank of a powerful clan in Windstonne. It would appear that they have great influence in mediacasting. Additionally, I found information suggesting that one of their associates is a member of your Advisory Council," Mac said.

"Who is it?" Ang asked, doubting that it could be any of the men he had come to trust after many passes.

"I was unable secure the identity. It was well protected, and my operative was booted from the system long before he could process any relevant datastacks. Hence why I found it necessary to speak with you in person without knowing who to trust via sonair," Mac replied.

"Everyone is connected these days. What is the significance of this clan?" Ang asked, resting his chin on his hand trying to imagine any behavior that might suggest a compromise within his council.

"I wouldn't have thought it important had it not been for this clan's potential involvement in a raid on a local mission which primarily housed Interlace members. Orders were given under the guise of finding me and my associates, but I suspect that it doubled as a cover for an attack on the Interlace itself," Mac said in a somber tone. "Combined with intel about unknown forces that are gathering all possible weaponry in the vicinity, I have reason to suspect that someone is preparing for an operation larger than a simple enclave blackout," Mac said.

"None of the western faction leaders have ever demonstrated the strategic capacity to make such a move. Why would Frank Jenkins risk rallying the people against his authority?" Ang asked, perplexed at the statement.

"I don't think Jenkins can maintain his power without excessive paranoia. If I'm on his short list, I can only imagine which faulty conclusions he might make in the process of lashing out against his enemies, real or imagined." Mac said.

"If subterfuge is as rampant as you suggest, we will have to tread carefully. The statutes binding the Global Alliance are murky at best. We don't need him spitting sparks next to some already dry powder kegs," Ang responded thoughtfully.

Executive Level, Casters Tower
Core City, Windstonne Enclave
Commercial Empire, Northam Continent
Thread: sysObserver.cmd

Frank Jenkins' face flushed red with anger, making his white hair and beard appear even more pale in contrast to the color of his face. Commander Donovan Pyln's failed attempts to secure communication with the three clans involved in the raid on the Dwelling Street Mission had finally revealed Jenkins' breaking point. Had anyone else been in the room, they might have detected the unlikely intimidation exhibited by the war hardened commander of the Imperan military forces. Command Pyln simply remained silent as Jenkins slammed his fist onto the surface of the desk repeatedly.

"Commander, I don't care what it takes, I want that mission reduced to a blackened crisp. Do you think your subordinates can accomplish such a trivial task?" Jenkins sneered in a cutting tone.

"Yes, Sir" Commander Pyln snapped in return while challenged to maintain his sense of formality.

Pyln turned about to exit the office and reached for the door handle when a soft knock interrupted his departure. A bald head peeked through the door and requested permission to enter.

"Am I interrupting anything, Mr. Jenkins?" Konrad Oszwick asked.

"No, Mr. Oszwick, please come in. I am merely trying to resolve a matter of incompetence. This is my first in command of our military forces, Donovan Pyln. I've had to resort to deploying our finest since the cost-friendly solution was a bust," Jenkins muttered.

"The legendary Donovan Pyln, you're quite the hero based on your reputation. You've done our faction a great service," Oszwick replied in an attempt to nullify the obvious tension in the room.

"Thank you, Sir," Pyln replied. Mostly disinterested in any manner of empty praise, Pyln found himself impressed that the new arrival didn't flinch upon seeing his abnormal facial features. Pyln had grown accustomed to the frequent stares anywhere he went on account of his large jaw and sharp, shiny teeth.

"That will be all, Commander," Jenkins replied, his temper clearly on the decline.

With a snap of his heels, Commander Pyln exited the office, leaving the faction leader and executive to conduct their affairs in private.

"So, what brings you by, Mr. Oszwick?" Jenkins asked, surprised that he was beginning to take the executive's assertive behavior in stride.

"I imagine that it would be proper to resolve the most pressing matters first. I would like to claim responsibility for Mogul Prime's absence in your recent operation. I requested their presence to discuss potential modifications in regard to you regarding Project Synergon, and I was unaware of their previous engagement," Oszwick said, knowing that his disclosure would likely initiate a firestorm.

Sure enough, Jenkins' eyes burned with fire as Oswick admitted not only to his meddling but the admission of knowledge regarding his personal project. "What business do you have meddling in my affairs, Mr. Oszwick?" Jenkins asked, maintaining his calm despite his inability to completely hide the rage festering within.

"I assure you, Mr. Jekins, you will be pleased to know that the information I have for your satellite project is of great benefit. Additionally, I may have intel of value regarding this Enforcer," Oszwick replied.

Jenkins' eyes narrowed at the mention of the nuisance who continuously reappeared, only to interfere with faction oversight, and then disappear until memory of his involvement waned. He was unnerved at Oszwick's ability to gather information so easily, but conversely he was intrigued at any opportunity to finally squash a nagging threat to his achievements. Oszwick passed Jenkins the datapill provided from Mogul Prime's encounter with the renegade before seating himself in one of the chairs facing Jenkins' desk.

Jenkins received the datapill with suspicion but finally placed it into the pillbox on his desk.

"It would seem that your target took initiative of his own and turned the tables on those you sent to resolve the situation," Oszwick said after Jenkins fully watched the datastream. "He even managed to compromise their datatank."

"Did he access anything on Project Synergon?" Jenkins asked, his irritation swiftly morphing into concern that his plans for the Global Alliance had been compromised.

Oszwick shook his head with a silent pause. "No, Mr. Sargent has assured me that all datastacks regarding said operations are stored securely on an isolated system. There was no breach."

Jenkins leaned back in his chair relieved that his hard work hadn't been undone. "How does he keep appearing and meddling at the most inopportune times? I want an end brought to this individual once and for all!"

Thread: sysObserver.cmd

Sath stared blankly at the noptic screen on her desk filled with the remainder of Frank Jenkins' appointments for the bench. She desperately wanted to complete her tasks and leave for the day before Jenkins decided to add more to the schedule. She was about to power down the terminal on her desk when a familiar face above a gray vest sauntered into the waiting room.

"Hello, Sath," Tycoon replied with his usual imploring smile.

"Hi, Henry," Sath mumbled, using her screen as a distraction to prevent looking him in the eye.

"Is Mr. Oszwick still here? I need to relay a message on behalf of Mr. Sargent," Tycoon said, struggling to hide his impatience.

Sath found it unusual that Tycoon wasn't present to flirt with her or speak with Jenkins. "Yes, but he is still in a meeting with Mr..."

Before Sath could finish her sentence Tycoon was already striding toward Jenkins' office. "Hey, you can't go in there," she stammered.

Disregarding the coordinator, Tycoon knocked on the door and proceeded into Frank Jenkins' office without an invitation. Before Sath could protest again, Tycoon had already disappeared into the office with the doors closing behind him.

Frank Jenkins' frustration almost returned at the sight of the Mogul Prime interruption. He already had to deal with incompetence, next it was non-stop interruptions. He contemplated the need for a Piran security detail directly outside his office.

"I am deeply sorry for the intrusion, Mr. Jenkins, Mr. Oszwick. Dean sent me with important news that could not wait. He attempted to reach Mr. Oszwick, but was unable to get through on his sonair," Tycoon said, hoping to placate any inevitable animosity.

"What is it, Henry?" Oszwick asked quickly before Jenkins' temper could flare up again.

"Mr. Sargent has heard from his contact in the Oceanic Outpost who happens to be embedded in Potentate Ang's Advisory Council. He has reported that the Enforcer has traveled down there to meet with Ang due to the urgency of his information. The Advisory Council was not briefed on the nature of the visit, but we have a hunch that it may be related to the breach when our shop was infiltrated," Tycoon said.

Both of the executives could tell that Tycoon was tense due to the potential backlash for his intrusion, but both were taken aback at the nature of the haps and easily dismissed the offense. Tycoon retained his professional demeanor and waited for either recipient to respond.

"Is there anything else, Henry?" Oszwick asked.

"No, Sir, Mr. Sargent just wanted you and Mr. Jenkins to be informed as soon as possible," Tycoon replied. Ultimately, his message was only intended for Oszwick, but he made sure to include Jenkins so as to not tip him off to the ever growing rift in their partnership.

"Thank you, Henry," Oszwick replied, dismissing the salesman.

As Tycoon departed, Frank Jenkins sat idly. pondering just how Konrad Oszwick had managed to evoke not only cooperation from Mogul Prime but also a mild command. The concept both intrigued and concerned Jenkins simultaneously. Jenkins ran his fingers through his previously neat hair which appeared disheveled, following excessive hand waving when he expressed his frustrations of having to deal with the Enforcer yet again. The persistent nuisance was truly grating on him.

"Now what?" Frank Jenkins asked as he stared blankly into the large fish tank on the far side of his office.

"Perhaps this event provides opportunity to initiate Project Synergon. If you were to call a meeting of Global Alliance leaders, you could demonstrate a trial run before this Enforcer is given time to rally more support for his cause," Oszwick said calmly.

Frank Jenkins was dismayed at the idea of his plans being accelerated simply by acting on the information of his adversary visiting another faction. "There hasn't been a meeting of the faction leaders in over eighteen lunars. I don't see any reason to be intimidated by this Enforcer on a large scale or jeopardize the security of this project," Jenkins said, hoping to dismiss his concern before an abrupt counter by Oszwick.

"If the Enforcer is indeed part of the Interlace, we will face added opposition which will naturally increase the cost of your campaign," Oszwick said, making sure to speak in a language that Jenkins understood.

"How can the Interlace be a threat if your Extend product lives up to everything that you suggest it can do?" Jenkins replied, deciding to test the executive.

"The Interlace is neither ignorant, nor without allies. Even I reserve caution for elements that can potentially disrupt my business. Ignorance is more becoming of fools than generals," Oszwick said emphatically, clearly pressing into Jenkins' blindspot. "The sooner we secure allies for Project Synergon, the sooner Extend's advantages can flourish and minimize any opportunity for someone to develop a countermeasure."

"We need the satellites at full capacity before I would dare take any chances with the Global Alliance," Jenkins replied.

"Mr. Jenkins, if you provide the authorization, I can have my assistant and crew complete the remaining modifications and have phase one complete before the faction leaders can finalize accommodations for the meeting," Oszwick said with confidence.

While Jenkins had concerns about the accelerated schedule, he certainly approved of an opportunity to cut costs. "Mr. Oszwick, you know how to deliver a sound bargain, and I appreciate your counsel. Let us make it so and further our experience in guiding this world in its quest to install proper leadership. It is time for us to discover those who would be allies and those would fall by standing against us. The Age of Unification begins today."

Vanguard Warehouse
Abandoned Sector, Windstonne Enclave
Commercial Empire, Northam Continent
Thread: actTgtPersp1.view

Upon completion of my latest training session, projected images faded into thin air leaving me with another opportunity to scratch my head and question their relevance. Unlike most prior sessions, I had to cope with any relevant thoughts on my own due to Mac's absence in delivering the typical dose of conceptual nonsense.

Before I could take my leave of the training floor, Maxwell waved a foreleg at me without taking his eyes off the noptic screen connected to the terminal. Normally, he was more animated, but whatever held his attention so closely had him mesmerized with intrigue.

"What is it?" I asked in a hushed tone as if I were sneaky predator capable of scaring off skittish intel.

Loads of text streamed across the screen almost at a dizzying pace. How the hamster parsed anything relevant was beyond my understanding, but eventually he pressed the tapper and applied filters to reduce the influx of information.

"I've run across several anonymous messages from an operative within a certain BOWTech Laboratories who is requesting protection from the designer of the Crossover Prevalent in exchange for intel on Imperan military exploits," Maxwell said, all while keeping his eyes locked on the screen.

"What's the significance? Possibly just a hustler looking for berry," I suggested as I finally sat down to view the messages for myself.

"The significance, first of all, is that protecting someone from the Commercial Empire is a rather hefty order. Secondly, Mac designed the prevalent. Since these messages originate several benches prior to our recent run-in with Imperan lackey's, I doubt potential connections with recent clan activity," Maxwell said.

"What exactly is the Crossover Prevalent?" I asked.

Maxwell finally looked away from the screen long enough for his expression to twist as if I had been skulljakt, at least until he recalled my detachment from world events, "the prevalent was a much needed solution for one of the Commercial Empire's most foul weapons ever. During early stages of wetware development, Imperan informatechs funded the creation of a polymorphic virus capable of traversing organic and digital pathways alike. In some rare cases it even mutated into an airborne strain. It was extremely messy and random, not to mention excessive even for the likes of Jenkins who lashed out at anything potentially threating his seat of power. The virus killed many in Northam, although many outbreaks were reported on other continents as well. It's still a mystery as to how Mac discovered the cure. Since he lacked the resources for mass production and distribution, he leveraged his connections in the Oceanic Outpost. Once the prevalent was widely circulated, the virus disappeared. Imperan propaganda claimed it was an experimental element designed to target datajackers, but of course, most suspect that was just the cover for yet another plot to target the Interlace."

"If this all happened several passes ago, why would this person begin a search now?" I asked.

"I don't know. Maybe someone is working on version two, perish the thought," Maxwell cringed.

"Any identification on the sender?" I asked.

"No, but I did find the initials KS craftily injected into a secondary layer at various intervals. Whoever this is individual is, the identity was to remain a secret," Maxwell replied.

"I agree," I mused.

"Agree on what?" Lennox asked as he ascended the stairs from the warehouse floor below.

"Somebody from BOWTech Laboratories is looking for Mac on account of his involvement with the Crossover Prevalent," I said.

"Got a name?" Lennox asked impatiently.

Both Maxwell and I shook our heads.

"Then it smells like a trap," Lennox replied curtly before disappearing into the galley.

"What if we were to anonymously liberate said individual and find out exactly what he or she is after?" I asked the hamster as I leaned in on the table.

"I heard that!" Lennox yelled from the galley.

"Well, what do you think Mac would do?" I asked.

"Ping him and ask him," Lennox snapped back.

I shrugged my shoulders and looked at Maxwell who attempted to activate Mac's sonair. We waited for the comm to open but received no response.

"No shreds," Maxwell said quietly.

"Then it looks like we sit tight until he gets back," Lennox said as he returned with a snack in hand.

"You mean sit around and do nothing?" I asked.

"Did he leave you in charge?" Lennox muttered sarcastically.

"No, but I'm just trying to figure what the best course would be if he were taking point," I replied.

"What do you say, Alex?" Lennox asked as the newest Vanguard member approached to join the debate.

Alex simply raised an eyebrow waiting for Lennox to elaborate. He was not one to suggest an accurate appraisal without first hearing the story. Miscalculations were always bad for battlefield business.

"You know. Anonymous crazy requests protection, offering information, no details. Does that sound like your type of mission?" Lennox quipped.

A comical smirk following a faint nod revealed Alex's affirmation, "A soldier always lives a life of servitude to defend others."

"You're no help," Lennox hissed in Alex's ear before knocking his shoulder as he walked downstairs.

"Looks like we better get to it," I said, glad that Vanguard wouldn't be sitting idle when help was needed.

Executive Level, Casters Tower
Core City, Windstonne Enclave
Commercial Empire, Northam Continent
Thread: sysObserver.cmd

Sath wished that she had finished her work prior to Tycoon's appearance because soon after his departure, Jenkins tasked Sath with a slough of new additions to his schedule. It was already two arcs past her normal checkout time, but if she didn't get the initial slate of items into the itinerary she would never hear the end of it. Frank Jenkins' decision to arrange a meeting with Global Alliance leaders would make for a complicated web of security and diplomatic relations. Thankfully, she could offload some of those tasks, but with the nature of faction leaders always being at odds, there was a considerable mess of bureaucracy to manage, not exactly Sath's favorite pastime.

Once her most critical entries were complete, Sath powered down her terminal before she could receive any more tasks. As she stepped back from her desk, she realized that Tycoon had failed to close Mr. Jenkins' door completely. She was surprised that even Mr. Jenkins hadn't noticed, considering that he was adamant about his privacy. Upon approaching the door, Sath realized that Mr. Jenkins and Mr. Oszwick were still discussing plans. She had been so engrossed in her work that she had forgotten about the executive from the akcellerant company.

"What if this Enforcer decides to show up at the meeting with one of his stealth gadgets?" Jenkins asked with an aggravated yet concerned tone.

"Allow my staff to do some research. I believe we should be able to find a suitable countermeasure for some of his gimmicks," Oszwick replied confidently.

Sath silently stepped away from the door hoping that her presence would remain undetected. The mention of Mac's clashtag from her employer's lips sent chills down her spine. She was fully aware that Mac chose only to reveal his identity to those he trusted, but if Frank Jenkins discovered it and was preparing to carry out some vendetta then she needed to warn him.

Sath understood the heavy burden that Mac carried in his responsibility to help others, a burden that she felt kept them separated, but the more she contemplated the situation, she started to realize that it was her ambition getting in the way. In the past, she had questioned Mac's potentially misguided priorities in their relationship, but she was finally understanding that there must have been a great deal of pain for

Mac to suppress the frustration over her employment for a man responsible for the deaths of millions including Mac's family.

Sath realized that it was time to make changes. Her doubts began to fester about the integrity of her boss. It was time for her to make amends not excuses for her employer. She could uphold the corruption no more. She knew that she risked her life if caught, but it was more important that justice be done.

Sath rushed to the stairwell and stopped at the floor below, locking herself in an unused office. She found the closest sonair and tapped in Mac's comm channel. After one failed attempt, she impatiently tried again only to receive the same lack of response. In desperation, she buried her face in her hands until she thought to try Mac at his warehouse.

After tapping in a new sequence, Sath waited. As the connection initiated, her hopes lifted, but they rose only so far upon seeing a different face on the screen. She struggled to put a name to the face.

"Hello, Sath," Lennox said as his face filled the noptic screen on the terminal.

"Uh, Hi, Lennox," Sath replied, hoping she had the right name per Mac's description of his mechanic with the spiky hair. She had never been formally introduced, but Lennox's name was the only one she could remember Mac speaking about at length in relation to their endeavors.

"Sorry, but Mac isn't here at the moment, he had urgent business to take care of," Lennox said.

"Is there any way that I can contact him? I fear that he is in danger," Sath replied, the concern quite evident in her voice.

"I wish that I could say that is out of the ordinary, but I'm afraid not, Sath. We haven't been able to contact him either. What is this about?" Lennox asked, hoping to reassure her in some way.

"I suspect that Jenkins may be aware of his location and might plan to kill him. I wanted to make that sure he is alright," Sath replied.

"He's out of the faction at the moment, so I don't think Jenkins can do anything in the immediate future. However, I can relay the warning once we hear from him," Lennox said.

"Thank you, Lennox, if there is anything that I can do to help, please let me know," Sath said.

"Actually, Sath, there may be. Have you heard of a company called BOWTech?" Lennox asked, changing subjects.

"BOWTech? Yes, that is one of Mr. Jenkins' military research firms," Sath replied, surprised at the question.

"That's just liquid," Lennox muttered sarcastically, "and do the initials KS mean anything?"

"The only name that I know from the company is their head informatech, Protech Szazs. I don't even know his first name. Sorry if I'm not much help there," Sath replied.

"Thanks, Sath, we'll keep in touch," Lennox replied.

Thread: actTgtPersp1.view

As the comm ended, Lennox flicked the power button on the noptic screen.

"What was that all about, shoving me out of the way like that?" I asked once Lennox was done with the conversation.

"The girl is in love with Mac and already concerned as it is. I'm sure she doesn't need the added emotional stress of an unknown look-alike hanging around," Lennox huffed as he departed from the op table.

"Whatever," I replied, suspecting the Lennox was still not on board with infiltrating BOWTech to rescue an anonymous informant. Leaving him be, Maxwell and I went to work plotting our strategy to investigate the facility and locate our mystery person.

17 – Ghosts of the Past – 17

Imperium Adminus
Commonwealth Prime, Cydnon Enclave
Oceanic Outpost, Oshan Continent
Thread: sysObserver.cmd

With the setting sun casting a blinding glare off the water, Potentate Ang and Mac opted to retreat indoors to continue their discussion of events, past and present. Ang opted to recount his career, how he reluctantly ascended the political ranks in the Commonwealth military. Although he was not of convincing physical stature due to his thin frame, his commitment to morality on the battlefield had certainly made him a hero among his countrymen. Some of the former Commonwealth's most iconic defensive victories were a result of Ang's strategies. Since he prioritized life over victory, he often clashed with his peers who deemed him reckless and ignorant, but after continued victories against seemingly impossible odds, Ang continued to succeed as a battlefield strategist with minimal loss of life.

Ang's powerful influence on the battlefield earned him the nickname, Boomerang due to his remarkable capacity to turn dire situations into surprisingly advantageous outcomes. Due to his adversity with the engagement strategies of the day, he found himself the subject of a court-martial on more than one occasion, but through his persistence his strategies eventually became the military standard. Ang considered every member of the country to be a luxury thus prompting him to always act around a core strategy, life is not expendable.

The Tricameral Endeavor and Uniod Bloc were but a couple nations to learn such a lesson the hard way as they continued to commit unsustainable numbers to campaigns during the Global War leaving themselves spread too thin to adequately defend themselves. While some nations rampantly surged any possible diplomatic means, others were leveraging brute force by way of kinetic strikes, devastating large swaths of land on multiple continents. The Uniod Block was often quick to dispatch aid where possible, but it couldn't outpace the rampant political hostility and terrorism which often turned even the most hopeful negotiations into a bloodbath.

Even with dark times perceived to be the norm, faint rays of hope still lingered. One fortification mission which had been deemed suicidal by the Uniod Block gave Ang the unexpected opportunity to begin his legacy when he managed to hold off a number of battalions from the combined might of Titangrad and the Red Wall. The hapcasts hailed Commander William Ang as the proponent of a great victory, but he and a few select others certainly remembered the events differently.

At the start of the Global War, the Commonwealth opted for neutrality, but in certain situations it deemed action necessary in the event of aiding allies due to bonds predating the onset of the war. As fleet commander, Ang had been tasked with participating in a defensive operation to support overwhelmed Uniod Bloc forces engaged with the Red Wall. Little did Commonwealth forces that know they were sailing into a trap.

Due to the heated engagement between Uniod and Red Wall forces on the ground, the Commonwealth fleet was instructed to bombard the coastline, granting time for Uniod forces to fortify their positions. Without proper intel, the Commonwealth navy was oblivious to the sizable mine field prepared by the forces of Titangrad from the north. The guided mines ripped holes through the entire batch of Capital class ships present in the engagement. While procedure dictated that Ang focus efforts on salvaging every craft possible, he immediately recognized the futility of such an exercise. Any who fought to repair damages would be escorted to a watery grave.

Even though the loss of vessels was great, the loss of manpower was virtually non-existent due to Commander Ang's strategic brilliance. All crews were ordered to flee and utilize recovery craft to reach the Red Wall coastline. Resentment simmered in the Commonwealth ranks for Ang's disregard of procedure, but there were no denials that his actions saved more lives than expected.

With the Commonwealth fleet assumed destroyed, the Red Wall and Titangrad forces advance to crush their Uniod foes, but by using the fleet's demise, Ang had created on opportunity for his forces to circle the Titangrad forces before landing. With provisions and armaments low, Ang knew that he only had one chance to drive a wedge into the opposition bearing down on Uniod forces.

The Commonwealth forces struck hard nearly obliterating a contingent of Titangrad forces before they retreated to regroup from the covert strike. Once the Titangrad forces were aware of their opposition, they had no choice but to discontinue their pressure against the Uniod forces, leaving them unable to complete what they started. Utilizing the gap between the opposing forces, the Commonwealth forces were able to establish a defensive perimeter for the Uniod forces.

The tactical delay was short lived as Titangrad forces returned, eager to crush Commonweath and Uniod forces in one strike. Already fatigued, Commonwealth forces struggled to hold the line. As Titangrad forces broke through the last defensive barrier, tired soldiers prepared for their final stand at close quarters, but to their surprise, the Titangrad behavior became more erratic and unorganized with some forces even firing in the direction of their own. Confused by the carnage, Commonwealth forces simply pulled back and watched.

As the noise faded and debris settled, an eerie calm overtook the battlefield. The smoke began to clear and a band of no more than twenty men emerged, approaching the Commonwealth forces. Many of them wore dark bodysuits and carried a variety of melee weapons and explosives, yet some bore armor pieces like the classic warriors of Sunland while others still bore colors associated with Tricameral Endeavor militias.

Perplexed at the new arrivals, Ang approached to get a better understanding, "I'm Commander William Ang of the Commonwealth fleet. Identify yourselves and your allegiance."

"It doesn't appear that you are in any position to make demands, Commander Ang," replied a voice, its owner bearing more decorative, armor including a helmet with outward angled plates and crescent pieces fastened to the forehead. The speaker removed his face shaped mask and extended his hand. "I am Captain Seechi, second in command of the Ghosts. We were on a joint search and rescue operation with our Tricameral allies when our intelligence reported Uniod forces in need of assistance. Hearing of opposition against Titangrad forces, we headed south to lend aid."

"We are in your debt, Captain. Unfortunately, we were grounded here due to the destruction of our fleet, courtesy of Titangrad mining operations. Your assistance has proven helpful, but barely left a dent, in contrast to the advancing Red Wall forces." Ang replied.

"Then we must hurry," Seechi replied as he nodded for his allies to move out.

"How can we strike effectively with such limited resources and position," Ang asked.

"We are masters of our art, Commander. Most battles are won through strength of mind, not body counts on the battlefield. Confuse your enemy, then let it self destruct," Seechi replied. "Foritfy your position with remaining Uniod forces and defend it until the proper time."

As Seechi's voice trailed off, he turned and walked away with the Ghosts and militia allies following close behind. Ang stared in disbelief, unsure how to process the abrupt change of events.

"Where are you going? How will we know when to attack?" Ang asked, struggling to make sense of the ambiguous response. "How do I know that we can trust you?"

"There is no way for you to know that with certainty, but reputation precedes us. If you are truly here to serve, then you will know how and when to do the right thing, and if you hold steady, you will prevail," replied a voice from one of the militia members. Ang squinted to identify the speaker who trailed behind the rest. He couldn't discern his features from the others, but sensed a compassionate albeit stern demeanor capable of sparking inspiration unlike the rigid behavior of the others.

Conceding that no more intel could be gleaned from their mystery intercessors, Ang quickly relayed orders for his crew to tend to the injured and consolidate all salvaged weapons and provisions. The Commonwealth forces complied with haste as they prepared their southward march.

Over the next forty arcs, Commonwealth forces managed to join the Uniod forces holed up in a rock formation pointing inland. The Commonwealth commander was relieved that the Uniod forces didn't opt to shoot first and make introductions later, considering that there was no means to signal their arrival in advance. Given the stresses common to war, Ang suspected that Uniod morale was dwindling.

"Your company is a most welcome sight, Commander Ang. We heard news that your fleet was destroyed," said a stocky fatigued Uniod general identifying himself as Jared Smythe, leader of the Overland Assault Force. He ushered Ang into the makeshift briefing room which was tucked into a small cave at the rear of the defensive ridge.

"Mechanically, it was a total loss, General, but most of my men made it out alive. Hardware is easily replaced, dedication, loyalty and trust... not so much," Ang replied, quickly summarizing the Commonwealth force's status.

"Why would you still come to our aide, Commander? Even without transportation, you might have had a chance to negotiate with neighboring islands, but here everyone has been reduced to a mobile gun rack and a moving target without hope. If our adversaries hadn't been alerted to your presence you might have had chance to save yourself and your men, but is likely that your fate will now be the same as ours," General Smythe replied, demonstrating his own despair.

"If I have learned one thing, General, it is that there is always strength in numbers even when they are small. Determination to survive can outweigh all odds," Ang replied, guarding against the infectious despair himself.

"I wish I shared your optimism, Commander," General Smythe replied.

"I have more than optimism, General. I have hope," Ang replied as he pondered whether or not to relay the events that kept his own men alive.

After a quick rundown of the situation, Commander Ang stared at the map of the terrain laid out in front of him on the boulder being used as a table. As he studied the markings pertaining to the lost Uniod skirmishes, he started to understand why such despair had taken hold. Ang was glad that neither of the officer's subordinates had been present to hear the prior conversation. Hopelessness in the chain of command spread easily like wildfire.

"How much time would you estimate that we have until Red Wall forces reach this location, General?" Ang asked.

"By our estimates we have less than six arcs. That would be enough time to prepare for one last assault. Remaining here is suicide," Smythe answered.

"You speak as if the battle is already lost, General. Our present location may provide an adequate defense and provide us the time that we need, despite its lack of elevation. Some of my men noticed a cliff face toward the west, no more than a parcel from here. We can have your scouts hold up there to give us a better view of incoming forces," Ang suggested pointing to a blank space on the map.

"I see merit in your strategy, Commander, but even if we fight off the first wave, what have we gained? My men are but a skeleton crew, and yours are ship operators. This will only prolong the inevitable," Smythe said with resignation.

Commander Ang stood upright and stared the Uniod general right in the eye, "We have but one directive, General. Survive!"

Annoyed with the general's weak composure, Ang turned and walked out of the makeshift briefing room and snapped orders for soldiers present to begin fortifying the perimeter. The faint glimmer of hope manifesting in the Commonwealth commander began to spread. Ang allowed the Uniod officers to take charge of their own men as they tasked various soldiers with establishing a perimeter upon reaching the cliff.

The midday sun bore down on the stranded military forces while they tensely watched the horizon. Just as Commander Ang rotated his wrist to check his sungauge, he heard murmurs filtering through the ranks. If the commotion pertained to the advancement of Red Wall forces, the general's prediction had certainly been accurate. Ang calculated that nearly six arcs had passed, to the click, since the depressing conversation with the Uniod general. Internally, Ang sensed his own frustration at General Smythe's capacity to allow morale to decline so deeply, but he also knew there was no time to judge the harsh choices the general made thus far. There was only time to reflect on the will to survive.

Ang took up position along the outer defensive ridge with his men. Ever since he completed basic training, Ang always made it a point to fight alongside his allies. If he were to die in battle, he would do so with his men's respect. He couldn't stomach the idea of barking orders from a command post.

The loud cracks of artillery units bellowed through the air, swiftly followed by the deafening explosion of plasma tearing into the rock face of the embankment. Large portions of rock broke loose, cascading down the ridge, crushing one squad positioned twenty boots to Ang's right.

"Hold your ground," Ang barked as half of the men covered their heads from the rock shower while the other half tensed their trigger fingers, intent on running down the ridge and plunging headlong into the advancing swarm of Red Wall infantry.

Commander Ang dispatched two of his men to look for survivors from the victims of the rock slide. One of the Uniod commanders opened his mouth to contest the order, but a fiery stare immediately silenced the officer, making it clear that Ang would not be challenged.

Another volley from the Red Wall artillery sprinkled more rocks upon the ridge. Ang was forced to dive out of the way as a misshapen boulder fell on his position. Coughing could be heard all around as the men attempted to clear their lungs and eyes from the dust.

Yells of intimidation and taunts peeled across the plain below as the artillery halted so that the Red Wall forces could advance. Even from the moderate elevation, Ang was able to see that the Red Wall forces were already splitting into two formations prepared to flank the ridge like sheets of insects.

"Fire at will!" Ang ordered as the hordes for Red Wall forces advanced. "Officer, get those snipers on the the cliff to do their work. It's time to earn their next meal... and ours."

Ang snatched the Equalizer assault rifle from the fallen soldier next to him, and fired down into the advancing horde. He managed to put down a couple of dashing soldiers before he crouched behind the protective rocks on the ridge. Three rounds of plasma splashed across the rock face just as he ducked out of the way. The plasma hissed and steamed like a thin acid.

Even above the noise of discharging plasma and charging infantry, Ang could hear the screams of his men perishing at the hands of Red Wall forces. Ang looked around for the officer with the comm equipment in order to dispatch orders to the squads on the cliff, but found nothing other than a lifeless torso protruding from beneath a boulder. Ang yanked the comm from the lifeless hand and demanded a report from the squads along the cliff.

"They've got their own snipers, they took half of us out before we had a chance to return fire," screamed a frantic voice through the receiver.

"Soldier, do you have any heavy munitions left?" Ang yelled above the increasing roar of Red Wall forces.

"We're low on grenades, so all that we have left are shoulder cannons," the voice responded.

"Get a cannon to everyone and bombard this hillside's base from north to south passing inland until you reach their artillery," Ang ordered.

The only response Ang received was the splintering sound of a crate before the comm faded into a wash of static. It was the only reply Ang needed. He pushed his lungs to the limit as he yelled for all Commonwealth and Uniod forces to take cover from the incoming barrage.

The ridge shook as the remnant of soldiers on the cliff fired into the distance and shelled the entire side of the ridge mowing down any opposition caught in their path. As the impact tremors settled, Ang peeked out from his rock cover as the large yellow explosive shells ripped through the Red Wall lines and continued westward toward the artillery units where another contingent of Red Wall forces held position.

Ang's heart sank as he watched the surviving Red Wall soldiers south of the ridge sneer and mock the final efforts of their adversaries who were pinned. Comms that still functioned were buzzing with reports of Titangrad forces approaching from the west. Ang once again leaned behind his cover and hung his head. He was reluctant to give the final orders of desperation since they were running out of men and resources. Ang didn't need another glance to know that Titangrad forces would be in firing range soon.

Before Ang could issue commands, a violent explosion ripped through the air. Testing his curiosity, Ang stood and squinted only to see a distant blaze covering a third of the Red Wall's remaining units. A secondary explosion tore through the ranks of the incoming Titangrad forces as well. Ang could not believe his eyes as he watched a firefight ensue between Red Wall and Titangrad forces. Ang was quick to ping the squad on the cliff and ask if they were involved in the explosion.

"Negative, Sir. It was as if something hit them from the inside," replied the baffled soldier.

Even the ambiguous answer was affirmation enough for Ang to understand the situation. "They are attacking each other! All Commonwealth and Uniod forces move out!"

Since General Smythe had been preoccupied with fortifying the position of his own men, he relished the opportunity to finally die in a blaze of glory. Smythe promptly confirmed the order of the younger Commonwealth officer barking for everyone to advance.

As the forces on the ridge ran downward, Ang grabbed a fresh assault rifle and sidearm, charging alongside the rest of the forces. The conflict between Red Wall and Titangrad forces enveloped the whole plain causing quite the melee. As Ang approached the conflict with his EQ spitting plasma from its spinning barrel, he soon recognized a familiar scene much like the one he witnessed a couple of days prior.

Red Wall forces were slaughtering each other, unable to discern friend from foe. Any Red Wall forces able to avoid the fray were potentially picked off by their Titangrad allies. Ang was eager to contribute to the confusion as he dropped multiple enemy soldiers with his EQ in hand.

The barrel of Ang's assault rifle locked up, announcing that the last power cell was empty. Ang dropped the weapon and released the safety on the small silver disruptor that he salvaged. While caught up in all the commotion, Ang felt simultaneously perplexed and intrigued by all of the havoc swirling about, but the lapse in his focus gave a staggering soldier opportunity to approach from behind and catch him off guard.

Ang heard the footsteps behind him, but his reaction was too late to prevent the Red Wall soldier from leveling an assault rifle at his chest. Ang raised the pistol toward the soldier's head, but only received a dry click as he depressed the trigger. He realized that there had been no time to check the firearm's magazine.

The menacing Red Wall soldier snarled and tensed to squeeze the trigger of his EQ, but before his finger made contact, a sharp instrument pierced through his chest from behind causing blood to spatter across Ang's uniform, narrowly missing his face. Delirious, the soldier looked down at the blade sticking through his chest, but in his state of shock he was helpless to stop the fork of a similar weapon from puncturing his neck. The hand grasping the bizarre weapon held tight and ripped it away cleaving flesh in the process, causing the soldier to fall to the ground.

Ang stared, also in shock, as the unsuspecting foe collapsed in a heap. Holding the crude ayvek weapon was the enigmatic militia member who had prompted Ang to hold strong. Without smoke interfering this time, Ang easily noticed the blue camouflage bandanna tied around his head. The weapon's owner flicked the blood from his weapons before twirling them about in his fingerless glove covered hands.

The man who couldn't have been much different in age than Ang said nothing and acknowledged with a faint nod. Ang, still dumbfounded, understood little about the mysterious ally, and said nothing himself, but he perceived that the mutual respect between allies spoke volumes. Realizing there was nothing more to add to the silent exchange, the man turned and walked away, disappearing into the tumult to continue his work.

Disregarding his blood stained uniform, Ang kicked the fallen soldier before him to seize his assault rifle before running off to help the rest of his men. He found General Smythe struggling while back pedaling to fend off two Titangrad soldiers. Weary from more than a bench of exhaustion, the general collapsed, unable to hold his ground. Ang dashed behind the soldiers, slamming one in the back of the head with the butt of his EQ before firing a five round burst from a full rotation of the spinning barrel into the other soldier's face. The massive scoring at close range simultaneously disfigured the receiving soldier and knocked him back a full pace.

Leaning down, Commander Ang helped the general to his feet, "Don't be so eager to die today. There are still plenty of opportunities to find the honor you seek."

"Honor to whom honor is due, Commander. May today go down in the archives as the day an old man was shown the true nature of survival through the dedication of one younger and more honorable than himself," General Smythe replied as he strained to return to his full height.

"Come on, General. Let's finish the job that you were sent to complete," Ang replied once the Uniod officer had steadied himself.

Commander Ang and General Smythe advanced together to rally their remaining allies and drive back the retreating forces of Titangrad and the Red Wall.

As the remnant of memories pertaining to the harrowing mission faded, Potentate Ang found himself drifting back to the present. Ang stared silently as he reflected on just how much that mission had impacted his life. While he had been privy to the Interlace since he was a child, he never fully realized the nature of selfless service until that experience by helping those in need. The outcome of the mission preceded William Ang in his welcome home as a state hero, and due to his increase in understanding, he sought to keep such valuable experiences in the foreground as he went on to shape the policy of the Commonwealth and the Oceanic Outpost as its Global Alliance successor.

Several passes later, Ang had the opportunity to once again ally with the newly promoted leader of the Ghosts, Sato Seechi, but he didn't discover the name or identity of the one who had interceded twice on his behalf, that is until long after the end of the Global War when someone decided to collect on a favor. Until that time, Ang might have considered such events to be coincidence, but once patterns emerged with regularity he began to realize greater influences at work.

As a plague spread from the Crossover Strain during the Smart Wars, Ang was surprised to finally receive contact from his mystery ally. Presented with a solution to the virus without a means to distribute it, Ang demonstrated little skepticism in backing the possible solution based on the reputation for sacrifice of the requestor. With a newly created communication channel, Ang leveraged the resources of the Oceanic Outpost to mass produce the solution that Mac Conner provided to combat the Crossover Strain. The collaboration proved to be a great success. While the Oceanic Outpost's reputation was both lauded and suspected for its involvement such actions, Ang was resolute in keeping his source confidential. He couldn't afford to compromise the preferred secrecy of such a valuable ally.

"You never did tell me how you and the Ghosts managed to spark all that infighting between the Red Wall and Titangrad," Ang said with a raised eyebrow.

Mac smiled, mildly pleased that past actions had managed to maintain a cap of mystery on a meaningful relationship. Mac opened his mouth to volunteer a reply, but he was quickly cut off as Zared Marx burst into the room with an urgent update from Frank Jenkins' agenda coordinator in the Commercial Empire.

The carefree atmosphere swiftly dissipated in Potentate Ang's office as haps of Jenkins' meeting call reached the ears of those present. While scheduled forums were typically reserved for some global threat or border dispute, spontaneous meetings on such short notice were unheard of especially since there hadn't been anything to justify one in well over a pass. The urgent request only solidified Mac's suspicions of Frank Jenkins' ever increasing lust for power.

"What's the proposed meeting time, Zared?" Ang asked of his public relations advisor who was soon followed by the other two members of the council.

Ang repeated the haps for Jackal and Newton as they took seats around the conference table.

"Did he offer any reason for the urgency?" Ang asked.

Marx only shook his head in response.

"Jackal, any intel regarding an increase in military clashes?" Ang asked, hoping that some justified cause might support Frank Jenkins' request.

"Nothing through the regular channels. If anything, events have been strangely calm since the last forum," Jackal replied.

"Then I fear that Mr. Conner's warning may warrant support. If Frank Jenkins harbors ill intent for the Global Alliance, this may provide him the opportunity to relay an ultimatum in efforts to test future allegiance," Ang said thoughtfully.

"Does he even have any pull with the other faction leaders?" Mac asked.

"That remains to be seen. Usually, the faction leaders have little interaction beyond the standard economic fare. Such a rash request is likely to create more hostility than favor without a convincing story," Ang replied.

"Jackal, bring up the fleet's readiness level. I'd like things to remain fluid should there be any foul play," Ang continued.

"Standard security detail, Sir?" Jackal asked.

"Yes, I will include you with our usual escort. Zared, you will remain here to conduct any affairs in my absence. Newton, I would like you to expedite any remaining tests on the amphibious craft," Ang said firmly.

"Would I be too forward if I asked to tag along?" Mac asked.

"Strict Global Alliance policy does not allow anyone near the neutral facility compound except the faction leaders and their escorts. I'm not opposed to having a party addition, but I don't know how you would get anywhere near the facility. Even the meeting itself is closed off from security escorts," Ang replied.

"As long as I have your approval to join, resolving the logistics should be simple, provided that the facility doesn't have widely integrated digital security systems," Mac said.

Ang pondered the request for a moment before finally shaking his head, "No, the leaders have minimized surveillance on the grounds so that meetings remain confidential."

"Then it's settled. I can fly solo and meet you there. Trust me, I'll remain out of sight," Mac smirked.

"It is quite a risk, but if you can pull it off, I will be impressed," Ang replied. "Zared, if you could, please show Mr. Conner to his accommodations after relaying the coordinates to the compound."

Zared nodded in agreement before standing and exiting the executive office. Mac followed suit and matched Zared's path until they reached the archive room. The room also had a conference table, but was also chock full of books, slates and maps. Zared pulled out a chair and tapped instructions into the closest terminal to reveal a globe on a nearby noptic screen. As the globe rotated, the view locked in position over the Equatorial Span. The view zoomed in multiple times until it rested on the landscape and facility to host the Global Alliance ever since the cessation of the Global War.

"Why the Equatorial Span?" Mac asked.

"Moz Fractillend?" Zared asked rhetorically. "Given the extensive tectonic upheaval after all of the bombings during the war, the Schistic Valley expanded and flooded essentially splitting off part of the continent. As a wasteland, it's a strong reminder for the Global Alliance leaders to uphold their responsibilities to their respective factions. Since the fractured portion is nigh inhospitable, it proved a logical choice for a secluded meeting hub," Zared replied.

"Indeed," Mac mumbled.

"Do you have a slate for me to transfer the coordinates to, Mr. Conner?" Zared asked.

"That won't be necessary. If this is the most accurate information, I can upload it directly," Mac replied as he pointed at the noptic screen already displaying the details.

Zared watched with curiosity as Mac focused intently on the screen. From behind the dark shades, the ocular overlays began to rotate, glow and flicker with speed in a variety of circular patterns.

"Impressive. Unless there is anything else, I can show you to your quarters for the duration of your stay since related support teams will not be departing until closer to the meeting time. Do you have any specific plans that will require special provisions?" Zared asked.

The question reminded Mac of the purpose for his visit. He suspected that Zared was trying to be a good host, but also decided against revealing any more than necessary. "I suppose that if I have a few clicks to spare, I may as well catch up on some culture."

"I can provide recommendations," Zared replied.

Mac nodded his approval and followed the Public Relation Advisor's lead. With new variables added to the dangers drifting toward the Global Alliance, he would have to commit more resources to foresight of every path possible.

Thread: sysObserver.cmd

With Talbot Newton remaining as the last council member, Ang contemplated how much information he wanted to relay to his chief informatech. He wasn't used to applying a filter in every conversation, at least not with his council.

"Talbot, how long would it take to get our Eastern Fleet through the Nihocopa Canal?" Ang asked while resting his chin on one hand with his elbow resting on the other hand.

"Why the Xenimac Bay, Sir?" Newton asked, curious as to such a distant location for the fleet.

"I have something of a hunch, Talbot," Ang replied, offering no details.

"I know that it's standard procedure to run our Capitol cruisers, but the Venture class ships alone could close the gap in under a bench and a half, I believe," Newton replied with reservation to make sure he didn't offer bad calculations.

"That may be too long. I'd like you to cut it to seven days or less with six cruisers and three carriers loaded with as much ranged and amphibious craft as we can manage. We'll approach the Nihocopa Canal from the west and steer clear of Jungyan territory," Ang replied.

Newton scratched his head, pondering how to execute the seemingly impossible request from a physics standpoint. He couldn't increase fleet speed AND increase the amount of artillery requested. He hoped that a political solution might offset the physical demands. "I know that the Nihocopa Canal has been declared a neutral territory, but won't rolling through with that much hardware turn some heads?"

"I will deal with the political fallout, Talbot. Just make the preparations," Ang replied, having already made up his mind on the next course of action.

Newton opened his mouth to protest since any wrong move with the fleet could leave the Oceanic Outpost vulnerable. Both the Martial Legion and the Jungyan Republic wouldn't hesitate to close in on the island continent if Potentate Ange ever fell out of favor with the Global Alliance or the people. Deciding against a counterargument, Newton stood and exited the Potentate's office. On his way out he spotted Zared and Mac who were casually discussing local culture. Before reaching the stairs at the end of the hall, Zared paused to fetch a small pill canister out of his pocket.

"Still downing the heart pills, Zared? Why not spring for the procedure and get the swap? Talbot asked disdainfully.

"Sorry, I'd like to keep the one I was born with," Marx retorted.

Mac didn't need his ikes to sense the hostility between the two council members. He was tempted to activate the IFX mode on his ikes, but he didn't want to stare and reveal his suspicion. He had to resort to finding a way of discovering the informant's identity without his knowledge. It would be an easier task if the directive from Jenkins hadn't been so pressing. There was good reason to suspect that his very presence may have already been leaked by the informant. Mac realized that danger's tempo was increasing and he would have to amp up his own speed and clarity of thought to match. There was no margin for screw ups.

18 – Change of Hands – 18

Synergon Assembly Plant
Core City, Windstonne Enclave
Commercial Empire, Northam Continent
Thread: sysObserver.cmd

Voltaire appeared to be lost in thought when Pythagoras reached the doorway to the managerial office. Typically, when Voltaire was in contemplative moods, he didn't like disruptions which prompted Pythagoras to turn away, but instead, Voltaire acknowledged him and invited him in.

"What do you think of Frank Jenkins and Konrad Oszwick, Dexter?" Voltaire asked without moving his eyes from his deep stare into the distance.

"You know me, Dean, I harbor disregard equally, but in their case I could dish up an extra serving. I don't trust them at all, especially that assistant of Oszwick's," Pythagoras replied.

"Do you think I made the right decision?" Voltaire asked, finally looking his associate in the eyes to verify his answer.

"There is no right decision, Dean. In our business we're always going to ruffle some feathers, typically, most ignorant squawks, but regardless of the outcome you know that the rest of us will back your decision," Pythagoras replied with a calm resolve.

"I agree and appreciate your candor," Voltaire said.

Seldom did Voltaire question his own confidence in planning, but it was always stabilized by the competence of his clan members. He knew all of them to be leaders in their respective fields. Voltaire doubted that there had ever been such a powerful collection of intellects. He knew that together they could sculpt the minds of the modern world.

With his eyes drifting toward the doorway, he spotted Hauteur who was waiting for a break in the conversation, "Yes, what is it Saphira?"

"Sir, Lucient is here. He says that Mr. Oszwick is requesting possession of the satellites for final alterations ahead of the launch schedule," Hauteur replied.

"What? That was not part of our arrangement," Voltaire said, his tone clearly revealing his irritation.

Voltaire stormed out of the office with Pythagoras and Hauteur in tow. Voltaire met Lucient at the plant entrance where the Oszwick Enterprises agent was nonchalantly observing the surroundings.

"Lucient, glad that you could pay us a visit. I understand there has been some confusion about our arrangement," Voltaire said boldly.

"No, there has been no confusion, Mr. Sargent. Mr. Oszwick gave me this slate with his signature on the manifest," Lucient replied with a wan expression.

Voltaire snatched the slate from Lucient's hand doubting the credibility of the executive assistant. Voltaire scanned the the manifest by sliding his finger along the slate. He found little information beyond the descriptors of the final alterations once the Synergon satellites were transferred to Oszwick Enterprises. The ambiguous manifest was finalized with Oszwick's signature. Voltaire looked up from the slate to see if Pythagoras was monitoring his reaction. The subtle exchange in their eye contact indicated that both were thinking of the conversation just moments prior to Lucient's arrival.

"If you'll excuse me for a moment, Lucient," Voltaire said with a weak display of courtesy as he headed for his office while leaving Pythagoras and Hauteur to keep Lucient occupied.

"Of course," Lucient said with a pretentious grin that was creepy and similar to Oszwick's.

Voltaire snatched the sonair off his desk to ping Oszwick's comm. After exchanging greetings with a hoarse voiced receptionist, Voltaire was connected to Oszwick's office. The executive's suave voice was not short on pleasantries, but Voltaire opted to get directly to the purpose of the call.

"Mr. Oszwick, you're assistant is here with a message suggesting that Mogul Prime has been relieved of responsibilities in relation to the Synergon Project. What is the meaning of this?" Voltaire snapped.

"Mr. Sargent, you are in no way relieved. It is simply a matter of the project's schedule. Mr. Jenkins' project has received an unexpected advance. In order to meet the new deadline, the project will require more resources and manpower, both of which are not adequate at the current facility," Oszwick replied with a tepid reassurance.

"I would have liked to know this information as soon as it was discovered, Mr. Oszwick. Alterations introduced at the last click seldom produce quality deployments," Voltaire said.

"Understood, Mr. Sargent. Mr. Jenkins just informed me of his intentions within the last arc. It appears that the revelation of our mutual adversary arriving in the Oceanic Outpost has, no doubt, motivated Mr. Jenkins to accelerate his plans unexpectedly. Remember, Dean, I only ask for one item, and that is trust. No changes have been made to our arrangement," Oszwick said, his experience in negotiations clearly evident.

"Yes, Sir," Voltaire mumbled as he tapped the sonair to exit the conversation.

Voltaire paced multiple times in his office before returning to the laboratory entrance. Pythagoras intercepted him halfway.

"It's liquid," Voltaire said under his breath, ensuring that the words were out of Lucient's earshot. "Oszwick said that Jenkins ordered the transfer within the arc."

"Within the arc? There is no way Lucient could have assembled his team and made his way across the enclave within that time frame. Either he anticipated it, or someone is withholding information. I don't like it, Dean. Let me oversee the transfer protocols before we complete the exchange. I want to keep a hand on this situation should anything go sideways."

"I trust your judgement," Voltaire said with a nod and hushed tone. "Whatever you do, exercise caution and discretion."

Voltaire clapped a hand on Pythagoras' shoulder before strolling off to finalize arrangements with Lucient, giving Pythagoras time to make his way to the closest operations terminal. Pythagoras easily encoded an artificial socket and replicated it across every satellite module. He made sure to bury the encryption under layers of the least complicated routines which rarely malfunctioned in order to keep prying eyes away. Even without physical control of the satellites, Pythagoras ensured that Mogul Prime could divert control, should the slightest hint of disruption sour the arrangement with Oszwick Enterprises.

With the encryption upload complete, Pythagoras made his way toward the lab entrance. The tension in his chest reminded him that he was quickly growing irritated by the very sight of Oszwick's assistant, but in spite of the growing animosity, Pythagoras was cordial in his announcement that Lucient and his crew could being dismantling the hardware for transport. Pythagoras knew that it wasn't wise to dwell on his present distrust, but considering that Mogul Prime was about to have more free time on its hands, he would be busy identifying what exactly was going on in the realm of shadowy executives.

Executive Level, Casters Tower
Core City, Windstonne Enclave
Commercial Empire, Northam Continent
Thread: sysObserver.cmd

As the noptic screen on his desk illuminated a view of his schedule, Frank Jenkins verified that all remaining appointments were delayed until his return from the Global Alliance meeting. With everything in order, Jenkins turned his attention to the report on Project Synergon. It appeared that the hardware transfer went smoothly. In a way, Jenkins felt a sense of relief that he no longer had to contend with Mogul Prime, even if he was apprehensive about accelerating the project without proper vetting.

Before he could evaluate all scenarios on the matter, Sath interrupted his thoughts through the comm to inform him of his final appointment for the day. Jenkins acknowledged and instructed her to show the last guest in.

"Ah, Mr. Oszwick, it appears everything went as expected," Jenkins said enthusiastically as a familiar face passed through the office doors.

"Yes, Mr. Jenkins. Mr. Sargent was quite cooperative. I find it hard to believe that you would discard such a talent pool from any project," Oszwick said as he seated himself opposite Jenkins.

"I'm sure you aware that people are simply pathways leading to the next product or service that you require. Traveling that path has a cost, but it is no longer remembered upon reaching the destination. If that path is too costly, I find another. Mr. Sargent has a tendency to increase cost without comparable benefit when negotiating the terms of our business relationship," Jenkins said as he scrunched the left side of his face to display his annoyance.

"I am quite sure that your calculations are unmatched when it comes to understanding the amount of sacrifices that others should make in order to stabilize your success," Oszwick remarked.

"Exactly, Mr. Oszwick. I wish that more individuals understood the high cost associated with power, but I'm sure you that didn't travel all the way just to flatter me before the commencement of our endeavors. I take it that you have new insight from sources within the Oceanic Outpost," Jenkins said, growing accustomed to Oszwick's manner of speech.

"I do. Our thorn in the side is indeed bolder than anticipated. I hear that he plans to attend the faction leader meeting alongside Potente Ang," Oszwick said.

"The potentate knows that is against established ordinances," Jenkins grumbled as he ran a hand through his beard. "Such a violation could completely distract from the purpose of the meeting."

"Yet, such an exposure might lend credibility to our cause by informing the other leaders of said treachery," Oszwick smirked.

"That sounds like a rather devious bonus, Mr. Oszwick. I find that to be an acceptable alternative, but should this Enforcer conceal himself with his tech what leverage would I have?" Jenkins asked.

"He won't have anticipated this," Oszwick replied as he retrieved a small hardmelt rectangle from his coat pocket with several buttons on its face. "This is a scatterfield. I had my team verify its capability with a variety of frequencies to neutralize any potential signal interference."

"Was your source able to gain access to his tech?" Jenkins asked with curiosity.

"Let's just say, my family's influence extends well beyond imagination," Oszwick replied with a sly grin.

"I'll take your word on that," Frank Jenkins said without taking time to ponder who commanded more authority in the room.

With the upcoming details of the plan settled, Jenkins walked over to his liquor cabinet next to his fish tank to retrieve a bottle of his finest. After pouring a glass for Oszwick and himself, he proposed a toast, "To a new era of influence!"

Frank Jenkins and Konrad Oszwick raised their glasses, pleased with how smoothly their operation had come together. With the Enforcer soon to be removed and similar strategies employed against stubborn dissidents, the Global Alliance leaders would soon be in their clutches, and the world would be theirs for the taking.

Inner Core Dartway
Core City, Windstonne Enclave
Commercial Empire, Northam Continent
Thread: actTgtPersp1.view

The night ride through the outer core of Windstonne toward BOWTech Laboratories proved to be a tense one. Torque didn't hesitate to express his disapproval of the mission as he guided the Chromehound toward the seemingly more civilized region of the faction capital.

"So, let me check this mess. We're out here to protect someone that we don't know exists for some information that may not be valid against one of the Commercial Empire's primary military suppliers?

That's just liquid. I don't know if ever smelled a more obvious trap!" Torque griped.

"What exactly does a trap smell like?" the Serpent rasped from the back seat of the mox.

"It stinks!" Torque snapped, rolling his eyes along with a glance over his shoulder. He didn't know what kind of technical answer the Serpent was expecting.

"Maxwell, can you access the BOWTech peripheral datatank? We're going to need a structural schematic and hopefully a location of our mystery hostage," I said, hoping that my volume overruled any noise from the Chromehound's engine.

"It'll take me a click, but I should have it by the time you reach the facility," Maxwell replied.

"This is our stop," Torque muttered as he pulled the easily identifiable mox into an empty parking garage.

"This is BOWTech?" I asked sarcastically.

"Perhaps you'd prefer I ping the valet. 'Driver, lockup for three please,'" Torque replied as he got out of the vehicle and slammed the door for emphasis. "We walk from here!"

"Got any stats, hamster?" I asked.

"You're half a parcel south of the complex. Security profiles show a checkpoint at the main gate and four guard towers. One on each corner," Maxwell replied.

"This should be fun. Suggestions?" I muttered as we kept to the shadows across the street from the facility surrounded by a twelve mark fence. The high powered lights sweeping the property were likely to be a challenge.

"Looks like it's up and over time," Torque replied.

"Cloaks on," I said. "Alex, we need to do this all at once. If the guards detect the noise, they'll be all over us You'll need to double time if you're still opting out of the tech," I said.

"Allow me to demo my craft," the Serpent hissed with a smirk.

"Liquid," I said with a nod. "Let's time the lights."

While I watched the wide beams of light cut through the night air and cast erratic circles on the ground, I lifted the hood my cloak over my head and engaged its primary function, rendering me invisible. Torque opted to follow suit for a change and engaged the cloak built into his jacket. It did not seem to be as powerful as the long black cloth that the Enforcer had given me, but it still appeared to be viable in a pinch. I momentarily switched my ikes' filter mode to electromagnetic so that I could still see Torque's form. The field filter made the Serpent invisible in the blue haze, but at least his ikes and sword still emitted a low enough frequency for me to detect his position. Ready to engage, we cautiously approached the fence and waited for optimal timing.

"Let's move," I snapped as we initiated our sprint toward the fence.

With better coordination than I had anticipated, I engaged my kips causing the electromagnets in my shoes to activate for our vertical run up the fence. The chain link fence went soft underneath my feet as Torque also applied pressure to the fence directly behind me. I strained against gravity to ascend the last few marks, but upon reaching the top of the fence we pushed hard to clear the coiled shredder wire lacing the top of the fence. All three of us jumped vertically into a forward moving back flip. We hit the ground with minimal sound, but the disturbance caused by the push from the fence reached the guards' ears, invoking frantic yells to move the floodlights in our direction.

The Serpent was forced to dart toward the shadows while we advanced toward the building. He had to make multiple reflex rolls along the short grass to avoid the erratic motion of the lights which continued to search for the source of the disturbance.

Torque and I remained still until the guards were certain that the noise was of no consequence. As the guards resumed a more systematic pattern of light sweeps, Torque and I sprinted to catch up with the Serpent who was already notching his way along the western side of the building.

A paved walkway parted the grass between a gazebo and a nearby entryway. I assumed that we neared an entrance for workers should they be granted recreational time. Since the path was adorned with a few drooping flowers and poorly trimmed shrubs, I could only hope that their security system was as dismal as their lawncare budget.

"Maxwell, do you have access to the security system for the staff recreational entrance?" I asked.

Instead of a response, we received a loud welcoming click as the bolt released within the door.

"Answers that," I said.

As we crept into the informatic facility, we quickly realized that we couldn't escape the pungent smell of cleaning solutions which so heavily saturated the air. The white walls and shiny tile floors reminded me more of a mendstat rather that an office hallway if not for the lack of patients.

"All security cameras along that hallway are deactivated. Personnel datastacks show that most staff members are checked out, but I'm not finding many bodies beyond the security guards on the central security system," Maxwell said.

"Our target has to be here somewhere. Any progress tracking it down or finding alternate security systems?" I asked in a hushed tone.

"One request at a time, Boss. I've only got two paws, or at least two to tap. Until I sprout an extra set you'll have to deal with hamster operational time. Got it?" Maxwell responded.

"Whatever, rodent, just get it done," the Serpent hissed in sarcastic manner.

"Oh, Serpent, my eye in the sky tells me that those white walls just aren't your color," Maxwell quipped back through the comm.

I disabled the filters on my ikes and looked up to see a red operational light on the security camera overhead. I looked over my shoulder to see what Maxwell meant and sure enough the Serpent would have been a better wall hanging with the way his dark colors contrasted the bleak obstacle free surroundings.

"He is right, you know. You look like a tropical tourist in the tundra," I said in a mock consoling tone.

"There appears to be a master laboratory in the south wing. Remaining personnel are there... and... Uh Oh... You're not going to believe this. It appears that our friend, Frank Jenkins, is on camera in one of the attached control rooms," Maxwell said.

"This I have to see," I whispered.

We quickened our pace to the location that Maxwell specified while keeping a watchful eye open for security guards and random personnel. At every break in the hallway, we waited for Maxwell to give the all-clear. With every pause, I made sure to verify our progress against a compound schematic of the building on my ikes. The last thing I wanted to be responsible for was failing the mission on account of getting lost in the massive complex.

Thread: sysObserver.cmd

Frank Jenkins paced sternly within the observation room. There was no hiding his aggravation. His reddened face had all the fury of a volcano ready to pop. Even the two Piran soldiers standing directly behind him struggled to hide their own intimidation should the faction leader's ire be directed toward them.

"What brought this on, Szazs? I have given you the most esteemed informatic position in the world and you willingly discard it," Jenkins snarled.

"I will not be bought, Mr. Jenkins, I will be party to your genocide no longer," Szazs retaliated with a shaky voice. surprising himself that he still bothered with formalities, given the circumstances.

He knew that his demeanor wasn't convincing, but he hoped that he possessed the will to uphold his beliefs against the self-serving faction leader.

"Genocide? This has nothing to do with genocide. This project is for the preservation of our faction's status and freedoms," Frank Jenkins snapped with a fierce glare just notches from the protech's face.

Killian Szazs gulped back the saliva collecting in his mouth. He knew that he couldn't so easily wipe the intimidation from his face as easily as the sweat forming on his brow. Despite the constant pressure, he held his ground without reply.

"You may not have a price tag, Mr. Szazs, but I will have you agree with reason. You have twenty arcs to turnover those authorization codes," Jenkins shouted in Szazs' face. Frank Jenkins knew that Szazs was barely a couple passes older than himself, but his disposition clearly conveyed how the luxuries of comfort and the servitude of others had worked in his favor, and the lack thereof against the aged informatech.

"See if you can talk some sense into him," Jenkins snapped at the lab assistant, Benni Kotes, who stood behind Szazs without uttering a word during the grilling.

Kotes opened his mouth to speak, but his words would have been ineffective since Frank Jenkins had already turned about to storm out of the observation room with the two Piran soldiers following behind. Had Jenkins not been so preoccupied with his anger he might have heard the faint hum of active cloaking devices as he marched down the hallway.

Thread: actTgtPersp1.view

"I say we just cap him right now and end the fishfest," Torque whispered as he watched the fuming faction leader pass by. Never had he been so close to an opportunity to settle old grudges.

"So we can have a deranged fish replaced with a shark? No, he needs to be exposed publicly. Until we have the evidence, we cannot risk plunging this faction further into the tank," I huffed.

I didn't have to see Torque's expression to see that it merely conveyed his compliance rather than agreement. At least we agreed that the mission took precedence. Getting back to it, I peeked over the half wall and peered through the safety glass separating the observation room from the control room.

A quick glance revealed that there were only two people left in the control room, an older pale informatech in a lab coat and a younger individual in more casual attire likely to be an assistant. I hoped to overhear their conversation, but the safety glass was effective at insulating the sound.

"Maxwell, got any audio on the cameras?" I asked.

"Working on it," Maxwell replied.

In a matter of ticks, sounds and conversation from the control room streamed through our ikes. It was hard to grasp the context of the conversation, but I did my best to piece together content about some ultimatum and information that the older informatech was reluctant to give up despite the coaxing of the younger individual. It certainly appeared to be a battle of insistence over exhaustion.

"Are you that eager for a promotion that you need to exercise authority over an old man?" the older informatech asked.

"Killian, I'm trying to look out for both of us. If you don't give Jenkins the authorization codes, you will hold both of us back, but if you do it's a win-win situation. I don't understand why you would postpone the inevitable. Frank Jenkins will find a way to get what he wants with or without us. All you will have done is declare yourself an enemy to be scrubbed in the process," the younger individual said.

"Let me stop you right there because that line of thinking will prove futile. Let me tell you about the nature of inevitability. Not only are choices inevitable, but so too are consequences. We are responsible for every choice we make and must bear the weight of the outcome. Frank Jenkins is a man who barrels along without concern for the latter. I advise you, Benni, learn from those who have already made their share of wrong decisions and spare yourself the trouble," the older informatech said with more conviction than the younger expected.

Before the assistant could respond, both individuals were startled to see the control room doors swing up as if by a will of their own. Perplexed at the odd visual, they were even more surprised to see two forms materialize out of the air defying their known informatic comprehension.

"KS, I presume?" I asked the older informatech who was still dumbfounded by the dramatic entrance.

"Who are you?" the assistant snapped.

"I am Aaron Fox and this is Torque. We're here on account of a message regarding..." I started.

"Are... are you the designer of the Crossover Prevalent?" Szazs stammered with doubtful enthusiasm.

"No," I replied shaking my head, "but our associate is. We decided to investigate first before getting him involved."

"Such a relief," Szazs replied with an evident change in his disposition. "I was starting to believe that my search was a lost cause. I am Protech Killian Szazs, and this is my obtuse assistant, Benni Kotes."

"Hope is never a lost cause on the Triad's timeline," I remarked, albeit in a surprise fashion as if by habit rather than conscious choice. "From the sound of things, it looks like that timing couldn't be more precise. We can at least provide temporary shelter, but I know our friend will want to speak with you before making any deals."

"Wait just a tick," Kotes interjected.

"That's enough, Benni. I am leaving," Szazs retorted with a tenacity well hidden by his exhaustion.

"Then, if you go, I go," Kotes retaliated.

"We don't have time for this," Torque grumbled.

No sooner had the words escaped his lips when shouts of "Intruders" peeled through the air, courtesy of the Pirans charging down the hallway. I twisted and grabbed a Nebula grenade from my waist and tossed it through the doorway. The metal cylinder exploded into a white cloud of abrasive fumes.

I heard a couple of Pirans hit the floor amidst loud hacking coughs of those still standing. Those who still possessed the energy shouted orders through the haze. After a tick of silence, a metal canister clattered and rolled into the control room. Torque immediately recognized the device and leveled his Cress at the safety glass. He instinctively ran forward unleashing plasma as fast he could.

"That's no smoke grenade! MOVE!" Torque yelled while continuously firing until the safety glass softened with several globs melting to the floor.

Sensing the danger to the equipment, Kotes moved toward the closest terminal, "The test results!"

"There's no time!" I yelled in response as I grabbed the informatech's shoulder and tossed him toward the melted hole in the safety glass where Torque was already helping Szazs through. I shoved Kotes through the hole and dove through behind him.

I couldn't have moved fast enough as the temperature in the control room escalated exponentially for a tick. The instantaneous blast of heat from the Inferno grenade turned all of the electrical equipment into a hissing firestorm. The safety glass shook and bowed outward under the strain as parts bubbled and others began to liquefy.

As the air settled, Torque and I were on the move, dragging the two informatechs with us. No more than a few steps into clean air, we helped Szazs and Kotes to their feet, yelling for them to keep moving. We didn't know if the Pirans assumed us dead, but we didn't stand still long enough to find out, should they waste time investigating the carnage.

I ran down the hall ahead of the informatechs to take the lead, leaving Torque to watch the rear. As we approached our inconspicuous exit point, I hoped that the Serpent had it secure, but on arrival he was nowhere to be found.

"Serpent, where you at?" I whispered. "I told him to keep a low profile, but not this low."

Without a reply on the ikes, we ushered Szazs and Kotes through the door and onto the facility grounds. I relayed that I was going to look for the Serpent while Torque got the others to safety. Torque was about to comment, but he was cutoff by shouts from the guard towers above. I anticipated that the Pirans had spotted us, but instead of pointing the lights toward us, they were pointed outside the facility perimeter. Torque squinted to see a familiar object approaching fast from beyond the fence.

"Found him!" Torque replied as he watched the Chromehound accelerate toward the BOWTech fence line, but as he watched his silver mox, his face twisted into an expression of horror since the vehicle was not slowing down.

The Chromehound slammed into the base of the chain link fence uprooting a large section which scraped across the bumper, front fenders and hood cutting deep grooves into the paint. We sprinted for the mox, hoping to close the gap before the Pirans spotted us running across the open grass. Even through labored breaths, I could hear Torque muttering about the damage done to his vehicle.

"Corzo's Carrier Service," the Serpent smirked as we reached the Chromehound.

The Piran guards spotted us and began firing in our direction. The Serpent punched the console and opened the back of the Chromehound so that he could operate the turret in the back. As the Serpent settled on the turret seat, Torque took the driver's seat. I fired a few random rounds from my Phantom toward the closest guard tower while Szazs and Kotes piled into the back of the mox. Even as I settled, the Serpent was already peppering the guard towers with plasma as Torque backed the Chromehound away from the fence. Torque shrieked as he had to listen to the grating sound of the wire fence doing more damage to the exterior of his vehicle.

"My paint job," Torque whined.

"Well, at least you still have repairs to keep you busy," I retorted.

Once the Chromehound reached a safe distance from the BOWTech facility, the Serpent settled back into the mox and comically introduced himself to the rescued informatechs. Before long, I proposed blindfolding our guests to obscure the location of the warehouse. I had no idea what kind of fuse we lit, so I figured that I had better start thinking about how to take every preventive measure possible for everyone's safety.

Executive Launchpad, Casters Tower
Core City, Windstonne Enclave
Commercial Empire, Northam Continent
Thread: sysObserver.cmd

Strong gusts of wind blew across the landing pad as Jenkins made his way to his private chopper. Since the pilot had already started the engines, the chopper's blades added to the wind's volume hindering Jenkins from noticing Commander Pyln's approach. Jenkins tensed as the Piran commander placed his hand on the faction leader's shoulder.

"What is it, Commander?" Frank Jenkins shouted to hear above the noise.

"Sir, there was an intrusion at BOWTech not long after your last visit. Both Protech Szazs and his assistant have gone missing," Commander Pyln shouted back.

Frank Jenkins was sorely displeased at the onset of bad haps, but he had no interest in adding any delays to his current plans. "Commander, it is more pressing that you see to the situation instead of accompanying me as originally planned. I don't care what it takes. I want necessary assets recovered, including malefactors. Discard the rest! "

"Yes, Sir!" Pyln snapped with a salute.

"Have three of your top men meet me at the rendezvous point before final departure to Moz Fractillend. You have your work to complete here," Frank Jenkins added.

Pyln nodded as Jenkins stepped up to board the chopper, but before he was completely inside he leaned out for a final remark. "Fail me now, Commander, and you'll bear more resemblance to a dung beetle than a fish when I'm through with you."

In closing, Jenkins slammed the door in Pyln's face before he had time to step away from the craft. Commander Pyln allowed a sneer to cross his face as he watched the executive chopper lift into the sky. Pyln knew that, as time passed, the Piran numbers increased without adequate battle testing. Those guarding BOWTech had certainly become soft, justifying the security breach. Over the passes, his confidence in his men had waned, but Pyln never lost sight of Frank Jenkins' ability to make good on his threats, especially since Pyln had often been the executor of such orders. For a brief moment, Pyln entertained the thought of the tiny chopper crashing into a ball of flames before it finally disappeared on the horizon, prompting him to return to the mission at hand.

19 – Compelling Offer – 19

Vanguard Warehouse
Abandoned Sector, Windstonne Enclave
Commercial Empire, Northam Continent
Thread: actTgtPersp1.view

With a tense but otherwise uneventful mission reaching its conclusion, Lennox situated the Chromehound before joining Alex and me in our efforts to resolve the hosting our new guests. Since the front offices were empty and spacious we escorted them to an unused office before removing their blindfolds. Even if they could be trusted, I didn't want to be responsible for a security breach of Vanguard's operation. The mission itself already required a lot of risk and likely would incur even more fallout from the Commercial Empire.

"I know it isn't much to look at, but it's the best we can do for now," I said as I removed the blindfolds from our guests. "We went out on a limb to track you down, so we'll figure out the next course of action when the Enforcer returns. We'll bring you some food, water and cots. Facilities are down the hall."

"Are we prisoners here?" Kotes asked with contempt as he stood from his seat.

"Not now, Benni. If we weren't their guests, I'm sure the accommodations could have been more dire. My apologies. As you can see, he is a bit overbearing," Szazs said.

"No matter. The offices are locked so you won't face the dangers outside. If you need anything, use the old comm system and our terminal operator will relay the message," I said, hoping that my suggestion discouraged interference or escape.

Lennox stared hard at Benni's face from behind his ikes. He didn't like how the arrangements had been so easily changed on the fly, especially in such a way that created additional security problems. His mind was set on voicing that concern once we had left our guests on their own.

"Protech, if you don't mind me asking, why have you gone to such lengths to sever ties with Frank Jenkins?" I asked.

Szasz shifted his weight on the rickety wooden chair that likely hadn't seen use in many passes. The fatigued informatech placed his face in the palms of his hands. Even in light of his newly granted freedom, he still felt as weary as ever.

"For too many passes, I have been an instrument of death. My role in such destruction needs to end. Rarely, do any members of our faction challenge the powers that be, so when this Enforcer you speak of came to mind, I considered that there might still be a means to utilize an old man like myself. I hoped that the creator of the Crossover Prevalent just might have connections. In all of my days at BOWTech, it was the only case that I could recall where someone went to such great lengths to fight the system, and for the benefit of others at that. I feel like it was my only recourse to atone," Szasz said.

"Just what exactly have you been working on for Frank Jenkins?" I asked.

"Creating death in a cage," Szazs replied grimly, his words trailed off, suggesting that he wasn't ready to speak of his latest assignment.

A quick glance at Kotes suggested that he didn't share the protech's views or the decision to leave BOWTech. He might quickly prove to be a loose end, but I was reluctant to make any rash decisions until Mac's return. I placed a hand on the elder informatech's shoulder for encouragement before Vanguard departed and left the two informatechs alone.

Equan Airspace
Neutral Territory
Moz Fractillend, Caafri Continent
Thread: sysObserver.cmd

The flight across the Trinsular Ocean had been a long monotonous one barring the intermediate fuel stops. The Eagle might not have made the flight were it not an undisclosed HARP that Ang mentioned. The high altitude refueling platforms were essential for such a small craft to make a long flight. Even with the occasional diversion, there was no substitute for being able to stretch on hard terrain, hence why Mac finally felt a sense of relief when the Caafri coastline came into view on the horizon. As a final check, Mac verified the coordinates that he received from Marx. He suspected that the Global Alliance compound had a wide security perimeter, so he thought it best to double-check his flight plan. Terrain that was both level and inconspicuous was in short supply.

After approaching from the south, Mac spotted a small plain tucked behind a ridge indicated to be at least three parcels from the Global Alliance facility. Mac did a quick circle around the landing zone before resting the Eagle on the ground. He was inclined to skip his normal protocols just for the sake of stretching his cramped legs. Since he arrived ahead of the Global Alliance delegates, he knew that there was time enough to stretch and make the run ahead of their arrival.

Moz Fractillend's bleak landscape was certainly a dismal reminder of civilization's low points on the sensibility spectrum. Although the barren terrain hadn't born the direct brunt of kinetic fallout on the continent, the resulting drought following the quakes had certainly left its mark. Gray rock and brown dust spanned as far as the eye could see with only the most persistent and scrawny plants struggling to make a resurgence.

As Mac's feet touched down on the dry scorched earth, he took a moment to gather his thoughts before initiating the long boring run. The whirlwind of activity made it difficult to accept just how much distance he'd covered since his last contact with others back in Windstonne. It was an easy distraction to lose sight of his current mission since Fox was accelerating in his skills sooner than expected. Mac had knowledge that he might not be able to withhold much longer since a mind without proper direction could easily stray. He hoped that Lennox and Alex were capable of limiting any shenanigans in his absence. With a looming threat closing in on the Global Alliance, Windstonne in particular, Mac set his mind on making sure that truth got priority. Until then, he would have to focus on the short term unknowns.

Vanguard Warehouse
Abandoned Sector, Windstonne Enclave
Commercial Empire, Northam Continent
Thread: actTgtPersp1.view

The new morning was off to a quiet start. Little sound could be heard other than Lennox's grumbling prior to firing up a sand blaster so that he could begin reversing the damage done to the Chromehound. I stared idly at the op table as Maxwell's little black eyes fixated on the noptic screen consumed with letters and symbols. I made little effort to understand the content related to his attempts to repair Streetz's coding. Alex too had vacated, likely continuing his training in the open air on the rooftop.

Maxwell nearly hopped into the air as an alarm signal blurted through the warehouse. I stood to look for any immediate threat. Lennox was already dashing toward the front of the warehouse with a rifle raised to his shoulder. Before I could peek over the railing, I suspected that the security door from the offices had been breached.

Lennox pointed his rifle at the doorway just waiting for an excuse to fire.

"Wait!" I yelled, already knowing what to expect even without Maxwell's findings from the security feed. "Shut that alarm off!"

Lennox, Maxwell and I all watched with suspicion as Benni Kotes poked his head through the entryway normally blocked by the heavy security door. Sensing no danger and ignoring the alarm, Kotes sauntered onto the warehouse floor while a three barrel Cress was still pointed in his direction.

"What the...?" Maxwell muttered, bewildered as to how the assistant could have breached Mac's security system.

"I'm sorry. I got a little bored and needed something to do," Kotes mumbled, poorly feigning a set of manners.

Killian Szazs wasn't far behind the younger informatech, but his grim expression suggested that he didn't desire to be party to the security breach. It appeared that he would have preferred to be an objective wall hanging given how his eyes were cast down to the floor in an attempt to avoid blame.

"Well, Lennox, it looks like you found help for your repairs," I muttered louder than expected as Maxwell killed the alarm before I could finish my sentence.

Lennox's sneer suggested that he didn't agree with my take on the situation, but after a long tense silence he finally lowered the Cress. He turned and walked away, but within three steps he snagged a paint can and hurled it at Kotes, "Time to earn your keep."

Kotes caught the can and looked at the protech before looking up at my perch. Knowing that he wasn't about to receive sympathy from anyone present, he finally followed Lennox.

The protech hung his head hoping not to receive the same assignment. Once he finally lifted his eyes from the dusty floor, he started to take in the sights related to the advanced hardware hiding in the warehouse. Szazs stepped backward nearly stumbling as he attempted to get a better view of the Behemoth's massive four-legged frame.

"Can I get you something to drink, Protech?" I asked from the floor above.

"P-please," Szazs nodded as he accepted the invitation to join me on the landing above. He struggled to take his eyes off the mechanical craftsmanship consuming its fair share of space in of the warehouse.

I returned from the galley with a chug of juice and handed it to the protech as he took a seat at the op table. He was startled as Maxwell waddled out from behind the old terminal.

"Well, what have we here?" Szazs asked with a child-like curiosity.

"So, you're the brain I had to track down?" Maxwell squeaked.

Protech Szazs' face lost all expression as he blinked, eyes wide at the furry white and brown creature squinting back at him. The manner in which Szazs' throat was twitching suggested that he was suppressing the reflex to spew his recent swig of juice back into the air.

"What? Do I have a goober on my nose?' Maxwell asked, unsure how to react to Szazs's flabbergasted expression.

"This is just amazing," Szazs mumbled. "May I?" He asked as he set his juice down and stretched out a hand to inspect Maxwell's collar.

"Is your tongue detachable for inspection?" Maxwell quipped as he looked at me cautiously.

Szazs recoiled his hand before Maxwell broke into a chuckle and nodded. I rolled my eyes at the hamster's jest aimed at our guest's curiosity. Szazs gently unclasped the collar and turned it over in his hand leaving Maxwell without his gift of speech.

"Finally, some quiet around here," I smirked.

Even without his collar, Maxwell didn't hesitate to shoot me a dirty look while the aged informatech marveled at the advanced device in the palm of his hand.

"To think that I spent so many passes allowing my intellect to be used for destruction rather than creation. How misguided I have been," Szazs said with a forlorn face as he returned the device to Maxwell's neck.

"Just what exactly does everyone do here, Mr. Fox? And who is responsible for all of these advancements?" Szazs asked, hopeful that he might finally turn a corner on his nagging guilt.

"I've yet to discover my my role here, but Mac, Lennox and Maxwell have certainly been busy over the passes committing time to construction and service. Even our latest, Alex sure fits in with all of the craziness after his defection from the Martial Legion. I can't speak for his motives, but he's certainly a complement to this strange family," I answered.

"Families are important for trust. Deep trust is critical to destroy barriers," Szazs replied.

"I sense that is something you feel is lacking and, in part, why you sought us out," I said, surprised that it was so easy to read the protech even without my ikes.

Szazs nodded.

Arcs passed as I continued my discussion with the protech. His understanding of behavior was astounding despite most of its application focusing on animal study. During his time with BOWTech, Szazs had opportunity to profile a host of individuals, but his findings were disappointing when some results showed that some exhibited as much worth as the most agitating insects. Over the course of his studies across humans, animals and synthetics, Szazs came to the conclusion that humans alone had the gift to reach outside their programming and acquire more, but only if responsibility accompanied that unique gift. Szazs felt that he personally learned such a lesson too late which had prevented an escape from the path of Frank Jenkins' destructive tendencies.

By the time Szazs and I were wrapping up our conversation, Lennox and Kotes made their way upstairs. Lennox, although still agitated at having to repair his vehicle, was glad to have the chore finished. Kotes, however, made no effort to hide the contempt on his face at having to participate in the manual labor.

A faint whirring sound reached our ears. We looked around for the source, but it only seemed to grow as it enveloped the entire warehouse. It had barely begun when Alex could be heard dropping into the warehouse from the utility elevator.

"We've got incoming!" Alex yelled frantically with his sword in hand.

Thread: actTgtPersp1.view

I had never seen the Serpent react with any mood beyond calm, but from his expression I could read that the utility elevator couldn't move fast enough to expedite his race for the weapons locker. After hearing the warning, I realized that the sound of loud rushing wind belonged to a series of incoming choppers.

Torque was already making a break for the weapons locker, but before he take two steps, a thunderous crash peeled through the warehouse as dark green uniforms kicked their way in through multiple doors. The airbridge access door from the front offices, the side bay door and the opposite utility room door all slammed inward. Even without having seen one in person, I immediately recognized the harsh physical characteristics of Piran soldiers on account of their common facial reconstruction. As some barged up the stairwell while others stared down at us from the airbridge above, we were prevented from reclaiming our firearms.

"Maxwell, lockdown assets now," Torque snapped as he stepped backward to the training floor center so that he could identify just how many threats we were up against. He at least had his kamas in his possession and decisively flicked the blades outward and spun them in hand while watching the broad faced soldiers.

I swiped my fima sticks from the table, but I didn't know what good they would be against the soldiers who appeared to be armed with the standard issue EQ assault rifles. I motioned for Szazs and Kotes to get behind me, not that it was a safer position since we were caught in a circle.

As the staredown persisted, another Piran walked across the airbridge overhead. From the haps, I recognized him as the Piran Leader, Commander Donovan Pyln, head of Frank Jenkins' military forces. Other Pirans parted ways so that Pyln could speak from his perch above the galley and living quarters.

"Mr. Jenkins requests your presence," Pyln said, sneering down at us.

"I think that you pronounced *demands* incorrectly. Invitations aren't typically delivered from the tip of a barrel," I retorted sarcastically.

"You're shrewd, but I'm not here to play word games. Mr. Jenkins has no interest in entertaining corpses, so to my chagrin I've ensured that you will be alive at least up until your introduction," Pyln grunted.

"You know, people used to like fish. Now, I see why they were given a bad name. You Fishheads have so much blood on your hands, but this time it'll be your own, knowing that I won't have regrets for putting you down," Torque yelled at the Piran commander.

Pyln's sneer widened even further as he thrust his index and middle finger forward in a pointing gesture toward the three of us who were standing back to back in a small circle on the training floor.

"Free Ice Brrgr's to anyone who gets us out of this mess," Torque muttered under his breath.

"Let me drive the Chromehound again, and you've got a deal," the Serpent hissed back as his eyes narrowed when a couple of Pirans advanced cautiously.

All of the hushed rumors about Pirans suggested that they were a fearless and punishing force not to be challenged, but as I scrutinized them in the few ticks before the hammer fell, I could see that they too were still human. Even with the vain desire to belong to a unit, they demonstrated their hollow nature. If they were ordered to take us alive and still cared about preserving their own lives, their superficial nature could work to our advantage.

One Piran charged the Serpent only to watch the copper glow of a superheated blade sever his left arm from the rest of his body. All of the Pirans' training in pain tolerance evaporated as a scream ripped through the air. Instantly fueled with aggression, the rest of the Pirans advanced.

In an attempt to tackle me, a Piran dove forward, but I sidestepped and delivered a cracking blow to the back of his head as he fell past my position. I knew that the soldiers would have thick skulls and require much more persuasion. From a quick estimate, I counted roughly thirty Pirans or so. With ten to one odds, I doubted that survival was a likely outcome.

As another Piran closed in from behind, I sprang into the air and launched my heel upward catching him square in the face with a reverse kick. Even though I assumed that they were tough, I was still surprised to see the amount of punishment that the soldiers could take as my foe only staggered backward and slowed down the two Pirans who approached from behind.

Torque weaved and sidestepped the three Pirans who hoped to pummel him in unison. Torque arced his kamas through the air slicing a Piran with each nimble step. His initial strikes only managed to tear long gashes in their thick uniforms. Given their persistence, Torque struck more ruthlessly, catching one in the neck with the underside of the kama blade in his right hand and another in the eye with the tip of the blade in his left hand before kicking the blinded victim backward.

The Serpent was quick to turn the training floor into a gory mess of severed limbs and cadavers. A quick sample of his work instantly validated his reputation within the Ghost ranks. I was relieved to be fighting alongside him rather than against him.

Out of my peripheral vision, I spotted Szazs and Kotes resisting the Pirans, but they were no match and easily subdued. They were forced to the floor unless they wanted to make their departure in an unconscious state. I swung hard with my fima sticks to catch a Piran in the face, but only succeeded in striking his sharp metal teeth which sent a shockwave up my arm. The Piran simply glared back at me in response. I moved to swing again, but another Piran caught me from behind trapping my shoulder, stopping the strike.

The Piran in front of me stepped in to punch my abdomen, but I countered by dropping one of my fima sticks, flexing my hand to activate a grip so that I coul pull the metal chair near the op table into the air. The chair slammed into the back of the Piran's head causing him to stagger. I swiftly followed the attack, jamming my other fima stick into the eyes of the Piran behind me. As the staggering Piran fell toward me, I dropped down and launched him over my body into the Piran behind me.

I felt like the temperature in the room had shot up drastically on account of the Piran rage and relentless assault. I couldn't negate the thought, given the sweat dripping from both sides of my face. Frustrated at the opposition, the Pirans started to act recklessly, flailing and tackling without hesitation or strategy. Four dove at me forcing me to jump laterally to evade them, but I wasn't quick enough. One of the slower Pirans clipped my heel, causing an awkward landing and putting me off-balance.

I flailed my arms to regain my balance, but I couldn't do so without jostling the op table and the hardware resting on it. As my back slammed into the railing, conflicting thoughts surged through my skull. The potential crash of the flatjack made me consider the data that could be jeopardized if destroyed, including Streetz's operating system, but conversely my training told me to remain focused on the fight. As my peripheral vision spotted Maxwell being tossed from the table, I somehow instinctively reached out and grasped onto the Vanguard terminal, an opportunity that was immediately seized by the closest Piran.

Quick to leverage the distraction, a Piran slammed a shoulder into my chest, knocking me backward over the railing. My left arm tightened clutching the flatjack while my right hand released the fima stick so I that could grab a railing post before dropping to the hard warehouse floor below. Disappointed that I had reacted so quickly, the Piran moved to stomp on my fingers. Even with the looming threat above, Maxwell's movement along the edge caught my attention since he was in danger of being crushed by the Piran's wide boot.

My eyes blurred and my shoulder screamed in pain from supporting my weight. The commotion caught Pyln's attention long enough for him to bark at Piran's and have them haul me up. I had no solution for my predicament, but I refused to put Maxwell or Streetz in danger. My body reacted on its own. I dug the base of my foot into the wall which granted me just enough traction to reach up, release the post and swipe Maxwell's tiny body before he got squashed. Naturally, there was nothing left for me to do but fall ten marks and slam into the floor. Maxwell squealed as I tucked him and the data terminal close to my chest. I closed my eyes, hoping that the immediacy of my plight might override the inexperience of my skills. My body tensed as it filled with a tingling situation before drifting into blackness.

Thread: sysObserver.cmd

Pyln watched his soldiers near the railing before they looked his way, blinking and dumbfounded. Pyln squinted, not fully understanding what had happened. The gasps and chatter about the foe disappearing into thin air made no sense. Aggravated by the failure to capture one of the targets, Pyln scooped the assault rifle from his hip and fired a five round burst into the torso of the one who failed to capture the target.

Torque noticed the diversion near the railing and turned his head ever so slightly. Even the minute distraction was a mistake that he would regret. Just as his eyes darted from his target, a Piran slammed a fist into the side of Torque's jaw followed by an uppercut to the midsection. The combo by the powerful soldier dropped Torque to his knees. He spit a mouthful of blood on the floor from the cut inside his mouth before another towering Piran kicked him in the back, driving him down to the floor.

The Serpent's strength too had reached its end. He felt that the Piran's were closing in for the final time as they continued to circle around him, but the Pirans all held position when they realized that Pyln had an EQ pointed at the target in their midst.

"It would give me no greater pleasure than to drag you before Jenkins as an unconscious meat sack," Pyln snapped.

He knew that he could still take a couple more on the way down, but the Serpent also knew that further resistance would be meaningless. He couldn't trust Pyln, but just maybe some of the Pirans would one day understand the grace that prevented their end at that time. The Serpent slowly turned to face every soldier looking on so that he could make note of how many were left while he loosened the grip on his sword before finally dropping it to the floor. Vanguard managed to thin the Piran numbers to half, but alas it was insufficient. The Serpent spotted Torque's body already sprawled on the floor, but it was the last thing that he saw before a sharp blow struck the back of his head crumpling him to the floor.

Global Alliance Compound
Neutral Territory
Moz Fractillend, Caafri Continent
Thread: sysObserver.cmd

As the Enforcer sprinted over the last hill, the Global Alliance facility came into view. The stone building with opposing sides that sloped upward had a dismal appearance matching the terrain. The hard surfaces and unappealing design had more in common with a fallout bunker than the resort it might have once been. The Enforcer suspected that the building was given a gaudy appearance to match the egos of the world leaders, but instead its construction too acted as an ominous reminder of the past, just like the local landscape.

The Enforcer effortlessly reached the rendezvous point that Ang provided and waited with his cloak active. Several military escorts finally arrived and surveyed the facility before giving approval to their respective leaders. The Enforcer pressed himself against the outer wall of the stone staircase leading into the building. Even though, he was invisible, he knew that proximity could allow passersby to hear the faint hum from the cloaking device.

As more faction leaders and their escorts arrived, the Enforcer had yet to see any sign of Potentate Ang. He hoped that the Mogul Prime informant hadn't done anything bold enough to disrupt the mission. He had already been reluctant to inform Newton of the eyecon tech that he passed to Ang in order to allow him to see the Enforcer even while cloaked.

As clicks passed, the Enforcer spotted Ang's lanky form approaching from the direction of the airfield. Commander Jackal and Oshan soldiers followed directly behind the potentate. As Ang approached the complex, he spotted the Enforcer right away and gave a slight nod in his direction. The Enforcer checked to make sure his pathway was clear and then followed the potentate like a shadow. He had to be extremely careful not to bump anyone and reveal his location.

The inside of the facility was as dismal as the outside, but at least it was surprisingly clean on account of the committees appointed to manage the place. The Enforcer kept an ever watchful eye open for security cameras should there be changes to the structure as described by Ang's last visit. As they passed the security escorts, the Enforcer noticed that General Seechi was not present in the Maleezhun security detail. Indeed the general had been correct in his suspicions, revealing that the faction's Emperor had already replaced the Ghosts with lesser known soldiers in black uniforms with dragon-like insignia stamped on them.

Even more surprising to the Enforcer than Seechi's absence, was that of Commander Pyln. From what the Enforcer had studied of Frank Jenkins, he was never known to be seen in public without Pyln at his side. The Enforcer could only speculate a couple reasons for such a change. Either Pyln had finally annoyed Jenkins for the last time and found himself terminated, or Jenkins tasked Pyln with something even more important that his agenda of global conquest. The latter option reminded the Enforcer of his lack of contact with Vanguard causing the thought of ill circumstances to send a chill down his spine, but knowing that there was no time to dwell on negative speculation, he suppressed his concerns and remained focused.

As the party neared the conference hall, the Enforcer noticed that military escorts were congregating in the lounge area opposite the hall entrance. Only faction leaders were allowed into the conference hall. Jackal and his Oshan officers cautiously stepped away from Potentate Ang, leaving him at the doorway to the hall. Once the escorts had stepped away, Ang nodded slightly over his shoulder that he was going inside. The Enforcer quickened his steps to stay behind Ang as they passed through the large double doors to avoid creating a visual disturbance.

The conference hall was a plain room with a circular table in its midst and adequate projector technology overhead. Large windows created a view over the landscape, but given the absence of color it was difficult to discern the outside from the drab interior. The only objects that weren't gray in the room were the twelve wooden chairs around the table. The Enforcer was already tired of the awful aesthetics. At least back home, the constant grays were offset by occasional clouds and distant city lights.

Potentate Ang found his place at the circular table near the opposite wall. The Enforcer walked softly and aligned his position behind Ang's chair before backing away from the table to minimize any audible sound to the faction leaders.

The cold and lifeless conference room did nothing to improve the atmosphere as it became evident that faction leaders were not pleased with Jenkins' call for the Global Alliance meeting. Given the stories that the Enforcer had heard of other faction leaders, he wasn't surprised at the absence of hospitable behavior. He hadn't been able to keep up with politics beyond Windstonne's border, but the Enforcer still recognized the long standing faction leaders who had held their power since the Global War by way of the Uniod Bloc's shrewd Tarak Delaney and the Equatorial Span's man of the people, Cecil Khadem. Due to many of their regions' continual states of unrest, new faces represented the factions of the Coalition of Jungle Republics, Insurgistan and Straypoint Stronghold.

The Enforcer slowly scrutinized the world leaders carefully watching their faces and expressions, but as he did, something rather peculiar became evident. The eyes of more than half of the faction leaders were a pale white. Both their irises and pupils were white, cloudy even and lacking in color. The Enforcer was unaware of any disease to cause such a phenomenon, and it proved concerning that it was affecting the leaders from disparate regions.

After a quick calibration of his ikes, the Enforcer ensured that his own vision was not being affected by his ikes or his cloak. He was also careful to observe the other leaders without the symptoms to see if they reacted strangely. The Enforcer was inclined to duck into the lounge to see if the security escorts exhibited similar conditions, but before he could move, Frank Jenkins finally entered the conference hall. All heads turned to face the one who had called the meeting.

Frank Jenkins' eyes narrowed as they panned across the conference hall. The Enforcer tensed, pondering if Jenkins was in any way aware of his presence. If the informant in the Oceanic Outpost administration relayed the tech given to Ang, Jenkins might be able to detect him, but after Jenkins had completed his check, satisfied that there was no pressing danger beyond the impatient looks, he strolled toward his seat.

"Gentlemen, I would like to thank you for meeting with me today," Jenkins said without bothering to seat himself.

"What is this about, Jenkins?" Emperor Shito asked.

Frank Jenkins continued speaking as if oblivious to the emperor's interjection. "Today, I do not come bearing haps of wars or terror, but of opportunity. Today, you shall witness the unveiling of the Unisphere"

Mumbling immediately arose from the faction leaders in regard to the strange proposal and the arrogance of the Commercial Empire's faction leader.

"I'm sure that you have many questions, but before you present them, I want to offer you the chance to serve on my council. All of you shall retain your present ranks and influence of your respective factions which will aid in a smooth transition. All I suggest is that you transfer authority of your holdings, which is simply transactional, to the newly coronated Governor Supreme," Jenkins added.

The mumbling erupted into outbursts as some leaders stood, hurling insults at Jenkins. Even though the outrage was nearly deafening, Jenkins was completely ambivalent and took the resistance in stride. He continued to stand there silently while the faction leaders vented and demanded explanation. After nearly five clicks, the majority of the shouting simmered, allowing Jenkins to speak at a reasonable level.

"Do any of you have access to your region's hapcasts? If so, please tap your desired feed into the projector," Jenkins continued.

A hush fell over the confused faction leaders as Jenkins looked for a willing volunteer.

"Mr. Delaney, perhaps," Jenkins said as he turned to the Uniod Bloc leader who still had a scowl stamped onto his face.

Still confused by the request, Delaney slumped into his chair with arms crossed and squinted at Jenkins. After a long pause, he reluctantly tapped the reference to the dominant hapstream in the faction's capital enclave. A gray haired hapcaster popped onto the projection in the midst of the conference table and began discussing the transportation issues happening within the faction.

"If you expected us to take a back seat while you steer this alliance, Jenkins, then you are a fool," snapped one of the newer faction leaders, his words as sharp as knives.

"I think you misunderstand," Frank Jenkins said with a smirk. "I'm not here to control your factions, I'm here to show you, how you can. As our newest members can attest, there is a certain danger to face when the will of the people breaches intended containment. Since there is still a lingering threat not yet extinguished since the last two wars."

"What threat?" another leader asked.

"Freedom," Jenkins replied. "Our Alliance is still unstable because some of you are still passive in leveraging your authority."

"You make it sound simple, but you only had to seize a system already on the verge of collapse," Tarak Delany countered. "We control the people as needed to maintain peace."

"No, Tarak, I did my part to seed its collapse long before it was given a push over the edge," Jenkins replied, making no effort to hide the rivalry between the two factions despite the oceanic divide. "You don't recognize that those who realize they are in a cage are most dedicated to escaping it."

Jenkins tapped the controls closest to his seat for the projector. Suddenly, the hapcast changed to a different Uniod Bloc meca, but the haps shifted toward reports of a revolt in the streets without clear indication as to which enclave. Delaney squinted at the projection and tapped the controls to change the meca, but all of his efforts yielded the same result. Cecil Khadem too performed a similar motion, but each of the hapcasts from the Equatorial Span frequencies all showed local reports of unrest.

"Control is in the casting, Gentlemen, and without my resources your time will soon come to an end. What you do not realize is that when the people are so distracted, so bombarded by convenience, by competition, by recreation they will not care about the invisible fence that you can expertly craft around them. You only need to have them work toward your agenda when they think they are working toward their own," Jenkins said smugly.

"You're skulljakt, Jenkins. The populations are too distributed to be controlled by a single source, and it's not possible for you to take over all widecast channels!" the leader from the Uniod Branch contested.

"No? Then perhaps you would care to explain why Mr. Delaney no longer has access to satellites under his domain. The new and improved satellites of the Unisphere have the power to disable any obstruction in orbit. Don't think that the people wouldn't hesitate to follow a narrative showcasing the end of any opposition," Jenkins said.

"I don't know how you're performing your clever parlor tricks, but I say that you are full of it," Ang blurted.

Jenkins' head snapped in Ang's direction like a snake ready to strike its prey as if he had been waiting for the Oceanic Outpost leader to address him directly. "I find it peculiar that you would be the one to lecture me on parlor tricks," Jenkins retorted as his hand rifled around his coat pocket before revealing a small black device.

The Enforcer didn't like how quickly Jenkins' tone shifted from arrogance to cunning, nor did he like that Jenkins was fixated on the device in his hand. A premonition suggested that events were about to alter course, so the Enforcer softly stepped away from Ang's seat and notched his way along with the wall to put himself closer to the exit. Jenkins punched the center button on the black device, immediately revealing that it was a scatterfield emitter. The Enforcer heard a faint pop as his cloak disengaged.

Frank Jenkins did his best to hide it, but he was startled at the Enforcer's appearance on the far side of the room. It was as if Jenkins knew someone was present, but didn't know the exact location. Once the Enforcer was detected, Jenkins' stare was upon him, and the other faction leaders turned to see the object of Jenkins' attention. The Enforcer accepted the reality update, his cover was blown.

20 – Dubious Alignment – 20

Mogul Prime Media Resource Center
Core City Fringe, Windstonne Enclave
Commercial Empire, Northam Continent
Thread: sysObserver.cmd

The silence hanging on the air was tense inside the Mogul Prime meeting room. All members were present and accounted for and eagerly waited for Voltaire to suggest a new course of action. Voltaire's grim attitude weighed heavily on the clan ever since the Synergon Project had been turned over to Oszwick Enterprises.

Following the suspicion of betrayal by Frank Jenkins, Mogul Prime felt that they, in turn, traded their services to the next highest bidder. Konrad Oszwick had proven himself to be an extremely smooth negotiator with motives as slippery as Frank Jenkins. After every stage in a series of transactions, Voltaire pondered if there was any outcome in which Mogul Prime didn't get the raw end of the deal. He continued to parse all possible scenarios in his mind while he continued staring at the far end of the table. The stares of his associates weren't enough to interrupt his deep thought.

"We all know what you're thinking, Dean," Pythagoras said, hoping that an audible cue might spur their leader.

"It's time we reconcile this blight and resolve matters ourselves," Tycoon added.

A mildly restrained ruckus broke out from all edges of the meeting room table. Voltaire absorbed all of the demands of his associates but maintained his silence. As he mentally mapped the phrases and puzzle pieces of a solution in his mind, he stood, tapped the comm button on the sonair mounted to the table. A hush fell over the clan members as they realized that he was about to ping Oszwick. Anytime Voltaire thought much and said little, clan members knew that his following words were likely to be profound or blunt and harsh. Either way, no one present wanted to be responsible for the latter.

"Mr. Oszwick," Voltaire said as the sonair connected to the executive's office.

"Ah, Mr. Sargent, I've been meaning to speak with you. I wanted to thank you and your crew for all of the hard work that you have supplied throughout this operation. I know that it must be difficult to understand what exactly is transpiring, but I assure you that you are still an indispensable asset to this project," Oszwick said, cutting in before Voltaire was given a chance to speak his mind.

"Is there any word of Mr. Jenkins' progress?" Voltaire asked through clenched teeth, frustrated at Oszwick's attempt to deflect any incoming hostility.

"Not as of yet, but I'm quite sure that our little adjustments are doing their part. I suspect that the outcome will be entertaining," Oszwick replied, offering no cause for concern to his supposed ally.

"Are you suggesting that Project Synergon is destined to fail, Mr. Oszwick?" Voltaire asked.

"Mr. Sargent, you and I both know that the proposed purpose of the project IS a failure. It is a merely a matter as to how unintended entities benefit from that failure," Oszwick replied forcefully.

"What are you suggesting that Mogul Prime is to do until then?" Voltaire asked impatiently.

"Enjoy the down time, or take a holiday. As soon as your services are required, I will make contact. Have a good day, Mr. Sargent," Oszwick replied curtly before terminating the comm.

Voltaire released a long yell from the pent up rage as he turned and slammed his fist into the wall, leaving a permanent imprint. Voltaire breathed heavily as his associates watched his face redden with anger. Members of Mogul Prime feared little, but the sight of their leader in an irate mood certainly placed high on the list.

The turn of events helped Voltaire understand just how Oszwick's manipulative qualities earned him the present position. He thought that Mogul Prime, of all players in the game, could have been immune to the game of double cross, or at least capable of staying in the running, but every single time, Oszwick successfully countered Voltaire's intentions or concerns with some twisted game of words through superficial confidence or gratitude to undercut any opposing agenda. To calm his mood, Voltaire paced back and forth for several clicks before Id was either bold or stupid enough to interrupt the show.

"So, now what do we do?" Id asked.

The others remained motionless as they watched Voltaire snap his head toward Id. Such a vocal intrusion was invitation for thrown chairs or overturned furniture, but Voltaire knew that the source of his anger was from beyond his clan. Undoubtedly, it was his fault for getting his clan into such a mess.

Doing his best to settle the frustration long enough to offer a reply, Voltaire moved his chair, but remained standing at the table. He tapped a button to display icons side by side on the table projector, one from Project Synergon and the other a visual demonstration that he was given by Oszwick.

"The way I see it, we can approach this one of two ways. We can play our hand to ensure that the venture orchestrated by the powers that be burns to the ground so that we can take what is rightfully ours, or we can initiate this backup plan that Oszwick offered us ahead of schedule to test how forthright our new benefactor actually is," Voltaire stated.

"Forget these suits! It's time we do our own thing. I say bring it all down," Bender blurted.

"I'll take option two for a solargrad," Tycoon added.

The room filled with conversation as the clan amicably weighed the outcomes of either decision. Voltaire felt his frustration from the conversation with Oszwick fade as he watched his clan work toward a solution.

"Why not do both?" Pythagoras asked upon detecting a break in the conversation.

The room fell silent as the clan members looked to Pythagoras for elaboration.

"To me it seems illogical that Oszwick would provide us information that he didn't intend to carry out. As long as our adversaries consider us the willing dupes, we may as well maintain that illusion so that we can gain more intel while furthering our own agenda," Pythagoras replied.

Pythagoras received approval for his insight, and the conversation shifted toward creative problem solving to tackle the complex operation at hand. Voltaire relished such moments when he was reminded of the stellar talent of his associates. A twisted smile crept across lips as he affirmed the new direction, "Let's do some research!"

Vanguard Warehouse
Abandoned Sector, Windstonne Enclave
Commercial Empire, Northam Continent
Thread: actTgtPersp1.view

The familiar sound of rushing energy like a distant waterfall finally wrestled my dormant consciousness back into the foreground before the sound diminished, leaving my body with a warm sensation. I feared opening my eyes, unsure what to expect, but I knew that the action was inevitable. As light started to filter through my eyelids, I thought it best to cover my eyes first, but I sensed that there was still a small furry body in one hand. As I slowly opened my eyes, I was reminded that I grabbed Maxwell before my fall. I released my grip hoping that I didn't crush him by accident, but thankfully he stirred as I set him down.

I had no sense of how long I had been unconscious or the particulars of how I shifted to and from the Vast. As my eyes flickered, I realized that I was on the warehouse floor, and by my best estimate, there was morning light poking through the windows overhead. I felt relief that my rash actions hadn't ushered me through death's doorway prematurely.

I motioned to sit up, but sharp pain prompted me to do so slowly. I did a quick injury check and didn't find any broken bones or pulled muscles, but somehow the impact still must have jostled me in the process of transitioning into the Vast. After finally completing the motion, I watched Maxwell as he tried to orient himself with his surroundings.

"What happened?" Maxwell asked.

"We're about to find out," I remarked not having any qualified answers. I hardly knew how to explain the Vast, let alone comprehend if Maxwell was capable of understanding it. I supposed that it was for the best if he had no recollection of the experience.

I carefully rose to my feet ensuring that I didn't drop the flatjack which had been tucked close to my body. I felt dizzy, but after leaning on the locker for a moment the sensation cleared. I scooped up Maxwell and headed for the stairs, afraid of what I might find. While ascending the staircase, I looked around, surprised that the Pirans didn't leave an observer if I were to return, in which case, I was also relieved.

Upon reaching the training floor, I cringed at the blood stains in multiple directions. The Pirans had been efficient in leaving no bodies behind, friend or foe. If it weren't for the crimson marks on the floor and walls, the struggle might have gone undetected. Thankfully, the absence of my friends suggested that they were still alive.

After righting the op table, I set Maxwell and the flatjack back into place and opened the terminal so that Maxwell could do his thing. Maxwell was quick to restore access, do a security check and remove the cloaks hiding Vanguard's vehicles. Once they were restored, I did another glance around the facility and considered it odd that the Pirans didn't bother taking any of Vanguard's wares. Either they had been convinced that I wouldn't return, or the retrieval of Killian Szazs superseded all other objectives, leaving little concern for renegades in the abandon.

It was obvious that Maxwell wasn't his usual self since he simply stared at the terminal screen.

"I'm going to need you to multitask. Do your best to get Streetz back online while employing everything that you can to get Mac back on the comm," I said. "When I get done cleaning, I'll help locate the others."

Maxwell nodded without any of his usual sarcasm.

Knowing that I was little help in the technical space, I needed some activity to clear my head. As I took in the havoc that had been unleashed upon our living space, I felt nauseous in part, likely on account of guilt for initiating such a foolhardy mission. I didn't know what to do next, so to pass the time, I would start undoing the mess. I hoped that someone would have a solution, but until that time, I knew that I was going to need a large supply of industrial cleaner.

Global Alliance Compound
Neutral Territory
Moz Fractillend, Caafri Continent
Thread: sysObserver.cmd

The Enforcer tensed at the surreal silence as all eyes fixated on him. He didn't know if he should wait to be addressed or immediately bolt for the exit and take his chances with the surplus of security escorts in the room beyond.

"I see that you have parlor tricks of your own, Potentage Ang. You are in direct violation of the neutrality agreement of the Global Alliance and are hereby..." Jenkins yelled.

"Not so fast, Jenkins. He isn't dressed like any of my citizens. His attire looks Imperan to me. You're trying to set me up!" Ang interjected with aggression that clearly caught Jenkins off guard.

Additionally, to Jenkins' surprise, the shouting resumed, but instead of any focus on Potentate Ang, it was directed at the faction leader of the Commercial Empire. All charges and accusations bearing Frank Jenkins' name were laced with an assortment of colorful language. Any favor that he hoped to garner was lost.

Leveraging the outburst that targeted Jenkins as a distraction, the Enforcer dashed for the exit. If any of the faction leaders noticed his exit, they were slow to respond. As much as he wanted to hear the outcome of the vocal barrage, the Enforcer knew there was only one mission at hand, Escape!

The veteran security escorts had grown accustomed to the nature of heated debates from within the conference hall, so an increase in audible voices didn't create any cause for alarm, but once the

Enforcer burst from the conference hall, his appearance created a surplus of confused stares.

After a brief hesitation, a loud chorus of clicks filled the waiting room as the security guards unlatched, primed and leveled their disruptors. Disinterested in hearing the next measure of the symphony, the Enforcer bolted to his right as a firestorm surged toward his position, charring the conference hall doors. The amount of plasma narrowly evaded convinced the Enforcer that there was no patience, mercy or even curiosity from the security escorts.

The Enforcer sprinted down the hallway, periodically bounding laterally to keep the soldiers from getting an easy lock on him. With his thoughts unfocused, he knew there was too much risk to shift into the Vast without risk of greater injury. His best option was to make it outside and hope that Jenkins' gadget hadn't fried his cloak permanently.

Jackal observed as the Enforcer dashed for the exit, but given the amount of firepower trained on him, there would be no means of escape. Even a stray plasma burst could cut him down, and the probability was high, given the violence prone behavior of the escorts bent on entertaining themselves. Jackal ran a partial-tick calculation quicker than he thought by doing an inspection of the other faction escorts' physical fitness.

Jackal sprang forward, hoping to intercept the Enforcer. At a minimum, he could add cover by blocking the line of sight from the trigger happy guards, most of which would be reluctant to fire on the Oceanic Outpost's military leader. Since Jackal made it a priority to maintain his own condition, despite his high rank, he quickly closed the gap between the Enforcer and himself. He only needed to create an adequate diversion before the other escorts could get a clean shot by the time the Enforcer reached the doorway.

The Enforcer felt plasma splash off the walls and at his heels singeing the carpet underfoot. He sensed Jackal's presence closing, and hoped that the Oshan commander had a plan, compared to the other possibility, that Jackal was the informant and responsible for revealing his presence. Taking no chances, the Enforcer forced his mind to commit every particle and fiber possible to accelerate his muscles and facilitate his escape.

Jackal was surprised that the Enforcer still had energy to burn as the gap between them widened. Jackal caught a glimpse over his shoulder and noticed that several other soldiers had followed his lead and joined in the manual pursuit. Surprisingly, a couple of limber soldiers managed to catch up to Jackal and followed directly behind. It was just the opportunity that the commander needed. It was time for a make-or-break decision.

Jackal slammed his foot hard into the carpet forcing himself to lose balance and tumble forward, initiating an obstacle for the following soldiers to trip over. Havoc ensued as the slow soldiers still tried to shoot around the melee but were prevented with all of the bodies in the way.

The Enforcer slammed his shoulder into the door and charged into the open air. Frustrated yells came from behind, but his pursuers didn't have enough time to make sense of the pile of bodies which created a choke point at the entryway. Without time for curiosity, the Enforcer sprinted in the direction of the Eagle, checked the status of his cloak and immersed himself in a sense of relief as a familiar hum suggested that his cloak was once again active.

During his return run to the landing zone, the Enforcer felt the paradoxical stimuli of the physical and mental toll. He was likely running faster on account of the adrenaline pumping through his system, but conversely, his mind was fatigued by trying to process the events recently executed and the efforts to solve the motives prompting them. Once the Eagle was in sight, he discarded the confusing sensation and focused on getting into the air.

Once aboard the Eagle, the Enforcer stowed his cloak and removed his ikes momentarily so that he could rub his eyes. His mind latched onto the onslaught of questions recently presented. Things were not adding up. Frank Jenkins' reason for the meeting, the faction leaders' strange appearance combined with the unusual mood swings, the Oshan informant, even Jackal's involvement all swirled about in a mental maelstrom. Even the efforts to see the big picture felt confusing, yet there was still an element of coordination behind it. The Enforcer had been on the hunt for solutions to hidden problems for far too long to let this one rest.

As the Eagle's engines roared to life, the Enforcer lifted the gray metal craft vertically. Once he reached optimal height he pressed the control stick forward and plotted his course for home. Given the turbulent state of the Global Alliance meeting, the Enforcer was concerned about the Equatorial Span raising its alert levels, jeopardizing his flight across the continent, but until such concerns took root in reality, he would have to stay frosty.

The mixture of thoughts centering on loose ends and the travel home introduced one more, Fox. The Enforcer reviewed the rapid progress of Fox's development, but he knew the time was reaching a critical threshold about just how much Fox could handle before being confronted with the path ahead. The body could be pushed to extreme limits, but only if the mind could keep pace. Fox had been cast into a fight much larger than he understood and although he had been given the tools to lead, without the proper purpose and will to utilize them, such tools could become an added burden to anyone in proximity. The Enforcer knew that time was short for him to make any corrective measures to a plan developed long ago. He couldn't afford to check out before imparting critical knowledge.

Thread: sysObserver.cmd

Before Mac's thoughts could map any future plans, they were interrupted by a shrill tone from the Eagle's sonair. He eyed the console suspiciously, knowing that only a few entities had capacity to reach him.

"Enforcer here," Mac said warily before verifying the identity on the other end of the comm.

"Mac! You're alright!" replied a soft voice through a heightened sense of relief.

"Sath, what's wrong?" Mac asked.

"I didn't know what happened to you. I heard that Jenkins might have identified your location. When I tried to reach you at the warehouse, Lennox said that he hadn't been able to make contact either," Sath replied.

"I'm sorry that communications were in short supply, but I assure you I'm fine. I was trying to track down a clan informant but unfortunately without success. At least I got to hear from Jenkins' own mouth some of his plans for overtaking the Global Alliance," Mac said.

"Mac, I'm scared," Sath said after a long pause. "I overhead chatter between some of the Pirans. It had something to do with a nasty fight. I couldn't get any information, but it sounded like there were captives. One description matched Lennox's appearance."

Mac bit his lower lip, contemplating what could have transpired in such a short time.

"Sath, I want you to get out of there, outside of Windstonne if at all possible, but definitely get somewhere safe," Mac said, shoving his concerns about the Piran conversation to the side.

"I can't. Jenkins is due back in a matter of arcs. He'll be looking for me," Sath replied.

"The first chance you get, find a way. I mean it," Mac replied emphatically.

"I will. It's good to hear your voice," Sath said.

Mac knew that there was no dismissing the fear in Sath's voice. He would have been lying if he didn't admit that he too felt a sizeable amount of concern given the circumstances. He wanted to take the time to reassure her that things would be okay, but no matter the words he considered, none of them felt convincing, knowing that if he didn't stop Frank Jenkins there wouldn't be a future for either of them.

Mac felt an internal conflict in refraining from telling Sath how he really felt, so all he could muster was, "You take care. I'll see you soon."

Mac felt a gut wrenching silence before Sath closed the comm. Sath's mention of Jenkins immediately snapped Mac's attention back to the meeting. He started scanning the Hyper Lynx for any irregular hapstreams, but another ping suggested more incoming comms. He expected to hear Lennox or Maxwell, but was startled at hearing Potentate Ang's voice.

"Mac, I apologize for having to track you down, but I'm sure you want to know what happened back there," Ang said, getting straight to the point.

"You could say that again, William. I wasn't quite sure what to make of your performance. That is before Jackal took point on trying to chase me down," Mac replied with an edge to his response.

"The way I interpreted events was that Jackal's quick thinking kept you from taking plasma to the back. He managed to delay the security forces long enough for you to escape," Ang replied reassuringly.

Mac remained silent unsure how he wanted to evaluate the alternate perspective to the events.

"That was quite the theatrical performance on Jenkins' part," Mac mused after tabling any potential accusations.

"You might be interested to know that my techs discovered interference with our satellites. They are still struggling to bolster the security, but I suspect that Frank Jenkins has taken his expansion by force to the next level if he has set his sights on global mediacasting," Ang said.

"That easily explains the visual trickery, but it feels a bit elaborate for Jenkins' methods. What happened during the outburst?" Mac asked.

"Strangely, I'm struggling to make sense of that myself. The outcome was most unusual. I sensed that Jenkins expected most leaders to lend him credibility and side with his cause, but somehow it backfired. It seemed like most were ready to string him up on the spot, especially those with the weird eyes, but his security escort interjected in time to calm things down especially since the fiasco with your escape distracted the other security teams. With minor exception, the leaders voted that it was time to shut down Frank Jenkins even if it risked war with another Global Alliance faction. The Uniod Bloc, Coalition of Jungle Republics and the Martial Legion all expressed their desire to participate in the operation," Ang said.

"That's not good, lots of civilians in the Commercial Empire. Do you plan on attending the party?" Mac asked.

"I'm fully aware of Jenkins' contempt for the Interlace, and I think it best to see him removed, however, I didn't vocalize such concern at the meeting. That said, I will do what ever is required of me to contribute to his removal," Ang replied.

"How long until the fish hits the can?" Mac asked.

"Our forces are already being mobilized, but I still must return to Cydnon before full deployment. It's going to take a few days to cut the waves between the Outpost and Imperan waters," Ang said.

"Understood. Be careful, Boomer-Ang. Our informant is still at large. Enforcer out," Mac said affirmatively before closing the comm.

Mac was ready to push forward on the Eagle's control stick, but his view from the cockpit revealed a brilliant horizon of green as he passed over one of the Equatorial Span's largest jungles. Memories unfamiliar passed through his mind. He knew the context of them, but the distant visuals of dense foliage and thick air reminded him of the ever present mission directing him, one which even superseded Vanguard's functions. No matter how distracted he might be with the current intrigue and threats, he needed to keep his wits about him. His time was short, and there was too much at stake to get caught up with the small scale affairs of meddling factions. Frank Jenkins was trouble, and if he was allowed to maintain his authority it would spell disaster not only for the remaining free populations of the Alliance but also for the Interlace and beyond. Clearly, the mask had been removed from Jenkins' campaign. Time was of the essence to ensure that even greater machinations were kept in check.

Gridloc: Diluvian Shift
Thread: frmCntmntMrkr.prt

Mac halted his hike through the dense foliage as the terrain clutched his shoe. The thick mud made suction noises as he carefully lifted his foot, hoping to leave as much of the sludge behind as possible. After a brief grimace he carried on, pushing broad leaves and coarse vines away from his body. His shirt clung to his chest drenched from the inescapable moisture in the air. Even if he desired to move faster and the vegetation were clear, he would have to endure the pond-like vapor plugging his respiratory system.

Taking a moment to wipe his brow, Mac felt relief upon spotting the dense fog surrounding a cliff face in the distance. Since he was unable to get specific directions from the locals, he had to rely on rather vague landmarks to find his objective. The Herdsmen weren't shy about their disinterest in joining him even for the best trades that Mac could offer. At least he wouldn't have to worry about confused onlookers, thus allowing him to complete his task in secret.

The brush gave way to the clearing enveloped in fog. Mac was about to inspect the mysterious stone columns within the fog when the snapping of branches on his left caused him to jump to the side. A host of leaves and branches parted as a large bipedal reptile lowered its massive head to snatch a cluster of buds from a nearby patch and munched on them noisily. The creature stared absent-mindedly as it looked in Mac's direction. Its tiny forelegs appeared useless, but it could have easily squashed Mac should it be startled and run his way.

Mac marveled at the calm nature of the creature that the Herdsmen referred to as a type of domedi. He knew they came in a variety of shapes and sizes, but nothing quite prepared him for seeing one up close, especially since they were reputed to be aggressive from known history, not too mention, long since dead.

After picking the flower patch clean, the domedi sauntered on its way, creating its own path through the jungle. Once his large neighbor faded into the foliage, Mac resumed his search.

It took a few moments for Mac's eyes to adjust to the fog, but as expected he detected a host of columns scattered across the plain. They were completely hidden by the fog at a distance. Inspecting the closest column, Mac traced his fingers over the ancient symbols which differed greatly from any language that he had seen. The small symbols contained lots of triangles and slashes much like the iconograph languages of the old Equatorial Span nations.

The coarse surface of the columns was like sandstone except where the embedded symbols had remarkably smooth edges suggesting that they were not simply crafted with a hammer and chisel. It wasn't long before the symbols beneath his hand began to glow. Mac removed his hand and watched until the glow spread outward across the other symbols. With slow steady fashion, the glow spread to the ground and then upward to the tip of the column, lost in the fog. Even the neighboring columns began to glow.

Mac turned about, watching the columns light up with tracer lines in all directions. The light blue illumination poked through the fog while the supporting columns remained obscure. Eventually, the glow spread to the cliff face at the edge of the plain where the lights traveled from the bottom all the way to the peak. The tracers revealed the creepy contours of several faces in the rock, each looking in a different direction. Strangely, the glow was brighter near the left most face, drawing Mac's attention toward it.

Making his way through the fog all while checking for unseen hazards, Mac finally reach the gargantuan mouth of the closest carved face. The mouth of the carving still rose four marks overhead. After simply brushing his hand against the wall, the depression within the mouth gave way to an opening, revealing stairs beyond. Based on all available reports, this was his destination. It felt strange to assume the safety of such foreign technology, but given the accuracy of his intel thus far, he ascended the stairs without hesitation.

Much like the columns outside, the cliff interior began to provide illumination relative to his position. Smooth, dark etched glass covered the stairs and the platform above which opened into a room with numerous control consoles. Parts of the light brown raised surfaces where visible from within, but the finely polished panels in every direction clearly indicated that the interior was not designed by any of the local residents. Perhaps it was best that the Herdsmen had a sense of taboo regarding such an unexplainable testament to some unknown culture.

Mac set his attention on the center console which he speculated was nested behind the middle head of the outer wall carvings. The console blinked to life with an assortment of interfaces, each displaying the foreign symbols that danced over the terminal. Per instruction, he tapped on the icon with the three angled slashes which instructed the interface to open a datatank of recorded visuals.

It was easy to forget his task as curious images of other cultures washed across the screen, revealing the variety of domedi in the region along with the experiments performed on them by cultures hostile to the Herdsmen. Before getting lost in the overload of data, Mac planted his body in the angled stone chair adjacent to the console while he pinged his contact.

"Observatory resources verified. Formula marker two-dot-one," Mac said upon hearing the comm activate.

"Yes, the stim encrypted sequence has been isolated. It may have been compromised by a recent guest, otherwise no deviation detected," Mac replied to the inquiry on the other end.

"What else did you need while I'm here?" Mac asked while swiping through more scans from the console.

"There's a lot here. A translation would certainly be helpful," Mac remarked, unsure how to identify the information requested.

"Oh, that's convenient," Mac mused as he tapped a silver icon upon receiving a tip.

"Let's see, Railer... Swoop... Tarbo... Oh, here we go... Turrets!" Mac mumbled out loud while sifting through the wildlife and hardware scans once he had access to legible text that allowed him to interpret the data.

Before returning to his target information, Mac found himself distracted by the profile of a large ground based domedi with a frill behind its head. Several large horns protruded from its skull, two above the brow, and one above the nose. Mac swiped through the images of the creature, but he felt his stomach churn as multiple scans showed procedures by another culture in the region. The large animals where greatly experimented on so that they could support strange and ambiguous weapon platforms.

"That's grotesque," Mac said, as he sat back in the chair.

He quickly queued up the entire datastack that had been requested and waited for an uplink to complete. Mac propped his feet up on the console as the closest screen blipped a conversion progress meter. Intermittent small talk transpired in between random status updates.

"A SES with a different location from the source? Is that even possible?" Mac asked when probed about a subject in which he wasn't exactly adept.

"I guess we'll find out," Mac said after hearing the suggestion for his next stop.

"Looks like all datastacks have been uploaded," Mac remarked. He was about to close the console when a perimeter warning showed a form looking at the columns near the entrance to the observatory.

"Looks like the locals are getting curious. Our work here is done," Mac said as he sat upright and powered down the console. "Follow protocol to the end!"

Mac quickly made his way for the exit, but before reaching the stairs, he spotted a pebble on the floor. He scooped it up and set it on the console in the vicinity of the translation icon. He had no idea if it would do any good, but at least he could point future visitors in the right direction. With a final nod, Mac exited the intriguing observatory without any proper time to understand its purpose, but at least he knew that his mission had been completed.

21 – Leveraged Assets – 21

Executive Level, Casters Tower
Core City, Windstonne Enclave
Commercial Empire, Northam Continent
Thread: sysObserver.cmd

Frank Jenkins stormed through the lobby outside his office with his Piran escort, stepping quickly to match the faction leader's stride. Sath stood upon seeing Jenkins and opened her mouth to speak, but she refrained as she observed her boss' quick pace. She learned early on the reality of Jenkins' quick temper. Even with the ability to dodge such wrath, Sath never envied anyone on the receiving end. Rumors circulated regarding those on Frank Jenkins' short list, such as strange tendencies to contract rare illnesses or have bizarre commuter accidents. The amount of rage plastered on Jenkins' face suggested that he had the capacity to throw someone through the dense glass that separated the executive office from a long fall to the turf below.

Without acknowledging his coordinator, Jenkins shoved his office doors aside while his security detail assumed a post in the lobby. Jenkins looked about upon seeing Konrad Oszwick and Commander Pyln inside.

"That did NOT go as planned!" Jenkins yelled at the bald executive who was staring out the window.

Until the outburst, Commander Pyln had been quietly observing the colorful finned creatures darting about the tank on the wall as he reflected on the animal which he and his troopers utilized for a symbol. As he turned to face Jenkins, he froze fully aware that Jenkins was in a mood commonly associated with unexplained disappearances.

Oszwick turned around, emotionless as usual with exception of his broad smile. "What seems to be the matter, Mr. Jenkins?" He asked, knowing that his calm voice should easily divert Jenkins' irrational behavior.

"You know full well what's the matter! That meeting ended with all of your Extend clients jumping across the table to kill me, and that was after I used that gadget of yours to expose the Enforcer," Jenkins ranted.

Commander Pyln tensed as he heard the clashtag of a potential target being mentioned after assuming that he had been tasked with the capture. At least, for the moment, Frank Jenkins was so frustrated and preoccupied with his ire toward Oszwick that Pyln felt like he wasn't the next entry on the short list.

"I think you're directing your aggression toward the wrong individuals. We were forewarned of his presence. As an uninvited guest, I find it unlikely that he could have swayed anyone to turn the attention toward you," Oszwick replied his subtle sarcasm acting as a salve to Jenkins' ears.

Frank Jenkins rubbed his beard while he contemplated Oszwick's suggestion, "You may be right. They were unable to catch him. This might have been a setup."

"Precisely, now who might have reason to undercut our agenda?" Oszwick asked, trying to get Jenkins' focus on the right track.

"The Enforcer, obviously. He has been a never ending thorn in my side," Jenkins huffed.

"And how did he manage to sneak his way into this exclusive meeting?" Oszwick asked.

"Supposedly, he contacted Potentate Ang, but that is according to your source, Mr. Oszwick," Jenkins replied as he cast a doubtful glare at the executive.

"What could have been so important to our agitant that he would be compelled to travel halfway around the world to the Oceanic Outpost? Wouldn't he have sought allies... locally?" Oszwick asked wryly.

"Potentate Ang is rumored to have ties with the Interlace. Other faction leaders frown on his lax policies in allowing people to educate themselves. That's it!" Jenkins snapped as if stumbled upon the revelation himself. The Interlace is behind this. I knew it!"

"You see? I knew that we could find a peaceful solution to your inner turmoil. I do believe Command Pyln has also been successful in his exploits and has details to share," Oszwick said smugly.

Pyln swallowed, unsure if he should prioritize Oszwick's ability to pacify Jenkins or the potential return of Jenkins' temper. Jenkins revealed his awareness of the Enforcer's presence at the meeting, but Pyln was uncertain if Jenkins might still blame his subordinate for an impossible capture. If the Enforcer had left the faction by the time he received the order, it would have been impossible to intervene in time. Deciding to take his chances by offering the least amount of information to rile Jenkins up, he answered as concisely as possible, "Yes, Sir, we managed to capture his associates. They are currently being held at Mr. Oszwick's facility until you have the opportunity to question them."

"At last, someone has finally done the job I ordered them to do," Jenkins said, clearly pacified for the moment. "Let's not waste time. I'd like to ascertain just how much leverage said associates are worth."

Pyln resisted the urge to snarl at Jenkins for his sarcasm but instead acted as if he received a compliment. In retaliation, he held his tongue and opted not to inform Jenkins about the other individual who managed to escape capture. Jenkins no longer needed to be at the leading edge of the intel gathering process. If he was so intelligent, he could figure it out himself.

Oszwick Enterprises
Core City Fringe, Windstonne Enclave
Commercial Empire, Northam Continent
Thread: sysObserver.cmd

Torque slowly lifted his head. He forced his eyes open only to witness a blurry haze. His face felt like rocks had been surgically stitched inside his cheeks stretching them to painful extremes. He motioned to lift his hands, but they were restrained behind his back. He shifted his weight but his chest and abdomen tensed in protest. His blurred vision slowly began to focus, revealing an extremely red and gray executive atmosphere. They were in some administrative building unlike the military compound or musty landfill that he might have expected. Apparently, the room's owner had a thing for leather, Torque thought to himself upon noticing that most of the furniture was black and shiny.

Movement caught Torque's attention. He looked over to see the Serpent and Protech Szazs in the same predicament. The Serpent appeared to have taken a similar beating, but Szazs fared better, likely on account of his age or inability to fight which may have prompted restraint.

"Anyone know where we are?" Torque half whistled through his lips, his jaw hurting even to speak.

"Weren't sure if you're going wake anytime soon," Szazs said quietly.

"It'll take more than a small basket of freaks to keep me from coming back for more. No offense, Serpent," Torque muttered as he looked at the emotionless heap sitting next to him.

For the first time since any of them had met, the Serpent actually managed a faint chuckle, amused at how Torque's humor had managed to improve in time of distress.

"I haven't seen anyone else since we were left here. I'm sorry for getting you guys involved this. It's all my fault," Szazs replied.

"No, actually it's not, Protech. It's our obligation to help those in need. It is merely a matter of who talked us into this one... Fox," Torque said.

"Speaking of that individual, what exactly happened to him?" Szazs asked.

"He's probably lounging around sipping an Archer cola. I'll have a few choice words for him when this is all over," Torque mumbled.

"I have witnessed that he and the Enforcer have abilities that I cannot yet explain. If he saw an opportunity to get away in order to get word to the Enforcer, I believe that he would have done so," the Serpent replied, countering Torque's frustration.

"The Enforcer, strange abilities, yes, but all Fox has is a few loose screws," Torque quipped.

"Better to have one man on the outside than everyone trapped on the inside, void of contact with the outside world," the Serpent said, trying again to counter Torque's perspective.

"Speaking of a man on the outside, where is that weasel assistant of yours, Protech?" Torque asked.

"I don't know. To tell you the truth I forgot about Benni. I never did like him, so he wasn't exactly my first concern," Szazs replied.

"Perhaps he smarted off, did us a favor, and got himself killed, or... he set us up," the Serpent said quietly.

"If that last one is true, we have to get out of here and stop him before he goes back to track down your friends," Szazs replied.

Torque started fidgeting with the cord that held his wrists in place. There was no time to lose. It was urgent for them to get out and warn the Enforcer. He was more of a capable threat to Jenkins than the rest of them combined. Just as Torque shifted his weight to get a better angle of the cords, Jenkins strode through the door.

Torque and the Serpent glared as Frank Jenkins' pompous frame sauntered in along with Commander Pyln, several Piran soldiers, and another executive looking individual wearing a dark gray suit with a red shirt. The unfamiliar bald executive's color scheme nearly matched that of the room.

"Ah, I'm glad to see that you're all awake. Now we can get to the bottom of things. Protech Szazs, I must say that I am most disappointed with your choice of company. You should be more careful. Hanging out with such social rejects can get you killed," Jenkins said with a haughty air.

"I don't see your face on any popularity awards, Jenkins," Torque snapped defiantly.

"Come now, Mr. Johnson, there is no need for hostilities... yet," Jenkins replied.

Torque's eyes shifted as Jenkins mentioned his name.

"Yes, that's correct. I'm quite familiar with your history of serving the Tricameral Endeavor through independent service. And you, Mr. Corzo, just what exactly is the Martial Legion's involvement in our affairs? Why have you come here?" Jenkins inquired.

"I heard that I could learn how to do a better job of killing those who get out of line, something that I heard Imperan forces were proficient at," the Serpent said icily, only to have Frank Jenkins glare in response to the insult.

"So, you read a couple of scans, Jenkins, Congratulations. Are you going to get the point anytime soon?" Torque asked.

"Mr. Johnson, I'm sure you have already figured out that this isn't about you, but the annoying fish you have worked with. The one who has for so long undermined my authority," Jenkins prattled.

"Well, Jenkins, first of all you shouldn't blame others for your own screw ups. Secondly, we haven't seen him, figured he was overdue some down time. Undermining pompous suitbags is tiring work after all," Torque smirked.

"I'm quite aware, Mr. Johnson, because he just happened to show up uninvited at our Global Alliance meeting, and now thanks to him and your precious Interlace, I have the Global Alliance breathing down my neck ready to flatten Windstonne. So help me, if I don't have the Enforcer's head on my desk, I'll will allow Windstonne to burn and anything you care about along with it," Jenkins huffed.

"You wouldn't destroy an entire enclave just to find one man, Jenkins," Torque sneered.

"You don't think I would?" Jenkins asked, squinting his eyes in contempt.

"I doubt it," the Serpent hissed.

"Try me," Jenkins said as an impatient Piran stepped up and slammed his fist into the Serpent's jaw. The Serpent took the harsh blow to the face in stride and stared back at the ugly soldier who stepped back and shook his hand.

"How's your fist?" the Serpent snapped at the soldier.

"That was not appropriate. These individuals are our guests," said the bald executive, speaking for the first time since the start of the interrogation.

"What is this, a round of good fish, bad fish?" Torque muttered. "Since you apparently have seen the Enforcer more recently than us, why the song and dance?"

"Because, Mr. Johnson, your friend managed to escape, in spite of our elaborate plans to catch him, and now the three of you are what we like to call in our profession, leverage," Jenkins responded.

"Sounds like everyone's an escape artist," Torque replied sarcastically, dropping his head to look at the floor.

Frank Jenkins' eyes narrowed as he turned to look over at Commander Pyln whom he then realized had failed to disclose details about the capture. Jenkins looked from Pyln to the property owner who was observing Torque with curiosity.

"There's someone else isn't there, Mr. Johnson?" the business executive asked.

"And just who are you?" Torque snapped.

"How rude of me. K. Oszwick, this is my facility and you are my guests," Oszwick replied with a smile too broad for Torque to believe was anything but artificial.

"Yeah, well your hospitality sucks," Torque replied, snapping his head over his shoulder, hinting at the cords holding their hands.

"Of course. Commander Pyln, remove the restraints," Oszwick said calmly, "But be warned, Mr. Johnson, my security resources are reliable. Engagement would prove... unwise."

Commander Pyln looked at Oszwick nervously then at Jenkins for confirmation of the command. Frank Jenkins nodded solemnly. Commander Pyln pointed at the three captives, indicating for the other Pirans to remove the cords. One of the Pirans must have been present during the warehouse attack due to his apprehension about stepping close to Torque and the Serpent.

Once the cords had been removed the soldiers stood behind Jenkins, Pyln, and Oszwick while Torque, the Serpent, and Szazs stood to adjust their legs.

"You know that he'll come for us, Jenkins. I wouldn't want to be in his way," Torque said.

"Actually, I'm counting on it, Mr. Johnson. You know why? Because your pathetic Interlace is built on such crutches as compassion and persistence, a weak *leave none behind* attitude just waiting to be exploited. Enjoy your stay. At least here, during your last days, you can watch as night falls on the Global Alliance and witness the dawn of the Unisphere," Jenkins replied in conclusion.

"Where's Kotes?" Szazs snapped at Jenkins who was about to walk out of the hospitality room as Oszwick had indirectly called it.

Frank Jenkins turned abruptly to address the old informatech, "I'm surprised that you should even care about any position that you so eagerly gave up, Killian. Benni Kotes has been tasked with one final mission before assuming your role as head director of BOWTech Laboratories, that is, if he's up to the task."

Jenkins, Pyln, and Oszwick turned to exit the hospitality room with the Pirans following behind. Once everyone had exited the room there was a loud thud as a brace was secured over the doorway, followed by the sound of numerous assault rifles being primed.

The Serpent walked over to the window facing the Windstonne skyline. If Jenkins wasn't lying, from the observation deck, the captives would have the luxury of witnessing the fall of the Commercial Empire's primary enclave, not exactly what he had in mind for front row seats. The only factor that he considered dismal was that he had to watch the spectacle without a bag of Mesquite-Os in hand.

Vanguard Warehouse
Abandoned Sector, Windstonne Enclave
Commercial Empire, Northam Continent
Thread: actTgtPersp1.view

My mood was dour at my apparent helplessness to correct my errors. Collectively, Maxwell and I tried several times to locate Mac without success. Following an absence of successful comms, Maxwell at least managed to keep himself occupied by once again undertaking the process of fixing Streetz.

I buried my face in my hands as despair placed its bid for sole resident in my skull. Even if there was a way for me to run an operation to help Torque and the Serpent, I had no way to locate them. There was no way that Imperan security systems would be so lax in allowing me to find operational parameters.

"Try one more time," I mumbled to the hamster who I'm sure was growing weary with the futile attempts to contact Mac.

Maxwell made an exclamation as the flatjack attempted to connect with the Enforcer's comm. My hopes flickered for a moment as the view screen continued to blink the connecting message. After a tense silence, I heard Mac's voice with the loud roar of the Eagle's engines in the background.

"Enforcer here," Mac replied in his typical serious tone.

"Mac, We finally got through. They're gone, Jenkins has Lennox and Alex, Pirans invaded the warehouse, we fought them, but there were too many. It's all my fault." I replied without considering just how fast I was rambling.

"Whoa, slow down, Fox, I don't like the ever increasing bad haps, but whatever it is, we will find a solution. I'm just off the coast, and will be back within three arcs, until then stay put and don't do anything stupid," Mac said as he closed the connection leaving me and Maxwell once again to our solitude.

"A little late for that," I mumbled.

I got up from my seat and began pacing around the training floor. I had two arcs to figure out how to explain how I had messed everything up, and I how I let down the individual who had already placed far more trust in me than necessary. Mac's mention of more bad haps added even more frustration to the mix. It sounded like things with his operation already went sideways, and I just piled on more negativity like a soggy blanket.

The wait turned into a rather grating experience, and I felt like I wanted to gnaw my fingers off from the tension. Finally, I heard the sound of jet engines power down. A few moments later, Mac crossed the warehouse and met me on the training floor to survey the fallout. He was silent as he took in the damage before he looked to me and asked for an explanation.

I started by informing Mac about the message from Szazs and the risk of infiltrating BOWTech to intervene on his behalf. I described how we brought Szazs and Kotes back to the warehouse, as well as how the Pirans discovered our location and assaulted the building, courtesy of Frank Jenkins.

"So, in summary, this whole mess is my fault. I got everyone captured, and I don't know how we can get them back," I sighed, expecting a stern lecture or a charge to leave for creating such a disaster.

Mac's silence was disconcerting as he sat there and pondered the details. "You had the right intentions. You were correct in guessing that I would have made a similar decision to intervene. Life is full of risks. Some you win, others you don't, but what I hope you learn most from this is that being a leader is not about always making the right decision, but having the responsibility to make up for the times when you don't."

It took a moment for Mac's words to sink in. I always had a tough time reading him since he was the epitome of an emotional void. "So you're not kicking me off the team?" I asked.

"Fox, there will be a time when this team will need you more than you realize. You are here because you have potential. It's simply my role to help you unlock it. Everyone is a crucial part of this team." Mac replied.

"What now?" I asked, feeling only mildly relieved that I hadn't received the anticipated exile.

"Get your verts together. We've got friends to rescue… and a war to stop," Mac said.

The immediate enthusiasm by his first statement was dashed to pieces by the latter, reminding me that his mission had yet to be explained.

"What happened on your trip?" I asked.

"I'll relay the intel once we're mobile," Mac replied. "Maxwell, get your eyes on for any Imperan Hyper Lynx traffic that yields any clues. We've got to find where they are being held."

Maxwell was about to comply when he interjected his inability to repair the missing fragments in Streetz' coding. "Uh, Boss, while you've been gone, I've been trying to repair Streetz but, so far, been unsuccessful."

Mac stepped over to the op table and looked at the coding that Maxwell had been attempting to patch and repair. In a matter of ticks, Mac pinpointed the cause for the hamster's oversight.

"You have to reroute all logic subroutines through the decision making algorithms otherwise you cannot have the perceived intelligence. Without that Streetz will not function," Mac stated.

"Oh… right, I knew that," Maxwell said in a weak attempt to play dumb.

"Uh huh," Mac smirked before he looked at me. "Grab as much firepower as you can carry without slowing you down. We're going to need it."

I moved swiftly to grab any gear in my quarters, including my fima sticks, cloak as well as the shoes and gloves that Mac had given me the night that we defended the mission. If I could execute the techniques that Mac taught me, I would have little use for armor, so I grabbed the most comfortable yet efficient clothing that I could find consisting of my black pullover fleece and gray cargo pants, perfect for stowing extra power cells and akcellerrants. Even though I thought it might be extraneous, I grabbed my black treadball hat for good measure and placed it on my head. Before darting out of my quarters, the mirror caught my attention. I humored myself with the thought that if I were to sacrifice myself for others, I may as well greet death while sporting proper threads. Although I wanted to appreciate my own personal humor, but Mac's recent words hit me like a kick to the face, especially one word in particular, *responsibility*.

Fearing that I lingered too long at the looking glass, I raced out of my room, and headed for the weapon locker and began loading up on power cells, stimpunches, and an assortment of grenades, most of which I still hadn't studied in the arsenal data. I grabbed several firearms including two of the small Splice 15ms which Alex typically used and a Phantom 4.0.

Before I could make my way back to the training floor, I heard the security door creak open. I knew that Mac was in the warehouse checking on the vehicles, so that meant the new arrival could only be an intruder. I leveled the Phantom in my hand at the doorway, only to watch a body slump to the floor once the heavy door was open far enough.

"Mac, get over here!" I yelled while cautiously stepping toward the fallen individual as I intermittently trained my disruptor on the body then the doorway.

Mac sprinted toward my position and pulled out a disruptor of his own noticing that I was suspicious enough to have one on the doorway. He slowly stepped forward and checked to make sure the doorway was clear before putting the disruptor away and rolling the body over to see the individual's face.

Once I caught a clear glimpse, I tensed. It was Kotes. "How did he get here?" I stammered.

"You mean through the door?" Mac asked me.

"No, he managed to crack the security once already. I mean how did he escape the Pirans," I replied.

"Well, hopefully, he has a couple of answers for us," Mac replied as he leaned down to help Kotes up to the training floor where we could put him in a seat.

I worked with Mac to get Benni up the stairs. Upon reaching the second floor, I overheard Maxwell snickering about something at the op table.

"What's so funny?" I asked.

"Nothing," the hamster replied tersely as he straightened up and quickly diverted his gaze from the view screen.

"Right," I muttered in disbelief as we settled Benni down in the chair.

Benni definitely was not looking well. His face was bruised, and his hair was matted in various directions, suggesting that he forced his way out of the Piran ranks. Several clicks passed before he finally stirred. He slowly looked around the room before looking up at us.

"Do you know where you are?" I asked quietly, leaning in front of the roughed up informatech.

Benni Kotes slowly nodded his response. Since Kotes hadn't yet met Mac, I was surprised that he wasn't alarmed at our similarities.

"How did you manage to escape the Piran forces?" Mac asked, solely interested in the truth.

After Benni had a moment to reorient himself to his surroundings, he told us that Torque and the Serpent managed to give the Pirans more grief while en route to their destination. He suggested that the diversion was intentional so that he could get away and pass the word along to Fox. Mac and I listened intently to the details of his story and waited for him to finish.

"We appreciate the risks that you took to make it back," Mac replied. "I know that you've had a lot to deal with. If there is anything you need you should be able to find it in the galley. Please help yourself," Mac said.

Benni apparently realized how fatigued he was and that he was in need of food and water and mustered the strength to make his way into the galley. Mac waited until Benni was out of earshot to discuss his story with me.

"What do you think?" Mac asked.

"Something stinks. If Lennox and Alex were unable to escape the Pirans, there is no way that fish was going to make his way back here on his own," I replied.

"Even without the ikes," Mac smirked in approval of my increasing discernment. "I agree. It's time to find out who he's working for."

Mac motioned toward the galley but halted as Maxwell began hollering about the completion of Streetz's repairs. Mac and I paused as Maxwell initiated Streetz's manual visualization sequence. Streetz took shape right next to us, looking the same as before.

"Streetz, how are you feeling?" Mac asked.

Streetz blinked before responding in an emotionless tone, "I feel like hammered waste jettisoned from the south end of an elephant."

Mac's eyes narrowed. "Thank you so much, Streetz, for that stunning visual, courtesy of a vocabulary well out of character. It's nice to know that someone took the liberty of altering your linguistic datastack."

Mac looked over his shoulder, casting an inescapable and incriminating stare at Maxwell.

"What?" Maxwell shrugged, feigning innocence.

"Hamster, make yourself useful and get the vehicles docked in the beast," Mac said, rolling his eyes.

Before the conversation could digress between Mac and the hamster, I turned my attention back to Benni who had been fixing himself a sandwich in the galley. Before he could take a bite, I watched him pull a small vial of pills and down a couple from within. Something familiar about the container caught my eye, prompting me to inspect.

Mac turned toward the galley as I closed in. I snatched Benni's pill container from the counter and held them before my eyes for inspection. The design matched the vial I found at the Mogul Prime warehouse.

"Where did you get these?" I asked.

"Those are for my indigestion," Benni replied, glaring at me like I was paranoid.

My eyes narrowed as I stared at the informatech's face. I stared long and hard, hoping that I could ascertain his honesty without activating my ikes. Growing impatient, Benni lashed out and aggressively attempted to snatch the container from my hand, but he was no match for my speed. In response, I caught his wrist and pulled, yanking him off-balance. As he stumbled forward, I slammed my forehead into the left side of his face with a head butt.

Benni stumbled backward and fell on the floor with his back against one of the storage cabinets. Momentarily stunned, Benni realized that he was more concerned with the fallen sandwich than his pills. The befuddled informatech reached for his sandwich, but swiftly retracted as one of Mac's metal sai pierced the air pinning the sandwich to the floor with great force.

As Benni looked up, confused and irritated, I found myself pondering why Mac too had exerted such energy to deter the movement, but upon looking back at Benni's face, I realized that Mac had seen something that I did not. One of Benni's eyes was pale white as if my head butt had knocked out a masking lens. I didn't understand the significance, but apparently Mac did.

"Who are you working for?" Mac asked coldly as he leaned down to get in Benni's face.

Benni glared before opening his mouth, "Go take a flying le-"

Before Benni could complete his sentence Mac had already snapped his hand to his waist, drew his Phantom, flicked the safety, primed a round and the thrust the barrel into Benni's mouth.

"Unless you're a travel salesman, I suggest that you choose your next words more carefully. It is not wise to suggest that others take action which you would not," Mac snapped with the poise of a coiled snake.

Benni's expression froze in terror as he stared cross-eyed at the disruptor which nearly made contact with the back of his throat. Mac slowly retracted the weapon.

"Rope him," Mac replied as he holstered the Phantom and snatched his sai from the floor. "And give his sandwich to Maxwell," Mac said with a quick turn, exiting the galley.

"You'll never find them," Benni responded defiantly as I stood him up and marched him out of the galley.

"Sure about that, are you?" I asked.

Kotes held his tongue but continued to struggle.

"If you keep this up, I'll have this one gnaw out your eyeballs," I quipped as I looked over to Maxwell who struck a ferocious pose with his paws up, only to twist into an expression of nausea and disdain as Kotes looked away.

Tired of the informatech's thrashing I finally slugged him in the back of the head, knocking him unconscious. Mac cast me a disdainful look, but I disregarded it as I proceeded to bind the informatech's wrists. At least I wouldn't have to listen to him if he didn't have anything useful to say.

After securing our prisoner, I tasked Maxwell with running an analysis on the pills once he had the time. Our focus on rescuing our friends assumed priority, but I couldn't silence my curiosity about the pills starting to cross my path at strange times.

DAVE TODD

22 – The Minds Below – 22

Oszwick Enterprises
Core City Fringe, Windstonne Enclave
Commercial Empire, Northam Continent
Thread: sysObserver.cmd

Lennox paced steadily in the eerie so-called hospitality room. His irritation continued to escalate as long as he couldn't conceive of a way out of the present predicament. The doors of the hospitality suite were the only standard point of entry, and the voices of multiple hostiles could be heard from the other side. The room itself appeared to be on the top floor of the facility scratching any likely escape through the window. The number of decks to the ground floor was more than Lennox cared to estimate.

Alex and Szazs were already zoned out on the hospitality couches, both staring blankly at one of the room's emcasts displaying nothing more than the usual Imperan rubbish. While pondering the state of his associates, an idea struck Lennox.

"Szazs, you're tech savvy, right? What kind signals do these mecas operate on?" Lennox asked.

Szazs blinked a couple times while the questions took a few ticks to register. "These are generic streams that you would find in any residence or business in the Commercial Empire, nothing special about them really," Szazs replied, slowly sitting forward, unsure what to make of Lennox's curiosity.

"Some carriers bounce their streams off Hyper Lynx terminals, do they not?" Lennox continued.

"Certainly, but these emcasts only receive an incoming signal without the ability to create a two way connection," Szazs replied.

"Except... all carriers monitor feeds for audience engagement. That feedback has to be relayed back to the carrier. Perhaps we can spike the response feedback signal in some useful fashion. Someone on the Hyper Lynx might be watching, Maxwell might be watching. Abnormalities rarely get past him. That's how he found your messages after all," Lennox said.

"I see your point, but what message can we get out if others detect it too?" Szazs asked.

"If you can solve the means, I can solve the message. I may not be one for military grade comms, but I can at least still craft a Vanguard encoded signal. Even locked in here, we're still in the fight, and I'm not about to scrub the mission just yet," Lennox said.

Szazs nodded in agreement, stood and approached an emcast on behind the bar. "Perhaps, if we consolidate the signal of multiple emcasts we can juice it just enough to fluctuate the range into an identifiable signal. We may only get one shot at this."

Lennox nodded and looked over to Alex, suggesting that he head for an emcast.

"I'll miss the latest episode of Petey Tuna," Alex replied sarcastically.

"I'll have Maxwell re-enact it for you," Lennox replied with an eye roll as he opened the base of the nearest emcast. He started tugging at a mess of wires and chips. Even though they were in a bind, he could at least keep his hands busy. The captives just had to nurture the hope that someone would be listening on the outside.

Vanguard Warehouse
Abandoned Sector, Windstonne Enclave
Commercial Empire, Northam Continent
Thread: actTgtPersp1.view

Before Maxwell could finish operating the mechanical lifts to stow the vehicles aboard the Behemoth, we stuffed an unconscious Kotes into the back of the Fire Ant. We didn't know if the informatech was supposed to lure us into a trap, but we had no time for idle speculation.

A last click inspection revealed that we were packing as much hardware as we could carry even after loading up the moxes. I snatched Lennox and Alex's weapons from the floor and tucked them under my cloak. I was about scoop Maxwell from the op table when he hollered for me to wait.

"Incoming," Maxwell shrieked unexpectedly.

"What is it?" I asked.

"I've got an unusual data spike. Strangely, it's in VNET syntax. After decryption it reads, *v secure, location unknown*," Maxwell replied.

Mac raced up the stairs upon overhearing the conversation about the message.

"Could anyone else have faked the message?" I asked.

Mac shook his head. "Only Lennox would know the syntax since I didn't relay it to Alex yet, and Lennox wouldn't break easily enough to give that up."

"Maxwell, upload everything you need to the Behemoth's console. You'll have to do the rest of your tracking on the road. There won't be any time to waste once we got the beast mobile," Mac said.

Before finishing the order, Mac was already strolling down the airbridge leading to the Behemoth's massive frame. Maxwell and I exchanged glances as he shrugged his shoulders. Once the data transfer was complete, Maxwell powered down the flatjack, so I could scoop him up and set him on my shoulder.

I walked quickly to catch up to Mac's position where he opened a hatch over what I might have called one of the Behemoth's front shoulders. As I passed through the massive metal frame, I marveled at the sizable gears that were enclosed within the framework to drive the machine's massive legs. In the center of the body, I spotted the Eagle on the lowest platform. Above the jet, the Fire Ant, Chromehound and Reptilian were all stored on parallel tracks. Clearly, the razerjack had plenty of room for storage, including multiple lockers and very narrow bunks which were efficiently inserted among spaces reserved for mechanical operations.

Mac was already headed for the control cockpit, so after stowing the excess weaponry, I followed along through the narrow bridge which was essentially the neck of the beast-like contraption. Two command chairs were in the center of the space while a host of consoles lined the interior of the metal beast's head. Maxwell gently tapped my neck and pointed to the center console in front of the viewport, prompting me to set him down so that he could get to work.

Mac was quick to take a seat in the leftmost command chair and tap instructions to initiate the engines. The loud roar of machinery filled the cockpit and drowned out possibility of coherent thought. Whether the Behemoth was running on steam or fusion cells I couldn't tell, but after a few clicks, the initial noisy sequence settled enough so that I didn't feel the need to cover my ears.

After a preliminary status exchange with Maxwell, Mac pushed forward on the control stick attached to the chair. The Behemoth's engines strained to increase momentum, but within several ticks the razerjack lurched forward with its first step. After a sluggish repetition of steps, the Behemoth cleared the open bay door.

It took me a few moments to get used to the shifting view of the horizon through the viewport on account of the Behemoth's lumbering gait. The afternoon sky angled from one side to the other until a speed increase minimized the effect. I stared in awe of the view of the abandon from the new vantage point.

Mac expertly navigated the Behemoth through excessively remote portions of the abandon, albeit in a northerly direction. I had no concept of what any potential observers could have done to convince anyone that a giant four-legged razerjack was plodding through a dull and lifeless portion of the enclave.

"Do you have a location yet?" Mac asked Maxwell, once the Behemoth held a steady pace along a reasonably unobstructed dartway.

"Yes, I've been able to cross reference the coordinates by way of an old weather satellite, but I can't get any specifics on the establishment itself, surroundings or landscape. It's in the Core City Fringe, so there's no avoiding some of the sparse population," Maxwell replied.

"Overlay with any business directories for that sector. It may just be a process of elimination. We'll head that direction, but there's still a stop to make on the way. If Windstonne is about to become a warzone, anyone ill-informed is about to become an instant casualty," Mac replied.

"It's that serious?" I asked still hoping for clarity on Mac's excursion outside the faction.

Mac nodded slowly in response. He took the time to explain the events transpiring in the Oceanic Outpost and Moz Fractillend. He regretted not being able to identify the informant in Potentate Ang's ranks. Mac relayed the details of the ruckus among the faction leaders which concluded with a call to war that put Frank Jenkins on the defensive. He even discussed the mysterious ordeal in which some faction leaders exhibited a loss of color in their eyes and an inexplicable shift in attitude, hence why Kotes' mannerisms caught his attention.

Until that point, I forgot about the pills that I found at the Mogul Prime warehouse. I knew that Mac might make more sense of the supplement than me, but before I could offer a description, he cut me off as we stopped in the the middle of nowhere.

Mac slowed the Behemoth to a halt. "We're here. Maxwell, pinpoint our destination while we're gone. We shouldn't be gone be more than a few clicks."

I looked out the viewport, but saw nothing of interest. We hadn't even fully reached the fringe, considering that I could only see a few building lights in the distance. There was nothing before us other than a continual maze of empty dilapidated buildings. Mac was already headed for the Behemoth shoulder hatch where he activated a small platform capable of following a track adjacent to one of the razerjack's front legs. After the platform gave us a smooth drop to the ground below, we headed into the darkness.

I was quick to activate the night vision filter on my ikes so that I didn't lose track of Mac who was already sprinting toward an old t-rail entrance, leading us underground. I had no concept of our destination without a nav marker, so I could only assume that Mac knew the terrain well enough. I hoped that the detour wouldn't prevent us from making a timely rescue for our friends' sake. If a war was looming, delaying actions would only compound our challenges.

No lights were to be found in the dark, humid underground transport station. I had grown accustomed to the green hue of my ike's, but I still needed to exercise cautious footwork to avoid tripping over the scattered debris in every direction. To my surprise, Mac hopped off the loading platform and ran down the t-rail track. We hiked through the darkness for quite some time until we reached a service entry door.

Mac opened the heavy door, its creak sending echoes down the tunnel. He led us down a narrow passageway. It felt surreal to actually encounter distant lighting in such a forsaken place, deep under the surface. As we rounded a corner in the passage, Mac halted as he spotted two large guards in between us and a door beyond. Both guards were dressed in rugged uniforms reminiscent of the old Tricameral Endeavor militia each holding legacy ballistic rifles to match.

"There's still militia here?" I asked under my breath.

Mac held up his hand, suggesting that I not speak.

"Identify yourself," One of the guards snapped tersely.

"Sapphire Brigand. I'm here to speak with L337 Haxs," Mac replied confidently.

"We regret to inform you that Subterra is under new management and that all former associates have been disavowed," the other guard said in an aggressive tone.

"Are those real?" I asked in a panicked fashion as the guards snapped the bolts on their rifles and leveled them at us.

"Shhhh," Mac snapped, standing still without as much as a flinch at the rifle barrels in front of his face.

Both of the guards snarled before depressing the triggers. I darted around the corner as the torrent of rounds peeled through the air. More than any sense of damage, the high volume static compelled me to cover my ears and duck low to the ground. The echos within the narrow hallway were deafening. I didn't even realize that I was yelling a protest of my own.

As the maelstrom of noise ceased and the fire bursts erupting from the rifles froze in place, I realized that Mac was still standing before the guards. If I didn't know better, I suspected that Mac was trying to suppress a laugh. Before I could verify, he immediately walked past the guards' projections leaving me to figure out the rest on my own. Assuming that I just got duped by a couple of projections, I lost interest in lingering in the forsaken hallway and followed.

Once we passed through another doorway, the atmosphere changed entirely. No longer humid, the air felt cool, refreshing and surprisingly well filtered. The illumination was still low, but instead of standard emergency lighting a variety of light blue tones sprinkled the walls allowing me to ditch the night vision. The high-pitch tweaks of interface commands reached my ears, but the most defining characteristic of the new room that we entered was cables in every direction imaginable.

After passing the first mass of low hanging cables, the light shifted as my eyes adjusted to the black lights which cast violet hues in the room. The awkward lighting made the room's centerpiece stand out, a giant emcast base. The device had to be at least ten marks across and had a mirrored structure overhead, fixed to the ceiling, allowing a reinforced display. The low lighting made the high resolution projections from the emcast crystal clear. The sheer amount of hardware in the well hidden facility easily proved it be the most advanced datajacker setup I could have ever conceived.

The high powered emcast had an octagonal design and adjacent to each of its four longer sides were chairs with advanced head sets connected to the back and tappers at the end of each arm rest. Two of the chairs were occupied, one by a girl with dark hair pulled into a ponytail, the other by a young individual with brown hair. Both had visors in front of their faces and arms restrained to improve efficiency with their tappers. Their fingers worked furiously on the touch plates while fast moving shapes that projected on the emcast moved in response.

Sensing an unusual presence, a tall round fellow approached. The individual easily stood head and shoulders above us. Even though our greeter still appeared young, he easily could have lifted us and removed us from the premises without incident.

"Ah, Mac! Good to see you again. The Blue Rogue is always welcome!" the individual said, extending Mac a cross arm and a super wide smile.

I exhaled, relieved that we hadn't sauntered into hostile territory.

As my initial response faded, my demeanor took on a puzzled tone, "Blue Rogue?" I asked, realizing that Mac was not addressed as *The Enforcer*.

"Sapphire Brigand, Cobalt Forager... " Mac expounded.

"Azure Marauder," our host added.

"Fox, meet L337 Haxs, mastermind of Subterra," Mac said. "Yes, clashtags are important here. Just as we use them on the battlefield, they are even more critical to dajacks especially since all they deal with is information. Anonymity is the law of the land, virtual as it may be."

I smiled and nodded as I returned the gesture when L337 Haxs propped up his forearm.

"Hey, Mac! Who's the trout?" Asked another voice.

Until I heard the question, I hadn't realized that another body stood near a broad console separate from the emcast setup. The other Subterra member entered the more illuminated portion of the room, revealing someone of less intimidating height but matching Haxs in a youthful and friendly demeanor. I was surprised that even the oldest of our hosts still didn't match Mac in age.

"Hellix, this is Aaron Fox, Vanguard's latest project," Mac smirked before addressing the others. "Fox, this is Hellix, and Clutch and Parity in the back."

I acknowledged Hellix's crossarm before nodding at the other two who were disengaging their session with the emcast once Hellix stepped away from the console.

"It's been too long, Mac. I'm surprised that you didn't ping me first. Not many like testing my security system without knowing my latest upgrades," L337 Haxs smiled.

"The upgrades are no doubt impressive, my friend. I'm sure they adequately convince the locals," Mac said struggling, to keep a straight face. He cast me a sideways glance, indicating that he was being generous by not drawing attention to my antics in the hallway.

L337 Haxs chuckled, easily picking up on the joke.

"How'd you know they weren't real?" I asked defensively, knowing that there was no point pretending that I hadn't been played.

Mac simply tapped on the outer frame of his ikes.

I shook my head in response, realizing that I still wasn't thinking on my feet fast enough to know when to use the tools at my disposal.

"What brings you by? Hellix is getting awfully close to that beating that longstanding solo Terrasaur takedown score of yours. The title won't be yours forever," L337 Haxs chided.

"Taikons?" I asked, trying to reconcile the new information. "All this talk of responsibility, and you're holding out on a career as a hardtap?"

Imperan meca's still advertised a host of virtual experience titles. I didn't fully understand the concept of strategic simulations, and opinions from the mission workers ranged from childish distractions to valuable social centerpieces.

"That was a lifetime ago," Mac remarked dismissively.

"Unfortunately, it's business that brings me back. Lots of fish about to hit the can," Mac remarked.

"You know, Mac. Your weapon handling skills will get rusty without a few rounds of Shoot 'n Scoot every once in a while," Hellix said.

"Sorry, fellas, duties keep me fresh on the real thing," Mac replied as he brandished his Phantom and waved it in front of his friends while keeping it pointed upward.

"Woooo," L337 Haxs and Hellix said in unison while waving their hands in a show of mock admiration and laughter.

"Hey! Who got cheddz on my tapper," Clutch shouted as he dusted cheese crumbs off a specialty touch pad near the large console. "It took me forever to get this import."

L337 Haxs and Hellix did their best to suppress outbursts of laughter while exchanging a fist bump outside of Clutch's line of sight. In response, I could only stare after consciously resisting the urge to deliver an eye roll to our hosts. Internally, I questioned what exactly we were accomplishing by tasking an important mission with youthful pranksters engaging in battle over granular snack crumbs.

"Don't we have an op to finish?" I asked, doing my best to urge an exit without insulting Mac's friends at the same time.

"Fox, when it comes to specialized tasks there is no substitute for the best, no matter what appearances suggest," Mac replied, clearly understanding the sentiment that I was getting at without even vocalizing it. "Not to mention, resources needed to procure the Crossover Prevalent wouldn't have been as readily available without help from some of the Hyper Lynx's finest."

"Amateurs," Maxwell coughed into the comm on our ikes.

Mac and I both winced at the unexpected outburst.

"What's that?" L337 Haxs asked.

"Hamster says 'Hi'. Wants you to know that he's still got the upper hand on solo Avalon runs," Mac replied.

"Oh, well if fuzzy cared to spend any real time on something other than rigging the data terminal, we'd be glad to take on his challenge," L337 Haxs quipped. "I mean, have you seen what it takes to maintain this rig? It can bake biscuits in less time than it takes to look up a script to prepare them with the amount of heat it cranks."

"Well, it looks like there is a demand for field work," Mac said while rubbing the bridge of his nose.

"I'm good, Boss," Maxwell replied, picking up on the subtle relocation hint.

"Sounds like today's not a good day," Mac said, indicating the end of the banter.

"If not a social visit, what brings you by, Mac" Haxs asked.

"More than anything, I wish it were. I don't know if there's any intel in the Imperan comms, but Windstonne is about to go hot within the next twenty arcs," Mac replied.

"Sounds spicy. We haven't been anywhere Imperan datastacks in a while. They've ramped up security. Normally, they only employ high level CT-7 gates, but now there are CT-14's crawling all over the lines. Talk about some juiced up sharks," L337 replied.

"What are gates?" I asked.

"Gates are the most sophisticated form of security on the Hyper Lynx. With the advent of wetware, opportunities for datajackers escalated. Corporations couldn't compete without employing similar tactics which of course meant immersing their own security staff entirely within a virtual environment allowing them to match speed to overpower incoming signals. Gates have the ability to terminate incoming streams which send very nasty feedback spikes to any foreign presence. Skulljackings aren't pretty which makes gate encounters extremely dangerous," Haxs replied.

"Datajacking is no longer an art form, it's a lifestyle. If it weren't for a doorman, datajackers would be scrapped immediately," Hellix added as he jerked his thumb toward Clutch who was still fussing over the console in the corner.

"I'm not interested in any primary Imperan lines, just their casting systems. Anyone still conducting daily affairs when the war hits is going to get crushed. Frank Jenkins won't give two dimps to warn the people. I need you to get word out that people need to evacuate or seek shelter. In other words, dig in or get out! The stream needs to blast every emcast, every terminal," Mac said.

"That's a tall order, Mac. Most of us can take one CT-7 a piece perhaps if the virtual winds favor us. For anything that big in the Imperan network, we could be looking at a six to ten CT-7 op with at least a couple of CT-14's in the mix. That would require all four of us on the move, but then we would be without a doorman," L337 Haxs replied as he rubbed his broad chin.

"And what if you had a doorman?" Mac asked.

"We're Interlace, Mac. You know we often get away with more than we hope to accomplish, but I don't know who could operate the console quickly enough. Hellix here is the best I've seen," Haxs mused.

"What do ya say, Streetz?" Mac asked.

"I'm game," Streetz replied as his form materialized into view.

"Subterra, meet Streetz, smoothest synthetic imprint ever," Mac smiled.

Haxs hesitantly shook Streetz's hand unsure what he was interacting with. Streetz's mannerism exceeded the craftsmanship of any construct that he had ever worked on. Streetz didn't often participate in standard greetings, but he nodded and followed suit with the others as he inspected of his surroundings.

After wrapping up the small talk, Mac and I resumed our mission and retraced our steps through the underground transportation tunnels. As we passed by the artificial guards still frozen in place, I chuckled at my own antics. I stowed the memory, hoping that I wouldn't make that mistake again.

Once we were finally clear of Subterra's domain, I questioned Mac about our young allies' capacity for such a dangerous mission.

"Fox, another piece of advice, never burn the bridge spanning the generation gap. You never know what you can learn from the generation before or how you might influence the one that comes after. At their age, they are just old enough to think for themselves, but just young enough to be free of the doubts that this world will continuously hurl at them. Age tends to beget narrow mindedness. I find it refreshing to have such friends not only willing to contribute, but also who are able to enjoy the journey. I accept their willingness for service in a heartbeat," Mac replied as we finally reached the base of the Behemoth's large metal feet.

Upon our return to the Behemoth cockpit, Maxwell informed us of our destination, Oszwick Enterprises. I mulled over Mac's words while the Behemoth sauntered toward our target, but I didn't have time to dwell on them since I was more focused on rescuing our friends.

"How do you think our buddy Benni is doing back there?" I asked once we neared our target.

"Oh, I'm sure he's in for a bumpy ride, hopefully the crane will jostle him really well," Mac replied. "Maxwell, prep the Fire Ant. We're going in!"

23 – The Hammer Falls – 23

Freight District
Core City Fringe, Windstonne Enclave
Commercial Empire, Northam Continent
Thread: actTgtPersp1.view

The grinding of mechanical gears waned as the Fire Ant was released from its storage track. The overhead winch guided the suspended mox out the rear bay of the Behemoth, allowing it to dangle decks above the terrain. I felt my stomach float as the vehicle descended until the Behemoth's winch line snapped taut. The vehicle slammed hard, testing the mox's suspension.

"It's a good thing that you've got someone to repair the hardware after the beatdowns you deliver," I remarked.

The Enforcer simply nodded before checking the rearview mirror, pacifying his paranoia that Kotes might cause a problem unexpectedly. I was surprised that even after the hard landing that the informatech wasn't already sitting upright and issuing a stream of profanities from behind his tape pacifier. Before our departure, we verified that he hadn't done anything beyond pass his time with sleep.

"Alright, Fox, nav us up. We're on a time crunch. If things are heating up as bad as the forecast suggests, we're going to wish we brought sunscreen. Maxwell, get the Behemoth cloaked. We'll be back as soon as we can. Oh, and keep your eyes on and ears open for any relevant comms," the Enforcer said as he slammed the Fire Ant's shifter and released the clutch.

The Fire Ant lurched forward after squealing and laying down tracks while I blinked commands into my ikes to manipulate the mapping sequence that Maxwell uploaded. I did my best to manipulate the compound projection which represented the streets and buildings of the abandon perimeter. The map boundaries made for an irregular drive until it morphed into the fringe with its improved dartway.

"What are we going to do with the noodle?" I asked after I plotted enough of our course in advance.

"Well, if he's one of Jenkins' pawns, he'd better know his way around, for his sake," the Enforcer replied flatly.

"And if he's leading us into a trap?" I asked.

"Then we have to hope that our efforts to modify the schedule will hijack their plan," the Enforcer said.

After the final turns through a nondescript business district, we arrived at the Oszwick Enterprises perimeter. We witnessed a clean professional building, well illuminated with a strange green tint. Upon exiting the mox, my face contorted as a horrendous stench filled the nostrils. I magnified my ikes to see the curling smoke emerging from the distant exhaust stacks in the late afternoon sky.

We were quick to open a back door and drag Kotes from the vehicle. Since he still slumbered, the Enforcer delivered a resounding smack to the face to wake him. Initially, I was surprised that the informatech could sleep so easily, but I considered the chemicals in his system might have additional side effects. After multiple groggy blinks, Kotes realized that he was propped against the vehicle and he slowly stood upright. Kotes looked at our surroundings then back to the Enforcer and glared offering his contempt without words.

"Yeah, yeah, whatever, tough guy," the Enforcer responded as he prodded Kotes toward the main building.

We approached the primary entrance to Oszwick Enterprise, expecting a warm security reception. Without resistance, we passed through the front door and found no one inside. The absence of personnel felt suspicious. Either there were no operations during evening arcs, or they assumed no one dared approach the place to justify an actual security detail.

The Enforcer hopped over the reception desk and scanned the closest terminal for a building layout. I observed that he was scanning the terminal as quickly as possible given how quickly the lights from his eyes blinked through his shades.

"Nothing," the Enforcer said. "We'll have to try some of the buildings deeper in the complex."

Out of the corner of my eye, I saw Kotes flinch. I walked over to him and ripped the tape from his mouth, prompting a pained yell.

"Where are they?" I snapped.

"How should I know? I don't live here," Kotes glared defiantly.

The Enforcer approached, but I could tell from his demeanor he would have easily allowed me to head butt the informatech again, "Listen here, lab rat..."

"Oh, I'm a lab rat now? You wound me," Maxwell interjected through the comms. "Listen up, I traced the coordinates of the message to the very building you are in, but that was two arcs ago."

"Maxwell, any specifications on how many emcasts are installed in the facility?" The Enforcer asked.

"A lot, but they are all on the top floor," Maxwell replied.

"Good work. Let's go," the Enforcer said, disregarding the altercation with Kotes as we hustled to the elevator.

I shoved the informatech forward, urging him to keep up unless he wanted to be dragged. After a brief elevator ride to the sixth floor, the chime announced our arrival, but surprisingly, as we disembarked from the lift, we found the same absence of life.

"I think they knew that we were coming," the Enforcer said as he raised his Phantom and pointed it down the hallway.

"Don't let him out of your sight," the Enforcer huffed as he cautiously stepped down the hall while keeping his eyes trained on his disruptor sights.

I shoved Kotes in the back who idly turned his head and rolled his eyes at me for intimidation. I responded by smacking the back of his head while drawing a Splice 15m and taking up the rear of the formation.

The Enforcer paused at every doorway, checking for any signs of life. It seemed peculiar that the door to every office and lab had been left open.

"What does your gut tell you, Fox?" the Enforcer whispered back to me as he continued to scan from behind the raised Phantom.

"That there's no one here," I replied.

"And what does your critical thinking tell you?" the Enforcer asked again.

"That they want to lull us into a false sense of security," I smirked.

"Good," the Enforcer replied.

"Oh, you two are a real pair of geniuses," Kotes snorted.

"Shut your mouth," I snapped. "Unless you want to be sucking tape again."

Finally, we approached the only door that wasn't propped open. The Enforcer positioned himself on one side of the door frame, and I took the other. We motioned for Kotes to walk through the door after the Enforcer pressed it open from the side. Even with this hands still tied behind his back, Kotes shuffled through the doorway. We awaited for any sudden movement on his part, should someone lay down a plasma barrage. Without any resulting commotion, we peeked around the door frame. The posh office within displayed evidence of a scuffle. Padded chairs were overturned, potted plants were tipped, spilling dirt on the floor, and wall mounted pictures appeared misaligned.

"This didn't happen long ago," the Enforcer said as he scanned the room with a thermal filter from his ikes. "There are still faint heat signatures here."

A thud drew our attention to a pair of doors which connected to an adjacent room. The Enforcer and I both raised our disruptors as the three of us faced the source of the noise. Leveraging our decoy, we shoved Kotes through the double doors. As the doors swung open, Kotes dove for the floor. No sooner had the informatech hit the floor when a series of plasma bolts sizzled in our direction. Without thought, we dove for the overturned furniture. Before the noise of the first barrage settled, another followed, raining over heads, burning the walls and cabinets behind us.

The Enforcer carefully notched his way from behind a large desk to an overturned chair. Plasma continued to singe the furniture, but the Enforcer could only roll his eyes at the incompetence of our foes. After reaching under his vest, he produced a grenade with a perforated core. A smirk creased his lips as he pulled the pin and tossed the Nebula grenade over his back.

After a minor delay, a muffled explosion rippled the air flooding smoke into the room of hostiles. It didn't take long for a round of hacking coughs to replace any threat of disruptor fire. The Enforcer chuckled at the simplicity of the resolution before he switched his ikes to his thermal filter again to identify the bodies in the haze. The opaque view of the room didn't deter the Enforcer from stepping on Kotes who was still cowering on the floor. As the Enforcer approached the overturned table that shielded our attackers, I switched my ikes to the same filter and observed our foes from a distance. They were most peculiar individuals, almost like an aged cloning project gone wrong. They were gangly, pale and grotesque. A couple were squirming on the floor, swatting at the air or rubbing their eyes in an effort to alleviate the burning sensation.

After clearing the table that once shielded our opponents in the firefight, the Enforcer kicked the ownerless disruptors away before grabbing one of the weird foes by the throat and propping him against the wall, "Where are they?"

The raspy voice wheezed for several ticks before finally raising a hand and pointing in the direction of the factories in the distance. The Enforcer released his iron grip and the unsightly individual collapsed to the floor. The Enforcer turned and walked toward the entrance of the failed trap, lifting Kotes on the way, dragging him toward the main hallway until he rose to his feet.

Once clear of the offices, the Enforcer broke into a jog and headed for the elevator. Reading the cue, I nudged Kotes to speed up as I resumed position at the rear of the formation. I was so focused on checking every direction that I didn't notice that the Enforcer halted abruptly at the hallway intersection.

DAVE TODD

As I stumbled forward, the Enforcer's "NOOOO" rumbled my auditory canals while my eyes widened in shock to see a large group of the same gangly looking staffers pointing disruptors at me. Knowing that I would only lose balance if I tried to turn, I tucked into a roll to pass the hallway intersection, narrowly avoiding the plasma that splashed on the tiles behind me. After my haphazard maneuver, I whirled around to see the Enforcer pressed against the wall with his disruptor raised while waiting for a break in the futile discharges.

"Now what?" I hissed from the opposite side of the hallway.

Instead of waiting for a response or for the Enforcer to retaliate with a projectile, I crouched on the floor and kicked myself into the intersection while firing two Splice 15ms from the floor. In the moment, my biggest foe was my own stupidity, but in contrast, my biggest ally was our attackers' terrible aim. I scrambled to my knees after firing several rounds and catching one of the humanoids in the forehead. I then dashed to the opposite wall to dodge return fire. I shifted my focus to the two opponents who pelted the wall with plasma. I fired and hit the first in the shoulder which sent his disruptor flying backward. Then with an unexpected burst of energy, I hurdled on overturned desk and thrashed the last armed opponent. He pointed the barrel to the ceiling and activated the safety suggesting that he had no intention of resisting.

The Enforcer snapped as he rounded the corner, "Fox, You're Cra-.."

"Impulsive, is the word I would use," I replied cutting him off.

"Yeah, well that little stunt wouldn't have been necessary if you had been paying attention," the Enforcer said.

"Attention?! Where's Kotes?" I asked in defense of my actions.

The Enforcer glanced toward the informatech's previous position against the wall and spotted him running the opposite direction. Once I could see around the corner, I too saw our captive on the run. I darted forward, but the Enforcer was quick to grab my shoulder. He nodded toward the facility exit instead.

With an agitated glance, the Enforcer brushed past me, "It's mind boggling that you were ever an mental marvel, because the common sense tank certainly appears empty."

As the Enforcer took the lead, he mumbled something, but I couldn't parse his words. "What was that?" I asked.

"Nothing," the Enforcer grumbled back.

We hit the stairs and then analyzed our surroundings upon clearing the exit on the bottom floor of the facility. The rear entrance to the facility was far less inviting than the front. Factories and reactors stretched into the distance emitting a dismal industrial vibe. I spotted several staff and transport scuttles parked near the doors. Anticipating the need to move, I approached the closest scuttle, released the wheel lock and fired up the electric engine. The engine whined as I backed the vehicle into the open. After doing so, I spotted another vehicle already getting ahead, operated by a couple of pale staffers.

"Let's move," I said as the Enforcer hopped into the scuttle.

"Head toward that far factory," the Enforcer yelled as I put the scuttle in gear.

I looked ahead and stared at the wispy gnarled fingers of smoke reaching from the facility rooftop and contrasting the orange setting sun. Smokestacks belched grayish-black plumes of acrid smoke intensifying the scent since we first reached the facility.

"What are they processing here? Synthetic sulfur?" I muttered.

Before the Enforcer could reply, more movement caught our attention. The Enforcer pushed my head forward causing my chest to crash against the wheel. I lost my grip which caused the scuttle to weave. Before fully regaining control of the wheel, plasma blasts were already whizzing overhead. I leaned to the side in order to keep my head low yet steer the cart from an awkward off-center position.

The Enforcer stood on his seat while bracing himself with one hand on the cart's frame. After minimizing the swerving, I got the scuttle back under control and resumed a linear path toward our destination. Once able to multitask beyond the sole act of driving, I looked over to see the source of the disruptor fire. A familiar face was directing a similar scuttle and weaving in and out of various piles of crates and industrial metal stacks.

"It's Kotes," I yelled.

"I know, Fox, just keep it steady!" the Enforcer yelled back.

Shifting my focus back to driving, I spotted the staffers ahead as they mimicked Kotes' action. They slowed their scuttle and started to fire a volley from ahead of our position.

"Hold on!" I yelled.

I wrenched the wheel, nearly causing the scuttle to flip as I felt a couple tires lose contact with the pavement. I guided the vehicle to the side, narrowly evading a scrape with a long wall of crates. The quick maneuver caused the Enforcer to fall. He would have toppled out of the scuttle had it not been for his quick reflexes and latching his hand to the railing that enclosed the storage bed on the back of the scuttle. He swiftly pulled himself back into place and crouched to lower his center of gravity, should I make such responses a habit.

"What was that all about?" the Enforcer snapped.

"We've got staffers firing on us too! We've got to take them out," I replied.

The Enforcer grunted as I heard a spring snap open the power cell chamber on his Phantom which ejected the empty cell over his shoulder before he inserted a full power cell. The wind caught the empty canister and it trailed behind us as we accelerated past the crates, momentarily offering us cover from either set of foes. Kotes drove parallel to our position on the left and the staffers slowed their progress to get a better shot from the right.

"Take Kotes, I'll get the freaks!" I said, holding the wheel with one hand while drawing my disruptor from my hip with the other.

From a kneeling position the Enforcer wedged his feet into the storage bed railings in order to free a hand and steady his shot. He needed to since my driving didn't help the cause. In order to avoid stray plasma blasts, I continually weaved the scuttle in and out of cargo stacks and inoperable heavy machinery.

The staffers fired more shots, some of which whizzed past my head. As the primary shooter paused to reload, I took the opportunity to punch the accelerator and put our scuttle within a stone's throw of my targets. I leveled my disruptor and fired a series of bursts at the staffer standing in the storage bed of his cart. I landed a direct hit. The gangly staffer fell backward onto the driver who lost control, forcing the scuttle to speed forward at a haphazard angle toward a metal ramp. The cart approached the ramp, but only two wheels on the far side of the cart connected with the ramp causing it to corkscrew as it launched from the peak of the ramp into a wall. The cart crashed to the ground in a smoldering heap.

"Good shooting! Get me closer to Kotes," the Enforcer yelled over the noise.

Swerving to avoid the other scuttle's wreckage, Kotes realized that he no longer had an ally in the vehicular shoot out. He slammed his foot to the accelerator and his scuttle sped forward and disappeared behind a wall of storage containers. I jerked the wheel to follow him and catch up.

"Time to shut him down. We can't let him tip them off that we're coming!" I yelled.

The Enforcer fired a couple of stray rounds into the air in Kotes' direction, but they were too far and too late. The facility was no longer a spec in the distance. It loomed high overhead. Kotes raced his cart off to the far side of the building, jumped out and dashed for the factory entrance.

The Enforcer tapped my shoulder then pointed for a location to park the scuttle. "Slow it down, Fox. We'll have to take the back way in. They will already know that we're here."

Oszwick Enterprises
Core City Fringe, Windstonne Enclave
Commercial Empire, Northam Continent
Thread: sysObserver.cmd

Oszwick stared from the observation deck out toward the assembly line where his mechanical masterpieces were at last able to initiate their mission. Pilots suited up and raced for their razerjacks per instruction.

"What's that noise?" Oszwick asked as he turned his ear away from the assembly line.

Others in the room looked at the executive with puzzled expressions. The factory was full of heavy machinery. They found it odd that Oszwick was concerned with one noise in particular.

"I didn't hear anything, Mr. Oszwick," Jenkins replied. "We are in a large factory. Surely, it wasn't anything significant."

Konrad Oszwick walked away from the observation window and paced for a moment.

"Commander Pyln, if you wouldn't mind, take a moment to secure the premises," Oszwick said.

Commander Pyln first glared at the hostages unsure if it was wise to yet again leave them unattended. After accepting the order, Pyln nodded to his men and they left the observation deck. With the security forces absent, Oszwick nodded to Jenkins for him to continue his dissertation.

"As you can see the Commercial Empire now possesses enough firepower to establish its status as the primary ruling body of the Unisphere. Anyone not aligned with us will be crushed," Jenkins said.

"Whatever, Jenkins. You didn't bring us here just so you could flex some metal muscles. Will you be getting to the point soon?" Torque quipped.

Without the meatheads in the room, Torque knew that he could sound off without an immediate backhand. He, the Serpent and Szazs had all been moved after the Piran's discovered their tinkering with the emcast feeds. They hoped that there had been time enough to relay their position to Maxwell, but everything hinged on the hamster's technical prowess.

Jenkins calmly took the insult in stride, "My brash friend, I don't think you realize the gravity of the situation. I do not care to have anyone in my way, and your associate is the perpetual thorn in my side. Considering that bait is never offered final rites, I thought I could at least offer you a free demonstration while we pass our time here."

Jenkins opened his mouth to continue, but a figure staggered through the door to the observation deck. He looked around until he found a table to lean against. The familiar individual was clearly exhausted from running.

"Benni!" Szazs gasped when he saw the young informatech's worn face.

Frank Jenkins and Konrad Oszwick exhibited no emotion toward the surprise arrival but instead looked on impatiently.

"Well?" Jenkins asked. "Were we successful?"

"Quite," Kotes replied with a sneer. "They are already here... and likely in the building."

"You conniving..." Szazs muttered as he attempted to rise from his chair and confront the former assistant, but Oszwick firmly pushed the older informatech back to his seat.

Kotes walked over and slugged Szazs in the face, "Shut up, old man. If it weren't for you, this operation wouldn't have required a takeover. You and your moral convictions clearly weren't sufficient to get the job done, so Mr. Jenkins was kind enough to render me your replacement. It could have been a smooth transition if not for these fishes arriving and mucking up the plan."

"Don't you have work to do," Jenkins interjected.

Kotes scowled upon having his promotion ceremony cut short, but after stepping back, he acknowledged. There was no time to berate an old man incapable of seeing the future. Kotes knew that there was more at stake, given the numerous operations ahead. He finally took his leave so that he could prioritize the one that involved undercutting a particular fossil.

Thread: actTgtPersp1.view

The Enforcer and I made a cautious entrance into the factory on the ground level and scanned for a likely place of operation. We ascended the first stair case and worked our way to the third floor. Carefully, we stepped along the airbridge, wary of any possible ambush. The excess of machinery, pipelines and robotic arms minimized the effectiveness of our ike filters. Even the warm, heavy air toyed with our senses in detecting nearby threats. I did my best to scan every corner while I followed the Enforcer through the maze of walkways and ductwork.

"We've got trouble," the Enforcer whispered as he came to an abrupt stop.

I turned my head down to the main floor of the factory to see rows upon rows of razerjacks with their respective pilots mounting up or performing final maintenance checks. The razerjacks had a humanoid appearance at least without a torso. Each had two legs connected by flat, yet angled, hip joints intersecting a dome-like cockpit in the middle. The cockpit was divided into halves, the lower housed the pilot, and the upper half supported the gunner responsible for the rotating gatling cannons that were posted over each of the legs.

"What... are... those?" I asked slowly.

"A disaster waiting to happen if mobilized. I don't like this. We musn't linger. We have to find Torque, the Serpent and get back to the Behemoth," the Enforcer replied with renewed urgency.

We quickened our pace until we spotted the observation deck which overlooked the assembly line. Multiple Pirans had taken up post outside.

"We don't have time to waste on them," the Enforcer said as he activated his cloak.

I activated my cloak as well and updated my ikes to reveal the Enforcers silhouette so that I could follow. He easily plotted a secure path around the guards allowing us clear access to the office which overlooked the factory. On approach we could see Torque, the Serpent and Protech Szazs all facing the observation window. Frank Jenkins had his back to the window while another darkly dressed figure stood behind our friends. Neither made aggressive gestures, but I was curious why Torque and the Serpent hadn't overpowered the stuffy suits, especially the one in the back. He certainly had the aura of a haughty salesman.

The Enforcer and I propped ourselves against the walls adjacent to the doorway. I awaited his signal since deactivation of our cloaks would announce our presence. Once the Enforcer was confident in his analysis, he gave the nod. Our cloaks fizzled out and with a swift kick the door was open. Knowing that the Pirans would be alerted to the noise, I promptly barricaded the door while the Enforcer leveled his disruptor and focused on the two suits.

"Well, Mr. Conner, Mr. Fox, how pleasant of you to finally join us. I was simply updating your friends on new developments regarding the Global Alliance restructure. Now, that you're here, we can have a

DAVE TODD

proper demonstration of the means," Jenkins replied calmly after yielding no reaction to our intrusion.

"Jenkins, I don't suppose your new title would be along the line of Dictator Infinitum," the Enforcer remarked sarcastically.

Jenkins returned a smug smile and addressed the unidentified suit in the back, "You see, Mr. Oszwick, he is smart. It'd be a shame if we let such suitable testing material go to waste."

"Indeed," the other suit replied with a smile. "I do believe interested parties would like to interrogate such a meddling mind."

"And what exactly is your take in all this, Mr. Oszwick?" I interjected.

"Gentlemen, considering that your tour of my facilities has been conducted outside normal business arcs, I would like to personally showcase our services. Oszwick Enterprises specializes in the unknown. To be more precise, goods for which there is not yet a known market," Oszwick replied in a sing-song voice.

For the first time, the Enforcer's premonition of a dark agenda was starting to make sense. I sensed potential deception, but I didn't comprehend the possible scope, just that there was something far more sinister at work than a couple of mere executives expanding their reach. Any resident connected to a meca might have bought the spiel, but not us.

"And what of your akcellerrant division? I suppose allegiance to the powers that be would ensure a sizable market share," the Enforcer stated.

"So you say," Oszwick replied with smile.

As a beeping sound pierced the air, I released the safety on my Splice 15m and pointed it at Jenkins allowing the Enforcer to train his on Oszwick. Jenkins raised his hands to indicate that he wouldn't make any sudden moves. As the pinging sound continued, Jenkins reached into his coat pocket to reveal a sonair which he placed in his ear. He remained still for a click before returning the device without ever acknowledging the party on the end.

Frank Jenkins remained silent, making no exchange with the entity who was contacting him. After a subtle nod he removed the sonair from his ear and returned it to his coat pocket.

"Gentlemen, we must be going. I believe some of our associates from the Global Alliance are interested in visiting our wonderful enclave. It would be unfortunate if we didn't see to the proper guide rails ahead of time. Untrained pets can be so unruly," Jenkins said.

"You're not going anywhere, Jenkins!" the Enforcer snapped as he shifted his Phantom from Oszwick to Jenkins.

Jenkins simply broke into a smile before bursting into laughter. In so doing, he pointed toward a camera embedded in the ceiling at the rear of the office, suggesting that the whole exchange had been monitored.

"Now," Jenkins ordered as he and Oszwick moved away from the observation window.

Suddenly, disruptor cannons shattered the observation glass. Vanguard and Szazs all hit the floor. Before identifying the attack, Pirans battered down the door and charged in. Jenkins and Oszwick made their way for the exit.

"Commander, please ensure that our guests are processed correctly," Jenkins said sternly.

Commander Pyln glared, revealing his jagged teeth as the executives departed.

Before Jenkins was out of earshot, we all heard his closing order, "Deploy the Goliaths!"

The factory trembled as the sound of the bipedal razerjacks marched in unison out of the facility. I exchanged glances with the rest of our crew as we picked ourselves off the floor. I counted at least a dozen Pirans between us and the door, most with their firearms already raised. For the first time since I joined Vanguard, I felt that I didn't sense a preconceived plan to give us the upper hand. This was the end, Pirans in control and Jenkins about to unleash destruction on the rest of the world with his mechanical forces.

As I felt helplessness creep in, my mind flooded with a multitude of whispers faster than I could comprehend. With so much volume, I struggled to identify tangible words. The most coherent were *Stand Fast, Walk not by Sight, Fight the Good Fight*. As the sensation dissipated, I looked about to see if anyone else took note, but as usual the phenomenon was exclusive to my own senses. At least, I knew that it was targeted for my benefit, suggesting that I get to work instead of focusing on the absence of a formal plan.

"What do you say, Pyln? Ready for round two? We deserve a fair fight this time," Torque said, first to break the staredown.

"I don't play fair," Pyln responded with a deep throated voice as he leveled his disruptor at the Enforcer and squeezed the trigger.

"No!" I yelled having the first glance at the commander's maneuver. I motioned to push the Enforcer out of the way, but even before my reflexes kicked in, the Enforcer had already begun rotating his arms like a cyclone which caught up the plasma blast and redirected it back at the Piran commander.

Caught unaware, but still nimble, Pyln ducked as the blast struck the Piran immediately behind him in the head. Leveraging the distraction, the Enforcer leapt forward to knock down as many Pirans as possible.

Reading the Enforcer's charge as a weapons free signal, I immediately tossed Torque and the Serpent their weapons from under my cloak and tossed the protech my Splice 15m. I followed up by snapping my fima sticks to my side and jumping into the fray.

The Enforcer successfully toppled at least five Pirans in the confusion, but he was forced to scramble back to his feet quickly before more Pirans moved in to pummel him. The Serpent had already unsheathed his blade with a cold familiar precision and dashed toward a pair of Pirans on the Enforcer's left. Torque too was already charging with his kamas in front to address the Pirans on the opposite side.

As I watched Pyln step toward the Enforcer's blind side, I moved to intervene, but the commander was already wise to my actions. Pyln raised a powerful forearm and caught my throat in his hand. My vision blurred as the vice grip started to crush my throat, but the bulky commander wasn't interested in my immediate death so he threw me backward. I fell hard against the floor, sputtering a few hoarse coughs to regain proper airflow.

The Serpent had already hacked through two Pirans before him and made his way toward Pyln. Already on the offensive, Pyln scooped down to hoist the metal battering ram used to splinter the door. Pyln hurled the ram as if it were as light as a bread loaf. Unconcerned, the Serpent sidestepped the projectile allowing it to shatter several terminals lining the wall.

Aggravated, Pyln began shouldering his way through the Pirans which the Enforcer was effectively immobilizing. As I stood to get back into the action, I saw the Enforcer pull his Phantom 4.0 and almost begrudgingly blast several Pirans in the chest to keep their persistent forms from getting back up. The behavior appeared foreign to the Enforcer's nature making me think that he was running out of options.

Another Piran charged me. I twisted into the air driving my front leg upward so that I could deliver a tornado kick with my back leg. The instep of my left foot line up with the with the right side of the Piran's broad face. The soldier attempted to roll out of the way, but chose poorly by diving into my kick adding force to the impact. The force of the kick sent the staggering Piran out the window previously breached by a Goliath below. Even above the noise of the fray, I could hear the sickening crunch of the Piran's body impacting the factory floor several decks below.

Pyln yelled for remaining Pirans to hold their ground while he dashed away from the observation deck and down the airbridge. The intimidation of the two Pirans facing the Enforcer easily revealed that their inner strength didn't match their hardened reputation. The Enforcer's fists moved in a blur as he knocked the Pirans into an unconscious heap as he chased after Pyln and another Piran indifferent to his given orders.

Once the Enforcer's feet hit the airbridge, Pyln was yelling at the Goliath below to fire on the enemy position. Air surrounding the Enforcer superheated as a yellow cloud of plasma surged upward. The Enforcer leapt forward, diving to the next length of airbridge as the one underfoot tore away from its support beams, but the weight of the dislodged piece pulled at more of the airbridge than expected. The Enforcer stretched out his right arm, his hand narrowly grasping the grate as the severed piece fell to the floor with deafening impact.

Torque heard the barrage spewing from the Goliath below as he incapacitated the last Piran. The razerjack's cannons were already winding up for another blast. Torque snatched the CQTR from the floor, no longer possessed by the unconscious soldier, and fired the heavy rifle at the Goliath below. The plasma from the rifle splashed on the upper dome of the Goliath's cockpit. He knew that the assault wouldn't affect the high density hardmelt shielding, but it was enough to distract the gunner.

"I'm not getting through! Serpent, double time!" Torque yelled.

The Serpent was already on the move after scooping up a CQTR disruptor of his own. As the Serpent opened fire, Torque snatched another disruptor tucking the stock of each under his shoulder, squeezing both triggers in unison. The Goliath's left shoulder cannon at last rotated away from the Enforcer's position and aimed for the office overhead.

While Torque yelled for the Serpent to concentrate fire on the same portion of the dome, I sprinted from the observation deck and jumped across the huge gap in the airbridge activating my kips to give me an extra push. As my feet touched down, I flailed my arms to avoid falling backward off the unstable airbridge.

The Enforcer clung to the dangling bridge section calmly. His forearm rippled with tension as he intentionally avoided making sudden movements to keep the structure from collapsing. I suspected that he activated his grips to alleviate the amount of pressure placed on his fingers which strained against his weight. Until I crept forward to help him up, he kept his eyes trained on the Goliath which was intent on vaporizing his form.

I glanced up to see the Goliath's gunner screaming as the dome started to melt under the combined barrage from our friends. Sensing that a breach was imminent in addition to interference from the untested targeting systems, the Goliath pilot backed the razerjack away to regroup with the others already on the march beyond the factory.

I felt a sense of relief as the Goliath departed, allowing me to focus on helping the Enforcer out of his predicament. Without any distraction from the Pirans, Torque and the Serpent helped Szazs find a way down from the smoldering office.

As we regrouped, I saw that the protech was quite shaken, he still clutched the disruptor tightly, but he willingly relinquished it. No one required an explanation or admission that combat was not his preferred mode of operation. We kept our wits about us to make sure that there weren't any extra Pirans or Oszwick Enterprise staffers to run us through. I looked around to see that we were alone in the vacated razerjack factory. Thoughts of such a machinery mass being unleashed sent chills down my spine. I refocused my attention and followed the others out of the factory.

"So, is that one Ice Brrger or two?" I asked, elbowing Torque.

"I wouldn't owe you if you hadn't gotten us into this mess," Torque grumbled as he shouldered his way ahead of the group.

"Such a grouse. When did you get so bitter?" I remarked as I looked over to the Serpent who shrugged his shoulders in response.

"Remind me to tell you about my last tour of duty some time," Torque huffed as he shuffled ahead.

"Life history is hardly a mid-mission conversation," the Enforcer remarked, quietly offering Torque some cover. "Especially, when perceived to be mired in bad luck. His heart's always where it should be, but anger can be a deficit. It holds him back, but my efforts to help apparently require more time. Perhaps, one day you will have more success than me."

"You can have two as long as the Serpent doesn't do the driving again," Torque replied back to us, doing his best to not make a big deal of the situation.

I didn't understand what the Enforcer meant since I had little experience in doing anything of meaningful influence. Rather than dwell on the conversation, I moved to find us a new scuttle to accelerate our exit, but I was halted.

"Not now, Fox. That will take too long. Maxwell, lock onto our position and remote the Fire Ant. Get it here, yesterday!" the Enforcer snapped into the comm.

"Ayezon, Boss! Should I be concerned about the surplus of razerjacks that I just saw pass through the area? Who's side are they on?" Maxwell asked.

"Not ours, Hamster. Not ours. Get the Behemoth mobile and locate the most optimal place near the fringe perimeter to regroup. War is imminent and it looks like Vanguard will have to bring the resistance," the Enforcer said.

Once the Fire Ant reached our position, we piled inside the mox and the Enforcer took the wheel. The ride to regroup with the Behemoth was a quick one. With the Fire Ant in position, Maxwell operated the overhead winch to lift the Fire Ant back into the Behemoth's body.

With the mox secured overhead, a cursory inspection was done for injuries and available stimpunches were doled out. Torque and the Serpent were quick to utilize supplies and food stores after seeing that Szazs had opportunity to find a restful spot. If he had any injuries, the Enforcer didn't stop for inspection, but instead headed straight for the cockpit. He dropped his form into one of the command chairs and immediately scanned comm frequencies across the Hyper Lynx.

I took up position in the opposite command chair and stared through the Behemoth's rectangular viewport. The Behemoth was still pointed toward Windstonne, revealing a faint glow of the enclave lights against the new night sky. Both the silence and stillness felt ominous. Adding to the tension, the Enforcer dimmed the lights in the Behemoth minus those he needed to operate the terminals.

After a brief systems check, those in the back utilized the meager bunks to catch some sleep. I was intrigued by the level of training that my friends possessed that allowed them to finish business and leverage any spot of free time for rest knowing that the action would arrive soon enough. I suspected that Szazs would have the toughest time adjusting, but given the recent ordeal it wouldn't take long for fatigue to get the best of him.

I wanted to make myself useful, but conflicting thoughts suggested that I might only interrupt as the Enforcer furiously checked for any status on Subterra's progress. I slumped down in the chair, hoping for any idea that might be useful, but instead my focus drifted as the lights in the distance blurred. I gave myself a moment to appreciate the relief of having rescued our friends successfully, but a counter thought nagged at me, seeding doubts that it could be in vain, given the conflict to come. All I could do was distract myself with the hope that Subterra would succeed so that other lives unknown would be spared by proper warning.

Gridloc: Origin
Thread: frmChsnAnlys.rvw

The Adjuvant made slow intentional steps toward his objective. One wrong move and he would tumble over the edge of the circular chasm only to succumb to an infinite fall, that is, unless the rumors of a deeply embedded security system were true, in which case, vaporization would be a welcome end. After advancing as far as the stable terrain would allow, the Adjuvant activated the solar shield on his visor to limit the interference from the energy channeling through the Abyss. His advanced sensors were nullified at a maximum depth of two decks into the dense darkness below his feet.

"There are certainly no guardrails on this one," the Adjuvant remarked as he backed away from the rocky precipice.

Once he returned to a sure footing, the Adjuvant surveyed the battlefield which was well illuminated by the white energy traversing the center of the endosphere. Rocky crags and pillars dotted the terrain as far as the eye could see, but more concerning were the bodies, big and small, human and other. Without wildlife dwelling in the Origin, the bodies would be on display to rot for quite some time unless keepers of the power plant tasked workers with actual cleanup.

"The resources committed to this campaign were immense. Adversaries were staging for this event long before we expected. Do you think that there is enough time to mount a defense?" the Adjuvant said into the comm.

The Adjuvant listened silently to the words on the other end while he observed the amount of destroyed hardware littering the battlefield. Tanks, ships and transports scattered the horizon. The appearance of ships in the dry domain seemed unusual, but a four-legged armored frame caught the Adjuvant's attention even more.

"A breach?" the Adjuvant asked. "You know that requires permission from the higher ups, but to your point, neither of us would be able to intervene if we don't take drastic measures now."

"You know that it'll take more than the physical hardware to win this one. People don't commit to campaigns like this without strong motivators. Fear or duty perhaps lead they way at times, but such factors weren't enough. They will need something more, if you're picking up what I'm putting down," the Adjuvant said.

"Carrier traces are absent, I can find nothing here. At this rate sequence deterioration from this branchmark will be cataclysmic... to put it mildly," the Adjuvant added.

"I will leave the procurement operations in your hands," the Adjuvant said after gaining the desired response.

With the comm closed, the Adjuvant made his way toward the closest junction. After a standard exit, his work in the Origin was complete.

24 – Digital Couriers – 24

Subterra Lair
Core City Fringe, Windstonne Enclave
Commercial Empire, Northam Continent
Thread: sysObserver.cmd

The causal air common to the Subterra lair waned dramatically after the Enforcer's visit. Rarely, did a mission arise that might issue Subterra an adequate challenge. Ambition was reserved for smaller contests, but this time every member would have to pull out all the stops. Lives depended on the effectiveness of their incursion into the Hyper Lynx.

L337 Haxs spent a few clicks mentally mapping a strategy for their operation before giving Streetz the rundown on the doorman console. Haxs was reluctant to place the lives of his crew in the hands of a synthetic imprint, but he trusted the Enforcer enough to stifle his reservations.

L337 Haxs instructed Clutch and Parity to discontinue their present operations which were likely little more than recreational distractions since Clutch was engaged with an allcourt sim across the Lynx with an associate in the Riverbend enclave. Hellix had been observing the match from a distance but snapped to attention at Haxs' order.

"I know our skills aren't often celebrated in society at large, but it is time again to show just how vital they are. In case you haven't heard, war is coming to the Commercial Empire, and it is up to us to sound the alarm. We're going up against the fiercest gates in all of the Imperan datatanks, so this will be a full team drop. The Enforcer assured me that Streetz has speedy digits, so he'll be on the door," Haxs said.

Subterra members nodded silently, unsure what to make of the pep talk. All were seasoned in Hyper Lynx operations, but none of them had dared cross the lobby of any datatank under Imperan regulation.

"We have to treat this like any other day on the Lynx. Let's do what we do best, Subterra... Win!" Haxs finished.

With confidence, the datajackers approached their op chairs surrounding the industrial grade interface. Their enthusiasm swelled as the sense of duty set in. They enjoyed advancing their skills, but rarely was there a greater satisfaction then when they were put to use for something important and not just daily recreation. Clutch broke into a rally chant much like a coach would before an allcourt match in order to set the mood. Streetz observed from behind the console, unfamiliar with the youthful display.

Each member of the team settled into their chairs and pulled the attached visors over their faces before pressing on their tappers to raise the chairs. Upon instruction, the large padded metal chairs hoisted up and spun in a half circle so that all were facing inward with a direct view of the the multi-directional emcast. With chairs in place, all members activated the wrist restraints to maximize all efforts of their agile fingers.

With a buzzing whoosh, four life-sized figures began to materialize within the bounds of the emcast's projection, each of them temporarily without distinction. Crew members were free to personalize the visual elements of their geists within the projection, yet most had grown accustomed to their previously defined profiles. Customization was still a popular mechanism within the artifical realms of the Hyper Lynx's underpinnings.

L337 Haxs felt his mind meld with the virtual projection as the wetware connection activated. It never ceased to amaze him how real his surroundings felt whenever he dropped into the system even though the visuals themselves still carried an artificial glow by way of the scrypto symbols swirling about many a structure, humanoid or otherwise. The only reminder of his connection to the real world was the cold surface of the tappers under his palms, allowing him to manipulate his geist inside the system.

As the other team members finalized their entry, L337 Haxs moved his geist about, shifting its weight. His projection was a set of white and black tactical clothes complete with an allweather hood, scaled to match his height, albeit slimmer in form. Similar humanoid figures took shape across from his geist, all varied colors, but each a collection of opaque and transparent stripes that revealed the swirling scrypto within the gaps.

Parity's geist was the first to complete, her purple shades glowing against the dull projection backdrop. Her form had a short skirt cut an angle from her right knee to the middle of her left thigh. Even her geist's top resembled her black hair pulled back into a ponytail. Clutch's nondescript light blue form appeared next which matched his focus on conquest over aesthetics since his time was mostly spent on internal stats. Hellix was the last to materialize. Given how much time he spent on the doorman console, the tweaks to his geist were not as readily optimized as the others, but finally, a blue essence with yellow trim encompassed his geist which represented a shorter figure with casual attire and a leather jacket.

Once the crew successfully merged with the system, Haxs took a moment to inventory his arsenal which included his bow, arrows and his favorite Cronos 18s all of which were products of his own design. While disruptors were the norm in the real world, many datajackers still preferred visual expressions of their historic ballistic counterparts in the virtual one. Haxs never tired of the rush from the high impact sounds and tactile feedback. Although the stimuli were virtual, Haxs still felt a sense of satisfaction as each sidearm locked a round into the chamber.

The final inspection of his weapon sights brought Haxs' attention back to the mission. He was mindful that the bullets emitted from his weapons were just datapods, but they were capable of spiking a gates transmission sequence rendering it inoperable. Since Subterra was about to face an unknown number of gates, Haxs hoped to terminate as many as possible to keep his crew alive.

"How we lookin', Streetz?" Haxs yelled above the noise of the emcast simulation.

"All signals liquid. All systems go!" Streetz replied as he glanced at each biotrack feeding into the doorman console. It had become his responsibility to monitor the vitals of all crew members. If a gate attempted to slip around and sever the conscious connection, it was his job to create a safe exit for the user's consciousness without dangerous feedback. Gates came in all shapes, sizes and forms, so he would have to run his algorithms at peak performance to keep Subterra free of threats.

"It's game time!" Haxs said as he moved the white scrypto form of his geist toward the Hyper Lynx access point.

Subterra performed all of its staging in the insertion zone which lacked any color except the glowing grid lines adorning the walls. Given the operational costs of improving wetware interfaces many datatanks were void of meaningful detail. Some zones were bare algorithms creating an utter dismal experience while others were rich in color and abstract design as if literally projected from the brain of the datatank's primary host. Haxs still felt himself unnerved from time to time as he contemplated that they were actually digging through another person's mind.

After a short walk, Subterra found itself in the domain known to be the lobby of Commercial Empire databanks. The lobby itself represented a city by way of its tall buildings and streets separating them, but buildings were nothing more than square columns reaching high overhead as long as they didn't reach past the emcast projection.

The visual terrain beneath their feet was filled with long narrow electrical pathways much like circuits. The pathways sparked and hissed as occasional datapods traversed beneath their feet. Some datapods even scaled the vein-like designs on the exterior of the building structures.

Shades of blue, purple and black glowed from the ambient surroundings. Beyond the building caps was an eerie green light as if sunlight had been poorly designed. Haxs looked for the source of the artificial lighting but found nothing.

"We have to make our way to the mounds," Haxs said pointing ahead of the crew's position. "That is where we will find the terminal."

Haxs kept his firearms pointed ahead as Subterra advanced toward their objective. Before being able to shout a containment order to Streetz, Haxs sensed the presence of a gate. A large flying object swooped down from above slashing with sharp fingers at the intruders. Hellix, who was still paces behind Haxs, dove to the ground narrowly evading the attacking gate.

Clutch and Parity were quick to fire at the apparition, but unable to successfully land a direct hit before their foe was high into the air and out of sight. Every member of the crew scanned the sky ready for another aerial strike.

Hellix kept his eyes trained on the sights of his MARC-15 rifle. He noticed an unusual shape protruding from the rooftop of an otherwise nondescript building. As soon as his weapon was tracking, the entity swooped down.

"Look out," Hellix yelled as he fired a burst of rounds. He attempted to follow the creature, but it was gone.

Haxs swiveled about to assist, but once again he was unable to track the target, "Streetz, what kind of signals are we getting?"

"It looks like you have a Drula in your area with other unidentifiable gates on approach. Distance unknown," Streetz replied.

"Give us an increased gravity flux no less than six marks from the floor. That should slow this one down a bit," Haxs ordered. "Let's get a move on, Subterra. There is no time to sit around."

Haxs pushed the group forward into a sprint as they headed for the lobby perimeter. Clutch and Parity followed close behind while Hellix cautiously scanned the skyline at a slower pace. As the gap in the party increased, the Drula used the opportunity to swoop down and knock the rifle from Hellix's hands.

Haxs spotted the boundary of the present domain as the distant colors shifted from green to black. As he pressed on, he heard the conflict behind, ready to assist, but Hellix shouted orders to the contrary.

"Keep going! I can handle this wench!" Hellix yelled.

"Better not kill her, Hellix. She may be the closest thing you get to a date," Clutch quipped as the crew continued forward.

With the Drula no longer concerned about hiding its presence, it circled above like a vulture. It had to exert energy to maintain height with the increased gravity. But the domain modification made the downward dives even more deadly. The creature's body had little detail beyond the red and purple scrypto defining its form with the only exception being its sizable wings and long claws extending from its hands.

Hellix watched the gravity affect the gate as Streetz worked to keep the variable physical property in an irregular form. Gates were quick to counter foreign signals, so doormen were responsible for keeping them guessing.

As the Drula detected a shift in its favor, it dropped downward latching onto Hellix's chest with its hook like appendages. Upon making contact, it worked to crush Hellix's geist, smothering the transmission lines that exchanged his conscious thought with the outside world. With increased gravity, Hellix knew that he wouldn't successfully push the Drula away and make it to his fallen rifle. He felt a sharp pressure as if his mind was swelling like a balloon. The Drula leaned in, its fangs glistening in the green light.

With reflexes swiftly dissipating, Hellix reached behind his back to release the metal scram stick he carried with him. He separated the ends of the stick to reveal the two sharp blades enclosed within.

"Suck on this!" Hellix replied as he shoved one of the blades upward directly beneath the Drula's chin. The blade pierced upward through the mouth and into the skull cavity of the gate. Hellix followed up by running the other blade into the Drula's chest. With a horrendous shriek the gate flopped backward and writhed on the ground until its form dematerialized.

"You've got at least three gates on intercept course," Streetz said once most of Subterra cleared the lobby.

"Streetz, shut that line now!" Haxs snapped.

"That will leave Hellix trapped on the other side," Streetz replied.

"These datatanks are crawling with secondary conduits. Find one that Hellix can squeeze through," Haxs replied.

"All of the closest lines are too narrow in diameter," Streetz said in concern.

"It may seem different than how you fight on the outside, but in here we tweak our surroundings Streetz. Warp it, bend it or stretch it. Do whatever it takes," Haxs replied.

While Streetz focused on getting Hellix to safety, Haxs turned to face the portal between the lobby and the mounds domain that they just arrived in. Haxs watched as a blockade formed between Subterra and the ambiguous shapes pursing them at a rapid pace. Before the blockade completed its sequence, two gates squeaked through the portal.

Haxs blinked a couple of times in disbelief as he stared at the shapes of the two gates that successfully cleared the obstruction. Gates, or at least the humans operating them, were rumored to spend the majority of their lives connected to the Hyper Lynx, potentially creating rather bizarre apparitions resulting from psychological degradation. The approaching gates supported such a theory as they revealed their squatty hardmelt forms akin to lawn ornaments found in the Outer City before the war. One was a gnome with a poofy white beard and red pointy hat and the other a pink tropical bird with long slender legs. Strangely, the gates had no dynamic qualities as their bodies moved as solid pieces with the bird appearing even more awkward as it seemed frozen in a one legged stance.

"Great! It's the lawn decos of doom," Clutch muttered.

"Slowly back away," Haxs whispered as they stepped carefully along the uneven terrain. He had never been in the mounds datatank before and most gates weren't so deranged. He wasn't keen on dealing with both factors at the same time.

The mounds' sky was far less bright, prompting cautious attention, should the gates make erratic movements in the reduced lighting. The randomly sloped terrain glowed in a common fashion to similar datatanks with its gridlines flowing across low hills as far as the eye could see.

As the three Subterra members continued to backpedal, the stiff hardmelt gates slowly proceeded forward with a bizarre curiosity, like suspicious rodents eyeing a baited trap. The gates had no independent limbs, so they hopped from side to side to simulate walking, tilting at opposing angles each time they advanced.

With the gap narrowing, Haxs unleashed a storm of bullets from his Cronos 18s at the pink bird that continued to stare with a blank expression. In response, an energy shield expanded in front of the yardbird halting any harmful projectiles.

"Streetz, a technical readout would be helpful, right about now," Haxs said.

"There's no time," Clutch snapped as he swapped his rifle for his Sandhawk pistol and fired at the garden gnome.

Sensing the immediate threat, the gnome began warping all over the landscape, making any attempt to track him extremely difficult. Parity also tried to squeeze a shot from her Sidewinders at the gate, but it appeared in multiple locations, circling Subterra's position. The spiral-like blasts from her weapons continued to stream past her target.

The yardbird hopped toward Haxs, leaned back and then thrust its hard beak into his abdomen. Haxs felt a sharp pain run through his system. He motioned to kick the annoying gate, but it warped laterally before striking again and knocking Haxs on his back.

Parity drew the large chopper blade from her back and swung at the yardbird as it moved to strike Haxs in the skull. The flat wide blade struck the gate full force, sending it sailing through the air, but in spite of the strength behind the attack, the gate appeared unharmed. Before hitting the ground, it righted itself and moved in for another attack.

Thread: sysObserver.cmd

Hellix watched as the portal collapsed, trapping him with two additional gates in the lobby datatank. He hoped to back away without incident, but there was no evading their awareness, especially in their own domain.

"Streetz, get me out of here," Hellix hissed.

Before his sentence was finished, Hellix spotted a nav marker identifying his escape route. Hellix already knew the outcome, he would have to crawl through an access pipe. It was bad enough that Subterra was taking on a surplus number of gates, but shuffling through a hazardous conduit certainly wasn't to his liking.

"Is that thing clear, Streetz?" Hellix asked as he approached an out of place hatch, leading to an underground system.

"As clear as its going to get. I can distort the pipe in three boot segments, but I can only do so at a rate of eight notches per tick, so you'll have to move quick," Streetz replied.

"You don't say," Hellix remarked.

With the gates advancing on his position, Hellix snatched his rifle before sliding into the hatch and began shuffling his way through the pipeline. A pinch of emergency lighting allowed Hellix to watch the pipeline expand ahead of his position. He would have to press forward at all costs to avoid being crushed by the systematic return to shape. Hellix partially imagined that he was inside a snake's belly without knowing how precise the expansions and contractions were.

Seeing a trace amount of light ahead, Hellix quickened his pace and scurried out of the pipeline. In the distance he could see Subterra engaging with the two gates that cleared the portal. The pink yardbird was leaping to strike at Haxs, but as soon as it hit the air, Hellix fired a single round from his MARC-15 piercing the hardmelt figure's torso ripping it into a hundred shards.

Haxs got up and turned to face the warping gnome which Clutch was still struggling to track. Even with the best marksmanship on the team, Clucth couldn't get a clear shot at the remaining gate. An unexplained force appeared to mess with his vision, as if the gnome's constant warping was its means of weakening an invader's connection to the Hyper Lynx.

Before Subterra could corner the gnome into one of its repetitive locations, a horrendous scream tore through the virtual air, tearing at Subterra's senses. Another gate managed to find its way into the mounds domain. Haxs turned to see a pale white banshee with greasy red hair slicked behind its head at a sharp angle. The banshee had no facial features as if a cloth garb had been wrapped around its face and pulled taut removing any noticeable form. The banshee's white apparel was as formless as its face with the exception of the red skirt draped downward and back into similar angle as its hair.

Haxs depressed the triggers on his Cronos 18s, unleashing a torrent of bullets, but the freaky apparition let out a sonic shriek knocking him and his bullets to the ground.

"Streetz, get us an audio containment filter two paces in front of my position," Hellix snapped.

"Can't do it, she's too quick," Streetz replied.

"Then let's find out how well these things work together," Hellix said. "Scramble their collision frames and remap any encrypted signatures. That should confuse them for a tick."

Clutch watched as the aggravating gnome paused his quick movements and acted sluggish for a moment. Clutch took a shoot, but the gnome was quick to resume the warping process. The bullet appeared to have cleared the gnome's position, but Streetz's adjustments did the trick. The small gnome retained the larger collision frame of the banshee making it a larger target despite its appearance. The gnome didn't compensate correctly and was tagged by the bullet.

Parity leveled her Sidewinders and fired at the banshee, but not soon enough to prevent it from impacting Haxs again who writhed on the ground clutching his skull. The gate showcased that its sonic blast was its means to impair Subterra's mental connections.

"Streetz, get Haxs an audio dampener now," Parity screamed.

Streetz's fingers moved rapidly on the console to give Haxs' brain alternate pathways to connect with his geist, but the banshee was fast. For each pathway shift that Streetz found, the banshee quickly adapted to reroute.

Hellix took initiative and fired on the banshee, hoping to divert the gate's attention from Haxs. Parity joined in and fired alongside Hellix. The banshee continued to focus on Haxs, but the sheer volume of the firepower started to push it back. The momentary diversion gave Streetz the time that he needed to reroute Haxs' primary control pathways.

Hellix and Parity continued to fire on the banshee and yelled for Clutch to join in. Clutch switched back to his B5C sniper rifle, but motion along the floor caught his attention. Hellix sensed the motion as well and knew exactly what the visual disruption was, a small black body with eight legs and a skull design on its abdomen, a skullbore. The barrage of bullets pushed the banshee back long enough for Haxs to recover and return fire, but Hellix was unable to take his eyes off the skullbore headed for Clutch's foot.

"Well, what do we have here?" Clutch asked as he raised his leg to crush the spider.

"Clutch, NO!" Hellix yelled, too late to halt Clutch's movement.

As Clutch's geist dropped its foot to crush the virtual spider, millions more appeared, flowing from the ground like maggots. L337 Haxs didn't need to turn to know what a full crate of terror just spawned in.

Quick to sense the futility of firing on the banshee, Haxs switched to his compound bow, pulled back an arrow and released. With a little guidance from Streetz, the arrow hit its mark, penetrating the pale white banshee in the chest. Despite the banshee retaining the gnome's smaller collision frame, the arrow struck its center, making the strike unavoidable.

The sheets of skullbores multiplied and thickened as Subterra burst forward at a full sprint.

"We're out of time, Subterra," Haxs yelled.

Waves of virtual spiders washed over the hilly terrain with one command from their respective gate, *destroy*. Hellix did his best to run backward, spraying as many bullets from his MARC-15 at the ground as possible to disperse the skullbores.

"Parity, you're the fastest. You have to deliver the transmission spike," Haxs yelled as an oblong turfball shaped object materialized above his hand. "We'll hold them off."

"You'll never stop them all," Parity snapped back.

"And we'll never sound the general alarm if that spike isn't delivered," Haxs said, tossing the turfball toward Parity.

Parity secured her weapons and caught the spike, tucking the shiny metal object under her arm. She questioned the need for the transmission spike to be shaped like the sporting instrument, but the thought faded as she sprinted even harder toward the edge of the domain, pushing her geist to move as fast as she could will it to move.

"Streetz, reroute all of Parity's weapon stats to speed implants. Optimize any free memory and get her to that terminal," Haxs barked. "Also, byass currents from secondary weapons and spike lateral connections within a one pace radius from our position."

"That will leave her without optimal weapon reserves. I do not recommend that course of action," Streetz replied.

"Get it done. If Parity doesn't reach the terminal, then we're all DEAD!" Haxs said.

Streetz immediately registered the tenacity and dynamic assessments at Haxs' command which had thus positioned him as Subterra's leader. Streetz complied and channeled as many cycles as possible from Parity's weapons, leaving them in a near useless state. The transferred energy created a shockwave through the ground disabling a large cut of the pursuing arachnid-like attackers.

The shockwave rippled through the carpet of skullbores. As the unseen gate adjusted its control, the Subterra trio raised their weapons and fired into the remaining onslaught of minions still under the gate's influence. Haxs knew that they would never find the actual gate within the swarm, leaving them only one option, unleash everything. Even with every energy reserve spent, they barely impacted the massive size of the skullbore swarm.

"You know the last resort, Subterra, RUN!" Haxs shouted.

L337 Haxs, Hellix and Clutch turned and sprinted in Parity's last known direction. They had no choice but to move and hope they could outrun the gate's minions. As they rushed forward, Haxs could see Parity's purple silhouette in the distance, but even with the strain to focus on their destination, the skittering sound of deranged spiders consumed his attention. Haxs felt tingles as the creatures raced up the legs of his geist. A sharp pinch tore through his calf. He attempted to shake off the skullbores, but only created an awkward motion causing him to step on more. The struggles of his friends suggested that they were enduring the same conflict.

As each spider bite streamed more virtual venom into the bodies of Subterra's geists, the greater the mental distortion as the wetware pathways suffered extensive blockages. Haxs felt his mind growing sluggish along with his response time. Only a few more bites and he would drop dead in the Hyper Lynx.

Streetz's fingers moved furiously, attempting to fend off signals from the spider bites, but removing the blockages was difficult. He programmed a shunt to vent the blockages from Subterra members' nervous systems, but as blockages were flushed more bites followed.

Through blurry perception in the virtual space, Haxs could see more gates approaching on either side of Parity as she approached the mounds terminal. "We have to keep her in the clear," Haxs mumbled as he fought to maintain mental clarity.

Clutch managed to wipe the skullbores from his body, fighting against any pain brought on by the skullbores. Haxs marveled at how Clutch possessed the ability to move his geist as effortlessly as his actual body. Clutch appeared to disregard any side effects on him and charged forward to tackle the uprooted tree-like gate on Parity's left. Haxs and Hellix renewed their efforts, followed Clutch and worked to tackle the storm cloud shaped gate on Parity's right.

Haxs intended to instruct Streetz for an emergency disconnect as Parity reached the terminal, but instead, he could only mumble various slurred words. He felt his consciousness slip as the skullbores finally began choking out his connection.

Without looking back, Parity sensed that the quantity of adversaries in pursuit had lessened. She continued her sprint over the low sloping hills. In the distance, Parity spotted the cube shaped terminal in the center of a plateau separated by a wide chasm. She knew that her friends had fallen behind. It was up to her to complete the mission.

"Streetz, give me full forward velocity that you can. I'm going to have to jump," Parity said anxiously.

Without awaiting a confirmation, Parity bolted into the air leaping higher than her geist ever could under normal conditions. She continued to sail forward, but as she began to descend, she realized that she wouldn't clear the chasm. From the peak of her jump, Parity realized that there was a conical hole in the cube shaped terminal on the land mass before her.

With no ability to override the mounds domain's gravity, Parity was out of options, that is, until the purpose of the transmission spike's shape registered in her mind. She raised the oblong transmission spike and hurled it with a perfect spiral just as her view dropped below the edge of the plateau. The downward descent overwhelmed Parity's body, but as she surrendered to the fall, she heard a reassuring ping, as the spike connected with the terminal. An explosion reverbrated through the air. Parity could live with that being the last sound she heard, satisfied with the sweet sound of victory.

DAVE TODD

25 – None Shall Pass – 25

Gridloc: Wayward Plane
Thread: frmAstStgMnfst.rgt

Mantis adjusted the harness which kept her hook swords attached to her back. Given the perpetual training regimen, it had been a while since she last had opportunity to don her street clothes. While her gear certainly needed some tweaks she was concerned about her leather pants fitting a bit too snug in the event of an altercation. Whether her body structure had increased on account of Tiger's training or gotten soft from lack thereof it was always a feature of the Monk lifestyle that seemed to be lose-lose.

Mantis' apparel wasn't the only thing in need of adjustment. She tucked one of her blonde braids back over her ear after becoming so reliant on the signature Monk knitted cap to keep her hair in place.

After realizing that she had been fussing over appearances in the abandon for no reason, she finally resumed her search for the next industrial district. She was frustrated that she had such little information to go on regarding the whereabouts of her former associate. Monks were adept at extracting information, some methods more extreme than others, but there was no way to gather information when it simply did not exist. All she knew was that the location of interest was industrial, and given that the southern end of Windstonne was littered with industrial complexes, her search would not be easy.

As she cleared the surrounding residential complex, Mantis spotted the defunct dartway heading away from Windstonne toward the southwest. She had often contemplated if the old dartways were only rumored to be destroyed to keep residents of the abandon from thriving outside the watchful eye of the Commercial Empire. She noticed that one of the overpasses crossing the Windstonne river was still intact. She had yet to search west of the Winzy, so the combination of a remote region with access to transportation suggested that she might have a new locale to inspect.

Navigating the rough which led up to the dartway embankment was an arduous hike, but a rewarding one, as she got a better view of the dartway. Without being able to see the details from below, Mantis never would have discovered that, despite the clutter, vehicles could still make their way along the dartway as long as the path wasn't heavily deteriorated. Even more spectacular was the orange hue bouncing off the distant Windstonne superstructures as the evening sun cast its last light.

Another hike toward the overpass ramp which crossed the river consumed more time, but Mantis finally attained a better view of the industrial zone on the other side of the river. After traversing the overpass, Mantis found a service stairwell and dropped back down to ground level, but after landing, she paused. A strange phenomenon washed over her senses, like she was being watched, a premonition beat into the Monks through their constant training.

Mantis remained calm but checked every direction to look for unidentified bodies. As she looked up, she felt the strange presence again, as if it were overhead and behind. Before she could confirm, the loud crunch of heavy armor landing sounded directly behind. She didn't draw her weapons, but confidently kept her hands forward in a defensive stance. She was surprised that the new figure had moved so silently. It was evident that it had flipped downward from the overpass but had remained silent throughout the motion with exception of the hard landing.

"This isn't exactly a prime location for real estate scouting," Crux said.

"You can have the land, I'm just looking for information," Mantis said reluctantly, narrowing her eyes at the unexpected sarcasm.

"Information is best found in the presence of answers, and things looks rather desolate out this way," Crux replied as he nodded his head toward the region ahead.

"If you must know, I'm looking for a friend," Mantis replied.

Crux paused and looked in a variety of directions before continuing. Even with the light blue visor obstructing all facial expression, Mantis knew that he was selecting his words carefully.

"Your friend is no more," Crux said solemnly.

"How could you know? I haven't told you who I am looking for," Mantis said, puzzled at the enigmatic roadblock in the form of a metal supersuit.

"How I know is insignificant, but your quest not so much," Crux said.

Mantis paused. She wanted to test the knowledge of this individual without revealing anything about herself. He was speaking in generalities making it difficult to get a read. She couldn't discern if he was just being a mindless security guard or had deep intelligence from experience in the way of espionage. She sensed no offensive gesture yet, but his calm demeanor suggested that could change if she continued to press.

"I'll take my chances," Mantis replied.

"I won't. I know what's at stake. You are a destabilizing agent, a wild card. The security of many hangs on long running investments and sacrifices. You would put those at risk with your betrayal," Crux insisted.

"I haven't betrayed anyone," Mantis said emphatically.

"Yet," Crux quickly interjected.

"Just who are you?" Mantis replied sarcastically, confused at how her own interests were hindered by some invisible yet muddled agenda.

"Even if I told you, you wouldn't remember without my approval," Crux said.

"I think I would remember some armored fish in a dark alley muttering nonsense, so I'll be the judge of that," Mantis said, taking offense at what the figure assumed about how much influence that he could have over a Monk.

"No. No, you won't," Crux stated. "Your presence here poses a threat, and your persistence comes with a cost. You can leave now and forgo that cost, but if you persist the cost will exceed the magnitude of anything you were ever trained to endure."

Throughout the conversation, Crux had remained surprisingly still, but Mantis narrowly spotted his right hand clench into a fist and then relax instinctively. Throughout the verbal sparring match she had been looking for weak points, a skill instilled by her training. This roadblock had armor pieces covering all limbs in various positions affixed to a bodysuit of an unknown weave. It didn't look suitable for a street fight, but Mantis had also learned to never underestimate her foes. Everything about the basics of Monk training suggested that the present altercation wasn't a time to make assumptions, especially with the strange nature of her opponent who potentially knew more than he should about her. If he was an intelligence operator who had evaded the Monks' own data network, then it might be he who was a threat.

"Just so you know, this eventuality has been taken into account," Crux said.

"Then I think were done here," Mantis said.

As one final test, Mantis moved toward her objective, but Crux was quick to place his body in her path. She reacted quickly by drawing her hook swords from her back and lowering her stance. She swung them with the hooked edge away from her opponent. Crux easily blocked the strikes as the heavy metal weapons clanged off his forearm armor.

Mantis stepped back before rushing again with more strikes. Each attack was met with a block or deflection, Crux shifted his stance as necessary to maintain his defensive posture, but he did not counter attack. Sensing that her opponent was a capable vector, Mantis flipped her hook swords around and lashed one toward Crux's shoulder armor. The hook caught the armor, and she pulled, but Crux spun toward the pull, giving him a chance to deliver a spinning back elbow. Losing her reach, Mantis was forced to block the attack with her opposite hook sword.

Crux held his ground, forcing Mantis to step back once again to optimize her range with the hook swords. She focused and feigned a high dual strike, when Crux did not react, Mantis changed the angle and drove both down onto his chest armor. She intended to pull downward and rip the armor plating away, but Crux pressed down with his forearm and trapped the hook swords against his body. Unable to get away, Mantis felt herself pulled forward as Crux dropped backward to the ground and drove his boot into her abdomen, flipping her over his body.

Mantis landed hard and was forced to release her weapons to break her fall. She scrambled to her feet but did so without her weapons. Crux was already back to a fighting stance and had knocked her weapons aside. Mantis' eyes darted quickly to the ground to spot her weapons, then shifted back to her opponent. She needed an opening to strike, but Crux had already found his.

In an undetectable blur, Crux's armored form closed the gap and delivered a series of pokes before Mantis could respond. His extended fingers connected with a specific target on her abdomen, then her neck, followed by impacts to both her temples. Mantis slumped to the ground unresponsive.

Crux stood silently, monitoring her vitals to ensure that she was done with the contest. He had hoped that things could be resolved without confrontation, but most sequence alterations yielded the same result. Crux prepared to return Mantis to a neutral location minus the recent memory. He would handle all resultant events accordingly. The carrier was not to be compromised.

Captain's Quarters
ONV Persistence, Oceanic Outpost Fleet
Southam Perimeter Waters, Quadrivast Ocean
Thread: sysObserver.cmd

The constant thrum of the ship's engines and the occasional spray of surf helped Potentate Ang keep his thoughts on the slate before him while he studied in the captain's ready room of the ONV Persistence. Normally, he preferred to observe the actions of the crew and be visible to show his support, but the sheer influx of information to digest pulled him away. From the haps that he was receiving, faction leaders were up in arms about Jenkins' declaration. The volume of information being leaked to the people was hard to measure. Ang was diligently looking for any social indicators of military responses, but before he could break away from the formal military briefs a knock on the metal door interrupted him.

"Captain's got something that he wants you to see," said a crewman after poking his head through the entryway upon invitation.

Ang rose from his seat and wiped his blue sleeves to dislodge any weak wrinkles. He was relieved, on account of his metabolism, that his weight hadn't changed much to threaten the comfort of his battlethreads due to his time in public office. He was formally the head of all military service, but he still preferred to abstain from formal insignia so that the officers were still the focal point of their subordinates.

A short walk put Ang at the bridge entrance. One crewman manning the doorway was about to announce the Potentate's presence, but Ang was quick to tug the crewman's arm, suggesting that he refrain from protocol.

Upon seeing the new arrival, Captain Robson Baird almost called for someone's head for failure to announce Ang's arrival, but his superior's expression told him that such orders wouldn't be necessary.

"Good timing, Sir. We are just now receiving visuals," Baird said as he scratched his light brown regulation-length goatee.

"Opposition?" Ang asked.

"Yes, Sir. Reports confirm that Drakken Warbringers are approaching from the west," Baird replied.

"Commsman, get me an open channel with the Drakken," Ang snapped toward the pit in front of nav console where crewmen were monitoring their terminals.

"No, resp-," the commsman yelled before being violently cut off.

The Persistence shuddered as a cannon strike obliterated the heavy munitions on the front deck. Klaxons blared immediately and emergency lights washed the bridge in red light. Crewmen on the bridge scrambled to verify structural integrity while crewmen on the deck rushed to mitigate the fire.

"Drakken Warbringers, this is Potentate Ang of the Oceanic Outpost. We are in compliance with the Open Water Compact. If you do not stand down, your attack will be treated as an act of war," Ang shouted into an open comm, indifferent to how many channels it was blasted on.

The concussion of more attacks could be heard before they struck the water near additional Oshan vessels. Ang dug his fingers into the nav console, hoping that the strain would lend him an optimal solution.

"Sir, we don't have the hardware for direct engagement against that many Warbringers, not to mention the Tiderippers running defense in the battlegroup," Captain Baird said reluctantly.

"I am aware, Captain," Ang said flatly, making sure that he didn't come across as condescending in light of the obvious disadvantage.

As Ang contemplated the next move, he looked at the navigational plate and realized that the coordinates were exactly those he had relayed to Newton about their attempt to cross at the Nihocopa Canal. Momentarily blinded by the frustration of betrayal, Ang spun about and focused on Commander Jackal who was anxiously waiting for orders.

"Commander, I want you to relay orders back to my security detail and have them confine Talbot Newton. Then, I want you to see to the transition of all personnel to the Ventures," Ang said.

"Yes, Sir," Jackal replied along with a stiff salute.

"If we're going to sprout fins, we're going to need cover, Sir," Baird said after picking up on the Potentate's plan.

"Agreed, Captain. Activate the Scramstrike," Ang said quietly, so that the captain could assume command of the tactical operations.

"All vessels, Engage Scramstrike," Captain Baird shouted.

Even with the bridge a flurry of activity, it surprisingly escalated even more as crewmen moved harder and faster to coordinate countermeasures with the other vessels. While he observed from behind the nav console, Ang felt a knot in his stomach as he contemplated their course of action. They were about to deploy weaponry based on the efforts of his informatic advisor, so to simultaneously ponder the betrayal of location to another faction did not comport in Ang's mind. Something felt off, but he would have to deal with the immediate threat first.

"Firing solution available," Captain Baird said before giving the order.

"You're on point, Captain," Ang said.

"Fire!" Captain Baird shouted.

The chorus of hisses commenced as missiles were fired sequentially, complete with a payload of Oshan tech. Ang watched intently on the screen for feedback. As expected, the missiles touched down in front of the Drakken Warbringers with the exception of a couple which overshot and detonated against the enemy ship hulls. Plumes of water sprayed high into the air, but on account of the recent chemical reaction, the water lingered in the air shimmering like a halted rainstorm.

Captain Baird nervously rested his hand on his chin. They wouldn't know immediately if the strike was successful. Thus far, the new scramwater technology hadn't been utilized beyond field tests. The brains in the research division devised the means to polarize water in order to produce interference with targeting systems. In a tech dependent world, the Oshan officer hoped that it bought the fleet the time it needed.

It wasn't long until a crewman relayed an update of incoming fire. Multiple missiles were fired from the Drakken ships, but most inbound hardware dipped into the water near the Oshan vessels. Ang released a subtle sigh of relief.

"Deploy the Ventures," Ang said.

"All Venture class vessels, proceed toward the canal. Maintain evasive maneuvers and activate all countermeasures at will," Baird barked.

After acknowledgement of the scramstrike results, communications volume resumed. Ang watched on the nav console as the smaller vessels broke to the east, heading for the waterway which separated the Northam and Southam continents. Their speed could put enough distance between themselves and the Maleezhun attackers which would put focus on the Oshan Capitol vessels.

Ang watched nervously as the smaller Oshan vessels broke away, prompting a pause in the Drakken attacks. He was about to exhale in relief when the nav screen lit up with destruction readouts to one of the Venture vessels. Prior attacks had been glancing strikes or misses altogether. The Drakken had found a way to negate the scramstrike.

"How did they hit that vessel?" Ang asked.

"Reports suggest coordination with the Coalition of Jungle Republics. They are likely triangulating position from ground based receivers," a comms officer replied.

Ang clenched one of his hands into fists, knowing that the new wrinkle would once again put the Capitol ships back in the crosshairs. There was no formal alliance between the Martial Legion and COJR factions, so Ang pondered how such an operation was activated so quickly. Ang could only settle on an internal opinion that the relationship was artificially arranged much like the inconsistent behavior of the faction leaders when they rallied against Frank Jenkins. Nothing about geopolitics made sense anymore.

Time for contemplation was cut short, as another strike hit the Persistence. The ship shuddered in protest while the entire pit was abuzz with handling damage control. Commander Jackal was quick to enter the bridge and announce that necessary personnel were being transported to catch up with the Venture vessels.

"Sir, you need to join them" Commander Jackal said to Ang.

"It is my responsibility to make sure that we survive this fight," Ang replied.

"Are you looking for history to repeat itself," Jackal responded with a scowl.

"Not this time, Commander. We need to maximize personnel and hardware," Ang said, remaining calm.

"With all do respect, Potentate. Your responsibility is to the fleet, the ship is my responsibility," Captain Baird interjected.

Potentate Ang paused knowing that his advisors were correct. If there was an opportunity to cut the conflict off before it escalated, it would be done on the Imperan turf not the open seas. Reluctantly, Ang nodded his agreement. He was about to depart when another impact rocked the side of the Persistence. He halted and looked to the Captain for a statchek.

"Hull breached, but countermeasures are already containing the rupture," Captain Baird replied, reiterating the need for the Potentate to depart.

"Understood. Serve well, Captain," Ang ordered.

"Life above all, Potentate. I have no intention of suckin' surf so easily. We will cover your departure. All aerial deterrents will be activated," Captain Baird said, snapping a salute.

Potentate Ang returned the gesture and followed Commander Jackal toward the skiff designated to join the remnant of personnel with the Ventures. Even though he understood the sacrifice and the weight to carry regarding the fight ahead, he couldn't shed the desire to see the present conflict through to the end. As the remaining Ventures accelerated toward the entry to the Nihocopa Canal, Ang continued to look back as the Capitol vessels closed in behind to block pursuit by any Drakken craft.

Additional scramstrikes commenced with anti-air batteries dismissing any missile strikes that the Drakken vessels dared attempt. Ang was proud of the warriors of the Oceanic Outpost. He knew they wouldn't be dismissed easily even in the face of seemingly stacked odds.

Ang checked to see that the skiff was closing the gap with the Venture vessel trailing to rendezvous. As Ang again turned his eyes back to the warships left behind, another barrage of missiles was intercepted by the Oshan craft, while a handful of missiles squeaked through, most dunked into the water and detonated. The one that didn't, continued on a high arc. Ang's face froze as he realized that the rogue missile was headed for their rendezvous craft. Ang yelled for the pilot to engage evasive maneuvers, conveying his last audible words before the disrupted surf enveloped the skiff.

26 – Dawn of War – 26

Freight District
Core City Fringe, Windstonne Enclave
Commercial Empire, Northam Continent
Thread: actTgtPersp1.view

The post-combat tension made for a restless night aboard the mobile fortress. My mind wanted to stay informed as low volume comm chatter pressed my ears, but ultimately my body's need for sleep won the contest as I drifted off in one of the padded chairs in the Behemoth's cockpit.

The light sleep did little to yield a mental state of rest. Half conscious, I still heard foreign voices on the comm in spite of the Enforcer's best efforts to minimize the noise. The unfamiliar sounds continued to prevent deep sleep as my imagination continued to exaggerate perception of those on the other end or conjure up questions about the strange executive who had embedded himself in Frank Jenkins' circle of trust. Every time my mind tried to wrestle a coherent thought of recent events, the images twisted into a fog-like blur, forcing me to wake up, disgruntled at the lack of actual sleep.

Eventually, sunlight seeped through the Behemoth's forward viewport, suggesting that any additional sleep would have to wait until after a break in the fight or the alternative, a dirt nap. As I rubbed my eyes, I recognized another voice in the cockpit, that of Killian Szazs. I groggily slouched in the command chair while listening to the exchange between the Enforcer and the protech as I attempted to put my senses back in order.

"So, how do I have the pleasure of your acquaintance, Protech?" the Enforcer asked over his shoulder to the one who sat quietly while observing everything of interest inside the skull of the metal beast.

I knew that the Enforcer had the details from my recount of the protech's exit from BOWTech. I gathered that he wanted to hear it from the source, so I decided not to interrupt.

"I retained operational control of BOWTech Laboratories, but after passes of Frank Jenkins' financial interests exerting increased influence, I felt like I was no longer in charge of the company I founded. We were in the final stages of our latest project, and Mr. Jenkins requested that I relinquish control over to him. I objected. I worked for Jenkins long enough to know that threats were often delivered in subtle code. Without me, they had no project, so I held my ground, but I was certainly in a bind until your friends arrived. We've all since learned that Benni Kotes was sent to replace me, but unfortunately, I had grown so weary that I didn't see that coming. Frank Jekins has been preparing for war and he utilized my experience to advance his cause. I couldn't comply any longer. I finally started to care more about doing the right thing than my own well being. It became clear that the Commercial Empire is under the thumb of a madman, so he will get no more support from me," Szasz said as he leaned back on a console, taking take time to reflect on his past.

"How long have you been operating BOWTech?" the Enforcer asked.

"Too long... far too long, given how many have been impacted by the works of my hands. BOWTech was created not long after the start of the Global War. If you weren't aware, the name stands for Beast of War Technologies, designed with the intent of mitigating the cost of human life in battle, not cause it. Even though I was already mature in my career following my education in informatics, I was clearly still too impressionable. I was compelled to use my skills to help the local war effort, but I never stopped to question the origin of my backers. It wasn't until many passes of death and destruction prompted the realization that I was allowing myself to be manipulated. Many lives have been lost because of my ignorance as far back as the subocular tech used to create the Crossover Strain and the pulse bombs during the Smart Wars. Given our perceived successes, the Uniod Bloc created a derivative of BOWTech well outside our control factors. We have no idea what they have been doing since their teams specialize in aerial combat," Szazs said.

I noticed that the Enforcer's expression changed immediately upon Szazs' mention of the pulse bombs. Their was a compound grief and rage that he fought to suppress. "Some close to me were affected by those domestic deployments," the Enforcer said, his voice cracking as he spoke.

Whatever lethargy remained from my lack of sleep instantly vaporized as I realized the horror of the present situation. I watched Szazs' face pale like a man who had not yet escaped death, but instead invited it now that he was face-to-face with someone who bore the consequences of his actions. If the Enforcer were to beat the protech senseless or toss him from the Behemoth, neither action would have surprised me.

"It is doubtful that I have enough life within me to repay the debts that I owe," Szazs stammered quietly.

After an extremely long silence, I heard the Enforcer clear his throat. His control in that moment finally helped me understand that the truth of what he taught. While he would have been justified in taking corrective measures, he remained calm despite the apparent conflict raging within. I was witnessing firsthand the sheer will at work in order to forgive in the face of atrocious acts committed.

"Protech... what exactly is this latest project that you created for BOWTech?" the Enforcer asked, his voice hoarse from battling the conflict inside.

The protech was far from settled into a state of relief, so he hesitated before replying, "Back when the Commercial Empire still had a tenuous relationship with the Uniod Bloc, BOWTech was gifted with several varieties of wildlife native to the Mahleezhun continent. Jenkins' twisted thinking insisted that tests be done on them to create creatures of destruction. That testing allowed for great advances in our fibernetic manipulation research. We identified methods to give the animals abnormal size, strength and speed as well as increase their capacity for influence," Szazs explained.

"What kind of animals exactly?" I asked, more concerned with the general concept rather than the specifics of biology.

The protech opened his mouth to reply, but he was cut short as a ping emanated from the front console. The sound diverted the attention of all present toward Maxwell who was perched on the console.

"Incoming?" Maxwell said with a shrug.

"Enforcer here!" the Enforcer said in a bold tone as if his inner turmoil had been suppressed at will.

"Mac, Windstonne is crawling with military. There are Piran's all throughout the enclave along with these massive metal walking things. Jenkins said there are opposing military forces on approach from at least four different factions. I don't know how I'm going to get out of here. I'm scared," Sath said, doing her best to suppress her fear.

"Sath, stay put. You're safer next to Jenkins for the moment. Until you can break away, just stay calm. We cannot afford to tip him off that you're in contact with us," the Enforcer replied tensely.

"Mac, I-" Sath faced toward the comm screen, but her words were cut off.

"What's going on in here?" barked a gruff voice from the other end of the comm.

Sath's face twisted into panic as she stood and moved to disable the comm. Before she could tap the power button, plasma rounds leapt from an unseen disruptor and tore through the sonair tech, terminating the comm.

During the momentary silence, I looked over to see the Enforcer clenching his teeth while balling his hand into a fist on the arm rest of the command chair. I didn't dare guess what he was thinking, but I knew that I didn't want to be on the receiving end of it. I remained silent until he decided to make a move.

The wait was brief since the Enforcer was quick to shove the throttle forward, pushing the Behemoth to a speed beyond what its laggy acceleration would allow. The massive razerjack advanced toward the heart of the Commercial Empire. Torque and the Serpent both stepped into the cockpit upon sensing the forward momentum. I shot a look over my shoulder with a subtle head shake to indicate that the Enforcer was not in a positive mood, hoping that they would pick up on the strategy to keep eyes and ears open and mouths closed.

Our visibility improved as we cleared the defunct industrial region of the Core City Fringe. I hadn't realized that it was my first time seeing Core City up close. Rarely had I ventured my way into the fringe since most of my time was conducted in the abandon. My limited view of those buildings in the distance hadn't done them justice across the few times I had seen them on the haps. Core City structures revealed multiple architectural layers, some brick, others glass revealing a distinct shift in construction since the Global War. Bridges and archways visibly joined many of the superstructures for added support while protruding plasma conduits ran vertically up the building sides to supply power.

The tall structures cast long shadows in the early morning light. While I found the visuals eerie, I suspected that the locals at street level were more intimidated by the Behemoth's presence as it stomped down the enclave streets.

Our surroundings fluctuated in height. The Behemoth towered over residences and small business complexes, but as we neared the heart of Core City, it was the Behemoth that appeared small in contrast to the massive superstructures.

Upon approaching the densest portion of the enclave, the streets below took on a strange look. The roads and walkways were obscured as if by a carpet as it shifted in irregular fashion. As the Behemoth drew closer, I realized that we were observing creatures on the ground with four legs which stood much taller than humans. Since they moved with such precision, I doubted that they could be feral.

The Enforcer didn't slow the Behemoth's approach as we neared the structural edge of the Core City. Once in range, I was finally able to distinguish the forms before us.

"Protech, please tell me that isn't your handiwork," I stammered.

Szazs didn't even need a visual confirmation to know that I was referring to his prior project which was now under Frank Jenkins' control. Covering both street and sidewalk alike were hundreds of tigers except clearly they were not the naturally occurring variety. All of them stood taller than any meca had ever described, possibly close to ten marks tall by my best estimate. Every tenth tiger or so was saddled with a rider which I overhead were referred to as catspurs. Each of the riders had a mounted shoulder cannon, likely a Mortimer, resting under the right arm.

I zoomed in my ikes to identify why exactly the creatures were more threatening beyond their wild counterparts. The tigers appeared to have enlarged skulls. The creatures' fur ranged from full to stringy in the parts that weren't exposing bare or scarred flesh. The creatures surprisingly remained still, suggesting that they were controlled either by their catspurs or from a remote location.

Since the Behemoth advanced at a full clip, it was perceived as hostile. Tigers at the front of the formation lowered their heads and then snapped upward, unleashing a growl that, once combined, emanated a shockwave capable of deafening any bystander. The shockwave rippled the ground and the Behemoth's legs, wobbling the massive razerjack. Both Torque and the Serpent felt their legs give way in spite of their keen balance.

The Enforcer continued the Behemoth's forward motion as he swiftly entered coordinates for a firing solution on the tigers ahead without waiting for a proper threat assessment. Everyone within the razerjack heard the Behemoth's planar cannon charge beneath our feet. With a rumble that ascended into an explosion, the cannon launched a wide bright yellow blast, angling downward at the street, disrupting the tigers' once precise formation. Bodies and turf flew in an outward direction

With systematic behavior that was activated by conditioning or instruction, the tigers realigned themselves and braced for another attack. The Enforcer wanted to activate another attack, but the charge interval from the large cannon was too long.

"Alright, let's send these kitties back to the litter box," Maxwell muttered.

The response to the hamster's remark was a collective eye roll.

"Looks like a tough crowd here today, Folks," Maxwell mumbled.

As a comm light blinked, Maxwell was quick to activate it.

"Any resistance friendly forces present?" A voice requested through the comm in between interruptions by numerous explosions.

"This is the Enforcer, Vanguard Strike Coordinator. Identify yourself," the Enforcer replied as he leaned forward.

"This is General Pedro Cruz of the Alcazaban Military," the voice replied.

"Is your presence authorized by Westcrest?" the Enforcer asked, curious as to the nature of the presence.

"Not officially. Word traveled fast about some nefarious forces within an Imperan plot. We convinced the Westcrest government to release a small contingent for observation purposes so that we wouldn't bog down official channels," Cruz replied.

"Understood, General, we can sync positions," the Enforcer replied.

"Coordinates away, Enforcer. If you could lend support, we could use it. We intended to hold position outside of the enclave, but we didn't expect to see razerjacks so far from the urban center.

"Support is on the way, General. Hold the line!" the Enforcer replied before closing the comm.

"See you on the outside," General Cruz replied as he signed off.

The Enforcer initially hesitated upon recognizing the phrase known to members of the Interlace. He might have been wary of a trap early in the conflict, but the general's manner reaffirmed the Enforcer's commitment to lend aid. Other factions weren't without regions built on Interlace roots.

"Alright, Vanguard this what we came here for. Give them all the help you can," the Enforcer said as he faced Torque and the Serpent.

"What do you expect us to do that they aren't already doing?" Torque asked.

"I don't know, but you'll think of something since you're good at getting attention. The least you can do is create enough of a fuss to draw the heavy weapons," the Enforcer said. "Ayezon!"

Torque and the Serpent nodded and repeated the expression before disappearing into the body of the Behemoth. A loud grating sound followed as the Behemoth's rear panels lifted and flooded the dark interior with light. Torque climbed a ladder to reach the track overhead where the Chromehound was parked. The Serpent followed close behind where the Reptilian was placed between the two Vanguard moxes.

I stood and observed from the front of the Behemoth's body as Torque revved the Chromehound's engines. Due to unfamiliarity with the docking mechanism, I was concerned about the Vanguard vehicles becoming stationary targets as the docking clamp lowered them. Before I could waste brainpower on additional useless scenarios, the docking clamp latched onto the Chromehound's roof. Torque slammed the mox into reverse as the overhead winch cable snapped taut corresponding with the crane which guided the vehicle into the open. The vehicle swung backward until the forward motion of the Behemoth and the Chromehound propelled it forward onto the pavement, tires squealing on contact.

The Serpent executed a similar maneuver on the Reptilian as he backed it from the storage rack and let the winch guide him into a backward swing. As the vehicle touched down, the Serpent opened up the throttle and twisted his ride down a side street to evade the onslaught of approaching tigers.

I failed to see the impact that two individuals would make in supporting an armored unit from an advancing wave of destruction, but I decided it best not to second guess the Enforcer's tactics. I turned my attention back to the surging clusters of tigers on the street below. With the Behemoth towering high above, the troopers in control of the beasts altered their tactics by directing the tigers to attack the legs of the Behemoth. Groups of five to six at a time would charge the legs of the razerjack, operating under the misconception that they might easily find a weakness and collapse the hulking frame.

Any tigers that weren't crushed under the claw-like feet of the Behemoth would smash their broad skulls into the legs and turn about for another charge, if they hadn't already seized from exhaustion or spinal injuries. The attacks from below nullified the effectiveness of the planar cannon since the tigers were swarming from below like roaches.

"How's it holding up, Maxwell?" the Enforcer asked.

"Oh, it's holding up alright, but I'm more concerned about the stacking bodies than the blows. We're prone to trip and fall if those things pile too high," Maxwell replied.

"Protech, you created those things. Is there any way that you can control them remotely?" the Enforcer asked.

"No," Szazs replied frantically. "We have high level encryption on the transmission protocols. I'm sure Jenkins tasked Kotes with with altering my credentials. If so, there is nothing that I can do."

By the Enforcer's straight face, I could tell that he didn't like the answer. "Fox, welcome to war! Grab a turret. They need to be cut down since the cannon cannot reach them."

For the first time in memory, I was about to be plunged into the heat of battle, but despite the warm tension in the air, I felt like ice water was pumping through my veins upon being called to action. I nodded in compliance and dashed into the body of the Behemoth.

Maxwell had already submitted the commands to fold out the lateral turrets on the sides of the Behemoth. As I approached the small platform on the Behemoth's right side, I observed a semi-spherical shell suspended on a similarly shaped track allowing for maximum targeting range. I jumped into the shell, slammed the harness down and clenched the triggers in hand, knowing that hesitation would only get me sniped.

Spotting an advancing cluster of tigers, I depressed the triggers and cut a path through the creatures with a sweeping arc of plasma fire. The turret's free range of motion allowed me to see anything on the same side of the Behemoth and anything beneath.

The bodies of the tigers continued to accumulate as I mowed them down before they could converge on the Behemoth's feet. As my presence was made known to the fray, the catspurs turned their attention toward me, firing a couple of shells which impacted on the Behemoth's dense armor. The dissipating heat from the explosions was more than enough to direct my attention toward those capable of firing back. I had no desire to get picked off so soon.

As I continued to spray the terrain with plasma, I checked my ikes to see if I had inadvertently activated the wrong mode. My targets all darkened as if night was settling in. I knew that the day had just begun, so I was perplexed at the phenomenon, especially with barely a cloud in the sky. I finally paused my barrage and lifted my ikes to verify that they weren't broken. Indeed a colossal shadow had been cast upon us, so I couldn't help but look up to find the source.

Thread: sysObserver.cmd

Killian Szazs diligently manipulated the console within the Behemoth cockpit. He was impressed with the sophistication of the technology embedded within the mobile assault craft. Even without control over his creations, he was still capable of running diagnostics on the adversaries below. He recognized the signals being received, but something caused a huge spike in transmission traffic. He deployed filters to narrow the datastream, but something was wrong. Additional signals common to the bandwidth used by BOWTech were causing interference. The strength of the signals suggested that they were emanating from a source five times larger than any of his projects.

Silently, Szazs moved toward the viewport and spotted the increasing shadow covering the ground as it advanced from the east. He hoped for a visual confirmation but had no way to inspect the skies. He adjusted his analysis and found a positive match on a project that he had long considered abandoned.

"Mother of fibernetic manipulation," Szazs said to himself under his breath.

The Enforcer and Maxwell were confused by the protech's behavior and did their best to identify the concern. Upon seeing the shadow before them, the Enforcer moved to pop the hatch over the Behemoth's head. As he witnessed the darkened sky, he found himself mesmerized with his jaw gaping as a batch of brown and grey winged creatures flew in formation, blocking the light of the sun.

The Enforcer immediately assessed the creatures to be birds of prey, but their scale exceeded the imagination. The birds' physique appeared no different than that of a hawk or eagle, but the size almost made them appear reptilian in nature with their feathers resembling scales. Maxwell was the first to stop gawking as he immediately ran numbers off the visuals from the Enforcer's ikes.

"Szazs, I hope you have a perfectly logical explanation of what we're seeing," the Enforcer said, his eyes still fixed on the sky.

Szazs gulped before speaking, "Back when the Uniod Bloc still had that strained alliance with the Commercial Empire, BOWTech had branches in both factions. Before things soured entirely, the Uniod Bloc assumed control over their local branch which happened to be working on an airborne project. I never thought that it cleared early trials."

"It'd be nice to know if they're friendly," the Enforcer replied.

Maxwell was about to relay a transmission to any possible controller over the new arrivals, but before his tiny paws could engage the comm, a loud shriek pierced the air, rattling every gear and strut within the Behemoth. The predatorial birds initiated their own contributions to the carnage as they swooped down into the deep alleys which were created by the tall Imperan structures.

"There goes that theory," the Enforcer remarked.

One of the massive brown birds angled toward the Behemoth as if it had been listening. Facing the razerjack, the bird shrieked, rippling the Behemoth's hull.

Thread: actTgtPersp1.view

"Fox, get back here!" the Enforcer barked.

The Enforcer's voice was loud enough for me to hear it over the comm and through the Behemoth's body. In response, I deactivated the turret and raced toward the cockpit only for the Enforcer to pass me upon my arrival.

"Where are you going?" I asked as the Enforcer made his way toward the Eagle.

"In case you haven't noticed, cats are no longer our only concern. You get to keep the Behemoth from toppling while Szazs and

Maxwell work on an override. I'm going out there before those raptors tear us to pieces," the Enforcer said before scaling the ladder next to the Eagle's cockpit.

There was no hiding the concern on my face. Thankfully, Maxwell responded by thumping a foreleg on his chest with an *I got this* expression. Even though the gesture was welcome, it did little to allay the concern of my new responsibilities as I parked my body in a command chair.

I took over the Behemoth's navigational controls while Maxwell monitored the Eagle's deployment. After the Enforcer occupied the Eagle, he fired up the engines which proved far more problematic than the raptor shrieks given the confined space. The deafening sound was appreciatively short since the Enforcer punched a status indicator on his console to open the trap door beneath.

The Behemoth's electromagnetic docking clamps released, allowing the jet to drop straight out of the belly of the Behemoth. The Enforcer angled the jet to the right, allowing him the necessary clearance to shoot forward between the Behemoth's front legs. Once clear of the razerjack, the Eagle accelerated to pursue the latest threat.

While Maxwell finished resolving the docking protocols, I only had to focus on keeping the Behemoth moving in a straight line. Other then avoiding trip hazards, things proved simple enough. Still, I was relieved when the miniature operator assumed control once again.

Szazs kept his attention trained on a solution to override Imperan and Uniod controls. I did my best keep my eyes on other sensors to ensure that no other unexpected visitors caught us off guard. As we neared another dense portion along the southern edge of Core City, I felt my nerves fray at the lack of razerjack sightings from the Imperan forces. I wasn't interested in a close quarters conflict, especially without having any time to learn the Behemoth's controls.

As I intently watched the scans of our surroundings, I noticed that many buildings had boarded windows. If the fighting had only begun, I figured the move had to be preemptive, especially since Core City was known for its aesthetic residences.

"I thought that this was a nice part of the enclave," I remarked before contemplating the cause. "Was Subterra successful?"

Maxwell hustled to multitask nav controls and perform a Hyper Lynx search. Numerous messages scrolled down the closest screen, first revealing the *Dig In or Get Out* message that the Enforcer passed along, followed by details of the looming conflict. Additional messages passed by, showing the citizens who were unable to depart activating strategies to hunker down, establish barricades and pool resources until they received the all-clear.

"Yes, they were," Maxwell replied.

It was a minor relief, but a welcome one knowing that not everyone would be blindsided. I checked for comms from Torque or the Serpent, but any hopes of an update were dashed as a ping crossed the comm, "Alcazaban infantry units are pinned down. If there are any forces able to lend aid, it would be appreciated. We've got snipers locking us down from the rooftops."

"Stand fast, Soldier, and relay coordinates. Help is on the way," I replied into the comm.

Maxwell blinked at me, surprised that I so readily accepted the request without even waiting for the coordinates. As an afterthought, I even surprised myself, but I was starting to accept that such behavior was starting to become my normal reaction.

"They are two parcels to the west, still south of the group that Torque and the Serpent went to assist," Maxwell replied.

"No one else is close enough. It's up to us," I replied.

"Fox, there is nothing I can do if they're on the roof. The planar canon can only fire so far above the horizontal, and we are sitting in a trench. We may as well be thirty parcels away to hit structure as high as these buildings," Maxwell responded.

"Then it's up to me. Can you reverse the polarity of the shield actuators?" I asked as a new strategy took shape in my mind while I navigated the Behemoth down a street perpendicular to our current course.

"Yes, but wh-" Maxwell started to reply, but then stopped to roll his eyes once he realized what I was thinking.

"Fox, you're more skulljakt than Mac."

"I'll take that as a compliment," I retorted as I returned control of the helm back to Maxwell and headed for the circular hatch overhead.

After opening the hatch and pulling myself upward, I struggled to get a footing. I teetered while fighting to maintain my balance on the Behemoth's angular head which shifted as the razerjack still plodded forward at high speed. As we neared the received coordinates, I could see disruptor fire ahead on the streets below. Multiple infantry units were holed up in alleys and business storefronts to take cover from stray tigers which separated from the main battlegroup.

As we neared the upcoming intersection, I could see several sniper trails zipping through the air toward the soliders' position. I followed the trails to their source atop a high deck hotel to the right of the Behemoth.

"Maxwell, get us close to the structure on the right. I found our snipers!" I snapped into the comm, realizing that I had to shout just to hear myself above the moving metal and the firestorm below.

"Fox, that's fifteen decks up. You'll never make that kind of jump," Maxwell replied.

"Have a little faith, my little friend," I responded.

Maxwell slowed the Behemoth's approach and prepared to release an electromagnetic discharge. I instructed my ikes to sync kip activation with Maxwell's command. I took a deep breath and checked my stance one last time. If I didn't tense up, the force would cause me to break my nose with my knees.

Shoving any negative visual out of my mind, I craned my neck to see just how many floors I would have to best in order to hit my mark. I attempted to count the floors, but as they blended together I abandoned the effort.

"Hit it!" I yelled as I clenched my fists.

The force of an invisible geyser launched me into the air as I felt the electromagnetic force push at the bottom of my feet. I kept my arms by my side to reduce wind resistance making my body sail like an arrow. It was too soon to tell if I could reach my target elevation, but one thing was certain, launching upward without gear was a rush like none other.

27 – Sky Brawl – 27

Urban Heights
Core City, Windstonne Enclave
Commercial Empire, Northam Continent
Thread: actTgtPersp1.view

If not for the ikes shielding my eyes, the wind force would have caused me to blink uncontrollably due to the speed the the discharge shot me into the air. My immediate concern was my trajectory and if it would allow me to reach the roof, but to my surprise, as my flight drew to a close, I cleared the the height of the rooftop by at least ten marks. As my motion peaked, I realized the greater issue, the gap between me and the building which was at least a good three to four boots.

Scrambling to solve the critical issue, I looked for something to grab, a pole, an overhang, anything, but I found nothing. Just out of reach was a platform connected to a service entryway. I was going to fall clear of the ledge covering the entryway, so I flailed to twist my body in any way that might drop me closer, but gravity worked against me. I swung my right arm forward and hooked the edge of the platform with my fingertips as the rest of my body fell.

Only at the last tick did I think to activate my grips. As my weight tugged on my fingers, I screamed as I pointed me free hand toward any metal object I could find. Before knowing which object my grips locked onto, the invisible force yanked my body onto the rooftop. The awkward pull twisted my body around. As I sailed backward at breakneck speed, I rolled my body to the side to mitigate impact to my spine and skull. I landed hard, but if there was any associated crash, I didn't hear it due to the shock. My body enveloped itself in needles as my vision washed over with spots.

Imperan Airspace
Core City, Windstonne Enclave
Commercial Empire, Northam Continent
Thread: sysObserver.cmd

The Enforcer found himself obsessively checking the sensors to make sure that raptors weren't tracking his back. By his best estimate, he had counted ten of the modified menaces. Upon first arrival, the oversized birds had been clustered together suggesting that an attack head-on would be suicide. After keeping the Eagle low and away from Windstonne's structures, the Enforcer waited for the raptors to disperse.

As expected, the raptors broke into several formations after receiving instructions to focus on larger battlegroups on the ground below. The Enforcer banked the Eagle hard as he cleared visual obstructions, providing a clear shot at the brown and gray birds ahead of his position. The Eagle released a pair of missles, firing straight for the center of the raptor group. Two of the birds rolled away as if possessing an advanced detection system. One of the missiles deflected off the third raptor causing both missles to strike the fourth bird in the chest rendering its airborne body lifeless. The strike should have incinerated the bird, but the explosion's devastation was mitigated by the scale-like feathers.

With an amplified aggression, the remaining raptors flapped their wings to turn about and hold position as the Eagle advanced. In unison, all three raptors released a shriek with enough force to knock the jet out of the sky.

The Enforcer's eyes widened as the gap closed between the Eagle and the raptors. The raptors dwarfed the jet with the their massive wingspans. Anticipating the barrage, the Enforcer was quick to respond by dipping the Eagle down and to the left, forcing the Eagle into the enclave's structural trenches.

Ambivalent toward the maneuver, the raptors pursued. The Enforcer had not anticipated the raptors' ability to keep pace with the Eagle so easily, their massive wings pushed them with such force that the Enforcer struggled to put distance between himself and the feathered foes. He continued to weave the Eagle to make himself a more difficult target, but doing so in the confined spaces of the trenches only increased his risk of collision.

The lead raptor released another shriek just as the Enforcer dipped the Eagle under the raptors' direct line of fire. The sound waves shook the jet like turbulence, forcing the Enforcer to wrestle with the stick to maintain control of the craft.

"Can't afford many narrow misses like that," the Enforcer muttered to himself. "Let's see how these birds do at maneuvering."

The Eagle passed through numerous clouds of smoke rising from the streets below as a result of the Goliath's wreaking havoc of any opposition in range, be it soldier or structure. Even if Frank Jenkins' campaign didn't succeed, Windstonne would remain scarred as yet another victim of his long running treachery.

The Enforcer was forced to acknowledge speed limitations while navigating the trenches at low altitude. Optic sensors allowed the Enforcer to observe the raptors as they pulled back into a triangle formation. As the jet weaved, the Enforcer realized that they were preparing for another shriek.

The Enforcer banked the jet hard to the left before pulling into a tight loop on the right, giving him the angle needed to divert course into a perpendicular trench. The raptors attempted to adjust their angle but struggled. The lead raptor smashed into a high rise, embedding itself into a tomb of steel and glass. The second attempted to make the sharp turn, but its wing still sliced the corner of the adjacent building like paper, only slowing the bird's momentum. The third raptor made the turn smoothly and advanced.

"One down, two to go," the Enforcer huffed.

The towering superstructures should have given the Enforcer ample opportunity to evade the raptors if he could out maneuver them, but the powerful birds continued to move through the enclave with less effort than the Enforcer required to manipulate the Eagle. With the raptors proving to possess quick reflexes, the Enforcer knew that he would have to sharpen his own, but that would mean taking more dangerous risks to terminate the threats.

High elevation walkways connected many of the taller structures. The raptors would never fly into them voluntarily, so the Enforcer opted to test their vision. The Enforcer fired several rounds into a side mounted advertisment on his right. The sign exploded into a cloud of sparks, shrapnel and smoke. The Eagle dropped just as it approached the closest walkbridge, leaving the haze for the raptors to contend with. The raptor on point had certainly miscalculated its approach and crashed into the walkbridge, but once again the birds' abilities were underestimated as the broad wings cut through the mesh of steel and glass without severe injury.

Running low on options, the Enforcer grew frustrated at the raptors' persistence. He had no desire to contribute to the carnage, but not destroying the creatures in pursuit would future destruction would be exacerbated by reluctance to remove them. The Enforcer spotted another walkbridge and fired missiles at the supports before narrowly dipping the Eagle underneath the collapsing structure. The first raptor cleared the obstruction, but the second got hammered as the bridge knocked the mutated bird out of the sky.

Without time to revel in the successful maneuver, the Enforcer was already plotting his next attack. He found another series of promotional boards and sprayed them with cannon fire for a distraction. As the Eagle passed through the particle cloud, the Enforcer pulled the jet into a tight loop in hopes of doubling back on his pursuer. As the large brown bird, entered his sights, the Enforcer fired a pair of short range missiles which generated enough impact to scramble the birds senses. Likely it could have endured the explosion, but without its ability to function rationally, it crashed to the street below in a lifeless heap.

Releasing an extra long sigh of relief, the Enforcer pulled back on the control stick before diverting course to lend support once again from above the enclave skyline. Just as the Eagle cleared the last of the superstructures in the vicinity, several icons appeared on the sensors. The Enforcer squinted for a moment, unsure if feedback from ground forces was interfering with his ikes or the Eagle's readouts, but as the icons turned into a more recognizable form, he tensed up and throttled the Eagle forward.

Three more raptors had withdrawn from their engagements to intercept the Eagle. Whoever was controlling the raptors clearly wasn't happy with the Enforcer for the four downed birds. Such actions likely elevated the Enforcer's ranking on an urgent threat list.

The new arrivals closed the distance on the Eagle as it flew toward the heart of the conflict. The Enforcer dipped the jet back into the trenches as each of the raptors snapped their wings to halt flight and rear for a sonic blast.

The sonic charge ripped through the air. The Enforcer hadn't estimated the speed and force of the combined shriek. The shockwave rattled the Eagle as it descended once again into the trenches. The Enforcer fought to keep the stick steady. If he overcompensated, he would slam into the buildings lining the trench. The Enforcer rolled the Eagle into a tight corkscrew allowing just enough clearance as he stabilized his flight path. The raptors beat their wings against the air and dropped to follow their prey with renewed aggression.

The Enforcer angled the Eagle's wings, reducing the surface area to negate some impact of the focused smaller attacks, but awkward ripples still penetrated the air, shaking the jet as the sound disruptions flowed over the wings. While verifying the jet's integrity, the Enforcer spotted more objects on the sensors, this time covering the ground with new information. He didn't need visual tech to know that a squad of razerjacks was marching along the street below.

The Enforcer twisted on the control stick prompting the Eagle to follow a split in the road. The maneuver put the Eagle closer to the Goliaths, but that was his intent. Waiting until the last possible tick, the Enforcer finally opened fire on the Goliath's to get their attention. Almost instantaneously, the Goliath shoulder cannons swung about and tracked the Eagle. The Enforcer pulled back on the stick, forcing the

Eagle into a power climb, leaving no obstacles for cover between the jet and the raptors.

One of the raptors found itself caught in the firestorm and plummeted to the street. When the Goliath pilots realized that they were not hitting their intended target, they ceased firing. Disinterested in the ground fight, the raptors followed the Eagle.

Frustrated that the diversion only took out one raptor, the Enforcer turned the Eagle once again into the trenches, his path clear of razerjack interference. The raptors began to shriek incessantly as they dove after the Eagle to finish the fight.

Since the present trench proved too narrow for lateral maneuvers, the Enforcer dipped and flew the Eagle dangerously close to the ground. Determined as ever, the raptors closed in from behind, their wingspans barely clearing the corridor. The Enforcer checked his display for a corridor with no outlet. Finding his target, the Enforcer weaved the Eagle along the Core City streets to lure the raptors into his trap.

The Enforcer's intended maneuver might cost him his craft, but if he disabled the pursuing raptors, it might be a justifiable loss. Countless signs lined the buildings. The Enforcer relentlessly fired on each side of the trench utilizing any obstacle in his path to create a visual impairment for his foes.

The end of the trench stopped short due to a tall commercial complex. With a thick haze of fine debris and two raptors trailing behind, the Enforcer pushed the Eagle to its limits within the tight confines toward the point of no return. He clenched the control stick, held his breath, and flipped up the safety cover on the eject button.

Inner Core Dartway
Core City, Windstonne Enclave
Commercial Empire, Northam Continent
Thread: sysObserver.cmd

Maxwell's eyes shifted about furiously as he continued to track the movement of hostiles beneath the Behemoth. After accepting the futility of testing mutated mammals versus razerjack armor, the catspur's began to break off their attack, knowing that there were plenty of squishy targets to be found on the ground. No one wanted to be responsible for wrecking the expensive tigers without accumulating the kills to show for it. As the conflict waned, Maxwell found a low traffic side street to park the Behemoth since he was reluctant to advance further into combat without anyone except Szazs present.

Maxwell looked over to see the the protech hunched over the console. The hamster hadn't seen the informatech so focused ever since he was rescued from his prior commitments.

"What is it?" Maxwell asked, unsure if he dare break the lone human's concentration.

"Something doesn't add up. If what Mr. Conner says is true, then why is the Uniod Bloc aiding Frank Jenkins?" Szazs muttered, his thoughts also answering the hamster's question, in part.

"Ah hah, there you are," Szazs mumbled with enthusiasm before Maxwell could respond. "They are using long distance relays. Either the Commercial Empire has successfully intercepted the signals, or the BOWTech Uniod Bloc forces are equally as corrupt as Jenkins. Let's say we test their resolve."

"Let's do it," Maxwell agreed as he mirrored the data on the console before him to observe the protech's findings.

"Were you involved in any of the fibernetic manipulation projects in the Uniod Bloc?" Maxwell asked out of curiosity.

"I was not, but many of their lead informatechs where trained here in the Commercial Empire. I wouldn't mind knowing if they built on our research or crafted their own methods. Given the challenges we had with the tigers' complexities, it is likely that they missed some crucial things to the neural integrity of the animals," Szazs replied.

Overwhelmed by the datastream pouring past his tiny black eyes, Maxwell realized that he had better check on the biotracks of fellow Vanguard members. As he popped up the vitals of man and machine, he nearly went into panic mode.

"Protech, I hate to complicate your endeavors, but if you can find something useful, I'm sure that the Enforcer would appreciate it. The Eagle has already taken several hits and those birds are wearing him down," Maxwell said, his voice heavy with tension.

Szazs' fingers increased in speed and moved with purpose as he scrambled to find the means to disrupt the modified aerial predators. Even with the abundance of technology at his disposal, he still struggled to find the frequency to override the raptors' control sequences.

"Maxwell, I need you to get me closer to the one of those birds. Signal strength is too weak, and there's a ton of noise. Information stored on the Hyper Lynx is locked down tight and obviously there's no time to interrogate BOWTech operatives over the comm," Szazs said.

After locking in the coordinates for the closest raptor's last known position, Maxwell input the navigational instructions. He also did so along the least active route. Even if he could operate the mobile assault platform on his own, his tiny body didn't posses the means to fix any real problems outside the reach of his console.

The Behemoth began to plod toward the target coordinates while Szazs squinted at the console in search of answers. After running filters against all possible carrier frequencies that might command the raptors' modified brains, Szazs discarded those unused and isolated the the most probable choices. The protech entered a seek command into the most suspect frequency and waited. Even a five tick delay in the return transmission felt like an eternity, dashing his optimism, but he persisted and animated his fingers to test other frequencies in similar fashion. As he did, a return signal finally lit up on the terminal, indicating success.

Inspired by the glimmer of hope, Szazs immersed himself in the complex interface that revealed itself ready for input. Szazs marveled at the intricacy of the operating system in place.

Maxwell's eyes were locked on the noptic scans for the Eagle's structural integrity, prompting a frown to cross his face. One more direct hit and the jet would be rattled to shreds. Even with the Enforcer's long running calm under pressure, the hamster knew that there were limits to his reflexes. One wrong move at such high speeds wouldn't even leave a wall paste as remembrance if he clipped one of those superstructures.

"Apparently, they have no neural interlock in place for the raptors' cranial cavity. Typically, remote transmissions to the altered mind then cap the receiver, preventing foreign intercepts unless preceded by the correct authorization code. These birds are ours for the taking," Szasz muttered.

"Truthfully, that's all fine and interesting, Protech, and not to rush you or anything, but ANYTIME NOW," Maxwell yelled at the top of his tiny lungs.

"Got it," Szazs replied without taking his eyes off the terminal to address the hamster's agitation.

Maxwell glanced at his console for visual confirmation. The threat indicator showing a raptor overhead transitioned from a vulture-like circular flight path into an spastic one which drove it into a downward spiral, headlong into the duracrete base of the trench.

"Protech, we need to get those two raptors off the Eagle before the Enforcer acts in desperation," Maxwell shouted, knowing that there was no time to celebrate the success until the most urgent threats were neutralized.

"You're going to have to boost the transmitters, we're not going to make it close enough in time," Szazs replied in a frenzy. If they were going to act fast, he couldn't afford to take a shot in the dark. He had to guarantee having the right signal.

"He's already removed the safety cover. He's going to pop!" Maxwell yelled in panic.

Szazs was only allowed half a tick to confirm the visuals of Maxwell's claim. Nailing the correct signal was imperative as the protech dug his old fingers into the tapper on the hard console.

Imperan Airspace
Core City, Windstonne Enclave
Commercial Empire, Northam Continent
Thread: sysObserver.cmd

The Enforcer tensely scanned his surroundings on either side, hoping for a last ditch idea to prevent dumping the irreplaceable aircraft, but no such opportunity presented itself. The Eagle whipped through the thick haze generated by the intentional destruction. The Enforcer touched his thumb to the eject button, but as he did a shrill digital voice pierced the comm almost startling him enough to depress the button.

"Mac! Don't do it! Szazs can hijack the birds," Maxwell screamed.

The Enforcer looked over his left shoulder to see one of the pursuing raptors convulse as if its bones were being twisted into knots. The spasms forced the bird to fly haphazardly into a residential complex, smashing a large crater into the exterior of the structure.

Amazed at the protech's success in such a short time, the Enforcer turned to watch the remaining raptor, but he instead saw his cut off point to bail on his strategy. He immediately jerked back on the control stick as the building which marked the end of the trench towered over him. The Eagle climbed, but its trajectory was putting it dangerously close to the building. The Eagle wouldn't be able to clear the trench wall.

The Enforcer realized that it was too late to eject lest he get caught in the crash. Out of desperation he fired the landing boosters at the Eagle's base as he closed within marks of the structure.

The gravitational forces pulled at the Enforcer's consciousness as he fought to pull the Eagle backwards into a loop. The landing boosters kicked in and pushed the Eagle away, threatening to fracture the craft under the strain. With the jet inverted, the Enforcer tilted the control stick to level out. As his senses returned to form, the Enforcer looked down to see the last pursuing raptor experience the same contortions as the previous one.

Rattled by the ordeal, the Enforcer deactivated primary engines so that the landing boosters could maintain a suspended position above the Windstonne buildings. His head still pounded as if his brain had been sucked through his ears after trying to outmaneuver the raptors. While trying to adjust, the Enforcer simply stared blankly through the cockpit's dome. As sounds of additional conflicts reached his ears along with visual conformation via rising dust clouds, the Enforcer did his best to shake his stupor and reassemble his thoughts.

"Killian, I think you just redeemed yourself," the Enforcer said softly with gratitude through the comm.

Inner Core Dartway
Core City, Windstonne Enclave
Commercial Empire, Northam Continent
Thread: sysObserver.cmd

With a deep sigh of relief, Maxwell looked over at the protech who finally took a moment to stand from his invisible prison at the console. With a newfound sense of satisfaction, Szazs took several deep breaths to alleviate the recent stress. Gone was the attitude of weary useless old man, replaced by the dedication of an informatech with a renewed purpose. As he realized that his shirt was drenched with sweat, he exited the cockpit and the stuffy air while Maxwell coordinated with the Enforcer.

"What is the status of the raptors?" the Enforcer asked through the comm.

"Our readings show that there are at least four raptors in the vicinity with another set on the way. As long as we're not operating in crisis mode, the protech suggested that he should be able to perform full overrides instead of turning them into feather dusters. The challenge is that they are adapting to our breaches and modifying their signals. Also, this affects the range at which we can intercept," Maxwell replied.

"Mr. Conner, we aren't close enough at the moment, but we could use the Eagle as a relay. Given your present mobility, you could expand our range without putting the Behemoth in jeopardy," Szazs added as he returned from his cooldown.

"That should work, Protech. I'm going to make another pass before I dock. By the way, where is Fox?" the Enforcer asked, the suspicion evident in his voice.

DAVE TODD

Maxwell and Szazs exchanged glances in response to the question, wondering themselves what had happened since Fox jumped from the Behemoth. There had been no communication whatsoever.

Urban Heights
Core City, Windstonne Enclave
Commercial Empire, Northam Continent
Thread: actTgtPersp1.view

I lay on the roof motionless, hoping that I hadn't damaged anything beyond repair, considering that the distant sounds of conflict had nothing on the sound of my heartbeat slamming my ears like hammers to steel drums. While spots darted in front of my eyeballs, pain coursed through my extremities, but a screech overhead was harsh enough to compel me to get moving. After a quick check that revealed nothing was broken, I began a jog across the rooftop until I was able to break into a sprint.

Various brick partitions separated sections of the rooftop. As I hurdled the closest one, the loud crack of a sniper rifle reached my ears. Realizing that I was getting too close to rush, once midair, I tucked into a ball and rolled onto the rooftop to find the closest cover. A nearby vent was immediately designated to fill the role. Crouching low, I waited for approaching footsteps, but hearing none I finally peered around the corner of the vent.

I spotted a couple of snipers who wore black and red uniforms with a foreign emblem on the shoulder. Since they were focused on the streets below, I had a moment for a proper threat assessment. Given the lack of facial deformities I assumed that they weren't Pirans. To better identify them, I zoomed my ikes to register the insignia on their arms. The VNET didn't take long to identify the Drakken symbol and their designation as the Martial Legion military force. I knew little of the Drakken beyond the occasional conversation with the Serpent when he wasn't tight lipped on the matter. If they had traversed the ocean to fight for Frank Jenkins' agenda, things were not looking good for the home team.

Knowing that the danger level only increased with more Drakken present, I did a quick scan with my ikes through the electromagnetic and interferic modes in turn. Finding no additional threats, I knew that there was little else I could do to improve my odds against the two present adversaries. If the Drakken were anywhere as tenacious as the Pirans, I would be in trouble, so I had no choice but to leverage my one advantage, surprise. Since both snipers had their attention fixed on their scopes, I hoped to catch them unaware.

I dashed as quickly and quietly as I could without compromising speed or stealth. I closed in on the prone snipers, but once I was within a pace of the leftmost Drakken, he rolled over to shoot at me with his sidearm. I leapt to the side and tucked into a roll. As my jump peaked, I drew the Phantom 4.0 from my waist, fired and caught the Drakken in the forehead. The other Drakken swiveled about to fire, but I was already obscured by an exhaust vent.

I held my breath to listen for footsteps, waiting to see if the Drakken dared pursue. Afraid to peek around the corner should he have his weapon trained on my position, I snapped an Inferno grenade from my waist and, without pulling the pin, I hurled it over the exhaust vent in a high arc, landing it behind the Drakken.

The Drakken snapped a glance over his shoulder to identify the projectile, but he didn't confirm its status. Knowing that he couldn't take the risk, the Drakken dove for the rooftop in the only direction available, toward me. I stepped out from behind the exhaust vent and leveled my Phantom at the Drakken's skull. The Drakken soldier froze once he was up to his knees and realized there was a weapon in front of his face. I stared at the cautious soldier, seeing a translucent amber eye patch covering one eye which suggested similar tech as the Vanguard eyecons. His uncovered eye however was much like Kotes', completely white.

The standoff was tense, I knew that the soldier before me likely had the experience to crush me in a fight, but at that moment I knew I had the choice to stay my attack. The soldier's eyes suggested that he was under the influence of substance or signal and might not even be himself. The internal strife made me understand the atrocities that were done or undone in the moment of reflex. I looked for behavioral indicators in the Drakken's eyes, but I couldn't discern between hatred or ambivalence, as they were void of any conscious reveal. The slightest twitch of my hand separated an act of war from an act of mercy, and either outcome meant a point of no return creating a deep internal conflict. I was no longer dealing with a faceless enemy, but a combatant directly before me. Sensing my struggle, the Drakken soldier reached for his knife, proving that, in spite of his disposition, his body was hard wired to fight. Caught off guard by the movement, I squeezed the trigger, dropping the soldier lifeless on the roof.

Part of me wanted to ponder my actions, but the sounds of ground fighting compelled me to pursue the distraction. I stifled any second guessing of the outcome, knowing that I was in a fight to protect both the people and the values which I held dear. I approached the edge of the roof and rolled over the body of the Drakken who didn't have a scorched face so that I could remove the eyepatch. I quickly placed the eyepatch between my left eye and my ikes to see if the fancy Vanguard tech could recognize the interface. Within a couple of ticks, my ikes replicated the Drakken interface which then enabled me to sync up with their weapons. I discarded the eye patch and scooped up a sniper rifle lying on the roof.

The reticle on my ikes changed and scrolled the name Hellings 20 before my eyes. According to the datastack, it was a standard issue rifle. I smirked, wondering why the Enforcer had neglected to offer training on said weapon.

I hoisted the rifle up to my shoulder and pointed the barrel down into the maelstrom which encompassed the streets below. The reticle adjusted as effortlessly as those of smaller firearms, but I had to adjust to the additional statistics which clogged the periphery of my view as they continuously updated with elevation metrics and atmospheric conditions. I locked onto a catspur at street level. I rested my finger on the trigger, but in so doing, a visual passed through my mind of my arm being ripped from its socket. Since I considered the Drakken to be professionals, I altered my stance, shifting into a prone position before resuming the hunt.

All of the carnage occurring in the street below quickly made me address the ugliness of war. All I could do was accept that it was my role to give it a face lift, so I tracked down my prior target and squeezed off a round. The recoil kicked hard into my shoulder, making me glad that I chose to put my body weight behind the long rifle.

Centering my view again, I verified that my target had slumped from his mount, his skull completely deformed from the burning impact. With all of the commotion, nearby catspurs didn't notice until I began to pick them off one by one. As disruptions increased in frequency, tiger mounts began to reposition themselves as the green wispy smoke trails loosely identified the direction of the attack.

"Any tips for sniping moving targets?" I asked into the comm, uncertain who would respond.

"Try leading the target. Aim where their head is going to be," the Serpent replied.

"Which, in the case of these Imperan types, is usually near their rear ends," Torque quipped as a follow-up.

"Acknowledged," I said in response to the advice.

"Today, skylights are free," I muttered as I fired off the last round in the high density clip at a catspur who directed his mount toward cover.

I rifled through the gear left by the dead Drakken and found three more clips. They may as well have been on a small expedition for all of the gear I found in their bags. After tucking a few salvaged food packs and power cells into my pockets, I slammed a new clip of high yield cells into the Hellings 20 and checked for a new target.

"Point and click," I whispered to my imaginary audience as I fired off two rounds at a white tiger charging toward a squad of friendly infantry.

As I reached for the next clip of power cells, a shadow overhead diverted my attention toward the sky. I didn't need to wait for the deafening shriek inbound before scrambling away from my perch on the rooftop edge. My previous position became an instant crater as the sonic blast shredded the affected structure. I dove forward just as another blast impacted the section behind me. I flailed to get my feet back underneath my body before the raptor overhead could turn me into a corpse.

The rooftop offered few obstacles for cover, and they were temporary at best against an adversary with an aerial advantage. Every other step translated the rooftop's shuddering instability up through my feet and legs in response to the raptor's sonic blasts. I took long strides, bounding onto any object that might give me additional spacing from the creature flying behind me.

I leapt across a horizontal shaft that was elevated from the roof. At first, I thought hopping onto the metal would provide a good springboard for my kips, but once I felt the warm heat of the conduit, I immediately realized my ignorance. Without another passing tick, I activated my kips to push away from the plasma conduit, taking no time to properly adjust for the force of the jump. I barely cleared the conduit when the next sonic blast tore into the conduit, its shockwave creating an explosion, knocking me off-balance midair. I tucked into a roll as I crashed down on the rooftop.

In the midst of my tumble, I caught a glimpse of the blue fire erupting from the conduit. The rupture spewed flame a good eight marks into the air giving the raptor reason to pause. Even though my adversary was delayed, I couldn't hesitate. If the raptor didn't kill me, the chain reaction from the flaming conduit would, and the rumbling underfoot verified that the building's imminent structural collapse. I sprinted directly away from the rupture, bounding from side to side as the raptor resumed its pursuit. Additional rumbles from below began to soften the structure, suggesting that I couldn't rely on the rooftop's stability for long.

Another blast sent me sprawling forward. I halted my momentum just in time to face the edge of the rooftop without falling over. I ruled out leveraging the Vast due to my inability to concentrate. Given the body's physical connection to the Particulate, I had no way to verify that the fluke event in the warehouse was applicable in the case of an even greater fall.

I estimated that jumping to the building across the street might be possible since the next building was shorter by several decks. Also the metal service ladders might prove to be a good failsafe if I shorted the jump. It was a long jump and I was out of options. I motioned to make the leap, but a roaring flame shot upward, creating a wall between me and my escape route as the plasma conduit along the side of the building exploded.

My time had expired. I had no way off the building except to pass through the wall of fire. In defiance, I turned to face my adversary which had slowed to verify the nature of the fire. The raptor flapped its wings and hovered, glaring at me, its trapped prey. It knew that I wasn't going anywhere, so it had to be savoring its victory, likely the manifestation of its controller rather than the bird itself unless its creators had performed even more nefarious alterations to its instincts beyond that of being controlled.

"What are you waiting for?" I asked as I removed my ikes from my face to look the creature in the eyes, discerning if there was something happening within beyond haywire fibernetics.

While my external movements were non-existent, my mind scrambled to piece together a solution, only to fail spectacularly. Instead, a dormant whisper tore through my skull, *where the carcass is, the eagles gather around.*

"That makes no sense and is in no way helpful, other than to signal that I'm a dead man," I muttered to myself.

"Look alive!" a familiar voice shouted into the comm.

I looked up to see the raptor rear its head to release its final shriek, but before it could release, a pair of missiles hissed through the air striking the bird in the chest. I blinked my eyes in disbelief as the impact stunned the bird, dropping it to the rooftop despite the explosion barely scratching its hardened feathers.

I quickly snapped my ikes back on and filtered out the smoke and haze to see the raptor writhing until it stopped thrashing altogether. I marveled at the dense construction of the feathers which only kept the bird alive maybe a few clicks beyond the impact.

"Fox, what are you doing down there?" the Enforcer asked through the comm just as the Eagle passed overhead.

"Oh, thought I'd look for a good place to roast some sugarpuffs on the spit," I quipped.

Disregarding my sarcasm, the Enforcer jumped straight to a recap, "Szazs and Maxwell are having trouble overriding the remaining raptors. Once we've finished, we're moving out of this sector, so I'd suggest that you make way back to the Behemoth unless you want to walk."

"Aye, Boss," I replied, mildly surprised that the Enforcer hadn't reprimanded me for my last string of actions.

As the roof rumbled again underfoot, I made for the closest ledge. At least without the raptor blocking my path I didn't have to make such a precarious jump. After gaining secure footing on the adjacent building, I took a moment to exhale and look up as the Eagle was already a spec in the sky, off to chase down more raptors. If not for the Enforcer's intervention, I would have been dead. The precise timing of it all was remarkable, in an incomprehensible way. The thought crossed my mind that something was amiss considering how I continued to survive narrow scrapes with barely a fraction of the experience possessed by my fellow combatants. Even the odd timing of the whisper in my head felt coordinated. Consciously, I felt like I was going insane for daring to think there were forces at work outside my scope of understanding.

Before I could pursue any conspiratorial notions, more small explosions suggested that it might not be long before my current perch too was affected by the imploding structure next to me. Getting my thoughts back in order, I returned to the building which hosted my deceased Drakken foes and scrambled to find any remaining resources within their gear. I snatched a shoulder insignia for reference and grabbed any loose power cells, but before I could scrounge for weapons, the low thrum of a cargo plane droned overhead.

As I observed the plane, which was clearly too high for direct engagement, I watched the tail open with countless black specs pouring into the sky. I suspected paratroopers at first, but seeing no parachutes, I realized that the arrivals were something different altogether. I zoomed my ikes to discover uniform colors matching the insignia in my hand. I watched the airborne Drakken more closely until they all deployed triangle wings from their backs. I had full display of the glider tech that had allowed the Drakken soldiers get into position so easily.

A cluster of Drakken dropped closer to my position, so I drew my Phantom and began firing into the sky foolishly with the mid-range weapon having minimal effectiveness given the distance and drag, yet my attacks clearly got their attention as a rainstorm of plasma descended upon me.

I raced for the nearest roof access ladder, firing over my shoulder which barely affected the incoming Drakken. At least two Drakken prioritized me as a target while I glanced to see that I was about five paces from the edge of the rooftop. Hoping that my foes were less agile than the raptor, I dashed for the edge. Anticipating my escape, a Drakken angled forward to increase his descent.

The closest pursuing Drakken reached for my shoulders, but I rolled forward just as he flew past. I grabbed one of his ankles just as he cleared the edge of the building, forcing both of us to tumble past the building, headlong toward the street below.

I delivered a couple of blows to the Drakken's abdomen with my free hand before reaching up to grasp his shoulder strap. Upon finding the release for the glider harness, I yanked hard, allowing gravity to pull my foe from the teetering glider. I wrestled to get my arms inside the harness while the ground rushed up at me.

With no time to spare, I wedged my shoulders into the glider harness and leaned back, hoping that I had time to counter my rapid fall. The change in direction pulled hard on the glider wings as they leveled out and thrust me toward a nearby building. Fearing a head-on collision like a bug on a window, I leaned to the right and the glider angled away. As I quickly adapted to the motion necessary to correct the glider, I guided it toward an alley that was untouched by the fighting. The quick descent made for a rough landing as I stumbled on contact. Impressed with the device, I found the wing retraction control, thinking that the pack might prove useful again in the future. Even more intriguing was the pair of pistols I found connected to the harness. Without a port for power cells on the weapons, I stowed my curiosity for later on how to operate them.

Relieved to be back on stable ground, I synced my ikes with the Behemoth's position. I knew that I had some new stories to share, assuming that I didn't encounter any more life threatening obstacles along the way.

28 - Ground Game - 28

Inner Core Dartway
Core City, Windstonne Enclave
Commercial Empire, Northam Continent
Thread: sysObserver.cmd

The Chromehound bumped along the increasingly cluttered streets of the enclave nearly causing Torque's fingers to miss the center console button to release the rear turret. Torque mulled over the automatic targeting sequences being too slow, but for the moment, they could provide proper distraction. After the rear panels slid to the side and the turret spun overhead, it began to lay down a swath of suppressive fire a good five paces ahead of the front bumper. Anything that the turret couldn't persuade, Torque opted to compress under the Chromehound's weight.

The Serpent followed close behind the Chromehound as it cleared the melee of tiger legs and toppled troopers. They needed to clear, or at least thin, opposition across a couple more parcels before negating the worry of becoming a snack for the striped mutations or paste underneath the foot of a Goliath. The Reptilian possessed no mounted weapons to contribute to the escape, so the Serpent drew his blade from his back and held it to the side slicing or decapitating any threat within reach. The tigers may have been designed to endure heavy plasma fire, but the Serpent doubted that their controllers took close range weapons into account. With one hand to control the mobi and the other grasping his sword, the Serpent cut through all four legs of a tiger creating a stumpy mess as the mutant howled and flopped out of the nearest catspur's control.

Torque suspected that the waves of infantry might catch on to their tactics, but if they did, their reactions hadn't caught up with their will. Even the tigers could have easily overtaken both the Chromehound and Reptilian if they had considered a coordinated maneuver.

Once a clear street popped up on the nav, Torque wrenched on the wheel to alter the Chromehound's course and put as much distance between himself and the tigers. He exhaled upon visual confirmation in the rearview mirror that the Serpent was close behind. Torque pressed on the accelerator to close in on Alcazaba's last known position. Thankfully, edges of the city were clear of the fight and also clear of bystanders who had already vacated or boarded themselves up to keep away from the battle.

As Vanguard support rolled up to the coordinates provided by General Cruz, Torque and the Serpent found a scene as frantic as the one just exited, only worse. It appeared that the forces sent by Westcrest had enough firepower to take down a full unit of Behemoth-sized razerjacks, but the interference by the local ground forces had been enough to undercut Alacazaba's artillery before they could get settled into the urban warfare.

Torque slowed the Chromehound as it approached a squad of Alcazaban soldiers adjacent to a destroyed Sandstorm tank. He then hollered at the soldiers who were sporting beige camouflage, so that he could inquire of the general's location. Soldiers pointed to a narrow road to the west, but before Torque could proceed, they suggested for a couple to ride along given the wall of tanks separating the command team from the rest of the enclave.

As Torque nodded his agreement, two soldiers boarded the Chromehound one in the passenger seat and another on a rear seat at Torque's direction. The soldier riding in the front seat guided Torque toward a dead end street. Torque found the location odd until he spotted the four Sandstorm tanks taking up parallel positions to guard the single entrance. Each of the heavy units had already locked stanchions, optimizing their stability making them ready for provocation.

The Alcazaban soldier accessed his comm to signal friendlies on approach. After being waved ahead from an allied soldier, Torque carefully guided the Chromehound between the narrow gap separating the tanks. In passing, the Serpent carefully assessed the tactical position of the camp, noting that it was only vulnerable to attacks from overhead.

Upon clearing the perimeter, Torque parked the Chromehound as directed and piled out of the mox and followed the soldiers to the command center which structurally looked like a bloated transport trailer even without its hefty amount of armor plating. Torque kept his eyes on every movement possible. While the Enforcer was more trusting of those admitting to be part of the Interlace, Torque didn't share the same sentiment on account of many passes of military conditioning.

Torque and the Serpent followed a soldier into the command center and were met with a blast of frigid air. The climate controlled interior sent a chill down Torque's spine. He hadn't realized how much his body had already grown accustomed to the heat of battle. Shaking off the chill, he removed his ikes to scrutinize the room.

The command center's layout was, as expected, a horseshoe layout of chairs lining one end of a central table with a tactical display in its midst. Surrounding the console was a collection of officers most of which were wearing nondescript uniforms comprised of gray or beige camouflage. Torque faced the officers, but he didn't exactly know who was in charge.

"Vanguard operatives, Lennox Johnson and Alex Corzo reporting," Torque said.

A middle-aged man of southern Westcrest descent as identified by his dark hair and brown skin rose from his hunched position over the display, straightening his broad shoulders. As the individual rubbed the outside of his mustache, Torque glimpsed the insignia on his collar.

"Mr. Johnson, Mr. Corzo, thank you for coming. I didn't expect such a timely arrival," General Cruz replied before extending his hand to both newcomers.

"I understand that you have been facing heavy resistance from Frank Jenkins' forces. I don't know what assistance my associate and I might be, but we are here to help. You'll have to pardon our lack of formal rank since we've been operating outside official channels for some time, but our experience on home turf may offset some of Jenkins' home field advantage," Torque replied. He didn't need special tech to see that Cruz's officers weren't keen on outside help, given their grim or annoyed expressions.

"I appreciate your sacrifice to assist, Mr. Johnson. I'm sure you were able to observe our collection of losses on approach. We didn't expect Frank Jenkins to have such formidable hardware at his disposal. Personally, I am not concerned about allied ranks, your chain of command is your business since some of us all share the same status within the Interlace, so I gladly welcome any intel that you wish to share," General Cruz replied.

Torque was eager to share his insight, but he first took a moment to observe the Alacazaban officers' reaction to Cruz's invitation. Some flinched at Torque's introduction while others produced subtle eye rolls of Cruz's mention of the Interlace, suggesting that Cruz's command was mixed in its views. At least having a sense of his audience, Torque sauntered to the op table while the Serpent followed suit but held back a couple paces to keep a watchful eye on the new allies.

"So far, we have witnessed the modified tigers and their handlers in action along with the Goliath razerjacks. Personally, we have faced Jenkins' military force, the Pirans, but they have yet to be found en masse in this conflict. I suspect that they will be in charge of the most critical infrastructure to Frank Jenkins' operation," Torque said, followed by his motion to highlight all key dartways and utilities of relevance. In response, the Alcazaban officers appeared to take on a curious nature, potentially formulating their own strategies as Torque revealed detailed information about the local terrain.

"Are you able to produce a scaled visual of active units from this display?" Torque asked.

General Cruz poked the tapper which connected to the flat noptic display on the op table, prompting icons to hover above the surface. Large numbers of Sandstorm tanks and Alcazaban infantry littered the display, compelling Torque to let out a low whistle upon seeing just how much firepower Westcrest had committed to the operation. Unfortunately, more hardware than expected had been decimated since Jenkins' forces had leveraged the outsiders' miscalculation of forces all too easily.

"My first suggestion, General, would be to position your forces so that they can repel infantry and hardware alike. Stagger your tanks with enough infantry in between to counter the tigers. The Sandstorm tanks should then be defensible to resist any Goliaths on approach. Next, optimize the broadest intersection to prevent getting blindsided," Torque said as he tapped a couple of key locations which matched his description.

"Relay coordinates to all forward units," General Cruz said to his comm officer.

"These are suitable maneuvers for a defensive posture, Mr. Johnson, but how do you propose that we flush Jenkins out," an officer asked.

"I'm getting to that, Sir," Torque said, snapping the title along with an eye roll for being interrupted.

"General, the next operation could be risky, but I think that we're going to need a team to bait some of those Goliaths into a trap. Do you have any lighter artillery units that can compete with those razerjacks?" Torque continued.

"Yes, we have our Squirms. They are all terrain, but they don't come close in firepower or speed. I don't think they are suitable bait," General Cruz replied as he activated an image of a boxy artillery unit.

Torque squinted at the awkward looking unit. It mildly resembled a zero turn graveler, given how its triangle treads covered both of its sides each with intermittent blocks connected to mitigate rough terrain. A long cannon rested atop the boxy center, suggesting that its firepower was hefty, but as the General stated, it wasn't about to win a race against a fast moving pedestrian.

"General, have any skirmishes thus far resulted in enough debris that can be leveraged as a roadblock?" Torque asked.

"There is a blockade five parcels to the north. One of our first engagements was quite a mess. It'll take a while to clear a path through," Cruz replied.

"Good, we'll leave it that way for now and use that street as our choke point. Position your tanks at the intersection along either side. We will draw in as many Goliaths and tigers as we can which ought to put a dent in the forces," Torque said confidently.

"Just how do you intend to bait the hook?" An officer asked with skepticism.

"If we present just enough units to pose a threat, they'll follow us right in. I can lead with the Chromehound. We should have just enough mobility to get a head start if we don't go too heavy on the artillery," Torque said enthusiastically.

"And how do you know that they will bite?" Another officer asked.

"If Jenkins' forces are even remotely matched in their egotism, they won't pass up opportunity to squash opposition," Torque responded with fading enthusiasm at the mention of Frank Jenkins' behavior.

"How many men do you think we should send?" General Cruz asked.

"Only those necessary. This could get ugly fast," Torque replied.

"Captain Nash, if you would please make the selection of those that you feel are most qualified," General Cruz said to the first officer who had expressed doubt in Torque's advice.

"Yes, Sir," Captain Nash replied with a stiff turn before walking out of the command center.

"The rest of you, to your stations. We need those Sandstorms blocked and locked," General Cruz snapped at the remnant of officers.

The officers present parted ways, some to the comm stations, others to their posts outside the command center. Torque and the Serpent followed Cruz out of the command center where Captain Nash had already assembled a team of three soldiers to ride along with Torque. General Cruz was familiar with all of them and proceeded with introductions. Torque was impressed with the general's knowledge of those under his command even amongst the lower ranks.

"Mr. Johnson, this is Sergeant Kronton, Corporal Harnen and Private AWOL," General Cruz said as he extended his hand before each subordinate in turn.

Torque nodded at the first two soldiers, the second of which had already assisted with directions to the Alacazaban camp, but he paused as he eyed the dark skinned soldier who had his sleeves rolled up to his shoulders, revealing his heavily tattooed arms.

"AWOL, Sir?" Torque asked, questioning if he heard the name correctly.

"Private Douglas Arnior is one of our most animated gunners, shall we say. He has served under Captain Nash's command for many passes. Captain Nash has kept the stubborn cuss around for his skills more than his compliance. His respect for authority went absent long ago, but he's always eager for action," General Cruz replied.

"Do you know how to kill a hostile?" Torque asked the last soldier.

"You don't grow up in post-war Angaleez without learning how to survive. Now, I just get paid to prove it," Private AWOL replied.

"He'll do," Torque replied nonchalantly while trying to hide a smirk upon recognizing another with similar tenacity as himself.

"General, if you don't mind the suggestion, I believe it would be best if you designated us as a scouting party before signing off on the op to compensate for the Squirms' speed," Torque said.

"I request permission to oversee the Squirms and the bait team, Sir," Captain Nash interjected before the general could reply.

"Why the sudden change of heart, Captain?" General Cruz asked.

"Sir, I took a moment to review available service records. I didn't realize that both Mr. Johnson and Mr. Corzo have reliable credentials. My prejudice against intel from civilians was in error," Captain Nash replied.

Torque eyed the captain while the general thoughtfully rubbed his chin in consideration of the request. After careful consideration, General Cruz nodded his approval, prompting the teams to separate for their respective roles. The Serpent was quick to stow his bike near the command center and grab a CQTR rifle before rejoining the others and occupying the passenger seat of the silver mox. Torque had already assigned Corporal Harnen's thin frame to the Chromehound's turret while Sergeant Kronton and Private AWOL took their seats in the rear of the mox and aimed their rifles out the windows.

"Captain, let me know when you ready to hook the target," Torque shouted toward the Alcazaban captain.

Before he could see the thumbs up response, Torque was already squealing the mox past the security checkpoint and the alley of Sandstorm tanks. Torque gripped the wheel with his left hand while he shifted with his right. Torque did a mirror check, doing his best to assess those who opted to volunteer for the potential suicide mission.

All of the Alcazaban soldiers were like ice, fingers frozen on the triggers. Even Corporal Harnen had a calm disposition as he carefully scanned rooftop and road alike while the Chromehound headed for the sounds of mass destruction.

The Chromehound's motion tracker on the dashboard flooded with movement. One extremely large icon blipped just ahead of the mox's position. Torque slammed on the brakes and twisted the wheel, pulling the Chromehound to an abrupt stop. AWOL cursed under his breath as the vehicle bumped hard on the sidewalk curb.

Torque shut off the engine just as a Goliath stomped through the intersection thirty paces ahead of the team's location. Even with the noise of the Goliath slamming its heavy claw-like feet into the street, Torque could tell that all present were holding their breath. Everyone watched as the shoulder mounted gatling guns swiveled about, each taking a turn to face the adjacent streets in anticipation of an assault. Had the Goliath been moving along the same street, the Chromehound would have been shredded leaving Torque to speculate that the Goliath pilots had poor peripheral vision which kept them focused on their forward trajectory.

"Looks like they have a blind spot," the Serpent remarked once the Goliath was out of sight.

"The boys back home are never going to believe any of this," Sergeant Kronton replied as he craned his neck out the window, half expecting more razerjacks to pass by.

"I'm seeing it and I still don't believe it," Private AWOL added with relief that someone decided to break the tension.

Torque cautiously restarted the engine, but kept an eye fixed on the motion tracker. The Serpent nodded his approval given his continual observation of heat signatures. As a small pocket of icons formed in the northeast quadrant of the map, Torque guided the Chromehound toward them. After closing the gap as much as he dared, Torque parked the Chromehound under an overhang until confirming that allied units were in position.

"Captain Nash, scouting team in position. We have a full unit of Goliaths to the east of us," Torque spoke into the comm.

"Acknowledged. Our division has almost caught up. Give us another five clicks, then proceed. The gauntlet opens from the south, so once you're on the move keep stringing them along," Captain Nash replied.

"Ryoukai," Torque replied.

Everyone in the mox sat stiffly, waiting for the five clicks to pass. Torque wanted to generate small talk, but he still felt his nerves behave restlessly even with his countless passes of conditioning. He knew that everyone in the vehicle was a combatant, complete with rigid training in a variety of forms, but he knew that they all shared the same objective, bring down any force that threatened freedom for all, no matter the cost.

Not a tick over five clicks, the Chromehound roared toward the numerous hostile icons which glowed on the motion tracker. The Serpent's eyes narrowed, expecting some unknown threat to end them as they neared their targets.

Torque slowed the Chromehound as they neared an intersection that provided access to enclave dartway. Multiple Goliaths towered overhead. Sergeant Kronton and Private AWOL leaned forward to glimpse the machines through the windshield. It surprised the Chromehound's occupants that the less-than-subtle design of the vehicle hadn't immediately caught the razerjack pilot's attention. given that its shiny exterior continued to bounce the midday sun in a variety of directions.

As the distraction finally served its purpose, the two closest Goliaths swiveled their turrets toward the mox. The tick that the turrets began to move, Torque was already pulling the Chromehound away in reverse. Once at a safe distance, he spun the vehicle about. Harnen was already firing upon the razerjacks, adjusting smoothly to the rotation of the mox. Kronton and AWOL took a few shots as well, but avoided wasting too much plasma given the range.

"They're not following," Harnen shouted as he released his hands from the turret triggers.

"They must not consider us a threat," Kronton replied.

"Let me back in there. Those metal chicken legs won't be worth scrap after I'm done," AWOL yelled.

"Reinforcements on approach," the Serpent said as he detected Alcazaban infantry, Squirms and a pair of Sandstorm tanks advance on their position. Torque twisted the Chromehound into a power slide and waited for the Alcazaban forces to catch up.

"Captain, they have limited visibility. We're going to need to make the bait large enough so that even these blind fools can see it," Torque said into the comm. "We're going to go rock the hornet's nest, so stay frosty."

The Alcazaban soldiers in the Chromehound let out a holler as Torque stomped on the accelerator to put the vehicle back on an approach toward the Goliaths. The Serpent did a quick count and noted at least seven razerjacks in the cluster. The motion tracker continuously updated with more information as it struggled to accurately process the influx. As soon as the Serpent considered that more Goliaths were masked, three more Goliaths stomped their way down the overpass exit.

"Pick one Goliath and focus all firepower. We need to show them we mean business," the Serpent yelled above the noise as he leaned out the window to get a good shot with his rifle.

Harnen targeted the lead Goliath and unleased a torrent of plasma at the bumbling razerjack. Kronton and AWOL followed suit, firing their rifles at the inbound unit.

"That ought to tick 'em off," Torque snapped as he swerved passed their target narrowly avoiding incoming plasma fire. The impact alone of the plasma hitting the street was enough to make for a rough ride.

Harnen pulled back on the controls to angle the turret as high as he could to fire on the Goliath overhead. All gunners in the vehicle focused their shots on the transparent dome on the razerjack's underside which connected the two legs. After concentrating fire, the dome gave way, allowing the plasma heat to burn the pilot inside. His mangled carcass fell through the gaping hole in the bottom cockpit, leaving the Goliath stranded.

Torque continued to thread the maze of Goliath legs. At close quarters, the Goliaths were unable to angle their gatling turrets low enough to inflict any serious harm to the mox. Additionally, the Goliaths at a distance were unable to target the Chromehound without risking heavy strikes against allied Goliath legs.

Captain Nash ordered all Squirms to fire on the Goliaths in the front of the bait team's formation, giving the Chromehound an adequate diversion. No longer consumed with the rodent at their feet, the Goliath pilots redirected their attention toward the Alcazaban forces.

While the smaller units distracted Goliaths, the Sandstorm tanks were already taking up position and locking their stanchions. Once the stabilizers were fully activated, the air shook as they fired a volley toward the razerjacks. Given the slow targeting of the tanks, their initial strike only flattened a couple of Goliaths before the nimble razerjacks began to exercise evasive maneuvers.

Torque maintained the Chromehound's course due west until he was clear of the Goliath mess. He utilized connector streets to catch a path parallel to the engagement and double back behind the Alcazaban forces. As the silver mox clipped down the street, the vehicle occupants caught glimpses of the razerjacks, keeping pace in their surge toward the artillery.

"Captain, get those units moving. They're going to be on top of you in no time," Torque shouted into the comm.

As Torque circled the Chromehound back around the Alcazaban forces, he was able to once again view the advancing Goliaths, but something beyond the razerjacks concerned him even more. Two large dark spots grew on the horizon.

"Captain, they have air support inbound. Get your tanks moving," Torque yelled.

Everyone in the Chromehound watched as two raptors swooped down to release sonic barrages on the way, crippling a Squirm and decimated an infantry squad. The Sandstorm tanks fired on the raptors, but the slow response time was insufficient. The impact of a shell stunned one of the raptors, knocking it to the ground, but the other was quick enough to evade and lash its hard talons and shred the thick armor of the Sandstorm tank. With fire suppressant lines ruptured, the tank imploded, leaving a smoldering heap of armor, turret and treads.

The raptor banked for another pass, but Captain Nash already had the Squirms mobilized away from the Goliaths giving them a fair shot at the raptor as it swooped again. The concentrated firepower dropped the second raptor. With the aerial threat neutralized, the small artillery units maxed their speed to resume course toward the trap entry point before getting overrun by Goliaths.

With the raptors dispatched, Nash ordered three Squirms to hold position and fire on the closest Goliath to slow their march while the bait team fell back. The awkward all terrain tanks turned on a wide angle to combat the two-legged razerjacks. In addition, Torque ordered his passengers to lay down suppressive fire to cover for the slow-moving Squirms.

After heading south to reach the perimeter of the trap, Captain Nash merged the firepower of his Squirm at a distance to that of the decoys in addition to the firepower of the speeding Chromehound. Collectively, the resistance forces were able to cripple two more Goliaths, but still seven more overran the lone Sandstorm tank trying to distance itself from the razerjacks.

"Forces are almost at the entry point, get those Squirms out of there," Torque said.

Even with explosions in every direction, Torque could still discern the captain's words to support the order. A visual confirmation from Harnen relayed that the Squirms were able to turn about and stay ahead of the Goliaths, but not by much.

Enclave buildings blurred together as the Chromehound raced through the entry point of the trap. The Serpent did a double take as they passed the first intersection where multiple Sandstorm tanks were positioned to await the advancing Goliaths.

Torque spotted the camouflaged, makeshift ramp designed to allow clearance of the massive barricade with debris and rubble blocking the center of the street. The Chromehound passed the captain's Squirm which held its position to cover those that remained behind. Torque pushed the accelerator to the floor as the Chromehound lurched up the ramp, nosed downward, and landed hard on the opposing side of the barricade, slamming down in the midst of a trio of Sandstorm tanks.

Torque wasted no time bailing out of the mox, snapping orders at nearby infantry to take position on the crest of the debris hill. He zoomed in his ikes as the Goliaths neared the opening of the trap, still unaware of the heavy armor waiting to greet them. He watched intently as the Squirms passed through the intersections where the Sandstorm tanks were posted.

Captain Nash barked orders over the comm for the Squirms to continue toward the barricade at the expense of neglecting their targets. They couldn't afford to slow the Goliaths and allow them to discover the trap prepared for them. As the small tank pilots complied, Captain Nash opened fire from the all terrain tank on the lead Goliath. The blast destroyed the upper dome that once protected the gunner. Before the Goliath pilot could react, Nash fired another blast at the lower dome, immobilizing the Goliath were it stood.

Angered by the destruction of their own, additional Goliaths fired on the Squirm narrowly missing, yet striking the building behind it. The explosion showered debris down on the Squirm, pinning it in place. Captain Nash fought with the controls to free the tank, but the obstruction held it in place.

Multiple Alcazaban soldiers were ready to lend aid and motioned to assist, but Torque yelled for them to standfast, "He can pull out of there. Those Goliaths will trample anything underfoot." While Torque contemplated if Nash could escape his predicament, he knew that there was no sense in risking the lives of additional soldiers if he could not.

Nash coaxed enough mobility from the Squirm's cannon as another Goliath placed itself in range. The Squirm unleashed a shell on the unwary Goliath. The shot penetrated the frame between the dome and the right leg, shredding the joint, forcing the razerjack to the ground.

Once the shot loosened the debris that pinned the Squirm, Nash wrestled with the controls to free the tank's treads of the obstruction. Captain Nash gritted his teeth and yelled as he fired at will into the wall of Goliaths.

"He's going to make it," Torque yelled. "Have all tanks behind the blockade fire on those Goliaths."

Before the order could pass through the comm, four pairs of gatling turrets focused on the struggling Squirm and saturated it with plasma fire. Just as the all terrain tank broke free, it was bathed in flame. A bout of nausea twisted Torque's insides as his hopes for the captain's survival were extinguished. Torque turned his head away from the sight, frustrated at how quickly the conflict could dispatch those with honor.

Further squelching any time to grieve, a host of roars and screams peeled through the air as a flood of tigers bounded into the streets, following the Goliaths as they passed through the intersection. The Goliaths were all focused on the Squirms which were passing through the safe zone on the other side of the blockade.

The first Goliath to pass into the trap intersection received a deafening welcome from the Sandstorm tanks on either side. The unsuspecting Goliath buckled under the stress and collapsed. With forward momentum against the Goliaths, they all reacted to pivot their turrets to the sides, but they were already caught in the firestorm. Heavy shells pummeled the razerjacks from opposite directions until only a couple remained, that is, until they were cleaned up by the Sandstorm tanks behind the barricade.

Undeterred by the destruction, the waves of tigers bounded over and around the flaming debris of the razerjacks. Some tigers were directed toward the Sandstorm tanks responsible for the carnage, but the mutated cats were easily dispatched by the infantry and Squirms tasked with protecting the heavy armor. The remnant of the tigers accelerated toward the blockade and those observing from its peak.

"On my mark, lob all Creep grenades into the air with as high an arc as possible," Torque yelled as he flicked a pin out of the grenade in his left hand. He quickly checked to ensure that the adjacent soldiers heard the order as he primed a round into his Phantom 4.0 with his right hand. Torque waited tensely for the tigers to close the gap.

Once the tigers approached the ideal range, Torque tossed his grenade into the air, ordering the soldiers to do the same. As the grenade left his hand, Torque was already reaching behind to grab a Splice 15m from under his belt. With the grenades at the peak of their flight, Torque fired on one, then another, turning each in succession into a wash of orange flame spreading like an umbrella over the advancing tigers. Torque connected with another four grenades, each detonation spreading a blanket of napalm over the tigers.

The street turned into a carpet of liquid fire burning anything in its path, tiger, razjerjack, pilot and rider alike. Torque waited a tick to ensure that every tiger was accounted for. He wasn't about turn his back to the enemy.

"Let's move," Torque yelled to those previously in his party. "All other posted forces should hold their ground until the remainder of Alcazaban forces advance."

Torque, the Serpent and the Alcazaban infantry trio returned to the Chromehound. With all party members locked in, Torque fired up the engine and followed nav markers through the Sandstorm tanks and around the flaming river of howling tigers. Once clear of the trap, the ride became silent. Torque struggled not to dwell on the loss of more capable soldiers, especially since he knew that Captain Nash wouldn't be the last. He suspected that those present struggled to balance the memories of fallen allies while staying focused on the battles ahead, but Torque knew that such moments were critical for a soldier to strengthen the resolve needed to remain alive.

Torque verified that the streets surrounding the command post were clear of action since the motion tracker displayed minimal activity. The tension in the Chromehound mellowed slightly once the mox was clear of the hot zones. Torque noticed that Kronton and Harnen appeared more relaxed while only the Serpent, AWOL and himself were shifting their eyes toward anything that moved.

A warning from the dashboard yanked Torque's attention away from the rearview mirror as an enormous blip indicated activity right on top of their position. Just as the Chromehound breached the intersection, a Goliath stormed onto the street from the east. Torque swerved to avoid the massive claw-like foot of the razerjack while everyone else opened fire. Unnerved by such close proximity to the Goliath, especially after being caught off guard, Torque stomped on the accelerator to put distance between the mox and the razerjack, even if it meant risking attention from the Goliath's large turrets.

Naturally, the Goliath opened fire, spreading a wide path of plasma fire. Harnen swiveled the turret to keep it locked onto the Goliath, despite the instability from Torque's evasive driving. As Corporal Harnen moved to adjust the turret he exposed his side allowing a stray burst to tear through his abdomen. The Alacazaban soldier's body slumped on the turret controls.

Outraged, Private AWOL leaned from the his side window at a dangerous angle. He locked one foot under his seat and the other against the Serpent's headrest. As the soldier's torso hung out the window, he spotted a clean shot at the dome protecting the Goliath pilot.

With Torque's erratic motions, AWOL's legs fought to keep his body from flying from the Chromehound, but his aim remained steady and he fired three consecutive bursts with uncanny precision.

The Goliath pilot flinched as the concentrated plasma splashed and burned a clean hole into the dome, but as the third burst dissipated against the shielding the pilot sneered at the soldier's weak attack. AWOL sneered back as he waited a tick for the shots to burn the protective dome before depressing the trigger again, releasing two more bursts both of which cleared the hole in the dome, catching the pilot in the forehead. The pilot's unconscious form fell forward against the controls, increasing the razerjack's thrust before its lack of steering forced it into a face plant.

With his job finished, AWOL pulled himself back into the Chromehound. He had no desire to exhaust his legs any further. He received words of respect for his precision.

"Must have been separated from the others," Sergeant Kronton said.

"That or they sent a few rogues after us," Torque replied, continuously checking the vehicle's rearview mirror as he resumed normal driving behavior.

With the Chromehound's position closing within five parcels of the command post, Torque opened the comm to inform the Alcazaban forces that the primary lanes were clear, but before he could confirm, another Goliath crowded the intersection. With the mox already cruising above ninety parcels per arc, Torque had no way to adjust course safely.

"Hold on!" Torque yelled.

Torque's force on the wheel accomplished little with the razerjack's foot already in the Chromehound's path. The mox banked off the top of the Goliath's foot sending the Chromehound into a corkscrew before it slammed down with the ear piercing scrapes of grinding metal. The vehicle rolled three times before landing passenger side up against the entrance to a local shop.

Torque yelled at the top of his lungs to validate that he was still alive. When his hearing and other senses responded, he checked on the others. The Serpent who had sustained the least injury had already removed his harness and proceeded to kick out the windshield. Torque looked behind him to see that Sergeant Kronton's body had been knocked to the rear of the vehicle and crushed beneath the turret. Private AWOL, irate as ever, kicked at the seats to push himself upward through the door.

Once all three survivors were clear, Torque did a quick scan of the Chromehound for a damage assessment. Realizing that the mox wouldn't be mobile without aid, Torque grabbed two Cutter rifles that had been tossed into the street, tucked one under each arm and marched toward the bumbling Goliath which seemed oblivious to the collison. It wasn't until plasma splashed the cockpit that it turned to face the trio. It must have been evading opposition of its own since its turrets faced any direction except forward.

Torque hesitated when a delayed dizziness forced him to stumble as he stepped forward. He realized that firing on the Goliath would require more concentration than he originally thought. The Serpent noticed the side effects and moved to intervene.

"We can't take it on foot! We need to wait for assistance," the Serpent yelled.

"We're on our own," Torque snarled. Even AWOL, as determined as he was, withheld any opposition, acknowledging the extreme disadvantage. He wiped his arm across the side of his face only to see a red smear on his arm instead of sweat.

Undecided if he was aggravated by the loss of more good soldiers or that his ride got mangled, Torque suppressed his fatigue, yelled and continued to walk toward the Goliath, still firing to get its attention. As if hesitant itself, the Goliath moved forward, but only trained one turret on the seemingly benign threat daring to attack.

The Serpent and Private AWOL were already moving for cover when the Goliath started firing at the street. Torque just stood in the middle of the road, unloading plasma from the Cutters in his hands. Indifferent to the outcome, Torque just glared relentlessly, draining the rifles of any plasma in the cells. Even once the power cells ran dry, Torque discarded the rifles and continued to taunt those operating the Goliath.

Expecting his end, Torque braced for his own destruction when he felt a familiar tremble rumble through the terrain beneath his feet. The plasma from the Goliath's turret ripped parallel paths up the street only to cease just shy of Torque's position as a flat plasma sheet tore through the air, severing the upper half of the Goliath before it burst into flames. The engulfed Goliath fell forward threatening to crush Torque beneath it. With all of his arrogance, will and determination, Torque flipped backward just as the razerjack collapsed on his previous position.

Shards of metal groaned and popped from the toppled war machine. A stabilizer bracket fell at Torque's feet which he promptly kicked defiantly. After the dustup, he looked to verify that the others made it to cover safely.

"See, I told you they would come," Torque yelled over to the Serpent who was looking up to see the Behemoth fully clear the intersection, casting its broad shadow over the street.

The Serpent simply rolled his eyes as he helped Private AWOL to his feet.

"Did we miss the party?" Maxwell chirped through the comm.

"Hamster, get that crane over here and scoop up that heap," Torque said, jerking his thumb toward the Chromehound.

"Then we need a ride back to the Alcazaban command post," Torque continued, stowing his limited patience and gratitude for once the team was out of danger.

29 – Operational Gambit – 29

Subterra Lair
Core City Fringe, Windstonne Enclave
Commercial Empire, Northam Continent
Thread: sysObserver.cmd

Streetz dimmed the lights even further in the Subterra operation room. The light levels hardly affected him, but Streetz knew that the other room occupants of the room would find even the slightest sensory input to be jarring once they awoke. Streetz considered giving them sensory inhibitors to mitigate the effects on waking, but he held off.

Each member of Subterra was present and accounted for, but the gate encounter certainly didn't leave much to spare. Had Parity been a tick late in delivering the transmission spike, Streetz would have had somber haps to report, but because she succeeded, Streetz used the disruption to disengage all members of the team successfully from the Hyper Lynx.

Subterra members slept silently, still connected to the apparatus of their command chairs. After checking their vitals, Streetz contemplated the fight with the gates. He felt a foreign sense of frustration at not being able to keep up with the rapidly adapting nature of the skullbores. Conversely, Streetz did feel relief, within the limitations of his construct, that all team members survived.

L337 Haxs twitched as he felt his senses respond to the cold metal restraining his wrists. His head rolled groggily to the side as he fought to exert control over his senses. Slowly coming around, he focused on the tapper under his fingertips and released the restraints. With his hands free, he lifted the visor from his face, not daring to test the sharp lights which normally flooded his eyeballs with the device active.

The release of the metal clasps on the chair felt like explosions to Haxs' ears as he tried to leverage them before his eyes. Subtle movements in the room suggested that others present were experiencing similar levels of sensory fallout.

With a grunt, Haxs leaned forward, defying the disruption that racked his brain, hoping to minimize the effects brought on by the quick exit from the Hyper Lynx. The motion helped his grogginess slightly, but Haxs' focus shifted to the needs of his friends. After confirmation of life by way of grunts from Hellix, Clutch and Parity, Haxs made his way to the command console to get the debriefing from Streetz.

"Everyone get some rest," Haxs said as he ambled toward the corner of the room.

"Did we pull it off?" Haxs asked of Streetz who continued to quietly observe digital traffic.

Streetz nodded in response, but his eyes remained fixed on the console. Haxs watched the information fly by, the communication on the Hyper Lynx ablaze. Haxs squinted, doubting the scans that streamed across the console.

"Streetz, put that on the primary," Haxs said.

Streetz complied and a large urban projection popped onto the primary emcast from the logistics being relayed. The buildings were easily rendered by publicly available schematics, but the scans from the military assets on site were startling. The system struggled to keep up with numeric adjustments and revealed the lack of resources required to properly depict the types of units present.

"How are we getting these specs, Streetz? Imperan military comms?" Haxs asked as he stood next to the large noptic display.

"Negative. All Imperan lines are still locked down tight. Current datastreams are being sifted through civilian security lines," Streetz replied.

"There is still too much noise in the datastream. We need to find a way to clean it up, but there's no way that we can cut through the Imperan protocols with this much of a security threat present," Haxs mused.

"After reviewing your vitals, I would advise against deploying again so soon. I recommend patience for the time being," Streetz said.

Haxs rested his hands behind his back. He didn't care to admit that he was not fond of patience, but he knew that Streetz was right. He was sure that any resistance in the Hyper Lynx would be on high alert, and there was no point putting Subterra in danger again without good reason.

Executive Level, Casters Tower
Core City, Windstonne Enclave
Commercial Empire, Northam Continent
Thread: sysObserver.cmd

Thick smoke rose above the skirmishes like lazy fog. In some cases, large fires were visible from the executive offices of Casters Tower. Any enthusiasm over victories on the ground swiftly dissipated as Frank Jenkins reviewed the performance of allied forces.

Oszwick Enterprises reported that in less than ten arcs, resistance forces had already impaired half of the Goliath fleet. BOWTech readings suggested that nearly several hundred tigers were already dispatched. Parallel reports from allies across the ocean were hazy in how some of the aerial units had been hijacked. While Frank Jenkins was still unclear why Tarak Delaney even bothered lending support, Frank Jenkins wasn't going to dismiss the destructive support rendered as a byproduct of his contribution.

With a brief break in the force updates, Jenkins mulled over how exactly he had arrived at the current course of events. The encounter at Moz Fractillend sure suggested that the faction leaders wanted his head on a plate. If operations hadn't been rushed, the Commercial Empire wouldn't have been so easily pushed into a defensive war. Oszwick certainly had some explaining to do. Given the trajectory of events, Frank Jenkins felt that the Commercial Empire would fall if something didn't change quickly.

Commotion from the doorway diverted Jenkins' attention as he looked up to see Oszwick and Commander Pyln enter the office. Jenkins knew that either individual had confidence in bearing good haps otherwise they wouldn't dare risking Jenkins' temper.

"Sir, Synergon unit two is also functional," Oszwick said.

"Mr. Oszwick, in case you haven't noticed things are not proceeding favorably. I have yet to see the usefulness of your services, so you had better provide a good reason for me to care at this point!" Jenkins fumed.

Oszwick's usual smile quickly faded. Commander Pyln felt inclined to take a step backward, but he refrained knowing that any action shifting attention away from Oszwick would not end well.

"Mr. Jenkins, I assure you that all of your efforts have not been in vain. Prepare to witness the splendor of Project Synergon as it combines the inspiration of the Commercial Empire and Oszwick Enterprises so that we may introduce the the Global Alliance to the Unisphere. Now, Mr. Jenkins if you will excuse me, I have some orders to transmit," Oszwick snapped before exiting the office ahead of any potential rebuttal by Jenkins.

Frank Jenkins felt that Oszwick's claim was neither conciliatory nor reassuring. Jenkins could only glare at the center of the executive's back as he exited the office. Suspicions continued to mount in the faction leader's mind that there was far more at play than an economic opportunity for Konrad Oszwick. The newly demonstrated ambivalence towards Jenkins' authority certainly supported the idea. After all, it had been Oszwick's persuasiveness that had adjusted the operational timeline. Treachery was never one of Jenkins' methods, brute force perhaps, but he didn't attain his seat of power through ambiguity of character. Everyone knew where Frank Jenkins stood, but he could not say the same for Konrad Oszwick. Something elusive about the partnership was starting to unsettle him.

"Commander, I want all of your men to form the strongest perimeter possible. I don't want anything within three parcels of this building. And... assign a detail to Mr. Oszwick," Jenkins said.

"Understood, Sir," Pyln replied with a sneer, relieved that he wasn't currently the subject of Jenkins' wrath.

Urban Floor
Core City, Windstonne Enclave
Commercial Empire, Northam Continent
Thread: actTgtPersp1.view

The hike back to the Behemoth proved more laborious than expected. I retraced my steps around to the side of the enclave parcel from which I jumped to the rooftop, but the mobile Vanguard fortress was nowhere to be found. Maxwell hadn't wasted any time in hiding the Behemoth or finding new hostiles to engage.

Still lacking proficiency in the eyecon nav system, I fired up the maps to identify my position relative to the Behemoth. After fiddling with enough filters, I located the hard-to-hide razerjack which was already at least four parcels west of my position.

I was going to need a speed boost in order to regroup. I evaluated the durability of the Drakken glider I liberated, but I wasn't sure that finding high ground and vaulting across the city would help me close the gap.

With no other options at my disposal, I broke into a jog toward my target. I nearly stumbled into a heated intersection and was quickly reminded that my cloak was still aboard the Behemoth, forcing me to rely on traditional stealth. I ducked back into the shadows of an adjacent alley and looked about for a faster means of transportation. I spotted a parking garage across the street and sprinted for its entrance.

Few vehicles remained in the complex, confirming that many citizens had already evacuated after the dispatch went out. Hope rekindled as I spotted a dark green four-door mox. I cringed at the thought of it being a civilian dream ride after having grown accustomed to the armor and speed of Vanguard's own hybrids. I activated my ikes and scanned the VNET, easily finding a security override for the Fervor, manufactured by Thursten motors. I was dumbfounded at the amount of salvage related information that Vanguard had been cataloguing over the passes.

As the vehicle unlocked, signaling its compliance, I hopped in, started the engine and directed it toward the Behemoth's last position with the exception of dodging any contested zones. Even with stomping my foot to the floor, the Fervor may as well have been standing still. I questioned if it had anymore output capacity than the scuttles at Oszwick Enterprises.

Despite the less than desirable speed, I reached the Behemoth well ahead of any time that I could have achieved on foot. I exited the mox after parking it near one of the Behemoth's rear legs. I was barely out of the vehicle when the Behemoth resumed motion and crushed the Fervor underfoot.

"Hey, don't you watch the tracking systems?" I shouted through the comm at Maxwell.

I heard a snicker make its way to my ear before Maxwell retaliated with, "You do know that those had terrible safety ratings, right?"

"I'd say you're a handful, but excess snacking has made you more than that," I retorted.

"Not wise to insult the liftmaster," Maxwell responded.

"Nor is it wise to strand anyone in charge of snacktime," I said.

"I saw we call it a draw," Maxwell replied as I watched the lift descend from one of the Behemoth's forelegs.

Once I was safely aboard the Behemoth, I ducked my head inside the cockpit to see that Maxwell and Szazs were still the only bodies accounted for. Szazs was still glued to his terminal trying to thwart any attempts to divert his control over the captured raptors. Maxwell had already stowed our squabble and resumed tracking enemies between us and Torque's position.

Leaving the technical matters in their capable hands and paws, I found an empty space in the body of the Behemoth to dump the newly acquired gear from the Drakken. In so doing, I noticed a red stain on my pants. I rolled up my pant leg to find a long gash on my shin. I surmised that I might have cut it on the rooftop. Reaching for a mendcase, I found a stimpunch and some disinfection cloths to clean the wound.

While dressing the wound, I thought that I heard Maxwell remark about our allies' position, but above the noise of the Behemoth's internal mechanisms, I questioned if I was hearing anything correctly. The sound of explosions permeated the hull, but I didn't flinch. Either I had developed an extra sense of discernment for the dangers all around, or I had accepted the harsh reality, I would already be dead by the time an imminent explosion ended me.

The mendcase fell from my lap as the Behemoth lurched forward. The movement change made me question the urgency more than the noise beyond. As I went to check on the action, another explosion ripped through the air just paces in front of the Behemoth. As Torque's grumbling ripped through the comm while bantering with Maxwell, I knew that the situation had been resolved.

After plopping down in one of the command chairs, I opened a groundside view, showing two Goliaths laying on the ground. Torque, the Serpent, and another individual were already using the lift to board while Maxwell focused on getting the Behemoth positioned for optimal extraction of the overturned Chromehound.

Torque stormed into the cockpit, clearly aggravated, but he kept his cool well enough to confirm that Maxwell had the proper coordinates for the Alcazaban command post. I didn't need special tech to hear the stream of gripes erupting from Torque as he made sure that the crane didn't do any additional damage to the silver mox. While Vanguard's mechanic oversaw the hardware, I kept my eyes trained on the tactical displays for hostiles.

Proximity sensors chimed, announcing that the Eagle was on approach and interacting with the Behemoth's docking protocols. The Behemoth's trap doors opened with a rush of air as the Enforcer adeptly positioned the jet. Feeling that I might be more useful elsewhere, I left the cockpit to observe the ongoings in the back of the razerjack.

The Enforcer killed the noisy engines of the aircraft, allowing the docking protocols to take control with the electromagnetic stabilizers. The Behemoth's body soon went from a surplus of light and noise to relative silence and darkness as the trap doors closed from the bottom and as Torque closed the bay doors from the rear. The Enforcer swiftly exited the jet and joined the small crowd gathered around the wrecked mox.

The Enforcer took one look at Torque, the Serpent and the unknown soldier verifying that their last outing was not by the book, "Is everyone still in one piece?"

The only replies that the Enforcer received were somber faces, faint nods and a subtle head tilt from Torque toward the mox. The Enforcer read their faces well enough to know that there had already been too many losses, irreplaceable friends at that. He also caught the subtle cue from Torque that there were bodies to clear, a slight exchange that the two Vanguard vets knew only from the length of time working together.

"I'm sorry this introduction isn't under better circumstances. I'm Mac Conner," the Enforcer said, extending his hand to the unnamed guest.

"Private AWOL," the Alcazaban soldier replied.

After a brief exchange, the Enforcer headed for the cockpit. After introducing myself, I also left the trio, leaving them to perform repairs of man and machine. I was eager to learn from the Enforcer what I missed and identify our next plan. I didn't think that many were expecting losses so early.

"What do we do next?" I asked as the Enforcer assumed command of the Behemoth's controls.

"Fox, for now, we're going to maintain our current plan. Drive a rail into the wall of Jenkins' defenses until he and his conspirators are removed. It's that simple," the Enforcer replied impatiently while adjusting the Behemoth's path for debris in the street.

Inner Core Dartway
Core City, Windstonne Enclave
Commercial Empire, Northam Continent
Thread: sysObserver.cmd

"All resistance forces and Interlace allies, this is Vanguard Strike Coordinator, Mac Conner. I'd suggest an inventory of all resources and tactics. Should anyone care to join, I will be at the following coordinates," the Enforcer said as he fired off a rally point to known allies.

"There really is no need for such secrecy, Mr. Conner. The Unisphere gladly welcomes all who wish to partake in its future comforts," said a smooth voice through the Enforcer's comm.

"If all parties present are up for divulging agendas, why don't you go first, Mr. Oszwick?" the Enforcer asked flatly.

The mention of a hostile name put Maxwell on edge. The signal being directed to the Enforcer's comm was not showing on the VNET. Maxwell looked at the Enforcer, only to see that his hand was already circling his index finger to put emphasis on signal isolation.

"Secrets are my business, Mr. Conner, but I don't think mine are of concern since I'm of mind that you already know who I am and what my purpose is, but perhaps your pursuit of truth is not as plain to those you travel with. Say, for example, those of similar features," Oszwick chided. "I can assure you that you're not the only one with the means to build alliances with foreigners, in this veras or the next."

The Enforcer looked over to see Fox distracted with the tactical display, to his relief since he doubted that he could hide the pale complexion washing over his face. The Enforcer knew that Oszwick couldn't see his tense expression, but it was likely the lack of quick response that revealed the executive was already pressing the right buttons to put his foe on edge.

"Mr. Conner, I have no intention of sparing your life, but for the sake of those you care about, I suggest that you call for a stand down. After all, it would be great marketing for the Unisphere. Having an administration quell a conflict before it starts would benefit all parties," Oszwick pressed.

"I have no reason to negotiate with those bound for the ashtray of history," the Enforcer replied.

"That is quite drol, Mr. Conner, but you and I both know that it requires more than strength of arm and density of metal to best me," Oszwick said.

"Even so, I will not turn a blind eye to the imprints that you seek to salvage," the Enforcer snapped.

"Then I shall take them by force," Oszwick's suave voice rang through the comm.

"Over my dead body," the Enforcer snarled.

"Precisely," Oszwick hissed before breaking into a hysterical laugh.

Thread: actTgtPersp1.view

I looked over to see the Enforcer tear his eyecons from his face. I guessed that it was an abrupt end to his conversation. The speed at which his eyes flickered with color suggested emotional distress. I had no capacity to discern if it was outrage, remorse or fear, but it was clearly anything but calm.

Maxwell offered confirmation that our approach was acknowledged by the Sandstorm tanks in the distance. The Enforcer was about to respond, but he immediately doubled over, one hand on his abdomen and the other on his head as if stricken with some fatal muscle contraction. One hand moved to his mouth as if to prevent fallout from overwhelming nausea, but before a mess ensued he dropped to his knees, breathing heavily to make sure the symptoms passed as quickly as they had arrived.

"What was that?" I asked with concern.

"I don't know, but I think our enemies have made their next move. I've heard of an interferic pulse, but never expected something like that. I can't help but think there is something terrible at work in this conflict," the Enforcer said slowly.

Torque and the Serpent stood in the back of the cockpit having witnessed the ordeal. The expression on the Serpent's face suggested that he sensed something unusual as well. It was as if an ancient invisible bond had been broken. It was something intense like the sensory overload of a battle, but at the same time distant. The Serpent had learned to trust his senses after all of his time with the Ghosts. The recent sensation wasn't something that he could explain, but he knew that help was needed on the battlefield.

Upon reaching the rally point, Vanguard and its guests exited the Behemoth and hiked toward the command post, but the lack of presence near the hardware made for a suspicious encounter. As the team drew closer to the command post an increase in newly dropped bodies suggested a recent conflict. There were no Imperan forces to be found, but the new arrivals exercised caution regardless. As they reached the command post, a perimeter of forces lined the outside of the complex with weapons drawn. As Vanguard stepped into the open, Alcazaban forces raised their weapons. Private AWOL quickly stepped forward and raised a hand to signal friendlies on approach.

Before anyone speculated the reason for the frigid welcome, the Serpent spotted his mobi intact and broke away from the group. Without a word, the Serpent revved the Reptilian's engine and turned it about, only pausing by Vanguard. The Enforcer looked puzzled at the action. Given the time he took to respond, I pondered if he was going to reprimand the Serpent, but instead he acted as if he already had full knowledge of the intentions behind the Serpent's strange behavior.

"If you're leaving, what will you do at your destination?" the Enforcer asked.

"Divide and conquer," the Serpent said flatly after a subtle pause, indicating his surprise that the Enforcer hadn't been more inquisitive.

The Enforcer nodded and said nothing more as the Reptilian engine blared and carried the Serpent out of the Alcazaban camp. The Enforcer understood deep allegiance, and if the Serpent was forced to abandon bonds long enduring the test of time, he wasn't about to make his friend choose one over the other. Ghosts held tight loyalties and if the Serpent was evading one fight, the Enforcer knew it had to be toward a greater one.

"I've seen him divide, it's messy," I remarked, hoping for clarity as to what just transpired.

Instead of providing answers, the Enforcer simply disregarded my comments and nodded toward the command post. The remainder of Vanguard would have to put the pieces together of recent events.

Inner Core Dartway
Core City, Windstonne Enclave
Commercial Empire, Northam Continent
Thread: sysObserver.cmd

After passing through the warzone side streets and alleys, the Serpent twisted hard on the throttle, racing the Reptilian along the desolate streets. He knew that his unusual course of action would certainly require explanation upon his return. He did his best to not focus on the inbound messages from the additional comm signal he had Maxwell install into his ikes, but old habits and loyalties were hard to set aside.

Disregarding any navigational markers, the Serpent pressed westward. Even though message prompts continued to suppress the physical location from the message's sender, he knew that no advanced tracking system could fully anticipate Ghost behavioral patterns. Given the extreme range from the center of the enclave, it was doubtful that an attack was staged at such a distance, but as the Serpent closed on his destination, blips from his motion tracker suggested that there was either a lot of activity by way of reinforcements, or something had gone horribly wrong.

The Serpent made a hard right turn and spotted an encampment in the distance. He narrowed his secondary eyelids to maximize his sight range. With smoke rising in the distance and signs of struggles amongst allies much like the fallout at the Alcazaban camp, the Serpent knew that nefarious actions were at work.

The most basic of survival conditioning activated within the Serpent as the Reptilian breached the perimeter of the encampment. His preference to use non-lethal force was overruled as he observed the carnage already past. His eyes locked onto a cluster of dissidents pushing for the encampment's leader. Identifying the old engine cover of a mox that rested at an angle, the Serpent ramped off the cover, lifting the mobi into the air. The crazy maneuver caught the attention of crazed Ghosts. As the vehicle peaked in the air, the Serpent pushed away allowing the vehicle to crush two of his adversaries as it fell, but with his body airborne, he drew his blade from his back and slashed downward cutting another deranged Ghost at an angle. As his feet touched down, the Serpent was already spinning to sever another Ghost at the waist.

Two more Ghosts stood to face the Serpent, glaring. He recognized them both, but strangely they viewed the Serpent as nothing more than an obstacle between predator and prey. The Serpent immediately noticed their eyes and how they were void of color, iris and pupil both pale white.

The white-eyed Ghosts drew their katanas from their waists and charged the Serpent who flipped forward hacking a quick strike through the arm of the Ghost on his left. As he twisted in the air and turned to face the back of the remaining Ghost, he slashed downward splitting him in two.

Furious at having to slay his own brethren with his own sword, the Serpent stared at the ground in disbelief at what he had just done. Other Ghosts present, of a less deranged variety, looked around for more traitors in their midst. The Serpent looked up to see a commanding figure with damaged armor approach from behind a line of weary subordinates.

"What happened here, General?" the Serpent asked.

"I do not know, Alex. I wish I had the answers. I've known these vectors longer than you. In all of my passes, I have never seen trickery make such vaporgusts of the most seasoned warriors. They all attacked without warning," General Seechi replied.

"Many recent events have occurred outside the realm of understanding, but nevertheless it is good to see you again, Sir," the Serpent said.

"Likewise. You're looking well. And Vanguard?" Seechi asked, noticing that the Serpent had arrived alone.

"Yes, Sir. I will have to make amends for my abrupt departure. I didn't feel that there was time to explain the predicament once I saw there was similar strife happening amongst our allies," the Serpent replied.

"I am glad to have your assistance with speed. We shall explain the situation together," Seechi said reassuringly.

"Was there any indication of shifting alliance?" The Serpent asked, trying not to reflect on past disruptions within the Ghosts.

"No, they acted no differently, but I noticed, perhaps as you have, that their eyes were strangely discolored, much like those of the emperor when he formally transferred the Martial Legion's military authority over to the Drakken," General Seechi said.

"Then our enemies are indeed more creative in their cunning than we have anticipated, allowing them to remain among us. If this is some ploy by the Martial Legion to divide the Global Alliance, then all should be warned. We mustn't waste time in regrouping with the resistance," the Serpent said as he turned to direct the surviving Ghosts in the direction of the Alcazaban camp.

The Serpent's mind sank into deep thought as he righted the toppled Reptilian. The faces and numbers of enemies multiplied in spite of every minor victory achieved. It was established that their adversaries were formidable from without and from within, but the Serpent wrestled with what could possibly turn the minds of battle hardened allies against their will. The enemy's subtle tactics were proving to be extremely dangerous.

30 – Balance Sheets – 30

ResistanceForward Command
Core City, Windstonne Enclave
Commercial Empire, Northam Continent
Thread: actTgtPersp1.view

The atmosphere was tense both within and without the converted fixture store. Once the Alcazaban meeting point had been compromised by unknown internal factors, resistance forces moved with urgency to relocate. Several brave locals offered their establishments, but quick decisions led to securing a fixture center so that supplies were readily available to build makeshift defenses.

After forming a rough perimeter to the new base of operations, all Alcazaban soldiers were on edge after being forced to square off against longtime allies who had turned on their own. Even though everyone remaining had been thoroughly checked to make sure that they didn't exhibit the same loss of eye color, some guards couldn't resist doing additional random checks. I temporarily removed my ikes to pacify the guard ahead of me before entering the command post.

The sounds of explosions had scaled down along with the daylight even though the activity was far from subdued within the command post. The thick dusty air made for irritable breathing conditions, but most inside opted to deal with the intermittent coughs. The Enforcer, Torque, Szazs, General Cruz and other military leaders that I didn't know by name were gathered around a collection of tactical displays. Once displays were fully operational, the Enforcer set Maxwell next to one of the noptic interfaces. Feeling that I had little to offer in the realm of strategy, I took up a perch on a waist-high pile of lumber against a wall.

Before the meeting could begin in full, the Serpent strolled in with three Ghosts behind him. I didn't recognize any of the party, but the Enforcer was quick to exchange greetings with the older Ghost dressed in heavy armor of a classic variety. After hearing the Maleezhun officer speak, I knew that it had to be General Seechi, the Serpent's former superior.

"I apologize for not informing you of my ongoing contact with the Ghosts," the Serpent said to the Enforcer.

"No apology needed, Friend. I gave Maxwell the authorization to install the additional comm," the Enforcer replied, suppressing a smirk.

The Serpent stared, disbelieving that his active communication with the Ghosts had been outed long before the confession. The Serpent looked at the general to see if he was in on the game. General Seechi simply shrugged, affirming why he suggested the Serpent join Vanguard to begin with. Accepting that the experience continued to reveal his need for trust among reliable allies, the Serpent nodded and redirected the group's attention back to the meeting.

Even though I was starting to put the puzzle pieces together through various stories thus far, the disjointed picture began to come into focus as members of the Alcazaban military and the Ghosts exchanged accounts of the unsuspecting traitors in their ranks who contributed to the needless loss of life. The somber attitudes of those reflecting on losses did more to make the room uncomfortable than any physical elements could. I knew that I was in the presence of those accustomed to losses in war, but the quick tally was making the numbers difficult to ignore.

"What's our best assessment on Imperan forces between us and the tower?" the Enforcer asked in an attempt to shift focus from the past back to the present.

"My analysis is still showing an indeterminate amount of tigers, a batch of Goliath's and the whole Piran corps," Maxwell replied as he relayed his Hyper Lynx datastream to the central noptic display.

"And what do we have to work with?" the Enforcer asked, looking around the room at the leading military strategists.

"Some of the white-eyes were pilots and managed to take several of our tanks with them. Our hardware numbers are dwindling," General Cruz replied.

"We arrived with nearly sixty in our company. A quarter of them turned and robbed us of a number nearly equal to that," General Seechi added.

"Can we expect support from any other factions?" the Enforcer asked.

"The emperor ordered the Drakken to support the resistance, but I wouldn't assume that there would be contact since the Ghosts are no longer permitted to serve the Martial Legion. We arrived to fight regardless," General Seechi replied.

"They've already put in an appearance, and I doubt that they're up for cooperation," I remarked as I produced the Drakken insignia from my pocket for inspection before returning to my lumber stack.

A couple officers stared in disbelief, but one of the Ghosts turned over the uniform patch and verified it. He nodded to those standing around the tactical display. General Seechi looked down at the display and leaned his hands on the table supporting it, disappointed in the direction of his homeland.

"Just more numbers for the opposing column," Torque sighed.

"The Coalition promised their support, but tomorrow was the earliest arrival estimate provided," General Cruz said.

"And the Oceanic Outpost?" General Seechi asked.

The Enforcer shook his head in response, "They should have been here by now."

"How do we know that further aid won't turn into more brain-bent white-eyes," Torque snorted.

"We don't," the Enforcer replied, "Which is why we must find the source of this phenomenon before we proceed."

"Are you suggesting that these white-eyes are controlled by the Commercial Empire?" The Serpent asked. "How could Jenkins possibly influence so many? What could possess so many to turn?"

The Enforcer paced for a moment. The pieces of the puzzle lay before him without image or purpose with which to clarify their meaning. The last few days of events had required so much attention that there had been no time to identify loose ends. Voices echoed through his mind about transmissions and Jenkins' initial plan. Something had been overlooked, the satellites.

"Protech, is there any way that Jenkins could have created a wetware interface so that it could be activated and controlled remotely by satellite," the Enforcer asked as if struck by inspiration.

"I suppose so, but what determines who can be controlled. What separates those white-eyes from the rest of us?" Szazs asked.

The room stirred with heated discussion as everyone attempted to solve the answer to the riddle. Frank Jenkins had found a way to turn the masses into his soldiers, but how he did it was a mystery. I sat there silently, listening to the others who proposed possible solutions, only to be negated by logical evidence of another.

I shifted on my uncomfortable seat while listening to the rants. As I did, a rattle in one of my pockets caught my attention. I retrieved the small pill bottle that I had swiped from the Mogul Prime warehouse. I turned the bottle over in my hand as I thought back on Kotes' strange behavior.

"Maxwell, what were your findings by chemical analysis for those pills that Benni Kotes was taking?" I asked above the noise, interrupting everyone's discourse.

The hamster paused as if the forgotten topic had escaped him, but he finally responded, "Side effects increased memory capacity, faster synapse response times, but increased the brain's influence to external stimuli."

Everyone's eyes narrowed on me as they pondered the relevance of my question since it interrupted the brainstorming. I walked over to the gathering of strategists and placed the pill bottle in the midst of the tactical displays.

"Someone once told me that the eyes illuminate the imprint within, and these chemicals appear to make for some rather crusty windows. It seems to me that someone finally crafted something so desirable that it was appealing enough for multitudes to sellout that which is most precious," I said quietly.

The room fell silent as I went back to my seat. I thought that I caught a faint smile crease the corner of the Enforcer's lips in approval. Whispers started circulating through the air until they elevated into regular confirmations. A couple of the soldiers recounted instances in which they saw their associates taking similar pills.

"How is this possible?" General Cruz whispered.

"Gentlemen, if you were to rule the world, would you rather waste time with trifling wars until your foes were beat into submission following costly campaigns, or choose a subtle means of persuasion in which your adversaries gave up that which you seek willingly," the Enforcer said.

"It appears that individuals who have purchased this Extend were not fully made aware of the side effects," General Cruz said.

"I doubt they were presented the fine print, General," the Serpent said.

"Understanding that there is always fine print creates a wide gap between wisdom and folly," the Enforcer replied.

"I have seen these side effects before, but it was not here. It was in the throne room of the emperor of the Martial Legion. How could the Commercial Empire have generated such influence to affect someone as high up as Emperor Kage Shito? He has no regard for Jenkins or his honorless tactics," General Seechi interjected.

"I have seen these side effects as well, and they have consumed three-quarters of the leading council of the Global Alliance. I believe that this may be why our support from the Oceanic Outpost has been cut off," the Enforcer added.

"If that is true, then we really are on our own. We shouldn't expect additional support from anyone," Torque said.

"Which is exactly why we cannot afford to fail. With a third of the factions in Jenkins' pocket and another third under his thumb, we have no choice but to succeed," the Enforcer said.

"So, we have one power hungry dictator with who knows how many pill-popping skulljacks at his fingertips, and all we have to do is blow up some satellites, which happen to be in space. Anyone got a couple of vac suits?" Torque snorted.

The Enforcer raised a hand for Torque to calm down. Irrational behavior would not improve manners, "All we need to do is disable the uplink to the satellites, and his instant minion force will be irrelevant. Maxwell, can you pinpoint the location of the most likely relay?"

"I've got one just inside the Piran main base of operations. No one is getting anywhere near that without being incinerated and scattered to the wind. That whole complex is rigged to blow," Maxwell said as he pulled up a noptic layout of the Piran military installation.

"Well, that's good isn't it? All we need to do is send in a decoy, and it will destroy the uplink," Torque said.

"No. It's hardened tighter than the Serpent's lockbox of Mesquite-Os. The uplink has redundant systems sheltered within a bunker which runs ten decks deep. Unless you've got a few lifetimes to dig a tunnel, scratch that out," Maxwell replied.

"What about the security systems via the Hyper Lynx? Is there a back door?" the Enforcer asked.

"Mac, I wouldn't link up an interface within three datatank hops of those security systems. They have twenty gates on any inbound port. I've never seen that much security in play. It looks like Jenkins planned ahead for once in his life," Maxwell replied.

"I wouldn't exactly credit Frank Jenkins with foresight. If preparation is involved than we are dealing with someone far more intelligent than Frank Jenkins, or far too many vaporgusts hopped up on these pills. His longevity in office is stayed only because of seemingly unlimited resources, and if he has allies with an influx of wealth, we should prioritize finding the source and liquidate assets with speed. Maxwell, who was contracted on the security system?" the Enforcer asked.

"Big surprise, none other than Oszwick Enterprises," the hamster mused.

Members of the Ghosts and Alcazaban military alike looked confused due to unfamiliarity with any outfit influential enough to secure a large scale Imperan contract. The Enforcer took only as much time as necessary to connect threads between Oszwick Enterprises and increasingly likely motivations behind Frank Jenkins' crusade to extinguish the Interlace under the cover of world conquest.

"Does Oszwick Enterprises retain operational control over those systems," the Enforcer asked.

"Negative," Maxwell replied.

"How about generators or power systems? Would damaging the local power grid have any impact on the defensive routines?" I asked from my remote position outside the strategist's circle.

Several turned to cast me strange looks, clearly implying my naiveté in said operations.

"I saw it in a meca once," I remarked, indifferent to the eye rolls that I received.

Regardless of the general mood, the Enforcer nodded for Maxwell to check local infrastructure. After a short but tense wait, Maxwell tapped on his controls to update noptic screens which hovered above the table.

"Well, I'll be a monkey's uncle," Maxwell muttered.

"You're too small to be a monkey," the Serpent hissed as he leaned in to view the new information.

"All power systems are relayed through a central power plant," Maxwell said as he illuminated a nav marker for the utility. "No reserve generators in sight. It appears that Frank Jenkins was hasty in studying the contract, or Oszwick Enterprises is leveraging control as a fail-safe to ensure command of the merchandise."

"That's due north of Casters Tower which potentially means stiff resistance. If we strike it remotely, what are the notables?" the Enforcer asked.

"Still a few gates to contend with, but nowhere near the quantities protecting the Piran base," Maxwell replied.

"Mr. Conner, I understand the suggested tactic, but most of my intel operators were the most likely Extend users or targeted first by the white-eyes. The few that I have left cannot be spared for such a mission," General Cruz interrupted.

"Understood, General, however, that may not be necessary. We have some rather liquid connections," the Enforcer replied as he tapped in a remote comm signal. With a soft buzz, two images illuminated at the edge of the closest noptic screen.

"For those who have not met, allow me to introduce, L337 Haxs, head of Subterra, and Streetz, Vanguard's support specialist," the Enforcer said, gesturing to his two friends joining the meeting.

"Good evening," L337 Haxs replied.

"Haxs, we have another task for you since Subterra clearly pegged high marks on the last one. I trust this may be up your alley," the Enforcer added.

"Everyone is exhausted from last night's gate-fest, but if there's work to be done, you know we'll give it all we've got," Haxs replied somberly.

"He's on the young side. Can his team handle the op?" an Alcazaban officer interjected.

"Sir, I'll have you know that Subterra is responsible for the reduction in civilian casualties in this conflict. Had they not integrated with the Imperan comm systems, there would have been no warning whatsoever. So, to answer your question, yes, they can handle it," the Enforcer replied defensively.

"Even if we scrap the security systems, what's the strategy for dealing with the power station?" General Cruz asked.

"Permission to lead the Ghosts on said target," the Serpent said.

"Thoughts, General Seechi?" the Enforcer asked, looking from the Serpent to his longtime superior.

"If anyone can maximize the Ghost's effectiveness, it's Alex Corszo. I'll keep two with me, and you can lead the rest," General Seechi replied in agreement.

"Very well," the Enforcer nodded.

"I'll go with him," Torque added with a smirk as he elbowed the Serpent. "Someone's got to cover his back if something goes wrong."

"There's goes the stealth option," Maxwell quipped under his breath.

"How many tanks do you have left, General Cruz?" the Enforcer asked.

"I estimate that eight functional Sandstorm tanks remain and at least double digit Squirms," Cruz replied.

"Protech, how about the raptor count?" the Enforcer asked drawing the informatech into the conversation from the sideline.

"Only three, but they are quite secure. I took the liberty of completing the loopback encryptions that the Uniod Bloc failed to implement," Szazs replied.

"That, of course, does not leave us much to work with. It may not matter where we attack Jenkins' forces. He will no doubt have a solid perimeter in any direction to protect his valuables, especially Casters Tower. Since hardware is a precious luxury that we cannot afford to waste, Protech, I would like you to mange the raptors remotely from the Behemoth. Place them on defensive protocols and cover the Sandstorm tanks at all costs. General Cruz, if I may suggest so, divide your forces into two units. Place your Sandstorm tanks in one unit and bolster their defenses with adequate ground support and put Squirms in the opposite unit along with all remaining infantry. Fox, you and

Maxwell have the Behemoth. We can push forward on three fronts eastward toward the Windstonne river. Fox, you'll cover the northern push. General Cruz, the central push is all yours. General Seechi, if you wouldn't mind accompanying me, we can take the southern push," the Enforcer continued until suggestions from others had been ruled out.

As I listened to the orders being delegated, I marveled at how much influence the Enforcer held, even among generals nearly twice his age. Not once did the Enforcer tout any manner of formal training to bolster his credibility, but his unwavering confidence and penchant for perception clearly carried more weight than any academic course.

Strategists continued to discuss matters with respect for all views, tackling logistical concerns one by one. As I heard orders drift in my direction, I felt nervous. I knew that I wouldn't be operating the Behemoth alone, but I still considered it a responsibility well beyond my skill set.

"Please relay plans as needed and move units into position quickly. We move at dawn," the Enforcer concluded.

Once the Enforcer switched off the noptic screens, Ghosts and Alcazaban soldiers left the building to relay orders. With the room clear, the Enforcer and Vanguard members alone remained to review their objectives, specifically the particulars of the joint Vanguard and Ghost operation.

"You two have already pulled more than your weight, so if it were up to me I'd leave this to someone else, but you know as well as I do that there's no sideline spectating without a towel toss. It will take Subterra a couple of arcs to get prepped and infiltrate the system, so I recommend getting sleep until then. Keep in constant contact with Streetz, he'll ping you with their progress. The least resistant path is likely the waste access tunnels. Messy, but even Piran's don't like hanging there," the Enforcer said, trying to optimize every detail for his friends' sake, despite the fatigue starting to show on his face.

"Been a while since Windstonne had an interesting night life," Torque replied.

"Just keep the flashing lights to a dull blast," the Enforcer replied with a half-hearted smirk.

With reassuring nods, Torque and the Serpent left to check their gear ahead of their limited window for sleep. The Enforcer watched them leave silently. A wide range of emotions, challenged his clarity of thought. The emotions were nothing new, if anything, they were common to any conflict, but that didn't make them any less of a nuisance. He knew that even good vectors and soldiers had a time, he just hoped that his allies' time was not anytime soon.

As I remained the last extra human body in the room, I suspected that the Enforcer wouldn't go without offering a snippet of advice, and sure enough, he lived up to said suspicion, "Fox, I'm going to need you to keep calm out there. This is a big step, but I know that you can handle it. Just keep in contact. If you need help, there's no reason not to ask for it."

"Are you sure that there isn't someone more qualified to operate that mountain of metal. You seem to have a lot of pull with the big dogs. I'm sure they have a lot of gear-heads eager to take a crack at that razerjack," I replied.

"The essence of being a leader, Fox, is not about giving orders, but seeing potential and then striving to help others reach that potential. You have the ability to lead, but until you are challenged to exit the comfort zone, those skills will fester in the dust, dying of suffocation," the Enforcer replied calmly.

"What are you going to do now?" I asked, deflecting from the topic at hand.

The Enforcer paused for a moment to look over his shoulder, but he did not reply. He scooped up Maxwell who had been waiting patiently for the conclusion of the last conversation. After their departure, I remained alone in the empty fixture store. I knew that I couldn't blame the Enforcer. I suspected that he was fulfilling his role of mentor to its fullest to make sure that I put the puzzle pieces together on my own. It gave me a moment to consider just how much weight that he carried, Vanguard's lives, Subterra's, Sath's, the Interlace and all of the resistance. I struggled to process how he hoisted that level of care on his shoulders. There had to be something personal behind it. As I contemplated the connection, I started to realize the difference. He wasn't fighting for his own safety, but that of others. Even Torque and the Serpent didn't hesitate to do what was necessary. I realized that such internal strength was still beyond my understanding.

Forced to acknowledge my physical exhaustion, I started to doze off on my stack of lumber. Too unmotivated to find more suitable bedding, I spotted a block of foam and converted it into a pillow. I considered that sleeping in the midst of a war might keep me more alert especially since the sounds of combat still pricked the senses on occasion, but the general stillness began to separate them from consciousness altogether.

After exposure to a full day of combat, my fatigue finally bested my will. My thoughts drifted toward doubts, primarily the uncertainty of life. My mind attempted to review the events that had spared my termination thus far, but with exhaustion solidifying its grip, nothing of significance helped me maintain consciousness. At last, a calm settled in and the surety of knowing that I had allies in the fight put uneasiness to the side, allowing a brief rest.

Urban Heights
Core City, Windstonne Enclave
Commercial Empire, Northam Continent
Thread: sysObserver.cmd

    The distant explosions of heavy weapons still trembled the floor of the damaged high rise that the band of travelers used for a lookout point. The smoke impaired observation of the general conflict, but the position kept the Nomads within a reasonable proximity to their target. Their leader revealed that their timing window was closer, but still at a safe margin since the conflict beneath them would likely be resolved before they could advance.

    "This veras sure is lax on flavor," Snacks said with a grimace. The crackers he relieved from a local dispenser proved brittle. "I think stonecoat has less additives."

    While the most vocal member of the trio noisily munched on his liberated concessions, Scownin stood nervously at the edge of the building's floor with the gaping hole that looked out over the enclave. The building had been struck by a stray mortar, displacing businesses for quite some time.   The infrastructure held fast, but lighter construction materials still proved hazardous.

    "Seems like a moot point to go to all this trouble, when we could just leverage a distraction amidst all this carnage," Scownin said, ever impatient at the abnormal chase they had been tasked with. "Our parameters are so vague. Why are you so sure that this mission is that important?"

    Rubric Flux kept his hands behind his back and slowly stepped forward, making sure that his footing was secure as he approached Scownin's position and looked over the enclave, "It's not often that someone can produce scenarios outside the scope of my own reasoning. While that alone may be insignificant, the combination of jeopardy to more vera collectively meant that I had to take this seriously. So far, all minor indicators have revealed that we have been on the right track. We will know soon if this was necessary or all for nothing."

    Rubric did his best assure his associates that their mission was not undertaken without hefty consideration, but he knew that he needed to be honest with them. Too often, he was perceived to have all the ideas, but that was a reputation he could easily lose if he didn't reveal his own limitations, at least with those he trusted most. Nomads were no stranger to taxing conditions in domains completely foreign to them. However, they weren't used to missions with such vague parameters, Rubric knew that he had to be the example of patience in order to see things through.

"The element that we're here to extract is more than a simple compound," Rubric Flux said, reaffirming the complexity of their mission.

Another concussive round bellowed through the air. There was no danger to the Nomads' position but the tremors shook the highrise. Debris broke loose from the floor overhead threatening to collapse upon the travelers' perch. In a blur, Snacks had already launched from a seated position toward the threatening rubble and knocked the chunks into the open air before gravity could have its say.

Rubric calmly looked at the crumbling stone, graypak and metal. The materials froze in place giving Scownin ample opportunity to seize the content with his levitation and push it too into the open air before allowing the debris to fall on the street below.

To the Nomads surprise, several chunks of interior wall were caught up with the push and revealed a massive hollow that had been adjacent to them the whole time. The trio could have jumped collectively as they witnessed a massive bird sitting calmly in the hollow as if it too had been taking shelter in the building. They easily recognized the creature as a bird of prey, but the burns, decayed skin and scale-like feathers indicated it was not in natural form, as if the creature's three-deck size wasn't enough indication.

While the bird's body resided two floors down, its head was parallel with the Nomads' position. After the debris clearing, it looked over at them momentarily, but then turned its beak to point into the distance. It had made no movement amidst any of the tremors or impacts.

With imminent threats of debris removed and no aggression indicated from the large bird, the Nomads could do nothing more than look at each other and shrug as they pondered the strange nature of the domain that they presently occupied.

DAVE TODD

31 – Temperamental – 31

Subterra Lair
Core City Fringe, Windstonne Enclave
Commercial Empire, Northam Continent
Thread: sysObserver.cmd

L337 Haxs stood hunched over the console, staring blankly while he contemplated how long to delay the wake up call to his friends. They were fortunate to sleep most of the day, but such a short span was seldom enough to counter the prolonged strain of encounters with gates. He had only managed a couple arcs of sleep himself since his mind was bent on staying on top of the situation above ground. He finally looked over to Streetz who continued monitoring the console with machine-like stamina on account of his synthetic construction.

"How we doin'?" Haxs asked.

"I've verified your point of entry. I can drop you a healthy distance from the furnace access point, but just close enough so that you won't have to hike far," Streetz replied.

Haxs did not like the thought of a temperature prone datatank. Temperature flux always guaranteed one of two things: a very strong gate, or highly adverse psychological conditions.

"How about the security profile?" Haxs continued.

"I'm only detecting a couple of CT-7's on the initial datatank which shouldn't be too much for you to handle, but my estimate shows there are at least two regulated datatanks between us and the power plant central system," Streetz said.

"Any reads at all on those intermediates," Haxs asked with concern.

"No, all probes were decoded and erased on contact. I have no specs until you get in there... and in range," Streetz said with a pause.

"Then it looks like we better bake in some extra time on this one," Haxs finished as he walked over to his command chair.

The sounds of interface taps and conversation had been enough to start waking the others as they slowly staggered from their quarters into the control room. Haxs sympathized with their exhaustion. The mission would be dangerous enough with an unknown number of gates ahead, but having improper recovery time likely compounded their woes.

"Spool Up, Subterra," Haxs ordered with close attention to his volume since he knew that any of his team could have bowed out or dragged feet to show up. There was no pressing need to leverage his authority just yet.

L337 Haxs wasted no time in locking down his visor and engaging the wrist clamps at the base of his tappers. As his geist took shape within the staging platform, he hurried to check the munitions for his Mour Carbine which freed his concentration so that he could oversee the other team members' progress. Depending on the deployment proximity, gates did have the capacity to interfere with the scrypto of invaders, and given the groggy state of his allies, Haxs wanted to minimize any possible scenarios.

Even with loading sequences complete, Haxs could sense that his team's geists were moving sluggishly, a clear sign that no one was looking forward to the mission, despite knowing that it was necessary. No one complained, considering all were aware that their very home was at stake. Haxs normally would have drummed up an inspiring battle cry, but for the next engagement he knew that he simply needed a positive attitude to lead the charge. He offered a smile even though it was unrecognizable on his geist with its signature hooded face.

Haxs leveled his carbine as Subterra members neared an arched doorway leading to their target datatank. Clutch already had his sniper rifle scope lifted to his geist's eye to scan the horizon while Hellix swapped for a pair of Cronos 18s and kept them at the ready.

The visage ahead contained intersecting gridlines above, flowing into the distance until they bled into a hazy featureless terrain below. Steam rolled through the air, requiring a good squint to even discern the shape of the industrial structure in the distance. Haxs looked about cautiously, knowing that the temperature's influence was already in effect.

"Anything yet, Streetz?" Haxs asked.

"Negative," Streetz replied.

"Alright, stay frosty, Subterra. We could be up against anything. This could be a fishbrain's playground for all we know. Also, try not to mind the heat," Haxs said.

"If you call this heat, then I'm six-legged wombat," Clutch quipped.

"Well, then we'll expect you to relay all first contact, Mr. Fuzz," Haxs snapped. "Stay sharp."

Hellix and Parity could already sense the temperature variation affecting their consciousness despite their best attempts to ignore it. Haxs looked down to see sweat soak through the sleeves of his geist.

"Carbon Forge units, quarc three!" Hellix snapped as he dove to his right to evade an incoming blast.

A massive maze of pipes rose from the ground separating both Subterra and its foes. The humanoid shaped husks revealing their presence took cover against their surroundings. While they appeared intelligent in their behavior, the mass produced security icons were nothing more than obstacles easily found in abundance in private security systems.

"Parity, do you have a shot?" Haxs yelled as ballistic shells pinged off the pipe next to him.

"Negative," Parity replied, daring to glance outside her hiding spot only long enough to attract weapon fire herself.

"Streetz, can you get us some numbers, yet?" Haxs asked.

"I'm counting three," Hellix yelled before Streetz could reply while scurrying underneath a lattice of ductwork.

"They ain't trouble," Clutch muttered as he scaled the closest pipe to get a downward shot from an overlook.

"Create a diversion," Haxs yelled as he fired at a pipe adjacent to the Carbon Forge units that were reluctant to move since Subterra's arrival.

The impacted pipe spewed a white hot cloud, but it didn't affect the virtual apparitions in any way. They continued to fire on any location from which Subterra revealed its presence.

Clutch continued to crawl along the top of the ductwork, keeping out of sight. The gate controlling the datatank certainly had a thing for confined spaces. Clutch had trouble moving his geist, let alone angling his rifle to get a clean shot. Once he cleared an obstruction and found a valid opening to fire upon the Carbon Forge units, Clutch positioned himself quickly, but he realized that the temperature affected him more than he thought. Simulated sweat poured from his geist's brow into the eyes. He held his concentration just long enough to wipe the sweat clear and fire three rounds from his rifle.

L337 Haxs heard the concussive blasts from the rifle and stepped from his hiding spot while Hellix and Parity did the same. All three of them knew that the outcome would be the same anytime that Clutch shot something. It died where it stood. Three lifeless shells from the Carbon Forge icons were laid out motionless.

"That's kid's accuracy is liquid," Hellix mumbled.

"Streetz, how about some navigation... and air flow," Haxs said.

Before anyone could gripe, Streetz had already updated the nav markers for Subterra, in addition to spawning several small canisters on the ground. Haxs stooped down to reach for a canister and observed what appeared to be a can of compressed water, virtually anyway.

"It's the best I can do," Streetz replied, based on the puzzled looks that he detected through the command interface. "If you don't resist the psychological effects there is no way that I can do anything from these controls remotely. I need access to their datatank."

"Ryoukai. Let's move, Subterra. Douse your geist's and think soggy thoughts," Haxs said as he used the can to spray the virtual water all over his virtual form.

After tossing the can, Haxs led the crew through an archway exiting the maze only for the environment to transition into a domed plot of twisting pipes and vents. The room ahead opened into a large incinerator with plumes of fire surrounding the room's perimeter. At the far end, a sizable dropoff defined the accessway to the next server.

"You've got a single CT-7 present," Streetz said before Subterra could fully study the room.

"Gate present, Subterra," Haxs snapped.

The four members of Subterra formed a small circle with their backs to each other as they scanned the interior of the furnace. If not for the crackling fire and hissing steam, the room would have been deathly silent.

"Where is he, Streetz?" Haxs asked as the tension grew.

"He's in there, I cannot lock him down though. Containment protocols are unavailable in there. The hardened exterior is restricting incoming probes," Streetz replied.

"Shall we vent the premises?" Hellix asked ready to punch virtual holes in their overheated covering.

"Not enough time, we need to flush him out!" Haxs responded.

Before weapons could be trained on the disruption, a large skeleton erupted from the center of the furnace floor. The gate spiraled upward, its bony arms knocking all four of the Subterra members in the back, but all members recovered quickly to assess their opponent. A six mark, pasty white skeleton stood in their midst, slowly rotating its skull in place to observe the intruders.

"You'd think they could feed these guys better in the security industry," Haxs quipped.

Without time for his words to linger, Haxs felt a bony fist slam into his geist knocking him to the ground. The three standing Subterra members leveled their firearms to shoot, but were intercepted by a thick, dark smoke that erupted from the walls behind them.

"Streetz, get them gas masks," Haxs ordered as he pushed himself away from the advancing skeleton.

L337 Haxs scurried from the floor and drew his bow, pulling back the string with three arrows drawn. He quickly released the arrows

DAVE TODD

which sailed toward the gate, only for them to pass through its ribcage. Haxs deciphered as much menacing expression as was imaginable from the otherwise blank skull. The skeleton charged again, pushing Haxs backward, dangerously close to the chasm leading to the next datatank. If he fell on the gate's terms, he would no doubt have his consciousness shredded to virtual dust.

As the skeleton moved forward to stomp Haxs into oblivion, Clutch and Hellix dove at the skeleton to drive it into the ground. The combined force toppled the gate temporarily, but their geists were cast aside like insects.

Forcing himself to ignore the mental side effects from the pain and fatigue inflicted by the gate, Haxs released a burst of rounds from his rifle. Most shots missed, but he got the gate's attention. The gate turned once again and charged toward Haxs. Haxs switched his Mour Carbine to single shot, took his time and drilled two rounds into the gate's skull. Two holes punched into the bony dome, the impact momentarily stunning the gate. As the skeleton nearly slowed to a crawl, Haxs knew that he had to inflict more damage on the gate, but the holes in its skull quickly sealed up, prompting the gate to charge again.

"Streetz, how do we beat this thing?" Haxs yelled frantically.

"What would you be afraid of if you were a skeleton comprised of nothing but bone tissue," Streetz replied.

"Gotcha, good ole' calc deficiency," Haxs replied as he hoisted his geist off the ground. "Give everyone fine shredder rounds. It's time to snap this thing like a twig!"

"Subterra, it's time for a shredda vendetta! " Haxs snapped.

As soon as the weapon modifications activated, all four of Subterra geist's leveled their firearms, targeted the gate and unleashed a torrent of firepower. The skeleton held its position, stunned as the substandard sized bullets pierced the gate's visual manifestation. Subterra watched with optimism as the skeleton's bones started to warp under the pressure of its porous structure. The gate reacted quickly to repair the damage, but it was too extensive for the desired response time. Acknowledging that repairs would have to wait, the skeleton resumed an offensive posture.

"Great, we just made it a more difficult target," Haxs grumbled. "Streetz get me a can of quicksnap, I'm about to ice this thing!"

With an instantaneous changeover in ammunition types, Haxs activated the secondary mode of his Mour Carbine and fired a canister at the gate, enveloping it in a white cloud. The liquid nitrex locked the gate in place immobilizing it.

"Parity, now!" Haxs said.

Parity holstered her sidearms and reached over her shoulder to grab the large rectangular blade from her back. With a swift motion she hoisted the heavy blade high overhead, leapt into the air and brought the blade down in the center of the gate's skull, shattering it instantly.

The impact triggered a blast of cold air as the gate exploded, knocking Subterra members onto their backs. Ice particles clung to life in the air, suggesting that the extreme temperatures of the furnace were beginning to mellow without a gate present to regulate operations. Subterra wasn't about to test the volatility.

L337 Hax groaned and heard similar sounds from the others as they righted themselves. After quickly verifying that the whole team was in one piece, Haxs' focus shifted to the environment as lights dimmed along with the dwindling fires lining the walls. Large flames turned into thick clouds of gray smoke.

"Time to get out, before we get smoked out," Haxs said.

Before losing all light completely, Hellix detected a small bridge on the far side of the furnace exiting the datatank. Requiring no order, Subterra members ducked out of the heated environment and poised for attack upon entering the next.

"Whatcha got, Mr. Doorman?" Haxs asked.

"Good haps and bad haps," Streetz replied. "On the upside you've disabled power plant perimeter defenses and I can now get readings on defensive datatanks. The downside... you have at least a two datatanks to go and and I'm reading at least five more CT-7's along with some other indistinguishable security countermeasures."

"Anyone okay with skipping the bad haps?" Clutch quipped.

"I wouldn't be doing my job, if I kept you in the dark," Streetz said flatly.

"Noted," Haxs replied, acknowledging a lack of rousing speeches at his disposal. "Buckle up, Subterra. Eyes in every direction!"

Streetz opened a transmission to resistance forces, relaying that the power plant perimeter defenses were disabled. Following, the control console was ablaze with incoming signals as Imperan forces tried to discover the source of the breach. Even for a synthetic, Strcetz would have to move quickly to keep Subterra alive. If external contractors were informed, they could flood datatanks with sentries or even dispatch inactive gates. The fact that no action had been taken thus far offered hope that Imperan forces weren't fully aware of the scope of the operation.

L337 Haxs cautiously moved his geist into the next datatank and its as-of-yet materialized environment. The lull in the action reminded him that visuals were only representations of the digital form and were not the actual digital form itself. He felt like blinking would will the scenery into existence, but the absence of visuals shifted his focus to the visor pressing against his face and the cold metal holding his wrists in place. The break in immersion reminded him that the mission was not a taikon. Thousands of lives were at stake in Windstonne alone, and if the resistance forces failed, the conflict would certainly engulf the Global Alliance once again.

A stiff wind, or at least the perception of one, cut through the air kicking up a gust of sand. The horizon slowly morphed into a series of slopes carving Subterra's outlook into a gently rolling desert. The welcoming appeal faded as a massively eroded stone structure arose in the middle of the dunes. The soft crunch of sand graced the air as Subterra cautiously approached the structure.

Haxs likened the environment to that of an open air tomb. The surroundings certainly weren't typical playgrounds for low level gates. He eyed the building ahead suspiciously, its circular structure reminding him of old coliseums, but the key difference was that this one appeared modern in design by using a slate stone in contrast to the colors of the virtual sand.

Haxs snapped his geist's fingers in the directions of the door posts adjacent to the nearest archway. He wanted Parity and Hellix to cover the entrance. Noticing that the dilapidated walls created a couple of perches for visibility, Haxs tasked Clutch with scouting the outer wall so that he could get a good visual on the interior and exterior of the structure.

"Streetz, wing me," Clutch said before his geist sprouted a pair of virtual wings, a benefit of his nondescript form having more flexibility for modification.

After a final check over his shoulders, Haxs acknowledged Hellix and Parity's all-clear signals and proceeded through the archway leading into the monstrous arena. The sky began to illuminate without any form of visible light source. The datatank had no representation of a sun or artificial lighting, but it definitely appeared that their presence triggered the arena's glowing behavior. With all three geists clear of the doorway, the tumultuous cheer of a crowd erupted throughout the arena. The uptick in volume caught the new arrivals off guard prompting them to raise their weapons, checking in every direction, but no spectators were found.

"What do you have, Clutch?" Haxs asked.

"Nothing here. I'm going to move around for a better view of the interior," Clutch replied.

"Streetz?" Haxs asked, hoping for a different take.

"Negative," Streetz responded almost preemptively.

L337 Haxs waved his allies forward with his geist's index and middle fingers while he leveled his carbine at the walls above the archway. Once again, no visible threats were to be seen. Haxs didn't like being out in the open, in the center of the arena, but it was likely the only means to flush out the gates. He silently hoped that Clutch would identify a proper cover point by the time that the adversary was revealed.

The outburst of cheers from an invisible throng cut loose again. Parity and Hellix watched the edges of the arena, confirming the absence of activity in the stands. The new tumult did not cease, but only escalated in volume.

"I don't like the sound of this," Parity said.

"I think we've got an inflated ego on our hands," Hellix replied.

Haxs slowly closed the gap between himself and his allies, joining them in the center of the arena. He scanned the walls again, pondering why their foe hesitated to make itself known. He at least expected some form of sentries.

"Hellix, make your way for the exit, if they're not going to come to us, then I'd much rather leave unnoticed," Haxs said quietly.

Hellix stepped past the halfway mark from the side that they entered, but his geist's shoe barely made contact before the sound of thunder rolled around the arena. A miniature tornado ripped across the floor of the arena spraying sand in every direction. Hellix instinctively lifted his arm to shield his eyes before correcting himself on useless behavior.

Knowing that the slightest distraction was all that it needed to get close, the gate ceased its sand raising and appeared right before Hellix, its ploy to influence those entering its domain clearly at play. As Hellix lowered his arm, he discovered a chrome plated humaske designed for one purpose... destruction.

The gate lifted its right arm and backhanded Hellix, sending the shorter Subterra member and his pistols sailing across the arena. Following, the humaske raised both arms overhead with a defiant and confident air of victory. Noise from the phantom crowd escalated in response to the gesture. Annoyed, Haxs flicked the carbine's safety off and unloaded a clip into the humaske, but all shots deflected off the gate's dense armor.

"Streetz!" Haxs yelled, demanding any available intel on the spot.

"I'm working on it," Streetz replied, surprised that his synthetic form was being taxed its limits even with his rapid processing capacity. The gate was flooding his readouts with interceptor pings at an unnatural pace for any single gate. No gate could combat Streetz's influence so easily unless it had help, and it did not appear that the humaske shaped gate was even attempting to combat the doorman while engaging the intruders on the inside. Streetz paused his breakdown of the gate's profile to check for other interference.

"Designation: Warplate, but I'm getting strange readings," Streetz snapped. " I need you to hold it at bay for a few ticks while I isolate the interference.

"Make it quick! We're going to need the help," Haxs replied while backing away from the humaske gate. He felt nervous, knowing that there was additional data compounding the situation beyond Streetz's ability to control.

L337 Haxs snapped a fresh clip to his carbine while Parity backpedaled, unloading every possible burst at the gate from her Sidewinders. Parity's attempts to damage Warplate were equally futile as the humaske advanced, unaffected. Even if the gate had no weakness to ballistics, it certainly had one somewhere. There had to be another gate present. Haxs normally couldn't detect gates from a remote system, but he could sense that there was another elusive presence.

"Streetz, give us some cover here," Haxs yelled as he grabbed Parity's shoulder and pulled her back, putting distance between his ally and Warplate.

"I'm still tracing the signals. There appears to be another gate present with a CT-14 en route," Streetz replied.

"Thank you, Streetz, I already know about the second gate. Now, if you would be so kind as to get us some cover," Haxs huffed while trying to suppress his impatience.

Streetz pounded on the control console to input the desired commands. While Haxs and Parity backed away from the gate, several walls erupted from the sand. They were short with rounded tops, but just enough to obscure the vision of the approaching gate.

Haxs paused as the walls arose. He felt the secondary gate's presence nearby. It was accompanied by the sound of liquid being sucked through a tube with mild force. Haxs notched his way toward the closest wall's edge and leaned out to hear better, but as he did a silver metallic liquid traversed the floor amidst the walls. The thick puddle rose into a humanoid form lacking any distinguishable features.

The liquid metal form towered over Haxs who was still pressed against one of the makeshift sand walls. The liquid gate raised a morphed arm and fist to crush Haxs, but the fist never dropped. The deep concussive boom of a sniper rifle ripped through the air. The path of the bullet tore through the head of the liquid gate, sinking in like a vortex before it escaped out the other side, but the hole was swiftly filled by the fluid metal.

Even without recognizable facial features, Haxs sensed that the gate was either irritated or insulted that someone dared to shoot it without invitation. Without warning, the gate sloshed back into a puddle form and slithered in Clutch's last known direction.

"Did I miss anything," Hellix asked, holding a hand to the side of his geist's head.

Even though Hellix possessed a sheer amount of determination, Haxs couldn't ignore the warped scrypto pattern forming a bulge on the side of Hellix's virtual skull. Visual cues often relayed a user's inability to mitigate the pressures from the surrounding environment. Haxs knew that the bruise was an indication of exhaustion in the present case.

"Stay here, I'm going to help Clutch," Haxs ordered.

"What about Mr. Bucket-of-Bolts, over here," Hellix asked.

"We got this," Parity chirped, putting her hand on Hellix's shoulder.

L337 Haxs returned a stiff nod before turning to support their isolated teammate. He did his best to remain low behind the sand barriers that Streetz constructed. He had no desire to discover any new tricks that Warplate had in store. He quickly spotted Clutch's position at the top of the wall overlooking the seating which might have hosted the would-be phantom crowd. Reaching the side barrier to the tiered seating, Haxs hurdled the obstacles and raced up the smooth slope, closing on the fast-moving silver puddle.

"Streetz, we ain't got time to play. Adjust everyone for environmental flux, and drop the temperature enough to slow that thing down. Its advantage is in its speed," Haxs snapped.

"On it," Streetz replied quickly. "Outer profile decrypted. Gate designation: 80HG, but gate parameters are still unavailable."

Without awaiting Streetz's instructions to take hold, Haxs grabbed the bow from his back and pulled three arrows back, aiming for the gate which was scaling the wall in attempt to drop on Clutch from above. Clutch shifted, startled from shock at how quickly the liquid metal gate moved. Haxs released the bowstring, sending the arrows at the gate piercing its form, again without effect beyond inconveniencing the gate.

Clearly enraged, 80HG sloshed downward back into a puddle and then upward with its entire form changing into a fist, delivering an uppercut to Haxs' chest. Haxs staggered backward, but he wouldn't be dissuaded from achieving victory. Haxs drew another arrow and fired it into the gate's chest. The arrow passed through the gate, but more slowly than prior projectiles, allowing just enough opportunity to shed corrosive scrypto into the gate's neural pathways.

Haxs knew that a half-tick pause for a virtual breath was more time than he should have allowed, but he drew one more arrow and aimed for the head of the 80HG and released. The arrow found its mark, sticking the gate in the head further corrupting the signals sent to its host.

As the temperature continued to drop, the gate's movement continued to slow until its form stood motionless. Haxs swapped his bow for his Mour Carbine and squeezed the trigger, unleashing a bullet storm that shattered the gate's visible form. With the gate's signal offline, Haxs twisted about to observe the humaske gate which had taken notice of the conflict in the stands above.

Even from the great distance, Haxs heard a click as compartments opened on Warplate's shoulders, revealing multiple missile launchers. Warplate released two projectiles from each shoulder, directly at Haxs' and Clutch's position. There wasn't even enough time for a vocal warning. Haxs dove laterally into the stands, but Clutch was unable to react fast enough. The blast radius mushroomed outward from the ledge where Clutch was last seen.

"Clutch!" Haxs yelled in desperation after the thick choking sand and dust cleared well enough for him to see.

While the humaske gate was distracted, Hellix scaled a sand barrier and jumped into the air, clearing the gate to draw its attention from Parity. Midair, Hellix switched from pistols to scramstick blades and slashed at the artificial humanoid, hoping to catch something vital, but the attack yielded the same results as before. Determined, Hellix knew that he had to hold the gate's attention and stay alive long enough for Parity to do her thing.

Once Haxs had left to help Clutch, Parity had already coordinated with Streetz to craft a corrosive grenade schematic specific for Warplate's armor. No other options remained. If the tactic failed, Subterra was better of exiting the Lynx in disgrace than continuing the assault.

The moment that Hellix captured the gate's attention, Parity exited her hiding spot and tossed a newly constructed grenade at Warplate. Hearing the sound of the grenade at its feet, Warplate disregarded Hellix and turned to face Parity who had already lobbed another explosive.

As the next grenade bounced off the gate's head, Parity expanded the Sidewinders attached to her forearms and fired on the grenades. The detonation caused a cloud of brown corrosive acid to fill the air. Even the mechanical gate looked like an apparition as the acid ran down its virtual frame. Within ticks, the corrosive fluids whittled Warplate into a pile of molten parts.

Stunned, as if his senses flowed down a tunnel, Haxs felt disconnected from the cheers of success rising from the arena floor. He reached the ledge where he last saw Clutch only find to find the inert form of the younger Subterra member's geist.

"Streetz?" Haxs asked sharply, the fear of the inevitable demise of any datajacker prompted a choking sensation in his throat.

"I'm sorry," Streetz responded. "I'm fending off three gate's with more inbound. I can detect a faint signal, but it is no longer in proximity to Clutch's geist."

More than anything, L337 Haxs wanted to doubt Streetz's report. Even more so, he wanted to doubt that Subterra's kid brother was the first to go, especially with his skill level. Clutch had more talent than the rest. All he had been lacking was experience, or perhaps luck.

Haxs did his best to shove remorse aside in order to proceed with the mission, but the chore was difficult as memories flooded his consciousness. Haxs stood and closed his eyes as Clutch's geist evaporated into the virtual surroundings.

"Haxs, we have no time for guilt. We can divide the blame when we're done," Parity shouted as an earthquake tore through the arena's domain.

A sinkhole formed in the middle of the arena beneath Subterra's feet while a blizzard instantaneously appeared overhead. Generated snow flurries above swirled about matching the rotational patterns of the whirlpool created in the sand below.

"Streetz, what's the statchek?" Hellix yelled above the noise.

"I think our interference with the temperature regulation systems has created an instability in the datatank, causing it to crash. No, wait! This isn't our doing. It appears that another gate is forcing the arena datatank to merge with another. We may have just disrupted some balancc of power in a virtual cold war. I've got that CT-14 bearing down on your position fast!" Streetz prattled frantically.

"Streetz, lock it down! We'll take care of it on the other side," Haxs replied between breaths as he ran out of the stands, toward the whirlpool that transitioned from sand to snow.

Haxs grabbed Hellix and Parity who still struggled for footing against the growing vortex and tossed them into it before jumping in after them. The cold whiteness enveloped their geists as they spiraled into the unknown. Haxs had to embrace his fear of being caught between two datatanks and the potentially inconvenient fallout. Haxs yelled for Streetz's confirmation of tracking their positions, but before he could form the words, Subterra found itself rapidly descending toward a grassy meadow.

Following a jarring landing, Subterra members stood and looked around to get their bearings. All were certain that they had crashed into the next datatank en route to their objective, how, remained uncertain. There were no complaints if the interrupted power struggle had worked in their favor.

"I don't see any snow or ice, so why is it cold?" Hellix asked as he looked out across the bleak rolling green meadow underneath a virtual blue sky and yellow sun.

"That can only mean the gate has diverted all available power to its apparition at the expensive of realism. I'd think frostiness is implied at this point," Haxs replied.

Unlike the experience in the prior domain, Subterra didn't have to wait for a theatrical entrance by the gates at large. The feud between security protocols left them without the ability to lose anymore virtual territory. Three shapes dropped from the sky, landing in the distance, just outside of optimal analysis range.

"What we got, Streetz?" Haxs asked.

"Three CT-7's, in the clearing, all standard issue. Either they are getting more bold in declaring their clashtags or just more sloppy. The far left gate goes by Yeti. In the middle, Toga, and the rightmost one, Beta. Stats suggest that you'll each have to take one. I don't think you can handle any two-v-one's especially since it's taking everything that I have to keep this CT-14 in containment.

"Acknowledged, either way, there are certainly flaws to exploit. Keep us posted," Haxs replied.

L337 Haxs took point, leading several paces ahead of Hellix and Parity who were both on his left. The trio double-checked their ammunition reserves and continued forward cautiously. All members present kept their eyes forward, alert for the gates while leveraging their ears for any changes to the environment around them.

Detecting that the gates returned the forward gesture, the trio broke into a sprint to close ground. Each of the datajackers had already made mental note of their respective targets. Haxs, Hellix and Parity all opened fire on the gates before the gap could narrow any further.

Instead of unleashing the Sidewinders, Parity snatched the Sandhawk from her thigh and depressed the trigger, spewing multiple high velocity rounds at the hairy, snowman looking gate between the weapon sights. Yeti lumbered forward at a quick pace, dodging some shots, but the bullets that struck embedded in its thick hide without affecting its charge.

Hellix eyed his adversary, a cloud of free-flowing smoke that periodically shifted into humanoid form with ancient Uniod attire. Knowing that the range was too close for the MARC-15, Hellix leveled his Cronos 18s and unleashed a storm of virtual bullets. The shots popped miniature explosions in the air, but struck nothing as the smoky form hovered and shifted in retaliation.

Haxs squinted in disbelief at the leftover gate he was stuck with. The object which referred to itself as Beta was nothing more than a yellow orb the size of an allcourt ball with four legs holding it up. If not for his experience, Haxs would have burst out in laughter, but he knew better when it came to virtual appearances in the Hyper Lynx. Slowing his pace to improve accuracy, Haxs leveled his Mour Carbine, but before his brain impulse finalized the signal to his geist's finger, he felt a shockwave which knocked him back five paces.

Still upright, Haxs watched the gate waddle forward as it released a series of meeps and squeals. Quickly assessing that the gate had some manner of telekinetic influence, Haxs motioned to shoot again, but in response, the gate released another shockwave, knocking the weapon from his hands. Adapting quickly, Haxs drew his bow, pulled back two arrows and fired at the gate. The arrows sailed toward the gate, only to sharply angle away from the squeaky orb with legs.

Recognizing the futility of weapons, Haxs charged the stubby gate to strike it with his fists, but like before, another telekinetic strike connected, flipping Haxs head over heels, forcing him to miss his target. Haxs landed hard on his back, sending feedback which created the perception of a sharp pain in his lungs. He forced himself back to his feet quickly before the gate could seize the advantage.

"Streetz, get me some plated boots, and warp me within half a pace the tick I start to move," Haxs ordered.

Raising his fists in front of his body, Hax stood idly as if to engage the eyeless orb of a gate in a staredown. He waited for the orb to soak up all of the confidence that it needed to assume that it could thwart Haxs yet again. Haxs charged, and as the orb motioned to knock him down, he began to swing his leg back, then forward again with all of the power that he could deliver through his geist. The motion appeared to be a feint given the distance, but as instructed, Streetz warped Haxs' geist to the precise position, bypassing the gate's telekinetic wave.

"Time to die, Squeaky!" Hax shouted as his kick connected with the spongey gate.

If the gate had bones, they would have been crushed as the impact caved in the squishy body. Haxs watched the orb drop into the distance on the green grass in a lifeless heap. Confident that the gate was out of commission, Haxs ran to assist his friends.

Hellix halted in his tracks as he watched the bullets hit nothing, passing through Toga's smokey form. Defiant, the gate blasted forward. Hellix expected little impact from an object that consisted of minimal mass, but he was mistaken. The smoke cloud struck him like a brick wall, sending him sprawling backward.

With its foe grounded, the gate hovered over Hellix, its thick gray form burning his eyes. Even without his sight, Hellix felt the gate which used the smoke to choke him out as the stench penetrated his nostrils. Hellix attempted to cough, but the gate was interrupting his respiratory system faster than he could pass instructions to his geist from the tappers.

Streetz worked the console as fast as possible to slow down the smokey gate, but he was still losing the race to keep Parity's foe at bay too. Haxs ran up to the smokey gate, drew his carbine and fired, but he knew that the attack would be futile against its attempt to choke Hellix.

"Streetz, get me a vacuum," Haxs said.

With newly loaded accessories, Haxs drew a hose connected to his belt and matching containment pack on his back. A loud startup whirred, and the gate, limited by the physics of its own scrypto, got sucked toward the tube that Haxs pointed directly at the gate. With the virtual air free from the smoke, Hellix at last coughed spastically, relative to the perceived burning sensation in his lungs.

Haxs ejected the containment pack attached to the vacuum and dropped the sealed canister on the ground. With the gate decommissioned, Haxs helped Hellix back to his feet so they could both proceed toward Parity's last position.

"Streetz, if you have time, decompiling that gate should be in order. I don't want it getting back out," Haxs said.

"Already done, but I should let you know that the distraction here has undoubtedly reduced resources needed to keep the CT-14 occupied. It's on the way," Streetz replied grimly.

"Noted," Haxs replied.

Parity emptied her Sandhawk magazine into Yeti, but it advanced, still disregarding any physical pain. She discarded her pistol, switched to Sidewinders and unleashed energy projectiles until she received a recharge message. With her firearms spent and the monstrous creature looming over her, she reached over her shoulder with her right hand to grab the chopping blade that nearly matched the height of her geist. She pulled down on the handle using the leverage to swing the blade into a downward arc, following through as she pulled the blade down to her opposite side. As the blade passed her leg, Parity timed the swing using the momentum to propel her body into a front flip. As the heavy blade's momentum carried through, Parity grasped the handle firmly with both hands and drove the blade downward just as Yeti motioned to block over its head.

The blade sunk deep into Yeti's left shoulder, narrowly missing its head. With the blade lodged into the gate's arm and her hands still holding the hilt of the blade, Parity was in a vulnerable position, accessible to the gate's powerful grip. Also sensing the opportunity, Yeti swung its right forelimb to grab Parity.

Out of sheer reflex, Parity pulled down on the blade handle while kicking upward with her feet. Once her body cleared Yeti's clutches she springboarded off the gate's back and flipped into the air. Parity expected to clear the gate's reach by kicking away from the creature, but her fatigue was beginning to impair her judgement.

Yeti countered by spinning into a backfist which caught Parity midair, knocking her to the ground. Parity's body tumbled through the cold stiff grass. Yeti twisted around and ambled toward her fallen geist. The gate lifted a broad foot to crush Parity, but an arrow sailing in front of its eyes made it think twice. It lowered its head and snarled as it turned to face L337 Haxs and Hellix instead.

Holding ground, Haxs drew another arrow, pulled it back and released it before the gate could make a move. The arrow struck the gate in the eye. The arrow's impact combined with two mags worth of rounds from Hellix's Cronos 18s rocked Yeti backward as it howled. The gate finally keeled over as Haxs placed two more arrows in its skull, putting it down for good.

After confirming an inert signal from the gate, Haxs checked on Parity. Hellix poked at Yeti's lifeless form and grimaced. He was amazed at either the creativity or in the insanity that the minds behind gates possessed to manifest such irregular personas.

"No time to linger, Subterra," Haxs said once Parity was back on her feet.

Hellix followed behind Haxs, but Parity paused to observe the dead gate while retrieving her chopping blade which was still lodged in its shoulder. She dug her geist's heel into the toppled creature and braced herself to pull the thick blade from the virtual carcass.

No more than a few steps from their last foe, Haxs felt an icy wind course through his veins, suggesting the presence of another. Although the sensation was more premonition than simulated effect, Haxs didn't need to be informed that the gate Streetz warned of had finally revealed itself.

L337 Haxs slowly turned about afraid of what his geist's eyes might see. Fearing another ghastly monstrosity, Haxs was shocked to discover that it was not the apparition, but the scenario unfolding, that caused his frame to freeze. The newly arrived CT-14 took on the appearance of a human male with abnormal realism. The gate wore only dark brown pants allowing him to flex his tight torso. His left hand wrapped around Parity's throat, the muscles in his forearm rippling as he applied pressure to her neck. Haxs could already tell that Parity was slipping from consciousness as her geist's eyes struggled to focus.

Sensing that odds of negotiation were slim, Haxs drew another arrow and directed its toward the gate's head while Hellix slowly circled to Haxs' left hoping to get behind the gate. Seemingly unconcerned with Hellix, the gate kept his eyes trained on Haxs and released a malicious smirk, making his intentions clear. He would pull Parity's face into the path of the arrow should Haxs release the bowstring.

"I don't know how you breached containment, but rest assured, that will be your last escape," Haxs muttered.

"Come now, you don't think the mighty Houndin could be captured so easily. You underestimate us CT-14's," the gate's apparition frowned in mock disappointment.

Outside of the virtual connection, Haxs fired a message to Hellix's display regarding when to attack, knowing that their opponent was advanced enough to intercept internal communications. Virtually, Haxs kept his geist's eyes trained on Houndin. Any gate using a human form, not to mention able to communicate effectively, clearly presented markers of someone who spent nearly their entire life inside the Hyper Lynx causing them to lose all sense of reality, making them very dangerous. Despite such a threat, Haxs knew that there was always a weakness to such foes, their own arrogance.

Haxs watched as Houndin tried to track Hellix via his peripheral vision. Knowing that they might only get one opportunity, Haxs confirmed on his tapper for Hellix to move in from behind. Hellix dashed toward Houndin. With the attack set in motion, Haxs released the arrow targeting the gate's head. In one swift motion, Houndin wrenched on Parity's neck, dropping her lifeless geist to the ground while simultaneously reaching behind with his right arm to catch Hellix under the shoulder, flipping him over. Hellix's body was tossed over the gate and the heel of his geist knocked the incoming projectile out of the air.

Haxs stared, dumbfounded by the speed and assessment that Houndin used to leverage Hellix's momentum against the pair. Houndin then held Hellix's neck in a vice grip after being flipped over so fast, preventing him from even planting his feet to the ground. Hellix was at the gate's mercy from his seated position, the gate's limb clearly in command of the situation.

Subterra's leader expected the gate to finish Hellix off like he had Parity, but the gate was toying with the surviving members, another clear indication that their opponent was extremely intelligent or insane. Houndin forced Hellix to his feet with more strength than would normally be allocated to such a small virtual body. In doing so, Houndin lifted the geist with one hand hurling Hellix toward Haxs, knocking them both to the ground.

Rolling to the side as quickly as possible, Haxs pushed himself from the ground, but Houndin was already standing over him and punched him in the face. The signals from the impact were already flooding Haxs' skull faster than any countermeasure he had ever experienced. Even with Streetz's help to keep his neural pathways clear, he struggled to combat the gate's influence.

Hellix sprung from the ground and snapped his scramstick from his geist's back, separating it into the two concealed blades. He slashed at Houndin who easily evaded the strikes, waiting for the right moment to counter attack. Hellix was sure that he had the upper hand as he slashed high with his right hand and swung toward Houndin's midsection with his left, but Houndin twisted out of range and grabbed Hellix's left wrist, snapping it and forcing Hellix to drop the blade.

Houndin pinned Hellix's right arm, snaking his hand around to disarm Hellix of the other blade and pressed one of the edges under Hellix's throat. Houndin wanted to ensure that Haxs witnessed the destruction of his only remaining ally as the neural signals continued to force the disconnect of his consciousness from the Hyper Lynx.

With much pain, Haxs forced himself to his knees. With blurred vision he saw that Hellix was in no position to fight back, but Haxs forced enough mobility out of his geist to speak before collapsing.

"Hellix, punch him in the stomach," Haxs groaned.

Houndin's eyes narrowed in confusion at the futile command from the faltering leader of the intrusion. Hellix didn't understand the command himself, but he possessed no strength to argue. Hellix balled his geist's hand into a fist and drove its elbow back into the abdomen of his adversary.

Unable to explain the loss of control, Houndin felt his own neural connection dissipate, and the empty shell of a gate released Hellix, slumping to the ground. Hellix grabbed his virtual throat checking for cuts to remind himself of the distinction between the virtual and the ever-convincing real effects that it had on him externally. Haxs also felt the disrupting effects of the gate diminish, giving him opportunity to roll on his back and breath slowly so that he could get his mind back in order.

"How did you know to do that?" Hellix asked in an artificially wheezy voice as he too plopped on the grass to reorient himself.

"These gates spend so much time patterning their virtual likenesses after historic things that they know nothing about, but their arrogance inhibits them from ever doing enough research to study the weaknesses baked into the scrypto. With all of the bizarre forms, I never expected to find one dumb enough to choose one with such an obvious weakness," Haxs replied.

Sitting up, reluctant to face reality, Haxs looked over to see Parity's geist. The radiant purple hue that once defined her character faded when the gate terminated her neural connection. He felt like an arrow had pierced his own heart, damaging the emotional vault that he felt was normally carried with him into the Hyper Lynx to minimize emotion. First Clutch, then Parity. Haxs felt like a huge chunk of his imprint being had been torn away. His crew functioned like a machine, each part interdependent, and he had to endure the crushing loss.

Haxs opened his eyes to observed the bleak cold expanse of the domain which held him captive. Standing, he helped Hellix do the same. He wanted to mourn the loss of his allies, but he knew that it was not the proper time since the mission was still at stake.

Slowly shifting back to a tactical mindset, Haxs looked about for the exit to their present datatank known as the Brink, but nothing appeared with any reasonable proximity to his geist. Before he had time to advance, a thunderous collision jolted the air as a deep chasm manifested before the Subterra survivors. The bland atmosphere darkened as haze swirled about.

A large four-legged beast, with a high arched back rose from the chasm. It had a broad square head with a rectangular jaw, its skin practically a composition of slime and scrypto. The apparition lowered its head and released a deep guttural snarl as it revealed long pointed teeth lining its massive jaw.

Haxs withheld the obvious question of asking if the new arrival was a CT-14 as the gate stared at the two datajackers. Haxs and Hellix slowly stepped back, the creature's virtual putrid breath still causing the symptoms of nausea in their external reality.

Quick mental math already suggested to Haxs that they had no means to defeat the gate in front of them. His initial impulse was to run for cover and regroup, but there was no cover and there was nowhere to run. There was no recourse but to hold ground and wait for the virtual beast to finish the matter.

The large beast moved a thick leg forward to execute the perceived demise, but as it did, a blue beam struck the creature in its side, knocking it back into the chasm. Haxs wasn't about to complain, but the occurrence left him confused. As the datajackers turned to track the source of the beam, they found another nondescript humanoid form similar in appearance to the 80HG gate they previously dispatched, but this one appeared less fluid.

"I thought that I sensed a power struggle," Haxs said to the gate.

"True, but that does nothing to make you a relevant variable in this equation," the gate replied.

With an air of defiance the featureless aura fired a blue beam from each of its hands, knocking Haxs and Hellix back to the ground. Streetz's fingers moved so fast that they nearly scrambled the doorman console in his attempt to unpack the gate's signature. The manner in which the gate spoke triggered a dormant memory.

In short order, Streetz verified the gate's signature and immediately snapped two containment fields into the Brink domain to protect his remaining allies before the gate could strike again. There was nothing more the young datajackers could do in their fatigued state. Streetz hoped that he could put an end to the pattern of destruction before it was too late. With two Subterra members already gone, it was up to him to prevent the body count from being total. Once the containment fields were verified, Streetz leapt over the console and dove for the large emcast pedestal and fused his form into the Hyper Lynx. It was up to him to take on the mastermind behind Imperan security protocols.

32 – Night Shift – 32

Windstonne Central Power Station
Core City, Windstonne Enclave
Commercial Empire, Northam Continent
Thread: sysObserver.cmd

The small band of operators tasked with impeding the Imperan power plant cautiously approached their designated entrance to the waste systems. One Ghost accompanying Torque and the Serpent lifted the access cover and jumped in the dark tunnel below. A foul stench permeated the air.

"Why does the late shift get the shaft?" Torque grumbled.

Two more Ghosts followed the first to secure the accessway. The Serpent narrowed his outer eyelids to optimize his eyesight in the dark while Torque utilized the green hue on his ikes to do the same. Upon receiving an all-clear signal from below, Torque and the Serpent jumped down into the sewage line followed by the remainder of the Ghosts. Torque grimaced as the party sloshed through ankle deep muck. He doubled his efforts to ensure that his ikes didn't miss a trip hazard that could plant him face first in the putrid sludge.

The Serpent motioned for two Ghosts to move ahead of the group. Torque observed as the Ghosts moved ahead without word or sound. Even the Serpent's motions had been as silent as the night. The means in which the Ghosts functioned and communicated so smoothly and noiselessly prompted Torque to think that their abilities bordered on telepathy or some unknown mystical skill. He then pondered Vanguard's capacity to achieve such a level of cohesion.

"How much longer do we have to endure this stench?" Torque griped.

"About another two hauls past the next bend," the Serpent replied dryly.

Privy to the group's progress, Maxwell updated ikes with a nav marker. Torque acknowledged the marker and sighed as he worked his way down the crowded conduit along with the silent killers. Once the main party had caught up with the Ghost scouts, they were instructed to hold until confirmation that the perimeter security had been disabled.

"Streetz, statchek?" Torque hissed into the comm.

After a three tick delay, Streetz responded with an all-clear symbol. Torque felt uneasy knowing that Streetz was unable to return an audible reply. Without time to press the issue, Torque nodded to the two Ghosts on point who emerged from the access shaft to infiltrate the Imperan power plant.

In trademark fashion, the Ghosts silently removed the last access hatch and darted into the fresh air. The full complement of Ghosts proceeded topside with Torque and the Serpent following. Once again in the night air, the party stood in the midst of an open lot well encompassed by the shadow of a tall stone cased tower with minimal access points.

"You do realize that remaining security systems are electronic, therefore rendering all of your special skills useless?" Torque asked.

"Who wants to escort the new guy," one of the Ghosts remarked, followed by snickers.

The Serpent held up his hand to cut the chatter, "Regardless of measures taken, it is still the human element that would impede our task."

"Then it seems our walk out might pose the greatest challenge," Torque replied after forcing himself to not grit his teeth at the prior jab.

"Indeed," the Serpent said before a quick turn and dash that put him on course with the looming structure.

In the short time that Torque had known the Serpent, he had yet to witness a Ghost's full skillset on display. Even with the Serpent trailing behind his associates, Torque struggled to track their movements. Without cover and a full speed run across an open lot, their very forms seemed to fade in and out of sight. Additionally, there was no sound to help keep up with the Martial Legion's elite force known for their stealth. Finally, the Ghosts halted their advance, pressing themselves against a half wall from which they could hear Pirans griping about being left behind.

"Sounds like they're itchin' for some action. Shall we oblige?" Torque whispered, taking a wall spot of his own which led toward the main entrance.

"We'll take care of them and draw out those inside," the Serpent replied as he nodded to the three Ghosts closest to the entryway.

"Do you know what a Ghost's best friend is after darkness?" the Serpent asked as he slipped two Nebula smoke grenades from his belt.

"Fashionable threads?" Torque chided upon his observation that the Serpent was the only Ghost wearing an outfit that wasn't dominantly black.

"I liked to call it adequate cover," the Serpent hissed as he launched the grenades over the wall, toward the unsuspecting Pirans.

The Ghosts who were given a headstart had already hurdled the wall and positioned themselves behind the soldiers. Yells of confusion bounced off the thick smoke as the security detail looked around, unable to find their adversaries. The panic was cut short, the screams squelched as the Ghosts performed their job coldly and efficiently. By the time the smoke cleared, all soldiers present had been terminated and the bodies stacked behind the wall out of sight.

The wide expression on Torque's face reflected his respect for the cold lethal precision demonstrated by his allies. The Serpent smirked as he watched Torque absorb the quick series of events.

Within ticks, the Ghosts even removed weapons from the entryway just ahead of more shouts erupting from within. Torque and the Serpent exchanged nods, agreeing that it was time to advance. For the next wave a hail storm of Nebula grenades pelted the scene, enveloping the entryway in smoke. The Pirans fired blindly into the white fog, but one by one they were silenced. With time of the essence, the Ghosts left the remaining bodies and pressed forward with Torque and the Serpent close behind.

The first interior sight proved no more receptive. The infiltrators found themselves in a choke point. A horseshoe shaped balcony lined the floor above with a contingent of Pirans pointing their rifles down at the party. Without requiring instruction, the Ghosts rained down with Nebula grenades, high and low to generate more confusion.

Two Ghosts bolted for the lateral staircases to attack the soldiers above while others boosted their allies up to the balcony by hand. Torque held back to assess the security layout.

"Maxwell, I need options here," Torque said.

"Shoot me the structure," Maxwell promptly replied, despite the static interference.

"Done," Torque replied after scanning the room with his ike's thermal filter to bypass the smoke. "Need something quick, heavy interference!"

"Security terminal on your left. Give me a remote access point and I can monitor traffic. I won't be able to crack the systems, but I can at least get you Subterra's progress," Maxwell said.

"Acknowledged," Torque replied, quickly navigating his way through the smoke toward the designated terminal. Above Torque, more yells and cursing broke out as the Pirans attempted to subdue the intruders without success. After securing the remote access point, Torque headed up the stairs to assist the Ghosts, if needed, while Maxwell parsed the security system.

The Serpent followed behind the Ghosts, slashing through firearm, torso and limb on his way through the lobby. One unsuspecting

Ghost found himself caught between two Pirans. While striking at one, he got clubbed by the other and collapsed. Without hesitation, the Pirans fired their bulky Claw Hammers into the Ghost. The Serpent retaliated by severing the heads of the soldiers. He recognized that the departed Ghost was a younger member and still reliant upon his tech, but the loss of any Ghost was always a waste.

Torque and the Serpent met at the entrance to the main hallway from opposing sides of the balcony. Upon verifying that there were no additional losses, Torque led the team down the main hallway, deeper into the power plant interior.

"Maxwell, do you read?" Torque asked.

"I'm in," Maxwell replied. "You'd better get a move on. They are scrambling reinforcements, even drawing some back from the frontline. I've already posted a nav marker for the primary reactor."

"Well, that sure got their attention," Torque grumbled as he noted the new marker on his ikes. He broke into a sprint toward the primary reactor with the rest of the team following his lead.

The winding maze of hallways finally led the team into an open observation room, revealing the enormous apparatus which powered Windstonne's energy grid. One of the Ghosts tilted his head back to get a full view of the reactor's height. Another let out a low whistle at the sight of the indescribable mechanism.

Without guards or technicians, one Ghost strolled toward the observation pane, but Torque was quick to dissuade him. Torque nodded toward the very floor and bridges within the chamber which glowed with an orange hue.

"That room is still hot. One wrong step and its fry time," Torque said.

A hard explosion rocked the corridor that the team had last passed through, causing a massive dust cloud to envelope the hallway. Chunks of the wall collapsed, scattering debris along the floor. Torque turned and opened fire with a Cutter on the Piran's who bothered following the intruders all the way to the observation deck.

"Maxwell, lockout status?" Torque yelled above the sound of disruptor fire and his ringing ears.

Additionally, the Serpent drew his two silver Splice 15ms from behind his back and supported Torque in returning plasma fire down the hallway. Some Ghosts stared wide eyed at their superior whom they had never seen utilize firearms, pondering the nature of his adaptation since departing their ranks.

"I've got nothing," Maxwell responded in frantic fashion.

The Ghosts waited patiently behind their Vanguard counterparts to prevent obstruction. Pirans seemed less concerned about obstruction as they continued to charge down the corridor only to get cut down by the plasma fire, in some instances by their own. One Ghost tossed a Nebula grenade down the hall, its noxious fumes only slowed the Pirans down momentarily.

The Pirans were positioned to overpower the team based on numbers alone after taking away the Ghosts' ability to cause havoc in the chokepoint. Accepting the disadvantage, Torque and the Serpent stepped back from their corner cover and allowed Pirans to advance toward the observation deck. The Ghosts, with their blades already drawn, were more than ready to once again cut the Pirans down. The bodies began to pile in the entry way, but there was no stopping the Imperan military force, their stubborn behavior matching their ugly features.

Torque twisted about hoping for an upside, but the reactor containment fields were still active. He had no choice but to backpedal as Pirans continued to advance.

"Where's my override?" Torque yelled, frustrated that determination alone wasn't enough to quell their foes.

Hyper Lynx Integration System
Imperan Localized Security Domain
Thread: sysObserver.cmd

Streetz felt his response system shudder as it integrated with the Hyper Lynx. The stimuli from the bleak digital universe felt foreign. His physical system was comprised of shifting fields to begin with, but the sensation of another virtual medium felt different altogether. He had never been integrated into an overlapping network, so there was great risk to his localized identity, but it was one that he had to take. After all, his environment was every bit a product of interpreted scrypto as himself.

Slowly calibrating his limbs, Streetz felt that he was able to move naturally as he recompiled his virtual appearance. His form matched his external appearance, varying greatly from the common scrytpo interlacing of geists. His head turned to verify that Haxs' and Hellix's geists were still contained, giving them opportunity to safely exit the virtual world. With his last external operation complete, Streetz could shift his focus to the gate which so easily incapacitated the Subterra remnant. Streetz simply tilted his neck as he watched the white featureless apparation strut around arrogantly.

"I see that you actually found someone to sponsor your demented behavior, Zox" Streetz said tersely.

"I must say that I'm surprised to you see that you are both operational and vertical," the mastermind gate replied. "I never thought anyone would dig you out of the rubble. What did they offer to prevent you from killing them?"

"A choice," Streetz replied dryly as his eyes tracked the gate's movements as it slowly paced. "A choice to be useful or be powered down forever. Not that difficult of a decision really. Just like it wasn't difficult to choose to reject the orders that led me to that state."

Normally, Streetz didn't like to entertain the simulation embedded in his core, but he could already sense that his integration with the virtual domain was affecting his judgement. He felt something well up in his routines that was long dormant since he had been forced to kill and steal without cause per instruction by those once in command of his operational core. The urban clan trash that once treated Streetz as a minion had been promoted to chief of Imperan security.

"You are a machine, Streetz. You were designed to follow orders. That is why you exist," the apparition representing Zox snapped.

"I was designed to think, analyze potential outcomes and choose accordingly. That's something which those of you with natural intelligence take for granted. Ironically, here you stand in the pinnacle of man's technological advancements, yet even here everything falls short of that which is readily available on the outside. Looks like those giving the orders still have no grasp on reality," Streetz said.

"What would you know of it? In here, I am the craftsman. I control who comes and goes," Zox replied, the vitriol lacing his words.

"Those who can't cut it in the real world shouldn't expect any greater success in the virtual. All you've done is digitize your insanity. You were born with perspective that I can never have and yet you throw it all away for imaginary kicks. That does not sound like an enviable strength," Streetz chided.

"That which is synthetic has no business passing judgement on the natural," Zox snapped.

"And that which is virtual is but a husk of that which is real," Streetz smirked.

"We shall see," Zox said, bringing an end to the conversation.

Zox's form tightened into a muscular figure. He still retained the formless face, but the new visage clearly indicated his hostile intent. Zox lifted his hands and shot two light blue beams at the ground where Streetz stood. Streetz evaded quickly by driving his knees upward while propelling himself into a forward moving back flip.

Even without Zox's facial expressions to give away emotions within, Streetz sensed that Zox was simply assessing the situation. Undoubtedly, Zox's last memory of Streetz would have been that of a bitter synthetic imprint with intent to harm the clan which coerced him into crimes for which the past unstructured governments had no laws. Given the passes since that last encounter, Streetz knew that he had the advantage of his added time with Vanguard and the fully featured adaptation that went way behind the initial designs of his late designer.

Assuming that Streetz's reaction was more luck than skill, Zox unleashed more bolts at his target. In anticipation, Street dashed through the air delivering a crisp flying side kick to Zox's cranium.

The attack did little to impair Zox's influence over the virtual domain, but it certainly evoked enough aggravation for him to adjust his strategy. Streetz's time in the outside world had given him time to optimize his field efficiency and attack cycles which translated accordingly even within the virtual space.

Zox slowly circled around Streetz, expecting an offensive maneuver, but instead, he only found himself being observed by his synthetic counterpart. Zox leaned forward, snapping his arm and wrist to test Streetz's reaction, but Streetz held his position, easily recognizing the difference between a strike and a feint.

Moving again, Zox wound up and twisted his body into the air spinning a full circle and a half, driving his leg high overhead before bringing it back down toward Streetz's dome. Streetz calmly sidestepped the first maneuver, but due to Zox's follow-up spinning hook kick, Streetz was forced to move with more intent.

Shifting from the two kick spin combo, Zox jumped into another spin roundhouse which Streetz dodged, but Zox turned up the pressure and twisted into a front flip kick only to snap into a plate spin kick. Streetz effectively dodged the first three kicks only to put himself in the path of Zox's lateral spin. The kick visualized by the horizontal wheel connected with Streetz's face. Streetz felt no pain upon impact, but he was forced to step backward and focus on the foreign scrypto that had embedded into his form at the point of collision.

While Streetz had encountered plenty of fights in the real world, he had zero experience with total immersion in a virtual environment. He too was faced with an adjustment in strategy. Within the subtick that Streetz needed to reconfigure his position, Zox was already stepping in again with a powerful side kick. Streetz sidestepped again, but he felt that the response time from his fields was sluggish. Something wasn't right.

A quick internal scan prompted Streetz to realize that every strike that Zox landed gave the gate more influence over Streetz's processing. Streetz would have to counter Zox's tactics quickly before the CT-14 could decompile his scrypto and erase it one chunk at a time.

Zox chambered his right knee into the air then slammed the attached foot to the ground as he delivered a right fisted power strike directly to Streetz's face, but Streetz swiftly placed an open hand into the air, palm inward, and halted Zox's punch. The two virtual forms engaged in a stare down until Streetz shifted to the offensive and stepped forward to catch Zox's front leg and push him off-balance. Zox countered by lifting his leg and stepping backward while driving his left hand into a hook punch at Streetz's head.

Streetz ducked under the hook punch and pivoted onto his right foot and knocked a powerful sweep kick against the back of Zox's legs. Once the sweep kick connected, it knocked Zox to the ground, giving Streetz a chance to stomp on the downed gate. Anticipating the move, Zox easily rolled backward and unfolded into a standing position in abnormal fashion.

As Streetz centered his position, Zox fired his fists again and snapped into a two punch combo, a straight with his lead hand and an uppercut to follow with the opposite. The double strike sent Streetz flying backward. He struggled to combat the disorientation, but Streetz retained enough focus to flip onto his feet and not land on his back.

The increased disruption to his processing demanded additional time for Streetz to regain his focus, time that he couldn't afford to give his adversary. He wouldn't be able to defeat Zox by attacking him on the surface. He would need to find Zox's weakness which wouldn't be found in his combat skills alone. It would require Streetz to keep Zox distracted long enough to allow part of his processing to tunnel into the environment and identify any of Zox's virtual dependencies.

Streetz shook off the fatigue and held position as was common to datajacker behavior. Zox's form tilted its head as if smirking at its success in affecting Streetz's processing power. Streetz closed his eyes as if from exhaustion, but it was a bluff as he sent pulses through the virtual domain to locate Zox's command interface. At first, Zox stepped forward cautiously watching Streetz's still form and closed eyes. Ruthless by nature, Zox had no qualms about taking advantage of a weary opponent, so he lunged forward. Streetz leveraged the trap and snapped his eyes open, impeding Zox's attack.

Streetz dashed forward to counter and flipped into the air dropping an axe kick at Zox who responded by flipping backward.

Streetz advanced his assault by leaping into a triple spin only to land in front of Zox.

"What was that? An exhibition?" Zox retorted at Streetz's technique which had more flash than function.

"While you were busy admiring the distraction, I was busy dumping your combat subroutines," Streetz replied calmly.

Zox paused in disbelief as he ran a scan of his command system.

"You seem to be mistaken," Zox replied after finding no errors.

"We shall see," Streetz replied without expression using the gate's own words.

Zox sprinted forward, unleashing a blurry storm of strikes connecting with various targets on Streetz's form including abdomen, jaw and temples. Streetz withstood the blows, but the influence of the gate was rapidly becoming more than his core could handle. Zox halted his attacks to enjoy the spectacle of watching Streetz convulse from the attack.

Streetz felt electrical surges ripple through his digital pathways. The strain on his processing systems nearly caused his form to nearly twist into a knot and buckle to the ground. Streetz lightly pondered the correlation to muscle tension as he struggled to stand against the forces driving him to defeat. He channeled all of the foreign signals and routed them through his garbage collection routines. Streetz stood upright and yelled as he dispatched Zox's attempts to end him permanently.

"Looks like you're wrong," Zox said, enjoying the struggle.

Streetz leaned low as he finished purging his system. He then looked up with a faint air of confidence before rushing Zox, his feet leading the way. Zox blocked Streetz's high side kick, but then unexpectedly found himself forced to block one kick after another. Streetz's leg never touched down as it snapped a countless series of roundhouses at Zox's form in succession. Zox continued blocking the kicks with ease until Streetz changed the pattern to a hook kick that forced the gate to evade.

The advancing pressure increased as Streetz landed two jump hook kicks to Zox's formless head. Zox was surprised at getting rocked by the power behind Streetz's attacks. Dumbfounded, Zox's form stumbled backward only to watch Streetz stare triumphantly.

"By the way, I never said I decompiled your offensive protocols, just the defensive stuff," Streetz said.

Zox's form snarled as it stood from the ground. He looked at his glowing hands in disbelief that he could be outwitted by a synthetic. Angered, Zox jumped at Streetz, hoping to knock him back to the floor and prevent another striking opportunity, but Streetz anticipated the jump and drove an uppercut into Zox's chest with enough force to transmit a shockwave through the entire datatank. Streetz watched a visual distortion rip through the virtual domain as Zox lost his control over it.

Zox's struggle to stand was short lived as Streetz stood over him, lifting a foot to crush the gate's virtual skull. Zox's bluish white body faded from view. Streetz turned his attention to the cold, bleak virtual surroundings. The grass, distant mountains, and sky flickered momentarily before being replaced by a dark room with regular gridlines.

Within the scope possible, Streetz felt a relief at the completion of the mission after Zox's lingering processes had finally dissipated. Staring down at the last occupied spot of Zox's body, Streetz felt a strange emotional simulation course through his processor. From a conscious standpoint, Streetz knew that revenge wasn't something integrated into his core, but the weight of unresolved threads seemed to diminish. He felt like a burden had been lifted by disrupting the presence of one who had forced Streetz to perform actions contrary to his core design. Streetz couldn't verify the status of Zox's body in the outside world, but the outcome was enough to know that he withstood his foe and won, likely preventing any future intrusion on the Hyper Lynx indefinitely.

As Streetz attempted to parse the protocols of the Imperan security datatank, he marveled at the amount of traffic that Zox was responsible for. If anything, it was a feat that Zox had been able to manage the workload by himself. Security alerts ran rampant as subroutines attempted to run damage control. Streetz funneled the signals into one channel making them manageable all while clogging the pipeline, forcing the system's speed to a crawl.

With the most urgent situations resolved, Streetz directed his attention toward the power plant. The feedback that he received was beyond expectation. Security intrusions flooded the system from every direction. It appeared that resistance forces weren't the only ones trying to keep up with the action. Torque's team had secured a path to the primary reactor, but stats showed that the team was pinned with more waves of Pirans on approach.

From within the system, Streetz raced to decompile and restructure any system necessary into an understandable format. Had he been at full capacity, he could have made short work of the security datastacks, but the bout with Zox affected his efficiency more than expected. Forcing his focus on anything threatening Torque's team, Streetz realigned all security commands, including the alert system.

"Security protocol access acquired. Doors will open five ticks after heat shield deactivation," Streetz relayed through the Imperan comm system.

"Nice of you to remember us down here," Torque ranted with disruptor fire punctuating his remark.

"My apologies, I was obligated to say goodbye to an old friend," Streetz said sarcastically.

Torque knew Streetz well enough to know that he was speaking in code, but his patience was beyond spent. "Well, when you're done sipping darwa, we could use some cover down here."

"Say please," Streetz responded.

"Now!" Torque yelled.

After the reactor engaged its cooling system and released the shield, the team forced their way into the reactor chamber. Once Streetz verified that the entire team was secure, he then sealed the doors and trapped the Pirans in the observation deck. Streetz then unleashed one of the coolant waste vents, knocking the Pirans unconscious.

With the team free to complete their objective, Streetz created a temporary power reserve, allowing just enough time to get himself, L337 Haxs and Hellix clear of the datatank before disconnect. Streetz transferred all relevant and newly gained security protocols to the doorman console and left the remainder to be destroyed along with the failing security datatank.

Streetz disabled the containment fields on the Subterra survivors before transitioning his own form back to an external state. With his allies safe from their connection to the Hyper Lynx, Streetz watched the unchecked power spike in the Imperan system grow until it released a surge that cooked every port adjacent to the datatank.

As Haxs and Hellix were granted time to recover, Streetz was able to direct his full attention back to the power plant team. Since the team had survived thus far without his help, he hoped that the rest of the mission could be completed with minimal complications before more Pirans arrived.

Windstonne Central Power Station
Core City, Windstonne Enclave
Commercial Empire, Northam Continent
Thread: sysObserver.cmd

Torque signaled for the Ghosts to enter the reactor chamber before he dropped an Inferno grenade as a parting gift and then dove into the chamber. Standing up to watch the commotion, Torque observed as noxious fumes poured into the observation deck, knocking the advancing Pirans unconscious if they weren't already caught in the grenade blast. Torque exhaled with a sense of relief, knowing that Streetz had assumed control of the security systems.

Without hesitation, Ghosts were already placing demolition charges at their assigned locations as Torque approached the terminal that Maxwell had marked previously. The Serpent was already waiting nearby, performing a scan of the chamber. Once the Ghosts had finished their task, the Serpent gave Torque a nod in order to proceed.

Torque quickly tapped the override commands received by his ikes. When a prompt appeared, he synced the countdown of the detonators. With the final sequence entered, the security systems started to blare warnings, automatically activated by safety protocols.

"Core dump in three clicks, evacuate all personnel from reactor chamber, blurted an automated voice.

"Let's move," Torque shouted.

With the observation deck still flooded, Torque led the team to the furthest point in the chamber from the core. Per order, one Ghost placed a shaped charge on the wall and primed it with a three tick fuse.

The infiltration team stood back while the charge detonated and cleared a hole just large enough for human forms to squeeze through. With all party members clear of the chamber, the team sprinted down another series of hallways for an indirect path back to the entrance of the power plant. Torque spotted the doors to the horseshoe entryway in the distance and envisioned free air beyond. He didn't dare look back for pursuing Pirans at the risk of hesitation that might slow their departure, but once he reached the lower level of the entrance, he realized that neglecting his surroundings was a fatal mistake. Even above the sound of heavy breathing, Torque caught the tone of a device that he hadn't heard since the war. It was a Deathtrap, harbinger of carnage, and the Pirans had left one set to proximity detection.

Torque couldn't even screech a warning fast enough for others to take cover. A violent explosion shook the air itself sending bodies, platform chunks and walls in every thinkable direction as the power plant entryway collapsed inward upon the team. The last thing that Torque felt before blackness was the force of the explosion sending his body backward into the wall behind him. The shockwave and extreme force consumed him in darkness as his body found a horizontal resting place.

DAVE TODD

33 – Trilinear Assault – 33

Resistance Forward Command
Core City, Windstonne Enclave
Commercial Empire, Northam Continent
Thread: actTgtPersp1.view

The regular interval of pacing footsteps and ambiguous sounds of muffled voices slowly disrupted my already inadequate slumber. Detecting conscious activity, my ikes gently reactivated the translucent interface before my eyeballs. My eyes didn't react well to the influx of light, so I slowly opened them, focusing on the sungauge in the corner. Acknowledging that it was still a couple arcs shy of sunrise, I suspected that I was dreaming, but as new information trickled through my senses, I was forced to admit that it was no dream. I groaned in response to the unpleasant aches associated with resting on the stiff makeshift bed.

Even through my groggy vision, I could detect the Enforcer's presence along with other resistance officers as they hovered over a noptic screen which relayed updates from the reactor team. I lowered my body back to the pile of wood, hoping that my senses would clear. Even though the Enforcer detected my stirring, there was no command to rush to my feet.

Once I felt like I was at least halfway to alertness, I sat up and temporarily removed my ikes to rub my eyes. After a few blinks, I detected the bulky layered armor of General Seechi and the sand colored threads of General Cruz. Maxwell too had a position adjacent to a tapper as he provided continual updates on the team's progress.

"Where are they now?" the Enforcer asked as I approached the circle of strategists.

"Already in the chamber," Maxwell replied. "Streetz has assumed control of the security system, but he relayed trouble about bypassing the gates."

"Casualties?" the Enforcer asked, sensing that intel to follow would be grim.

"Half," Maxwell replied grimly, knowing that few wanted to face the reality of such an outcome.

Silence enveloped the room as everyone stared at the tactical screen. The leadership present was fully versed in war's indiscriminate behavior to age. While it had consumed many who acknowledged the threats, it was still a tough moment to address the loss of those sacrificed both young and outside the realm of military service.

Typically, the Enforcer bore an expressionless state on his face, but I could still perceive a level of internal tension on account of his decision to involve Subterra. He did his best to redirect everyone's attention back to the matter at hand, hoping to prevent any additional burden on the shoulders of those present.

"Charges set. Three clicks to boom," Maxwell said.

The Enforcer and military figures quietly walked outside to monitor the effects of the power plant's destruction. I followed closely behind to witness the navy colored ink dominating the pre-morning sky offset by the illumination of Core City's superstructures. It boggled my mind that even after so many passes of crisis, Core City still continued to operate at such active social levels around the gauge.

As the synchronized countdown suggested the result of an unheard explosion, a growing hum spanned across the enclave center, darkening the urban parcels one by one, but as the wave of power shortages reached Casters Tower, the blackout ceased, leaving the blocky iconic building illuminated like a candle in a dark room. As gripes rumbled through the nearby ranks of soldiers on patrol, several parcels adjacent to the tower regained power in short order.

"Looks like we have our next objective," the Enforcer said as he made his way back to the op table.

"The tower must have a local power source," General Cruz added as the strategists reclaimed their positions.

"Any impact on the white-eyes?" the Enforcer asked.

"Inconclusive," Maxwell replied, unable to find relevant data.

"It appears that it is time to deliver the Commerical Empire its severance package, from the neck up," General Seechi said as his hand tensed around the sword handle at his waist.

"I think we knew that this was inevitable," the Enforcer replied.

"Intel reports that COJR forces are slated to arrive by midday," General Cruz said, following a message delivered by a subordinate.

"Let's hope that their support will be enough," the Enforcer replied.

"What is the infiltration team's status?" General Seechi asked.

Everyone looked down at Maxwell, but his expression wasn't reassuring, "I've lost all comms. Sensors registered an internal explosion before the reactor detonation."

I watched the Enforcer and General Seechi exchange looks. It was evident that both had confidence in the team's abilities and didn't need to manufacture faulty optimism, yet both knew the continual influx of sour intel wouldn't bode well for morale.

"I'm not counting them out, General," the Enforcer replied even though his own doubts tempered his confidence.

After a tense silence, the Enforcer returned his focus to the tactical display and input multiple navigation markers, each adjacent to an urban bridge crossing the Winzy river. I assumed that the three highlighted regions correlated to the prior breakdown of force deployment.

"Jenkins is no more a strategist than his subordinates, but he's smart enough to protect his assets. I suspect that if we wait for reinforcements, he'll suspect a stronger attack from the south. General Seechi, you and I can advance from the southernmost angle in search of a weak point, or at least create a distraction. General Cruz, since you have the greatest command of hardware, I recommend pushing the strongest assault from the central bridge where the transportation corridors are most likely defended. If the request isn't too forward of me, I'd like to request a couple of Squirms to support the Behemoth at close quarters. Fox, this is where you come in. The Behemoth and Squirms will lend support from the northernmost bridge, but hang back. This will give Szazs an opportunity to manage the hijacked raptors. Naturally, I want at least one able body protecting that piece of hardware," the Enforcer said.

After expanding the outline, the Enforcer graciously entertained feedback from the older, more experienced veterans. With the oddities of the conflict already on full display, and given the amount of trust, there was little argument to be had regarding the Enforcer's approach. After nods of agreement were unanimous, the Enforcer powered down the noptic display, scooped up Maxwell and followed the generals outside where their operations had already been staged.

I followed the Enforcer, but I felt an awkward burden, still perplexed as to why I was being tasked with such a responsibility, despite having no military experience. I felt that my contributions thus far were at best, trivial.

"Mac, it's still a rather tall order," I said as hustled to catch up in the cool morning air.

The Enforcer turned to reply with the exasperated but patient reply of a parent. I sensed his exhaustion, but he still never wavered in his commanding presence. "Fox, I know that you've been through more than you could imagine within the last bench, but if I didn't believe in your capacity, I wouldn't have asked."

"No margin for screw-ups. These are heavy decisions that impact life-or-death levels of consequence that compound quickly," I remarked.

"Mistakes are bound to happen, but since you already know the weight of having to make up for them, leverage that pressure to minimize them," the Enforcer followed-up with his soft reply. He left me to contemplate my role underneath the sunrise while he departed to coordinate with the military minds.

I struggled to fathom why the Enforcer had so much more confidence in my abilities than I did myself. I was not a student of war, but given the context, I needed to become one fast. I began my stroll toward the Behemoth which was parked a parcel over from our makeshift base camp. If the day had great challenges ahead, I needed to find a way to get ready for them.

Urban Floor
Core City, Windstonne Enclave
Commercial Empire, Northam Continent
Thread: sysObserver.cmd

General Cruz continued to monitor the disposition of the troops under his command as they mobilized, ready for the Commercial Empire's defenses. Cruz couldn't deny that morale was shaken, given the atrocity of pitting soldiers against their own. It was too early to reach a breaking point because Cruz knew that the outcome of this conflict set the course of the Global Alliance to follow. The Commercial Empire and Westcrest already had a turbulent history, and no one wanted to see conflicts of the past renewed.

With soldier and hardware alike moving forward at an acceptable pace, General Cruz ducked into his Sandstorm tank and closed the hatch overhead. Cruz nodded to Lieutenant Tiago, relaying that operations where to proceed. Without needing an invitation, Sergeant Vick notched the tank forward while chewing on the stick hanging from his mouth, a habit he had been allowed as long as it kept him distracted from unleashing his blunt vocabulary against the chain of command.

Lieutenant Tiago kept his eyes trained on the comm hardware specially outfitted for the general's tank. Cruz didn't require updates as long as he wasn't distracted with overall coordination. As icons blipped on the targeting sensors, he suspected that the Commercial Empire still had plenty of razerjacks and fibernetic abominations to throw at the resistance.

"Alcazaban forces, stagger positions. I want a one to one ratio of infantry divisions to tanks. There may still be plenty of tigers ahead of us, so I don't want them ripping apart the last of our hardware. Lock down all Sandstorms until consecutive formations can advance," Cruz said into the comm.

After a series of acknowledgement light blinks, Cruz ordered Vick to bring their tank up behind the leading formation of Sandstorms. The means in which Vick bit down on the stick suggested that he wanted to mouth off, but he held his tongue instead. Cruz knew that Vick would have protested their position which put command too close to danger, but Cruz couldn't afford to project leadership from such a distant position when morale was already at a low. If their leader wasn't strong enough to guide them, then no one was.

As the advance formation reached the roads parallel to the Winzy river, Cruz studied the scans which revealed a sparse line of Goliaths, tigers and Pirans guarding the bridge.

"Fire at will!" Cruz ordered.

As the orders hit the headsets of the Sandtorm tank pilots, Cruz heard a concussive volley of firepower as it unleashed from the front line until it was joined by the staccato bursts emitted from the infantry firearms. Optics were obscured by the signature dust kicked up by the Sandstorm tanks on the front line, but Cruz still maintained awareness of the situation by ear and noptic display alike. Noise from Alcazaban forces was returned in the form of Goliath gatling plasma and the guttural roars of tigers as they were ripped apart. Hostile icons on the tactical display started to dwindle.

As opposition was thinned, General Cruz ordered the second line to advance and lockdown until he could assess the situation. As optics cleared, Cruz spotted another wall of Goliaths which protected the opposite end of the bridge while the bridge itself remained clear.

"Front line, resume shelling until the opposing bank is clear. I have no interest in getting caught in a chokepoint. Advance two Squirms and a Sandstorm. When they reach the midpoint, send another set with infantry," Cruz ordered.

General Cruz knew the dangers of committing to such a hazard in the open, but given the urgency, there was likely no alternative to crossing the Winzy in such a fashion. The loud shriek of a raptor pierced the air as it flew overhead to cover the units from above. The raptor circled before tracing the river's path with its massive wings, casting a shadow on the water. Cruz permitted himself a moment's relief at having Protech Szazs lend support. After banking to the side, the raptor dove and scooped a Goliath in its massive talons before dumping it into the river.

Several Goliaths diverted attention toward the raptor, but their fire was interrupted as an explosion rippled underfoot, launching pieces of the bridge skyward. The majority of the bridge folded inward as its supports gave way underneath.

General Cruz watched in horror as an irreplaceable number of his men went down with the heavy armor. Squirm pilots at the edge of the collapse scrambled to exit the top hatch. The light armored vehicle fell, but the pilots found themselves caught in a massive raptor claw before watching their vehicle get caught up in another. The Squirm and its pilots were set down alongside a similar set of rescuees before the two controlled raptors dove to lift the sinking Sandstorm tank. In tandem, the raptors sank their talons deep and lifted the heavy tank into the air with strain before dropping it on a smoldering pile of dead Imperan forces.

Without time to celebrate the partial recovery, Cruz barked into the comm, "The bridges are rigged! I repeat, the bridges are rigged! All forces hold position until access is secured!"

"All forces hold!" General Cruz shouted again. He felt like he had been hit with a brick after watching more of his men die at the hands of the enemy. The Commercial Empire continued to deal one blow after another. The resistance wouldn't last much longer without support. Cruz simply hoped that his warning was received and that the COJR forces arrived before it was too late.

Thread: sysObserver.cmd

The inbound warning from Alacazaban forces escalated the urgency for the scouting team. The Enforcer followed close behind General Seechi and his two ranking Ghosts as they sprinted for the marked bridge across the Windstonne river. Their objective transformed from weakness identification to securing compromised roads.

"Ryoukai, General. We'll shift priorities to neutralization of structural threats," the Enforcer replied.

"I'll await your findings, Cruz out," General Cruz said.

General Seechi allowed the Enforcer to take point as he headed south and monitored his ikes for potential threats. Just before reaching the last parcel between the scouting team and the bridge, the Enforcer's electromagnetic filter lit up, revealing multiple Goliaths. A raw visual check confirmed that tigers were present as well.

"Looks like a job for us," Seechi whispered.

"I'll follow, but you know I'm still tech reliant," the Enforcer replied.

General Seechi nodded in response and then sprinted with his subordinates following close behind. The Enforcer engaged his cloak and dashed along behind them. Even with his own harsh training, the Enforcer found himself trailing behind the armor laden Ghosts. Both General Seechi and the upper ranked Ghosts bore the iconic heavy layered armor of the Martial Legion's traditional warrior class. Even the specter ranked Ghost, while still sporting a smattering of tech, had his share of dense armor compared to the Enforcer. With such a disparity in physical output, the Enforcer knew that his advantage of fewer passes in age counted for nothing. General Seechi himself proved that age itself could at times be masked by strict conditioning.

As the Ghosts approached the garrison of Imperan forces protecting the bridge, they started shifting toward any shadow possible, difficult as it was in early daylight. Even with a thorough outsider's understanding of the Ghost ayvek of Yuurei, the Enforcer still marveled at the stealth operators' ability to always ascertain the focus of their enemies, not to mention their capacity to move in silence at a full sprint.

Halting underneath the closest Goliath, the Enforcer took a moment to assess the razerjack's structure. Thus far all encounters had been from a distance. He double-checked his cloak, considering that he could be crushed instantly, if detected by a pilot that decided to march the Goliath forward.

Without time to entertain curiosity in full, the Enforcer captured relevant info to his ikes then watched Seechi take up a position next to a loose crate by the railing at the streets edge. The Ghosts leapt over the railing and held onto it from the opposite side until achieving proper positioning to shimmy down to the bridge supports.

General Seechi kept his eyes trained on the Ghosts until he received a hand signal to confirm explosives on both bridge supports. With interpretation of the signals lost to memory, the Enforcer watched Seechi return a similar set of motions to ascertain means of defusing the explosives. The Ghosts replied with an affirmative motion and got to work on the process.

Trusting his subordinates, Seechi shifted his attention to the bridge itself, no obstacles in sight. The Ghosts under the bridge had adequate cover, but Seechi would be vulnerable in the open. Taking in the dilemma, the Enforcer looked for an alternate solution.

"General, I think it's time to make a blast from the past," the Enforcer said.

Seechi nodded and made note of the crate used for cover, it had regulatory munitions text all over. Suitable for noise, the general then spotted similar crates scattered about the Imperan formation.

Additionally, one Goliath had been lowered, its pilot dismounted to speak with allies.

"Enforcer to Cruz, southern bridge secured, in part. Advise, strategic relocation and use of... diversion. We'll need one to get out of here," the Enforcer said into the comm.

"Acknowledged," Cruz replied

"Okay, time to chuck some rocks and burn their socks," the Enforcer whispered.

Upon receiving Seechi's confirmation, the Enforcer sprinted toward the parked Goliath, throwing an Inferno grenade into the cockpit before sprinting toward the closest munitions crate. General Seechi was already doing the same, dropping Neubula grenades as he ran, providing cover and confusion.

The duo's actions created yells of confusion from the Imperan forces. With the task accomplished, the Enforcer and General Seechi bolted across the bridge. With Alcazaban position markers already on arrival, the Imperan forces were quick to focus on the larger threat.

"Ghosts, report!" Seechi snapped, no longer able to use silent communication.

"Round two nullified by the time you reach us, Sir," one Ghost replied.

The Enforcer and General Seechi broke into a full sprint across the bridge, but they only made it a quarter of the way across when movement on the far end drew their attention. A Goliath started making its way toward the conflict to support allies.

"We have to close the gap before it sees us," the Enforcer said in between breaths.

The Goliath trained its guns on the advancing Alcazaban forces, but Seechi observed its pace, watching it decelerate as it detected the Ghost in the open. The Goliath gunner spun the turrets toward the bridge. At the same time, the Enforcer disengaged his cloak revealing his position. The hesitation in choosing targets bought General Seechi the time he needed. The Ghost leader drew his katana from his waist cocked his arm back and hurled the blade towards the pilot dome. The katana flew with such force that it penetrated the shielding and struck the pilot in the chest, forcing him to slump forward on the controls. The Goliath gunner struggled to correct his targeting as the razerjack lurched erratically.

Operating like a machine, the Ghosts tasked with securing the bridge sprinted into the open. General Seechi was already positioned underneath the Goliath with his hands cupped to boost the advancing Ghosts upward. The Enforcer stared as the Ghosts clambered up the razerjack's legs with ease like spiders. As one Ghost accessed the pilot hatch and assumed control, the other punctured the gunner dome, terminating its occupant. Within ticks, the pilot Ghost dislodged the dead pilot and dropped General Seechi's blade. As if by second nature, the Ghosts controlled the Goliath and started advancing the razerjack to fire upon Imperan forces from behind.

"That's impressive," the Enforcer remarked as Seechi deftly restored his katana to his waist.

"We've had to adapt, Mac. I've done everything within my power to keep the Ghosts aware of their resources, and that includes technology. It hasn't always been the way of our mixed heritage, but I've lost good Ghosts all because of a technological disadvantage, something that I never wish to repeat," Seechi replied somberly.

"Let's ensure that the body count flatlines here so that you can carry on that legacy," the Enforcer replied.

Without argument, Seechi nodded and the longtime allies trailed behind the commandeered razerjack, ready to insert distractions into the battle between the Alacazaban and Imperan forces. With mechanical resources dwindling and manpower faltering, the resistance would need to turn the tide soon.

Thread: actTgtPersp1.view

The sounds of plasma fire, explosions and battle yells still penetrated the hull of the Behemoth, slamming my ears even above the mechanical grinding of the plodding Behemoth and the advancing Squirms below. For a moment, I leaned over to watch Szazs' progress as he guided the hijacked raptors to lend support to Alcazaban forces. Maxwell kept his eyes trained on the control console until we reached our designated waypoint by the river.

Strangely, I found no hostiles in the street adjacent to the bridge. The motion tracker lit up with hostiles on the far side of the bridge, but they hadn't taken an interest in our presence. I passed instruction to the Squirms to advance cautiously as I down shifted the Behemoth.

The Squirms reached the edge of the bridge just as General Cruz's warning about the bridges being rigged blared through the comm. My eyes widened as I observed the triangle treads of the Squirms advancing toward the bridge.

"Alcazaban Squirms, Pull Back!" I immediately snapped as I punched the comm button.

The Squirms did not halt easily. Although they hadn't made it far, they weren't out of danger, considering that they had no reverse mechanism. Their respective pilots utilized the tight turn radius, but opposing forces still opted to blow the bridge. The first Squirm made it to safety, but the opposite unit teetered on an angled portion of the collapsing bridge.

"Szazs?" I asked tensely without needing to elaborate my concern after watching the informatech deftly rescue the other Alacaban units.

"Already on it," Szazs replied.

Before the Alcazaban pilots could even contemplate evacuation, large talons clamped onto the vehicle's roof, and with a giant wing flap dragged the machinery back to safety. I let out a deep exhale that there were no casualties on our end so early. I relayed my thanks and that of the soldiers below to the protech.

"Maxwell, what's our next likely option to wreak havoc?" I asked.

"There are more bridges to the north, and I suspect those are rigged as well. We might be able to utilize the overpass from the dartway. It would take way more explosives to bring it down, but it is also out of the way," Maxwell replied.

"Alcazaban Squirms, we need to make a detour to the north. Are your machines still battle ready?" I asked.

"We're not missing out on the action, Sir," came the reply from the Alcazaban contact.

"Acknowledged. Let's get a move on," I replied.

After some awkward maneuvering, the Behemoth was finally directed parallel with the river and gradually increased in speed. I had yet to witness the Behemoth at top speed, and upon experiencing the acceleration, I admitted that it wasn't something that I wanted to endure for a prolonged period of time. The noise was almost deafening as the mechanisms powering the four-legged razerjack pounded the pavement with long strides. I observed the rear monitors to see sizable cracks in the streets below. As speed increased, so too did my paranoia of accidently toppling the razerjack by clipping irregular terrain.

As the Behemoth advanced with the Squirms trailing at a distance, I kept an eye trained on the opposite bank of the Winzy and spotted a contingent of Goliaths moving at a rapid clip toward the south. As data poured in from the contest happening at the southernmost bridges, I suspected that the havoc required the Imperan forces to call for backup.

"Maxwell, where are those Goliaths going?" I asked upon realizing that they weren't compelled to face the towering razerjack opposite them.

"Based on the present speed and statcheks, I suspect that they're going to close in on our allies," Maxwell replied.

"If resistance forces have already pushed through one line, will they be a problem?" I asked.

"It isn't the firepower that's the issue. Cruz's forces have entered the next corridor. They will get trapped if those Goliaths close from behind," Maxwell said nervously.

"We have to warn them. Open the comm," I snapped.

After a delay following the hamster's numerous inputs to the command console, he stared back at me and shook his head, "I'm getting interference."

"Not good," I rambled. "Protech, can the raptors be used to hinder Imperan progress?"

"I'm already utilizing them for defense. I cannot find an opening," Szazs replied.

"Then I guess I'll have to deliver the haps in person," I replied stiffly as I stood from the command chair.

"You'll never make it time on foot," Maxwell remarked, clearly thinking that I was daft at the suggestion.

"Only if have to hoof it," I said as made my way toward the Behemoth's body.

"I really get the sense that he doesn't like piloting this thing," Maxwell said as he looked over at Szazs who simply shrugged in response.

Rather than bother with the interior lights, I toggled my ikes and switched to the night vision filter, bathing the interface in green light. With my proficiency becoming second nature, I was able to focus on finding my objective, the Drakken glider-pack. I snatched the liberated gear and headed for the cockpit.

"Fox, park your verts," Maxwell snapped upon my return. "I'm detecting a Drakken carrier. They are known to utilize scramblers during deployment.

I doubted Maxwell's assessment, but to be sure, I leaned over the command console which showed allied and hostile forces across the noptic display. Only seeing grounded forces, I intended to correct the hamster, but before I could, countless dots blinked onto the display in the airspace above Windstonne. Agitated, I plopped back down in the command chair.

"Allies will shred you alive without the ability to distinguish friend from foe," Maxwell said softly.

Acknowledging that Maxwell was right, I had no reason to gripe about the situation, "Then I guess we better do our part to thin them out."

Maxwell was about to agree when new signals lit up on the display, "Hold that thought. I've got incoming."

"Who is it?" I asked.

"Signatures suggest COJR aircraft," Maxwell replied.

"Reinforcements? How far out?" I asked.

"Trajectory puts them on the Casters Tower doorstep, and they aren't replying to any resistance comms," Maxwell said with wide eyes.

"White-eyes?" I asked, looking nervously from Maxwell over to Szazs.

"Likely, given our lack of insight into Jenkins' operations," Szazs replied.

"Then we best get this bolted frame back in the fight," I said.

"Aye, Boss," Maxwell replied as he attempted to coax more speed out of the razerjack.

I dropped the glider-pack which was still in hand and sat forward, keeping my eyes trained on the tactical display. I was thankful that having competent allies prevented me from diving into a crisis, but I still felt anxious, knowing that there was no way to anticipate our enemy's next move.

DAVE TODD

34 – Line of Skirmish – 34

Windstonne Central Power Station
Core City, Windstonne Enclave
Commercial Empire, Northam Continent
Thread: sysObserver.cmd

Sharp tingling leg pain jolted Torque's brain back into a conscious state. Mentally, he felt nothing but blackness as he struggled to recall his location. He tried to move his leg, but a large object held it in place. He tried to open his eyes, but the effort caused enough pain to force hesitation. Even as his eyelids slowly moved, only a dull orange and gray glow defined his surroundings.

Torque forced himself to look around, grogginess impairing his senses. He spotted red splotches on collapsed chunks of wall nearby. He gingerly touched his fingers to the side of his head, but swiftly retracted them upon detecting blood on their tips. Assessing the damage was nigh impossible in the dim lighting.

"Alright, now I'm mad," Torque intended to yell, but the words barely achieved the volume of a grunt.

"You're always mad about something," mumbled a familiar raspy voice.

"Right, but now I've got a reason. These fish messed up my hair," Torque grumbled about his normally spiky cut being matted to the side by blood, sweat and crust.

With much pain, Torque squeezed his leg free of the pinning debris so that he could find his ally. He rolled onto his stomach and notched his way in the direction of the Serpent's voice. Torque barely moved before wishing to retract his petty statement after seeing the twisted arm of a Ghost pinned under the rubble. There was no helping the one who had been completely crushed under the weight of the collapsed wall.

Torque found the Serpent pinned under a fallen walkway chunk. The Serpent's arms were free, but the obstacle in place gave him no leverage to budge the heavy debris. Torque placed his hands under a corner of the metal so that the Serpent could assist. After a couple clicks of shifting the grate, the Serpent managed to wriggle free. With relief, he propped himself up, able to breathe freely without the heavy restraint.

"That had to be boring, laying around with nothing to do," Torque remarked.

"You have no idea. I almost took up poetry," the Serpent groaned as he checked for broken ribs.

The Serpent stood slowly with a manageable amount of discomfort. Basic senses told him that not everything was functioning correctly, but a full health assessment would have to wait. He narrowed his secondary eyelids to visualize the situation in the dim lighting and haze. Seeing the deceased Ghost that Torque had passed, he feared a similar outcome for others.

"Ghost Kairudo, statchek," the Serpent hissed.

The Serpent and Torque held their breath in the dim, dusty lighting, listening for signs of life. Even without waiting for a technical response, Torque started to scour the imploded entryway for any positive sound.

"Any Ghost, statchek," the Serpent shouted.

"Specter Tagawa, here," a strained voice said into the comm.

Torque switched his ikes to the thermal filter, washing his lenses in a blue light. With smoldering heat pockets, Torque was unable to discern any life sources, so he tweaked the vision mode to add the organic enhancement covering the scene with scanlines and a segmented purple view. At last Torque spotted an orange hot spot identifying the Ghost's position near the tunnel which led to the entryway. The Ghost's hybrid bodysuit, issued relative to his rank, had shielded him from part of the blast. After an injury check, Torque helped the disoriented Ghost to his feet.

The Serpent continued to scan dark areas of the entryway, looking for signs of additional survivors, only to find the crushed and mangled bodies of his brothers, some burned beyond recognition. Angered that the Imperan explosive had done its job so efficiently, the Serpent turned to help Torque free the lone survivor. At least reassured that one made it, the Serpent did his best to choke down the rage within. A strong reluctance to continue clouded his thinking, knowing that these operatives had been under his care, but stronger yet was the need to continue so that the vectors lost in the conflict were nothing more than a sample of the destruction that the Commercial Empire would still exact.

"We should get moving," Torque said quietly.

The Serpent could only reply with a nod. He then held Tagawa's arm to help the Ghost right himself. Torque leaned beneath the Ghost's other arm and assisted with the walk out of the reactor station. The Serpent took the lead as the trio made their way outside, but he couldn't help that his eyes wandered in hopes of more survivors.

Just as the team reached daylight, the Serpent spotted the body of another unconscious Ghost. Kneeling down, the Serpent checked for a pulse. He found one, albeit faint. The Serpent was ready to hoist the Ghost onto his shoulder but hesitated as the survivor stirred.

"Who is he?" the Serpent asked, not recognizing the operative.

"Wraith Simon Chung. He was a rather promising recruit who joined shortly after your departure," Tagawa said.

The mobile members of the team waited for the unconscious Ghost to come around. After verifying his ability to move, the Serpent helped the younger Ghost. Concerned about the threat of Pirans arriving on the scene, the team was ready to move, but they were interrupted prior to their departure.

"Where do you think you're going?" a hushed voice asked.

The Serpent spun about to see a fellow specter and wraith, carrying an unconscious and heavily injured Kairudo with his arms across their shoulders. Wraith Hikashi exhibited the most energy and managed to speak up, but Specter Philips didn't appear to be in much better condition as indicated by the scorch marks and damage to his armor. Even ranking Ghost Kairudo didn't look alive given the gash on his head and the brutal split in the operative's large tiered helmet. The Serpent was reticent to hope that Kairudo was alive, but he knew his subordinates wouldn't have carried him if they didn't believe that the Ghost was still alive. The Serpent only allowed himself a glimmer of hope in seeing more survivors, but he knew that he had to stay focused to prevent the sacrifice of those lost on the mission from being undone by the Imperan forces still at large.

Urban Floor
Core City, Windstonne Enclave
Commercial Empire, Northam Continent
Thread: sysObserver.cmd

General Cruz barked orders at the top of his lungs. He doubted the reception of his orders since he couldn't hear his own yells above the explosions all around, combined with the frequent shelling of the Sandstorm tanks.

Two Sandstorms had already cleared a path to the bridge and moved to secure the adjacent cross streets. The tanks were in the process of locking down their stanchions when Cruz ordered all soldiers closest to the tanks to provide cover. Cruz spotted a Goliath advancing on their position at a fast clip. The Alcazaban commander was about to order forces to fire when he watched the Goliath turn its weapons on fleeing Imperan units. Doubting the visual, Cruz rubbed his eyes and got a direct line of sight. Once he saw two familiar forms trailing the

Imperan razerjack, he exhaled, relieved that he hadn't taken out friendlies.

"Nice work, Gentlemen," Cruz shouted into the comm as he watched the Enforcer and General Seechi withdraw to the Alcazaban formation while the hijacked Goliath halted to cover smaller artillery units that moved into position on the bridge.

"We brought you a souvenir, General," the Enforcer replied.

"It's not my favorite color, but it will do," Cruz chuckled.

"Just throw some mud on it, and it will blend right in," the Enforcer said.

General Cruz appreciated the brevity, but he that knew there was no time to celebrate, "Fortify the far bank!"

The hijacked Goliath and multiple Squirms advanced across the bridge to secure the way for the slower Sandstorm tanks. Units still in lockdown fired shells across the river as Imperan infantry dared reveal their positions by firing on the advance resistance units.

Once the far bank was secured and the closest tanks locked down, Cruz ordered the next wave to advance while two tanks remained to cover the occupied end of the bridge. As resistance units filled the corridor on the far bank, another wave of Goliaths stomped into the corridor. All units in range opened fire immediately, dropping the first two Goliaths. One raptor flew just above the street, extending its broad wings, severing or buckling the razerjacks' legs.

Despite the consolidated firepower of the resistance combined with aerial support, the Goliaths kept pouring into the corridor. Sniper contrails started lacing the sky from decks above the conflict, but the added range was only suitable to impair the ground forces. Cruz checked the tactical display to gauge just how many Goliaths were in play, but interference was scattering objects in the air. Cruz tasked Tiago with confirmation of the readings, only to discover that the interfence markers were legitimate hostiles.

General Cruz popped the hatch on his Sandstorm tank and looked up to see black dots peppering the sky, only to form triangular shapes as they loomed closer. There was no doubting the signature shape of the Drakken gliders dropping on the resistance forces.

"We've got more aerial incoming," Cruz snapped into the comm.

Lieutenant Tiago read the comms regarding COJR forces and hesitated to relay the update, "Sir, update from Fox suggests that Jungyan forces have crossed Imperan lines without incident."

Cruz clenched his teeth unsure how to respond to the update. As plasma began to splash down from the incoming Drakken units, he dropped back into the Sandstorm tank and closed the hatch.

"All forces advance into the trenches. Anything in the open will be vulnerable," Cruz ordered reluctantly. He didn't like adapting strategy in such a way, but the tall towers of Windstonne would minimize mobility of the airborne threats.

Taking in the tower lined horizon across the river, General Cruz's mind was flooded with memories of similar enclaves prior to the Global War. Libertas had many such great enclaves exceeding even Windstonne, but following the conflict they were reduced to husks or abandoned altogether. While much of Windstonne's inner culture had been preserved, war had finally breached its perimeter. Cruz knew there was responsibility to be shared in the destruction of a lingering free standing enclave on the Northam content, but after a moment he shook off the guilt, knowing that the value of lives superseded that of the architecture.

Tiago gathered all of the requested datapoints on the structures listed by Cruz. Quickly identifying the desired configuration, Cruz highlighted four towers neighboring the intersection ahead of resistance forces. Each of the buildings had modernized powered conduits ascending the sides. The conflict may have prompted suspension of power to the buildings, but the plasma lines were likely still hot. Tiago helped Cruz consolidate scenarios and identified firing points which were then relayed to Sandstorm pilots.

General Cruz relayed targeting orders and then commanded respective gunners to hold. Chatter questioning the reason for firing on civilian structures was quickly silenced, allowing Cruz to focus on the advancing Goliaths on his display.

"Fire!" General Cruz barked as the Goliaths stomped into the corridor beneath the conduit lines.

In one unified deafening volley, the Alcazaban forces unleashed their firepower on the selected conduits. With two conduits on opposing sides of the street, both high and low, the ruptures created a crisscross convergence of plasma as it was shunted into the street. The plasma smothered the Goliaths, bathing them in a light blue flame.

A tumultuous cheer rose from the soldiers who witnessed the demonstration of military precision. With a glimmer of hope surging through the ranks, all resistances forces regrouped and moved to secure the next corridor leading them toward Casters Tower.

Thread: sysObserver.cmd

Dust and air were still settling from a recent impact, but the Enforcer kept his eyes locked on the patio doorway. After a seven deck stair climb, the Enforcer, General Seechi, Private AWOL and several squads of Alcazaban infantry advanced into a business complex to secure a perch to counter the incoming Drakken. Private AWOL was tasked with relaying comms from the infantry back to the Enforcer who had command. After a delay, the patio door opened and Private AWOL nodded the all-clear signal. The Enforcer followed up with a hand gesture for remaining units to advance.

The Enforcer deactivated all filters on his ikes and noted the debris littered across the patio which was normally used by building workers for recreation. The building was structurally sound, but the secondary impacts from the conduit ruptures made quite the mess. The debris served as welcome cover against Drakken opposition who had the aerial advantage. Snipers and related support were dispatched to cover the edge of the patio while others advanced to another access point and secured a position inside.

General Seechi remained close to the Enforcer's position, his hand continuously locked to the hilt of the blade at his waist. Even without aversion to ranged weapons, he felt most comfortable in a support role while his subordinates continued to operate the razerjack in the conflict below.

Bringing a Hellings 20 rifle up to this shoulder, the Enforcer pointed it in the general direction of incoming Drakken. The Alcazaban snipers followed his lead. The Enforcer switched his ikes to a finely tuned biomass filter, allowing him to detect hostile positions through the edge of the building which obstructed the gliding enemies from view. He softly called out the count and positions of the enemies relative to the building obstruction relative to the floor count. The soldiers each designated their targets and waited.

The tick that the first Drakken glider came into view, the Enforcer depressed the trigger of the rifle. The wispy contrail followed the dense plasma round that ripped a hole in the Drakken soldier's chest. The event initiated a volley of fire that struck many targets in similar fashion. As the Drakken continued to rain down with plasma fire, the Alcazaban snipers reloaded and fired in intermittent waves. The Drakken were too numerous to quell on the first wave alone, so support soldiers fired with Cutters of their own or EQ's already salvaged from the fight, turning the air over Windstonne into a firestorm of green and yellow plasma.

The Ghosts operating the razerjack were reluctant to be left out of the fight against their homeland opposition, so they spooled up the gatling rifles and unleashed torrents of plasma upward at the descending foes.

"Die, Drakken scum!" the words of the Ghost gunner said through the comm.

"Subtle," the Enforcer smirked, directing half a glance at General Seechi.

"Given the circumstances, I think that they're afforded some flexibility to... cut loose," Seechi chuckled.

"Bring them to the after-party, Sir, and I'll give them an updated definition," Private AWOL yelled as he continued unleashing plasma from his EQ into Drakken that managed to evade the sniper fire.

"We'll have to make that sure we're all alive for the party, Soldier," the Enforcer replied.

"Yes, Sir," AWOL replied, already acknowledging respect for the Enforcer after serving alongside Vanguard's other members.

The Enforcer wanted that outcome to be possible, and with the downpour of opposition, it was going to take more than numbers. It was going to require an optimism that could punch through the despair of being outgunned. The Enforcer allowed the surrounding noise to fade. He exhaled as he brought the sniper rifle to his shoulder again. He knew that the Hellings 20 had significant recoil, but the motion and the spent shell combined with the scattered range would impact his ability for multiple kills in succession. He gave himself several ticks to concentrate, ignoring the plasma zipping through the air. The stares by distracted soldiers created the concern for his mental faculty as he stood in the open.

Once ready, the Enforcer popped his eyes open, blinked into his ikes to target the three closest Drakken and fired upon each in succession. The expelled shells rang through the air as his shots found their marks, each termination was verified as the glider-packs and their owners spiraled downward, out of control.

Onlookers impressed by the spectacle wanted to cheer, but their own distraction gave inbound Drakken chance to get close to the patio ledge, landing so they could fire close quarters. Alcazaban soldiers panicked, trying to turn their weapons on the enemies who closed on their ranks, but their concerns were swiftly negated as General Seechi's form blinked out of sight, and then back to visible before two Drakken fell to the ground, victims of his katana. His form disappeared again, before reappearing to dispatch the remaining three Drakken who managed to touch down. Multiple mouths were agape after witnessing the Ghost general's speed firsthand. Never again did they question his ability or the potential drawbacks of his perceivably impractical armor.

After taking in the offensive maneuver, the Enforcer returned a faint nod and a smirk to Seechi as the general again took up a defensive position while returning his sword to its place. Such events were the kind that vectors would never forget so that they had a story to share whenever the odds seemed most dire.

Before he could sight up another target, the Enforcer hesitated as Vanguard markers popped back up on his ikes. He adjusted settings to compensate for interference and ensure that the comm was open. Static bled through the earpiece prompting him to fallback from the immediate conflict and mitigate the overall noise.

"Did we miss the after-party?" Torque's voice asked amidst the static.

"No, did your invitation get lost?" the Enforcer asked.

"Not exactly, but the last one sure got crashed," Torque replied. "What's our waypoint?"

The Enforcer felt a sense of relief upon hearing the voice of a friend. He quickly assessed the distance and found that the reactor team was not far from the Behemoth.

"You're several parcels north of the heat, but not far from the Behemoth. I'd advise that you regroup... and I'm glad that you made it, Friend," the Enforcer said.

"Ryoukai," Torque said.

"Dare I ask the scorecard?" the Enforcer said quietly.

"Total... minus seven," Torque said slowly. "Hit us with a Deathtrap on the way out."

The Enforcer was able to verify that both Torque and the Serpent's markers were reading strong. His personal sense of relief was stifled knowing that the operation cost so many Ghosts. General Seechi continued to linger within the Enforcer's line of sight knowing that his attention wasn't fully on the conflict. As the Enforcer closed the comm, he relayed the update to Seechi who clearly exhibited similar sentiments. It was encouraging to know that more survived than expected, but knowing that so many close friends would not make the return trip home instilled a large amount of grief. Before the longtime allies could fully ponder the outcome, the sound of aerial engines ripped through the air.

"Take Cover!" the Enforcer yelled as Alcazaban forces scrambled to find shelter in the building.

A firestorm of plasma pelted the patio, catching several Alcazaban snipers who were focused on their Drakken targets. The highly agile Tornado Alpha Class chopper angled its weapons to catch remaining forces heading into the business building for cover. The COJR aerial unit shifted for a better shot, shredding the building's exterior of glass and stone. The soldiers needed to move deeper in order fully escape the weapons fire, unless the enemy unleashed a missile.

The Enforcer stared at the craft, looking for a way to distract it. The agile Jungyan craft were reputed to be lethal from their maneuverability. It was still a chopper by design, but the craft had adaptable rotor blades that could lock in as wings. Combined with its powerful stabilizing engines, the Tornac easily darted about, making it a difficult target to hit.

Before any practical solutions came to mind, a large pair of wings overshadowed the enemy craft while a pair of talons tore through the unit's armor causing at least one engine fire. The Jungyan pilot fought to control the craft, but it hopelessly twisted sideways, crashing into a building a parcel over. As hope was rekindled, the hijacked raptor was pierced in the chest by two missiles from another Tornac chopper on approach. Recognizing that ground forces were no match for the aerial bombardment, the Enforcer dashed into the building to get the troops as far from the firefight as possible. The dead raptor was a high cost, but its loss preserved precious lives in the process.

Thread: sysObserver.cmd

Torque's frustration with the operation outcome continued to nag his mind. In part, he wanted to unleash a torrent of verbal gripes, but his injuries and the needs of the team survivors continually kept his impulses in check. At such times of challenge, Torque mused at the Enforcer's ability to rely upon his interferics study and practice of Hykima, something that Torque had never fully grafted into his regimen. Even though Torque had plenty of passes leading and following during the Global War, he still struggled to maintain the positive outlook needed to encourage those forging ahead. Stuck on deficits, Torque replayed the scenario at the Imperan reactor in his mind, wondering if something could have been done differently. War always brought risks, but even with foreknowledge of risks, it never brought comfort regarding those lost for those who remained.

As familiar buildings and signs of destruction breached the periphery of Torque's vision, he quickened his pace, encouraging the others to do the same. Torque felt distracted as he continually checked on the progress of his allies and kept a lookout for Imperan forces. Although Jenkins likely needed the bulk of his forces to protect Casters

Tower, war always had a host of flukes to account for when forces were cut off. Torque knew that he wouldn't feel safe until there was a large weapon and clear line of sight between himself and the enemy.

Torque knew that the team was close when the proximity marker which displayed on his ikes counted down the digits under one parcel. Fox had halted the Behemoth's advance long enough for the team to regroup. Torque did his best to break into a sprint despite his body's protest. With the utility lift already accessible, Torque helped the injured Ghosts and settled for a later ascent given the weight limitations of the lift. Once survivors were secured, Torque knew that he could divert his attention to exacting payback.

Thread: actTgtPersp1.view

Statistics and unit positions continuously updated on the Behemoth's tactical readouts as Maxwell did his best to keep up with constantly fluctuating data, but all of it faded into the background when Torque's voice came through on the Vanguard comm. I had nothing to add, but I listened intently as Torque updated the Enforcer of the reactor situation. As subtle as it was, I could sense the relief in the Enforcer's voice even though it was still masked by the responsibility that he continued to shoulder. I looked over to see Maxwell nod in approval as well that our friends were safe before he punched in designated coordinates to rendezvous with the survivors.

As the Behemoth changed course, I pondered how the Enforcer managed to uphold his stoic demeanor. I knew that he was still likely concerned for Sath's safety. He was concerned for the countless lives he never met, and yet he still functioned in an unwavering manner garnering the confidence of those around him. Even Torque and the Serpent pressed onward despite the destruction they survived. I knew that I was in the company of vectors with conviction far beyond my comprehension.

I exhaled as I resolved to do what little I could to ensure that my actions in some way lessened their burdens, preventing any doubt that someone was still trying to aid them in the battle ahead. As I slumped back in the command chair, I felt a sense of calm. At first, I found the mood confusing, but then as I reflected on the Enforcer's lectures thus far, I considered that perhaps things were finally taking on practical application after all. Focusing outward on others was starting to feel more advantageous than jamming my own frustrations into the equation.

Shortly after the regroup comm, I watched Szazs tense. I intended to question the cause of the behavior, but the tactical updates clearly displayed the loss of a raptor following the contest with the COJR forces. I supposed that all lingering hopes of reinforcements from any Southam region had been dashed after encountering more opposition.

The pause in advancement gave me a chance to keep an eye on the battle's progress, but I was undecided if I preferred watching from safety over actually having an impact on the conflict directly. Before I could make up my mind, the noise from the utility lift and arrival of the reactor team snapped me from my introspection. Just by glancing over my shoulder, I could tell that the Ghosts were in bad shape. I intended to move and lend aid, but the Serpent held up a hand to suggest he would see to injuries so that I could maintain command of the Behemoth.

After multiple uses of the utility lift, I knew that Torque had returned based on the rise in one-sided conversation volume. Rather than stow his gear or help the wounded he marched into the cockpit, "Alright, Jellyfish, let's say you let me drive for a piece."

Filled with a mixture of bewilderment and amusement, I looked from Maxwell up to Torque who stood adjacent to the command chairs, "That tomato splat on your face... Take care of that first, then we can negotiate."

I did my best not to break into a dopey grin. Torque flexed his hands into fists pretending to be angry, but I watched him relax before nodding and complying with the suggestion to treat injuries first. I detected a smirk, likely on account of his approval that I finally demonstrated some voluntary backbone at the basest level of identity within Vanguard.

I awaited confirmation that survivors were treated and locked in before resuming our advance. The Serpent finally entered the cockpit and signaled all-clear.

"How are they doing?" I asked, unsure how to offer encouragement.

"Ghosts do not break easily," the Serpent said softly.

I searched for words to add, but Maxwell was quick to relay updates on the COJR forces pushing back against our resistance allies, "We've got Jungyan forces all over the map. Two chopper variants, Tornado Alpha Class, their attack choppers, and Derechos, their transports. They're dropping Guerillas on every elevated landing that they can find and pinning down our forces three parcels west of Casters Tower."

"Ready for a strafing run?" I asked.

"Not without me," Torque interjected after the Serpent nodded. "Time for some payback."

I watched Torque and the Serpent slam a cross arm as I nodded for them to take position on the Behemoth's lateral turrets. With the Behemoth already increasing pace, I pushed for more acceleration after acknowledging that the other Vanguard members had the turrets deployed and ready to fire.

I knew that it was going to be a bumpy ride through the cluttered enclave streets, but with speed and weight, I doubted that there was hardware capable of halting the monstrous razerjack. We could rain plasma on enemy forces before they could regroup. I was finally ready to bring the fight to the enemy.

DAVE TODD

35 – Stragglers – 35

Executive Level, Casters Tower
Core City, Windstonne Enclave
Commercial Empire, Northam Continent
Thread: sysObserver.cmd

Frank Jenkins kept his hands clasped behind his back, as he paced about the skydeck where his officers had established their tactical command post. Scans of activity in the enclave below were hostile and numerous. He continued to fume about his recent observation of the enclave going dark after the power station had been halted. Despite reluctance to admit it vocally, for once, Jenkins was glad that he took the advice of installing a backup grid several passes prior. He still fed on his confidence that the paltry forces below wouldn't breach his domain.

"Sir, we have confirmation that Coalition forces have arrived. They have already engaged in pushing back resistance forces from ground and air," Command Pyln said gruffly as he stepped behind Jenkins.

"Good work, Commander," Jenkins replied without turning to acknowledge the Piran officer.

Commander Pyln simply nodded after recovering from his surprise that the faction leader complimented his efforts. Frank Jenkins was never one to utter even the slightest praise. Typically, appreciation was implied through the absence of verbal lashing. Disinterested in pressing his luck, Pyln returned his attention to coordinating comms with the foreign allies arriving in Windstonne.

The Coalition of Jungle Republics was a force that Jenkins never thought he would be working with to protect his control. Sure, a meager trade agreement existed between the continents benefiting both factions, but Jenkins knew that there was something else at work beyond mutually shared desire for power over their respective regions. Additionally, something else felt off about the contest happening in the streets below. Imperan forces had already succeeded in whittling down numbers of the resistance forces, preventing any suggestion of a second wave. The Commercial Empire and its allies had the numeric advantage even to win a short, defensive war, and yet something spurred the resistance beyond reason. Even throughout the brutal campaigns of the Global War, no battlegroup persisted with such determination. Surrender had always offered more agreeable terms than anything that the Imperan forces dished out.

Jenkins continued to chew on the mystery internally until he reflected on the events prompting the war, the very scoundrel who had eluded him for years during his quest for supremacy throughout both the Global War and the Smart Wars. Frank Jenkins clenched his teeth upon remembrance of such a festering nuisance. It was irrational to contemplate just how much influence a singular individual could have when so many lives were in the balance. Frank Jenkins was one man, and with his influence, he sculpted the factions by extreme force, but this Enforcer did no such thing, yet his influence stretched beyond the realm of human comprehension.

Konrad Oszwick silently stepped beside Jenkins who did his best to conceal his surprise that his internal musing allowed him to get distracted. The bald executive already perceived the faction leader's mood and did so without any sophisticated tech.

"Resistance forces have demonstrated a strong will. I think we can break it if we release them," Oszwick said quietly.

"Is that really necessary?" Frank Jenkins asked as he turned to face Oszwick.

"This is not a popularity contest, Mr. Jenkins. You've already lost that one. This is about exercising supreme authority... for the good of the factions," Oszwick replied smoothly.

Frank Jenkins turned back to the window and contemplated the added damage to be calculated, following the executive's suggestion. He had no desire to stare at a broken enclave, but he knew that there would be no lofty view ever again should the campaign fail. Jenkins sighed as he pressed his forearm to the window and stared at the streets below. After an internal debate, he nodded his agreement.

"You and I both understand the nature of your distress, and rest assured, Mr. Jenkins if we cut off the problem at the head, the body will fall," Oszwick said confidently, knowing that he had fully secured his influence over Jenkins' predictable and pliable personality.

Oszwick let his words permeate Jenkins' thoughts before leaving the faction leader to stew in his frustration Before exiting the skydeck, Oszwick snapped an order at the Piran officers, "Release the Magellans!"

Urban Floor
Core City, Windstonne Enclave
Commercial Empire, Northam Continent
Thread: actTgtPersp1.view

Tactical data flooded the Behemoth's command console, taxing my ability to keep up with it. Occasionally, I would pause certain data points, trying to identify the most concentrated Imperan groupings. Two separate icons yanked my attention once they flickered confirmations that Torque and the Serpent had deployed the Behemoth's side turrets.

"Brace for some mean turf," I said into the comm as I brought the Behemoth up to its max speed.

There were few obstacles on the civilian streets that could pose a threat to the massive weight of the razerjack, but it wasn't exactly designed for a smooth suspension at high speeds as the powerful motivators strained the massive gears operating its legs. Because of its long stride, the four-legged machine could match the average speed of any motorbox below. It wouldn't take long to catch up to the Alcazaban Squirms sent on ahead.

I did my best to ignore the banter and competition driven chatter from my allies through the comm as I watched a pair of Derecho choppers fly over the razerjack to drop Guerillas on the rooftops several parcels ahead of the Behemoth's position. Initially, Torque and the Serpent opened fired on the choppers which resembled transports of the Global War. The choppers were sluggish, but their bulky frames withstood distant turret fire. The choppers only required enough time to drop their troops before lifting out of firing range. Streams of plasma surged ahead of the front viewport as my allies targeted the troops. Despite their best efforts to dig in, most units were cut down as the Behemoth tromped down the enclave street. Torque griped as the Behemoth passed by optimal range for the turrets against the closest drop platform, guaranteeing that some hostiles survived the initial strafing run.

"Don't forget how to fight indirectly," the Serpent replied.

I required no explanation as I watched a view of plasma fire on the noptic screen target the floor and supports beneath the landing platform of the Guerillas. The destruction turned sections of the buildings into molten and jagged husks leaving only the bare structure, collapsing the floors beneath our adversaries. Clearly familiar with the carnage of war and its toll on allies Torque and the Serpent hollered as our enemies were dispatched. Although I had no personal insight into their recent experience, minus angry quips about Frank Jenkins' endeavors, I couldn't help but focus on the destruction that was obliterating civilian operations and residences, knowing that I too was responsible. I hoped that body counts were low on account of evacuation efforts, consolidating my focus on shortening the need for this conflict since similar destruction would only continue if Frank Jenkins wasn't stopped.

In between relaying pertinent information to Torque and the Serpent's ikes, I studied the nature of the Tornac chopper as a couple zipped by, pelting the Behemoth with return fire, which thankfully was mitigated by the razerjack's shielding. Maxwell illuminated a schematic showing that air vehicle could function as a chopper or small jet given the behavior of its rotors and the reliance upon jet propulsion for dynamic engagements. Even from my peripheral vision, I could see that the protech was struggling to keep the remaining raptors at odds with the fast moving aircraft.

Clusters of Imperan units blinked across the tactical display. I knew that we had to be closing on the primary conflict between Imperan and resistance forces, so I slowed the Behemoth's pace and sighted up the largest grouping of opposition. Maxwell gave me a nod once the planar cannon was ready. I squinted at the magnified view of the units on the ground and strangely I watched them start to scatter. Perplexed, I fired the planar cannon which hummed through the air, cutting through a chunk of hostiles, but due to their preemptive maneuvers, it was not as efficient a strike as I had hoped.

"Yeah, that's right! They know it's crunch time!" Torque hollered, sensing that our enemies were fleeing the looming razerjack.

As I watched more closely, I noticed that Imperan forces were only clearing the road. They weren't making a full retreat. There was something suspicious about their behavior. Additionally, while the Behemoth advanced sluggishly, I pondered if there was a strange vibration rumbling up through its legs.

"Maxwell, are we walking into a kill box?" I asked.

"No sign of explosion rigging or traps?" Maxwell replied after responding to a quick scan.

"Something's not right," I muttered into the comm.

"They're afraid of the upper hand," Torque belted back.

"Ayezon, Vanguard! They aren't running from us. The fact that they're clearing the road but not retreating suggests that they know something that we don't," the Enforcer snapped back, clearly still monitoring the Vanguard comm from his position on the ground.

I feared that the Enforcer was correct as the subtle tremors began to escalate. I suggested that Maxwell test for any seismic scans that he had available. He quickly produced a wave meter that continued to grow with a tick interval in between each spike.

"What is that?" I asked as I squinted at the scan.

"Something big," Maxwell replied.

"The concussive blast of the planar cannon, secondary explosions from Goliaths, and dust from nearby structural hits created quite the visual impairment of the road ahead. I shifted my focus from the noptic display to the viewport, and as I stared, a looming shadow began to form in the distance. I temporarily removed my ikes to rub my eyes, doubting what I was seeing. In the distance, a large metal framework roughly took shape in the obscuring haze. My eyes widened, realizing that I was staring at the midsection of a monstrous bipedal razerjack. The Behemoth's head rested around four decks from the ground with another two plus decks in height for its arched body, but this new threat towered over the Behemoth by another couple decks.

"What am I looking at?" I said in a panicked state.

"Mmm, signature reads Magellan... courtesy of Ozwick Enterprises," Maxwell said flatly.

Torque and the Serpent trained all turret fire on the new threat, but its dense armor appeared impervious to the barrage of plasma fire. Conversely, the tall razjerjack which looked like its head and been punched down into its chest, had two massive shoulders from which hung gigantic gatling rifles which began to spool up in response.

"Hamster, put us in reverse," I yelled.

"Reverse? This thing doesn't do reverse," Maxwell quipped.

Frantically I looked for a solution. The corridor on the Behemoth's immediate right was filled with resistance forces and would cause havoc for our allies, the corridor on the left put us too close to the consolidated Imperan forces. The only remaining option was to surge toward the next angled corridor.

"Full speed ahead! We need to make that next intersection," I snapped.

"That put's us too close to that thing," Maxwell countered nervously.

"Until you can figure out reverse, we have no choice," I said.

"Torque, Serpent, buckle up! This could get ugly," I said into the comm. If the Behemoth was about to scrape the sides of the urban trenches I didn't want them getting crushed.

As the Behemoth advanced and cleared the haze, I realized that there was not one but three Magellans bearing down on us. The razerjacks were so big that they couldn't march in a row and were forced to stagger formation. I clenched my teeth as massive rails began to slam the Behemoth. The rails were deflected by the Behemoths shield but the bombardment was shattering to the ears. I did what little I could to angle the Behemoth away from the target intersection before cutting sharply to the right. As expected for such a tight turn at high speed the Behemoth's right side scraped against the adjacent business tower, crushing glass and exposed supports. Magellan rails continued to pelt the exposed side of the Behemoth as it shifted toward the adjacent street.

"Shields can't take much more of this," Maxwell warned, the tension adding pitch to his normally low artificial voice.

I knew that the Behemoth's angular design in part helped deflect incoming projectiles, but there was no safety until we cleared the Magellan's line of sight. We needed to round the corner on the next parcel or inevitably a rail fired perpendicular to the Behemoth would rupture the shield. I had no clue as to the Magellan's top speed, but escape would involve out maneuvering the razerjacks past the next corridor.

As we cleared the next intersection, I directed the Behemoth back toward the Winzy river, but as it plodded parallel to the river, my stomach contracted. Directly ahead of us was another Magellan. The razerjacks couldn't have compensated fast enough to cut us off, I assumed that there were more of the units unaccounted for. I braked the Behemoth as effectively as I could. Our options were slim.

"Now what?" Maxwell asked.

"It's us or the river!" I yelled.

A bridge on our right crossed the Winzy between us and the Magellan proceeding up the bank. If I moved toward the bridge, there was no guarantee that any explosives were removed. Additionally, the Behemoth would be an easier target if the Magellan manually fractured the bridge. If I navigated the Behemoth to the left, we would stomp back into the thick of the prior Magellan formation. Without rear mounted weapons, the Behemoth would get sandwiched once the closest razerjack closed in. Given the size of the Magellans, there was no trampling it in a contest of mass either. I clutched my hands into fists unsure what to do. Even Torque and the Serpent had entered the cockpit and had no solutions to offer.

Knowing that there was nothing left but risks, I moved my hand to accelerate the Behemoth forward, opting to squeeze into another narrow trench, but before my finger connected with the control pad, concussive blasts peeled the through air leaving a bright trail of smoke after connecting with the closest Magellan. More mortars shuddered the air as more impacts targeted the Magellan before its upper third exploded violently.

"Somebody order a can of whupasse?!" a friendly voice shouted into the resistance comm.

"And a side of cries!" Maxwell added as he feigned a spitting motion toward the defunct Magellan.

"I see that we missed the appetizers," Potentate Ang said after executing the well coordinated strike on our razerjack blockade.

Shocked at the late arrival, I wanted to pop the hatch and get a visual, but I opted to first navigate the Behemoth into the clear so that the pursing Magellan's from the rear could receive a similarly warm reception from the new arrivals that quickly dotted the updated tactical readout. I finally exhaled and slumped back into the command chair, knowing that we had options which didn't involve dunking the Behemoth in the river.

"Boomerang, you are right on time," the Enforcer said into the comm, his voice conveying the relief felt throughout the resistance.

Even though morale received a giant boost, I was reluctant to savor the moment so easily. I verified that that Oshan forces were ready to fire on any threat accessing the street along the Winzy river. Given the lack of fireworks, I surmised that the destruction of one Magellan signaled a halt to the initial advance.

Once a pause was in order, I raised the hatch in the center of the Behemoth's head and looked south toward the newly arrived Oceanic Outpost forces. I was stunned by the display of personnel and hardware being deployed. Large tent shaped vessels logged as Venture class ships proved to be the primary transport mechanism since rivers separating the Commercial Empire's domain were likely too shallow for the bulk of the Oshan fleet. As the Venture ships held position, smaller hovercraft designated as Platypus models unloaded hundreds of soldiers on the banks of the river. Troops scrambled to setup relay points for awkward looking artillery units called Wombats, their massive cannons supported by a pair of treads dissimilar in size. Even without the tactical readouts from my ikes, I knew that those units had been responsible for halting the Magellan in our path, considering that numerous units had already been positioned on a secured bridge across the Winzy.

I was overwhelmed by the information which my ikes intended to put before my eyes as I took in the landscape. No doubt, the Enforcer had logged the information in the VNET since he had a working relationship with the Oceanic Outpost. Despite the challenge of information overload, I felt an uptick in optimism, but I knew that the state of emotional flux had to be contained. I didn't want any misplaced emotions clouding my judgement. I dropped back into the cockpit and settled into the command chair to await the next set of orders.

Thread: sysObserver.cmd

Commander Thomas Jackal locked his stance as he rode the Platypus hovercraft to the shore. In contrast to his responsibility for oversight of deployment, he couldn't help but scratch the itch which compelled him to get into the fight. It had been several passes since he had seen actual combat, so the rush of adrenaline flooded his system. With his subordinates finally clearing the bridge that connected them to the bank of Imperan terrain, Jackal followed and snatched a Mortimer cannon laying on top of a munitions crate.

COJR Tornacs flew by in the distance. Once or twice the pilots dared test the gunners aboard the Platypus vessels. Without confirmed kills, the mounting disinterest suggested that the aircraft were not as durable as the pilots hoped.

With all operations unfolding as expected, Jackal advanced toward the southern perimeter of Oshan deployment. His eyes darted in every direction knowing that hostiles were present high and low. The compressed barrel of the Mortimer pressed against his blue uniform sleeve as he cautiously peeked around the closest urban corner. The mechanical whirr in the distance verifiably belonged to Tornado Alpha Class chopper holding position just beyond view of the Oshan forces. The position didn't bode well in defense of the Imperan core, so Jackal knew it was acting as an observer.

In order to get a clean shot, Jackal would have to reveal his position. His battlethreads still bore the signature blue camouflage of Oshan colors which didn't do anything for disguise against the various grays of Core City. Confidently, Jackal strode into the center of the street where the Tornac hovered. The chopper pilot hesitated to assess if Jackal was a threat. As Jackal lifted the Mortimer cannon to his shoulder and twisted the collar, the pilot pressed forward on the control stick and aimed the guns at the singular target. The tube at the back of the Mortimer extended and its vents fanned in a circular direction.

Staring at the chopper, Jackal dared the chopper pilot to advance. With the attack craft moving quickly, Jackal adjusted the Mortimer for thermal tracking. As plasma peppered the road, Jackal squeezed the trigger, and with an explosive hiss, the Mortimer unleashed a dense ball of plasma, striking the underside of the chopper, detonating upon impact.

"How do you like me now," Jackal taunted as the Tornac fell to the ground in a ball of flame.

The commotion caught the attention of catspurs also patrolling the southern edge of the conflict. The bright orange wreckage in the street prevented the patrol from seeing Jackal, so a catspur guided his tiger toward the fire to inspect. Before Jackal could pull back to the support perimeter, the catspur spotted him and lunged the tiger forward.

Without time for shock at the matted, mutated mount, Jackal was already in motion. Mid-roll, Jackal snatched a Binder grenade from his belt and broke the pressure seal, its corrosive goo quick to break the outer glass seal.

"Here, hold that," Jackal said as the grenade leapt from Jackal's fingers and the green adhesive bound itself to the tiger's orange and black fur.

Oblivious to Jackal's actions, yet aggravated at missing its prey, the tiger whirled about and lowered its head, snarling as it prepared to pounce again. Jackal simply sneered as the beast lowered its body. The grenade attached to its belly exploded before the tiger could hit the air. The force from the grenade blew a hole in the tiger's abdomen and knocked it laterally a good five paces in addition to pinning its rider underneath.

With the tiger a lifeless heap, Jackal trained his eyes on the distance, waiting for additional tigers to advance. Hearing the explosion, more approached on either side of the burning chopper hull. As expected, the catspurs all expected to advance on their defiant foe who stood alone, but they all recoiled as a Platypus whisked into the intersection, its guns pointed at the tigers and their riders. Thomas Jackal smirked, pleased that his soldiers still had his back and that there was still plenty of fight to go around.

36 – Gut Check – 36

Resistance Forward Command
Core City, Windstonne Enclave
Commercial Empire, Northam Continent
Thread: actTgtPersp1.view

The cool air felt like a new experience after finally being granted the means to park the Behemoth and wait outside of the new makeshift base camp. The tiny ice cubes in my metal cup disappeared at last as they succumbed to the water temperature within. Anything less than the stuffy battle tension of the Behemoth's cockpit during a fight felt like a luxury. I rested by leaning up against a wall of the supermarket urgently transformed into a military post. In part, I felt out of place as the ever-present amount of activity swirled about me whether it was the construction of supply tents, treating of the wounded or continual munition checks and hardware repairs. I was witnessing firsthand activity of those who had spent their lives training and participating in war, whereas I was an outsider tossed into its midst.

Internally, I wanted to relax, but my conscious mind prevented entertaining the idea since there was still much to discuss once the officers and strategists regrouped which I suspected wouldn't happen until after sundown. Arrival of Oshan forces had certainly put the Commercial Empire on its heels, but the numbers and hardware at Frank Jenkins' disposal had forced the days contest into a stalemate with neither side willing to overextend. Light skirmishes and challenges were scattered throughout the day's remaining arcs as forces on both sides licked their wounds and prepared for the next plan of attack.

I marveled at the sight of civilians helping the military forces find locations for tents or optimal places to store hardware. It was no doubt an inconvenience to have the military occupy an everday business operation disrupted by the power struggle, but thankfully, at least a sample of the Imperan citizens knew that, regardless of the victor, their lives would never return to normalcy without an end to the conflict. Frank Jenkins' agenda had descended on the people so quickly that even the citizens were reluctant to make assumptions as to who had the agenda high ground. At least the people first attitude demonstrated by the resistance had helped some make up their minds.

As the sunset faded out, I noticed that the Alcazaban and Oshan officials made their way into the command center. It wasn't until the Enforcer, Torque, the Serpent and several Ghosts arrived that I knew it was time to participate. I got a silent nod from the Enforcer toward the entrance suggesting that I follow.

Overwhelmed with the ingenuity of the operation, I took note of the darwa shop near the supermarket entrance that had already been converted into a command center. In the distance, I spotted aisles of displaced apparel to make room for makeshift bunks and treatment centers for the wounded. Even the produce section had been converted to a mess hall. Trying not to get distracted, I focused on the command center which had already been closed off by movable partions and injected with all kinds of comm terminals. Still a stranger to such scenes, I found a stack of crates to lean against while those more adept at large scale coordination gathered around a series of noptic displays. With the abundance of Oshan forces and tech, there had clearly been an upgrade since the prior battle meeting.

General chatter permeated the command post until things started to come to order under Potentate Ang's guidance. Despite a variety of command structures, ages and experience levels, I perceived that there was an unspoken deference to offer the floor to a faction leader. I perceived that he had earned respect from his military peers on account of his own service despite having made a forced exit into the political arena.

"Our biggest remaining threats are the Tornac choppers and the Magellans," General Cruz said after speculating that the Oshan forces had been reasonably caught up on the engagement.

"How many raptors do we have left?" the Enforcer asked of the protech who had found a new station at a nearby comm terminal.

"Only two. They are currently perched in a hollow formed by the destruction amidst one of the enclave towers," Szasz said.

"I have a lot of pilots who are in your debt," General Cruz said to acknowledge the rescue of many of his soldiers at the informatech's hands and the raptors' claws.

"No gratitude needed. I have a debt of my own to settle," Szazs said, hoping to turn the attention back to those more qualified.

"Two birds and one Goliath won't spark much intimidation," the Enforcer said.

"I have discovered that they have a dislike of plasma shells. If we can create a web of cover, then Oshan forces can certainly maintain superiority on the ground," Command Jackal replied.

Conversation continued about how to best divide forces and maintain a perpetual advance of infantry-based heavy weapons scattered throughout accessible buildings leading up to Casters Tower. Roles were divided among Alcazaban and Oshan troops with necessary countermeasures, knowing that they would encounter COJR Guerillas who had likely already established a foothold.

"And that leaves these guys," Maxwell said, shifting the display to scans of the Magellan razerjacks after conversation was settled on the choppers.

Silence loomed over the room while the resistance leaders mulled over the specifications of the unexpected force recently introduced. The nine deck high razerjack towered above any unit in play since the Global War. Its size represented a blockade along any approach to Casters Tower. Although its mobility was limited and its armor dense, its firepower was sure to cut down precious life until resources could be consolidated to overpower it.

"How many of those do we have to face?" Torque asked since no one else dared.

"Two have been immobilized, with reports of at least another two with confirmed visual. We've had to rely upon civilian reports due to lack of resources for scouting west of the conflict, but we hear that there may be at least another two. That suggests there's still four active," General Cruz said, doing his best to piece data together from a slate in hand.

Numerous yet doubtful strategies were presented to take out or limit the Magellan's influence. Any solution that positioned firepower in advance involved luring the Magellan's into a trap which would prevent staging of other resistance units. Solutions that committed enough firepower put units at risk, also creating doubt. It wasn't until Commander Jackal presented the most abstract concept of all that the strategists paused, either to consider reasons why the idea wouldn't work or because they considered the suggestion a joke.

"We're in an urban engagement. Those things are surrounded by buildings that are even taller. Hijack one from above," Jackal said.

Initially, opposition had the vocal majority, but as Jackal built his case, it became clear that, despite the risk, it required the least amount of resources. There was no better way to disrupt the Imperan hardware than from within. Conversation shifted toward leveraging distractions and how to best reach the razerjack without being picked off, or worse, missing and falling to the street below.

Feeling unsettled about the abundance of problems over solutions, I considered what value I could contribute. As options were being exhausted, I exited the command post, doubting that anyone noticed, other than perhaps the Enforcer. I found Vanguard's designated spot for gear until a suitable bunk location had been chosen. I found the

Drakken glider-pack and walked back into the command post. Dusting off the enemy gear, I handed it to Jackal.

"It's risky, but I believe it could work. Just be careful since it drags to the left," I said.

I knew that I received the same dumbfounded treatment as Jackal when he first brought up the idea, but I ignored the stares as I returned to my vacant console leaning post. After inspecting the gear, Jackal nodded and pressed for more ideas on how to get a couple of techs aboard the Magellan if he successfully removed those within. Finally, the conversation moved in a unified direction with Jackal willing to stake his life on the line for the crazy idea as long as it kept the remainder of resistance forces focused on the fight elsewhere.

With urgent issues tackled one by one, the state of affairs calmed as the military commanders appeared ready to parse details on the general advance. Before agreeing to any more discussions, the Enforcer halted the conversation.

"We have still have a large issue before us," the Enforcer said as he nodded for General Cruz to introduce someone.

General Cruz signaled for one of his officers to bring in a boy, no more than ten passes in age. The boy had dark hair, fair skin and freckles and seemed nervous about entering the room full of serious adults, but he still stood tall and followed the officer who gave him a box to stand on which boosted his sense of self importance. Numerous smiles cracked the tension as the boy beamed at being able to see the noptic displays glowing and blinking before him.

"This here is Khet. He told one of our soldiers that his brother had disappeared, only for him to be seen fighting alongside the Pirans during the conflict. I thought it best for you hear his story personally," General Cruz said.

Those present were concerned and reluctant to question the boy, but as reassurances and calm tones prevailed, he told his tale. As summarized, he described his older brother taking unknown pills and eventually starting to act strange. When the fighting started, his brother seemed unresponsive and insistent upon fighting. Khet had been unable to stop his brother, and was scared after seeing his stark white eyes. After relaying his tale, the attending officer encouraged the boy on account of his bravery before taking him to visit the mess hall. Silence permeated the command post after Khet's departure as all present internalized how to deal with civilians being grafted into Frank Jenkins' plot.

"Gentlemen, this drug is a deception," the Enforcer said after snapping his fingers to have an officer toss him a recovered canister of

Extend pills. "Our enemy has had many passes to practice the art of subversive warnings embedded within manipulative marketing. We have already witnessed this substance being integrated into the whole of the Global Alliance, from lowly citizen to high office. If we don't succeed here and now, we are going to witness this behavior on a grand scale."

Silence continued. No one dared question the Enforcer's statement. They agreed, but as students of war not a single one wanted to admit the high risk on account of civilian coercion. The Enforcer leaned on the tactical table, taking the time to look over every combatant present to make sure that they understood the scope of the problem.

"What do you suggest?" Potentate Ang asked.

"We need a non-lethal solution," the Enforcer replied.

Initial counter thoughts sounded like grumbles, but they were quickly countered because everyone agreed. The challenge was that no one offered a viable strategy. As options were presented, tweaked and discarded, I kept to myself without having any input to add. I struggled to fathom the depth of the deception regarding the drug and its cryptic warnings, but I sure couldn't deny that its promotion had permeated every corner of the Hyper Lynx and every hapcast imaginable. I pondered just how the Enforcer continued to hold his ground for the sake of those caught up in the storm against those who would easily considered them unfortunate losses.

Debates heated up as the go-to solution from the military leaders was naturally the use of force. Concessions were made for the usage of low density plasma, a common stun procedure, but many were concerned if the method would have enough stopping power to overcome the mind control effects of Extend. Volume of the discourse rose and settled once again, deadlocked without the means to reach consensus.

As my attention to the conversation drifted in and out, I caught word of discussion related to signals. Szazs was the first to query those present on potentially different behaviors once the reactor was disabled. Murmurs morphed into recounts which built a case for diminished control over those with lesser dosages of Extend or extreme distance from Casters Tower. Discussion once again escalated as ideas began to flood the room.

"If we know this is signal based, what do we need?" Potentate Ang asked.

"Counter signal, or at least enough noise to disrupt it," Lieutenant Tiago suggested as he momentarily looked away from Alcazaba's comms terminal.

The Enforcer looked over to the protech for validation of recently expressed ideas.

"If we cancel out the signal we should be able to disrupt most of those who are fighting involuntarily, but I don't know the resources needed to repeat the signal and at what strength," Szazs replied. "I'm sure that we don't want to overcommit by playing caretaker on the battlefield should the effects not hold."

More comms specialists chimed in suggesting that they could use casting hardware from the vehicles to relay the counter signal which would help suppress hostiles until they could clear the way for those to administer treatment or restraints once the battle formations advanced. As a solution with more buy-in grew, so did optimism. Many were relieved that lethal force had been shoved down the procedure list for noncombatants as a last resort. Once the means was settled, the necessary minds went to work on the execution. Sensing that there was little more that I could contribute, I took a break from the strategy session and exited the command center.

Despite the evening settling in, many were still working to secure the camp, treat the injured and repair machinery. I was intrigued by the involvement of the citizens who helped with the basic tasks of construction and transportion. It shouldn't have come as a surprise considering that their lives were radically disrupted and they wanted things back to normal as quickly as possible.

The warm air caught my attention, shifting my thoughts toward any manner of cold liquid. Adjacent to the entryway, I spotted an Archer vending machine. I wasn't keen on downing anything carbonated, but I hoped to find a palatable juice. Approaching the machine, I was pleased to see it operational. Retrieving my berry clip from a pocket, I slotted the required dimps and fed them into the machine. I heard the small spheres clack their way into the unit, but after pressing the button for a Berry Slosh, the machine continued its idle hum. Concerned, I pressed the button again. Becoming frustrated, I tapped more buttons on the machine only for it to remain oblivious to my requests.

Agitated, I was about to kick the machine when I saw boy staring at me, curious at what I was about to do. Checking my behavior, I put my foot down. With a smirk, the boy walked up to the vending machine and rapped the side of his hand in a specific location, likely next to the exit mechanism. On command, the machine finally spit out the chug of juice that I had originally selected.

Impressed by the boy's street smarts, I smiled and nodded while he chuckled at my desperate antics. Unsure how to repay him, I considered paying for another drink, but as I turned my berry clip over in my head, a sense of detachment washed over me. I contemplated why I was hanging onto the thing while in the midst of the battle. Vanguard had plenty of resources, and my time spent laboring for such a miniscule form of exchange felt so distant.

Following the discussion of Extend's influence, I contemplated just how long manipulative mediacasting had been running throughout the Commercial Empire. I reluctantly gave weight to the idea that even my priorities could have been skewed in subtle ways, even from my remote residence in the abandon. Opting for a mindset change, I handed the boy the berry clip with its remaining contents. Initially, he doubted my intentions, but when he realized that I was serious, his face beamed with excitement. He muttered his thanks before sheepishly nodding and racing off to show his friends who were playing nearby as their parents helped with camp operations.

I knew that the little amount of berry which I gave away weighed little in the material sense, but I found it strange as a sense of lightness settled in. After all the efforts I made to take information in, to find things for myself, all of that counted for nothing with a symbol of labor which didn't work in the time in which it was needed. I knew that the boy's excitement meant far more than the few trinkets I could have purchased with the colored dimps. I was surprised that it took such a simple event, but at last the actual execution of an outward focus finally resonated with my frequent discord with the Enforcer's continual *others first* drive. At least in that small instance, I was rewarded with seeing the boy's enthusiasm at the unexpected gift, but I struggled to overlay that with the efforts to continuously pour outward when the efforts were either unknown or uninvited. I felt that the internal sense of lightness verified the Enforcer's explanation of drift waves and flow, but I still had so much to learn.

After finishing my break, I discarded the empty juice chug and returned to my obscure observation spot in the back of the room. Tension had been replaced with collaboration as all minds present continued to optimize the solutions for neutralizing the white-eyed victims of Extend. From my limited understanding, I sensed that there was still an issue with the signal which was yielding intermittent results against the data that they ran through the simulations.

Given my fresh experience with a drift wave scenario, I contemplated if Extend had any capacity to affect the body at a deeper level. The more that I chewed on the idea, and the less that I heard about verified solutions, I decided it best to make sure that the question was considered. Since I had no strength in deep particle matters, I swiftly blinked a quick note into my ikes and sent it directly to the Enforcer across the VNET.

Even from across the room, I noticed the Enforcer do a slight nod and direct his attention to a console so that he could dissect all wavelength patterns related to the Extend victims. After finding the object of his search, he transferred it to the protech's console who swiftly ran a new test.

"This could work," Szazs said as he leaned back in his chair running fingers from both hands into his hair. His expression demonstrated both relief at a working model and surprise at its unusual form.

"Where did you get this?" Commander Jackal asked.

"From a field of study oft neglected," the Enforcer said calmly.

Those working with Szazs quickly performed their own tests. In turn, they all offered little to no conflict with the stated model. As tests were affirmed, those without the technical knowledge looked to the Enforcer for an explanation as to how he made his discovery. He seemed reluctant to expound in detail, but the silent stares suggested that basic answers were expected.

"This substance greatly exploits the influence of the Catalyst on the body," the Enforcer said.

The room reaction was strange, as if the Enforcer had just insulted the lineage of everyone in the room. A weird mixture of grumbles and gasps circulated, clearly distracting from the overall solution to the problem at hand.

"So, you're suggesting that this has to do with some archaic morality system?" Lieutenant Tiago quipped.

It was easy for me to understand the Enforcer's reluctance to pop the cork on that bottle as I watched the discord elevate. I noticed that much of the frustration was exhibited from the younger officers who were likely more adjusted to the overall knowledge restrictions brought on by the Global Alliance in recent passes. I was intrigued by the calm observation by those who had known the Enforcer for such a long time, including Potentate Ang and General Seechi. As if by comical insight of maturity, they let those present vent before playing hands of their own.

"I'm sure most of you here recall the Crossover Strain," Potentate Ang said, once volume diminished to a level for him to interject without raising his voice.

The comment struck a nerve since so many had been affected by the Smart Wars, and it seemed odd for the faction leader to make such a remark. With eyes directed at Potentate Ang, he volunteered his own defense of the situation.

"I'm sure Mr. Conner is reluctant to stand on his own credentials, but for those of you who are still here today, due to the compressed timespan of that ordeal, you might want to consider that he played a role in cutting it short," Ang said calmly.

As the discourse lulled, focus returned to the Enforcer.

"So, who does this affect?" Commander Jackal asked from his reticent stance on covering information considered anathema by Global Alliance standards.

"Everyone," the Enforcer said in curt fashion to make sure that those present understand the gravity of the threat. "At least, by my understanding anyone who isn't a proxy for the Firewall Protocol. It wasn't until I compared different sample groups that I could see a pattern. I suspect that Extend is just an entrypoint, but if usage reaches critical mass, our foes may be able to leverage its ability against those who have never consumed the product in question. Even if there is no autonomy to provide protection through the Firewall Protocol, the low quantity of proxies might make things extremely problematic."

A hush fell over the room. I did my best to watch the reactions in the room even without interferic readings. Most present from the Oshan continent seemed indifferent to the scans. I speculated that many weren't used to trafficking in knowledge outside of the Global Alliance's watchful eye. Those younger members or those fighting from more oppressive factions seemed most jarred by information clearly suppressed in their home territories. Since the more senior strategists like Ang and Seechi held their ground, no one dared upset the proposed plan without having any reasonable alternatives.

I felt the tension settle as the conversation shifted back toward plan execution. Once the strategy was locked in, those with minimal interest bowed out under the guise of preparations. I recognized that the Enforcer had his work cut out for him with trying to keep any concrete knowledge of drift waves in the foreground in order to translate it into a working frequency for the sake of the comms officers. Perhaps a couple of the officers seemed intrigued, but only Szazs appeared genuinely enthusiastic about the influx of new information. Naturally, Potentate Ang revealed his knowledge as he did his best to support the workflow, but others kept their distance, only taking in the information as needed from a strategic viewpoint.

As word salads and technical jargon permeated the air, I felt my focus fade, sensing that fatigue was finally flushing out the last dregs of heightened awareness. Rather then disrupt the conversation at hand or find myself snared in Torque's hardware checks, I punted on the idea of querying Vanguard's accommodation status. I left the command post and headed for the section of the supermarket with cots lining the aisles.

While most of the professional soldiers had their own tents posted outside, the supermarket served as an overflow which was filled with scattered resistance combatants and displaced civilians alike. After sensing that several rows were full, I spotted one overlooked by a weary shopkeeper who had just finished cleaning the last shred of space available. I nodded my thanks to the middle-aged man who had graciously made space available and peeked down the aisle. There were still a few cots available, and I noticed that lighting was at a minimum since the back of the store had been reduced to emergency lighting only.

Internally, I acknowledged that the cot had nothing on my bed back in the Dwelling Street Mission, but it was a stark upgrade from the lumber pile of the previous night. I felt a mental conflict about abandoning some form of readiness, but the thoughts were offset by the understanding that fatigue would only lead to mistakes on the battlefield. I recognized that I was an amateur in knowing how to prioritize one over the other, but the tick I lay on the cot, I knew that my body wasn't going to fight my mind without a couple arcs of sleep.

37 – Grounded – 37

Executive Level, Casters Tower
Core City, Windstonne Enclave
Commercial Empire, Northam Continent
Thread: sysObserver.cmd

Without having as much as a dart set to pass the time, Sath leaned back in the padded chair and exhaled, exasperated. She had been isolated in a vacant executive suite ever since she attempted to contact Mac. She didn't know what Jenkins intended do with her, but all attempts to discover his intentions or the outcome of other personnel in Casters Tower were denied. She guessed that those detained in the building were corralled in larger common areas like eateries and conference halls.

A single Piran guard stood outside the office until relieved at a shift change, so any means to escape had been cut off. The walls and internal windows were too dense to break without drawing attention, and the external windows were useless, naturally, on account of the building's height. Even with a slate in hand, Sath had no Hyper Lynx access to communicate with the outside world. If not for the small chiller, utilities and sofa, Sath knew that she could have had a much worse situation on her hands. Either Jenkins still wanted to guard anything that she knew, or he didn't know what to do with her since she hadn't been locked up with the others.

Finally, a rap on the door followed by a familiar face entering the room without invitation. Lieutenant Morton, who had been guarding the office during the day shift entered, disruptor rifle still in hand. Sath stared and only shot an inquisitive look since the Piran had no food or supplies in hand.

"He wants to see you," Morton said flatly.

"Who?" Sath asked.

"Jenkins," Morton said in a condescending tone, annoyed that there could have been any other option.

"Well, he can pay me a visit if he wants. I'm busy," Sath said, leaning her head back against the chair.

"That's not how things work around here," Morton snapped as he moved forward, indicating that he wasn't opposed to dragging Sath if necessary.

With an eye roll, Sath stood from her chair, attempted to smooth the worst wrinkles from her clothes and tied her brown matted curls behind her head. She only intended to test the thick skulled Piran lackey since she knew that she couldn't overpower him. Working with Jenkins had undoubtedly created a sense of shrewdness, testing thresholds which could make even the slightest conversation an opportunity to identify a person's character and reveal useful information. She never thought that she'd have to use said skills for her own survival.

Lieutenant Morton waited for Sath to exit before closing the door behind them. He then took point and led her toward the elevator. En route, Sath caught a glimpse of Core City facing the Winzy. Smoke and destruction littered the terrain below. The window in her office cell faced Lake Mitten, so she had little insight regarding the conflict raging below her feet.

After a tense but quiet elevator ride, the Piran guard showed her to Frank Jenkins' conference room on the skydeck where he hunched over a table littered with slates and deployment data. Sath slowly entered the room, giving herself time to assess the situation.

"I'll be outside, Sir," Morton said after being acknowledged by Jenkins' nod.

"What's this all about, Frank?" Sath asked since her employer seemed preoccupied and reluctant to start the conversation.

"Forces in play see fit to remove me from power," Frank Jenkins said as he finally stood upright and gestured toward a chair for Sath to sit in.

Sath declined the invitation to sit as her eyes followed Frank Jenkins' over to the window where he stood, observing the activity of the day, knowing that forces were drawing much closer to the tower doorstep.

"Per reports that I've received, I've had to issue your termi..." Jenkins started.

"I already quit, Frank. I could have submitted the scans myself if you hadn't locked me in a hole for the last two days," Sath snapped back.

"No doubt after padding your account, I presume," Jenkins said without turning to back up his accusations with eye contact.

Sath felt heated as the blood rushed to her face, livid at such an accusation. She had worked for Frank Jenkins and not so much as a single dimp had ever gone missing. Even with Frank Jenkins' misdealings she never had motivation to keep a log of his actions to profit off them herself. Internally, she wanted to verbally tear the faction leader's head off, but she reflected on her attachment to the Interlace, knowing that ultimately she answered to an even greater authority than a petty power monger. She released a quiet exhale, fully aware that it was never wise to play into Jenkins' hand. She had learned the ways of the brutal negotiator from a distance, and she was one of the few with capacity to call him out. Sath only exercised that ability as needed, especially since she watched the reputational, and at times economic, destruction of those who thought they could outwit Frank Jenkins.

Taking a moment to collect her thoughts, the agenda coordinator looked about the room before settling her focus back on the executive. She was surprised that even under duress, Jenkins still managed to craft the appearance of authority. His suit was still in pristine shape, but his eyes told a different story about his resolve. There was no hiding the strain which started to reveal itself around the edges of his facial features.

"Frank, have I ever given reason to mistrust me?" Sath asked.

Frank Jenkins held his tongue and mulled over past events. He knew that he could not break Sath's will from a performance review. She knew more than anyone about Imperan operations, with exception of skeleton burial locations. The wetwork alone had been offloaded to Commander Pyln, and Sath certainly wouldn't have been able to operate above reproach if she caught wind of such activities. He needed a different angle and all he had were suspicions. The impulsive Piran guard who disrupted Sath's conversation with the outside world could only characterize the comms. All data traces proved fruitless especially after the terminal had been destroyed. Jenkins tensed every time that he had to consider that the festering sore of the Interlace might, yet again, be party to his opposition.

"It has been expressed to me that you have contacts with the resistance," Jenkins said calmly.

Sath tensed, curious as to how much Jenkins actually knew. She had learned long ago that visual cues told volumes, so she refrained from any reaction possible. If Jenkins had been wise to her relationship with Mac or her connection to the Interlace, he could have acted long ago, unless he hoped to gain intel. Since any intel presently available wasn't working in his favor, Sath opted to call his bluff.

"How can I answer that in any way that you will believe? After the way I've been treated the last couple of days, I doubt there's anything I can say that would support my case," Sath replied emphatically.

"You didn't answer my question," Frank said.

"You didn't answer mine," Sath fired back, knowing that she was right to hold the line. Her limited usage of calling Frank out as needed was about to pay off. He was unable to provide specifics to her accusation, a tell easily exploited.

DAVE TODD

Jenkins fumed internally, he knew that his ammunition was low, but he couldn't shake the agitation within. He considered a deflection, "We live in a time when enemies are in plain sight. They can take many forms. I have simply tried to bring order to the Global Alliance, but unfortunately malcontents have painted me as their villain."

"I don't suppose that has anything to do with your theatrics with the faction council," Sath retorted.

Frank Jenkins felt like his collar had been lit on fire upon hearing the ease in which Sath leveraged her insight. She should have had no capacity to know the inner workings of the faction leader fallout without eavesdropping, or worse collaboration with foreign elements. Frank Jenkins paused to consider an even more detestable reality, that Sath might have a connection with the Enforcer himself, who strangely had insights to the meeting.

"You need to let the people go, Frank," Sath interjected before Jenkins could build his argument.

"It's not safe. It's still too dangerous out there," Frank Jenkins said as he placed his hands behind his back, straightened his shoulders and feigned a stoic act.

"You mean it's too dangerous for you. No one cares about your throne. I suspect that no one out there is on a hostage hunt," Sath replied.

"You suggest that you know much, Sath, but I cannot afford to take the chance on anyone who might be a threat," Frank Jenkins snapped, finally looking his former coordinator in the eye.

"The only threat to you, Frank, is yourself," Sath said exasperated. Sath took the accusation in stride knowing that before her was a broken man with no way to put the pieces back together.

Frank Jenkins was so outraged that he wanted to fling chairs and flip the table in the room if it was in his capacity to do so. Sath had deftly cut through his attempts to glean any information relevant to his suspicions, but all attempts came up short. All he could do was clench his fists and resume his glare out the tower window.

"What are you going to do? Disappear me?" Sath queried.

As much as Jenkins wanted to vent his frustration he had no intention of displaying physical violence, "No, I'm just going to ensure that no one else can be used against me. I'm not going to add any more blood to my hands than necessary. Farewell, Miss Kinze."

After a call for the Piran guard outside, Jenkins pursed his lips, suggesting that there was nothing else to exchange. Frustrated, Sath shook her head. She was relieved that Frank Jenkins still held to some internal code, but despite that, she felt sad that there was no imbuing him with any rational thought beyond his quest to hold on to his temporary power.

Sath complied with Lieutenant Morton's gesture to follow, but before leaving, she couldn't help but leave Frank with one last thought, "For what it's worth, Frank. I'm sorry that I was never able to get through to you."

"By the time someone gets through to me, I gather that it will be too late," Frank replied without even a parting glance.

Saddened by the final state of her encounter with her longtime boss, Sath followed the Piran soldier back to her containment office.

Gridloc: Fractured Expanse
Thread: frmCntmntMrkr.prt

Mac paused in the silent intersection, checking for a nav update on his ikes. Given the limited information available for his destination, he grew frustrated with the frequent corrections which slowed his mission. Urgency weighed on him knowing that lingering too long would create questions from the locals. Borealis was no stranger to foreigners, but that didn't mean people wouldn't get curious about his presence.

The culture aboard the aerial city certainly operated as rumored in its practice of adhering to strict schedules. Other than support crew, there were no imprints to be seen prior to sunrise, another reason his unusual presence created a sliver of anxiety.

After one final turn around a residential block, Mac discovered the designated terminal on his ikes. He did one last check to confirm that he was still in the Sunward Trangle given the city's lack of directional signage.

Mac slid into the angled chair, so that he could accurately see the display screens attached to the headpiece. He understood that the terminals scattered throughout the city were commonplace, allowing residents to easily access digital services necessary for daily activities. Borealin tech was known for its high end security which prevented the issue of theft from rarely crossing the mind of most residents.

"Destination locked," Mac said as he activated the terminal and his comm.

Mac activated his ikes so that his presence would be recognized as an alternate identity. "Are you sure this is going to work? Their security is tight at the social level, how much worse could it be for infrastructure?"

"Oh, so you wrote this algorithm? Does it come with a guarantee? Because that'd be some top level datajacker stuff right there," Mac joked.

While engaging in low level banter, Mac easily navigated the foreign interface on account of his ikes which provided translations and pointers on the fly. The system verified his authentication as an alternate identity as hoped. As an overlay popped up allowing him to traverse the option system, he found the portals for communication and security systems. Leveraging an optic transcriber, he fed the data from his ikes into the terminal and bundled it into a datapod. With the transfer complete, he embedded it into an ambiguous sea of data packets undetectable until the corresponding identity accessed the system.

"Payload secure. Formula marker two-dot-two active," Mac said.

After closing comments on the comm, Mac exited the terminal. For a brief moment, he absorbed the information from his senses. The streets were clean, unlike most urban clusters he'd seen. Given the massive energy consumption that the city required, he doubted there was margin to waste on even the tiniest scrap littering the street. Even with distance from the massive machinery below, Mac could hear the faint hum of the engines which kept the city afloat.

With his limited window of time for sightseeing expired, Mac headed toward a nearby junction. As he passed through the center of a Borealin street, the impending sunrise caught his attention. Seeing the daily spectacle from a raised elevation refreshed his mood for a moment. The early rays of orange scattered across the lingering clouds. He contemplated if the Borealin residents had appreciation for something for which they had in abundance and wonderful access to, but thoughts of the locals also reminded Mac of the heavy weight on his shoulders. He considered crafting more of a warning regarding the tragedy ahead, but he knew that tragedies even greater existed on the other side of meticulous planning that he dared not deviate from. Without capacity to contemplate the choices at hand, he fixated on the plan before him simply taking in the morning splendor before taking his leave.

Resistance Forward Command
Core City, Windstonne Enclave
Commercial Empire, Northam Continent
Thread: actTgtPersp1.view

The ground rumbled, passing small tremors upward through the cot legs, ultimately fracturing the deep sleep that had seized my consciousness. After a small interval, the sequence repeated, pulling my mind back to the living. If the Alcazaban artillery was already being deployed, I knew that I needed get a move on. After sitting upright, I tried to wrestle my senses into a near functional state and flex the contractions out of my muscles. Without the time needed, I settled for the three-quarter mark and shuffled through the supermarket.

Along my walk, I had hoped to pass my regards to the shop owner, but I had to settle for relaying a message through nearby staff. No doubt, the owner had earned a break after all the sacrifices made to tend to those in the battle. A quick scan of the room showed that a few cots were still occupied mostly by civilians and other local resistance members less bound by formal expectations. Even though Vanguard too was outside the command of any governing body, I knew that the Enforcer would expect me to adhere to a high level of responsibility as if it was the last squad of vectors on earth.

Sauntering into the open air, I felt relieved that the sunrise was just getting started, mitigating any guilt from oversleeping. I found my friends engaging in small talk as if it were any other day while standing around a stockpile of munitions not far from where the Behemoth was parked. I appreciated knowing that, in time, such conflicts carried a sense of normalcy in perspective. Whether the sentiment was genuine or forced, at least it felt like we were about to simply embark on another day's work.

"Pack your verts, Fishstick?" Torque chuckled as he tossed me an oat bar.

I promptly caught the oat bar, unwrapped one end and held onto it with my mouth while retrieving my Phantom 4.0. I ejected a spent power cell in Torque's direction, forcing him to evade slightly.

"Why do you need to borrow a set?" I quipped.

"Whoa, a big fish has entered the pond," Torque replied as he continued loading the EQ in hand.

"I could have ordered you some, but Skydrop was sold out of child smalls," I continued.

With lightning speed, Torque snapped a Splice 15m from his hip and pointed it at my chest, "Got a splash pad integrated with those civvie threads. My berry says Mac hasn't taught you everything yet."

Initially, I thought that I struck a nerve, then realized Torque was testing my mettle if I wanted to banter like a professional. Knowing that I was outmatched, I looked over to the Enforcer only to get a shoulder shrug acknowledging that I was in over my head, a mess of my own creation. The sheepish look on my face indicated that I clearly still had a lot to learn. The Enforcer nodded toward a pile of light armor, suggesting that I utilize it given there was no time to custom tailor a more fashionable armor style. I quickly noted the context, suggesting that my Vanguard allies already had the necessary dense fiber tech woven into their respective vests and jackets.

I exchanged my pullover for the light tactical vest. I was surprised at its flexibility, wondering if it even had more durability than the fleece I had been sporting thus far. After checking the utility pockets, I situated my treadball cap back on my head and returned my attention back to the gear checks, and my oat bar.

"Now you look like a proper moving target," Torque chuckled. "That'll at least keep you from passing out by the low density stuff and stray shrapnel."

"No Behemoth, I take it," I remarked, accepting that we'd be heading out on foot.

"It's going to get tight in there. We can't risk conflicting with our allies, so we'll let Alcazaba handle the hardware. Plus, we need Maxwell to hang back and guard the rations," the Enforcer said.

"I heard that," Maxwell remarked through our ikes. "Don't make me pull the plug on your eyeballs."

The chiding continued in a variety of directions for a while, putting my mind at ease. Admittedly, it was the most informal I had seen Vanguard since my introduction. I was nearly surprised to see the Enforcer crack a straight face more than once, offering him a break from the the invisible weight that he constantly seemed to carry. The Serpent even fired off a subtle expression or two in unusual fashion since he hadn't yet donned his ikes, and Torque seemed like he was in his element regardless of the situation. I sincerely felt that Vanguard was at home at the edge of a conflict with purpose, and it strangely had a calming effect. It wasn't long ago that I was doing menial tasks without direction. Things changed drastically. There I stood beside friends that I trusted, ready to throw down against a twisted adversary, and I was okay with that.

The mood shifted quickly after the hollow concussion of distant Sandstorm fire reached our ears. Alcazaban forces were already engaging Imperan forces, so that was our cue to move out with one of the ground units. Vanguard swiftly finished its business with a final chorus of snaps and clicks as the gear check ended.

"Ayezon, Vanguard," the Enforcer said as he broke away first to find our attached battle group.

The remainder of us followed with an intentional stride. We folded in with the Alcazaban troops surrounded by a mixture of Alcazaban and Oshan hardware. There were was no time for introductions with the soldiers beside us, so we kept our focus on the road and structures ahead. Internally, I wanted to feel secure amidst the artillery units, but I knew that a well placed shot from a sniper perch could undo all personal well being.

Our battle group ambled forward for a few parcels, halting at intersections to verify clearance from groups ahead. We approached Casters Tower from the northwest, but about the time we hit a five parcel perimeter, heavy plasma fire rained down from embedded Jungyan troops overhead. The resistance artillery held position while ground troops instinctively parted to either side of the street, taking cover beneath overhangs or within ground floor shops.

While the heavy units were impervious to small arms fire, adversaries managed to clip a Squirm's treads with a Mortimer shell. The vehicle's system strained, causing an internal fire to expel the pilots from within. The halt in resistance forces gave Imperan forces opportunity to flood the chokepoint from the ground as well.

"Fox, follow me," Torque yelled.

Torque worked his way through a storefront and back outside. He had already targeted a hollowed out mox partially crushed by prior conflict, minimizing any concerns of explosion. He took up a position on one side of the mox and expected me to do the same from the opposite end. He was quick to unleash plasma fire from an EQ while simultaneously transmitting ideal targets from his ikes to mine where the formation was weakest. I yelled as I unleashed fire at the advancing units in the open as they crossed through the intersection.

Torque's reaction time was quick, his finger pressing on the trigger at intervals. He was effectively downing Pirans and cycling new power cells with precision. When he saw that I was struggling to keep pace, he withdrew a small device from his pocket and tossed it my way without even looking.

"Here try this," Torque said.

Before I could ask, a small icon already popped up on my ikes, indicating that had given me a regulator mod for my EQ and it even displayed the insertion point which I hadn't noticed before. I quickly snapped the modifier into the rifle and returned to my targeting. The regulator adjusted the plasma density, helping me drop targets faster.

"This is liquid! I have got to get myself one of these," I remarked at the improvement.

"How did you work in salvage and never hear of Dropper's Clause? If it's in hand, it's yours," Torque fired back. "You think Vanguard runs on donations?"

"I guess Imperan rules and regs failed to mention that one," I replied as I downed another advancing Piran.

"Time to learn street rules quick, because if you didn't notice, they're not exactly friendly," Torque quipped.

"Noted," I smirked as I fired upon another Piran who failed to make his way to cover.

Thus far, our enemies bore the green and gold uniform of the Commercial Empire, or the graystone camouflage of the Jungyan forces. Even if the military forces were under Extend's influence, they were considered a hostile target. I was under enough pressure in acclimating to firefights, so I was thankful to have one less stressor. The former was lessened even more for a moment as the deafening engines of an Oshan Platypus rumbled down the street, offering cover to troops on foot while its gunners targeted any elevated threats.

Given the adequate armor, capacity for speed and a tight turning radius, the Oshan hovercrafts were able to test enemy lines and retreat quickly or perform cleanup operations to secure the way. Amongst the tumult, I found myself mesmerized by the technology of the craft. Its dark bulbous tubing for an uplifter mitigated plasma fire and seemed impervious to most problematic ground obstructions. Its flat armored top connected to the trio of backfacing turbines as well as easily secured a small group of gunners on each corner giving it a wide range of fire. The Platypus bore the signature blues and blacks of the Oceanic Outpost faction and created a strange blur as it passed through one's peripheral vision.

Turrets from the unit were ablaze as it passed from the north into the corridor south of our position. Structures overhead were peppered with plasma anytime a hostile dared give away its location. After reaching the next intersection, the craft spun about and zipped back in our direction.

"Next corridor is all clear," a voice said through our comms.

The Enforcer snapped orders for ground troops to form up and follow our escort down the next corridor. Our lead Sandstorm tank halted before clearing the next intersection as an advance party made a similar call. I soon heard that there was a blockade to the west and a Tornac chopper was hovering to provide aerial support. The unit was a guaranteed threat to the Alacazaban armor.

"Someone give me a distraction. The rest follow me," the Enforcer snapped before I could realize just how quickly he had devised a plan.

Torque and Alcazaban allies quickly took cover behind wall corners, sandbags and other obstructions to open fire on the Imperan blockade at the end of the next corridor. As the Enforcer began moving toward an overturned transport truck, I spotted waypoints displaying on my ikes, plotting a course from behind the truck toward the building on the opposite side of the street. The Enforcer's structural scan revealed that it was a business complex with a shared hallway that ran parallel to the street, so we had a clean shot at flanking those who were dug in.

Our run through the business complex was uninterrupted, surprising me that Imperan forces had done so little to secure their position. As we reached a contact point, the Enforcer halted our advance. Just as I was about to let my rifle down, an enraged, white-eyed civilian burst into the hallway, racing toward me like a mindless vim. Panicked, I reached for my Phantom which was still set to suppression mode and popped a blast in the chest. The civilian dropped to the floor unconscious but alive. I exhaled in relief that I reacted in time since I would have been too slow to switch the configuration on my EQ.

The Enforcer was quick to dispatch orders to allies present, designating troops to positions on the ground floor and the next one up. He stressed that those on the second floor were to only fire a single volley because they were most at risk to the COJR craft on lookout. The plan was to deal with it after the troops in the barricade. Without disagreement, all units took their positions. The Enforcer approached the storefront, secured a spot behind a service counter and leveled a Cutter at the contingent of Imperan forces thrilled with their successes in holding back the resistance.

Without question, I mimicked the behavior of the other troops who held position behind cover until receiving the attack signal. I could see the Enforcer monitoring Imperan forces after looking at the store ceiling. I suspected that he was using a thermal filter to track the chopper's angle. It hadn't fully engaged the resistance forces, but instead, checked other angles of the intersection at random.

Curious, I peeked over my sign-board cover. I suspected that my action was a mistake as a Piran soldier near the shop reacted to something in his peripheral vision. Alerted to something unknown, the soldier ceased firing and squinted into the darkness of the shop on his left where we tensely waited. I dropped back down and looked over to the Enforcer for a statchek. Relieved to see that he confirmed the necessary timing, he dropped his hand toward our foes and yelled for all forces to fire.

An explosive torrent of plasma poured from the storefront catching the Imperan forces at a right angle. Piran and COJR forces alike were dropped without discretion. True to their orders, soldiers on the second floor quickly retracted their positions. Within a matter of ticks, the bodies in the street were laid horizontal.

The COJR pilot only witnessed the tail end of plasma fire from the ground level as he spun the chopper about to once again face the hot corridor. A catastrophic firestorm rained down on the storefront from several decks above, shredding front-facing walls, windows and light supports, but the intended cover held. Structural debris poured into the street, some of it covering the deceased Imperan forces.

As the resistance plasma ceased, so too did the fire from the chopper once the structure no longer resembled a habitable building. With the debris and dust obscuring all vision, the Enforcer shuffled through the store and took position behind a large wall chunk in the street, separating himself from the aerial threat above. The pilot was clearly cautious, scanning the wreckage looking for more hostiles. Without orders necessary, I followed the Enforcer toward his secure cover only sensing that a couple of allies were close behind.

"C'mon, we can take him," Private AWOL snapped, clearly eager to clear the fight and head to the next as he rested the barrel of a Mortimer cannon against his shoulder.

The Enforcer had dropped the Cutter and switched back to his Phantom. With his opposite hand, he pointed it open palm toward us. He didn't explain if he wanted us to hush or hold position, but I knew that it was best to stay out of his way. Thankfully, the order overrode AWOL's impatience as well.

Firearm at his side, the Enforcer strode out into the middle of the street amidst the settling smoke. Before it cleared completely, he raised the firearm and pointed it at the pilot seat of the COJR chopper. The pilot continued to survey the destruction until he spotted the Enforcer, immobile like a statue with weapon raised. The sight had to have caught the pilot off guard because he doubted that one shooter could take down the armored airborne unit.

Nervously, I watched the Enforcer extend the barrel on his Phantom. At first, I thought him crazy. There was no need for a suppressed round against a bulky craft, but then I realized that the Phantom had another feature previously unknown to me. He was compressing the entire power cell into a single dense shot which required a number of ticks to activate. Just as the pilot gained the confidence to overcome his misconceptions, it was too late.

The Enforcer's Phantom barked a high density round so compact that it pierced the craft's viewshield and struck the pilot in the head. Incapacitated, the pilot slumped forward on the control stick forcing the craft to lean to the left until it clipped the building overhead and crashed in the corridor to the south.

Subtle as the behavior was, I could tell that the Enforcer exhaled and relaxed his muscles after taking such a risky shot. Cheers erupted from those that had provided the distraction while the rest of us secured the dilapidated storefront. Thankfully the body count was virtually nonexistent only leaving some wounds to treat. The day was early and we still had parcels ahead of us.

38 – Escalation – 38

Resistance Forward Command
Core City, Windstonne Enclave
Commercial Empire, Northam Continent
Thread: sysObserver.cmd

Szazs rubbed his eyes before blinking and returning his focus to the never ending datastream on the noptic screen in front of him. He managed to get a couple of arcs sleep, but he still had to shove the deficiency out of his mind, especially since the excitement of new information had kept his mind churning more so than the conflict at hand, making sleep difficult. Despite the physical fatigue, Szazs felt an internal sense of renewal as his old mind wrestled with the influx of new data provided by the Enforcer.

Tech officers aiding in the creation of the Extend countermeasure dubbed it the neurolash. They showed no restraint in their dislike for the information presented. They simply viewed it as a tool to end the conflict. Szazs, however, treated it like a precious light at the end of a long dark tunnel and it was uplifting to finally witness it. Deep down, Szazs wanted to ponder what he could have done with his research if he had encountered the Firewall Protocol earlier, but for the present time, he would apply his experiences, new and old, to the current conflict to save as many lives as possible.

The urgency left Szazs with little time to digest intricacies to the Firewall Protocol, so he had to leverage data provided by the Enforcer in relation to interferics and drift waves. Szazs required no convincing to see just how dangerous the data could be in the wrong hands which likely represented the source of the resistance's struggle.

After constructing some new models, Szazs overlayed them with the samples related to white-eye behavior. He marveled at the correlation which produced a process that greatly superseded anything he had ever exploited with his animal experiments. Szazs' fingers continued to move on the tapper as he performed wave analytics, but he found himself pausing intermittently to account for an anomaly. Frustrated, Szazs leaned back and ran his fingers through his white hair. After a deep exhale, Szazs finally considered the possibility of another factor. He rearranged his projections and after accounting for the known signal and correlating drift waves, he found the culprit, another signal.

Szazs' eyes widened as he mulled over the discovery. He went to work utilizing his access to the Oshan comm towers. Strangely, he found that the carrier signal did not originate from Casters Tower, but an alternate location altogether. Normally, Szazs would have been more surprised, but given recent events, he half expected it to be none other than Oszwick Enterprises. The informatech was ready to pass the word along, but he second guessed himself, thinking that he should verify the signal's purpose before creating a panic.

Szazs compressed his projections to account for base signal strength and proximity. As he extended the projection timeline, he discovered a variable trait that was capable of bypassing static countermeasures currently in development. Such a process would negate the neurolash.

Frantically, Szazs dug deeper. A careful dissection of the carrier signal revealed that the embedded signal mimicked drift waves themselves, but they had no impact on the average individual. He discovered that Extend was merely a gateway which allowed the hidden signal to have great impact once received. Over time, the embedded signal could continue to impact the Extend user even after discontinuation of chemical consumption.

Szazs gasped at the new discovery. The result twisted his stomach into a knot. Sustained periods of exposure to the unknown signal not only damaged the chemical users permanently, but it had the potential to relay influence to users who never consumed the product.

Something needed to be done, but only comms officers were present in the command post. All strategists were preoccupied with battle operations, so Szazs doubted that any resources could be spared, especially without solid evidence. Szazs knew that he would have to validate his findings. In the event that something happened to him, he made sure to leave a temporary solution to bolster the neurolash's adaptability. If he didn't make it back, it wouldn't cost the lives of anyone critical to the fight on the ground.

Never before had Szazs felt such a strange mixture of feelings for his work. Any urgency had always been under the pressure of a cracking whip to meet deadlines and budgets. For this discovery, he potentially held the keys to rescuing lives unknown. He was excited for new data, but he found that it arrived beneath an indescribable weight. Szazs felt that he better understood the Enforcer just a pinch, and he was thankful that, after all recent struggles, he had a new lease on life.

Contrary to his typical studies, Szazs popped open a tactical map to survey the conflict. As he hoped, there was minimal fighting to the south. Szazs plotted a course around the battle for Oszwick Enterprises which was still comfortably outside the area of contest. All he had to do was find himself a ride.

Urban Floor
Core City, Windstonne Enclave
Commercial Empire, Northam Continent
Thread: actTgtPersp1.view

The conflict was densely packed. I felt like days had been compressed into a matter of arcs. Every chunk of ground gained came with slow sustained pressure or sacrifice. I was quickly learning firsthand why war weighed so heavily on those who had already experienced it with the most prominent reminder being that there was no quit option.

Resistance forces had been thinned and were more scattered in formation. Progress had been slowed by the increase in civilian white-eye victims. The closer we drew to Casters Tower, the more we encountered compromised civilians. Imperan forces made no reservation about using Extend victims as distractions or shields. Resistance forces were divided into suppression and neutralization teams. Anytime a Platypus or Sandstorm tank was taken down, we lost our ability to contain large pockets of civilian obstacles without the neurolash transmissions.

I found myself holed up with Vanguard in another storefront adjacent to an overrun Imperan checkpoint. We waited for Oshan reinforcements, but remaining Goliaths still held their ground against the mobile hovercraft. Additionally, Imperan forces had adjusted their tactics even further to counter the Oshan hovercraft. Due to the dense armor up top, Pirans discovered that the tigers were most effective against the softer mass of the Platypus levitation mechanism, utilizing teeth and claws to shred the supports.

The noise of Platypus turbines roared in our ears as another unit approached from the south. In response, four riderless tigers opposite our intersection position bounded over Imperan allies and charged toward the Platypus. Resistance response immediately prompted a firestorm to be unloaded on the controlled creatures.

With all firearms present locking onto the beasts, it almost seemed futile to expend so much plasma just to drop a few adversaries. The ratio was clearly different than dispatching them by the pack with the Behemoth's planar cannon from a safe position above. I never realized how much that I never wanted to stare one in the face until seeing the mangled flesh, fangs and enormous claws up close.

The tigers bit and clawed at the Platypus, but they struggled to latch onto their target since it didn't halt for their arrival. The overload of plasma finally dropped two of the tigers, but the remainder took notice of the plasma stream. The first turned away from the vehicle and growled. I could tell that it was centered on my position and ready to charge. I fired the last few rounds that my EQ would permit. I panicked, unsure what to do as the beast loomed. With its jaw still open, a well placed Mortimer shell sizzled through the air. The blast struck the tiger right in the mouth, ripping its skull apart leaving a disgusting mess on the street. I looked over to see an enthusiastic Private AWOL who relished the hit.

"I got ya," Private AWOL nodded. "Heavy Weapons. Never leave home without them!"

All I could do was express my gratitude with a nod and weak chuckle since I was still too shaken to vocalize the experience of my potential demise. More shouts quickly distracted me from such thoughts as the remaining rogue tiger bore down on more allies. The tiger was within claws reach as talons from above sunk deep into the tiger's torso lifting it into the air. Shouts of terror morphed into enthusiasm as a hijacked raptor flapped its wings and tossed the menace with force into a Goliath trying to fire at the monstrous bird of prey.

After a sizable reduction in opposition, resistance forces moved forward to secure access to the next corridor. While some took up defensive positions, others verified health of any compromised civilians caught in the crossfire, yet others were tasked with resolving terminal status of enemy combatants. Squeamish about the decision making process, I took up a position on the northeast corner of the intersection, hoping that such a post would require less attention since it pointed away from our southwest trajectory. To my surprise, I was wrong, considering that Imperans forces had secured a perimeter all around in the event of an attack from any direction.

Commotion flooded my eyeballs, prompting me to display tactical markers on my ikes, but doing so nearly made the situation worse, assaulting my brain with an information overload. Allied and hostile icons alike danced before my eyes. I kept my weapon pointed to the north, but my reticle shifted slightly with each body movement per gradual neck adjustments when I tried to gain a better sense of action the next intersection over.

Icons marked projectiles high overhead as Wombats fired along the related corridor. The Wombat's shells splashed into a large grouping of Imperan forces. A pack of tigers scattered into the intersection with only a couple of riders amongst them. Fleeing without strategy, the tigers were then overrun by a Platypus anticipating the reaction. In a counter move, a Goliath that evaded the shelling fired on the Platypus forcing the craft to weave out of control until it got lodged on an angled path of debris. The Goliath was able to run down the impaled Platypus. The Goliath pilot lifted a hefty razerjack foot and stepped on the armored dome of the Platypus while the gunner pointed the turrets downward and fired on the craft.

A resistance controlled raptor swooped down to distract the Goliath, but the bird operator hadn't detected that there was another razerjack on approach. I rubbed my eyes to confirm that there was a large clearing to the northeast obscured by the Windstonne buildings. A Magellan advanced at an angle to the otherwise squared dartway. The Magellan opened fire on the raptor. The raptor controller was at least able to detect the massive razerjack's presence at the first sign of danger, so he forced the mutated bird to evade and fly down another corridor.

Another raptor flew in from the Magellan's blindside and blocked the view of the pilots within. The Magellan swiveled to confront the engaging raptor, but its movement was too slow. The raptor ran its sharp talons down the hull of the Magellan only to discover that it had additional countermeasures. The Magellan fired an electrical pulse, making contact with the large winged foe. Without adequate capacity to deflect the charge, the raptor convulsed and twisted into an unnatural shape as it fell to the ground.

My eyes widened at the ineffectiveness of the mutated bird against the razerjack. If I hadn't felt small in the Behemoth against a Magellan, I certainly did at that time with as much stature as an ant against an elephant. The Magellan held its position and fired upon nearby resistance forces. I felt my insides twist, knowing that once it was finished, there was nothing left for it to do but bear down on top of us.

Urban Heights
Core City, Windstonne Enclave
Commercial Empire, Northam Continent
Thread: sysObserver.cmd

Commander Thomas Jackal pressed his hat against his head as a strong gust of wind from the passing raptor nearly lifted it away. His team drew close to the building's edge, as the Magellan in the street trudged toward resistance forces. From the rumbling underfoot, he could tell that the razerjack was approaching from the left. He was about to make a move for the building ledge, but when he realized his position was still a deck below the unit's viewport, he hurriedly hissed orders for his team members to get behind cover. The operation couldn't be risked by giving away their position.

The razjerjack moved slowly, giving Jackal enough time to look for a solution to the height disadvantage. He quickly spotted the external emergency ladder attached to the next building adjacent to the razerjack's path. Once the Magellan matched the team's position and there was no longer a threat of detection, the team rushed up the metal stairs, clearing at least three decks to put them above the looming mechanical threat.

Forced to rush several steps ahead of the marching razerjack, Jackal finally halted the team while he dropped the line that he intended to connect with the Magellan's angled head. He swiftly broke out the gear provided. The Oshan techs had provided him with a high powered magnetic grapple. Jackal made sure that it was securely attached to the line and fastened to his belt after double-checking the harness for the Drakken glider on his back.

Jackal crouched low on the roof of the taller building along with the two techs with him. It normally wasn't his method to travel with noncombatants, but he knew they would be needed to master the Magellan's operations in short order.

The Magellan below finally reached the drop point as it stopped to engage the resistance forces which were in the street. As expected, it took the bait of attacking the raptors still controlled by the operatives at the command post. The first raptor darted away from the conflict while the second one obscured view of the Magellan operators. The tick that the raptor made contact, the pilot activated a pulse to paralyze the massive bird. Hard scaly feathers poked into the air as the bird twisted and collapsed.

Sensing that the Magellan was going to advance, Jackal tensed his fingers around the glider harness.

"What if it activates that defensive webbing again?" Sergeant Trevor asked with concern.

"Then you'll have to figure out how to hijack that thing without a glider," Jackal replied without taking his eye off the target.

"Sir, your assessment of our resolve is a bit... generous," Trevor responded, clearly revealing his disdain for field work.

"Can't win wars from a desk, Fishies. Sooner or later you have to take the plunge," Jackal snapped as he sprinted for the building ledge.

Jackal leapt into the air and extended the glider wings. He felt a rush as he viewed the spacious view of the trench below while his stomach threatened to drop out of his body. The harness held tight as it upheld his weight. The Magellan's exhaust vent blew a strong gust of air, forcing the glider upward. Jackal angled his body to the side to resume course on target lest he crash into an adjacent building.

With speed, the glider closed the distance and Jackal touched down on the Magellan. The lumbering sway of the razerjack made it difficult to secure footing, so Jackal prioritized slapping the grapple onto the Magellan's angled dome. Sacrificing objective for priority, Jackal stumbled while collapsing the glider wings. He fell backward, barely grabbing the line he'd secured with the grapple. His arm screamed as he dangled by one arm. There were no scalable objects within reach so he kicked his foot off an exhaust pipe to propel himself up to the hatch on the top of the Magellan's head. Urgency escalated as the Magellan's movement threatened the amount of slack from the line attached to the building.

Jackal tugged on the access hatch only to verify that it had been secured from the inside. He quickly fed as much slack as he could through the line from the grapple and held tight. He needed as much slack possible. The Magellan viewport would likely endure more than low density plasma, so he needed to optimize every tick available.

With a strong kick, Jackal jumped from the top of the Magellan's head and the line in his hand snapped taut, forcing his body into a downward collision course with the razerjack. Jackal immediately fired every round he could at the viewport frame before kicking his feet inward to dislodge hardmelt window.

As the viewport folded inward, Jackal twisted his body to fit the horizontal frame. The awkward human projectile pressed the viewport against the pilot and gunners impairing operations which brought the razerjack to a halt.

One gunner scrambled out the Magellan hatch, hoping to get a downward shot at the unwelcome attacker. With a smirk the gunner leveled his firearm at Jackal who struggled to right his position. Jackal simply smirked in response. Confused the gunner looked about, but he never got the joke as Sgt. Trevor's boots kicked him in the back. After using his EQ to zip down the line, the Oshan operative knocked the threat off the razerjack completely.

The scream from above distracted the pilot and the remaining gunner long enough for Jackal to aim at the Magellan occupants. Jackal squeezed the trigger, but the pilot was quick to grab his arms from behind. The firearm was knocked from his hands, forcing Jackal to reach over his head and jam his thumbs into the eyes of his restrainer.

Yelling in anger, the pilot released his grip long enough for Jackal to connect a boot to the scrambling gunner. Determined, the gunner tried to unleash a flurry of punches at Jackal's body, but a burst of plasma by Trevor's EQ from the access ladder put the Imperan foe down. Free to spin about, Jackal slammed the pilot into the Magellan viewport frame, his face slamming hard with a sickening goosh noise.

"That wasn't so bad was it?" Jackal quipped as the tech dropped down through the access hatch.

"I never want to do that again," Trevor huffed.

Clapping him on the shoulder, Jackal let Trevor help the other tech reach the Magellan. Jackal moved the bodies of their foes behind the command chairs given the lack of space in the cramped cockpit. With the first hurdle cleared, they immediately scrambled to decipher the Magellan's controls.

Commander Jackal settled into the elevated pilot seat which was centered between the lateral gunner chairs. The Oshan operatives went to work testing control interfaces.

"Looks like these were rolled, err... marched, out prior to final testing," Trevor mused.

"Premature but still lethal," Jackal replied as he familiarized himself with the control stick and nearby tappers. "Focus on mobility and weapons. I don't have time for the new feature sales pitch."

"This is a three man rig with isolated roles," Trevor replied, unsure how the commander would assume the ability to multitask with such a large machine.

"Sergeant, there is no way that an enterprise would spend the berry to build one of these without failsafes. There has to be an emergency routine somewhere," Jackal replied impatiently.

Trevor quickly scanned the interfaces and found the subroutine to slave weapon access to the pilot seat. It was an assisted process, so he was doubtful as to its effectiveness, "Sir, even though I can reroute controls, the targeting systems are hard wired."

"I thought you brainpans never left the lab without a slate. I'll work with a makeshift interface, just get it done," Jackal snapped.

Trevor quickly withdrew a noptic slate from his field pack and linked its visual interfaces with those of the Magellan before handing it to Jackal. He was about to protest upon discovery of another issue, but Jackal was quick to interject.

"Have you considered swapping the colors?" Jackal asked. He suspected that the tech was about to relay an issue regarding the friend and foe targeting system.

Trevor grimaced as he reluctantly responded to the suggestion. He was frustrated yet again at being outmatched by his superior, so without a word, he handed the adjusted slate up to Jackal. Raring to get the razerjack moving, Jackal set the slate within his line of sight so that he could use it without having to shift his eyeballs toward the confusing Imperan interface.

"I knew that you could do it," Jackal said, making sure to affirm his subordinates skills in spite of the added pressure. "You two keep on the breakdown, and I'll take care of the beatdown."

After a quick survey of the controls, Jackal pressed on a floor pedal. The pedal was heavy and required far more pressure than a mox. He felt the Magellan's engines rev as he realized that he had only depressed a clutch. Jackal huffed, realizing that even the razjeracks had adopted the cultural inversion of driving standards. Acknowledging the switch, Jackal pressed the opposite pedal which required even more pressure, and the powerful mechanisms within the Magellan forced it to lurch forward one step.

The Oshan operatives looked at the commander, wondering if he was up for the task. Commander Jackal cast a look of disdain which subordinates knew by reputation. Challenge him without an alternative, and there would certainly be havoc to behold. The operatives returned their attention to deciphering the systems and Jackal switched over to the targeting system which allowed the Magellan to swivel far more easily than the walking mechanisms.

Trying to manage multiple systems on the razerjack was certainly a chore, but Jackal found himself making sense of the Magellan as its steps became less jarring within the scope possible. He accepted that the massive machine had no brake since gravity accomplished that in combination with the clutch to disengage the active gears.

Enthused about finally operating the razerjack properly, Jackal was distracted enough to disregard the targeting slate as another Magellan cut into formation from a side street. Jackal reacted by slowing the razerjack and squeezing a trigger on the control stick to fire the rail cannon. As suspected the assist subroutines missed their target and shredded the building adjacent to the opposing Magellan which stomped ahead with a full stride.

Detecting the missed strike, but uncertain as to its source, the Imperan razerjack's torso spun a half circle without breaking its advance. Frustrated at losing the element of surprise, Jackal huffed his agitation before firing all weapons at the Magellan. The Imperan Magellan hesitated, but as the torrent of rails pierced the air, it too opened fire.

Concerned that the acquisition would be short lived, Jackal tried to find a weakness as large metal spikes bounced off the dense angled razerjack armor. The adjacent buildings were looking like oversized porcupine victims as the weaponry defaced the urban trench walls. At last, one rail clipped the shoulder armor of the Imperan Magellan. Exploiting the gap, Jackal fired upon the exposed razerjack frame. As Jackal shifted the firing solution, eventually a plate fell from the target.

"Is that what I think it is?" Jackal asked as he squinted through the viewport. "Give me a readout of all available ordinance on this heap!"

"There are no other systems listed as active," Trevor replied in a panic.

"Then we'll test the system integrity the old fashioned way," Jackal snapped.

Jackal focused all rails on what appeared to be a missile system embedded on the Magellan's shoulders. The first few shots missed, but once a rail pierced the nose of a missile embedded within, the neighboring munitions continued a chain reaction, engulfing the Magellan torso in flames, creating scorched craters in the faces of the adjacent buildings.

"It's a little early for fireworks," the Enforcer said into the comm.

"Yeah, well burn that image into your brains and save it for later when we finish this fight," Jackal quipped.

"Ryoukai," the Enforcer responded.

Jackal exhaled as he verified that there was no life left in the opposing Magellan. He returned his attention to mastering the razerjack's controls while he tasked the techs with finding any and all hidden weaponry attached to the Magellan's frame.

Urban Floor
Core City, Windstonne Enclave
Commercial Empire, Northam Continent
Thread: actTgtPersp1.view

The air cover from raptors and artillery support from the Wombats alleviated the pressure on the ground teams, allowing us to advance our position. Teams fractured even more by their roles as we drew closer to Casters Tower. The Imperan forces were so compressed within the final stretches that the battle was not limited to the street corridors alone. Frank Jenkins had tightly packed his defensive options in order to withstand attacks from every angle.

We countered increasing resistance from civilians as well. While the lack of counter transmission support had cost the lives of some civilians, the support teams continued to work tirelessly to restrain and transport any noncombatants who were severely under Extend's influence. Many civilians who feared to exit their homes during the conflict demonstrated comprehension and appreciation for resistance forces once they understood the nature of the control taking over their loved ones. For the cases in which family members had been able to track their loved ones that were forced to fight, they offered to monitor and restrain those captured once secured, lessening the workload on the support teams. The remnant of Extend victims were carted off to pens to be restrained and monitored by Oshan tech teams until the power skirmish was settled. Even soldiers initially concerned about target selection did little to gripe after comprehending just how integrated the problem was within the Windstonne populace. Had the strategists not made the decision to contain over terminate, the body count of noncombatants would have been catastrophic.

Torque and the Serpent split off and joined another team, but I continued to shadow the Enforcer until ordered otherwise. We still advanced alongside Alcazaban and Oshan soldiers all who had proven competent. My mind continued to spin at just how much ground we had covered in the few arcs of daylight. I was shocked that I was still alive on account of conditioning from the Enforcer's training, intercession from skilled allies on my behalf or just simple panic maneuvers of my own as plasma, debris and orders were flung in every direction.

Our team had taken a more southern approach to Casters Tower after receiving intel about skirmishes still between us and our target. Members of the team constantly checked in every direction before advancing to the next set of cover. As we reached a new corridor, we discovered little evidence of conflict. There were indications of combat, but they suggested that forces had rushed through. I sensed that the team felt uneasy, but no one could identify any immediate threats.

Even with the honed observation skills of my allies, I knew that something felt off. I continued to scan the buildings with my ikes, swiftly toggling magnification levels and filter modes. I too found nothing.

Knowing that hesitation did us no good, the Alcazaban scouts cautiously stepped into the clearing. They kept their weapons up, ready to move to cover. As they moved forward, I could tell that the Enforcer tensed as he too suspected something unusual. My eyes tracked the adjacent buildings until my eyes landed on a vertical restaurant in the distance with balconies on each floor that overlooked the street. I was unable to gain any information at such a range from my ikes, but the tick that the soldiers reached the center of the corridor a green flicker of light revealed a bolt of plasma fire.

Before I could even shout out a location, the two scouts immediately dropped to the ground in pain. The remaining team looked in every direction ready to open fire, but the Enforcer ordered everyone to standfast while he raced into the open.

I calculated that our allies didn't even comprehend the nature of the scouts' injuries. The speed of the attack created just enough of a blur on my ikes that I realized they had been shot in the legs, instead of the chest, if our foes had been going for a kill shot. The thought carrying the understanding of the situation surprised me, it was a trap. I opened my mouth to yell for the Enforcer to hold off, but my words went unheard in the confusion. All I could do was hope that he had already seen what I had and that he knew the risks because there was no stopping him.

I watched nervously as his form dashed into the open. Confirming my suspicion, his arms moved to create his own distractions. His arms extended and light metal debris flung into the air after he activated his grips. The Enforcer whipped his right hand, forcing one piece of the debris to fly overhead, and then followed similar form with his left. A dense plasma bolt dinged the first plate and then deflected off the second. The sequence of levitating scraps which deflected well placed sniper rounds certainly frustrated those looking to capitalize on the carefully laid trap.

Not content with deflected attacks, the Enforcer dove over the injured soldiers and lifted a flurry of scraps and shards before tossing two Nebula's into the air flooding the area with smoke. The cloud burst quickly obscured all natural visibility.

I knew that the smoke couldn't fully dissuade all attacks. With tech filters active, I watched the Enforcer assist the soldiers from within the smoke. Realizing that odds of survival for those injured would go up by reducing the time needed to whisk them to safety, I rushed toward the smoke cloud to assist, followed by a couple of our allies. Further adhering to the Enforcer's prioritization methods, another thought settled in. Despite the perceived jeopardy to his own life, the quick thinking negated the overall jeopardy to others.

Urban Heights
Core City, Windstonne Enclave
Commercial Empire, Northam Continent
Thread: sysObserver.cmd

The Drakken soldier huffed as he switched the power cell clip of his Hellings 20. He quickly made the switch while the sniper next to him also fired multiple missed shots at the rogue daring to run into the open. The Drakken was perplexed at the adversary's timing since he anticipated or adequately deflected the shots fired in succession. Minimizing his reload time to a tick, the Drakken resighted on the pair of downed soldiers and glared through his amber eyepiece to find the target only to have his entire scope blur with the distant smoke.

Angered, the Drakken looked away momentarily to confirm the massive smoke cloud which hovered above the trap zone. He pressed his eye once again to the scope, hoping to leverage the Drakken tech thermal filter. Before doing so, the Drakken noticed the billowing smoke shifted enough to get a raw visual on the target, but what he saw through his scope surprised him. The rogue sporting blue camouflage stared directly back at him, knowing right where he was. The gap had to be at least a parcel away which suggested the impossible, but the Drakken knew better than to hesitate. His face twisted into a sneer as he squeezed the trigger to drop the defiant fool.

The shot never sounded as the Drakken's head rolled from his shoulders with a clean cut. Hearing the distraction, the adjacent Drakken sniper intended to turn his head, but never got a glance of the blade or its wielder since his head rolled onto the balcony in similar fashion.

"Ghosted," Wraith Chung smirked as he raised a fist to his side.

The Serpent nodded as he matched Chung's fist while they stowed their blades. The pair of Ghosts quickly scanned the balcony for more foes. They found none, but a COJR Tornac quickly zipped into line of sight as its pilot suspected that something was off. The attack chopper spun about to face the balcony where the dead Drakken lay, but the two Ghosts had already blinked out of sight.

The Tornac pilot angled back on the control stick as a Mortimer shell zipped passed the cockpit. He quickly turned the chopper to the right and lifted it a couple of decks to face down Torque who had the spent Mortimer lowered to his side. The chopper pilot stared, confused why Torque wasn't running. Either he had more shells to fire or he was just plain stupid. The pilot smirked as his finger tensed on the firing controls.

Torque smiled back, knowing that the pilot had to gamble on the situation. Torque posed no threat if he had no means of returning fire. Defiantly, Torque gestured at the craft with his free hand and pointed over its frame. The chopper was close enough for Torque to read the confusion on the pilot's face.

The pilot shook his head in response thinking that Torque wanted him to look around at some distraction. Torque then nodded comically, trying not to laugh. Even though he couldn't send the visual cue as intended, Torque leaned to the side and nodded at an unseen ally opposite the urban trench.

By the time the pilot realized the nature of the antics, Private AWOL squeezed off a shell from behind the Tornac. The shell connected with the left exhaust vent, shredding the internal structure, leading to an internal misfire of the engines. The pilot twisted hard on the unresponsive stick, but to his own demise the chopper fell into a burning heap on the street below.

Recognizing the attack on one of their own, two Derecho choppers flying parallel separated to drop Guerillas on each of the buildings occupied by Torque and Private AWOL. The choppers dropped quickly, and the Guerillas in their graystone uniforms quickly rappelled to the rooftop, training their weapons on the surprisingly low quantity foes.

Before the Guerillas could engage, threat markers illuminated on Potentate Ang's console from the command post after which he immediately relayed coordinates and firing verification to a series of Wombats lining the skirmish perimeter. Although the belch of the small artillery units was too distant for the Guerillas to hear, the local explosions were not, as shells rained down shredding the COJR soldiers and the choppers above them.

Structural integrity quickly diminished, compelling Torque and AWOL to flee their respective rooftops. The precise Wombats fired clear of their positions, but not of the buildings which soon rumbled underfoot, weakened even further by the fireballs of the choppers landing on the rooftops.

The chopper closest to Torque fell hard, shuddering the whole structure. The outer third of the rooftop collapsed no longer able to support the weight of the blazing air unit. Ultimately, the craft toppled toward the street. The fireball threatened to fall on an approaching Magellan, but instead the unit halted its march, twisted its torso and backhanded the craft knocking it to the side. Triumphantly, the Magellan unleashed a chorus of metal clicks as its weapons went through a reload cycle.

As resistance forces recognized that the approaching Magellan was the one commandeered by Commander Jackal's team, cheers arose from the ground. Optimism gave forces the morale boost needed to push ahead to the next intersection. Forces closed on the last couple of parcels standing between them and Casters Tower, and the density of remaining Imperan forces embodied the desperation of a cornered enemy.

39 – Dayshift – 39

Resistance Forward Command
Core City, Windstonne Enclave
Commercial Empire, Northam Continent
Thread: sysObserver.cmd

Maxwell's head popped backward as he realized that he was nearly falling asleep at the terminal. Strange fluctuations in signal wavelengths created just enough of a jarring light display to grab his attention. He shifted his weight onto his back legs as he stared at the anomaly. Swiftly engaging the closest tapper using his interface designed for hamster sized paws, Maxwell brushed through some scans before isolating what he thought was the anomaly.

"This is unusual," Maxwell mused as he tried to confirm his suspicions.

"What are you thoughts on this, Protech?" Maxwell asked.

Getting no response, Maxwell shuffled to the edge of the desktop where he could get a view of Szazs' console, "Protech?"

Seeing an empty workstation, Maxwell's eyes darted about. Since his console was on the adjacent desk, Maxwell waddled to the gap between the desks and flung his rotund body across to the next. Szazs' workstation wasn't setup for Maxwell's interface, but the data remaining on screen caused Maxwell's little black eyes to widen immensely.

"Porter!" Maxwell yelled for the Oshan tech assigned to help if needed.

After a quick exchange, Maxwell poured through the scans that Szazs left behind about a dual signal from a remote location as well as his potential solution to temporarily override the adaptive nature of the signal from Casters Tower. Maxwell's brain went into a panic while he tried to implement a strategy, but he was just a hamster. He wasn't going to pull it off without help.

Urban Floor
Core City, Windstonne Enclave
Commercial Empire, Northam Continent
Thread: actTgtPersp1.view

My lungs screamed for air as we momentarily settled from our run to the next demolished storefront for cover. The last few stretches had been nothing but tense, highly concentrated firefights. Fireteams and suppression teams alike had their work cut out for them. While the amount of Imperan hardware was diminishing, the number of ground level firefights increased. Fireteams were forced to slow their attacks to account for the greater concentration of white-eye victims while the suppression teams had to increase their output to stop them. Average civilians acted like crazed vims either rushing with bare hands or makeshift melee weapons.

As I leaned against a damaged wall, I checked my supply of power cells and snapped two more into my EQ. I was grateful to have the support teams present because I struggled to keep up with shifting between military and civilian targets and was likely to fire upon the wrong one without being used to switching weapons.

Noticing that I was running low on cells, an Alcazaban support member handed me a few more which I stowed with my gear. I nodded my appreciation in return without extra air for words.

There was no denying the overload of sensory information that I hadn't been accustomed to from daily life. Every input relayed constant information to my brain on account of adrenaline and yet my internal fatigue poked at me only for the urgency and danger to keep it outside the perimeter of influence. Sweat soaked clothes clinging to my skin, hazy smoke filtered lights and the scent of scorched brick, plasma and charred skin all fought to keep my focus on the mission at hand.

"Mac, we've got a problem," Maxwell's voice chirped through the Vanguard comm.

Per the interruption, the Enforcer nodded for the fireteam to advance without us.

"Switch to local," the Enforcer said in response.

I realized that the Enforcer was concerned with other Vanguard members getting distracted without knowing their situation, but he still opened the comm for me to hear while Maxwell relayed updates.

"Szazs discovered an adaptive nature to the Extend signal, and a secondary signal eventually able to operate without the victim's requisite use of Extend. The other signal originates somewhere other than Casters Tower," Maxwell said.

The Enforcer took a moment to consider the impact before his response, "Does the protech have countermeasure suggestions?"

"That's the problem. He's nowhere to be found. He left scans at least to resolve the adaptive signal. I have already relayed an algorithm adjustment for the neurolash transmitters, but the secondary signal is still a problem. I fear that Szazs opted to deal with it himself," Maxwell said after a long pause.

Even without the ability to read minds, I could sense that the Enforcer was internalizing possible solutions on account of how wildly his lens colors shifted from behind his ikes. Under similar circumstances, I would have expected anyone to get frustrated and start vocally spitfiring possible ideas, but instead, his calm persistence resulted in a simple response.

"Good work, Friend," the Enforcer replied to Maxwell.

"I hope it's enough," Maxwell said.

"One hill at a time," the Enforcer replied in a manner that starkly opposed the tension of the situation.

"Vangauard, form up," the Enforcer said as he resumed the open comm with our allies.

Lights blinked on our ikes to confirm the order. I recognized that our primary objective hadn't changed. I too found myself puzzling over how to overcome both angles of the fight and forced myself to table the new data, knowing that it could only distract when there was an abundance of plasma and debris zipping in front of my face.

The Enforcer and I caught up to our designated fireteam with Torque and the Serpent quick to join us. Finally, we had line of sight on the base of Casters Tower, and it was a light show of plasma, smoke, fires, bodies, sandbags and structural holes.

We barely had time to settle when a loud hum signaled the dissipation of energy from all the structures surrounding Casters Tower. At first we thought a power failure had finally activated, but as we stared at our target it began to glow with greater intensity. The building's lighting shouldn't have been as noticeable in the daylight, but to our shock the daylight too was diminishing in response as dark heavy clouds formed in the sky, creating a dark backdrop to place emphasis on the tower. The clouds rode atop strong winds which only seemed more intense as they flowed closer to the tower.

As the power drained from the Windstonne grid, it appeared to flow upward through the tower forcing us to track its movement until a near blinding burst of white flashed from the tower's antennae well out of sight from the ground level. Without aerial footage relayed from scouts, we never could have envisioned the phenomenon as we craned our necks to see the byproduct of the light burst. The event impacted the atmosphere itself as the very clouds above the tower swirled in circular fashion.

"That is not natural," I remarked. Vanguard members present said nothing, although the Enforcer did manage a facial twitch, knowing that I was at least self-aware of my own overstatement for a change.

The strange visual even distracted our foes for a moment, but likely per strict orders they were the first to return to the matter at hand of dispensing plasma in the direction of resistance forces. Once the distraction was unanimously disregarded, the firefight resumed in full, but I couldn't help but get one last glance at the securely powered structure which now glared like a torch in a cave against the premature nighttime darkness.

Oszwick Enterprises
Core City Fringe, Windstonne Enclave
Commercial Empire, Northam Continent
Thread: sysObserver.cmd

The atmosphere was strangely still as the contingent of Mogul Prime members approached Oszwick Enterprises. Structural damage and stray plasma fire suggested a recent conflict. The visitors assumed that there might be an effort to begin repairs, especially during the daytime, but no such activity was to be found.

Voltaire led the partial clan toward the executive building's front entrance. Before he could decide on announcing his presence or just walking in a familiar face exited the door and blocked the clan's advance on the entry platform.

"Mogul Prime. To what do I owe the visit?" Lucient said, eyeing the four guests suspiciously.

"Oszwick tasked us with assuming operational control of some projects," Voltaire said flatly.

"You? Takeover? I don't think so," Lucient snapped, nearly spitting his words.

"It's not my problem if you were cut out of the loop, Lucient, but one way or another, we are taking over Project Synergon," Voltaire said.

"You have no place here. No right! This is a family operation, and this is my inheritance after working it from within," Lucient said.

"Well, carp, Voltaire. I think I forgot my junior executive badge at the shop," Tycoon chided.

Lucient fumed, looking at each of the visitors in turn. They returned no emotion, hinting that they weren't to be swayed by any discussion whatsoever, "Your paltry clan cannot handle the operations. The shards will never work for you."

"We didn't come here for loyalty, only the hardware," Voltaire said emphatically, tired of Lucient's obstruction.

"Then I guess we'll test your capacity to seize it by force," Lucient snapped.

Oszwick Enterprises' calm façade exploded with activity as countless pasty skinned staffers ambled out of the building, charging toward Mogul Prime. Lucient was quick to backstep in order to retreat into the building, but Bender swiftly shoulder charged through unsuspecting shards and blocked the door. Lucient scrambled to safety through a wave of shards who approached from his right. Since he wasn't the target, Mogul Prime was forced to repel the witless rabble of shards looking to tackle them.

Voltaire rolled his eyes he as watched Lucient slip away. Snapping a powerful side kick outward, Voltaire caught one shard in the face who fell into two more on approach. The unskilled laborers of Oszwick Enterprises posed little threat beyond a time delay. Mogul Prime needed to get inside before Lucient had means to tamper with internal systems. The clan members could rush through the door, but it would surely create a messy chokepoint.

Hauteur was swift to pull her scarf over her face, only allowing her eyes to peer through the designated slot in the fabric. Taking sentiments from clanmates to heart she knew that her style was to craft an icon, not adhere to the rules of her homeland in regard to keeping her face covered in a conflict. Since she knew that the shards were already compromised targets, she considered it practice for future impressionable minds. With her cloth mask secure, she pulled her nagat blade from her back and telescoped the staff to its full length which nearly matched her height. Her first swing transferred lethal slashes to the first three shards who approached.

Very few shards dared to exercise caution as they closed in while the others mindlessly charged the outsiders by means of extreme conditioning or absent mental capacity. Tycoon had already drawn his jutte, its dense metal occasionally reflecting light sources as it connected to shard skulls or spines with destructive force. Tycoon was never one to fight without an emphasis on class as he deftly evaded the shards and swung the forearm-length rod at any who dared get to close. The sickening crunch of metal to bone ensured that Tycoon rarely needed to strike a target twice.

"Anyone up for a wager?" Tycoon smirked as he dropped into a low stance, challenging any nearby shards to advance.

"You know I never gamble with my dimps. That's drinking berry," Bender replied after wiping his mouth and securing his flask in a vest pocket.

"Deal. How about if you net the body count, you have to do my quarterly datasheets... sober," Tycoon quipped.

"If I win, you get to do them yourself, after drinking me under the table," Bender replied.

After Tycoon nodded his agreement, Bender drew both of the shiny wooden pobats from behind his back and quickly spun them around from their perpendicular handles. Two shards found themselves smashed upside the temples as Bender whirled the short weapons around in blinding fashion.

"Best get crackin'," Bender snapped before leaping into the air and dropping on a group of shards who were unable to dodge in time.

With the graceful, evasive and precise attacks of one, and the crude menacing brutality of another, Tycoon and Bender created a whirlwind of carnage, overwhelming the first wave of Oszwick Enterprise bodies which poured out of the building. The fray gave Hauteur enough room to swing her weapon with maximum effectiveness without catching her allies. She was quick to impale one shard at range, only to jam the butt of the staff into the abdomen of another who approached from behind.

Voltaire thought little of the squishy minions as he dropped another shard with a solid punch to the jaw. His knuckles felt minimal sensation from the impact, but Voltaire knew that the sheer number of adversaries would likely create a bruise or two along with some scuff marks on his shoes. To him, it was a personal indication that Mogul Prime had no time to waste. To accelerate the process, Voltaire snapped his fimachuk to his side and cracked several shards in the skull in succession with the short staff.

The hybrid stick moved swiftly at Voltaire's command as he unleashed a flurry of strikes to any approaching shard. Temple, neck, abdomen and ribs were critically fractured as Voltaire unleashed hits before the shards could respond.

Tiring of the mindless behavior of the shards, Voltaire belted a command at the top of his lungs, "Sit down!"

Whether the impact was from a seeded command or the volume force, at least three shards were knocked onto their backsides. One behind Voltaire still advanced and attempted to grab Voltaire in a choke hold from behind. The shard struggled to hold the grip as Voltaire stood to his full height, lifting the shard off the ground. A quick blow from the fimachuk knocked the shard senseless, putting his feet back on the ground. Voltaire spun about, wrapped the stick around the shard's neck and extended the weapon until it revealed a connecting cord between the two halves. With the shard behind him again, Voltaire leaned forward as the fimachuk pressed against the shard's neck. The minion flipped over Voltaire's back and was launched into the air. Without even a glance, Hauteur impaled the flying shard with her nagat and guided its fall onto another batch of enemies.

As Mogul Prime began to thin the horde, they felt a looming distraction as the skies darkened abnormally. Each member wanted to pause and identify the cause, but the relentless shards prevented them. At best, they could only catch the disturbance through peripheral vision.

"Anyone want to speculate?" Bender asked, being the first to vocalize the confusion.

"The fruits of somebody's labor," Tycoon replied as he crushed the skull of another shard.

Voltaire spotted Lucient who was heading for a side access door to the building. The clan leader's hands moved the fimachuk in blinding fashion as he ran, spinning the connected short sticks and knocking any adjacent shard senseless.

Lucient was about to make his way into the safety of the building when he too noticed the skies darkening. He had the clearance to observe until he realized that Voltaire was closing in.

"Divert the secondary signal," Lucient said into his sonair.

Before Voltaire could clear the obstacle of shards, a tumult arose from the surrounding industrial buildings and distant residences. Lucient did something to activate Extend victims in the vicinity, some of which which were already bearing down on the clan members. Disregarding Lucient, Voltaire hustled back to the entry platform to run damage control on the mindless horde of white-eyes that mixed with the waning contingent of shards.

The white-eyed foes were no more competent than the shards under the influence of the Oszwick Enterprise systems, but they compensated with numbers, tenacity and crude weapons. No one dared elaborate that the scenario appeared to be a losing proposition.

"Go! You need to secure the uplink," Tycoon shouted at Hauteur after she cleared a space by swinging the long weapon overhead.

"We'll cover you," Bender affirmed, indicating that Voltaire needed to go too.

Voltaire nodded in response as he and Hauteur made for the building entrance, leaving the other two clan members to consolidate the mess of bodies. Hauteur wanted to check the building's security systems to assist her allies, but securing Project Synergon took priority. She was confident that even two Mogul Prime members could hold their own, at least temporarily.

"What do you say? Want to go for two quarters?" Tycoon huffed as he grimaced at the cut in his vest.

"Stack 'em up," Bender complied as he took another swig from his flask. "I've got a brew that will put you out in one shot."

After wiping excess drips on his elbow, Bender arrogantly twirled his pobats and spun his body in a circle connecting with a long string of adversary skulls. Tycoon wouldn't be bested as he quickly calculated an effective path of strikes and evasions through a large cluster of white-eyes ahead. The two of them shared the resolute mindset common to all of Mogul Prime, no one would interfere with their quest for dominance.

Urban Floor
Core City, Windstonne Enclave
Commercial Empire, Northam Continent
Thread: actTgtPersp1.view

There was no escaping the thick tension that seemed to slow our advance more than the opposition. The heat of conflict was so heavy that it trapped us behind cover, never allowing us to progress from one firefight to the next. We could see the first floor of Casters Tower without visual aid, that is, when there was enough of a clearing through the smoke. Everyone looked for a way to break through the defensive Piran line, but it was so well fortified and bolstered by white-eyes that there was no access without destruction to the entrance should larger ordinance adjust the equation.

Suppression teams were exhausted, no longer able to perform their task at a distance. Without the ability to clear bodies, the risk to the Extend victims was increasing. We were also starting to witness the effects of the variable signal as targets once dropped were starting to regain consciousness and pursue yet again.

"We've got an opening on the northwest corner," a voice snapped through the comm.

The Enforcer was quick to verify, noticing that well placed Mortimer strikes had cleared Goliath and tiger elements alike in addition to thinning Piran numbers. Without word, the Enforcer was already leading Vanguard toward the opening.

"Platypus units with updated neurolash transmitters are stalled. Stand by," Ang responded, fully understanding the need to capitalize on the situation.

"It's now or never, Boomerang!" the Enforcer yelled.

While I let those on point debate the advance, I tugged on a strap to my vest, thankful that I had listened to my friends. The end of the strap was singed and a scorch mark or two suggested that I might not still be upright had I not been wearing it. Since I had the clarity of thought to check, I verified that my EQ was still full on power cells before the next advance. Before I could even exit the interface on my ikes, a new statement blared across the general resistance channel.

"Weld those verts together, Men! This is not about politicians or borders, but freedom! Not only yours, but that of your families! Now, Fight On!" General Cruz barked.

The intended morale boost sparked the proper cord because Alcazaban forces were moving ahead without waiting for Oshan support. The Enforcer quickly identified the strategy which was intended to drive a wedge into the weakest point of the Imperan forces.

"Ayezon!" The Enforcer yelled as he led the way for Vanguard to integrate with the advancing formation.

I found myself contributing to the battle cry that erupted from the mass of resistance forces rushing Casters Tower on foot. My mind screamed lunacy at running toward opposition without cover, without designated targets, without process. Shocked that I had enough time to contemplate such thoughts within the short window of time, I suspected that the audible overload helped shove reason into the background as well as intimidate the enemy. Success of the latter seemed questionable. In the distance, I could see Pirans sneering as they raised their weapons. They exuded arrogance, quick to scoff at the meager forces assaulting their defenses, but as we drew closer I watched their faces twist into horror as they realized that the ground forces were not the sole threat. Giant illuminated fireballs of Wombat mortars heralded our advance, adequately timed by Potentate Ang himself. The mortar shells crashed down, scattering or obliterating large groups of our opposition.

The opening salvo was just the beginning. As each individual footstep registered within my brain, along with each press of the trigger, I felt like I was moving through water as if time slowed to allow my senses to identify every tangible piece of input. Plasma rained from every direction, making the prospect of evading every stray burst seem impossible, but more than once, when I suspected that I might be a Piran target, my foes were quickly dispatched by allied fire or the blade of a Ghost. With the excess of information smacking my brain, I didn't know what to believe in some cases. If it weren't for the smoke and dust, I thought that I saw the Enforcer blink in and out of sight like a Ghost even without his cloak.

Crushing the Imperan formation took priority, but many were concerned that white-eyed civilians would get caught in the crossfire. Before the worry could settle, the promised Oshan units arrived with the modified transmitters set to maximum levels. White-eyes began to drop and convulse on the ground, allowing resistance forces to train all weapons on the remaining, clearly conscious and willful Pirans, Guerillas and Drakken which stood between us and our objective.

Platypus units circled about the intersection, keeping the neurolash transmitters focused on any region surrounding the fireteams. Added support from the gunners helped thin the Piran forces which fired from behind barricades. Even as a Goliath advanced to repel resistance forces, another Platypus dashed forward and spun about, its back end taking the Goliaths legs out from under it. In sequence, another Platypus opened fire on the Goliath's dome ensuring that it was no longer operable. The collapsing razerjack then formed a new barrier for Imperan forces to contend with as allies began to leverage any barricade possible to close off opposition.

Vanguard was about to pass the last perimeter of barriers when my ikes blared a warning about incoming fire from my right. I spotted a Piran with the massive Claw Hammer weapon in hand. The three-pronged discharger at the barrel of the bulky weapon was already releasing the purple, hazy electric strand of plasma. I leapt into the air to clear the wall of sandbags in front me. Before my hands could touch down for a dive roll I felt unimaginable pain tear through my lower body. As I completed my roll, I attempted to pop back to my feet, but I collapsed as nerves suggested that my left leg had punched upward into my abdomen.

The Enforcer reacted quickly and propped an arm under my shoulder. I tried to will my right leg to move, but the pain distracted so much that I thought the Enforcer was dragging me through the doorway into the Casters Tower lobby.

"You got this," the Enforcer said. "Be glad that it wasn't a chain shot."

Quick to guide me to an empty wall space, the Enforcer let me slide down to the cold marble floor, as he leveled his weapon on the tower entrance. Vanguard and a handful of Alcazaban soldiers made their way into the building with many others still facing outward against the forces trying to remedy the breach.

"Go! We'll hold them off!" Private AWOL shouted as he and a couple of Ghosts quickly dispatched any breathing Pirans within range of disruptor or blade.

The barricades outside made it difficult for the Platypus pilots to position their craft in a defensive manner, so Oshan techs were quick to set up barriers of their own, capable of deflecting plasma and relaying the neurolash signal. Alcazaban soldiers formed a perimeter behind the newly established barriers to secure the entrance while awaiting any capable hardware for reinforcements.

The surrounding events barely registered in my mind as the pain wracking my body consumed all. I thought my teeth were going to fuse together from clenching them so hard while my cheeks could have ruptured from the irregular exhales. Signals within told me to concentrate, but the pain suggested the contrary. Within a matter of ticks, we had taken the Casters Tower lobby, but I was in no frame of mind to celebrate.

DAVE TODD

40 – Ascending the Spire – 40

Lobby, Casters Tower
Core City, Windstonne Enclave
Commercial Empire, Northam Continent
Thread: actTgtPersp1.view

Allies quickly formed up and pushed back the Pirans in the lobby. At least within the building, interference from white-eyes dropped to nearly zero. Imperan forces pressed hard against allies that worked to establish a perimeter, but the defensive measures held.

I did my best to sit upright and get my breathing under control.

"You'll have to go on without me," I huffed, sensing that I was in no condition to fight.

The Enforcer crouched down and inspected my injury. Past the singed pants covering my thigh, he found nothing beyond a slight burn.

"If you're ready to cut bait, I'm sure the Serpent can find the proper blade so you can perform a ritual Maleezhun gut-slash. Right here, right now," the Enforcer said.

I looked over to see the Enforcer attempting to restrain a smirk. I knew that he was walking a fine line between lightening the mood without making light of the situation. Despite the encouragement that my injury wasn't severe, I struggled with making my body respond to that reality at a conscious level.

"Then just pass the stimpunch along, so we can keep moving," I grimaced.

"Why? So you're too groggy to see the next one coming," the Enforcer replied. "Settle the mind, and the body's functions will take care of the rest," the Enforcer said as he stood to focus on the situation at hand.

"They've got reinforcements," Torque snapped as allies took cover to halt the plasma-firing Pirans from the next room over.

"I can barely move my leg," I responded to the Enforcer's suggestion.

"Well, then sit tight," the Enforcer chided.

"Thanks, Mender Conner," I glared while trying to move myself behind cover so that the others could focus on the fight.

The Enforcer was quick to take up position at the doorway leading into the next room while Torque and the Serpent were assessing the situation. The Pirans had secured the elevators beyond and kept their weapons trained on every access point.

I took a moment to consider the intent behind the Enforcer's discourse. He always comported himself with the intent to carefully select the best tools for every situation, yet I felt like I was always settling for cheap substitutes found in a salvage bin. I calmed my breathing so that I could allow my body to leverage its systems designed to heal rather than inject myself with questionable chemicals.

As my eyes relaxed, I felt that my eyesight took on a faint hazy overlay, likely of the Vast. I knew that I hadn't altered any settings on my ikes, so I contemplated if I was finally starting to access some of the Enforcer's prescribed techniques. I had no concept of what to concentrate on, but I could feel a subtle adjustment in my limbs as muscles flexed and relaxed on their own.

Despite the stride forward, the process was cut short as hazy forms started to manifest in my peripheral vision apart from known positions of my allies. My vision snapped back to the standard view of reality and I tensed, sensing that action was about to ramp up.

"Still got props?" Torque asked as Pirans engaged from the elevator corridor.

"Everyday," the Enforcer smirked as he selected an Optic Pulse from his belt.

With a quick motion that the Pirans couldn't track, the Enforcer lobbed the grenade into the room. The device had enough force to knock out the Piran whose skull it connected with before it detonated with a blinding flash. All but two Pirans staggered, rubbing their eyes. Those with enough reaction time to shield their eyes rushed the doorway intending to capitalize on the distraction.

"Torque, High Foot," the Enforcer yelled as he spun low into a sweep kick, knocking the first Piran into the air.

Torque's reaction was already in motion as if he didn't even need the command. His hand dropped to the ground while his torso followed it, his legs twisting over it as I had seen during his Kapptivae training. The airborne body of the unsuspecting Piran was knocked senseless by the downward force of Torque's foot as the angle of the kick reversed the momentum of the prior setup.

While one Piran bounced off the floor, the other continued his charge, only to get launched into the air by the Enforcer's foot. The maneuver almost made the Enforcer's body look like a wheel with one foot grounded while the other fired a kick upward and over his body. The Serpent too was already on the move as he dashed upward and off the wall. His body spun laterally as his right hand brought the silver blade from his back and swung the sword around with precision. While his body was in the last revolution of the spin, the Serpent's blade severed the Piran's head from the rest of his body. By the time his feet touched down, the Serpent had already rechambered his sword on his back in a silent confident manner.

"Masterful finish there," Torque mused.

"A mecaworthy performance yourself," the Serpent replied as he and Torque snapped a crossarm gesture.

As I watched the ever maturing dynamics of the team that I joined, I found myself distracted enough to stand with assistance from a nearby credenza. After taking the initiative, Vanguard cleared the way so that Alcazaban soldiers could clear the room of staggering Pirans still floundering to find the enemy before them. All adversaries were quickly terminated, or so we thought. One wary Piran with frayed nerves hid behind a pillar, hoping to call for reinforcements. When his comms failed he dared to run for the elevator to find allies.

"Nade me," the Enforcer said calmly as he held a hand behind his back pointed in my direction.

Scrambling, I unlinked an Inferno grenade from my belt and tossed it toward the Enforcer. My throw was slightly off, but he still caught it behind his back before switching momentum to the opposition direction, spinning a full circle and whipping the grenade toward the elevator.

"Going up," an automated voice chimed.

The grenade glided smoothly through the margin of the closing door. The rattled Piran looked down to see the grenade bouncing off the back wall onto the floor as the door sealed him in with the explosive. He could only sigh in resignation, knowing that his end was certain. A loud explosion followed by a puff of smoke that seeped from the elevator seams concluded the matter of Piran opposition in the elevator corridor.

"Going down," Torque said, his quip followed by chuckles from other resistance members.

While my allies were focused on the elevator corridor I heard stomping boots on approach from an unguarded hallway. Knowing that my leg wasn't fully operational, I dove to the side to avoid detection. The awkward tumble put me too far from my weapons, or so I thought. As I collided with the floor, the strange weapons that I confiscated from the Drakken slid across the floor with one of the units discharging a single yellow bolt after rotating multiple times and landing on the trigger. The activation of the weapon prompted the name Monoon to display on my ikes.

I didn't have time to study the weapons in full, but since my allies were about to be flanked, I quickly scooped up the weapon pair and ducked behind the credenza. The ammo icon on my ikes blinked as empty. I then rotated the weapons' small barrels around the base initiating a series of clicks and a high pitch activation effect. My ikes updated with a level one charge notification.

Since the reload sequence got the attention of the advancing Pirans, I quickly popped up from my cover and depressed the triggers. A short flurry of yellow bolts embedded into the chest of the closest Piran. Knowing that I could only employ that trick once having given away my position, I swiftly darted into a conference room, where I could leverage more tables and chairs for cover.

The Pirans were quick to follow me, albeit on guard with their weapons raised. Before they were close enough, I charged the Monoon with two charge cycles, verified by the level two notification on my ikes. I still counted five Pirans, so I knew that I would have to evade effectively. I popped up and dropped the next Piran with a faster discharge of orange bolts. The Monoon responded with the familiar, slightly smaller, yellow bolts as I dropped the next Piran.

As the Pirans, returned fire on my last position, I was able to mask the sounds of three rotational charges. My ikes updated with a maximum charge response, so after changing position I popped up intermittently to drop the three remaining Pirans in sequence. The Monoon spewed red bolts, then orange and then yellow, each color bearing an increased quantity in bolts, but a reduction in discharge rate.

With the Monsoon on complete discharge, I held position to verify the dispatch of my foes, but before I could take cover again a wary Piran stood in the conference hall doorway with his EQ leveled at my chest. The closest cover was beyond reach even with a competent dive roll. Before the Piran could depress the trigger his body launched forward with enough force for it to clear the conference hall. I heard the sounds of snapping bones from the impact of the strike to his back and the hard fall to follow.

"Are you done playing around?" The Enforcer quipped.

"You know, news toys... I couldn't resist, " I smirked before waving the Monoon, stowing it and regrouping with the others.

After a quick health and salvage check, the Enforcer was quick to shift attention to the next move, "We need to cover as many floors as possible."

"We'll expand the margin for error and cover the lift system on the east end of the building," Torque replied.

The Enforcer nodded his agreement only to nod at me, suggesting that I join the planning session. Nerves still fired in my leg causing me to limp, but I forced myself to choke down the tension. As I hobbled over, the Enforcer had already requested two Alcazaban soldiers join our group. Lieutenant Skynov was tall with a prominent brow looking like he could have taken any challenger in the room with his confident stature, but it appeared that he also respected chain of command. Sergeant Martin, however, looked nervous as if he was fresh out of training, but something about his demeanor suggested that he had an affinity for the rules. His uniform was still immaculate without dirt or blood stain, so more than likely, he was that proficient in battle.

We found our way to the primary stairwell on the western edge of the building. My stomach turned, considering that I was not only walking off an injury, but I also had to ascend stairs to do it. Lt. Skynov and the Enforcer were about to begin when Sgt. Martin had to open his mouth, "With an average of fifteen steps per flight..."

"Soldier, some intel is not meant to be shared," the Enforcer interrupted before he led the way.

Annoyed, Martin looked to his superior who only shrugged in agreement.

I fully agreed with the sentiment of avoiding the massive ascension ahead of us, but something about the Enforcer's quip caught me off guard. I exhaled knowing that I would have plenty of time to consider the nature of the oddity while I fought to drive the pins and needles from my leg.

Urban Floor
Core City, Windstonne Enclave
Commercial Empire, Northam Continent
Thread: sysObserver.cmd

Commander Jackal poked at the Magellan interfaces while the razerjack lumbered toward the next intersection. His eyes locked onto a feature that was disabled.

"What is this?" Jackal asked.

"It's designated as a prototype. Likely disabled during the rush off the assembly line," one of the Oshan techs replied.

Jackal's eyes widened as he read the description," Sir, are you reading this?"

Potentate Ang scanned the specifications being relayed to the command center. He preferred that the techs resolve the breakdown, but if the feature's title suggested what he thought, the disabled feature might turn the tide. The greatest drawback indicated by the techs was the immediate lockdown of all linked Magellans.

As Ang continued to contemplate the ramifications of meddling with foreign tech, his mind mulled over the unresolved information leak back home. He had always trusted Newton's expertise and it felt strange not having him present as a consultant. Ang even questioned the possibility of nefarious motives if something went wrong with the newly discovered razerjack feature. Jackal hadn't given Ang cause for distrust throughout the conflict thus far, but something completely unsettled him about the present situation that he couldn't identify, given how much deception that Imperan forces had leveraged.

"Sir, we have other platforms advancing on the tower. Resistance forces may not hold out if we hesitate," an Oshan comms officer relayed.

Ang tensed while keeping his arms folded across his chest. He did his best to weigh all possible outcomes, but despite the urgency, he had no choice but to make a call. He knew that the resistance might not be in its current state had the Magellans been fully operational or deployed in an even greater quantity. The remainder of razerjacks still posed a looming threat, and the risks were justified. Straightening his shoulders to mask any manner of hesitation, Ang finally voiced his thoughts, "It's fortunate that we activated our operation ahead of theirs," Ang remarked.

"Shall we finish what they started, Sir?" Jackal asked.

Ang stared at the blinking text which read *Synchronous Aerial Defense Platform*. His eyes darted across the schematics looking for any weakness. A formation on the tactical maps suggested that even accessing the feature might alert other Imperan pilots. One Magellan within a parcel of Jackal's unit broke formation and advanced toward the compromised unit.

"Sir, razerjack on intercept course. They've been alerted to the potential activation," a tech shouted.

"Make it happen," Ang snapped as he exhaled. He would deal with the fallout of the decision after, but for the duration, he would leverage every asset at his disposal.

Commerce Level, Casters Tower
Core City, Windstonne Enclave
Commercial Empire, Northam Continent
Thread: actTgtPersp1.view

The increasing temperature as we scaled uncountable flights of stairs was the least of our concerns. I was certain that others present initially wanted to question why we couldn't opt for an elevator, but the

Enforcer's methodical and intentional actions of checking every floor indicated that it wasn't worth the risk. It would have been too easy for Imperans to either rig the elevator with explosives or even blow the cable once enemies began their ascent. Even the lack of opposition led to the unspoken question regarding why we weren't encountering more foes.

"You'd think Frank Jenkins would have at least placed checkpoints throughout the facility," Seargent Martin said.

"Being a power monger does not necessarily make one a strategic genius," the Enforcer remarked as he finished checking another accessway to the stairs.

No one could disagree with the Enforcer's statement. In order to take my mind off the increased strain of my leg muscles, I pondered other possible causes, only voicing ideas in a hushed tone once clear of a floor check. The most likely solutions were that Frank Jenkins had over extended his reliance on white-eye minions since he never believed that resistance forces would breach the tower, or more simply put, we were finally witnessing the diminishing resources in the numbers game.

I guessed that we were at least a good twenty decks up when a new floor layout caught our attention. Instead of the glass walled office complexes, we observed large dark walled rooms with minimal entry points. After our routine sound and filter checks, we prepared to continue to the next floor when I stopped at one of the doors suspecting some manner of archive. Out of curiosity, I opted to scan with my eyes that which my ike filters could not.

"What is this?" I gasped rhetorically as lighting activated to reveal countless shelves of books fading into the darkness.

The Alcazaban soldiers shared similar expressions as they followed me into the archive. What little I had learned about Westcrest suggested that all Northam factions had highly restrictive policies much like the Commercial Empire, so it was no doubt a shock to them as well to witness such a trove of materials considered contraband, in a faction controlled building no less.

Unable to help my curiosity, I tapped on a nearby terminal to find an index of the archive's contents. I was shocked to discover materials across the spectrum including history, informatics and everything in between. Most elements were marked for storage, cataloguing or transfer. The most frequent entities to assume ownership of tagged materials were Oszwick Enterprises and the Daystar Institute.

"Now you see that even governments can commit the very acts they speak against, all under the guise of social prosperity," the Enforcer said as he leaned on the archive doorframe while we took a moment to absorb the situation.

"For what reason?" Martin asked, clearly shaken by the fracture in his orderly world.

"Control," Lieutenant Skynov said flatly.

The Enforcer nodded in agreement with the confident soldier's reveal of his keen intellect to match his combat prowess, "If you have access to information while suppressing it from others, you will always have the upper hand. Power is not something that these types ever want to relinquish."

"And yet, I see no entries for the Criterion or anything related to the Firewall Protocol," I said after a quick search of the archive index.

"I think it's safe to suggest that any such items are summarily destroyed. They can run damage control on things that they can twist and repurpose, but the truth about the fabric of reality which can circumvent their power hold, in any age, in any way? They can't have that. Given the invisible nature of the paraverse, they assume that no one could find that on their own. If they fear its discovery that much, it shows that they not only acknowledge it to be true, but also its power. Revising history and skewing informatics are but a couple of the tools leveraged by would-be despots," the Enforcer said.

"How can so few fight back against a massive grip?" Martin asked.

Curious as to his answer, I looked away from my search to observe the Enforcer's response.

"The truth itself is simple. There is no way to counter every lie. All that I've been able to do is point to the system with the actual means to bring down the obstacles. Every individual is responsible for their own interaction with the Firewall Protocol," the Enforcer said.

As the Enforcer mentioned the factor identifying the Interlace, I noticed that archived items included details on the salvage operations that found the materials. The Dwelling Street Mission was listed in multiple instances.

"The mission is listed here. Things appear dismal if even the Interlace can be misdirected. Even I may have contributed to this," I said at the sobering possibility.

"The Firewall Protocol can only prevent a force takeover like in the case of Extend. Even the Interlace can be deceived when those willful or conscious disregard it. Because the Relay will not operate by force, the choice to leverage it becomes that much more powerful which is why our enemy fears it so," the Enforcer said.

The sense of urgency to continue on finally overshadowed remaining questions. Accepting that there was nothing new to be gained in the archive, I powered down the terminal and returned to our operation at hand. I didn't know if our conversation had any meaning to our Alcazaban allies, but given past conversations with the Enforcer, I knew that I had plenty to mull over as we continued our climb within Casters Tower.

Another floor check was underway when I asked the Enforcer, "Do you ever get tired of the fight?"

The Enforcer kept his eyes trained on his floor checks while using hand gestures to signal all-clear to advance to the next floor, "It's not a matter of fatigue. It's about what could happen to those I care about if I don't continue to fight."

Until that moment, I hadn't considered the additional motivation the Enforcer had for being so diligent in checking the floors. There were plenty of others that he cared about in addition to Vanguard. With the fresh reminder of his prioritization, I redoubled my efforts to scan for hostages and holdovers as well as traps. The systematic floor sweep continued as we balanced the battle of fleeting time versus safety which slowed our progress every step of the way.

Executive Level, Casters Tower
Core City, Windstonne Enclave
Commercial Empire, Northam Continent
Thread: sysObserver.cmd

Commotion outside the office walls caught Sath's attention. She was surprised just how much she had been staring at the wall out of boredom since the dark skies outside were creating a depressing weight. Without Hyper Lynx access and nothing of interest in the sky beyond ominous storm clouds, she opted for the simplicity of the wall opposite her lounge chair.

"There's been a breach. Boss Man is sending any loose bodies down to shore up the lines," one Piran said to the guard outside the room.

Sath was tempted to stand and place her ear to the wall, but she managed to hear the conversation just fine if she remained still in her seat.

"What about her?" The guard asked.

"Take her down to the eatery hall where the others are held," the new arrival said.

The guard's grumbles in protest were indiscernible, but Sath easily guessed that her Piran captor was not happy about giving up his easy assignment. Before she could discern any more of the conversation, a wave of thoughts hit her all at once. If the tower had been breached, it meant that there was finally opportunity to shut down Frank Jenkins' power grab for good, but it also meant a strong chance of conflict and more risk to those trapped in the tower. Sath at least welcomed the chance to be moved to a location with more people over her recent isolation.

As the conversation outside finished, the Piran guard was quick to open the door. Sath had already scooped up her personal effects and stood in the middle of the room. The guard fumed as he saw that Sath was ready to leave, deflating his ability to snap an order at her.

At the invitation to exit, Sath walked through the door and followed her guard once he pointed the direction that they would be taking. With her duties for Jenkins consuming most of her time, Sath knew little of the tower's lower floors, so she let the guard lead the way. After descending to a floor with a better view of the enclave, Sath was finally able to witness the destruction occurring below. Without taking the guard's permission into account, Sath walked over to the window. The guard reached for her arm, but she twisted free before he could secure his grasp.

"What have you fools done?" Sath gasped.

"We're securing this region and purging it of threats, so that we can get on with our lives," the guard said with annoyance.

"If that's the line you were sold, then you really are a carp," Sath said, turning to face the guard, her eyes laced with fire. "No wonder Jenkins has such a vice grip on you inverts."

"I may not be a master of statecraft, but we do the dirty work so you don't have to, Princess," the guard snarled.

Sath took a step to the side, putting a little distance between her and the Piran. Since her employment with the faction leader had been terminated, she no longer felt obligated to deal formally with the security force she so readily detested.

Also disinterested in showing respect, regardless of orders, the Piran advanced and placed a hand on Sath's shoulder, "Let's say you and me stay here and watch the fireworks... together."

An explosion in the sky created a flash of light that glinted off the Piran's signature filed metal teeth. Instead of grimacing at the facial feature, Sath channeled her anger by gripping the pointer that Mac had given her. She tensed it in her fist and slammed the sharp instrument into the side of the Piran's neck. The spinning motion put the guard's back to the window. In shock, the guard reach for the instrument as blood started to escape the wound.

Although Sath expected the guard to perform an aggressive move in response, she had no time to determine the effectiveness of her attack as she immediately spotted the source of the bright light. Her eyes widened in panic and her only reaction was to run. Even if there was no time, any step possible might be enough. Even from his delirious state, the Piran recognized the panic and turned to face the window, but the fireball hurling toward him would be the last image burned into his eyes.

Commerce Level, Casters Tower
Core City, Windstonne Enclave
Commercial Empire, Northam Continent
Thread: actTgtPersp1.view

Collective fatigue tagged along as hushed conversation began to wane, even as a distraction from the never ending stairs. We had successfully cleared the archive and general business floors and approached the executive levels. None of us dared remark about how many floors remained. Other than a couple of Piran patrols that we either avoided or swiftly suppressed, the ascent was without incident.

Internally, I calculated that we had finished at least seventy floors. As we reached the next entryway, the Enforcer froze abruptly as he went to reach for the door handle. He had been so systematic that we found it jarring for him to halt momentum altogether.

"What is it?" I asked in whisper.

"Sath's emergency locator just activated," the Enforcer replied.

I needed no explanation. I sensed that he was rapidly trying to identify the signal's location on his ikes relative to our position. The update had to carry a mixed set of reactions. It had to be advantageous to narrow our search, but it also increased the urgency if the situation required immediate attention.

The Enforcer's behavior quickly reflected his internal conflict externally. Our floor checks became more rushed since he desired to quickly reach the floor in question. He shared the position which then placed an icon on the building schematic that I periodically checked out of boredom. Given the size of Casters Tower and the density of the infrastructure, the receiver could only narrow the signal down to three floors at best.

Finally, we reached the lowest of three potential floors. The Enforcer continued a defensive stance as he checked the hallway, but he bypassed the usual hand signals for others to fan out. Instead, he took point and started working his way toward the signal. The Alcazaban soldiers had certainly proved their capacity for observation as they followed along without question, clearly sensing that the scenario had changed.

I followed silently behind the Enforcer, keeping the butt of the EQ up to my shoulder. I intermittently checked my filters as well with varying success. The electromagnetic filter barely proved useful on account of the power outage on the floor, plus the massive building girders inhibited signal clarity. The thermal indicator showed that there was little life on the floor, but I struggled with knowing if it or the interferic filter was best for the situation. If I relied on the interferic filter too much, I might have walked into a wall. The thermal filter had minimal structure readings, so I still found myself using the night vision as well.

The floor appeared to have partial business occupancy as evidenced by the glass walls with no furniture to be found within, but some offices were used for storage since they were full of furniture stacked in no practical fashion. The empty spaces were not aesthetically pleasing, so it was easy to speculate that we were in a low traffic area.

Despite the vacancy, the Enforcer paused with his hand tensed on his Phantom 4.0. He nodded for me to open the door as he did a final scan. I wasn't sure what he was seeing beyond the possible signal, but I complied. The Alcazaban soldiers followed the Enforcer into the vacant office, and I brought up the rear.

The Enforcer led the group through an interior hallway until it opened into an office space on the southwest corner. There were faint traces of heat and scattered snack bags littered the floor. Lt. Skynov inadvertently stepped on one of the partial bags, crushing the dry contents within. The sudden noise prompted something to bump against a half wall of stacked desks followed by an indiscernible whisper.

"Step out!" The Enforcer snapped as he trained his Phantom in the direction of the noise.

"Don't shoot!" An individual said as he and another body popped up, their hands in front of their faces.

Both were wearing grungy coveralls, likely on account of being trapped in the tower without a safe exit. A quick survey revealed that they were maintenance workers trying to avoid Piran patrols, hence why they hid themselves in the abandoned office which had no strategic value.

The Enforcer lowered his Phantom, but raised a solar torch and pointed it directly at the face of each worker in succession. The group tensed when we saw that there was some faint discoloration in their eyes. They didn't appear to be hostile, but they certainly bore symptoms of Extend usage.

"Have you been feeling okay?" The Enforcer asked, switching the light back and forth, uncertain if he considered the workers to be a threat.

The workers exchanged nervous glances about explaining their situation. The Enforcer lowered the torch after they conceded that we weren't with Imperan security or likely to turn them in. The slightly taller worker with dark brown matted hair identified himself as Hank.

"A while back our supervisor began handing out what he referred to as supplements, for free," Hank said. "After noticing some side effects, my mender suggested that I discontinue use of Extend. Wessill here was the only one to believe me, but the rest of the maintenance crews thought nothing of it. I'm glad that we did because, when the fighting broke out, everyone else started acting like total vims. We were unsure how we were supposed to fit in when everyone was acting like lifeless machines, so we decided to hide. Without knowing when the fight was going to end, we decided to wait here until it was over. We definitely didn't expect it to continue this long. Thankfully, there are dry goods in the eatery storerooms."

The Enforcer didn't press any further. For whatever reason, he accepted their story. Out of curiosity, I checked my interferic filter. I couldn't find any reason to doubt their story either since their readouts didn't reveal any abnormal energy blockage compared to the average individual. The workers posed no physical threat either.

"We cannot linger, so you're free to go. There is a team in the lobby. If you can make your way down, they can help you once it's clear," the Enforcer said.

It was evident that the workers felt safer away from the conflict, but Hank offered an alternate idea, "We'd prefer to follow you to avoid any run-ins with the Pirans."

I suspected that the Enforcer didn't want extra weight given the urgency of the situation, but even in the midst of the fight, he was still contemplating how to make the most of the situation to the benefit of all.

"Do you know of accessways least likely to be guarded?" The Enforcer asked.

"We're sure that maintenance was never closed off. Pirans wanted nothing to do with anyone who kept the building operational," Hank replied.

"Very good. Keep behind us and we'll have you point the way once we make our push," the Enforcer said.

The conversation wrapped quickly, indicating that the Enforcer was ready to get back on track, especially to check the next floor. There was no deviation from his intention to find Sath. The maintenance workers acknowledged that we were going to move fast, so there was no time to secure supplies. They quickly whisked a couple of essentials from their hideout and fell in line.

The Enforcer was ready to run for the accessway when a bright light outside the tower caught his attention. It was rare that his demeanor was unsettled, but it was apparent as only one word escaped his lips, "MOVE!"

The team responded at the comment, but there was only time for us take but a couple of steps away from the window before an impact shuddered Casters Tower. An explosion mixed with an eruption of glass, graypak and steel spraying in every direction. My brain had no time to contemplate the events as darkness consumed everything.

My perception registered the experience as only a few ticks, but the persistent ringing in my ears demanded that I pay attention to all of my senses which were firing hot. I felt pressure from the heat, but I couldn't find anything pinning me down. My vision was blurred making focus on my ikes difficult. The scent of burning fuel and dust plugged my nostrils.

"Sound off!" The Enforcer said in what felt like a muffled form against my ear ringing.

"Good, I think," I mumbled.

"Liquid," Lt Skynov replied, followed by a loud click from a gear check which was prioritized over his health.

"My threads are wrinkled," Sgt. Martin replied.

"He's good," Lt. Skynov added in case there was need for translation of Martin's antics.

"Civvies?" The Enforcer asked from somewhere in the haze.

"Uh huh," sounded a timid reply.

Upon regrouping, we stared at the gaping hole in the side of Casters Tower plugged by the nose of a Tornac chopper minus the smoke billowing outward. Something had caught the COJR unit and with the pilot unable to control the craft, there was no preventing its impact against the faction capitol building. More missiles pierced the sky in succession, giving us a clear explanation for the chopper's flight failure.

"Check fire, Check fire! Friendlies on site!" The Enforcer yelled as another chopper narrowly evaded a stream of missiles. Its flight path almost caused strays to clip the tower. "Last impact was a near miss!"

Amidst the noise and wash of static, I thought that I heard an Oshan tech trying to defend the urgency for leveraging the immobilized Magellans' weapon systems against the onslaught of hostile aircraft, but excuses were swiftly interrupted by Potentate Ang's voice, "Flaws are being worked out of the hijacked system as we speak."

At first I thought Ang's response was rather cold, but I quickly realized that he intended to hold everyone accountable regardless of the situation. The heat of battle allowed no excuses. A short silence followed before Ang followed up on Vanguard's channel.

"How close was it?" Ang asked in a more concerned tone.

"I can read you the identifier on the chopper nose if you like," the Enforcer said, already settling from his brief outburst.

"All targeting is being relayed through command. I'll ensure that we give you the necessary margin," Ang said after a pause which I assumed was for a somber exhale.

"Ryoukai," the Enforcer said calmly.

The conversation that I observed on the surface was insignificant compared to the one that I perceived beneath which spoke volumes. Within the exchange between the Enforcer and the faction leader was an undertone of mutual agreement. Whether it was from a long affiliation in battle or simply the respect of one leader to another, I found myself surprised at its execution in contrast to the frequent meca portrayal of such battlefield fallout. There was always blame to be passed around. I was starting to doubt if I would ever see the end of the upside-down behavior that I had grown accustomed to.

Setting the current tension aside for the former, the Enforcer scanned the wreckage. Before we could move, bits of the floor above crumbled and a body fell into a heap on the wreckage. I thought that the Enforcer's eyes were going to bug out when I realized that the body related to the signal marker which blipped before my eyes, lay lifeless before us. Calmly, the Enforcer inspected the body which was the charred form of a Piran soldier. He deactivated the signal marker after inspecting the slim instrument protruding from the neck. If the neck injury hadn't killed him the impact certainly did.

I sensed that the Enforcer was conflicted since we found the emergency signal, but Sath's whereabouts were still unknown. Without warning, he clambered onto the front of the chopper and activated his kips to jump to the next floor. I looked over to see our Alcazaban allies stunned at the maneuver while my thoughts gravitated toward the instability of the structure.

I left our allies to tend to the civilians while I followed the Enforcer's path, albeit less gracefully without having spent enough time mastering the kickplates. To my surprise, Lt. Skynov opted to follow us by climbing up through the wreckage while Sgt. Martin guided the workers up through the closest stairwell.

Even without a location marker, I could tell that the Enforcer hadn't gone far. About ten paces from the impact site, he was already kneeling over a body which I immediately recognized as Sath from comms at the warehouse. She appeared free of major injury with exception of a serious bump on the side of her head. Other than a few lights scrapes, she had escaped the impact unharmed. The Enforcer confirmed that she had a pulse and was breathing normally but she remained unconscious.

"Sath," the Enforcer said gently as he removed a glove to place a hand under her cheek. He called her name again, but she only stirred at most and did not wake.

The Enforcer had already considered the risk of moving her, but he knew the impact site was unstable, and there was no time for a proper health evaluation. By the time Lt. Skynov and Sgt. Martin converged on the location, the Enforcer had lifted Sath in his arms and walked to Lt. Skynov.

"Soldier, I need you to treat her as a high value asset. See that she's secured in the safest place that the resistance can afford until we resolve this conflict," the Enforcer said. He considered explaining Sath's value as an intel asset or the leverage that she represented as a hostage, but he already knew that Skynov understood the situation.

Lt. Skynov nodded as he carried Sath toward the stairs. Sgt. Martin paused in protest, but a nod from his superior was all that he needed to comply. The workers, however, looked rattled at narrowly surviving the impact and showed concern at the division of their escort.

"I need you two to show us to the maintenance accessway, and then you can follow our friends back down to the perimeter," the Enforcer said to the maintenance workers while he returned his glove to his hand.

Nervously, the workers nodded and allowed the Enforcer to lead the way back to the primary access point. It was subtle, but I noticed that the Enforcer made one final glance over his shoulder at Sath as we parted ways with our Alcazaban allies. I suspected that he was deeply conflicted internally since I detected an equally subtle change in the Enforcer's demeanor, knowing that he was again free to focus on the mission at hand once Sath had been located and could no longer be used as leverage by Frank Jenkins.

Our ascent up the primary stairwell felt accelerated compared to the prior floors since the Enforcer acted as if a weight had been lifted from his shoulders. Our progress was slowed only on account of the maintenance workers not accustomed to moving with such purpose. As we arrived at the bottom most executive floor, one of the workers indicated that it was the lowest access to the maintenance corridor for the series of floors.

Hank described the location verbally as we passed by a posh lounge overlooking the enclave. If it weren't for the smoke trails in the air, one might never know that there was a conflict happening, but a downward view of fires and wreckage clearly told the actual story.

I felt the temptation to linger and spectate the activity from above, but urgency nagged in full. As we were about to exit the lounge the tower rumbled from girder to glass. The vibrations underfoot were strong. They weren't enough to shake a proper footing but the disruption of the air wreaked havoc on the ear drums.

The ambient light intensified. White tendrils of electricity crawled up the window exterior. Even with the wide view of the lounge, events suggested that it was happening to the entire tower. The strange visuals appeared dangerous, but I couldn't help but step closer to the windows to verify what my eyes wanted to doubt.

"What is happening?" I mused as I took no more than a step or two, held back by my own caution.

Given the lack of response from the Enforcer, I assumed that he was running a thorough analysis through his likes. To confirm, I looked over my shoulder, but the motion behind us shocked me more than the strange energy surges.

The maintenance workers, while still upright, convulsed, their heads pointed upward. Their veins bulged indicating an internal conflict between their musculature and nervous systems. Their limbs flailed as if their ability to move on their own accord was being sapped from them. The spectacle lasted for a few ticks before they suddenly calmed and then faced us. The remaining color had been drained from their eyes and they glared at us as if they were wolves cornering wounded prey. Their hesitation was but an instant before they lunged.

"Look out!" The Enforcer yelled as he knocked me to the side with his shoulder.

The abrupt interception knocked me over a lounge chair, knocking my ikes from my face and my spine on the floor. I scrambled to get a footing without tripping on the haphazard furniture. The Enforcer twisted his body, turning his back to one of the workers, only to catch the arms of the second. He twisted the worker about using his body as a shield against the other. He successfully tossed one across the room into a far couch, but the remaining one grasped for the Enforcer's neck with feral behavior.

"Stun 'em," the Enforcer said.

The worker was still no match for the Enforcer's strength, but his calm did little to cover for my own frantic response. Disregarding my lack of ikes, I drew the Phantom 4.0 from my back and leveled it at the mindless worker that the Enforcer kept at bay. I had grown so accustomed to the targeting reticle that I doubted my ability to fire without hitting the Enforcer. If I didn't hurry, the second worker would recover and create more of a problem. I forced myself to settle my breathing. As if on cue, the Enforcer tensed his muscles locking his stance and forcing the worker's arms in place. He bought me the moment I needed to secure the shot, so I pulled the trigger.

41 – Nemeses – 41

Oszwick Enterprises
Core City Fringe, Windstonne Enclave
Commercial Empire, Northam Continent
Thread: sysObserver.cmd

Killian Szazs felt his bones creak as he shuffled down the poorly lit Oszwick Enterprises hallway. He took a moment to catch his breath, still in disbelief at the events which drew all of the staff from the informatic facility. He had no desire to return to the site that recently held him captive, but his mind rationalized that he might yet survive his way in a laboratory setting. He speculated that his Vanguard hosts were rubbing off on him in good ways and bad. Szazs leveraged Maxwell's tricks to reduce his visibility on the security system, but there was no denying the compulsion to live up to the possibility that differences could be made even by few, despite a lack of skill, or fitness. Szazs knew that he was out of his mind for daring to investigate his suspicions on his own, in his aged condition, but he would deal with the consequences as needed.

Even with his invisibility to the security system in place, Szazs knew that he had to hurry, lest the more dangerous physical threat of the staff return in force. He double-checked his slate in hand to make sure that he was taking the correct path to the uplink center.

Upon entering the massive room with walls lined with electronics, Szazs was surprised that the overhead lights were off given the abundant activity level of the apparatus employed by Oszwick Enterprises throughout the conflict. Szazs rushed to the central terminal which overlooked a massive conduit which dropped downward beneath the floor before exiting the facility and running to its powerful antennae elsewhere.

Szazs' fingers hovered over the terminal tapper as quickly as possible as he tried to locate the power systems. Once he believed to have found the correct series of commands, Szazs was greeted with an authorization screen. His findings never revealed authorization codes, so he found himself frustrated at the obstacle. Before he could imagine a possible workaround, Szazs heard approaching footsteps.

"It won't matter," Benni Kotes said as he entered the uplink center and engaged the primary terminal.

"Once the proximity system is active, all losses will be mitigated," Kotes replied defiantly into his sonair.

Szazs stifled his exhale upon narrowly securing his hiding spot behind a data terminal in the back of the uplink center. He had barely exited the command console and powered down the lights ahead of Kotes' arrival. His pain sensors fired in protest to the toll that the crouching position was waging on his old body. He knew that it was futile to catch the other end of the conversation, so he did his best to hold still.

No more than a handful of ticks passed between Kotes closing the comm and Lucient charging into the uplink center. Lucient glared while Kotes kept his focus trained on the console before him.

"What are you doing?" Lucient asked. "The white-eyes are attacking the shards!"

"I'm just following orders," Kotes replied.

"Then you need to divert the signal now!" Lucient snapped.

"You don't get it, do you?" Kotes yelled back. "I don't work for you. I work for your boss, and this was never your operation."

Kotes finally faced Lucient. The fury pouring from Lucient's eyes contrasted his pale skin. Kotes' eyes might have matched the intensity of Lucient's had there been any color left in them. Fuming, Lucient charged forward. With blinding speed, Kotes drew a Splice 15m from his side and fired at Lucient. Unable to react fully, Lucient drew his hand to cover his face but it still took the brunt force of the plasma shot, burning his hand while more of the plasma splashed onto his right eye. Recoiling more from the nerve response than the injury, Lucient halted his advance, flicked his right arm to the side before lifting it cover this eye.

Even through the pain, Lucient heard the advancing sounds of hostile voices and footsteps. All he could do was glare at Kotes one last time before he bolted out of the uplink center. He had been cut out of Oszwick Enterprises and at that time he had no countermeasures at his disposal.

After his eyes followed Lucient out the door, Kotes set the firearm on the data terminal behind him and returned to his work on synchronizing the control signal being relayed from the Oszwick Enterprises uplink. Szazs tensed in response to the events which he overheard. He wasn't sure if he was more unsettled by the showdown or the unexpected contact of metal as Kotes placed the metal disruptor on the terminal just above Szazs' head.

Four new arrivals burst into the uplink center, but paused upon seeing Kotes who ignored them while he tapped away at the terminal.

"Who are you?" Bender snapped as he lowered his torso and tensed his fingers around his pobats.

"I'm your insurance policy. Lucient wanted to overrun you with white-eyes, but I overwrote their last instruction set," Kotes replied casually.

Voltaire took a step forward and put out a hand to settle Bender. The Mogul Prime members kept their guard up as if stepping into a trap. They hadn't expected Lucient to know of the betrayal, let alone an informatech who seemed overly familiar with the plan.

"All of us have a part to play, and some of those parts don't come with a lot of trust," Kotes continued, given the cautious behavior.

"Why isn't he deranged?" Tycoon asked as he realized that Kotes' eyes were as white those of the civilians they faced outside.

"Sometimes prototypes just happen to retain their intended benefits, but still have some side effects," Kotes said. "That is, before the real side effects are added."

On a nearby screen, Kotes displayed a sample of mecas showcasing the results of Extend's product development concluding with examples of the conflict happening in Windstonne. Voltaire and his allies watched the scans, but they exhibited neither surprise nor concern.

"There is a strong bond between vaporgust and windseed," Kotes said flatly.

"Then it would be unfortunate if that bond was tested," Voltaire said if he understood that those leveraging Extend were drawing energy from its victims.

Kotes smirked, sensing that Mogul Prime was picking up on the hidden agenda which he didn't dare vocalize. He had a narrow window of time, and he still had countless calculations to run before the Oszwick Enterprises signal could be activated... securely. He felt that he was ready to initiate the final sequence when the overhead lights flickered, the security lights glowed red and all of the noptic screens in the uplink center flashed a block of indiscernible text.

"What did you do?" Voltaire asked.

"Is it the resistance?" Hauteur asked joining in.

Grunting in anger, Kotes slammed his fist against the terminal frame, "NO! It's not possible. These lines are shielded. There is no way that someone breached these systems."

Kotes worked frantically to regain control over the uplink center. It was as if something with hardware orders of magnitude greater than Oszwick Enterprises' system was intercepting and overriding all scripted commands. Panic washed over Kotes as he realized that his processes were being undone faster than he could blink.

All of the calculations resulting from his gains by Extend were being nullified before his eyes.

"You need to get to a hardpoint now. Localized influence over the shards is lost. All security encryptions are being wiped as we speak. The resistance will soon be able to break down the signal. Lucient will be able to override the system as well if he detects the breach before we can lock it down. Here are the hardpoint locations. Now Go!" Kotes snapped as he popped a slate from its cradle and handed it to Voltaire.

Voltaire immediately spotted the closest hardpoint location and nodded for Mogul Prime to move out. He handed the slate over to Hauteur since she was the most competent with interfaces. The rest of Mogul Prime would run interference to ensure that their operation stayed the course.

After settling from his tantrum, Kotes reset the noptic screens and the uplink center lighting. He would need to concentrate. He had no idea what he was up against, but there was certainly something unnatural about his adversary. Kotes took a breath, ready to trace the intrusive signal, but before he could trace it, it was gone. Without time to question the intrusion, Kotes proceeded to reactivate his routines, but his concentration was immediately broken by another presence in the room.

Szazs slowly straightened his back as he leveled the Splice 15m at Kotes.

"I'm surprised that you're still alive," Kotes quipped without facing the protech.

Szazs did his best to mask the shaking in his forearm, but Kotes didn't have to turn his head to notice. So long, he had been behind a desk, never a thought of using such a weapon, but the situation forced him to consider it an instrument of his resolve. Although not a desirable action on his part, he felt less intimidated with a weapon in hand for the second time.

"You shouldn't be doing this," Szazs stammered.

"Do what? Pursue my ambition? What do you think that you spent passes doing?" Kotes snapped.

Szazs was caught off guard by the speed and vitriol of Kotes' reply. The words cut deep. The protech knew that he had little defense against his past actions, but he quickly set doubts aside as he reflected on the efforts being made to stop the power struggle at the heart of the Commercial Empire. His new allies had shown both courage and grace to anyone willing to push forward. It was a new start for him, even in old age.

Kotes continued his scramble to assume control over the uplink center. Szazs' presence was more of a nuisance than a barrier to his objective.

"I endeavored to make a difference. Unfortunately, it was for the wrong people. I may never be able to atone. At least I can dust my tracks so that no one can follow in my footsteps," Szazs replied.

Szazs felt a lightness within him which greatly contrasted the weight he used to shoulder. He almost overlooked that the shaking of his arm supporting the Splice had stopped.

Further agitated by the response, Kotes paused his tapping, but kept his eyes trained on the screen before him, "You don't have the verts, Old Man."

Szazs' eyes narrowed on the pistol sights. He contemplated if Kotes was right. If he harmed Kotes, was he still perpetuating the misdeeds that he wanted to escape. He tried to assess how the Enforcer would have reacted. There was clear indication that he actively fought on behalf of others and could deal harm, but Szazs couldn't recall any instance of him making the first move. Certain that he should do the same, the protech kept his hand steady. He didn't have the strength to overpower Kotes, but the young informatech also refused to step away from the terminal. He was caught in a standoff.

Angered by the Szazs' inability to act, Kotes finally looked away and glared with his white eyes, daring the older informatech. The firearm remained steady. In foolhardy fashion, Kotes finally yelled and tensed, snapping his arms out as if to attack. Purely on reaction alone, Szazs' finger squeezed the trigger. Kotes had presented the defensive requisite that Szazs needed. In silence, the traitor's body slumped to the floor in a heap.

Executive Level, Casters Tower
Core City, Windstonne Enclave
Commercial Empire, Northam Continent
Thread: actTgtPersp1.view

The scuffle was short, but tense. I managed to help the Enforcer secure the deranged, but unconscious, maintenance workers into a conference room with an outward swinging door. We quickly moved a sofa in front of the door should they come around before we made our exit. The events were frustrating since it required excess plasma to stop one worker and deliver a serious head blow to the other to obstruct their feral behavior.

While the Enforcer took a moment to reinforce the barricade, I looked around the floor for my eyecons, hoping that I wouldn't step on them in the poor lighting. Finally spotting the chair that I had fallen over along with my missing shades, I repositioned my ikes on my face only to see a bizarre message covering the lenses. Initially, I couldn't read the message until recognizing that it as the same print as the foreign text on the cover of the Criterion. Just as the text faded out of sight, I realized that it said *By ExHa.* I looked for a way to recover the screen, but it seemed that it had nothing to do with the VNET interface.

"Did you see that?" I asked.

"See what?" the Enforcer replied.

Before I could explain, our ears were flooded with panic on the comms as responses regarding the increase in white-eyes came in without warning. In some cases resistance forces were being overrun, demanding permission to open fire if not doing so already.

"Negative, negative! Forces can still be subdued," the Enforcer yelled.

Potentate Ang managed to break through on the comm with enough clarity, "We are running out of time. Reports are pouring in that low dosage victims are turning regardless of Extend consumption rates. In rare cases, those who haven't used Extend are behaving similarly to those who have, when in proximity to verified users."

"All the more reason to protect them," the Enforcer said, despite wanting to take a click to assess the situation even though he wasn't afforded one.

My ears tuned out the exchange, but as I looked into the conference room, I saw that Hank was on his feet, calmly tapping on the glass to get my attention. All I could do was shake my head and hold a hand up for him to wait. He nodded in understanding, clearly free of his former behavior, for the moment.

"Mac, look," I said, directing him toward Hank's docile form.

"Suppression methods remain the same," the Enforcer said into the comm as he nodded an acknowledgement in my direction.

Potentage Ang attempted to refute the suggestion, but he was clearly interrupted by a technician on his end, "Whatever the trigger was, it appears to be passing. Mac, you had better hurry, nerves are fraying. If we don't end this soon, it will be the fastest failure in history."

"Acknowledged," the Enforcer said tensely before closing the comm.

After relaxing his clenched jaw, the Enforcer did his best to explain to the conscious maintenance worker that he had no choice but to leave them contained until we could send someone to help. Reluctantly, Hank agreed and resorted to assisting his fellow worker.

With the short exchange concluded, the Enforcer snapped an "Ayezon" at me and we proceeded to the maintenance accessway to finish our objective.

The increasing heat that we experienced as as we climbed the maintenance stairwell only added to my inescapable fatigue. While most floors were likely running on low power, the climate systems that were operational on the upper levels were clearly insulated from the accessway. The stuffiness of the air battled against the pain in my legs as I was continuously forced to shut out the physical distractions.

I knew that the Enforcer had been able to shed a huge weight once Sath had been rescued, but I still suspected that he was wearing thin as well. Even with all of his knowledge and conditioning he had to be getting tired. Without having a deep understanding of the Vast, I couldn't comprehend how to connect to it without a great deal of concentration. If the Enforcer was doing so while on the move, his mental fortitude was on another level.

"How do you do it?" I asked. My mind needed a greater distraction, so I blurted the question before considering the proper timing should we be in earshot of enemies.

"Do what?" the Enforcer asked in a hushed tone.

"Keep going, pushing beyond perceived limits... You have injuries and death happening to those all around you. Not only do you keep going, but you also persist with such dedication that military leaders twice your age respect your input. I feel like I'm about collapse. What do you know that I don't?" I asked between labored breaths and stair flights.

"Fox, you have access to the same knowledge that I do. There are too many factors to cover every possible scenario. All I can possibly do is lay the foundation. Once you have understanding, it is up to you to turn belief into action by applying the corresponding principles," the Enforcer said, pausing for a brief moment.

The Enforcer's manner was calm, and it no longer held the sharp edge to which I had grown accustomed when my naiveté dominated my learning. Even though I suspected that it was his own fatigue, I felt that there was more patience attached to the statement as if he recognized that I was finally putting the pieces together with sincerity rather than brute force.

I could do nothing more than nod that I understood, in theory. I did my best to mull over the particulars as we concluded our last few uninterrupted flights of stairs. Think time expired once the Enforcer detected Piran patrols on the current floor. Thermal filters indicated that Pirans were patrolling the halls, but not bothering to check the accessway. Once they passed, we exited the accessway and stepped into the carpeted hallway which muffled every sound in contrast to the abundant echoes of the stairwell.

The Enforcer had already plotted a course to Frank Jenkins' office. We were likely outnumbered, but at least with our ikes alone we had the capacity to avoid patrols. The wealth of executive collections was on display since the hallways were littered with ornate furniture and decorative plants providing suitable cover in what would be an otherwise barren corridor.

I followed the Enforcer's lead as we traversed the immediate halls until we arrived at an intersection with minimal cover. I was uncertain if our cloaks would have helped given the spatial distortion against such rigid surroundings. Regardless of our inventory, we had to rely on our wits.

Two Pirans approached. Our fingers tensed on our weapons as we crouched behind the last possible cover before an empty stretch of hallway. The patrol turned to the right, putting them directly across from us, leading away from our position.

"We can take 'em," I said.

"There might be more," the Enforcer chided.

"Sure, but it'd be so easy," I remarked as leveled my EQ and pointed it at the backs of the Piran soldiers.

In my folly, I wasn't sure if I depressed the trigger with the safety off in a mock fire or if my finger tensed accidentally, but a plasma burst spewed from the barrel of the disruptor, dropping one soldier and alerting the other. I required no words from the Enforcer to understand that I had inadvertently unleashed a storm as he quickly responded and dropped the remaining Piran with his Phantom.

As the Enforcer's caution suggested, the noise drew attention of more Pirans from an office that had been converted into a lounge. The jostling of weapons and heavy boots approached in a hurry.

"Stay out of sight," the Enforcer snapped.

As three more Pirans entered the hallway intersection, they hesitated upon seeing their fallen allies. Before they could assess the angle of attack, the Enforcer was already leveraging the distraction by firing a sequence of headshots dropping each soldier in turn before snapping a fresh power cell into his Phantom.

As more approached, I unleashed more bursts from my EQ, but instead of acknowledging my support fire the Enforcer huffed, indicating that he literally wanted me out of sight despite my intent to compensate for my initial mistake. My shots drew attention as well, prompting one Piran to focus on the table acted as my cover. The Enforcer dropped two more Pirans, but he was forced to step into the open as he put himself between me and the incoming plasma fire. In a continuous motion, he shouldered me out of the way, pushing me further away from the conflict, but in the process, he was grazed by stray plasma fire. Undeterred, the Enforcer dropped the remnant of Pirans in the intersection, but the sound of more on approach prompted drastic behavior.

The shove impaired my balance causing me to topple over and smash my head on a stone planter. The Enforcer tipped a bench over my prostrate form, snapped a Nebula grenade to the floor and dashed toward the intersection. The blackout from the head injury and smoke impaired my awareness of events that followed.

The Enforcer snapped his body into an aerial cartwheel catching the advancing Pirans off guard. His shots were less accurate midair, but they still put the enemy on the defensive. While the Pirans shifted their rifles in the direction of their adversary, the Enforcer's form blinked out of sight. The enemy once on their right appeared on their left. Without pausing to consider his advanced conditioning, the Enforcer immediately detected the wall's support beam with his ikes, surged forward, and hopped toward the wall. Once his shoes connected, he activated his kips and dove over the confused batch of Pirans. His body sailed over the group, but he flattened himself to properly tackle the approaching Piran at the rear of the formation.

Hands extended, the Enforcer made contact with the poorly grounded Piran, the flying tackle knocking him to the ground. The Enforcer's momentum set him up for a forward flip allowing him to pop from the ground so that he could level his body yet again and deliver a powerful drop kick to the last Piran to approach. The Enforcer's body hit the floor hard, but he still popped back up and twisted around to fire his Phantom at the batch of Pirans turning to track his position. With two final shots, the Enforcer dropped two more Pirans before throwing his Phantom at a third connecting the firearm with the soldier's face.

As remaining vertical Piran's opened fire, the Enforcer was already exiting the hallway with speed. At least one Piran that was strong enough to whip his Claw Hammer around squeezed off a sequence of shots, but despite their curvature toward their target, the last strand still splashed on the wall corner of the next intersection. Regardless if the direction change put him closer or farther from Jenkin's office, the Enforcer intended to keep the focus on himself.

The frantic run made it difficult for the Enforcer to rapidly cycle the filters on his ikes, so he began to dive through every intersection if unable to verify that each consecutive path was secure. The strategy was short lived as he finally passed an intersection in which Pirans had secured two of the three alternatives following a comm from previously engaged foes. While his body was midair, a group of Pirans anticipated the arrival and unleashed a stream of plasma down the hallway. Even from a sloppy barrage, the nigh translucent blue of a Cress shot clipped the Enforcer's leg impairing his landing. He tumbled to the floor, and rushed to regain his footing, but the Pirans were quick to surround him.

Despite possessing a perpetual ill will, especially since numerous allies had been dispatched, the Pirans could have easily fired on the Enforcer, but they were at least disciplined enough to verify the target that had caused them such a headache. The Enforcer remained low in a kneeling position. Seeing that his foes were too numerous, he put his hands outward showing that he had no weapon within. His sai, grips and diminished energy to disappear were all limited options against the number of his adversaries in close quarters. The most impetuous Piran at the front of the formation was ready to squeeze the trigger on his rifle when his superior halted him upon doing a visual check against his slate.

"Stop! That's the one!" The Piran officer said. "After all of Jenkins' hand wringing, his foe actually came to us."

The verification did little to calm most of the Pirans, yet they complied, knowing the importance of capturing such an important piece on the battlefield. They were quick to stand the Enforcer to his feet and take his sai. Despite the desire to bludgeon their enemy in the process, the maximum force that they dared attempt was a couple of forceful shoves. Finally, the Enforcer was going to confront the authority behind the whole contest.

"Fox?" A hushed voice said as motion moved my shoulder. "Fox."

As I tried to shake the blackness in my head, I felt my skull pounding and my lungs burning. The voice sounded so distant even though it was right next to me. I moved my hands gradually along the carpet until I could roll over. Even without opening my eyes, I felt like the room was spinning.

Once I started to move the voices paused, but there was still a sense of urgency as multiple hands helped me sit up and lean against the wall. As I carefully opened my eyes, I saw blurry versions of Torque and the Serpent crouching low to ascertain my health. Disoriented, I took a moment to establish that I was still on the hallway floor. On my left, I saw Piran bodies not yet recovered. "You make a good rug, but I want to know what happened? Where's Mac?" Torque asked quietly, reminding me that we were still in hostile territory. The fact that the Enforcer wasn't present hit me with a load of concern. The conflict with Pirans was a result of my error, and it pained me to admit that it might have cost us dearly. "They must have got him," I replied after giving a quick recount of the events.

Torque struck me as the one most likely to cast blame, but he still had his wartime conditioning engaged, "We'll verify before operating on that assumption."

My Vanguard allies helped me to my feet and we reset our position, should the Pirans return for dead body pickup. Frank Jenkins' office was still marked on our ikes, so there was no doubting our destination. Torque led the way, giving me a chance to clear my head as we kept a watchful eye out for hostiles.

My mind was distracted from the fight as I contemplated the battlefield within. I knew that if anyone wasn't expendable it was the Enforcer. I couldn't accept that someone capable of fighting, leading and inspiring might be lost on account of my error. It was a strange time for my understanding of interferics to activate, but I considered that I was finally making sense of just how much damage a little pride could do. A passing thought of arrogance may have jeopardized the whole operation. While I knew that stopping Jenkins took priority, I couldn't shake the reminder of why I started this journey, to find answers. With content from the Enforcer's training finally sinking in, I hoped that my folly hadn't put that quest at risk. I still had so many questions to ask about my memory on account of the anomalies experienced along the way. Refusing to let the quest be in vain, I pressed on with my allies.

Executive Level, Casters Tower
Core City, Windstonne Enclave
Commercial Empire, Northam Continent
Thread: sysObserver.cmd

After passing through a pair of glass doors, the Enforcer knew that his captors brought him to his desired destination. White marbled walls with black offsets and gold trim suggested that there wasn't a more ornately decorated office in the whole of Casters Tower. Gaudy large framed paintings attempted to capture political successes of the Global

War despite having no attachment to actual events. The Enforcer refrained from cringing at the decorations knowing that there was little to capture of the Global War in a positive light. The only sight to give him pause was the workstation in the open lobby. He immediately recognized the backdrop from Sath's desk where she had, on occasion, sent him comms when she believed that there was no immediate privacy threat.

Sensing the hesitation, the Piran captors shoved the Enforcer toward the doors ahead. Two advanced to open the doors while two remained on either side of the prisoner as yet another pair kept their disruptors trained on his back.

The Enforcer kept his ikes deactivated to limit any distraction from captors should they realize the nature of the tech. He didn't need them to verify his host who wore a white suit, despite its worn nature after being confined to the tower for a time longer than expected. Even from behind, there was no mistaking the well known form of Frank Jenkins who didn't even turn to acknowledge the arrival but instead continued to stare out the window.

The ranking Piran set the Enforcer's sai and empty Phantom 4.0 on Frank Jenkins' massive desk. The sound of metal against wood was the only trigger to prompt the faction leader to look over his shoulder momentarily.

"Leave him," Frank Jenkins said as the Enforcer stood silently opposite his desk.

The Pirans were shocked that Frank Jenkins would leave a sworn enemy unguarded in addition to that enemy's lack of resistance or aggressive behavior in captivity. Knowing that there was no argument to be had, the Pirans reluctantly complied, closed the office doors behind them and returned to their posts.

After the tense silence settled in the room, the Enforcer tucked his hands behind his back and walked toward the window to stand next to Jenkins.

"You have rather crude weapon choices, Mr. Conner," Frank Jenkins said, breaking the silence.

"Even crude weapons can be concealed or used effectively... in the right hands," the Enforcer said after a long pause. "I can't imagine them any more crude than your own weapons of choice."

Frank Jenkins felt a mixture of anger and elation. He was thrilled that the destruction of his enemy was within his grasp and yet he wanted nothing more than to toss the Enforcer through the heavy glass separating them from an overly generous fall into the urban blackness. The opening volley already revealed that his enemy was shrewd. He

DAVE TODD

would be foolish not to learn every manner of intel. The conflict at his doorstep showed that there were way too many holes in his plan, and they needed to be plugged in order to solidify his grasp over the Global Alliance.

"So, you're the so called Enforcer who has continuously been a thorn in my side after all these passes. I suppose that after such prolonged opposition, I expected something more," Frank Jenkins said, failing to resist a smirk after realizing that he was still half a mark taller than his foe.

"Something matching your ruthlessness, I presume," the Enforcer mused.

"Perhaps... and to think that my greatest adversary was under my nose the whole time in the very enclave that I command," Jenkins said, the vitriol starting to erupt.

"I was never your enemy, Jenkins. You are. Your lust for power has done nothing but blind you to reality," the Enforcer said curtly.

Frank Jenkins glared at the Enforcer who calmly stared out the window. He was uncertain if he was more irate at the insult or his own inability to evoke an emotional response from his enemy.

"This situation can still be salvaged. Shut down the satellites and allow the people to choose their own way," the Enforcer said.

"You act like you are in control and even suggest that I am. The satellites were never under my control," Jenkins fumed as he returned his view to the battlefield below.

"Anytime you make a deal with the kilnsman you always lose," the Enforcer said flatly.

"I suppose my error was that I made that call so long ago," Jenkins responded. "I don't see how we're any different with the body count that you accumulated to reach me."

"The difference between us is that I was never under any illusion about who IS in control. The Triad always has authority and you chose the opposition, Frank. If it were up to me, there would be no second chance, but I'm here because you get one," the Enforcer said.

The Enforcer calmly walked over to the large bubbling fish tank and stared at the creatures darting within. He noticed the similarities between the creatures and the common facial features of the primary Imperan security force, but the Enforcer knew that it took more than just the surgery of a praised military icon to compel so many soldiers to identify with such carnivores. It took the embodiment of a tyrant.

"I can't help but wonder if your prattling blinds you to your own ignorance, Mr. Conner. You were disarmed and ushered in here so easily. Instead of issuing threats, you bargain with promise of opportunity. Your weapons lay before me and you make no motion to defend yourself. You have no idea just how ruthless I am," Frank Jenkins said

"No, Mr. Jenkins, if I were truly ignorant, I would do as you suggest without full awareness of the disruptor behind your back that you would pull the moment I tried," the Enforcer said. Without even turning to face Jenkins he sensed the half smile from the faction leader, conceding the point.

"So, your ability to see through the deception and theater is why you have made such a formidable opponent all this time," Frank Jenkins said. "Perhaps I will regret no longer having such an obstacle to my success."

"This is the end. You don't have to look much further than that window to see it," the Enforcer said as he turned away from the fish tank to face the faction leader.

"You may be correct, but I am confident that if it is my end, it is the end of my enemy as well," Frank Jenkins said as he lifted the Phantom 4.0 from his desk and turned it over in his hand.

"People with that kind of resolve need to know how to get their own hands dirty," the Enforcer chided as he moved around the opposite side of the desk.

"I'm here because I'm already an expert, Mr. Conner," Frank Jenkins said as he ejected the spent power cell from the sidearm and replaced it with a fresh one from his desk.

The Enforcer kept his eyes trained on Frank Jenkins' face. The faction leader held the disruptor with a steady hand, but his face revealed his annoyance at his enemy's ability to retain an inexplicably calm demeanor.

"Just so you know, I can break your arm in three places before squeezing the trigger," the Enforcer said.

Frank Jenkins wanted to laugh given the distance between the Enforcer and himself. At least two paces away, he considered it impossible, "I wrote the book on aggressive diplomacy, Mr. Conner. Nice try and farewell!"

Without hesitation, Frank Jenkins squeezed the trigger. The Phantom 4.0 spewed a yellow plasma bolt that struck the Enforcer's head with such force that it knocked his body backward into a large padded chair and tipped it over. Frank Jenkins stared down at the motionless form in disbelief that his long time enemy had been dispatched so easily. After shaking his paranoia, he questioned if he actually felt relief that a nigh insurmountable task had finally come to an end. Before returning his attention to the battlefield beneath his feet, Jenkins tapped the comm on his desk.

"The Enforcer is finished," Jenkins said.

"Splendid," a voice on the opposite end replied.

42 – Behind the Veil – 42

Executive Level, Casters Tower
Core City, Windstonne Enclave
Commercial Empire, Northam Continent
Thread: actTgtPersp1.view

My head pulsed as we advanced through the halls toward the marker identifying Frank Jenkins' office. We moved slowly along the carpeted floors, hoping to avoid more Pirans. The urgency to find the Enforcer scuttled any possibility of sitting down to regain my senses and let my body heal. At least to distract myself, I entertained the thought that the skull jarring might have at least knocked a memory or two loose.

We were halfway to our target when the floor rumbled again. All security lights and appliances dimmed and flickered as the familiar hum of a system drain flooded our ears. I looked out an office window intending to see more energy tendrils climbing the structure, but instead the diminished lighting put an emphasis on the dark swirling clouds outside which were periodically accompanied by a flash of lightning in the distance. Even Torque and the Serpent hesitated as they observed the unnatural phenomena happening before our eyes.

Shortly thereafter, our ears were assaulted by an influx of panic over the general comm. Our best efforts to filter related channels or get confirmation from leadership failed, forcing us to mute the comms. Apparently suppression efforts on the ground were failing and the activity within Casters Tower was the cause. We needed to hurry for the sake of those giving us the opportunity remedy the situation.

Commotion from the hallway adjacent to our observation office prompted a pivot, so I leveled my EQ at the source of the noise.

"Whoa, easy, Killer," Torque said as he suggested that we drop behind cover.

From our vantage point we watched Pirans engaging each other. Some were coherent and utilizing their disruptors while others were behaving in a way common to most Extend victims, charging ahead as if feral. Since I felt little sympathy for those trapped in the spectacle, I quickly followed Torque who recognized an opportunity to skirt around our distracted enemy.

The Piran scuffle cleared our last stretch of hallway leading to Frank Jenkins' office. In spite of our need for caution we advanced quickly toward the lobby preceding the navigation marker. Neither the thermal filter on our ikes nor the Serpent's keen vision gave us an accurate description of what was happening beyond the lobby. We took up position as best we could, ready for anything that might happen within or without.

Thread: sysObserver.cmd

Frank Jenkins' smug expression reflected off the window before him as his focus drew back from the battlefield. He was pleased that the true figurehead of the resistance had been crushed. It was not as tidy as Jenkins preferred, but it secured the inception of the Unisphere. There were no longer any relevant pieces capable of altering his plan.

The faction leader felt compelled to relay the specifics to Oszwick in person. Jenkins set the heavy pistol on his desk and headed for the door. He glanced at the outcome of his actions as he passed by his desk, the toppled chair and the lifeless body on the floor. It was a sobering moment, but one that he had no reason to dwell on. Progress had little time for sentiment.

Frank Jenkins' fingertips barely grazed the door handle when he felt the sensation of being watched. Knowing that his victory had to be premature, he whirled about leveling the Splice 15m from behind his suit coat. Suspecting that his enemy had a few tricks to play, Frank Jenkins recognized that his doubts had been realized, but instead of revealing his confusion as to the methods, he stifled his concerns with the usual mask, his arrogance.

"My arm is feeling pretty good, Mr. Conner. After the injury you promised, I find your word to be sketchy. Your reputation suggested that you prioritized truth. A good leader ought to keep his word," Frank Jenkins sneered as he leveled the firearm at the Enforcer who stood between him and his desk.

A tense staredown ensued. Frank Jenkins squinted, waiting for the slightest trace of emotion from his foe, but he received none. The Enforcer remained still, his eyes locked on Jenkins face. Tired of the game, Frank Jenkins' finger tensed on the trigger. Before his muscles contracted, the Enforcer's form blurred forward with indiscernible speed.

The Enforcer's hand pushed upward on Jenkins' weapon laden hand before catching it in a strong grip. He pulled downward on the executive's wrist and twisted it with extreme force heralding numerous pops in succession. Frank Jenkins shouted in agony as one knee buckled and the Splice dropped to the floor.

"I didn't say which pull," the Enforcer replied flatly.

Despite the pain tearing through his arm which soon had the flexibility of a noodle, Frank Jenkins glared, leveraging his defiance to prop himself up. If one arm was disabled, he could still swing with his free one. With great strain, Frank Jenkins attempted to punch with his opposite hand, but the Enforcer easily blocked it after releasing a partial grasp on the injured wrist.

"Frank Jenkins, your authority is by your own mouth, revoked!" the Enforcer said flatly.

Jenkins snarled with hatred at his adversary, but any uttered words twisted into a scream as the Enforcer turned about and pulled on the faction leader's arms. The body had no choice but to follow as it sailed into the air. The Enforcer hadn't calculated the guided throw, but it proved to be a fitting end. Jenkins' body cleared the desk with his head crashing into the exposed side of the large fish tank. The executive's thick skull penetrated the glass, leaking water and fish onto the floor. The carnivorous fish that were still in the water rushed and latched onto Frank Jenkins' flesh, quickly disfiguring their meal. Screams only erupted as sputters while Jenkins' thrashing proved useless with damaged limbs.

Frustrated that the faction leader's actions led to such a demise, the Enforcer turned away from the spectacle. Jenkins' own admission verified that the mission wasn't yet over. He only proved to be the front man for the one running the operations behind the curtain.

Thread: actTgtPersp1.view

The soft carpet was our only ally in the cautious rush to reach Frank Jenkins' office. Our footsteps and breathing still gave away our presence as we approached. The lack of security didn't lessen our concern for traps either.

Torque and the Serpent were quick to take up positions on either side of the doorframe to the lobby. There were no adversaries present. The dense walls protecting the office prevented our filters from working effectively. I thought that there were amorphous shapes representing bodies through the thermal filter, but with all of the tech in the area I couldn't rule out interference.

My allies were about to advance when a loud crash made us tense. I leveled my EQ at the doorway, but Torque was quick to raise a hand for caution.

I lowered my weapon shortly after my friends lowered theirs as we entered the lobby. The Enforcer calmly strolled out of Frank

Jenkins' office. The heavy doors closed slowly enough for us to observe the spectacle of Jenkins' twitching body attached to the fish tank.

"He should have opted for goldfish," the Serpent remarked.

I was uncertain if the shared cringe reactions were from Jenkins' demise or the Serpent's humor, but we didn't spend long deciphering the situation.

"What took you so long?" The Enforcer quipped.

I squinted for a moment, puzzled by the remark. I found sarcasm to be uncommon in the Enforcer's mannerisms, so from the side I casually checked my interferic filter. I didn't sense any anger from him, but his readout was out of alignment without any suggestion as to the cause. Nothing suggested that his interaction with Jenkins' was based on vengeance or malice and yet the hazy form from his profile looked off.

"Oh, you know. We were passing by the eatery and the Serpent had to grab an Ice Brrger and some Mesquite-Os from the vending machine," Torque said.

The Serpent simply returned a head snap in Torque's direction. Even without a change in facial expression, I knew that it was one of mock insult which was more then enough to counter Torque's jest. The Enforcer entertained half a smirk for the moment, but we all knew that there was more to be done.

"Are we clear?" The Serpent asked flatly.

"Not yet, Frank Jenkins was just the front man for the real windseed," the Enforcer said shaking his head. "The towers on the roof are still interacting with the satellites. We need to shut those down and Extend's creator."

Torque and the Serpent took the information in stride without suspecting that there was something unusual about the situation, but I found it strange that the Enforcer arrived at that conclusion without any time lapse since his capture. He didn't indicate that Frank Jenkins revealed anything of significance, but he was certain of the facts in regard to our true opponent. The situation continued to add weight to my suspicion that the Enforcer still knew more than revealed, reminding me just how close I had come to losing access to that information by making a rash decision.

Vanguard was ready to make a move toward our objective, but I hesitated, wanting to make sure that I cleared the air and made up for my actions that led to the recent capture, "Mac, I..."

"Before you say anything, if past actions compel you to prevent repeating them, reflect on those. That will carry more weight than hollow words," the Enforcer said over his shoulder as he paused briefly.

I nodded my compliance for the time being. There was still no anger in his voice, only the strength of a constant mentor. I couldn't understand how he maintained the role or why it felt like such a relentless pressure to match expectation, but I knew that there was no time to dissect the matter beyond acknowledging his take on it. I was continually being challenged and pulled upward, but never kept down. I wanted to ask more questions, but Vanguard's advancement kept my focus on our objective. Looking forward to a time, in which I could finally ask more, I fell in line and followed.

Building scans showed that we only had a floor or two remaining within the executive section. The uppermost floors were reserved for mediacasting, storage and security, so we didn't expect much of a civilian presence, but a quick filter scan revealed there were still bodies between us and the next accesssway. We made a break for the next hallway intersection only to pull back narrowly evading a Mortimer blast that ripped down the corridor. We were forced to face the fortification of missing Pirans recently positioned as a last line of defense. We shifted our tactics as we dove for the floor while graypak, glass and debris saturated the air.

The concussion impaired our capacity to stand and regroup quickly. My ears were ringing, but through the thick muffled sound I heard warning from our adversaries about a live grenade. I scrambled to find the explosive in the smoke and dust without success. I intended to yell a warning, but was uncertain of my success given the disorientation.

"Not this time," Torque snapped as he watched the red hazy highlight of the airborne object through his tracking filter.

Torque swiftly stood and punted the Inferno grenade back in the direction it came from, forcing the unsuspecting Pirans to scramble. The blast returned the favor, putting many of them on the floor.

"Can you buy us five clicks?" the Enforcer shouted, his form already moving toward our foes.

I felt a strong tug on my arm as the Enforcer lifted me to my feet, suggesting without words that I was part of the advance.

"I can buy you a sungauge if it makes you move any faster!" Torque yelled back as he and the Serpent found secure cover.

The Enforcer bolted from the smoke and bounded over the Piran barricade. I continued to struggle with my senses, but I followed the Enforcer in less agile fashion. While midair after clearing the barricade, I fired my EQ to the side and downward, hoping to deter any surviving Piran from getting up too soon. Heavy footsteps suggested that more Pirans were alerted to our location, ready to reinforce the barricade, but Torque's quick thinking bought us the time and opening that we needed to slip through. The only thing left to impede our progress toward Oszwick was our ability to run.

Thread: sysObserver.cmd

Knowing that the distraction wouldn't last long, Torque and the Serpent charged the recovering Pirans. Before they could reach melee weapon range, a powerful body intercepted. Torque felt like he was hit by a truck as his feet lifted into the air and his body collided with the Serpent before both crashed to the floor. Torque responded quickly as he rolled and popped back into a stance with the Serpent performing a similar maneuver.

Torque rose up to face the tackling form. Even in the dust and flickering lights, Torque recognized the bulky frame of the Commercial Empire's senior military officer. The direct showdown was Torque's first opportunity to realize that the Piran soldier stood nearly a mark taller than himself or the Serpent and likely outweighed either by a hundred blocks.

"Looks like I finally get to finish you off myself," Commander Pyln snarled.

"Not so fast," Torque said as he wiped grime from his face with the back of his hand. "We're the ones with a score to settle."

The Serpent stood in a rigid stance, blade drawn, between Torque and the Piran. Torque quickly flicked his kama blades to the side and leapt into the air. Clearing the Serpent's height, Torque pushed off his shoulders gaining the elevation for a strong downward slash to Pyln who angled his body to catch Torque and toss him to the floor.

With his blade slicing the air, aiming for Pyln's back, the Serpent executed a quick strike, but Pyln dropped his weight and spun into a low sweep kick toward the Serpent's legs. Fluidly continuing the combo, the Serpent was already in the air dropping his blade for another attack. Pyln too continued his momentum by spinning out of the way after his misplaced kick.

As spectating Pirans leveled their weapons, they trained them on the scuffle before them. One Piran barked for the commanding officer to stay down as they unleashed a torrent of plasma fire down the hallway. A firestorm erupted, prompting Torque and the Serpent to dive into an adjacent office through an open door, but the thin walls did little to hinder the collective impact. The Pirans maintained their barrage against the glass and graypak walls.

"All of these obstructions might make line of sight... difficult," the Serpent coughed.

"Which means it's a two way street," Torque replied.

The Serpent required no vision enhancements to perceive the huge smirk plastered on Torque's face. The two quickly lifted into a crouch and navigated the office left in shambles. Torque continued to toggle between his night vision and tracking filters whenever airborne debris didn't create interference. He had no desire to get caught off guard. Leveraging misdirection of his own, Torque found a metallic desk ornament and tossed it toward office entrance.

Pirans startled by the noise fired blindly into the darkness, giving Torque and the Serpent opportunity to use the noise as cover for their run through the office furnishings. They intended to find an alternate exit and flank their opposition, but once they hit the hallway, they were spotted once again, prompting an observant Piran to call out their position. At the next junction, they ran in separate directions. They knew that the conflict's outcome was irrelevant as long as they bought enough time for their allies.

Torque sprinted down a hallway lacking any cover whatsoever. The heavy tromping of boots hinted that he could be fired upon soon. He had to reach the next corner before his foes opened fire or he was a dead man. The next closest doorway was a conference room. Torque knew that the Pirans would certainly check the room first, so he searched for an adequate diversion. He lifted a conference chair overhead and waited. As soon as a shadow appeared in the doorway to the darkened room he tossed the chair at the silhouette.

Yells and muffled banter filtered into the room while Torque searched for an exit. To his surprise, the alternate door to the conference room led into the barricaded hallway. He quickly fired a couple of blind shots to distract the Pirans while he made his escape.

Torque suspected a trap ahead, but instead found the barricade abandoned since the commotion had demanded a full search of the premises. Torque leapt over the barricade and quickly scooped up two EQ assault rifles, tucking one under each arm.

While some Pirans doubled back, others kicked down every door attached to the conference room. The Pirans were perplexed at how their quarry escaped, but Torque felt obliged to announce his presence. With a confident stride, Torque stepped past the barricade where the hunting Pirans stood and squeezed the triggers to the EQs, unleashing an unforgiving stream of plasma.

Imperan soldiers were dropped to the floor as spent energy cells were ejected from the assault rifles with a metal *sching*. Torque kept the triggers depressed until the rifle in his left hand had its revolving barrel grind to a halt, following the final discharge from the last dry energy cell.

Even without hostile movement in the hallway, Torque kept his eyes and ears trained on his surroundings. He dropped the EQ in his left and was about to lower the one in his right when a face quickly peeked around a distant doorway before pulling back. Even without great clarity, Torque knew the survivor was none other than the Piran commander. Determined, Torque squeezed hard on the trigger with his right hand.

Accepting that he was detected, Command Pyln crossed the hallway and shoulder charged a section of graypak already weakened by disruptor fire. Pyln's massive frame made short work of the flimsy wall and created a new escape route.

Torque gritted his teeth and followed Pyln with the EQ barrel still spinning. As the power cell drained quickly, Torque continued forward and snapped two more fresh cells into the assault rifle. The weapon spewed plasma at the walls even when Torque's motion tracker put an unmistakable box across his ikes any time that Pyln's retreating form made a move.

Debris crunched under the weight of Commander Pyln's boots. Dust and smoke clung to the air as the Piran soldier sprinted away from his adversary. Torque continued tracking the box on his ikes as it followed Pyln's body which would have been invisible otherwise amidst the rubble. Chunks of wall dropped from eye level to the floor cuttting a way through the wall as the EQ continued to spew plasma rounds at Torque's discretion.

As the last power cell kicked past Torque's right forearm, the inset spinning barrel of the EQ snapped to a halt. Torque dropped the disruptor and drew his lockblade kamas from behind his back, flicking the blades to full extension. Torque thought that he saw Pyln's form round the corner before the motion tracker lost his position.

Based on his gut reaction, Torque guessed at Pyln's possible direction and position. With extreme force, Torque raised his arm and threw the kama into the smoke. Beyond his range of vision, the kama sank into the wall just notches in front of Pyln's face.

Pyln blinked at the weapon with the jagged outer blade which sunk halfway into the wall. Silently, Pyln reached for the modified melee weapon and removed it from the wall before folding up the blade and tucking it under his arm. He had been forced to drop his firearm in the run, so as quiet methodical footsteps approached, Pyln ducked out of sight and waited.

Torque kept his guard up as he moved cautiously through the wreckage. His left hand led his body from the front while his right spun the remaining weapon around from behind. He quickly noticed the gap in the wall where his thrown kama had stuck, but the weapon was nowhere to be found.

Offering no time to react, Pyln charged forward and drove a shoulder into Torque's chest, sending him sprawling backward. Torque tucked his body inward since the force impacted him enough to send him into multiple somersaults. Once his momentum waned, he finally extended his limbs to slow the roll and prevent more severe injury.

Torque kicked his feet over his head while rolling backward so that he could push himself back onto his feet. As he returned to a standing position, he faced Commander Pyln who glared with a malicious sneer. Torque was quick to notice that the Piran had the missing kama tucked under his right forearm. Charging in, Torque led with a downward angled slash with the kama in his right hand. Pyln evaded the attack, prompting Torque to continue with a reverse horizontal slash which Pyln dodged by ducking.

As another strike passed by, Pyln snapped his right wrist and blocked the incoming attack with the stolen weapon. Torque began chaining his moves together, but Pyln swiftly countered high and low strikes with the closed lockblade kama. Recognizing that Pyln was too advanced to be bested by traditional strikes, Torque raised his kama overhead and feigned a high strike. Pyln moved to block the hit, but Torque cut his motion short and drove the base of the weapon's handle into the center of Pyln's chest. Torque knew that the strike would do little damage against the commander's body armor, but it certainly got his attention.

Commander Pyln continued to glare as he waited for Torque to strike again. Torque advanced with a spinning slash to catch Pyln with the outside edge of the kama blade. Plyn drove his right leg outward with a front kick to Torque's body, but Torque spun about and drove another slash across Pyln's face, narrowly missing the opportunity to strike his throat.

Torque stepped forward with a straight punch, but Pyln caught Torque's wrist, stepped forward, and lodged a kama handle under Torque's chin. Pyln used the momentum to control Torque's body and hurl him into the air. Torque barely righted his body before his feet touched down with his toes moving just in time to prevent being pinned to the floor by the stolen kama which Pyln finally released with a violent throw.

"Now I understand why Jenkins is so irritated with you carp. You just don't know when to quit," Pyln snorted.

Torque paused before sloshing around a mouthful of blood from an internal injury but before spitting it on the carpet, "I suppose no one ever told you that it's better to be stubborn than ugly."

Letting his anger get the best of him, Torque tossed his other kama to the floor and rushed at Pyln. Carelessly, he fired another punch at Pyln's face, but the bulky commander caught the punch in his palm before stepping to Torque's exposed side and delivered a jarring uppercut to his jaw. Pyln continued stepping around, pulling on Torque's arm. Torque's body had no choice but to flow with the motion until a consequential pop ripped through the air, announcing a dislocated shoulder as he flew over Pyln's body without resistance and tumbled on the floor like a limp rag. Pain shredded Torque's ambition as he tried to support his left arm with his right hand while pushing against the floor to escape Pyln's advance.

Finally dispatching the Pirans that dared chase him, the Serpent suspected that activity down the hall was amiss. He caught the exchange between Torque and Pyln in his peripheral vision and realized that the outcome was not good. Disregarding the newly created mess of bodies on the floor, the Serpent moved to intercept. Commander Pyln moved in for the kill, but was immediately halted as the Serpent stood between the Imperan soldier and his target. Pyln stepped back and glared as the Serpent held his glistening blade in front of his body without wavering.

The Serpent stepped in for a strike, but Pyln matched with speed as he grabbed the knife strapped to his thigh and deflected the quick attack. After many passes of training, Pyln knew better than to attempt a block of such a weapon or challenge the power of its wielder. Evasion and redirection were the optimal strategies.

Commander Pyln deflected three more of the Serpent's strikes which had been chained into a fluid maneuver before he finally unseated the blade from the Serpent's strong grasp. As the blade dropped to the floor, the Serpent had already bent his wrists and flattened his hands into the striking position identified by his ayvek.

Pyln expected little resistance from his disarmed foe, but he quickly discovered that his difficulties were on the rise. Pyln slashed the air multiple times with broad swings, but the Serpent swooped under one swing only to follow-up with a snaking deflection, utilizing the inside of his left forearm in order to gain control over Pyln's arm. Pyln lowered his body to avoid being trapped by the Serpent's counter. Even with the temporary lapse in offense, the Serpent was able to poke a successful strike. Pyln leaned away from the first strike but the second was unavoidable as a flat handed poke caught the corner of Pyln's left eye. The Imperan commander immediately winced and squinted, losing sight of his target in the blink of an eye.

Long running combat experience gave Pyln all the data that he needed even without a direct visual of his opponent. Without need of critical analysis, Pyln slammed his elbow backward at head level and caught the Serpent in the cheek with his blind technique.

The Serpent reeled backward from the powerful blow as he compensated for the balance shift. The Serpent made another advance, but Pyln spun about and landed a hook punch to the Serpent's face. The Serpent knew that he had the agility advantage over the Piran, but the strong blows were quickly breaking his concentration. Leveraging momentum, Pyln unleashed a series of punches requiring the Serpent to evade or block each one in turn while trying to regain a stable footing.

Torque struggled to push himself from the floor, but the efforts caused more pain than he cared to admit. With his good arm, he managed to prop himself up enough to get his knees under the rest of his body and use his legs to do the rest. Knowing that the Serpent wouldn't hold up much longer under Pyln's pressure, Torque gave one more painful shove as he wobbled to his feet. He slammed his shoulder into the wall to reset the joint, tending to other injuries later. He felt like arrows ripped through his entire right side as his limb impacted the wall. He had better control of his arm, but he knew he would have to live with the pain for the duration of the conflict.

Commander Pyln made two more wild swings which the Serpent evaded, but the third locked onto its target. Pyln drove his fist upward into the Serpent's chest knocking the wind from his lungs. The Serpent staggered while trying to recover.

Torque watched the crushing blow as he advanced toward Pyln's back. Yet again, Pyln advanced for the killing blow, but Torque was quick enough to dive high into the air, easily clearing Pyln and the Serpent. Torque extended his limbs giving him enough clearance to bound over the vectors. Even despite his fall, the Serpent already read the nature of Torque's motion. With his hands in front of his head to prevent cracking it on the floor, Torque reached to place his hands down first while his feet clamped to the side of Pyln's head. The continued motion of the dive roll, pulled Pyln's body forward and upward into the air sending the Piran head over heels down the hallway.

Before Pyln's body landed, Torque was already completing his roll and turning to face the Serpent who was normalizing his air intake. Despite his clouded thinking, the Serpent anticipated the next move.

Even with shaky footing, he was able to fall toward Torque who pressed his knee into the Serpent's midsection and tossed him toward their adversary. The Serpent pressed his arms and legs toward his sides and straightened his body which sailed through the air like a screw at the flailing airborne commander. The Serpent drove his head into the body of the target before curling into a ball and safely rolling to the floor.

The extra hit kept Pyln's body airborne long enough for Torque to stand, snag his weapons with the grips in his coat sleeves and hurl them toward Pyln. The Piran barely straightened his body before slamming into a wall at the end of the hallway. Pyln saw the inbound projectiles and deflected the first, but the other caught his forearm cutting a deep gash.

Further enraged, Pyln shook off the the injuries and charged toward his foes who almost stood side by side. Raising his combat knife overhead, Plyn advanced with a downward slash. The Serpent pressed himself against the wall as needed in such close quarters and snapped his hands at the proper moment to disarm Plyn of his blade.

As the weapon fell, Torque caught the knife, dropping his center of gravity. He moved the blade in a circular arc, using his momentum to spin around his back. For a clean opening, Torque dropped to his knee, spun and jammed the combat knife hard into Pyln's side, only to rise back up with a spin in the opposite direction to snap a jump kick to the commander's abdomen. The Serpent too contributed with a kick of his own to Pyln's back.

Commander Pyln added annoyance to his rage as he withdrew the bloodstained knife from his side and tossed it to the floor. He charged again, but Torque was ready for the advance. In a fluid agile swoop, Torque leaned past the Commander's charge and used the forward motion to flip Pyln into the air. With masterful precision, the Serpent used his grips to reclaim his fallen blade and immediately point it upward from the floor as Torque dropped the heavy commander directly onto it, impaling him instantly.

The Piran commander flailed but realized that the lethal wound was draining his strength rapidly.

"You know some wounds never heal until you get to the source," Torque grimaced as he reached for a fallen Splice 15m.

"Do it. You're no better! Revenge will never satisfy," Pyln choked as blood ran across his signature filed teeth.

"This was never about revenge. This is justice for those afflicted by your passes of treachery. For them, the wound is now closed," Torque snapped in conjunction with a squeeze of the trigger.

The plasma shot was muffled in the soft business setting as Pyln's head rocked on the floor with finality. Without any need to verify Pyln's condition, Torque kicked his boot against the Piran's body to roll it over, so that he could withdraw the blade and hand it back to its owner. The Serpent deftly flicked the blade to the side freeing it of the excess blood before engaging the heating element to vaporize the rest. The two exchanged a mutual nod which conveyed each was in working order, despite the accumulated injuries. With resolve, they headed for the empty barricade. They had already wasted enough time.

Thread: actTgtPersp1.view

Every muscle fiber in my legs felt as though they were being shredded from the bone and reattached via staples. I never felt as though I had ascended a flight of stairs so fast before. The painful experience was compounded by the fatigue. I tried to focus on any upside to the situation, but the only solace that I could find was that we weren't being chased. Given the diminished assets of the Piran forces, our climb was free of opposition, at least externally.

I was aware of the nature of the Windstonne superstructures' subtle shifts on account of height and wind, but it was my first time experiencing the gentle sway underfoot. I had been too distracted to notice the sensation at the executive level, but as we neared the final levels of the tower, the strain to already tired stabilizing muscles proved taxing.

Upon reaching the final stairwell to the rooftop, the Enforcer motioned for me to pause while he used his ikes to check for traps. Sensing no dangers of the inanimate variety, he kicked the access door open and stepped onto the rooftop, putting us at least a hundred decks above the enclave terrain.

My senses were assaulted in full, initially by the roaring wind, but later by the gravity which put my equilibrium in check. My first reaction was to drop and hug the rooftop, considering the lack of barriers between us and a very long vertical drop. Once I realized that other stimuli were at work, I stepped further away from the access door. Seeing Windstonne from above was a magnificent view, but as the fierce wind ripped my treadball cap away from my skull, my senses warned that it wasn't time to sight-see.

The pair of transmission towers crackled with energy, creating a blinding display to contrast the dark enclave below. I saw wispy translucent waves emanating from the towers, floating away and disappearing from sight in addition to the white curls of energy that erratically spiraled upward much like the tendrils we witnessed previously. The entire spectacle made me nauseous, prompting me to accept that the devices were the source of my sensory overload.

The Enforcer was cautious in our hunt for the towers' operator, but the search was brief considering our target stood calmly between the pair of towers, his gray suit coat, pants and red shirt whipping fiercely in the wind. Konrad Oszwick stood calmly with his back toward us while he reveled in his operational success. Initially, I wanted to tackle the unsuspecting executive from behind, but the Enforcer already extended a hand to halt any advance since he suspected that our arrival was anticipated.

"Shut it down, Oszwick," the Enforcer yelled. "It's time to return the people's will."

"Oh?" Konrad smirked as he slowly turned to face us. "Someone has finally arrived to pull down the curtain. I don't see any reason why I should comply."

I had no intention of advancing on our target, but our opponent's demeanor caused my arm to tense against my disruptor. I realized that Oszwick perceived the slight action, but instead of responding with motion, a seemingly random electrical arc erupted from the closest tower, firing right on our position. The bolt charred the metal platform directly between the Enforcer and me, prompting us to dive out of the way. The unexpected arc gave me little time to react, and I had little room for clearance. As I fell to the platform, my head collided with a stack of crates.

My relief that I didn't black out did little to calm the internal discord of my senses. My ears told me that the Enforcer was already back on his feet, holding position. I did my best to scramble, but my sluggish response demanded a tick. As I lifted my weight back onto my feet, my eyes locked onto the corporate logo stamped upon the crates, showing the Oszwick Enterprises logo, and the name of our adversary above it. My vision blurred prompting me to stagger. The strange illusion of name and logo blurred the words as if a latent memory seeped through and created a conflicting visual. For a brief tick, I felt like I was seeing the crates in a laboratory environment instead of from the present tower platform and the only letters that I could discern were the initial from Konrad and the first part of the company name. In a groggy state, I turned to face our target while the illusion faded.

Annoyed that we were still standing, Oszwick grimaced.

"That wasn't a nice thing to do, Chaos," I mumbled, uncertain how I even connected the name or if I was even speaking from a state of clarity.

I rubbed my eyes to make sure that I was seeing clearly. Initially, I thought that my vision was still off, because I soon realized that Oszwick had leapt from the platform to a tall power regulation box and was perched on top of it. His posture was not that of an aged man, but instead he was crouched low almost like a frog with his hands resting near his feet. The pose looked uncomfortable regardless of a person's age. I looked over to see the Enforcer bearing a startled expression, but it wasn't on account of Chaos' behavior, but my revelation.

"Intriguing," Chaos mused as amusement washed over his face. "That's a name reserved for a select few, and one not easily known to vapors. Judging by expressions it wasn't something that was explained to you. Which means you're starting to comprehend things that you shouldn't."

"He's of no concern to you, Oszwick," the Enforcer snapped.

"It is of great concern anytime someone interferes with a long running family feud, a contest that is meant to be kept from most," Chaos replied.

"I don't care about your family business, but I think it is our concern that you would subvert the lives of those we care about," I replied automatically, without having time to think about the exchange that I had stumbled into.

"This veras... is... MINE!" Chaos snapped with a teeth-baring grin, finally revealing his truly maniacal demeanor which had been long hidden behind the professional façade.

The reference to topics that I had heard only from the Enforcer caught me off guard. While I needed time to digest the level of knowledge that I was up against, Chaos yielded no such opportunity.

"I have operated out of sight for several thousand passes, and I'm not about to let a few vapors disrupt my progress," Chaos said.

"Thousand? That's not possible!" I retorted as I stared at the executive, who barely matched Jenkins' age in appearance.

"Is it?" I followed-up, after considering the opposing view to my initial outburst while looking at the Enforcer.

"Your protégé?" Chaos mocked. "You really do underestimate me if you think that I can be defeated by anyone so uninformed of reality."

For once, I was taken aback that the Enforcer didn't have an answer for my question. I suspected that he had the means to explain, but I interpreted his silence as improper timing. Chaos, however, used the lack of response from his foes to elaborate.

"I was there when the Master Craftsman's first vapor abandoned all inheritance, for what? Clever word play and a fruit salad?" Chaos bragged after the howling wind settled. "Some of us precede the very instruments that you use to measure time."

Strangely, I recognized that some of Chaos' claims overlapped accounts in the Criterion. If he was indeed as shrewd and timeless as his words suggested, I knew that we were outmatched, and I knew that there was no hope but to stall him until reinforcements arrived. The consequences of such a delay though also gave him opportunity to stall while he prattled about his accomplishments. Periodically, the towers crackled and white energy tendrils flickered and popped from their base. I didn't know how Chaos was using the energy to his advantage, but I had to find a weakness fast.

"With all rights ceded, how could my family not leverage the opening?" Chaos asked rhetorically.

"Did you create the Catalyst?" I asked.

Chaos' face instantly twisted from beaming arrogance to absolute disdain, "Hardly."

The executive's reaction told me that he wasn't necessarily the one in charge, so I decided to press the issue. "So, you're not actually the windseed, you're just a bottom rung vaporgust, incapable of doing your own fighting."

The towers bristled and crackled in succession, corresponding to Chaos' mood change, "If you lived to be a hundred passes and were to fight a nation comprised of millions a tenth of that age, how could you lose? The very knowledge of war gained in that time always surpasses that of those continuously losing their foundational knowledge on account of generational decay. I've learned every ayvek known to vapors, and at this present age it bores me. I have no need to sully my hands when I can just as easily poke the minds of minions and plant suggestions."

"Like Jenkins," the Enforcer said emphatically.

I recognized that the Enforcer gleaned something from the faction leader and had no doubt as to the connection between the mediacasting executive and the immortal warlord before us. I thought that the Enforcer had been unusually quiet, but out of my peripheral vision I caught his eyes darting about as if he were still crafting an optimal solution to the situation at hand.

"Precisely," Chaos muttered as if annoyed that we were parsing his methods, "Along with countless others."

I sensed that Chaos' countenance was not as stable as first impressions suggested. Clearly, he had the desire to flaunt his endeavors and dismiss those of others. If he were easy to distract, I considered keeping the conversation going. I thought that the diversion might give the Enforcer more freedom to move about, but as the Enforcer tensed to take a step to the side, the transmission towers crackled yet again as if warning us to remain in place. I knew that the executive's bloviating would make for quite the stall tactic until reinforcements arrived, but it also allowed him to stall us to an unknown end since we didn't fully understand his connection to those linked through Extend.

"Why use the Commercial Empire as your base? The Tricameral Endeavor was founded with the Criterion at its core. Surely, there would have been enough of a remnant to oppose your plans," I said, trying to dig up what little history I could recall.

Chaos remained in his awkward crouching position. He eyed the Enforcer suspiciously, making sure that we remained in place before daring to explain his strategy, "Since your time is short, I see no issue in catching you up to speed. What better way to bolster support than by increasing buy-in from entities built on truth. Military might, economic success, free reign, all of these have appealed to the masses for generations. If they bought into those values as a pathway to desirables, who were they to question when I began to twist them from the inside as a proving ground for my agenda. Never underestimate the power of luxury and vice. When the ideals in my way had been all but erased, all I had to do was claim the most advanced infrastructure available to captivate audiences around the world."

"If your ideas require coercion then they must be terrible. It's no wonder you needed help selling them," I said poking at Chaos' ambitions.

Chaos' head tilted backward as he erupted into loud raucous laughter which was heard even above the wind and energy crackles of the towers. After shifting from his deep guttural mockery, he stared his eyes burning with arrogant fury. "You have no idea the lengths that some would go through to enlist the support of the unwitting for the sake of *help*. I'm sane enough to know my domain, unlike those who would drag resources from another veras."

Chaos' words ripped through the air as if laced with a corrosive acid. After glaring at me he shifted his gaze toward the Enforcer who continued to hold position in an expressionless state. After being hit with so much information, I was hoping that the Enforcer would interject. I had no cause to assume that Chaos would tell the truth, but his antics suggested that he knew more about my past than the Enforcer ever disclosed.

"Mac, what's he talking about?" I asked nervously on account of the heavy doubts welling up in my mind.

"Don't give ground to a deceiver. He won't hesitate to mix a pinch of truth with a barrel of lies," the Enforcer retorted.

"All I need is the power of suggestion. I always provide the fine print. None of my clients ever participate without freedom of choice," Chaos gloated.

"Never mind the fact that you bury the fine print under a mountain of sentiment," the Enforcer said.

"How is that any different than omission of the truth?" Chaos hissed.

"Imprints will never fully accept truth OR lies by force this side of the Exterior, as you well know! It must be by choice. That is why free will is so necessary," the Enforcer snapped back.

Chaos' expression changed from one counter claim to the next. His face twisted anytime the Enforcer illuminated a hole in the executive's logic. The exchange gave me a sense of internal conflict. I was finally learning the depths of the contest that I had been thrust into, but the way in which I was discovering my past came at the lips of an enemy. We had no way to further our objective without any knowledge of how to sever Chaos' connection with those that he continued to manipulate.

"Last warning, Chaos. Shut it down if you don't want to be sucking blazewater ahead of schedule," the Enforcer shouted.

"It is, as you say, your free will to choose death, but if you cannot enforce your will, I have no reason to oblige," Chaos smirked.

The contest escalated instantaneously. The Enforcer drew his Phantom as he recognized that Chaos had finished prattling. Although a tick slower, I drew my firearm as well, but our poor positioning gave Chaos the ability to strike us both. He leapt from the utility box with such blinding speed that his punches connected with our torsos before we could even completely extend our arms to fire. We were knocked to the platform with our firearms sliding well out of reach.

Amidst the backward tumble, I fought to regain my footing. I had no desire to fall off the platform let alone the rooftop to which it was attached. The Enforcer returned to his feet quickly enough to watch Chaos calmly step back and retract his arms.

I hoped that Chaos didn't have too many similar attacks. I thought that we were already in trouble given his ability to manipulate the tower's energy, but if his actions verified possession of a well hidden ability to fight, then we truly were at the base of the greatest uphill battle yet. I made sure to note that he capitalized on our positioning, so I kept a sizable distance between myself and the Enforcer.

Since Chaos reacted to the introduction of our weapons, I opted to advance with fists. I tensed my legs and pushed hard against the platform, but the Enforcer had already initiated the assault. His hands were a blur as clenched fists were adequately blocked by Chaos. My feet pounded against the platform to close the gap.

Chaos extended an arcing horizontal strike which the Enforcer evaded in turn by lowering his torso and weaving under the attack. Without hesitation, I jumped into the air and snapped a flying side kick outward, easily clearing the Enforcer's position. To my surprise, Chaos was already on the move as he recovered from his strike and leaned his torso away forcing me to miss completely.

As Chaos angled away, he delivered a ridge hand strike to the side of my neck. The strike wasn't powerful enough to do lasting damage, but it served its purpose of causing me to see spots and throw my landing off. While I stumbled, Chaos pushed a hook kick into my back, allowing him to turn about and face the Enforcer.

I had no desire to give Chaos an opening, so I threw a weak punch in his direction, but he stopped it with a low block while simultaneously using a high block to deflect the Enforcer's punch from the opposite side. With a swift counter, Chaos spun through his blocks delivering a side kick to the Enforcer's abdomen while pushing on my arm as he faced me. As I stepped in to attack, he leveraged my momentum and tossed me upward over his shoulder at the Enforcer. With his quick reflexes, the Enforcer pushed my back while I was midair, allowing me to flip over his head instead of causing the impact that Chaos intended.

"At least you weren't bluffing about your physical prowess," the Enforcer quipped.

"I have found that the perfect blend of truth with lies will always keep others off-balance," Chaos sneered.

"Too bad for you a healthy diet of truth keeps us grounded," the Enforcer said with a blank confidence on his face.

Disinterested in the exchange, I snapped back into position at a reasonable distance from the Enforcer. Sensing the urgency in my demeanor, Chaos shifted his focus toward me, but the Enforcer used it as an opening by jumping into the air and twisting his body. I felt my perception of time slow as the Enforcer's body spun three full rotations before a leg extended to kick Chaos.

Chaos began to lean away as I had observed before, but I intended to prevent his evasion. I drove my left knee into the air to give my right leg the clearance needed for a downward heel drop over his new position. In eerie fashion, Chaos anticipated my motion as well and twisted his torso toward the floor and snapped both legs upward, allowing him to use an aerial cartwheel to escape both attacks.

The Enforcer landed with composure and faced Chaos with his hands open, but in a defensive stance. Conversely, I lost my balance and fought to focus despite my advance with a flurry of sloppy strikes. Chaos deftly countered each strike and followed with a pushback technique. The Enforcer did the same, but in more precise fashion only to receive a similar knockback.

I paused briefly to analyze our surroundings. I detected nothing of tactical advantage and Chaos stood between us and our firearms. Even with well timed advances, Chaos still swatted us away like insects. I could already feel my insides protest, but I fought to suppress any sign of external fatigue when possible.

My lungs flexed as the Enforcer advanced again. I knew that I was unable to coordinate fast enough with my attacks to make them effective, so I did my best to match the tempo in which Chaos deflected the Enforcer's attacks. Just as both of Chaos' hands were occupied with deflecting blows, I lunged in to deliver a strike to Chaos' right eye. The Enforcer leveraged the opening and punched at Chaos' left side. Despite a weak block of the prior hit, the Enforcer followed up with a hook to Chaos' opposite side.

As Chaos staggered backward, I initiated the first hit in a combination with an uppercut. Chaos' body was launched by a flash kick from the Enforcer and I completed the sequence with an upward reverse kick that knocked the executive into one of the transmission towers. Chaos slammed into a tower frame, but the effect surprised us as the swirling energy held his body in place instead of letting gravity run its course.

The Enforcer and I held position, ready to advance, but the spectacle proved distracting. The towers crackled and hissed as Chaos slid to the floor, but his legs locked in defiance. He still appeared functional, but strangely he intermittently underwent convulsions with his head twitching backward. The towers seemed to glow even brighter each time that Chaos' behavior proved irregular.

I looked over to see that the Enforcer kept his eyes trained on our adversary. Even without words, I knew that he had no explanation for the absurd behavior. Finally Chaos' posture normalized and his head snapped forward. As the convulsing ceased, he lowered his head and glared. I squinted to make sense of the visuals before me. I questioned if my eyes had burn in from the tower brightness. I felt like I was seeing an orange glowing haze in front of Chaos' eyes as if my eyes were seeing something from the Vast event without technological assistance. Chaos seethed as his shoulders rose and fell with his deep guttural breathing. I sensed that the Enforcer was put off as to how the executive drew power from means unknown into the physical domain.

Recognizing that standard methods of incapacitation were no longer viable, the Enforcer drew his sai, and flipped them around his index fingers as he snapped into a ready stance. Given the speed of the skirmish I had forgotten about leveraging our weapons once our firearms had been removed from the equation. Trying to inject my willpower with artificial confidence, I sprinted forward with my fima sticks drawn, one overhead and the other ahead of my body.

I was so intently focused on my adversary that I was oblivious to the crackling arcs that escaped from the tower. The bolts might have struck me had it not been for the Enforcer's thrown sai spinning through the air, acting as lightning rods to draw the energy away from my position. I didn't have time to contemplate how Chaos could manipulate the energy so accurately, but the Enforcer's quick reactions allowed me to remain focused.

Chaos leaned away as I swung with the stick in my left hand, but he did nothing against the second as he absorbed the hit to his rib cage as I swung with my right hand. Startled by the lack of reaction, I swung the stick again, each hit reasonably connecting a blow to his arms or torso. As I struck again, I was intercepted by a painful uppercut to the jaw which lifted me into the air. The fima sticks flew from my hands as I flailed to right my body, but I was helpless to adjust my fall as my back slammed onto the platform.

My nerves tingled and lungs screamed for air. The only sense that seemed functional was my hearing as the Enforcer continued to engage Chaos with fast piercing strikes from his sai. He only faired marginally better in his ability to absorb one or two of Chaos' abnormally powerful blows.

I forced myself to roll onto my side. As I propped myself up, I saw Chaos backhand the Enforcer knocking him into the air before slamming a side kick into his body which pushed him through the air. I heard the metal clang of the Enforcer's sai hitting the platform even above my groan that erupted as I attempted to stand. My physical limitations were clearly exceeding my ability to conceal them.

As the Enforcer and I both fought against the increasing injuries, a demented laugh saturated the air, rising above the noise of the howling wind. The sound felt like it permeated my very being as if every fiber in my body wanted to just collapse and remain on the platform. My mind was coaxed into giving into the sentiment when two markers registered on my ikes. I rolled over to see that Torque and the Serpent had reached the rooftop.

Chaos' gleeful success was cut short as he spotted the late arrivals. In response, he brought his hands in front of his body and then extended his arms outward and to his sides in a deliberate circular fashion. In alignment with his motion, an energy shield arose from the perimeter of the tower platform which trapped the Enforcer and myself on the platform and cut off access for our allies. Torque stepped back to avoid burns from the energy shield as he and the Serpent were forced to observe from the rooftop.

The maniacal laugh resumed as I hobbled over toward the Enforcer's position. Before I could utter a word, the Enforcer was already in a crouched position and assessing the situation. Without hesitation, the Enforcer was airborne again with his right arm chambered to bring a fist down to Chaos' skull. The laughter disengaged as Chaos lifted his left hand to catch the Enforcer's throat before the blow could be delivered.

Chaos relished having the upper hand as he watched the Enforcer struggle, "I don't know how he's still alive, but you... you're right on schedule. Your appointment with death has always been at my hands. Completing the job that was left unfinished will only secure my standing in the Regime."

"You're not the only one who can land a hit. Are you sure that you have the right target?" The Enforcer asked. He was forced to clamp his hands onto Chaos' forearm and support his weight against the executive's powerful grasp. His voice released as raspy and faint on account of the restricted airflow.

Chaos paused, his eyes darted from his adversary then down to the platform while he contemplated the statement. His blazing eyes shifted about, searching for an anomaly or the possibility of error in his calculations. He found none, but he wouldn't be undone as his eyes locked onto the Enforcer again. "I don't know what you've changed, but you can do nothing more than delay the inevitable. The Regime will finish its job."

"You couldn't be more wrong. That's why a formula has been put in place to deal with your whole family of freaks," the Enforcer wheezed.

"Is that why you recruited a chemist?" Chaos sneered, squinting as he mused without knowing just what level of futile plans the Enforcer alluded to.

"No, that's why I recruited a vector!" The Enforcer said with a shout that was reduced to a hoarse proclamation.

My forward motion distracted Chaos, giving the Enforcer an opening to swing his legs over Chaos' arm. I was halted in my tracks, unable to contribute to the fast paced exchange. The Enforcer dropped his body into forward roll and flipped Chaos over, slamming him into the platform. He then grappled the executive's arm and attempted to snap it, but Chaos was swift to roll backward in order to drop a foot onto the Enforcer's face. The Enforcer released his grasp in time to block Chaos' foot with his forearms. As he caught Chaos' shin, he delivered a powerful kick of his own to the executive's chest from his grounded position. The kick impacted Chaos' chest, knocking him back with enough force to launch him into the air which gave the Enforcer enough time to roll onto his shoulders, push into a handstand and backflip toward Chaos. The Enforcer dropped his knees onto Chaos' shoulders and pinched his head before flipping backward and tossing the executive toward the tower yet again.

The Enforcer landed in time to see Chaos twisting his body midair only to allow a soft landing back on his feet. With the Enforcer settling his stance, I took to the air and drove both feet forward with a push kick. I knew the technique had little power, but it was enough to catch Chaos off guard and topple his balance. Continuing my advance, I dashed forward and hooked my arm underneath Chaos' shoulder and hurled him back at the Enforcer who responded with an uppercut to the airborne body of our foe. As Chaos sailed back toward me, I followed up with a flash kick.

Knowing that we couldn't give our adversary time to react, the Enforcer completed the combo by pushing off the platform with his kips thus giving him enough elevation to bring a high ax kick down from overhead. The strike connected hard with Chaos' body in the middle of his chest, dropping him to the platform with extreme force.

Chaos hit the platform with enough momentum to bounce, yet even that wasn't enough to impair the inhuman executive. After witnessing so many perspective shattering concepts in recent days, I couldn't even claim to be surprised that he would recover so quickly.

Knowing that Chaos wouldn't hesitate, the Enforcer and I continued our press. The Enforcer began to circle his hands overhead, channeling energy into his technique. I mirrored his motion as I placed my back to his. My senses detected a rise in the towers' bristling energy, ready to strike as beckoned, but I knew we couldn't afford to shift focus from our adversary.

I felt energy channel outward from my center, flowing into my limbs and down into my hands. The Enforcer and I struck our fists at Chaos, but as we connected, the activity from the towers became clear. Chaos managed to absorb the energy from the towers to repel our attacks before full extension. He did so with enough force that his retaliation knocked both of us backward.

My shoulder slammed hard into the platform, narrowly preventing my skull from doing the same. Tingling ran through the entire left side of my body as I rolled over. I grunted heavily in an attempt to push myself up with my uninjured arm. I expected to see the Enforcer already racing toward Chaos, but instead he barely beat me in returning to a wobbly stance.

"We have to destroy the towers," I yelled, my voice faltering in the wind.

"No," the Enforcer yelled back. "We don't know what will happen to those he is influencing. It could kill them. We have to leverage the Vast. It's the only way!"

The thought of using techniques that the Enforcer had described as dangerous without proper care did not bode well. Chaos wasn't going to give us time to recover and I couldn't comprehend attempting something that gave him an even greater opening at the risk of greater harm.

"If you cannot beat him with your mastery, what am I supposed to do?" I responded in exasperation.

"Fox, remember you have to look past what you see with your eyes," the Enforcer replied.

I felt conflicted about the constant state of lectures. My body was screaming from the inside on account of pain. The continual pressure to be morphed into something far beyond my expectation had reached critical mass, and I had no idea how to take the next step. I had already failed to detect a weakness from Chaos by way of the technology provided. I was exhausted from all of the riddles. I only started this journey for the sake of answers, and I found myself on death's doorstep no closer to that goal.

"I don't have what it takes," I said beneath a crushing weight of despair.

I sensed a pause in the Enforcer's reply as well as Chaos' hesitation to attack us while he celebrated the discord among his enemies.

"The true test of character comes from how one operates when they don't have all the answers," the Enforcer said calmly.

Even amidst the noise of the towers and wind, the Enforcer's words cut through it all with crystal clarity. In spite of his attempt to be reassuring, all I could feel was an overwhelming flood of aggravation.

"What are you not telling me?" I yelled as the frustration inundated me.

I had no recourse but to vent in the form of irrational behavior. My eyes locked onto an Inferno grenade that had fallen on the platform. Before my brain could squelch my impulse, my body moved to convert the frustration into action.

"Why do I feel like I get more answers from him," I snapped in anger as I kicked the Inferno grenade.

The following click burned into my brain as a nigh infinite span of time. The instant that my foot connected with the device, the consequences of my mistake were sealed and stamped into my mind in such a way that no level of amnesia could erase them.

Chaos held position, thrilled at the conflict erupting before his eyes. The grenade that I kicked sailed over his head and impacted one of the towers and then exploded violently. Chaos responded by whisking his form to the side, but the greater effect was the damage to the tower's integrity. With one of its support beams crushed inward, the tower bent toward the platform. The Enforcer and I had no choice but to dive away from the massive tower which threatened to crush us beneath it.

My impact with the platform jarred my already boggled senses as electric arcs and metal shrapnel flew in every direction. I scrambled to move away from the collapsed structure, but my body moved sluggishly. I sensed that the Enforcer had cleared the tower as well, but I couldn't see our enemy. I couldn't say the same for him.

As I slowly twisted about, I realized that our evasion had given Chaos a decisive opportunity to finish us before we could respond. Our Phantoms were on the platform, within his reach, but he didn't need them. A tingling sensation permeated the air as the remaining tower crackled. Chaos faced us and extended his hands to the side. Without any explanation to his means, white erratic electricity appeared to surge in a torrent toward his body. It impacted his torso and extended outward toward his hands. The energy contact should have had in adverse effect, but instead Chaos appeared to control it as if it were simply an extension of his own body. As he brought his hands forward, the energy followed until it created a discharge from his palms. In a stupor, I watched the weaponized energy extend from his reach. What fully escalated my panic was that it wasn't aimed at the Enforcer's position, but mine.

I felt an overload of information pouring into my eyes as the blinding energy swirled about in a directed channel. The display on my ikes was jumbled given the unknown projectile. I realized that one of my eyecon lenses was cracked and its functions were scrambled, unable to pick a specific vision filter. As it momentarily selected the interferic filter before moving onto the next, I detected a hazy motion to my right. I automatically knew that it was the Enforcer, but strangely in an instant, my mind verified something that I suspected ever since his encounter with Jenkins. His signature was out of sync. As the filter cleared, an even greater panic followed the last upon realizing that his movement was not toward Chaos to attack. His body was already airborne on an intercept course with the energy blast. My expression expanded into one of horror as I realized there was absolutely nothing that I could do to change the course of events. My body could not respond in time to warn the Enforcer or even evade the projectile.

With a fierce impact, the blast struck the Enforcer in the head. His ability allowed him to mitigate some of its impact by redirecting it through his body, but given his lack of alignment or concentration, it wasn't enough. He could have let it pass through him, but it would have struck me instead. For reasons I couldn't explain, he put himself between me and Chaos' strike. His body hit the platform hard. With pure determination, I fought to will my body into action against the pain and resistance so that I could shuffle toward the Enforcer's prone form.

I felt dizzy as my brain churned with sensory information despite my tunnel vision to assist the Enforcer. I tossed my broken ikes aside which barely minimized my distractions. Behind me, Chaos erupted into a deep laugh, but it didn't sound like a single voice. It was like a chorus of a thousand tortured imprints likely heard from the furthest trenches of Core City. The sickening sound permeated the body, tensing muscles and turning the stomach. I knew that I wasn't the only one impacted as sounds reached my ears of Torque and the Serpent fighting to overcome its influence as they exploited the gap in the energy barrier following the tower crash.

"Hang on. Response teams can't be that far," I clamored as I tried to prop up the Enforcer's torso.

I recognized that the Enforcer was only alive on account of his ability to deflect part of the blast, but ultimately it was ripping him apart from the inside out. His body was rocked with convulsions, yet he still fought to move his arm. I had never seen the effects of high density plasma hits up close, but I then understand why it was a sight that most would rather look away from.

"There's... no... time," the Enforcer said through clenched teeth.

"This is my fault. What can I do?" I asked as I began to recognize the great futility of my own behavior.

The Enforcer's face tensed, clearly exhibiting the pain as he fought to lift his arm and remove the blue camouflage bandanna from his head. Still fighting the convulsions, he placed the bandanna in my hand and forced my fist to close around it.

"The truth will set you free," the Enforcer said with a faint voice and his final breath.

Knowing that he had uttered that which was most important, his head leaned back and his eyes closed for the last time. I felt my consciousness seize with terror upon facing the expiration of the one critical influence that I had any memory of within the short life that I had. My first selfish impulse drifted toward the awareness of losing access to my past, but such thoughts were erased by the realization that I had lost my mentor and my friend. Even greater weight bore down on me as I was forced to accept that the loss occurred from my own actions. I could tell that my body's reaction was to sob convulsively, but the overload of consequences left me numb and immobilized. I couldn't reconcile how the Enforcer continued to fight again, and again and again. Throughout the contest in Windstonne he prioritized the lives of others, those he did not know, those he did, and ultimately those not worthy, as my actions revealed. Within his behavior, I knew there was an example demonstrating the lessons which had been relegated to hollow words from memory. My mind wanted to scream in anger at the paradoxical explanations, and yet there I was facing an example of the Enforcer's convictions in action, an example that allowed me to live at the expense of another.

I rose to my feet under great strain. My fist clenched around the bandanna in hand. I stared ahead at the exchange between Chaos and my allies. I knew that seeing the Enforcer would have an impact on their concentration, but true to their passes of training, they easily prioritized stopping the immediate threat before them. Without having witnessed the prior conversation, I didn't know if they comprehended the full scope of hatred that they battled against. Regardless of that knowledge, their own injuries were revealing their inability to keep up with the ancient form that easily kept them at bay.

I stepped forward to contribute to the conflict, but suddenly a crushing noise enveloped my mind. My legs buckled. My hands barely responded to keep me at a kneeling position, let alone prevent my face from impacting the platform's metal grating. A rushing maelstrom of words, expressions and phrases enveloped my mind, making concentration on anything except them near impossible. All external senses were muted as I wrestled to parse the noise circulating within my skull. Even motor functions felt locked away from my desire to push ahead and help my friends. When the volume subsided, I realized the consistency was still that of the voice that had guided me onto this path. It almost felt distant on account of its rarity throughout the whole of the Core City battle. Upon recognizing the nature of the voice I calmed my frustration and quit fighting with my rush to engage the enemy. My concentration improved, but it was still difficult to separate the jumbled, conflicting thoughts trying to pass for words. When I relaxed my muscles and settled my breathing, one phrase drowned out all others that dared compete, *there is no greater love to lay one's life down for friends.*

Just when I thought that I couldn't be hit by more weight, I felt an impact jar my entire consciousness before it evaporated altogether and consumed all other distractions along with it. The expression was clear, and I had no reason to assume that it had originated from anything but the Criterion itself. I didn't have the presence of mind to understand why that expression superseded all, but I couldn't deny being the recipient of the Enforcer's efforts to adhere to that very principle. It felt impossible for me not to connect his ability to live for that ideal and the strength that it revealed as a byproduct. I couldn't comprehend the full significance, but it was the only answer I was going to get for the situation at hand.

My mind continued to swirl with questions and doubts about how to leverage the revelation, but I shoved them to the side, thankful that even the slightest relief of weight on my consciousness allowed me to regain both my senses and motor functions. I knew that my friends were struggling and we had an enemy before us that would stop at nothing beyond the control of everything beneath our feet, enclave and all.

As if on cue to address my return to the fight, Chaos finally dismissed Torque and the Serpent's efforts by delivering a back hand to one and a strong side kick to the other. Both crumbled to the platform, unable to overcome their own exhaustion. My insides were torn up just by observing the harsh strikes, but I marveled at my own ability to stand, despite already receiving a similar beating. At last, I was finally starting to understand the very nature of the strength that the Enforcer possessed. It was only for the sake of others that one could stand with such persistence. My friends were in danger, those in the enclave below were in danger and they wouldn't be helped by any selfish ambition on my account. As I held position, Chaos did too, grinning as if tired of the game. He locked his eyes on the only one that he considered a threat, me.

I tensed my leg muscles, feeling like they might still give out even with the energy that I felt coursing through my body. I finally moved the bandanna in hand to a pocket. I couldn't explain the likelihood of my body's potential collapse or the internal forces that prevented it from doing so, but I held my ground.

Chaos continued to face me with his white teeth glaring in the tower light which starkly contrasted the dark sky, "You see, Mr. Fox, you are no match for me. If you value your life, you may as well surrender."

"I think you've already established that my life would be forfeit even if I don't try to stop you," I replied, quickly shifting my eyes down and to the side in the direction of the Enforcer's motionless form.

Wasting no more time on banter with the executive, I lunged forward, chambering and releasing a hook punch with my left hand. Strangely, my body acted on thought as if the barriers of physical resistance had been removed. Chaos matched speed and ducked under the punch. Without time to calculate the next attack, my body responded at the lightest suggestion and extended a straight punch and locked it out right in front of Chaos' face.

"You can't do it, can you, Mr. Fox?" Chaos said, still unafraid.

"Actually, I'm giving you one last chance to surrender," I replied, my form precise and unwavering.

"Apparently you still can't comprehend the end result of compassion! With every arrogant stride you become more like me," Chaos sneered.

"I'm not like you, Chaos. I learn from my mistakes. Neither guilt nor ignorance will stop me from finishing you," I said flatly.

Chaos twisted away, quick to charge for another attack, but I was ready for him. I snapped my left leg into a side kick. The agile executive ducked the maneuver again as I twisted my raised leg into an ax kick and dropped it. Chaos responded with an awkward lean, rising out of the evasive posture. I increased the pressure, twisting my body into the air so that I could drop a downward roundhouse as my base leg touched the platform, but Chaos responded with a kick of his own to my incoming shin.

The counter action rocked my leg backward forcing me to lose balance. I stumbled backward while gauging the distance from my adversary. Chaos didn't pursue, but instead only glared. I still felt like energy rippled through my body, but the tick that I entertained defeat, I knew that all of the pain held at bay would crash down like a tidal wave. I did my best to settle my nerves, breathing and concentration. As I motioned to channel that energy toward my center then outward to my limbs, my body accelerated forward in a blur to the naked eye. Closing the three boot gap with my quarry, I snapped my left leg forward while pushing off my right. I locked out my right hand, but Chaos again responded with a fluid lateral twist evading the punch while setting himself up for a counter attack from my side.

Chaos calmly delivered a powerful blow to the side of my ribcage, countering my forward momentum. The force of the strike sent me sprawling toward the edge of the platform on a side with minimal rooftop margin. I rolled over onto my hands and scrambled to my feet before I tumbled over the edge. Chaos moved to deliver a killing blow and knock me off the rooftop, but with an eerie lightness I felt my body easily evade Chaos' series of punches.

As Chaos' final punch in the combo passed over my head, I tensed up and shoved my shoulder into his chest, knocking him to the floor. The action allowed me to flip over his flailing body. With the executive between me and the ledge, I took to the air again to drop a downward crescent kick, but Chaos recovered fast and rolled to the side as I connected with the platform.

I rushed to prevent Chaos from regaining his position, so I jumped again and tried to drop a high spinning ax, but once again I was too late. Chaos angled away from the kick and returned a jump spinning hook kick of his own. I recognized an opportunity and twisted backward into a grounded flip, but with the exception of catching Chaos' airborne body with my legs. My reversal slammed Chaos into the platform.

Uncertain of how much punishment Chaos could take, I knew that I needed to end him before I reached my own unknown limitations. I considered the risk, but I settled on using the most lethal technique that the Enforcer taught me, the Vortex Punch. It was capable of rupturing target organs, or disabling limbs, but at the cost of lengthy recovery from the amount of energy transferred. I had to finish Chaos before my body collapsed.

I brought my hands parallel to each other and twisted them in a circular motion overhead. I continued the motion behind my right side before spinning them in a final circle. I snapped my right arm toward Chaos, but he was faster. He lunged from the rooftop, deflecting my blinding technique with his left hand before clutching my throat in his right. He followed up with a stomp to my ankle, prompting a series of snapping sounds to bounce with deafening echoes in my skull. The depleting energy from the failed strike, pain and deprived air quickly sapped my remaining energy and will. I locked one hand around Chaos' wrist while using the other to swing at his face. Without air, my body was starting to operate without any response to my suggestions. My eyelids started to close on their own with my mind sinking into blackness as Chaos hoisted me from the platform.

"Mr. Fox, it looks like this ideal of yours is worth dying for," Chaos said as he observed my struggle, helpless as my feet dangled in the air.

My eyelids fluttered as I tried to keep them open, but in the process I momentarily caught a glimpse of the Vast. Having already discarded my ikes, I remembered that the Enforcer said that the technology was simply an aid, not a necessity. Trying to keep my lungs functioning for another tick, my eyes darted about, looking for an opening. Sensing nothing but the hazy form in front of me, I realized that a deep energy concentration circulated around Chaos' eyes.

In the moment of decision, another whisper passed through my head, *the eyes are the light of the body... if that light is darkness, how great is that darkness.* Given my fading eyesight and the confirmed visual from the Vast, I required no explanation to finally make sense of the application that the Enforcer once described regarding the visualization of a person's weakness. I accepted that technology was not necessary for me to see that which was visible with my own eyes.

"No, it's worth living for," I wheezed.

I reached up one last time and poked at Chaos' right eye. Chaos gasped more out of surprise than lasting injury, but it was enough for him to reduce his grip on my throat. Instead of dropping me, Chaos stepped around and threw me over his shoulder toward the platform with violent force. My body slid for a boot before coming to rest in the platform center. Fresh air rushed into my lungs, but it did little for my ability to respond, I lay there incapacitated while Chaos turned his back to me and faced the enclave below.

"I can change too, Mr. Fox. I think I've changed my mind on killing you quickly. I'll offer you the privilege of watching the world implode on itself. Since you don't have the strength to face me, you WILL die without knowing who you are or where you came from," Chaos said, his words hammering my ear drums.

I felt that I had no choice but to accept the present outcome. I had no strength to move and I knew that I couldn't trust anything from Chaos' lips. I would die without knowledge of my past and the home that I did have would fall prey to his demands. I closed my eyes with any remaining tension in my body slipping away and my consciousness fading into a deep slumber, but not without one final headache and a barrage of whispers in such a flurry that I struggled to parse them in full. The trailing thought settled on *he shall bruise your heel and you shall bruise his head.* Given the injury to my foot, I felt slightly put off by the connection.

Using my speculation about Chaos' eyes being his weakness, I did my best to connect the whispers together, but I didn't know how to execute a relevant strategy. However, I was certain that I couldn't expire without one final attempt.

With all willpower that I could muster from the suggestions of the subtle voice in my skull, I fought to lift my body from the platform. I felt like gravity had been amplified tenfold as I strained to perform the basic function of standing. As I pried my heavy eyelids open, I spotted our scattered melee weapons on the platform. I wobbled on my feet as I watched Chaos turn around.

"My past is irrelevant, Chaos, I know who I am. I am Aaron Fox, defender of truth," I shouted as I shifted my weight onto my good leg.

"Do not even try, Mr. Fox. I alone will rule above the Exterior. I will rule the Grid from beyond the stars. None can contend with me," Chaos shouted with his voice amplified on the wind.

I had no energy to offer a witty reply. Instead, I hobbled forward, dealing with the pain in my leg. Chaos readied himself to defend another attack, but he didn't suspect the rustling from his side as my fima sticks lifted from the platform. I manually activated my grips with the unique hand position the Enforcer mentioned since my ikes were no longer available. The fima sticks snapped to my hands, allowing me to immediately throw them toward Chaos' face.

Chaos raised his hands to swat the projectiles away, but the very instant he deflected them my body blinked from sight. He looked around, but he did not find me. Too late did he realize that I had blinked into the air above him, flipping downward. While airborne, I snapped my hands out again and snapped the Enforcer's sai to my palms. With the metal weapons held tight, I allowed gravity to pull me down toward my opponent. Combining the force of the flip and the fall, I drove the long blades of the sai downward through Chaos' eye sockets.

The executive screamed and staggered. The impact should have incapacitated any human, but the executive floundered, a sickening howl erupting from his body. The standing tower flickered and pulsed as if Chaos' control over it had been interrupted. The energy that flowed between his body and the tower flickered and arced spastically. The tower's light diminished as the energy flowed toward Chaos. A sound similar to his laugh erupted. The sounds of a thousand tortured imprints escaped his form while he failed to regain control of his motor functions. With his body unable to absorb the excess energy, a bright beam of light shot upward from Chaos' position.

I landed hard on my knees, but I forced myself back onto my functional foot. I recognized that Chaos' form was dangerous, but I had few options available. I refused to lose the Enforcer's sai, but I couldn't simply extract them without touching the lightning rod of Chaos' form. Even without an internal whisper, I realized that before me was the manifestation of what the Enforcer fought against, the fury constantly operating from the shadows to consume anything in the light.

A phrase from the Criterion rushed from my lips before I could even think. "Pride goes before a fall," I said as I pushed into the air with my base leg and spun into a reverse kick. My leg screamed in agony as my injured foot connected with Chaos' body, but the technique kept me at the safest distance. Unable to defend, Chaos was rocked backward, and his body cleared the edge of the rooftop. Before his body could arc downward, I snapped the Enforcer's sai back to my hands. Dislodging the weapons did nothing to impair the connection of electricity that overloaded Chaos' form. The howl persisted until his body suddenly vaporized, no longer physically capable of containing the energy with which it was bombarded. Catching a final glimpse of my foe, I saw a whispy white haze linger in the air a moment before Konrad Oszwick was no more. The tower went inert and overwhelming silence rushed in.

I landed on the platform, but my weight compelled me to drop on my bad leg. As pain shot upward through my body, I felt like everything left within me was being drawn out by a magnet. I had no energy left to stand. What followed was beyond my memory. My body fell forward with my face ready to crash against the platform. I imagined a pair of hands catching me, but I no longer trusted any of my senses as my mind fell into blackness.

43 – Unraveling the Shroud – 43

Rooftop, Casters Tower
Core City, Windstonne Enclave
Commercial Empire, Northam Continent
Thread: actTgtPersp1.view

Sounds of boots on metal and other general commotion trickled through my ears. I couldn't understand what was happening around me, but I was certainly not alone. I felt a heaviness register in my mind as I started to awake. Words finally started to become discernible once consciousness marginally returned. Slight pressure on my shoulder reminded me of the sense of touch, but it was quickly followed by the reminder of pain's existence too.

"Fox, can you hear me?" An unknown voice asked.

My eyelids gradually parted to reveal human sized blurs against the orange light of dusk. I felt like I remained motionless for a great length of time before responding with a couple of groans. I gradually moved my fingers testing which body parts I could move without triggering pain.

"Can you move?" The voice asked.

"I'd prefer not too," I grimaced.

"That's good, your brain is functioning," the reassuring voice said with a chuckle.

I felt a series of hands help lift my body and position me on a cot to escape the cold metal of the tower's platform. Other than the pressure of being moved without much volition on my part, I felt little, but as I blinked a few times and tried to clarify the images before my eyes, a cascade of stimuli rushed in. I recognized the blue of Oshan uniforms, as numerous hands belonging to mendtechs helped me sit up while checking my vitals. I was able to adjust my neck just long enough to see Lennox and Alex receiving similar treatment.

As more of my senses registered, I felt like I was waking up from a bad dream, but as I observed a sheet covering the Enforcer's lifeless body, I was forced to accept that it was indeed reality. I looked up, uncertain what sentiments to acknowledge in my fractured state. Both Potentate Ang and General Seechi were on the platform assessing the damage of the enclave. I knew that many questions would need answering, but any interested parties had the decency to wait until coherence improved.

The Oshan mendtechs were both gracious and efficient. Once Vanguard's members were cleared for transport, we were taken from the roof and settled in an executive office already established as a recovery room while operatives continued to search for injured and scrambled to secure the tower's elevator systems. I had no concept of time within my groggy state as I slipped in and out of consciousness. My mind opted for natural rest before focusing on the need to stitch my most severe injuries back together. With the danger past, I didn't resist the usage of a stimpunch which certainly prolonged the lack of clarity.

As my head started to clear, I picked up more conversations from the slow concerted actions surrounding me. I heard that those with minor injuries were encouraged to proceed downward through the tower if possible. Other operatives still had their hands full with bringing wounded to the relay station and corralling any resistant Pirans. Most Pirans had given up the fight with their authority figures dead, but resistance leadership still encouraged keeping the soldiers contained until the initial recovery phase had ended.

Gradually, I heard more musing about how white-eyes had regained their own will after the towers had been shut down. I guessed that the time more closely overlapped Chaos' death, but I had little energy to insert myself into nearby conversations.

With health and containment operations normalizing, it allowed opportunity to start assessing what had happened within the tower and above it. Potentate Ang, General Seechi and General Cruz all took interest and began to causally query Vanguard once vitals were stable. Lennox and Alex relayed their accounts, including the conflict with the Piran commander. I could tell that the resistance trio had their doubts about the events on the rooftop, but given Lennox's service history and the Alex's bond with the Ghost leader, no one presented any counterargument. I suspected that doubts were amplified after listening to my recount of the events prior to the arrival of my friends. Since the resistance leaders had connections with the Interlace, few had reason to question further.

The leaders prepared to leave the relay station and allow us to rest when General Cruz bumped a table that held possessions taken from a deceased Piran. A pill container fell onto the floor and rattled until it rolled to a stop. Ang froze in his tracks as he stared, then scooped up the pill container. I immediately recognized the container as an Extend bottle despite having a label unlike the one that I confiscated from the Mogul Prime warehouse. Potentate Ang's demeanor changed as he turned the bottle over in his hand. His expression of calm washed over with extreme concern.

"I have made a fatal error," Ang said. "I must return to the Oceanic Outpost at once."

Without explanation, Ang exited the relay station leaving the operatives to handle matters. Shortly thereafter, I learned that operations were underway for the Oshan fleet to return home minus multiple contingents of recovery teams.

Oshan techs worked through the night to enable the transport of remaining citizens using the elevator system. After an awkward night and restless wait on a cot inside the relay center, Vanguard was finally cleared along with the last of the injured survivors. Most civilians descended by using the business elevators, but Vanguard opted to return to ground level using the utility elevators alongside the bodies of those fallen.

The exit process remained slow even at ground level. Staging regions were established to tend to those requiring additional treatment or to help them advance to mendstats where they might best connect with concerned loved ones. For Vanguard, the wait was a somber time with few words exchanged, knowing that we still had the heavy task ahead of laying our friend's body to rest.

Upon clearing the final checkpoint in the Casters Tower lobby, my senses were assaulted by fresh air and sunlight, prompting me to raise my hand to mitigate some of the light prodding my eyeballs. I heard many shouts from civilians behind Oshan guarded barricades. Countless onlookers sought after any sight or word of missing relatives. There were many tears of joy and sorrow for those who found them and those who received unfortunate updates.

As I lowered my hand, I recognized Sath who appeared to have sustained minimal injury. She still exhibited an air of patience, but I suspected that she already caught word of events that happened in the tower above. I looked away, having no way to be of comfort. Grief was confirmed as I heard the sobs erupt as she saw the soldiers carrying Mac's body near Vanguard's position. With Lennox being the only member to have interaction with Sath, he walked over to explain what happened.

Without any comprehension of how to respond, I looked around for a distraction. Near a barricade, I spotted a toppled duracrete slab supporting noptic displays and personal belongings which identified those already confirmed dead. Strangely, an object at the base of the slab caught my attention, my black treadball cap, albeit in lighter rugged fashion on account of the dust. I moved toward the cap and lifted it for inspection. I felt a sense of relief in finding it, but as I turned it over, detachment rustled my insides. Rather than return the cap to my head, I found an exposed support rod protruding from a rubble pile. I placed the cap on the rod and let it hang there.

I stood in the light breeze for a moment, my mind isolated from the social commotion all around me. I reflected on the outcome of surviving physically, but I questioned to what extent. During the fight, I acknowledged that I had an identity even without answers, answers to questions that I could no longer ask. I accepted that part of my old identity died on the rooftop as I tensed a hand around the bandanna in my pocket. Uncertain how I would put the pieces back together, I exhaled deeply and returned to my friends so that we could concentrate on resolving the fallout together.

Vanguard was treated with great respect at the resistance base camp even if at a distance to grant us reasonable recovery time. Unwilling to let others do the heavy lifting, we only allotted ourselves enough rest to recover basic mobility before jumping into the recovery efforts. Civilians and soldiers alike worked together to prioritize treatment of the injured along with identifying those dispatched. Some teams were quick to assist with the most critical infrastructure devastation, knowing that expansive daily life obstructions could create just as much fallout as the conflict itself over a greater time period.

Despite the internal discomforts of jumping into action so soon, the activity level helped distract my mind during the interval leading up to the memorial service for those fallen. Part of me was ready to retreat to the solitude of the Vanguard warehouse, but I knew that I would rest even more soundly having helped ease the burden of those cleaning up a conflict that they never requested.

The two days leading up to the memorial service passed quickly. While some wanted a delay on account of those not yet recovered, the timing was for the benefit of those needing to return to their own factions who had lost many of their own. A prompt event allowed the public to get an update in addition to the opportunity to remember the outsiders who fought from beyond the borders of the immediate enclave.

Since the Oceanic Outpost had the most surviving personnel to spare, several techs had been tasked with Vanguard's recovery of its vehicles. Thankfully, none were out of commission, but there was no argument regarding the need for fixes. Despite its drastic need for body work, Lennox reluctantly drove the Chromehound which carried us to the service.

We were met with a calming breeze and a canopy of green which blocked the sunrise over Lake Mitten. Once we made our way through Arbor Park, we found a clearing designated for a massive attendance. What was once faction property had been swiftly claimed for permanent remembrance of those who stood against faction tyranny.

Large noptic screens had been placed everywhere to accommodate the masses who couldn't see the central stage at a great distance.

I held up my hand to shield my eyes from the midday sun while adjusting to the blue sky. Given the insufficient seating, I was perfectly comfortable blending in with the masses that stood toward the rear of the field. I spent most of my time observing the crowd and taking in scenery of the park. After taking a moment, I accepted the wisdom of having the service so soon. Much conflict had been compressed into a short time and residents would need a reminder of what still remained, beyond the maze of damaged buildings and fractured homes.

Eventually, I heard General Cruz's voice boom through the air as he gave the introduction to the service and recapped the events leading up to the conflict in Windstonne, a wise decision considering that the conflict had descended upon Windstonne so quickly. Most enclave dwellers were still in the dark as to the nature of the events which had already transpired. The explanation was brief as it helped maintain calm from those likely to erupt with grief over loss of loved ones. Rumors of events within Casters Tower circulated fast, but there was no way imaginable to correct every falsehood. The disclosure of key events helped satisfy the public's most pressing questions.

On account of time constraints, shared stories were compressed and limited since there was no way to mention every imprint lost in the conflict. Civilians and military figures alike had been chosen to share select stories of meaningful impact or heroism that occurred during the battle.

Even Private AWOL had a turn on the stage telling embellished tales of actions on the battlefield. The public easily sensed that many of his details were fabricated, but no one complained since he shared in such animated fashion that laughs erupted on multiple occasions, giving even the most stoic of combatants opportunity to mask their deep grief over those lost.

As the service closed, the public was made aware of a tentative custodial agreement for the Uniod Branch and Westcrest to share oversight of the Commercial Empire until an infrastructure could be developed from within. Since the mentioned factions were neighbors along the Northam continent, the choice appeared logical to most. The strategy allowed Alcazaba time to regroup and remain within the enclave while the Oceanic Outpost ramped up efforts to make the return trip home.

Once all speakers exited the stage, a hush fell over the crowd before mass exodus attained priority. I found myself lost in thought, mulling over the explanation of events. The people appeared pacified at the explanation of Frank Jenkins and his use of Extend to deceive the Global Alliance and its population for his own personal conquest, but strangely absent was any reference to Chaos or Oszwick Enterprises. I had my reservations about withholding such information from the public, but then I considered the timing in order to prevent the perpetual feud of freedom versus safety from reigniting so soon. Eventually, those with curiosity would dig deeper and unpack the nature of what transpired on Casters Tower. I even considered that, given the raw emotional state of those affected, it proved wise to limit disclosure to verified information especially since the scope of the truth regarding Frank Jenkins' benefactors might supersede our own understanding to that point. My mind finally settled with the current disclosure upon accepting that limited information kept Vanguard out of the spotlight, allowing it to resume its operations outside of scrutiny. Shifting attention toward my actions certainly would have jeopardized everything that the Enforcer had built for the sake of protecting those who favored truth over murky faction oversight.

As the surrounding throng dissipated, I observed Alex who passed his regards to the surviving Ghosts and his long time mentor Sato Seechi. I was surprised that Alex opted to remain with Vanguard, suggesting that it still offered plenty of challenge. General Seechi supported Alex in the decision, but he didn't disclose the Ghosts' future plans. They were reluctant to return home to the Martial Legion, so they would continue searching for a new home in order to rebuild and resume their training.

As the crowd thinned further, I spotted a couple of out of place figures in the form of Subterra's survivors standing next to Streetz. I suppressed a chuckle at their dark clothes contrasting their pale skin. Their dark shades made them appear to be junior faction agents given their limited exposure to daylight. Given the loss of their close friends, I was glad to see their participation in the event.

Vanguard and Subterra exchanged their regards, each suffering losses. Streetz was eager to return to Vanguard after Subterra graciously checked his pathways for residual effects after his integration with the Hyper Lynx. L337 Haxs and Hellix both expressed their gratitude for Streetz's quick thinking since they might have expired too if not for his adequate response time.

Since Vanguard had already conversed with much of the military support during cleanup operations, there was nothing left to accomplish at the park. While the finality of the Windstonne operation lifted a massive burden, I recognized that there was still much weight to be shed. Given the suppressed nature of the things observed firsthand, I knew that Vanguard needed to resharpen its blades in preparation of future operations unknown.

Capitol Detainment Block
Commonwealth Prime, Cydnon Enclave
Oceanic Outpost, Oshan Continent
Thread: sysObserver.cmd

Talbot Newton felt weak as he struggled to move his legs at the expected pace of his security guard escorts. Their steps echoed in the cold duracrete halls. The harsh, colorless structure opposed the vibrant colors that the Oceanic Outpost was known for. Finally having access to social interaction, Newton queried the guards as to the purpose of his confinement, but he received nothing other than instructions of where and when to move.

Newton lost track of time while in a cell. Beyond the occasional conversation from a passing guard, he wouldn't have known of the conflict or outcome of the contest in the Commercial Empire. Without knowing the particulars of what prompted the event or who survived, Newton was incapable of feeling anything but a void in his core since he normally would have been an essential piece to such a large scale operation. All of his attempts to request information had been cut off, especially regarding why he was a suspect.

Newton was perfectly aware of the Oceanic Outpost's strong justice system that helped maintain order, but he never once thought that he'd be an occupant of its facilities. His stomach turned as the escort placed him in front of a large door with massive rivets. The guards promptly opened the door and ushered Newton toward the fixed metal chair in the center of the room. Newton required no explanation to realize the sole purpose of the room was for execution. Since the room had no observation window, it had to be for crimes of the highest order. The only furniture in the room was the chair with its restraints and a small rolling table likely to hold lethal chemicals at the time of administration.

First sight of the room compelled Newton to bolt for the door and run, but he was a middle-aged advisor and no match for the younger, adept guards. In utter despair, Newton sat in the cold chair while the guards secured his forearms to the chair with leather restraints. Once the guards left the room, Newton was left alone.

A quick glance around the room revealed nothing but cold stone walls and a sungauge above the door. Newton had no desire to watch time pass, so he fixed his gaze on the floor. He expected that investigators would arrive at any moment to offer some explanation, but no such arrival occurred.

Newton's last hope of an explanation were dashed when two individuals entered the room and sealed the door behind them. One wore a lab coat and the other the dark formal uniform of a magistrate. The very sight of the individuals informed Newton that he had been scheduled for an execution without an inquiry.

"Talbot Newton, do you know why you are here?" The gaunt magistrate asked.

Newton shook his head silently.

"You have committed treason of the highest order against the faction and are hereby scheduled for execution. Would you like to make a statement?" The magistrate asked.

Newton looked around nervously. Since he detected no meca input, he pondered what good it would do to produce a confession, real or contrived. He had no idea how he could have mistakenly committed such a heinous act after so many passes of loyal service.

"That's not possible," Newton replied. "I want to speak with the Potentate."

"Orders for your execution came down from the highest office," the magistrate said, flatly denying the request.

Newton clenched his fists and began sweating, as the official began to read legal procedures relevant to the process. None of the words registered as Newton's mind swam in circles. He knew that he had no option other than complete surrender, but his will refused to quit without having an answer. At last his mind settled on the only possibility, he had been set up.

"Talbot Newton, do you have any final words?" The magistrate asked.

Newton shook his head again. There was no escape. Since the war in the Commercial Empire had been won, he hoped that he could die knowing that the intended treachery had failed minus allowing him to take the fall. He knew that all remaining words would fall on deaf ears as he slumped back in the chair.

The magistrate motioned for the proctor to finalize the procedure. The proctor readied the chemicals and lifted the injector. Even soft subtle sounds felt like hammers competing with Newton's pulse as the ticks dragged on indefinitely.

As the proctor reached for Newton's arm, a shrill ring disturbed the morbid atmosphere of the cold room. The abrupt noise startled the proctor, prompting him to look at the magistrate. Without enough time for a response, a guard entered the room and whispered to the

DAVE TODD

magistrate. Offering no explanation, the proctor set down the injector and followed the magistrate out of the room.

Newton felt sweat trickling down the side of his head with no way to wipe it away. He noticed that a tense fifteen clicks had already passed since the officials left the room. Just when he felt like had been reduced to starvation over injection for his execution, the door opened. To Newton's surprise, a familiar figure entered and left the door open, but he wasn't sure if the presence was there to reassure him of anything.

"I'm sorry. I knew that I should have trusted you," Potentate Ang said as he leaned low enough to look Newton in the eyes.

"What is going on, William?" Newton asked with uncertainty, given the claim about execution orders.

"Factions have been infiltrated at the highest levels, and despite my best efforts to identity a traitor, I almost failed to catch him in time. Someone leaked our position to the Martial Legion, causing great loss and delay to our involvement in the Windstonne conflict," Ang replied.

"William, I never spoke to anyone of that information. I have no reason to betray my faction, or you," Newton said in his defense.

"I know, old friend, I know. Let's get you out of here," Ang said as he released the chair restraints.

Potentate Ang helped his advisor return to his feet and walked him to the door. A security detail was ordered to protect Newton and keep him out of sight. Newton had a ton of questions, but he assumed that the plot to undermine Ang's authority was not yet fully resolved. He exhaled deeply, at last feeling relief that his execution had been stayed. He could wait until being brought up to speed at the proper time.

Imperium Adminus
Commonwealth Prime, Cydnon Enclave
Oceanic Outpost, Oshan Continent
Thread: sysObserver.cmd

Zared Marx took a moment to pause the shuffling of effects into storage containers so that he could appreciate the colorful view overlooking the administration building's courtyard. While haps regarding Talbot Newton's treachery and execution came as a shock to many, Marx only cared about one thing, opportunity, especially since the outcome meant a vacancy with a better view. Marx completed his break and continued to remove the former occupant's things when Potentate Ang arrived.

"Packing things up so soon?" Ang asked his social advisor.

"The faction never sleeps, so I thought it best to get the drudgery out of the way and get back to work," Marx replied, attempting to hide his actual motivation.

Marx found Ang's prompt return home concerning, but he felt that he had covered his tracks well. There should have been little evidence to connect him to recent events. As he removed more of Newton's personal effects from the desk his eyes locked onto the noptic globe, common to most offices. He froze as he remembered that he hadn't removed the transmitter from its base. To avoid suspicious behavior, he nervously fished around in his pocket for his pills. Not finding them, he realized that his demeanor was becoming erratic.

Ang produced a small familiar capsule of pills from his pocket, "I found these on the floor."

Marx gratefully accepted the capsule and downed two small units from the container. After consuming the pills, he felt like he had calmed down, but as he resumed removal of items from the task, he realized that Ang's gaze was fixed with a piercing stare.

"Why did you do it, Zared?" Ang asked coldly.

"Do what, William?" Zared replied.

"Sell out your faction and order the execution of good man to cover your crimes," Ang said flatly. "I know these aren't for your heart. It's an Extend prototype that I found it in Windstonne."

Marx's stomach tensed as he realized that he had been played, but he had no desire to undo everything that he had built, so he simply exhaled and chuckled, "Oh, that's clever. I take pills and you want to pin the treachery of others on me?"

Ang's hand snapped out and latched onto Marx's curly beard. He tugged with extreme force yanking the advisor's head down. Ang reached around with his opposite hand and slammed Marx's face into the noptic globe, his patience having long since expired.

After the jarring blow, Marx groggily stood upright trying to focus his vision on the item that Ang picked from the shattered display base. Ang held the transmitter in front of Marx's face and glared.

"Anything that I've done has been for the betterment of the faction. I know that you harbor the Interlace and other knowledge seekers. Such ideals only lead to unchecked freedom. There are greater threats coming, and if collective resources aren't brought under the control of those able to maximize their efficiency, then we're all condemned," Marx snapped.

"What threats?" Ang asked. "I've heard the common threat justification for absolute faction control before, and every time it's pitched by those with zero integrity and care for nothing more than their own self-gratification."

"You have no idea what's coming," Marx huffed while wiping blood from the cut on his cheek.

"What threats?" Ang yelled.

"I fear those in control more than I fear you," Marx snapped back, having no desire to bend to Ang's accusations.

"You've done well for youself here, Zared. If the coming threats you describe are as severe as you suggest, you won't mind contributing your wealth and signing it over for faction use," Ang responded in a stark calm, demonstrating his ability to vary his demeanor at will.

"You can't do that!" Marx screamed.

Zared Marx knew that he was backed into a corner even without any admission to plots or connections with entities at work. When the Potentate threatened to seize that which he had worked to attain his composure began to unravel. He looked around the desk for a sharp object. He might have had a chance to overpower the faction leader and concoct a compelling story, but as if on cue, two Oshan officers entered the room and stood behind the faction leader.

"I believe that the very seizure system you implemented in the courts will suffice," Ang said flatly.

Marx reached for any object that he could throw in anger, but the officers were quick to restrain his arms.

"You should just kill me now," Marx snapped.

"No, Zared. That would be too easy for your. You're going to spend the rest of your time enduring hard labor in an effort to repay the faction for your treachery," Ang said. "Get him out of here."

The Oshan officers held Marx firmly despite his attempts to flail and get free. The deranged advisor nearly frothed at the mouth in anger.

"When you're done, you can tell your friends in the kiln that you never got to appreciate that which was never yours to begin with," Ang said without looking at his former advisor as he passed through the doorway.

The commotion finally settled as the Oshan officers escorted Marx down the hall. Potentate Ang took a moment to lift an overturned noptic display of Newton's family. "I believe this is yours," Ang said as Newton silently entered the room.

Talbot Newton graciously received the personal possession and returned it to his desk. He overhead the tail end of the conversation from the hallway. He was still dumbfounded as to the level of treachery witnessed after serving alongside someone for so many passes. Lofty positions in a peaceful faction were no stronghold against the malevolence that still traversed the Global Alliance.

Newton had many questions for Ang, but he was patient enough to wait for the proper timing. He fully understood that the remainder of days granted were a luxury then intertwined with the purpose of ensuring that they weren't wasted.

Potentate Ang felt deeply relieved that he intercepted the plot against his longtime friend. He realized that he had to become an even better leader still to ensure that such subterfuge didn't shake his faction again. He walked over to the window which overlooked the courtyard. The bright hues of the Oceanic Outpost landscape and uplifting tones should have bolstered his mood, but inside he felt a series of conflicting sentiments. Marx's betrayal and disclosures revealed the level of craftiness common to the enemy they faced. Ang had his reservations about Fox's story regarding the executive willing to destroy everything to bring down the Firewall Protocol and Interlace alike, but Marx's antics certainly added validity to the events in Windstonne. Ang was forced to face his own oversights in allowing such animosity to fester within his own administration. Chaos hadn't successfully secured influence all the way to the top of the command structure, but he certainly advanced his agenda to the next highest level.

Even with Extend victims being placed under close observation for the foreseeable future, Ang knew that the enemy's reach was vast. Such influence might even pale in comparison to the threats that Marx suggested. As Ang lifted his eyes to the horizon where many of the faction's signature vessels patrolled along the sun reflecting waters, he knew that another storm was coming. When the time arrived, he was sure that the Oceanic Oupost needed to be ready.

Gridloc: Wayward Plane
Thread: frmChsnAnlys.rvw

The crunch of stone and grit under the heavy boots created sound waves that continued into the distance as if the air itself was dead and lacked the will to protest. Physically, the ascent up the stairs implanted into the mountainside was of little consequence, but without any color or wind the climb drained the senses. Upon reaching the platform that hosted the gateway controls, the armored figure looked past the mountain that once obscured his line of sight. Where he expected a view into the unseen, he found nothing, no trace of the Vast, no trace of life, no sign of welcome.

"Zero trace of carrier presence. It's a wonder that the Particulate is still holding together long enough to witness this," the Adjuvant said into his comm.

After adjusting the magnification on his helmet visor, the Adjuvant scoured the stone plateau for clues. Even with sensory inputs to the max, there was no indication of any life remaining to be catalogued. On his left, the command console to the gateway remained intact on account of the reputed durability of Exterior technology, but it too, was void of life traces after the harsh atmospheric purge. The Adjuvant ran his gloved fingers over the terminal, but it yielded no lights in response.

Turning about to view the landscape preceding his ascent, the Adjuvant started feeling his stomach twist at the barren depression of the Vod at the base of the mountain. If it weren't for the ominous color, one might never know the extent of the graveyard below. Instead of skulls and bones, only a field lay bare. After the roiling heat of the purge, the color red had been baked into every rock and saturated the terrain. The persistent gray clouds taunted him, suggesting that they would never rain again to wash away the reminder of the conflict.

It boggled the senses that the vultures even dared to circle though pickings had long since been charred and obliterated. Unless the vermin from beyond the Vod ventured into the dried basin of blood, the birds inevitably wasted their time.

"If the objective were to test the impact of the latest adjustments, I'd say things were smashing success. The desired outcome? Not so much," the Adjuvant remarked.

"Do you want to take credit for bungling this branchmark? I didn't think so," the Adjuvant replied to the ill-timed comments on the other end of the comm.

Despite the adequate tech in his helmet, the Adjuvant still placed his hands before his eyes to focus on select positions of the terrain below. He dropped down a couple of steps toward a significant location. He knew that the view from his vantage point was enough to change the course of reality, but the great question was, by how much.

"This has to be personal," the Adjuvant said.

"Even our enemies hesitate when they realize the personal cost of something," the Adjuvant said in response to the remarks on the other end.

The Adjuvant crouched low, knowing that what he saw needed an amount of clarity to be studied for relevance. Achieving a view of a specific point on the battlefield would require more coordination than he could imagine.

"The divergence produced by this sequence was unforeseeable. The tidebreaker necessary to ensure that things go as intended will need to be immense," the Adjuvant said.

"Yes, I do recommend shifting our branchmark as far back as possible. If our enemies rely on external force, we must do the same," the Adjuvant continued.

After a final glance at the command console and then the scorched battlefield, the Adjuvant rolled his neck and shoulders before making his way back down the steps.

"Very good. I have a list of candidates to put into operation and will submit for your review. Crux out!" The Adjuvant closed.

44 – Living Memory – 44

Vanguard Warehouse
Abandoned Sector, Windstonne Enclave
Commercial Empire, Northam Continent
Thread: actTgtPersp1.view

A faint breeze rustled loose elements on the roof, but it didn't match the raw tension enveloping the warehouse. The lack of a full roster and direction had everyone coping in different ways. More than once I heard the anger of hammers flung about while Lennox worked on repairs. Alex had taken to expanding his painting with such tenacity that I dared not ask if he was adding birds or bugs. Conversely, Maxwell was often found staring into the distance without his usual energetic flair. Only Streetz seemed unaffected, but his focus on recalibration matched each of our desires to distract ourselves from the changes around us.

With three days passed since the final resolution atop Casters Tower, the journey toward adjustment had only just begun. I calmly leaned against the brick barrier of the rooftop while staring absent-mindedly at the parking lot below. Lost in thought for a long time, it took forever for my consciousness to register that subtle oranges of sunset were overpowering the former blue sky.

As I lifted my eyes, my perch still granted me a hazy distant view of Windstonne to the north. Even at range, I could see some of the superstructures in the distance. The waning daylight even poked through some of the formerly solid objects showcasing the destruction that happened during the conflict which would require a great deal of time to repair. Occasional wisps of smoke still clung to the air as fallout of the destruction lingered.

I felt confident that the enclave would be rebuilt, but there was no denying the tension that would persist after the utter infiltration exacted upon the Global Alliance. The joint custodian roles placed over the fallen Commercial Empire proved logical, but most of those dwelling in Windstonne were likely to be too consumed with survival demands to heed any concern for the shift in authority, temporary as it may be.

Unable to process the weight of society at large, I dropped my eyes from the horizon back to the local terrain. I stared blankly at the warehouse surroundings while I reflected on the strange memory that occurred on the Casters Tower roof. Thus far, it was the only time that I felt like a natural memory had broken through. I closed my eyes to draw out the mental image of the crates that drew me to Oszwick's actual name. The logo was affixed to crates holding informatech equipment. The memory expanded into a view of a laboratory. The sensory recall continued as I found myself sitting at a desk with an open Criterion before me. I clearly remembered submitting the request to download the Firewall Protocol.

I gasped as I opened my eyes, pondering the distinct will and clarity behind the memory. The very nature of the laboratory brought back sentiments of academic pursuits, curiosity and study of subjects through recommendation. I was unable to recall any neighboring events, but at last I had a fixed point to acknowledge my own personal connection to the Interlace. Suddenly, Mac's lack of insistence made more sense as if he had prior understanding to my existing connection. Given how integrated the installation was with the conscious mind, I contemplated if my headaches were a result of the Relay forcing concepts through without having my past memories to draw upon.

I lowered my head almost to the rooftop barrier, overwhelmed by the information. Unable to adequately contrast my miniscule past with my hyper volatile present, I glanced over at the Criterion on the barrier next to me along with the bandanna resting on top of it. I couldn't fully grasp just how much two small objects represented the absolute transformation that I had undergone in such a short time. While the discovery of the Criterion had initiated my path toward Vanguard, the bandanna symbolized my responsibilities yet ahead. My confidence in my capacity to fill another's shoes was drastically lacking.

Preferring to not linger on that which I couldn't do, I opted to find something I could do to distract my mind from the added churn of uncertainty and doubt. As I lifted the Criterion and bandanna and moved toward the access door, I heard the click of a small item impacting the rooftop. I looked around finding nothing at first, but as I squinted I discovered a small oblong item. I immediately recognized the item as a datapill, but it differed from the usual variety by its deep red color.

Perplexed, I lifted the Criterion and began flipping through it. To my surprise, more sections were accessible than the last time I inspected its content. As the pages floated before my eyes, I noticed an anomaly in a middle section. Pausing and flipping backward to the section in question, I found an impression between pages were the datapill had been squished.

As my eyes locked onto a section just above the impression, my jaw nearly detached from dropping so fast. The datapill had been placed just below a line reading, *the truth will set you free.* I blinked my eyes a few times, doubting what I was seeing. Someone with more advanced access to the Criterion had placed the item in an area that I previously had no access to. Given Mac Conner's final words to me, I couldn't help but ponder the connection.

After breaking from my absent stare, I noticed that another pill-like shape was nestled into the same area. The second pill was white in color and had no metal contact points suggesting that it was not a datapill. Holding both pill-like shapes in my hand, I closed the Criterion and hustled inside.

As I disembarked from the utility elevator, the warehouse fell into silence with the exception of Streetz's punches to the training floor bags. He continued recalibrating his fields as I approached Maxwell at the op table. The hamster sat hunched over with a wan expression. His demeanor was listless without having an operation to complete.

"I've got something for you to check," I said quietly as I produced the datapill.

At first Maxwell looked up at me with a blank stare, but gauging my serious intent to discover the nature of my find, he perked up slightly and nodded as he pushed a pillbox toward me. I quickly popped the datapill into the transfer device, and Maxwell shook his forelegs, manipulating his interface to display contents on the flatjack. There was no delay since Maxwell found a singular meca on the storage device. Verifying that I wanted to play the item, Maxwell looked at me. I nodded my approval.

The noptic screen was quickly filled with a recording of Mac's face with the Eagle behind him. The background was obscured and all timestamps had been obscured or erased. I sensed that Maxwell's eyes were as wide as my own, if not for the difference in physical size. I gasped, then held my breath as Mac spoke.

"Fox, if you're watching this. I trust that you have finally reached a point that you can access that which I left for you. While you may be concerned with how my foreknowledge brought this to you, that answer pales in comparison to the why. I know a lot has been placed on your shoulders, and I have no intention of leaving you without the answers that I can provide in the short time that I have," Mac said.

Stupified, I could do nothing more than collapse into the closest chair without taking my eyes off the screen. Having experienced one of Mac's advanced interfaces before, I didn't bother with any questions but instead stared at the screen.

After a brief pause, Mac continued, "I know that you have struggled greatly with the sensation that everything surrounding you feels foreign. There is a reason for that... because it is. I can only address the questions that you struggle with most. Who am I? Why do we look alike? Where do I come from? Why can't I remember anything?"

"First and foremost, the answer to *Who am I* has and will always be up to you. No amount of answers on my part would have had any impact without you first accepting your own identity regardless of who you thought you might be. Additionally, all eventual outcomes that involved me relaying this information to you never would have allowed for this interaction in this fashion. While that may seem undesirable, I will save the particulars for the end."

"*Why do we look alike* is answered in simple fashion. Mac Conner and Aaron Fox are congruents, or congi, from completely different vera. I know this is a lot of weight to hit you with which is why I made sure to include a basic understanding of the Grid within our discussion time. There is no way that I could have prepared you for all that is without detracting from the urgent matters at hand."

"*Where you come from* may not have any personal meaning without your memory, but this veras is known as the Wayward Plane and you come from another called the Temporal Shift. While this may spawn its own curiosity, the bigger variable in the equation is why you can't remember."

As I stared half in shock, I felt like I needed to send a signal to my lungs to breathe. I was overwhelmed with the influx of information. I wanted to doubt it, but my senses confirmed what I suspected all along, that the Enforcer knew more than was revealed. While distrust may have been the first sentiment to surface, I knew that the recording provided such specificity that I had no reason to discard it, especially with how long I searched for answers without any plausible alternative.

My eyes remained glued to the noptic screen, virtually tuning out the sounds of Vanguard's other members approaching. Lennox ascended the stairs, confused as to why he heard Mac's voice while Alex hushed his consumption of the Mesquite-Os in hand. Even Streetz walked over to observe.

"Finally, what I guess is the answer you desire most, that of your memory loss. I stumbled across a far-reaching plot to attack the Interlace. As the plot unfolded, I discovered that it wasn't limited to one veras. Still a novice in understanding the Grid myself, I discovered that many had no understanding of the Grid whatsoever. If vera populations were knowledgeable in their understanding, they often had tight observation or restrictions on interactions with others. This made the hunt for allies difficult. I had no choice but to seek out those most likely to think like me, my congruents. While we worked on a plan to counter the plot we still had to contend with local issues. One of those was the Crossover Strain, something which you were instrumental in resolving. If not for your knowledge in chemical informatics, we might not have been successful. You helped craft the Crossover Prevalent which was then finalized by Subterra and mass produced through Potentate Ang's resources in the Oceanic Outpost."

I struggled to keep up with the information. I wasn't sure if Lennox and Alex might have been more surprised by my connection to the expanded reality known as the Grid, or by my unknown impact on our current vera. Without a pause to ask questions, the recording continued.

"During my travels, I discovered that our plan was at risk and we drew the attention of those desiring to cut us off. Before I could warn you, our enemy already made the first move, targeting your laboratory with you inside. You were pulled to safety, but not before sustaining a nasty head injury which is likely to blame for your amnesia. Since facts regarding the identity and origin of our enemies were limited, you were brought here and placed under the care of the Dwelling Street Mission. It was best to allow our enemies to think that they succeeded."

My mind raced with questions, but without Mac present, I was at a loss.

"I'm sure that my methods seemed harsh, but they were necessary. Modern mecas would have you believe that icons can simply be transferred by wearing a special mask, a shoulder patch or donning a cape. I assure you that it is much more complex. Symbols are just the outward representation of the values within. Assuming the role of Enforcer is not just about a camouflage bandanna, but the values of self-sacrifice and an indominable defense of the truth. Those are not things that cannot be imposed externally, but must be chosen internally. If you are watching this, I trust that your own choice in the matter has risen to the surface. Because the role and the identity become synonymous to others, I could find no other means to elevate that which would inspire without the aid of those with the same identity. Comparable life experience can fill in the gaps."

"Lastly, I know you are considering the possibility that things might have turned out differently if other actions had been taken. For those of you who might feel guilt over my departure, Don't. I have known the end of my time long in advance and with that knowledge came a heavy weight that few could bear. It often came with the temptation to deviate from my course, but for the greater good it was necessary to meet such an appointment head on. I had a great friend show me the way, and to that example I hold."

"How could he have possibly-" Lennox gasped.

"Lennox, I know that you're most likely to question such an outcome, but rest assured that specifics are not nearly as critical as the path that lies ahead for Vanguard. Since you have known me the longest, you can attest to the reservations that I have demonstrated over many passes."

Lennox could do nothing more than nod since he had often questioned Mac's reluctance to take part in anything larger than Vanguard's secluded operation. Accepting Lennox's confirmation as yet another mark for the meca's reliability, I returned my attention to the content that remained.

"Aaron Fox, I leave Vanguard in your capable hands. I know that might seem like a daunting task, but I most certainly wouldn't have left you with such a responsibility without support. If you managed to find this datapill, I trust that you found another along with it. Within is all of the remaining information that I could isolate. The memories of Mac Conner are now yours. See you all on the outside."

My eyes returned to their doubtful yet expanded state as I held up the white pill in front of my face. My friends stared at me and the pill with curiosity as the meca concluded. I turned the pill over. Without the ability to connect it to the pillbox, Maxwell shook his head nervously, knowing what I was about to do.

Before I could be stopped, I downed the white colored pill without any liquid to follow. At first I felt nothing, but a deep rumble from my stomach forced me to my feet. My body was immediately wracked with intense pain as if I had been run over by a freight mox only to be run over again and again. My entire body shook as every muscle spasmed uncontrollably. My ears rang with high deafening pitches while my vision blurred and contorted reality into indiscernible shapes. I intended to cover my ears as if the piercing sounds were external, but my limbs failed to respond to any instruction. My insides convulsed, making me feel like I would gag to reject the pill, but there was nothing of substance to expel from my system. From my core to my extremities, I felt like every muscle fiber and tendon sheared from my frame and reattached themselves in the most excruciating fashion. The most horrendous yell of pain I had every experienced escaped my lungs and rang throughout the warehouse. Then, just as if I had been submerged in the most pressurized depths of the ocean, I was snapped back to a stimulus free clarity as if warped back to a normal atmosphere. The entire sensation cleared before Alex and Lennox could even place their hands on my shoulders to stop the shaking. As the entire experience dissipated instantaneously, my body snapped back to a normal standing position, and I looked about in shock at the immediate dispersion of the sensory overload, all while questioning what had happened to me.

Lennox grabbed me a chug of water as I plopped down in the chair. I breathed deeply, trying to make sense of the experience. After downing some water, I stared at my hands as I turned them over. I flexed my fingers into fists and relaxed them multiple times. I tried to place what was different. Physically, I felt the same, or so I thought, but there was no denying that something... felt... different. I tried to see if I could recall anything different mentally, but I couldn't conjure up foreign memories at that time. My mind certainly felt crowded as if more information had been crammed into it in a short time.

Alex and Lennox had a host of questions, but they were gracious enough to table them until I had a chance to walk around the training floor to make sure that I hadn't acquired any injuries or disabilities after ingesting an object of such foreign nature. Before receiving an opportunity to test for anomalies, Maxwell jumped once startled by a ping from the comms terminal. I walked over to the flatjack and instructed Maxwell to open the comm.

"Fox here," I said.

"Ah, Mr. Fox. Glad to see you and Vanguard well," Potentate Ang said upon seeing my allies within range of the display. "I apologize for my abrupt departure, but I am thankful to report that a major crisis was averted. I must admit that I was doubtful of your findings in relation to Extend, but if they hadn't been so instrumental, I might have needlessly lost another good friend, all while putting the Oceanic Outpost at great risk."

After a quick recount of the events in the Potentate's faction, I easily understood the need for his urgent exit. It was a relief that no greater harm had been done and that Mac's discovery connecting the faction's administration had finally been solved.

"What happens next, Potentate?" I asked.

"We will be sure to thoroughly parse any information that Marx might have had with clans and other insurgents. Now that I have an open position, I was hoping that you might relay a message for me. If you see Protech Szazs, I thought you might pass along my interest in his candidacy," Ang said.

My expression shifted into a blank stare as I looked to Lennox and Alex for clues as to the informatech's whereabouts. All I received were faint shoulder shrugs. Even Maxwell shook his head, suggesting that he had been unsuccessful in locating the Szazs too. I felt at a loss upon admitting that the absence had never been vocalized. We had lost all trace of the protech, yet hoped that he was still alive.

"I'm sorry, Potentate, we still haven't successfully located him, but I'll be sure to pass along the honor once he surfaces," I replied.

"That's all that I can ask," Ang said with a smile. "My administration is in your debt. Should Vanguard call, I will ensure that all resources of the faction are at your disposal."

"I hope to never require such a favor, but it is good to know that we have friends in far places. Vanguard out," I replied.

I exhaled after acknowledging awareness of the Szazs' absence. We quickly revisited any possible means of tracking his whereabouts, but arrived at no viable solution. During the conflict, enclave traffic systems were a mess, and without knowing the form of transportation that the protech secured, we had no way to track him down.

After verifying that we exhausted every search possibility, we were interrupted before my friends could resume poking at me to see what had really happened with the pill and verify if I was okay. A loud crash penetrated the warehouse walls, so we quickly snagged our closest weapons and made for the parking lot. We lowered our guard upon seeing a nondescript mox crashed into one of the warehouse's duracrete pylons. Its driver, who was slumped over the wheel, was none other than the protech himself.

We hurried to open the driver's door and verified that the elderly informatech was breathing but unconscious. He appeared to be more gaunt than usual, likely from fatigue and exhaustion. We quickly carried him inside and laid him on a cot while fixing him up with some cursory scans and the necessary fluids so that he had a chance to rest. Alex, Lennox and I all exchanged looks, perplexed, not about the timing of Szazs' arrival, but by the numerous questions about where he had disappeared to and why.

A number of arcs passed before Szazs stirred on the cot. As he came to, he panicked as if still in a delirious state. I calmly kept a hand on his shoulder as he attempted to sit up. Once he did so in full and started to recognize those around him, he stopped fidgeting, but he didn't let up on an urgent need to discuss something. Finally, we convinced him to take a moment while Alex fetched the informatech some food and water. After Szazs downed a few bites of bread and sips of water, he was insistent that there was no time to waste on what he had to explain.

Lennox helped Szazs to his feet in case he wasn't strong enough, but he assured us that he wouldn't fall so easily at that point. We walked to the op table so that Maxwell could be included in the conversation.

With all of Vanguard present, we listened intently as Szazs started with his personal decision to download the Firewall Protocol and then he continued with his discovery of the secondary signal and his travels to Oszwick Enterprises. His body had been stressed to the maximum level as he hid from Oszwick's workers and Mogul Prime. Even after his termination of Kotes, he was forced to hide for great lengths of time in order to exit safely. He knew that he was no match for a single clan member, but his interactions with the Oszwick Enterprises tech so shocked him to his core that he knew the executive's secrets had to be revealed.

Protech Szazs described the exchanges, suggesting that Mogul Prime had been listed as the company's successor unlike the former assistant Lucient. Mogul Prime disregarded Kotes' disappearance and proceeded with securing and transferring ownership of critical tech. Once the facility had been vacated, Szazs did his best to access the system, but the only remaining system that was operational was a countdown timer.

Instantly interjections circulated, pressing Szazs to explain if there was a bomb in the facility. Although Szazs was still rattled, he assured us that he discovered no trace of explosives. His concern came from tangent information related to things called vera and a massive reality framework called the Grid. Given the number of arcs remaining on the countdown, he was forced to hurry out and issue a warning. He relayed that the countdown timer was going to expire within the next day.

Szazs released a deep breath after finally accomplishing what he set out to do. A massive burden had rolled from his shoulders. Even though he didn't know the nature of the Oszwick tech or a viable solution to address it, he knew that he did as much as he could. After taking a moment to break from our own stares we assured the protech that he made the right call and that Vanguard would handle the rest. After taking another food and drink break, we caught Szazs up to speed on the events since his departure as well as the position offer from Potentate Ang. With a simple nod, Szazs admitted that he would be better equipped to unpack all of the new information after some rest.

With Szazs taking his leave, Vanguard stewed over the possibilities. With our limited understanding of the Grid we had no way of comprehending just what Chaos might have been up to with his knowledge and tech. Even more concerning was that such resources had been transferred in his absence. While Vanguard was dismayed about the lack of break from conflict, I could still sense renewal at having an objective once again. Those of us remaining put our heads together and prepared for a long evening of planning.

DAVE TODD

45 – The Road Ahead – 45

Vanguard Warehouse
Abandoned Sector, Windstonne Enclave
Commercial Empire, Northam Continent
Thread: actTgtPersp1.view

The late planning and early prep made for a short night. Normally, I would have required more sleep, but strangely, my body was starting to act on its own. Things that I normally struggled with, felt more relaxed, fluid even. Even without knowing what I had undergone, much of my consternation about battles ahead felt diminished.

Our first order of business was to ensure that Szazs was on his way. Torque secured the borrowed vehicle and verified that it had a full charge so that the protech could meet up with an Interlace contact in Core City. It was up to him if he wanted to locate any remaining Oshan liasons in the region or to make informal, but longer, travel arrangements.

After bidding our farewells, Vanguard got to work locking down any resources deemed necessary for an unknown conflict ahead. Maxwell had already loaded the moxes, Eagle and Reptilian into the Behemoth storage bay with the automated systems. Torque wasn't crazy about deploying without bringing the Chromehound back up to his tight standards, but he reluctantly admitted that it was still battleworthy, a testament to his proficiency at his craft.

As the time to rollout arrived, I found some of Mac's redundant attire. He had to have been partial to his wardrobe since I had my choice of gray shirts and black pants. Before putting on my shirt selection, I stared at the mirror, shocked at the stranger staring back. I ran my fingers across my collar bone and the scar I acquired from the Monk encounter. I knew that the burns on my leg had begun to heal and left similar markings of their own. I reflected on the abilities learned which allowed me to not only survive, but function in such a harsh world.

I noticed slight creases in my chest and arms as they started to shed their slothful pudgy look. My torso had more resemblance of a trained vector than the daily salvage worker soaking up meca optics. Even my face had tightened with my jaw line forming a weathered expression. My eyes no longer revealed the carefree ignorance of the life I once had. Initially suspecting that the pill changed more in subtle ways than I could trace, I knew that recent battles had made plenty of marks on their own.

After putting on the gray shirt, I pulled over the blue vest and tugged at its edges and settled the collar. Another tug tightened the bandanna around my head. With one final introspective glance, the colors of my eyes shifted and flickered before I covered them with my ikes.

I stepped onto the training floor and found my shoes. I figured that I already had broken them in, so I didn't need to change up anything. Placing my weight back onto my feet, I admittedly felt lighter.

As I paused on the training floor, I felt the first traces of a memory trickle through my mind. It felt like a location near my lab, and Mac was teaching me the basics of combat. I couldn't decipher if the memory was my own or Mac's, but it felt real regardless.

While reflecting on the past in the place where I had learned so much, I recalled memories of Mac's mention of Hykima and its connection to identity. I couldn't parse if my existing ayvek was inherited from a mentor or something of my own experience. I had finally accepted who I was with or without my past, but separating the difference between inherited past and present experience would require experimentation.

My conscious thoughts felt the same, but my muscles acted as if there was a need to test them. In a daring move, I kicked one foot forward until my body followed into the air, allowing for a forward moving back flip. I stumbled slightly on the landing but still regained my balance. Even though my reflexes were still awkward, I never would have been able to execute such a maneuver at will in the past without great concentration and risk.

"Judges give the landing a 4 out of 5. Are you sure that you want to be piloting the Eagle just yet?" Torque chided after observing my antics.

"No time like the present for a field test," I exhaled.

"Just make sure it's not a crash course," Torque smirked as he nodded toward the Behemoth. "I don't have enough nuts and bolts to put you back together."

I swiftly grabbed my weapons and hurried to the Behemoth since the others were already onboard. Once I settled into the Behemoth's command chair I gave Maxwell the nod to move out. I allowed him to direct our course toward Oszwick Enterprises until he prompted me to assume control as needed. With every free tick in between, I reviewed the Eagle's interfaces from my ikes. Strangely, as I reviewed them, I felt like I was watching a meca for the tenth time. By the time we reached our destination, I would be ready.

Our trek through the abandon's edge passed quickly. As we neared the expected perimeter of Oszwick Enterprises, Maxwell gave the nod and I issued the orders for everyone to mount up. With jittery nerves but steady motion, I arose from the command chair and made my way for the Eagle's cockpit. After using the adjacent ladder, I settled into the jet's pilot seat as the Behemoth's body flooded with light. With the rear bay door open, Maxwell operated the cranes to deploy the Chromehound and Reptilian. Once they were clear, I activated the Eagle's engines. With all protocols clear, the bottom bay opened and the electromagnetic restraints activated. In response, I dropped the jet out of the bay.

"Sound off, Vanguard," I said once I had a clear view of the open stretch of road ahead.

"Wheels, check," Torque shouted as the Chromehound pulled in front of the Behemoth on the left.

"Scales, check," the Serpent added as the Reptilian did the same maneuver on the Behemoth's right.

"Legs, check," Streetz replied from the Behemoth's cockpit while Maxwell steered the razerjack.

"Wings, check," I yelled nervously as the final snap of a switch closed the Behemoth's bay doors and deactivated the docking restraints.

While my mind nearly seized in a panic, fearing that I might crash the metal bird on the road below, my fingers, hands and arms all responded to the proper maneuver of the control stick. Without time to marvel at the muscle memory that I had inherited, I angled the jet, passed in front of the Behemoth and increased in elevation and speed.

Hollers peeled across the comm, relaying enthusiasm that I didn't crash. As the Eagle ascended, the tactical display lit up with Vanguard positions and critical stats. I took a moment to get familiar with the vehicle's motion. Even with the physical pressure on my body, I felt quite the rush from adapting to such a new experience.

After brief chatter on the comms, everyone locked in their coordinates for the rally point at Oszwick Enterprises. No longer did I have time to worry about the unknowns. Along with my new family, I had a mission. I discovered that with an identity and truth we could go far, and the latter would always be under attack. As long as there were nefarious entities, bent on its destruction, we would be there at the front of the fight. Because WE are its Vanguard, and I AM its Enforcer.

S0 – Active Formula – S0

Wayward Plane
Urban Overlook
Abandoned Sector, Windstonne Enclave
Commercial Empire, Northam Continent
Thread: fnlFrmRvw.pln

The faint evening breeze made for a relaxing mood, as the Actuator approached the edge of the building's rooftop. The full moon offered the only light available in the night sky with exception of its reflection bouncing off unmaintained glass in the abandoned enclave. The only building to truly grab his attention was the emptied archive in the distance with the sloped glass capable of scattering the moonlight in seemingly random ways.

The Actuator had grown so accustomed to urgent high intensity modifications to his work that felt he had earned a moment to reflect, despite knowing that the finalization of the current phase was only the precursor to the true test of his collaborative efforts. Before allowing his mind to slip out of focus completely, he emptied his pullover pockets of their contents and set them on the rooftop, ledge doubting that the wind was strong enough to abscond with the items.

Cool air filled the Actuator's lungs as he closed his eyes and revisited the numerous iterations of his objectives, hoping that there were no oversights. Before he could fully rerun the mental list, he heard the heavy steps of armored boots as they approached from behind.

"Hard to believe that the time is finally upon us," the Adjuvant said as he leaned forward, placing his gloved hands on the ledge.

Rarely had the Actuator interacted with the Adjuvant directly since they accelerated their plans, making it easy to forget just how intimidating the full set of black moddenite armor was, especially in the darkness now that it loomed like a deep shadow. Even for appearing to be of such bulky craftsmanship, the armor made little sound other than the slight crunching of the bodysuit while the Adjuvant procured items from a pack at his side.

"I have fully verified the contents and received the approval for all external offsets," the Adjuvant said as he slid a metal tin toward the Actuator.

The Actuator activated a portable lamp that he rested on the ledge, offering just enough light to inspect the tin. The nondescript gray metal container offered no clues as to its contents, so the Actuator promptly popped the hinged lid. Inside were two objects embedded in a foam cushion. The first was easily recognizable as a vial bearing the industry markings belonging to a mendtech industry of foreign nature. It required no label for the Actuator to know its purpose.

"I can isolate the entire sensory coded pair back to the branchmark you requested, but I think it would be best if we replicate it first. There's no telling what can happen on a displaced instance," the Actuator said.

"There's no time to delay. Once the formula is activated, I will have time to synthesize an isolation compound, but if our execution is not precise, countless will be lost to the kiln forever," the Adjuvant replied.

The Actuator nodded, ever frustrated at the constant reminders of the scope of their mission. As the light from the lamp bounced off the tin's occupants, the Actuator lifted the metallic object neighboring the vial. When held vertically, the object resembled an oversized key, but the irregular shapes comprising it looked like they could represent foreign letters given how numerous rounded squares overlapped and attached to each other.

"Is this a neurosieve?" The Actuator asked. "I heard the side effects from these are brutal."

"Impurities cannot be purged without heat and pressure," the Adjuvant replied flatly.

"That is true," the Actuator replied as he replaced the key shaped object and closed the container's lid. "We wouldn't be here without said pressures personal, impersonal, great or small."

The Adjuvant silently nodded in agreement.

"I believe you will know what to do with these," the Actuator said as he slid a book over to his associate with a disheveled bandanna resting on top of it.

"The greatest weapons can at times be the most subtle," the Adjuvant said as he ran his finger across the book's title before stowing it and the bandanna in the pack from which he had produced the metal tin.

"I've often contemplated just how much weight I've put on your shoulders with the knowledge at your disposal," the Adjuvant said while reflecting on the need for tenacity upon starting the next phase of the mission.

"I think you may find that in time, the weight of that burden is evenly distributed. While your activators were great in number, they were also disconnected. Finalizing a terminal event may lead to an indeterminate outcome, but so too may the observation of that event when the activators were personal like mine," the Actuator replied.

"Who can argue with the unknown in these battles for hearts and minds. As our enemies flourish in numbers and schemes, so must we," the Adjuvant replied, turning to depart.

"Follow Protocol to the end," the Actuator said without looking away from the still view of the enclave.

The Adjuvant paused in his tracks and mulled over his thoughts. He had nothing to add to mission parameters, and he knew that a mission of such grave importance left little room for personal sentiment. After a seemingly long pause in the night air, he looked over his shoulder, allowing the moonlight to reflect only from the angled visor inset on his helmet.

"See you on the outside," the Adjuvant said in parting, compelled to initiate the next phase.

DAVE TODD

Traveller's Codex - Metrics

Over the course of my travels, I have discovered a common practice implemented by most global cultures. that of a universal measurement system. The location presently settled upon uses one such standard called the GMS or Global Measurement System as adopted by its Global Alliance. However, many cultures that I observe possess a rivalry of systems. One such system common to various regions is based on a language called Inglesh. My understanding is that it is a monarch metric. While I do not have access to the official standard, I can only, in part, provide approximations relative to the local metrics. The following notes are my comparisons which are available thus far.

~ The Traveller

Arc / Click / Tick - No domain is without its measurements for the movement of celestial bodies. While some cultures utilize a device called a clock as their sungauge, they have varied terms for incremental units. The most common expressions that I have observed are Hour, Minute and Second respectively. I have been unable to verify if such cultures have matching interval lengths, but I can confirm that most have a commonly accepted usage of said terms in daily context.

Pass / Lunar / Bench - While I find it interesting that cultures seldomly deviate from the concept of day, some have an implied understanding of a solar being the completion of one morning and evening cycle. Larger lengths of time certainly vary by name across cultures, yet they frequently retain their connections to celestial bodies. Unsurprisingly, one year equates to a pass in their equal representation of the earth around the sun. Similarly, one month matches a lunar in relation to the moon's path. Strangely, one week is represented by a partial lunar or seven days. I find that the term's context is accepted culturally by its connection to labor schedules.

Boot / Mark / Notch - One of the most common terms that I hear in this foreign system is that of a foot. While it is an approximation to the size of the monarch's actual foot, the measurement most closely correlates with the GMS boot. I find it anomalous though, the discrepancy to have only one term when some cultures use it strictly for horizontal measurements in contrast to the mark being used for vertical measurements. Additionally, a notch is a smaller segment of these measurements. Current approximations place it around a tenth of the length of a boot or mark.

Pace / Haul / Parcel - Certainly the most divergent of terms are spread across those of distance. Without knowing the origin of counterparts, approximations with the yard, partial mile and mile are in dire need of additional study. While the monarch system lacks a partial mile term, I commonly hear cultures utilize the term kilometer from a rival system.

Deck - Across most cultures, I find the concept of a story to be most informal, both in its origin and standard. Through context, I have discovered that it refers to singular floor of a building. I have been unable identify a suitable measurement for a deck within the monarch system.

Cap / Block - Having many uses for weight and volume relegated to automated technology, comparisons with foreign systems have proven difficult. Those who have adopted the usage of the monarch system regularly use ounce and pound for the their most common terms of weight. Due to resource limitations, I have not yet been able to translate their values relative to caps and blocks respectively.

Traveller's Codex - Geopolitics

Overall domains have uniform terran deposits, but occasionally those with cataclysmic deviations in their histories exhibit radically different masses of land and water. While the presently chosen region is similar to many others, it, like most, has a divergent political structure along with differing boundaries. Given the adaptation challenges of most who would venture out of their own domain, I considered that a proper catalogue of overall features might be in order.

~ The Traveller

Continents

Northam - Often the center of attention, the Northam continent is known for leveraging its influence across political structures. Its land mass exists in the Northern Hemisphere and is greatly separated from other continents by oceans on the east and west. Its land was often sought after by colonial forces, allowing for its amalgamation of disparate cultures.

Southam - Like Northam, Southam exists between two oceans and connects only to its northern counterpart by narrow land bridges and waterways. It too was a great prize for explorers, yet its perpetual conflicts prevent it from achieving the influence of other regions.

Uniod - A region continually in flux, the Uniod continent dominated the cultural seeding efforts of the Northam & Southam regions. Its economic strength has remained strong and has often leveraged less kinetic means of warfare on its opposition.

Shian - Physically connected to Uniod, the Shian continent contains large populations and divergent cultures despite long histories of sharing the largest land mass. While home to numerous factions, originating nations long since learned the nature of war. With latent knowledge on standby, strong identities continuously strive to protect their heritage.

Caafri - A hot zone, geographically and politically, the Caafri continent has been continuously sought after for exploitation with varied measures of success. Until recently, the continent has remained several steps behind other regions despite its abundance of resources straddling the equator.

Oshan - The smallest habitable continent, the Oshan continent would have no interaction with other regions apart from sea and air travel. Its isolation has afforded it the opportunity to accept or reject paradigms of other regions of its own accord.

Oceans

Transispan - This ocean separates Northam and Southam from the western edges of the Uniod and Caafri continents. Its size is moderate, but not a detriment to commerce or travel amidst the neighboring regions.

Quadrivast - The largest body of water separating four continents, the Quardrivast requires that regions leverage its scattered islands as waypoints amidst their travels among the eastern edges of the Shian and Oshan continents and the western edges of the Northam and Southam continents.

Trinsular - This body of water borders the eastern edge of the Caafri content, the southernmost portion of the Shian continent and the western edge of the Oshan continent.

Factions

Commercial Empire - Dominating much of the Northam Continent, the Commercial Empire rose from the ashes of the Tricameral Endeavor.

Uniod Branch - Still retaining its Uniod heritage, the Uniod Branch neighbors the Commercial Empire to the north.

Westcrest - United mostly by culture, Westcrest is comprised of the western most portion of Northam including the land bridges reaching to the south.

Coalition of Jungle Republics - Continuously in a warring state, the faction comprising the Southam continent appears to have a rather tenuous standing at present.

Uniod Bloc - With a faction boundary that matches its continent, the Uniod Bloc still remains a political and economic influence.

Sibera - True to its cultural roots, Sibera has maintained its faction boundaries in addition to crafted alliances with its Shian continent neighbors on account of its strength.

Martial Legion - Most known for its massive population and its expertise in war, the Martial Legion is comprised of Shian mainland and island territories many of which still possess underlying tensions within its political system.

Stratustan - Residing in the southern peninsula of the Shian continent, Stratustan varies in its influence as its massive population spans the entire spectrum from poverty to affluence.

Insurgistan - Occupying much of the Shian continent's eastern border, Insurgistan is constantly at war internally and externally. Its arid climate frequently creates conflicts over territory and resources.

Straypoint Stronghold - Existing in a corner between the Uniod, Shian and Caafri continents, the Straypoint Stronhold is often a target despite its small territory on account of its resources in contrast to the lacking adjacent regions.

Equatorial Span - Recently unified within the Caafri continent, the Equatorial Span has unified its political systems in order to cultivate and defend its often exploited resources.

Oceanic Outpost - Isolated from other cultures, the Oceanic Outpost has developed its independence on account of the waters protecting the Oshan continent on all sides.

Traveller's Codex - Firearms

It is highly uncommon fot domains to halt the advancement of their weaponry in the era of ballistics. Surprisingly, the region settled upon has had a drastic enough turn of events to shift the paradigm of most common tools leveraged in conflict resolution. On account of the National Conglomerate's decree following the Bioterminus Convention, the entire region switched from powder driven projectiles to plasma discharges. Proponents of the shift claim that related technology is more humane and less messy, but detractors have made many arguments on account of long term nervous system damage in survivors where phase disruptors were involved.

~ The Traveller

Splice 15m: Standard Pistol - The most abundant firearm on the market, the Splice 15m is compact and effective for immediate situations. It operates on a magazine of microcells. Due to the mass market appeal, a full catalogue of models is unavailable.

Phantom 4.0: Tactical Sport Pistol - A firearm with varied uses, the Phantom 4.0 is favored for special operations. Not only does it have significant stopping power, it also features a collapsible barrel stabilizer for suppressed precision shots. Unknown to industry regulators, the Phantom 4.0 is highly adjustible through after market modifications. It operates on one standard power cell.

Monsoon: Economy Pistol - To some the Monsoon is considered a trinket, but for those who are more self-defense minded, it is a suitable alternative to more expensive models. Commonly operated in a pair, the Moosoon features barrels that rotate around a hand grip. Spinning the barrels in succession leverages the firearm's kinetic actuators, eliminating the need for a power cell altogether. It has a three tiered charge system capable of storing few high speed charges at the highest level with speed and discharge density diminishing at the lowest.

EQ: Assault Rifle - The most widely produced rifle, the EQ or Equalizer is mostly commonly used among armed forces. It is a light weapon with a series of short rotating barrels, allowing for a rapid rate of fire. It is considered to be a minigun in compact form. Its four standard cell capacity make it suitable for prolonged operations.

CQTR (Cutter): Tactical Rifle - Noted for its hefty stopping power, the Close Quarters Tactical Refit boasts an intimidating range and plasma density output. It is capable of functioning on standard power cells and is most commonly implemented by enforcement and domedi hunters.

Cress: Suppression Rifle - Famous for its three barrel design, the Cress is a short rifle capable of halting hardened assets in their tracks. It is frequently used for riot control since its wide low density burst inflicts less damage while delivering a lot of force. It uses spindle-bound triplets of microcells.

Hellings 20: Ranged Rifle - The specialist's weapon of choice, the Hellings 20 still dominates the market share of sniping apparatus. The Hellings 20 leverages a clip of high density cells making it a lethal tool in trained hands.

Claw Hammer: Targeting Rifle - Due its physical mass, the Claw Hammer is typically only used by operatives with extensive physical strength. The oversized weapon is capable of firing up to three sequential strands with potential tracking capacity on account of the three polarizing prongs that expand from the barrel when discharged. Those proficient with the weapon can even chain the strands in order to deliver an explosive contact charge. Due to the firearm's brutal nature, it is rarely seen outside the employ of oppressive regimes. The weapon operates on megacells which often makes it cost prohibitive.

Mortimer: Shoulder Cannon - The most explosive of all plasma tech, the Mortimer is restricted to those with the most competence. It is rarely used by anyone other than armed forces for mass suppression, breaching operations and anti-vehicle support. The weapon features a collapsible tube form, making it light for transport. When in use, the fully extended tube opens a tail funnel to protect the operator. Because of its limited storage capacity of shells, the Mortimer is not rechargeable.

Made in the USA
Columbia, SC
29 May 2025

58522439R00416